☆ ☆ ☆ ☆ ☆ ☆ ☆

THE PICADOR BOOK
OF CONTEMPORARY

# AMERICAN
# STORIES

Also by Tobias Wolff in
Picador:

*The Stories of Tobias Wolff*
*This Boy's Life*

# THE PICADOR BOOK
## OF CONTEMPORARY
# AMERICAN
# STORIES

☆

EDITED BY
TOBIAS WOLFF

PICADOR

# ACKNOWLEDGMENTS

☆    ☆    ☆    ☆

I would like to thank Peter Straus for his tireless enthusiasm and good counsel in seeing this project through, and, for all her help – once again – my wife Catherine.

## For Raymond Carver, 1939–88

This collection first published 1993 by Picador

a division of Pan Macmillan Publishers Limited
Cavaye Place London SW10 9PG
and Basingstoke

Associated companies throughout the world

ISBN 0 330 32530 2

Introduction copyright © Tobias Wolff 1993
This collection copyright © Picador,
a division of Pan Macmillan Publishers Ltd, 1993

Pages 720–724 constitute an extension of this copyright page.

1 3 5 7 9 8 6 4 2

A CIP catalogue record for this book is available from the British Library

Typeset by Cambridge Composing (UK) Limited, Cambridge
Printed by Mackays of Chatham PLC, Kent

# CONTENTS

☆  ☆  ☆  ☆

# INTRODUCTION

☆  ☆  ☆  ☆

Anyone who has traveled across this country knows that the West was never really won. The spaces are too obdurate. Nowhere is this more true than in North Dakota, where the incidental and provisional nature of our tenure is inscribed on a landscape almost bare of human habitation. A few years ago I met a wheat farmer from that state and couldn't stop myself from asking him how he kept from going crazy in all that windblown solitude, a question he did not seem to find peculiar.

I listen to stories, he said.

It sounded mystical, after the fashion of holy men who dance to the music of trees and rocks. But that wasn't his meaning. He told me that when he was out in the fields he brought along a Walkman and listened to short stories. He had a collection of several hundred, some bought through catalogues but most of them taped from collections and anthologies he borrowed from the library. He and his wife read them aloud to each other, and to their tape-recorder, at night and during long winter afternoons when the snow kept them housebound. They kept the stories they liked and erased the rest. He named some of his favorites, and from the way he spoke about them it was clear that they had become part of his life. I have to admit I was embarrassingly grateful to hear a title of my own on the list. Seldom have I been more hungry for a sign of favor. It had something to do with the image of a finger hanging over a STOP button – like death, but personal.

And there was more to it than that. Jack Yeats described writing as "the social act of a solitary man." The same is true of reading. It requires isolation as the price of the best society. Writers can never be sure, in the act of writing, if anyone will pay that price for the company of their words. We proceed on faith but in doubt, dreaming uncertainly of readers who will justify this lonely work by passion equal to our own; readers who live as much for us as we for them. It's always an astonishment to meet one.

I don't know this man's name. In true old-West style, he never gave it. And in this too he remains the ideal reader, perfect stranger and perfect intimate. I had him in mind when I put this anthology together, him and all the people I've seen lost in good books on busses and subways, in restaurants, in military barracks and rest areas, at reception desks, in toll booths on empty highways late at night. The surrender of their attention to the words before them seems to me truly gracious – made freely, out of love, no strings attached.

Almost all the stories gathered here were published during the last fifteen years or so, during the perod of what has been termed a short-story "renaissance" in this country. To judge by the respectful attention this renaissance has received from reviewers and academics, you would think it actually happened. It did not. This is a rhetorical flourish to give glamor, even valor, to the succession of one regime by another.

The problem with the word "renaissance" is that it needs a dark age to justify itself. I can't think of one, myself. The short-story form has reliably inspired brilliant performances by our best writers, in a line unbroken since the time of Poe. But among writers of the recent past there have been rough similarities and rough dissimilarities sufficient to give those who require such drama the sense of witnessing a contest.

The dominant impulse of American literature has been realistic, and never more so than in the first half of this century. Realism was not a school that writers defined themselves by joining or attacking; its spirit was too pervasive for that, and too generous. Writers as different as Flannery O'Connor, John Cheever, Katherine Anne Porter, J. D. Salinger, Bernard Malamud, Paul Bowles and Eudora Welty, who must have thought themselves very unlike each other, still belonged recognizably to the same family. They were storytellers rather than scholars. Their work was impelled not by formal preoccupations but by their interest in the human, in the deeds and possibilities of that sad animal.

But in the 1960s we began to see a different kind of story here, resolutely non-realistic, selfconsciously literary, scholastic, concerned with exploring its own fictional nature and indifferent if not hostile to the short story's traditional interests in character and dramatic development and social context, except when used ironically to expose the naiveté of the reader willing to believe in the world of a story as if it were actual. John Barth's "Lost in the Funhouse" is the perfect example of this art, wherein a tender coming–of–age story is dissected by the narrator even as he tells it, and is shown to be an assemblage of hoary tropes and rhetorical devices and antique narrative conventions. In the end, though, the story does not entirely dismantle itself; the tenderness survives the narrator's seeming attempts to expose it as trumpery. And this, too, is by design.

The works of the Postmodern or Metafictionist writers have come to be discussed *ensemble*, as if Donald Barthelme, William H. Gass, Robert Coover, Ronald Sukenick and John Barth were all the same. I've probably gone too far in that direction myself. Of course they aren't the same. John Barth, for example, is complicated, intense, philosophical, his rich language and formal playfulness reminiscent of the eighteenth–century novelists, especially Lawrence Sterne. Robert Coover is terse, ironical, clever, with a weakness for farce, the lower the better. The work of all these writers is quite distinct. It is generalization enough to say that they share a certain impatience with the inherited forms and assumptions of realistic fiction.

But in at least one of these writers this impatience amounts to ferocity. He cannot stop himself from letting you know that what you are reading is *made up*, is *fiction*, that the sentence that just broke your heart is nothing but a series of ink marks on a flattened piece of wood, and the woman you've fallen in love with only a crude variation on the old harlot–queen figure that shows up as Helen in the *Iliad* and which Homer himself borrowed from an earlier epic whose beginnings can be traced to a cycle of drinking songs popular in Ur just before the Flood.

I recently had a chance to watch this Village Explainer in action, at a writers' jamboree. For three days he spoke tirelessly about the fictionality of fiction, the textuality of text. Then one night his presence gave rise to an interesting situation – interesting, at any rate, to me.

We were driven to an old mill in the countryside where we were to have dinner and watch a play. We ate outside in the courtyard; then went into the theater. The Explainer arrived late, no doubt from a talk he'd been giving. The play was divided into two long acts. The first act had just begun, and there was no way for him to get in without disrupting the performance, as the doors also served as entrances to the stage. The courtyard, now empty of diners, had become the back-stage. Here the actors changed costumes between takes – it was a comedy, the humor of which depended on a series of lightning transformations – put on and took off their make-up. The stage-hands trundled props back and forth, worked the lights, made the sounds of thunder and rain, sent out for pizza and drank up the beer in the cooler. The Explainer was stuck out here in the midst of all this clanking machinery, forced to bear witness to the play's complete artificiality while the rest of us happy idiots sat in the dark and had a good laugh.

When the Explainer mentioned later that he'd been caught outside, I thought, not for the first time, of Isak Dinisen's hymn of praise, "As the heavens are higher than the earth, O Lord, so are Thy short stories higher than our short stories." What a perfect, yea, divine epiphany of the Explainer's situation – the perpetual Back-stage Johnny, all wised up to the scene behind the scenes, but unable to enter the play.

The question comes down to this: Does it show culpable innocence in us that we can freely and with pleasure lose ourselves in a contrived, artful world? If you think it does, then subversive irony is inescapable in your role either as audience or artist. My own guess is that the capacity for belief in imagined people and circumstances, whether on *General Hospital* or in *The Great Gatsby*, is evidence of a kind of receptive gift that can easily be destroyed by bitter knowingness, such as that of a boy who, discovering his mother uses make-up, decides she isn't really beautiful after all. The democratic nature of this gift is understandably infuriating to those who have rejected it, and may account for the tone of mandarin scorn in which the Postmodern ironist not infrequently addresses his readers.

The new thing becomes the old thing, and the old the new. Now, I can't imagine anything more quaint than a scatological retelling of some nursery tale, or a fiction about a writer writing the fiction you are reading. In recent years the freshest, most powerful stories we've seen in this country are the kind that were supposed to have been rendered obsolete by the preceding avant-garde – stories with plots and characters, stories inextricable from time and place and historical consequence.

Some of the writers I've gathered here have been filed and cross-filed as Minimalists, New Realists, Dirty Realists, even Neo-Realists, a term that makes me think of clenched fists and badly spelled manifestos. The truth is, they are no more alike than the so-called Metafictionists, from whom, it can at least be said, they differ more radically than from each other. But their work is not reactionary; they haven't set out to overturn or oppose another way of writing. In the end they have gone where their own interests, talents and voices have led them, in ways hard to speak of generally.

Many of them write about the difficulties between husbands and wives, fathers and sons, sisters and brothers. So much is true. But you can't go on from that observation, as some have, to say that contemporary fiction is driven by unprecedented anxieties about "the family." Family life has always been great theater, and always will be, like war. If these writers give evidence of having thought about problems of gender, race and class, it's still impossible to speak of them as united by some new political consciousness. Some aim to prescribe, edify, transcend; to come up with answers. For others it's enough to set the problem. You can find work in here that will satisfy Frank O'Connor's famous description of the modern short story as the chronicle of misfits trying to break out of "submerged population groups," but you can find more work that doesn't.

What these writers do have between them is an exuberant, unembarrassed faith in the power of stories to clarify our sense of reality. They do not seem to believe that literature is of necessity self-referential; their narrative art, however complex and sophisticated, tends to efface rather than make an issue of its principles and mechanics. Their gaze typically goes outward.

Chekhov says of one of his characters, "He had a talent for humanity." It is this quality, above all, that puts these writers on common ground – the ability to breathe into their work distinct living presences beyond their own: imagined Others fashioned from words, who somehow take on flesh and blood and moral nature. This is, I believe, miraculous in itself, and miraculous in its consequences. These presences pass through time as if it wasn't there, cross the appalling spaces between us to fill the solitude of the dreaming girl, the nurse on her lunch break, the farmer in his empty fields. They make our expensive choice and suffer our fates before we do, even as we look on. They live and die and yet do not die. We know that Tolstoy's Napoleon isn't "real," is a confection of language, but when we think of him, how do we fill the name except with an essence, a soul? Where does that soul come from? Which, finally, if not more real, is more real to us, the opaque Napoleon of that myth called history or the Napoleon of *War and Peace*?

We writers are too careful not to romanticize our calling. We're afraid of sounding soft-headed and self-indulgent. The idea is to make it seem a job like any other. Well, it isn't. Nobody would do it if it were. Romance is what keeps us going, the old romantic Frankenstein dream of working a miracle, making life where there was none. That's what these writers are after, and if they were after anything less, why should we read them?

Tobias Wolff
*May 1993*

DOROTHY ALLISON

☆ ☆ ☆ ☆

# River of Names

At a picnic at my aunt's farm, the only time the whole family ever gathered, my sister Billie and I chased chickens into the barn. Billie ran right through the open doors and out again, but I stopped, caught by a shadow moving over me. My cousin, Tommy, eight years old as I was, swung in the sunlight with his face as black as his shoes – the rope around his neck pulled up into the sunlit heights of the barn, fascinating, horrible. Wasn't he running ahead of us? Someone came up behind me. Someone began to scream. My mama took my head in her hands and turned my eyes away.

Jesse and I have been lovers for a year now. She tells me stories about her childhood, about her father going off each day to the university, her mother who made all her dresses, her grand-mother who always smelled of dill bread and vanilla. I listen with my mouth open, not believing but wanting, aching for the fairy tale she thinks is everyone's life.

"What did your grandmother smell like?"

I lie to her the way I always do, a lie stolen from a book. "Like lavender," stomach churning over the memory of sour sweat and snuff.

I realize I do not really know what lavender smells like, and I am for a moment afraid she will ask something else, some question that will betray me. But Jesse slides over to hug me, to press her face against my ear, to whisper, "How wonderful to be part of such a large family."

I hug her back and close my eyes. I cannot say a word.

I was born between the older cousins and the younger, born in a pause of babies and therefore outside, always watching. Once, way before Tommy died, I was pushed out on the steps while everyone stood listening to my Cousin Barbara. Her screams went up and down in the back of the house. Cousin Cora brought buckets of bloody rags out to be burned. The other cousins all ran off to catch the sparks or poke the fire with dogwood sticks. I waited on the porch making up words to the shouts around me. I did not understand what was happening. Some of the older cousins obviously did, their strange expressions broken by stranger laughs. I had seen them helping her up the stairs while the thick blood ran down her legs. After a while the blood on the rags was thin, watery, almost pink. Cora threw them on the fire and stood motionless in the stinking smoke.

Randall went by and said there'd be a baby, a hatched egg to throw out with the rags, but there wasn't. I watched to see and there wasn't; nothing but the blood, thinning out desperately while the house slowed down and grew quiet, hours of cries growing soft and low, moaning under the smoke. My Aunt Raylene came out on the porch and almost fell on me, not seeing me, not seeing anything at all. She beat on the post until there were knuckle-sized dents in the peeling paint, beat on that post like it could feel, cursing it and herself and every child in the yard, singing up and down, "Goddamn, goddamn, that girl . . . no sense . . . goddamn!"

I've these pictures my mama gave me – stained sepia prints of bare dirt yards, plank porches, and step after step of children – cousins, uncles, aunts; mysteries. The mystery is how many no one remembers. I show them to Jesse, not saying who they are, and when she laughs at the broken teeth, torn overalls, the dirt, I set my teeth at what I do not want to remember and cannot forget.

We were so many we were without number and, like tadpoles, if there was one less from time to time, who counted? My maternal great-grandmother had eleven daughters, seven sons; my grandmother, six sons, five daughters. Each one made at least six. Some made nine. Six times six, eleven times nine. They went on like multiplication tables. They died and were not missed. I come of an enormous family and I cannot tell half their stories. Somehow it was always made to seem they killed themselves: car wrecks, shotguns, dusty ropes, screaming, falling out of windows, things inside them. I am the point of a pyramid, sliding back under the weight of the ones who came after, and it does not matter that I am the lesbian, the one who will not have children.

I tell the stories and it comes out funny. I drink bourbon and make myself drawl, tell all those old funny stories. Someone always seems to ask me, which one was that? I show the pictures and she says, "Wasn't she the one in the story about the bridge?" I put the pictures away, drink more, and someone always finds them, then says, "Goddamn! How many of you were there anyway?"

I don't answer.

Jesse used to say, "You've got such a fascination with violence. You've got so many terrible stories."

She said it with her smooth mouth, that chin nobody ever slapped, and I love that chin, but when Jesse spoke then, my hands shook and I wanted nothing so much as to tell her terrible stories.

So I made a list. I told her: that one went insane – got her little brother with a tire iron; the three of them slit their arms, not the wrists but the bigger veins up near the elbow; she, now, *she* strangled the boy she was sleeping with and got sent away; that one drank lye and died laughing soundlessly. In one year I lost eight cousins. It was the year everybody ran away. Four disappeared and were never found. One fell in the river and was drowned. One was run down hitchhiking north. One was shot running through the woods, while Grace, the last one, tried to walk from Greenville to Greer for some reason nobody knew. She fell off the overpass a mile down from the Sears, Roebuck warehouse and lay there for hunger and heat and dying.

Later, sleeping, but not sleeping, I found that my hands were up under Jesse's chin. I rolled away, but I didn't cry. I almost never let myself cry.

★

Almost always, we were raped, my cousins and I. That was some kind of joke, too.

*What's a South Carolina virgin?*

*'At's a ten-year-old can run fast.*

It wasn't funny for me in my mama's bed with my stepfather, not for my cousin, Billie, in the attic with my uncle, nor for Lucille in the woods with another cousin, for Danny with four strangers in a parking lot, or for Pammie who made the papers. Cora read it out loud: "Repeatedly by persons unknown." They stayed unknown since Pammie never spoke again. Perforations, lacerations, contusions, and bruises. I heard all the words, big words, little words, words too terrible to understand. *DEAD BY AN ACT OF MAN.* With the prick still in them, the broom handle, the tree branch, the grease gun . . . objects, things not to be believed . . . whiskey bottles, can openers, grass shears, glass, metal, vegetables . . . not to be believed, not to be believed.

Jesse says, "You've got a gift for words."

"Don't talk," I beg her, "don't talk." And this once, she just holds me, blessedly silent.

I dig out the pictures, stare into the faces. Which one was I? Survivors do hate themselves, I know, over the core of fierce self-love, never understanding, always asking, "Why me and not her, not him?" There is such mystery in it, and I have hated myself as much as I have loved others, hated the simple fact of my own survival. Having survived, am I supposed to say something, do something, be something?

I loved my Cousin Butch. He had this big old head, pale thin hair, and enormous, watery eyes. All the cousins did, though Butch's head was the largest, his hair the palest. I was the dark-headed one. All the rest of the family seemed pale carbons of each other in shades of blond, though later on everybody's hair went brown or red and I didn't stand out so. Butch and I stood out then – I because I was so dark and fast, and he because of that big head and the crazy things he did. Butch used to climb on the back of my Uncle Lucius's truck, open the gas tank and hang his head over, breathe deeply, strangle, gag, vomit, and breathe again. It went so deep, it tingled in your toes. I climbed up after him and tried it myself, but I was too young to hang on long, and I fell heavily to the ground, dizzy and giggling. Butch could hang on, put his hand down into the tank and pull up a cupped palm of gas, breathe deep and laugh. He would climb down roughly, swinging down from the door handle, laughing, staggering, and stinking of gasoline. Someone caught him at it. Someone threw a match. "I'll teach you."

Just like that, gone before you understand.

I wake up in the night screaming, "No, no, I won't!" Dirty water rises in the back of my throat, the liquid language of my own terror and rage. "Hold me. Hold me." Jesse rolls over on me; her hands grip my hipbones tightly.

"I love you. I love you. I'm here," she repeats.

I stare up into her dark eyes, puzzled, afraid. I draw a breath in deeply, smile my bland smile. "Did I fool you?" I laugh, rolling away from her. Jesse punches me playfully, and I catch her hand in the air.

"My love," she whispers, and cups her body against my hip, closes her eyes. I bring my hand up in front of my face and watch the knuckles, the nails as they tremble, tremble. I watch for a long time while she sleeps, warm and still against me.

James went blind. One of the uncles got him in the face with home-brewed alcohol.

Lucille climbed out the front window of Aunt Raylene's house and jumped. They said she jumped. No one said why.

My Uncle Matthew used to beat my Aunt Raylene. The twins, Mark and Luke, swore to stop him, pulled him out in the yard one time, throwing him between them like a loose bag of grain. Uncle Matthew screamed like a pig coming up for slaughter. I got both my sisters in the tool shed for safety, but I hung back to watch. Little Bo came running out of the house, off the porch, feet first into his daddy's arms. Uncle Matthew started swinging him like a scythe, going after the bigger boys, Bo's head thudding their shoulders, their hips. Afterward, Bo crawled around in the dirt, the blood running out of his ears and his tongue hanging out of his mouth, while Mark and Luke finally got their daddy down. It was a long time before I realized that they never told anybody else what had happened to Bo.

Randall tried to teach Lucille and me to wrestle. "Put your hands up." His legs were wide apart, his torso bobbing up and down, his head moving constantly. Then his hand flashed at my face. I threw myself back into the dirt, lay still. He turned to Lucille, not noticing that I didn't get up. He punched at her, laughing. She wrapped her hands around her head, curled over so her knees were up against her throat.

"No, no," he yelled. "Move like her." He turned to me. "Move." He kicked at me. I rocked into a ball, froze.

"No, no!" He kicked me. I grunted, didn't move. He turned to Lucille. "You." Her teeth were chattering but she held herself still, wrapped up tighter than bacon slices.

"You move!" he shouted. Lucille just hugged her head tighter and started to sob.

"Son of a bitch," Randall grumbled, "you two will never be any good."

He walked away. Very slowly we stood up, embarrassed, looked at each other. We knew.

If you fight back, they kill you.

My sister was seven. She was screaming. My stepfather picked her up by her left arm, swung her forward and back. It gave. The arm went around loosely. She just kept screaming. I didn't know you could break it like that.

I was running up the hall. He was right behind me. "Mama! Mama!" His left hand – he was left-handed – closed around my throat, pushed me against the wall, and then he lifted me that way. I kicked, but I couldn't reach him. He was yelling, but there was so much noise in my ears I couldn't hear him.

"Please, Daddy. Please, Daddy. I'll do anything, I promise. Daddy, anything you want. Please, Daddy."

I couldn't have said that. I couldn't talk around that fist at my throat, couldn't breathe. I woke up when I hit the floor. I looked up at him.

"If I live long enough, I'll fucking kill you."

He picked me up by my throat again.

*What's wrong with her?*
*Why's she always following you around?*
Nobody really wanted answers.

A full bottle of vodka will kill you when you're nine and the bottle is a quart. It was a third cousin proved that. We learned what that and other things could do. Every year there was something new.

*You're growing up.*
*My big girl.*

There was codeine in the cabinet, paregoric for the baby's teeth, whiskey, beer, and wine in the house. Jeanne brought home MDA, PCP, acid; Randall, grass, speed, and mescaline. It all worked to dull things down, to pass the time.

Stealing was a way to pass the time. Things we needed, things we didn't, for the nerve of it, the anger, the need. *You're growing up*, we told each other. But sooner or later, we all got caught. Then it was, *When are you going to learn?*

Caught, nightmares happened. *Razorback desperate*, was the conclusion of the man down at the county farm where Mark and Luke were sent at fifteen. They both got their heads shaved, their earlobes sliced.

*What's the matter, kid? Can't you take it?*

Caught at sixteen, June was sent to Jessup County Girls' Home where the baby was adopted out and she slashed her wrists on the bedsprings.

Lou got caught at seventeen and held in the station downtown, raped on the floor of the holding tank.

*Are you a boy or are you a girl?*
*On your knees, kid, can you take it?*

Caught at eighteen and sent to prison, Jack came back seven years later blank-faced, understanding nothing. He married a

quiet girl from out of town, had three babies in four years. Then
Jack came home one night from the textile mill, carrying one of
those big handles off the high speed spindle machine. He used it
to beat them all to death and went back to work in the morning.

Cousin Melvina married at fourteen, had three kids in two
and a half years, and welfare took them all away. She ran off
with a carnival mechanic, had three more babies before he left
her for a motorcycle acrobat. Welfare took those, too. But the
next baby was hydrocephalic, a little waterhead they left with
her, and the three that followed, even the one she used to hate so
– the one she had after she fell off the porch and couldn't
remember whose child it was.

"How many children do you have?" I asked her.

"You mean the ones I have, or the ones I had? Four," she
told me, "or eleven."

My aunt, the one I was named for, tried to take off for
Oklahoma. That was after she'd lost the youngest girl and they
told her Bo would never be "right." She packed up biscuits, cold
chicken, and Coca-Cola, a lot of loose clothes, Cora and her new
baby, Cy, and the four youngest girls. They set off from
Greenville in the aftenoon, hoping to make Oklahoma by the
weekend, but they only got as far as Augusta. The bridge there
went out under them.

"An Act of God," my uncle said.

My aunt and Cora crawled out down river, and two of the
girls turned up in the weeds, screaming loud enough to be found
in the dark. But one of the girls never came up out of that dark
water, and Nancy, who had been holding Cy, was found still
wrapped around the baby, in the water, under the car.

"An Act of God," my aunt said. "God's got one damn sick
sense of humor."

My sister had her baby in a bad year. Before he was born we had
talked about it. "Are you afraid?" I asked.

"He'll be fine," she'd replied, not understanding, speaking
instead to the other fear. "Don't we have a tradition of bastards?"

He was fine, a classically ugly healthy little boy with that shock of white hair that marked so many of us. But afterward, it was that bad year with my sister down with pleurisy, then cystitis, and no work, no money, having to move back home with my cold-eyed stepfather. I would come home to see her, from the woman I could not admit I'd been with, and take my infinitely fragile nephew and hold him, rocking him, rocking myself.

One night I came home to screaming – the baby, my sister, no one else there. She was standing by the crib, bent over, screaming red-faced. "Shut up! Shut up!" With each word her fist slammed the mattress fanning the baby's ear.

"Don't!" I grabbed her, pulling her back, doing it as gently as I could so I wouldn't break the stitches from her operation. She had her other arm clamped across her abdomen and couldn't fight me at all. She just kept shrieking.

"That little bastard just screams and screams. That little bastard. I'll kill him."

Then the words seeped in and she looked at me while her son kept crying and kicking his feet. By his head the mattress still showed the impact of her fist.

"Oh no," she moaned, "I wasn't going to be like that. I always promised myself." She started to cry, holding her belly and sobbing. "We an't no different. We an't no different."

Jesse wraps her arm around my stomach, presses her belly into my back. I relax against her. "You sure you can't have children?" she asks. "I sure would like to see what your kids would turn out to be like."

I stiffen, say, "I can't have children. I've never wanted children."

"Still," she says, "you're so good with children, so gentle."

I think of all the times my hands have curled into fists, when I have just barely held on. I open my mouth, close it, can't speak. What could I say now? All the times I have not spoken before, all the things I just could not tell her, the shame, the self-hatred, the fear; all of that hangs between us now – a wall I cannot tear down.

I would like to turn around and talk to her, tell her . . . "I've got a dust river in my head, a river of names endlessly repeating. That dirty water rises in me, all those children screaming out their lives in my memory, and I become someone else, someone I have tried so hard not to be."

But I don't say anything, and I know, as surely as I know I will never have a child, that by not speaking I am condemning us, that I cannot go on loving you and hating you for your fairy-tale life, for not asking about what you have no reason to imagine, for that soft-chinned innocence I love.

Jesse puts her hands behind my neck, smiles and says, "You tell the funniest stories."

I put my hands behind her back, feeling the ridges of my knuckles pulsing.

"Yeah," I tell her. "But I lie."

TONI CADE BAMBARA

☆ ☆ ☆ ☆

# The Hammer Man

I was glad to hear that Manny had fallen off the roof. I had put out the tale that I was down with yellow fever, but nobody paid me no mind, least of all Dirty Red who stomped right in to announce that Manny had fallen off the roof and that I could come out of hiding now. My mother dropped what she was doing, which was the laundry, and got the whole story out of Red. "Bad enough you got to hang around with boys," she said. "But fight with them too. And you would pick the craziest one at that."

Manny was supposed to be crazy. That was his story. To say you were bad put some people off. But to say you were crazy, well, you were officially not to be messed with. So that was his story. On the other hand, after I called him what I called him and said a few choice things about his mother, his face did go through some piercing changes. And I did kind of wonder if maybe he sure was nuts. I didn't wait to find out. I got in the wind. And then he waited for me on my stoop all day and all night, not hardly speaking to the people going in and out. And he was there all Saturday, with his sister bringing him peanut-butter sandwiches and cream sodas. He must've gone to the bathroom right there 'cause every time I looked out the kitchen window, there he was. And Sunday, too. I got to thinking the boy was mad.

"You got no sense of humor, that's your trouble," I told him. He looked up, but he didn't say nothing. All at once I was real sorry about the whole thing. I should've settled for hitting off the little girls in the school yard, or waiting for Frankie to come in so we could raise some kind of hell. This way I had to play sick when my mother was around 'cause my father had already taken away my BB gun and hid it.

I don't know how they got Manny on the roof finally. Maybe the Wakefield kids, the ones who keep the pigeons, called him up. Manny was a sucker for sick animals and things like that. Or maybe Frankie got some nasty girls to go up on the roof with him and got Manny to join him. I don't know. Anyway, the catwalk had lost all its cement and the roof always did kind of slant downward. So Manny fell off the roof. I got over my yellow fever right quick, needless to say, and ventured outside. But by this time I had already told Miss Rose that Crazy Manny was after me. And Miss Rose, being who she was, quite naturally went over to Manny's house and said a few harsh words to his mother, who, being who she was, chased Miss Rose out into the street and they commenced to get with it, snatching bottles out of the garbage cans and breaking them on the johnny pumps and stuff like that.

Dirty Red didn't have to tell us about this. Everybody could see and hear all. I never figured the garbage cans for an arsenal, but Miss Rose came up with sticks and table legs and things, and Manny's mother had her share of scissor blades and bicycle chains. They got to rolling in the streets and all you could see was pink drawers and fat legs. It was something else. Miss Rose is nutty but Manny's mother's crazier than Manny. They were at it a couple of times during my sick spell. Everyone would congregate on the window sills or the fire escape, commenting that it was still much too cold for this kind of nonsense. But they watched anyway. And then Manny fell off the roof. And that was that. Miss Rose went back to her dream books and Manny's mother went back to her tumbled-down kitchen of dirty clothes and bundles and bundles of rags and children.

My father got in on it too, 'cause he happened to ask Manny one night why he was sitting on the stoop like that every night. Manny told him right off that he was going to kill me first chance he got. Quite naturally this made my father a little warm, me being his only daughter and planning to become a doctor and take care of him in his old age. So he had a few words with Manny first, and then he got hold of the older brother, Bernard, who was more his size. Bernard didn't see how any of it was his business or my father's business, so my father got mad and jammed Bernard's head into the mailbox. Then my father started getting messages from Bernard's uncle about where to meet him for a showdown and all. My father didn't say a word to my mother all this time; just sat around mumbling and picking up the phone and putting it down, or grabbing my stickball bat and putting it back. He carried on like this for days till I thought I would scream if the yellow fever didn't have me so weak. And then Manny fell off the roof, and my father went back to his beer-drinking buddies.

I was in the school yard, pitching pennies with the little boys from the elementary school, when my friend Violet hits my brand-new Spaudeen over the wall. She came running back to tell me that Manny was coming down the block. I peeked beyond the fence and there he was all right. He had his head all wound up like a mummy and his arm in a sling and his leg in a cast. It looked phoney to me, especially that walking cane. I figured Dirty Red had told me a tale just to get me out there so Manny could stomp me, and Manny was playing it up with costume and all till he could get me.

"What happened to him?" Violet's sisters whispered. But I was too busy trying to figure out how this act was supposed to work. Then Manny passed real close to the fence and gave me a look.

"You had enough, Hammer Head," I yelled. "Just bring your crummy self in this yard and I'll pick up where I left off." Violet was knocked out and the other kids went into a huddle. I didn't have to say anything else. And when they all pressed me later, I just said, "You know that hammer he always carries in his fatigues?" And they'd all nod waiting for the rest of a long story. "Well, I took it away from him." And I walked off nonchalantly.

Manny stayed indoors for a long time. I almost forgot about him. New kids moved into the block and I got all caught up with that. And then Miss Rose finally hit the numbers and started ordering a whole lot of stuff through the mail and we would sit on the curb and watch these weird-looking packages being carried in, trying to figure out what simple-minded thing she had thrown her money away on when she might just as well wait for the warm weather and throw a block party for all her godchildren.

After a while a center opened up and my mother said she'd increase my allowance if I went and joined because I'd have to get out of my pants and stay in skirts, on account of that's the way things were at the center. So I joined and got to thinking about everything else but old Hammer Head. It was a rough place to get along in, the center, but my mother said that I needed to be be'd with and she needed not to be with me, so I went. And that time I sneaked into the office, that's when I really got turned on. I looked into one of those not-quite-white folders and saw that I was from a deviant family in a deviant neighborhood. I showed my mother the word in the dictionary, but she didn't pay me no mind. It was my favorite word after that. I ran it in the ground till one day my father got the strap just to show how deviant he could get. So I gave up trying to improve my vocabulary. And I almost gave up my dungarees.

Then one night I'm walking past the Douglas Street Park 'cause I got thrown out of the center for playing pool when I should've been sewing, even though I had already decided that this was going to be my last fling with boy things, and starting tomorrow I was going to fix my hair right and wear skirts all the time just so my mother would stop talking about her gray hairs, and Miss Rose would stop calling me by my brother's name by mistake. So I'm walking past the park and there's ole Manny on the basketball court, perfecting his lay-ups and talking with himself. Being me, I quite naturally walk right up and ask what the hell he's doing playing in the dark, and he looks up and all around like the dark had crept up on him when he wasn't looking. So I knew right away that he'd been out there for a long time with his eyes just going along with the program.

"There was two seconds to go and we were one point behind," he said, shaking his head and staring at his sneakers like they was somebody. "And I was in the clear. I'd left the men in the backcourt and there I was, smiling, you dig, 'cause it was in the bag. They passed the ball and I slid the ball up nice and easy 'cause there was nothing to worry about. And . . ." He shook his head. "I muffed the goddamn shot. Ball bounced off the

rim . . ." He stared at his hands. "The game of the season. Last
game." And then he ignored me altogether, though he wasn't
talking to me in the first place. He went back to the lay-ups,
always from the same spot with his arms crooked in the same
way, over and over. I must've gotten hypnotized 'cause I
probably stood there for at least an hour watching like a fool till
I couldn't even see the damn ball, much less the basket. But I
stood there anyway for no reason I know of. He never missed.
But he cursed himself away. It was torture. And then a squad car
pulled up and a short cop with hair like one of the Marx Brothers
came out hitching up his pants. He looked real hard at me and
then at Manny.

"What are you two doing?"

"He's doing a lay-up. I'm watching," I said with my smart
self.

Then the cop just stood there and finally turned to the other
one who was just getting out of the car.

"Who unlocked the gate?" the big one said.

"It's always unlocked," I said. Then we three just stood there
like a bunch of penguins watching Manny go at it.

"This on the level?" the big guy asked, tilting his hat back
with the thumb the way big guys do in hot weather. "Hey you,"
he said, walking over to Manny. "I'm talking to you." He finally
grabbed the ball to get Manny's attention. But that didn't work.
Manny just stood there with his arms out waiting for the pass so
he could save the game. He wasn't paying no mind to the cop.
So, quite naturally, when the cop slapped him upside his head it
was a surprise. And when the cop started counting three to go,
Manny had already recovered from the slap and was just ticking
off the seconds before the buzzer sounded and all was lost.

"Gimme the ball, man." Manny's face was all tightened up
and ready to pop.

"Did you hear what I said, black boy?"

Now, when somebody says that word like that, I gets warm.
And crazy or no crazy, Manny was my brother at that moment
and the cop was the enemy.

"You better give him back his ball," I said. "Manny don't
take no mess from no cops. He ain't bothering nobody. He's

gonna be Mister Basketball when he grows up. Just trying to get
a little practice in before the softball season starts."

"Look here, sister, we'll run you in too," Harpo said.

"I damn sure can't be your sister seeing how I'm a black girl.
Boy, I sure will be glad when you run me in so I can tell
everybody about that. You must think you're in the South,
mister."

The big guy screwed his mouth up and let one of them hard-
day sighs. "The park's closed, little girl, so why don't you and
your boyfriend go on home."

That really got me. The "little girl" was bad enough but that
"boyfriend" was too much. But I kept cool, mostly because
Manny looked so pitiful waiting there with his hands in a time-
out and there being no one to stop the clock. But I kept my cool
mostly 'cause of that hammer in Manny's pocket and no telling
how frantic things can get what with a big-mouth like me, a
couple of wise cops, and a crazy boy too.

"The gates are open," I said real quiet-like, "and this here's a
free country. So why don't you give him back his ball?"

The big cop did another one of those sighs, his specialty I
guess, and then he bounced the ball to Manny who went right
into his gliding thing clear up to the backboard, damn near like
he was some kind of very beautiful bird. And then he swooshed
that ball in, even if there was no net, and you couldn't really hear
the swoosh. Something happened to the bones in my chest. It
was something.

"Crazy kids anyhow," the one with the wig said and turned
to go. But the big guy watched Manny for a while and I guess
something must've snapped in his head, 'cause all of a sudden he
was hot for taking Manny to jail or court or somewhere and
started yelling at him and everything, which is a bad thing to do
to Manny, I can tell you. And I'm standing there thinking that
none of my teachers, from kindergarten right on up, none of
them knew what they were talking about. I'll be damned if I ever
knew one of them rosy-cheeked cops that smiled and helped you
get to school without neither you or your little raggedy dog
getting hit by a truck that had a smile on its face, too. Not that I
ever believed it. I knew Dick and Jane was full of crap from the

get-go, especially them cops. Like this dude, for example, pulling on Manny's clothes like that when obviously he had just done about the most beautiful thing a man can do and not be a fag. No cop could swoosh without a net.

"Look out, man," was all Manny said, but it was the way he pushed the cop that started the real yelling and threats. And I thought to myself, Oh God here I am trying to change my ways, and not talk back in school, and do like my mother wants, but just have this last fling, and now this – getting shot in the stomach and bleeding to death in Douglas Street Park and poor Manny getting pistol-whipped by those bastards and whatnot. I could see it all, practically crying too. And it just wasn't no kind of thing to happen to a small child like me with my confirmation picture in the paper next to my weeping parents and schoolmates. I could feel the blood sticking to my shirt and my eyeballs slipping away, and then that confirmation picture again; and my mother and her gray hair; and Miss Rose heading for the precinct with a shotgun; and my father getting old and feeble with no one to doctor him up and all.

And I wished Manny had fallen off the damn roof and died right then and there and saved me all this aggravation of being killed with him by these cops who surely didn't come out of no fifth-grade reader. But it didn't happen. They just took the ball and Manny followed them real quiet-like right out of the park into the dark, then into the squad car with his head drooping and his arms in a crook. And I went on home 'cause what the hell am I going to do on a basketball court, and it getting to be nearly midnight?

I didn't see Manny no more after he got into that squad car. But they didn't kill him after all 'cause Miss Rose heard he was in some kind of big house for people who lose their marbles. And then it was spring finally, and me and Violet was in this very boss fashion show at the center. And Miss Rose bought me my first corsage – yellow roses to match my shoes.

# RICHARD BAUSCH

☆ ☆ ☆ ☆

# *All the Way in Flagstaff, Arizona*

Sitting in the shaded cool quiet of St. Paul's Church in Flagstaff, Walter remembers a family picnic. This memory is two years old, but nothing ever fades from it. It takes place in a small park called Hathaway Forest, on Long Island, one Sunday afternoon in early summer. He and his wife, Irene, spread blankets on the grass next to a picnic table and a brick barbecue pit; it is a warm, clear-blue day, with a breeze. Irene has insisted that they all go, as a family, and so soccer games, trips to the movies and to the houses of friends, have been put aside. Because Walter is hung over, he tries to beg off, but she will not hear of it; she will not cater to his hangovers anymore, she tells him. So they all go. He and Irene sit quietly on the blankets as, in the grass field before them, the children run – William, the oldest, hanging back a little, making a sacrifice of pretending to have a good time: he is planning for the priesthood these days, wants to be Gregory Peck in *The Keys of the Kingdom*. He saw the movie on television a year ago and now his room is full of books on China, on the lives of the saints, the missionaries, the martyrs. Every morning he goes to Mass and Communion. Walter feels embarrassed in his company, especially when William shows this saintly, willing face to the world.

"I wonder if it would help William to discover masturbation," Walter says. "He's at that age, isn't he? Don't boys start at fourteen? When did I start? I guess I should remember."

"I forgot the baked beans," Irene says. "I left them sitting in the middle of the kitchen counter." She has this way of not hearing him when she wants to avoid a subject; she will not talk about William. "You want some lemonade?"

"No, thanks." He makes a face; she smiles. He can always make her laugh.

The children form a ring, and begin to move in a circle. Susan, the second child, orchestrates this, calling in a kind of singing cadence as they contract and expand the ring by raising and lowering their arms. They are playing well together, co-operating; even William seems to have forgotten about heaven and hell for the moment, moving a little too fast for the youngest, the baby, Carol, to keep up with him. There is something mischievous about the way he causes the girl to falter and lose her hold on him.

"You should light the charcoal, honey," Irene says.

"Certainly," he says. He is anxious to please. He knows she will again have to ask her father for money, and she will again use the word *borrow*. There is always the hope that something will change. He stands over the brick barbecue pit and pours charcoal, while she pours more lemonade, not bothering to ask him this time if he wants any. In the car, in the space under the spare tire, hidden by a half-used roll of paper towels, is a fifth of Jim Beam. He thinks of it with something bordering on erotic anticipation, though his head feels as if it were webbed with burning wires. As he sprinkles lighter fluid on the coals, he begins to plan how he will get to the bottle without the others knowing he has done so.

"Dad."

It is William, standing a little apart from Susan and the younger children. He holds up a Nerf football, wanting to pass it.

Walter smiles. "I'm cooking. I'm the chef of the day."

William wants to get a game up, boys against the girls; he wants Irene to play. She refuses, cheerfully, and so does Susan, and the younger boys begin a desultory game of keep away from Carol, who begins to take it seriously, crying and demanding that she be given a chance to throw and catch the ball. William and Susan walk off toward the far edge of the woods, talking, William pausing now and then to pick up and throw a stone or a piece of wood. Irene sits reading a magazine, with a pad and pencil on her lap. She likes to write down the recipes she finds, and keeps the pad for this purpose. In fact, she doesn't read these magazines as much as she ransacks them, looking for things to save. She's a frugal woman; she's had to be. She controls the money now, what there is of it. Since the last hitch in the Army, Walter has worked seven different jobs; now, at forty-six, he's night clerk in a 7-Eleven store.

"That's enough," Irene calls to the two younger boys, Brad and James, who have tormented Carol to the point of a tantrum. Carol is lying on her stomach, beating her fists into the grass, while they toss the ball above her head, keeping it just out of reach. "Brad! Bra-a-a-a-d! James!"

The two boys stop, finally, walk away scuffing the ground. In a moment they are running across the field, and Carol has come crying to her mother. Because she is the youngest and the smallest, she has learned to be feisty and short-tempered; she seems somehow always dogged, face into the wind, dauntless. "Don't pay any attention to them," Irene is saying.

Walter lights the fire, stands watching it.

"You go on, now, and play," Irene says, and Carol whines that she doesn't want to, she wants to stay here. "No – now, go on. Go have fun. I don't want you hanging back all afternoon. Go on – go."

Carol wanders over to a little play area near the car; it is, in fact, too near: it will be hard for Walter to get anything out of the trunk if she stays where she is, riding a sea dragon on a corkscrew-like metal spring.

"I don't like her being over there by herself," Walter says.

"She's fine," says Irene. "Let her alone."

He sits down, rubs his hands; he wants a drink.

"You want to put the hot dogs on sticks?" Irene asks.

"That tire's low," he says.

"No, it's not."

"It is – look. Look at it. It's low. I better change it."

"You're in no shape to change a tire."

He gets up. "I think it's low."

"Walter."

"I'm just going to look at it."

"Hi, Daddy," Carol says as he approaches.

"Go see your mother."

"I'm riding the dragon."

"Your mother wants you."

"I don't wanna."

"Come on," he says, "I have to look at this tire." He lifts her from the dragon, puts her down on her feet, or tries to: she raises her legs, so that he comes close to falling forward; he lifts again, tries again to set her down, and it's as if they dance. "Stop it," he says, "stand up." She laughs, and he sets her suddenly, with a bump, down on her rear end. "Now you can sit there," he says. She begins to cry. He walks over to the car and stands gazing at the right rear tire, which is not low enough. Even so, he opens the trunk, glances back at Irene, who is lying on the blanket like a sunbather now, her arms straight at her sides, her eyes closed. Carol still whines and cries, sitting in the dust in the foreground.

"Go on," Walter says, "you're not hurt."

"Carol," Irene calls without moving, "come here."

Walter is already reaching into the little well beneath the spare. The Beam is wrapped in a paper bag, and carefully he removes it, leaning into the hot space. In almost the same motion, he has broken the seal on the bottle and held the lip of it to his mouth, swallowing. He caps it, peers out at Irene and Carol, who are frozen for him in a sort of tableau: Carol beginning to move toward her mother, and Irene lying face up to the sun. He leans in, takes another swallow, caps the bottle again and sets it down, rattles the jack, stands back slowly and puts his hands on his hips.

"Walter."

"It's okay," he calls. "I guess it'll have to do – the spare's no better." He looks at Irene, sees that Carol has reached her, that she is involved with Carol, who wants her to fix and bow her hair. So he leans into the trunk again, swallows more of the whiskey. Then he recaps the bottle one more time, puts it back in its place, retrieves it almost immediately, and takes still another swallow. He closes the trunk hard, walks steadily across to the blanket, where Irene and Carol are busy trying to get Carol's hair braided and bowed. He sits down, looks at the flames licking low along the whitening coals. When Carol asks him to look at how pretty her hair is, he tells her she is the most beautiful little girl he ever saw. He reaches for her, pulls her to him, and hugs her. "You are my sweet sweet sweet sweet thing," he says, "you are my sweetie-pie. My little baby love darling boost-a-booter."

"I love you, Daddy."

She removes herself from him, dances, for his benefit, in a circle around the blanket. Then she runs off to meet William and Susan, who are coming across the crest of the field.

"It could be like this all the time," Irene says.

He says, "Yeah." He gets up, stands over the fire. "The coals are almost ready."

"What's the mat—" she begins.

He has swayed only slightly; he pretends to have simply lost his balance on an unevenness in the ground, looks at his feet, lifts one leg, puts it down. It is a beautiful blurred world, and he believes he can do anything.

"It's brave of you to come out today," she says.

"I wanted to."

"You know, Walter, I am going to leave you."

"Right now?"

She ignores this. "I don't want to. I love you. But I really am. You don't believe me, Walter, because you've never believed me. But this time you're wrong. In a while, very soon, I'm going to take the children and go."

"But don't you see?" he says. "I'm going to quit. I'm never touching the stuff again."

"No," she says.

"Come on, kid," he says.

"Let me tell you, dear, what you were thinking all the way here, and what you finally got your hands on a few minutes ago. You were thinking all the time, weren't you, about the bottle of booze you had stashed in the trunk of the car."

"What bottle of booze?"

"I believe it was Jim Beam?" She looks at him.

He wonders if she can see the color changing in his face and neck, the blood rushing there. "Jim Beam," he says. "Jim Beam."

"It won't work, Walter."

"You think that's it? You think I've been – you think that's what I've been doing, huh." He is nodding, looking away from her, trying to control his voice. "You think – on a beautiful day like this, when I'm with my family – some – a bottle of booze in the trunk — "

"Forget it," she says.

"I didn't know – I didn't even know if there was a bottle of booze in the goddamn spare-tire well."

"Please," she says.

"You think I've been thinking about a goddamn bottle of booze in the trunk of the car."

"All right, then."

"That's what you think of me. I mean – we've come that far – that you'd think I could be standing here on this nice day thinking about sneaking drinks like there's some – like there's a problem or something — "

"Walter," she says.

"I mean like it wasn't just – you know, a drink in the afternoon or something — "

"Don't say any more," she tells him.

"Just something I found and – you think I haven't been sick at heart for what I've done, Irene." He has never meant anything more. "I didn't even think anything about it, honey – you think I'd do anything to hurt you or the kids – something – some bottle or something that's supposed to be hidden or something. Like I planned it or something. I swear I just remembered it was there – I didn't – didn't want to worry you, Irene – Irene — "

"The sad thing," Irene says, "is that I could've stopped you today – just now. I knew what you were doing – after all, Walter, you've become a bit sloppy in your various deceptions and ruses. They've become pretty transparent. I could've stopped you, only I just – I just didn't have the energy."

"I don't know what you're talking about," he says. He looks at his children, all of them coming now from the crest; they seem somehow not together, though they come in a group, no more than five feet apart.

"I wish I could feel anything but this exhaustion," Irene says.

"It's not anything like I'm drunk or anything," Walter says. "I just need to get calmed down, honey."

"No," she says.

"You know me, Irene. I always – haven't I always come through?"

She looks at him. "I think – now – that you think you have."

"I just need a little time," he says.

"Walter."

"That's all, honey. Just let me get straight a little." He doesn't want to talk anymore. He drops down at her side. "I'm nervous, kid. I get real bad nervous – and – and I'm not going to drink anymore. I'm simply – absolutely done with it. Forever, Renie. Okay? I'm going to pull it together this time." As he gazes out at the field, at his children returning, he is full of resolve, and courage. Irene sighs, pats his shoulder, and then takes his hand into her own. "Poor Walter," she says, "so sick."

"I'll be all right," he says. "I just need to be calm."

The children are there now, and the picnic is made ready: William puts hot dogs on the grill, and Susan dishes out potato salad, Jell-O, bread, pickles. There is a lot of vying for attention, a lot of energy and noise. It all rises around Walter and his wife, who do not look at each other.

Anyone walking into St. Paul's at this hour will see a man sitting in the last pew, hands folded neatly in his lap. He sits very straight, with dignity, though his clothes are soiled and disheveled. In his mind are the voices of two years ago, the quality of light on that day, and how the breezes blew, fragrant and warm. He can hear the voices.

"Oh," William says, shortly before they start to eat. "We forgot to say grace."

"It's too late now," Susan says.

"It's not too late. It can't ever be too late."

"It's too late."

"It's not too late – that's just silly, Susan."

"Daddy, isn't it too late?"

"It's not too late," Irene says. "William, go ahead."

"Bless us, O Lord, and these Thy gifts which we are about to receive from Thy bounty, through Christ our Lord, amen."

"I still say it was too late," Susan says.

Irene says, "Susan."

"I've decided I'm going to be a nun," Susan says.

"Susan – that's nothing to joke about."

"It's not a joke. I'm going to be a nun and wear inky black clothes and have my hair cut off at the roots and sit in church with my hands open in my lap and sing off tune like Sister Marie does."

"That's a sacrilege," William says.

"What's a sacrilege?" Brad asks.

"It's when you talk like Susan," says William.

"A sacrilege," says Susan, "is when you take Holy Communion with a mortal sin on your soul."

"And when you say you're going to be a nun when you're not," William says.

"Come on now, kids," Walter says, "let's get off each other a little. Let's talk about something nice."

"I know," says Brad, "let's talk about Pac-Man."

"Who wants to talk about *that*," says Carol.

"All I said was I was going to be a nun," Susan says, "and everybody gets crazy. Mostly Saint William. You should've heard Saint William a little while ago, planning his martrydom in China – shot by the Commies. Right, William?"

"That's enough," Walter says. "Let him alone. Let's everybody let everybody else alone. Jesus."

"Have mercy on us," William mutters.

"Oh, look," Walter says, "don't do that. Don't pray when I talk."

Irene says, "Let's just eat quietly, all right?"

"Well, he keeps praying around me. Jesus, I *hate* that."

"Have mercy on us," says William.

"When're you leaving us for China, son?"

"You don't have to make fun of me."

"Okay, look – let's all start over. Jesus." Walter spins around, to catch William moving his lips. "Jesus Jesus Jesus Jesus Jesus," he says.

William crosses himself.

"Amazing. The kid's amazing."

"Let's all please just stop it and eat. Can we please just do that?"

Susan says, "I've changed my mind about being a nun. I'm going to be a priest."

"Oh," William says, "that *is* a sacrilege."

"William," says Walter, "will you please pronounce the excommunications so we can all go to hell in peace?"

"I don't even like this family," the boy mutters.

"Perhaps you should've asked your Father in heaven to have chosen another family for you to be raised in on your trek to the cross."

"Have mercy."

"I don't believe I used any profanity that last time."

"Have mercy on us," William mutters.

"All right!" Irene shouts. "We're going to eat and stop all this arguing and bickering. Please, Walter."

"You might address your displeasure to the Christ, here. Or is it the Vicar of Christ?"

"Have mercy on us."

"I'll be the first lady priest in the Catholic Church," Susan says, "and then I'll get married."

Walter says, "Don't pay any attention to her, William. Think of her as a cross to bear."

"Walter," Irene says.

He stands. "Okay. Truce. No more teasing and no more bickering. We are a family, right? We have to stick together and tolerate each other sometimes."

They are looking at him. He touches his own face, where his mouth, his lips are numb. His eyes feel swollen.

"And then," Susan says, "after I'm married, I'll become Pope."

Walter bursts into laughter as William turns to Susan and says, "You are committing a mortal sin."

"Susan!" Irene says.

Walter says, "Judge not, lest ye be judged, William, my boy."

"I know what a mortal sin is," Brad says.

"Everybody knows that," says James.

"Look for the mote, William. When you see the gleam, look for the mote," Walter is saying.

William mutters, "I don't even know what that means."

"Walter, sit down," Irene says. "Let him alone. All of you let him alone."

"Let's all leave each other alone, that's right," Walter says. He sits down. They eat quietly for a while, and he watches them. Irene wipes mustard from Carol's mouth, from the front of her dress. William's eyes are glazed, and he eats furiously, not looking at anyone. He has been caught out in his pride, Walter thinks, has been shown to himself as less perfect than the glorious dream of a movie he wants to live. It dawns on Walter that his son probably prays for him, since he does not go to church. He wonders, now, what they all think of that, of the fact that he is, by every tenet of their religion, bound for hell. This makes him laugh.

"What?" Irene says. "Tell me."

"Nothing. I was —" He thinks for a moment. "I was thinking about this one," pointing to Susan, "planning to be a married lady priest."

Susan beams under his gaze.

And then he looks at William, feels sorry. "It's okay, William," he says, "it's all in fun."

The boy continues to eat.

"William."

Irene touches Walter's wrist.

"No," Walter says, "the kid can accept somebody's – a gesture – can't he? My God."

William crosses himself again.

Walter stands. "That's the last time."

"Father Boyer, at church," William says almost defiantly, "he told us to do it whenever someone used the Lord's name —"

Walter interrupts him. "I don't care what Father Boyer said. I'm bigger than Father Boyer. I can beat the *shit* out of Father Boyer."

"Not another word from anyone!" Irene shouts.

For a moment no one says anything.

"Well," Walter says, "aren't we a happy bunch?"

James says, "What do you expect?"

"Why don't you explain that one, James?"

The boy shrugs. He is always saying these mysteriously adult things that seem to refer slyly to other things, and then shrugging them off as if he is too tired to bother explaining them. Last year, at the age of eight, he announced to Irene that he did not believe in God. It was a crisis; Irene feared that something serious was wrong. James has since revised himself: he will grant the existence. Those are the words he used. Walter looks upon him with more than a little trepidation, because James is the one who most resembles him. More even than William, who, now, with his heart in the lap of God, is hard to place. Even Irene, for all her devoutness, finds William irritating at times.

"I am going to be a priest," Susan says now. "All I have to do is get them to change the rules."

"You," says Walter, "are the saint of persistence. You know what a wolverine is?"

"Some kind of wolf?"

"The wolverine kills its prey by sheer persistence. I mean, if it decided it wanted you for dinner, you could take a plane to Seattle, the wolverine would meet you at the airport, bib on, knife and fork ready, licking his chops. Salt and pepper by the plate, oregano, parsley, a beer . . ."

Susan laughs.

"Daddy's funny," Carol says.

"When I'm the first lady priest and married Pope, I'll buy a wolverine and keep it as a pet," Susan says.

"Have mercy on us," says William.

"All right," Walter says, "let's drop it, please, William. No more prayers, please. We're all right. God will forgive us, I'm sure, if we all just shut the fuck up for a while."

"Walter!"

"I'm sorry, I'm sorry," he says.

They are quiet, then, for a long time. The youngest ones, Brad and James and Carol, look at him with something like amazement. He makes two more trips to the trunk of the car, not even hiding it now, and in the end he gets Carol and James to laugh at him by making faces, miming someone sliding off a bench, pretending to be terrified of his food. Susan and William laugh too, now, as he does a man unable to get a hot dog into his mouth.

"You clown," Irene says, but she smiles.

They all laugh and talk now; the afternoon wanes that way: Walter tosses the football with William, and Brad and James chase a Frisbee with Susan and Carol. Irene sits on the picnic table, sipping her lemonade. It grows cooler, and others come to the field, and finally it's time to leave. They all work together, gathering the debris of the afternoon, and Walter packs the trunk. He's bold enough to take the bottle of Beam out of its place and drink from it – small sips, he tells Irene, offering her some. She refuses as she has always refused, but she does so with, he is sure, a smile. It strikes him that there is nothing to worry about, not a thing in the world, and he clowns with his children, makes them laugh, all the way home, Irene driving. He calls to people out the window of the car, funny things, and they are all almost hysterical with laughter. They arrive; there is the slow unwinding, getting out of the car and stretching legs and arms, and Walter begins to wrestle with Carol, bending over her, tickling her upper legs, swinging her through his own as she wriggles and laughs. Brad jumps on his back, then, and he pretends to be pulled down, rolls in the grass with the boy, and then chases him, bent over, arms dangling, like an ape's. He is hearing the delightful keening sound of his children's laughter in the shadows. It is getting dark. He chases Brad and James around to the backyard, and they are hiding there, just beyond the square lighter shape of Irene's garden. He crouches in the shadow of the house and makes an ape sound, *whooo-hooo, whooo-hooo hah-hah-hah-hah*. He can hear them talking low and he thinks, Why this is easy, this is fun. Carefully he works his way closer, seeing William and Susan running along the back fence, their silhouettes in the dusky light. *Whoo-hoo, whoo-hoo.* And now he makes his run at them, changes direction, follows Brad, while the others scatter. When he catches Brad, he carries him under his arm, kicking and struggling, to the house, the screened-in back porch, where the others have gathered and are huddling, laughing in the

dark. He comes tumbling up onto the porch and he has them,
they are trapped with him. He puts Brad down in the mass of
struggling arms and legs; he engulfs them, kneeling; he has them
all in the wide embrace of his arms; he's tickling a leg here,
pinching or squeezing an arm there, roaring, gorilla-like. He
catches one of them trying to get away, then turns and grabs
another. He's got them all again, and they are yelling and
laughing, there is light on them now, a swath of yellow light,
and he looks up to see Irene's shape in the doorway, everything
speeding up again, until there is a long shout, a scream.

And he stops. He stands, sees that they are cringing against
the base of the porch wall, to the left of the door, cringing there
and shaking, their eyes enormous, filled with tears.

"Kids?" he says.

They are sobbing, and he steps back, nearly tumbles backward out the screen door and down the stairs. "Kids?" he says.

Nobody moves.

"H–hey. Kids?"

Irene steps down, bends to help William rise. They all get up
slowly, looking at him with the tremendous wariness of animals
at bay.

"H–hey – it's me," he says, holding out one hand. "Kids?"

"Come on," Irene is saying, "don't be silly. Your daddy
would never hurt you." She makes each of them kiss him, then
ushers them inside. "Susan, will you start the bathwater?" The
door closes on them. Walter looks at his hands and says, "God.
Oh my God." He doesn't really hear himself. And in a moment
Irene opens the door and steps out lightly, closing it behind her.
All around, now, the insects are starting up. Irene's voice begins
softly: "We've been through so much, Walter, so much together
– and I simply can't do it anymore. I don't know what to say or
do anymore. I love you, but I can't make it be enough anymore."
She kisses him on the side of the face, turns, and is gone.

Yet it takes more than a year for her finally to leave him. She
gives him every chance. She waits for him to put it together as
he keeps saying he will. He tries for a while, in fact: he goes to a
doctor, a psychologist specializing in family counseling, who

tells him he has not broken with his father, and instructs him to find some ritual way of making the break. So he goes back to Alabama to stand over his father's grave. At first, nothing happens. He feels anger, but it is only what he expected to feel. And then there is a kind of sorrow, almost sweet, welling up in him. It makes him wince, actually take a step back from the grave as if something had moved there. When he was seven years old his father took him outside of the house in Montgomery and made him urinate on his mother's roses. He tells himself, standing over the grave in Montgomery, that children have been through worse; indeed, he himself has. Yet it takes all the moisture from his mouth, remembering it. Perhaps it is the fact that it was done to him not for himself but to get at his mother – there is something so terrifying about being used that way, merely as an instrument of wounding. In any case, it has haunted him, and now at the gravesite he spits, he rages, he tears the grass. It all seems simply ordained. It is a role he plays, watching himself play it. It exorcizes nothing.

He returns from Alabama with a sense of doom riding him like a spirit, a weight on his neck, the back of his shoulders. He visits the psychologist, who seems slightly alarmed at the effect of the journey on him. He is determined, vibrant with will, and hopelessly afraid. The psychologist wants to know what his exact thought was the first time he ever picked up a drink. Walter can't remember that. His father never drank. He believes he wanted at first to show his freedom, like other boys. He says finally he wanted it to relax and be kind, to relieve some of the tensions that build in him. And so the psychologist begins to try to explore, with him, those tensions. They are many, but they all have the same root, and there is no use talking about childhood trauma and dreams: Walter is versed in the canon; his hopes are for something else. He can tell the psychologist the whole thing in a single sentence: he has always been paralyzed by the fear that he will repeat, with his own children, the pattern of his father's brutality. What he wants is for the psychologist to guarantee him that this won't happen, tell him categorically that there will be no such repetition, and of course this can't be done. Life must be lived in the uncertainty of freedom of choice, the psychologist says. The problem is that Walter is afraid to take responsibility for himself. It is all talk, and it is all true. Walter's father had a thing he liked to call "night dances," in which, for the benefit of Walter, for his correction and edification, Walter's father became a sort of dark gibbet that Walter danced beneath, held by the wrist within the small circumference, the range, of a singing swung belt whose large buckle was embossed with the head of a longhorn steer. This all took place in the basement of the house in Montgomery, before Walter was ten years old. There was no light at all in the basement, and so it was necessary for the boy to dodge blindly, and to keep from crying too loudly, so he could hear the *whoosh-whoosh* of the belt. Walter trembles to think of that. He tells the psychologist how his father would swing the belt calmly, without passion, like a machine, quiet in the dark. He shakes, telling it. He talks about the ancient story: the man who, in the act of trying to avoid some evil in himself, embraces it, creates it.

The visits end. He is dry for about two weeks, but falters, and Irene finally does leave him.

This is what has happened to him. He is in Flagstaff, Arizona. He sits gazing at the small stained-glass windows on either side of the church, where in a few minutes he will probably be talking to a priest. God, he thinks, Flagstaff, Arizona. There is no reason for it. Perhaps he will go somewhere else, too. There is no telling where he might wind up. Irene and the children are all the way in Atlanta, Georgia, with Irene's parents. He has not had anything to drink today, and his hands shake, so he looks at them. He wonders if he should wait to talk to a priest, if he should tell a priest anything, or just ask for some food, maybe. He wonders if maybe he shouldn't tell the priest about the day of the picnic that he has been remembering so vividly, when Irene came out on the porch and told him she couldn't make it be enough anymore. He wonders if he should talk about it: how he walked out to the very edge of the lawn and turned to look upon the lighted windows of the house, thinking of the people inside, whom he had named and loved and called sons, daughters, wife. How he had stood there trembling, shaking as from a terrific chill, while the dark, the night, came.

# ANN BEATTIE

☆ ☆ ☆ ☆

# *A Vintage Thunderbird*

Nick and Karen had driven from Virginia to New York in a little under six hours. They had made good time, keeping ahead of the rain all the way, and it was only now, while they were in the restaurant, that the rain began. It had been a nice summer weekend in the country with their friends Stephanie and Sammy, but all the time he was there Nick had worried that Karen had consented to go with him only out of pity; she had been dating another man, and when Nick suggested the weekend she had been reluctant. When she said she would go, he decided that she had given in for old times' sake.

The car they drove was hers – a white Thunderbird convertible. Every time he drove the car, he admired it more. She owned many things that he admired: a squirrel coat with a black taffeta lining, a pair of carved soapstone bookends that held some books of poetry on her night table, her collection of Louis Armstrong 78s. He loved to go to her apartment and look at her things. He was excited by them, the way he had been spellbound, as a child, exploring the playrooms of schoolmates.

He had met Karen several years before, soon after he came to New York. Her brother had lived in the same building he lived in then, and the three of them met on the volleyball courts adjacent to the building. Her brother moved across town within a few months, but by then Nick knew Karen's telephone number. At her suggestion, they had started running in Central Park on Sundays. It was something he looked forward to all week. When they left the park, his elation was always mixed with a little embarrassment over his panting and his being sweaty on the street, but she had no self-consciousness. She didn't care if her shirt stuck to her body, or if she looked unattractive with her wet, matted hair. Or perhaps she knew that she never looked

really unattractive; men always looked at her. One time, on
Forty-second Street, during a light rain, Nick stopped to read a
movie marquee, and when he turned back to Karen she was
laughing and protesting that she couldn't take the umbrella that
a man was offering her. It was only when Nick came to her side
that the man stopped insisting – a nicely dressed man who was
only offering her his big black umbrella, and not trying to pick
her up. Things like this were hard for Nick to accept, but Karen
was not flirtatious, and he could see that it was not her fault that
men looked at her and made gestures.

It became a routine that on Sundays they jogged or went to
a basketball court. One time, when she got frustrated because
she hadn't been able to do a simple hook shot – hadn't made a
basket that way all morning – he lifted her to his shoulders and
charged the backboard so fast that she almost missed the basket
from there too. After playing basketball, they would go to her
apartment and she would make dinner. He would collapse, but
she was full of energy and she would poke fun at him while she
studied a cookbook, staring at it until she knew enough of a
recipe to begin preparing the food. His two cookbooks were
dog-eared and sauce-stained, but Karen's were perfectly clean.
She looked at recipes, but never followed them exactly. He
admired this – her creativity, her energy. It took him a long
while to accept that she thought he was special, and later, when
she began to date other men, it took him a long while to realize
that she did not mean to shut him out of her life. The first time
she went away with a man for the weekend – about a year after
he first met her – she stopped by his apartment on her way to
Pennsylvania and gave him the keys to her Thunderbird. She left
so quickly – the man was downstairs in his car, waiting – that as
he watched her go he could feel the warmth of the keys from her
hand.

Just recently Nick had met the man she was dating now: a
gaunt psychology professor, with a black-and-white tweed cap
and a thick moustache that made him look like a sad-mouthed
clown. Nick had gone to her apartment not knowing for certain
that the man would be there – actually, it was Friday night, the
beginning of the weekend, and he had gone on the hunch that he

finally would meet him – and had drunk a vodka Collins that the man mixed for him. He remembered that the man had complained tediously that Paul McCartney had stolen words from Thomas Dekker for a song on the *Abbey Road* album, and that the man said he got hives from eating shellfish.

In the restaurant now, Nick looked across the table at Karen and said, "That man you're dating is a real bore. What is he – a scholar?"

He fumbled for a cigarette and then remembered that he no longer smoked. He had given it up a year before, when he went to visit an old girlfriend in New Haven. Things had gone badly, they had quarreled, and he had left her to go to a bar. Coming out, he was approached by a tall black round-faced teenager and told to hand over his wallet, and he had mutely reached inside his coat and pulled it out and given it to the boy. A couple of people came out of the bar, took in the situation and walked away quickly, pretending not to notice. The boy had a small penknife in his hand. "And your cigarettes," the boy said. Nick had reached inside his jacket pocket and handed over the cigarettes. The boy pocketed them. Then the boy smiled and cocked his head and held up the wallet, like a hypnotist dangling a pocket watch. Nick stared dumbly at his own wallet. Then, before he knew what was happening, the boy turned into a blur of motion: he grabbed his arm and yanked hard, like a judo wrestler, and threw him across the sidewalk. Nick fell against a car that was parked at the curb. He was so frightened that his legs buckled and he went down. The boy watched him fall. Then he nodded and walked down the sidewalk past the bar. When the boy was out of sight, Nick got up and went into the bar to tell his story. He let the bartender give him a beer and call the police. He declined the bartender's offer of a cigarette, and had never smoked since.

His thoughts were drifting, and Karen still had not answered his question. He knew that he had already angered her once that day, and that it had been a mistake to speak of the man again. Just an hour or so earlier, when they got back to the city, he had been abrupt with her friend Kirby. She kept her car in Kirby's garage, and in exchange for the privilege she moved into his

brownstone whenever he went out of town and took care
of his six de-clawed chocolate-point cats. Actually, Kirby's
psychiatrist, a Dr. Kellogg, lived in the same house, but the
doctor had made it clear he did not live there to take care of cats.

From his seat Nick could see the sign of the restaurant
hanging outside the front window. "Star Thrower Café," it said,
in lavender neon. He got depressed thinking that if she became
more serious about the professor – he had lasted longer than any
of the others – he would only be able to see her by pretending to
run into her at places like the Star Thrower. He had also begun
to think that he had driven the Thunderbird for the last time. She
had almost refused to let him drive it again after the time, two
weeks earlier, when he tapped a car in front of them on Sixth
Avenue, making a dent above their left headlight. Long ago she
had stopped letting him use her squirrel coat as a kind of blanket.
He used to like to lie naked on the tiny balcony outside her
apartment in the autumn, with the Sunday *Times* arranged under
him for padding and the coat spread on top of him. Now he
counted back and came up with the figure: he had known Karen
for seven years.

"What are you thinking?" he said to her.

"That I'm glad I'm not thirty-eight years old, with a man
putting pressure on me to have a baby." She was talking about
Stephanie and Sammy.

Her hand was on the table. He cupped his hand over it just
as the waiter came with the plates.

"What are *you* thinking?" she said, withdrawing her hand.

"At least Stephanie has the sense not to do it," he said. He
picked up his fork and put it down. "Do you really love that
man?"

"If I loved him, I suppose I'd be at my apartment, where he's
been waiting for over an hour. If he waited."

When they finished she ordered espresso. He ordered it also.
He had half expected her to say at some point that the trip with
him was the end, and he still thought she might say that. Part of
the problem was that she had money and he didn't. She had had
money since she was twenty-one, when she got control of a

50,000-dollar trust fund her grandfather had left her. He remembered the day she had bought the Thunderbird. It was the day after her birthday, five years ago. That night, laughing, they had driven the car through the Lincoln Tunnel and then down the back roads in Jersey, with a stream of orange crepe paper blowing from the radio antenna, until the wind ripped it off.

"Am I still going to see you?" Nick said.

"I suppose," Karen said. "Although things have changed between us."

"I've known you for seven years. You're my oldest friend."

She did not react to what he said, but much later, around midnight, she called him at his apartment. "Was what you said at the Star Thrower calculated to make me feel bad?" she said. "When you said that I was your oldest friend?"

"No," he said. "You are my oldest friend."

"You must know somebody longer than you've known me."

"You're the only person I've seen regularly for seven years." She sighed.

"Professor go home?" he said.

"No. He's here."

"You're saying all this in front of him?"

"I don't see why there has to be any secret about this."

"You could put an announcement in the paper," Nick said. "Run a little picture of me with it."

"Why are you so sarcastic?"

"It's embarrassing. It's embarrassing that you'd say this in front of that man."

He was sitting in the dark, in a chair by the phone. He had wanted to call her ever since he got back from the restaurant. The long day of driving had finally caught up with him, and his shoulders ached. He felt the black man's hands on his shoulders, felt his own body folding up, felt himself flying backward. He had lost 65 dollars that night. The day she bought the Thunderbird, he had driven it through the tunnel into New Jersey. He had driven, then she had driven, and then he had driven again. Once he had pulled into the parking lot of a shopping center and told her to wait, and had come back with the orange crepe paper.

Years later he had looked for the road they had been on that
night, but he could never find it.

The next time Nick heard from her was almost three weeks after
the trip to Virginia. Since he didn't have the courage to call her,
and since he expected not to hear from her at all, he was surprised
to pick up the phone and hear her voice. Petra had been in his
apartment – a woman at his office whom he had always wanted
to date and who had just broken off an unhappy engagement. As
he held the phone clamped between his ear and shoulder, he
looked admiringly at Petra's profile.

"What's up?" he said to Karen, trying to sound very casual
for Petra.

"Get ready," Karen said. "Stephanie called and said that she
was going to have a baby."

"What do you mean? I thought she told you in Virginia that
she thought Sammy was crazy to want a kid."

"It happened by accident. She missed her period just after we
left."

Petra shifted on the couch and began leafing through
*Newsweek*.

"Can I call you back?" he said.

"Throw whatever woman is there out of your apartment and
talk to me now," Karen said. "I'm about to go out."

He looked at Petra, who was sipping her drink. "I can't do
that," he said.

"Then call me when you can. But call back tonight."

When he hung up, he took Petra's glass but found that he
had run out of Scotch. He suggested that they go to a bar on
West Tenth Street.

When they got to the bar, he excused himself almost immediately. Karen had sounded depressed, and he could not enjoy his
evening with Petra until he made sure everything was all right.
Once he heard her voice, he knew he was going to come to her
apartment when he had finished having a drink, and she said that
he should come over immediately or not at all, because she was
about to go to the professor's. She was so abrupt that he
wondered if she could be jealous.

He went back to the bar and sat on the stool next to Petra and picked up his Scotch and water and took a big drink. It was so cold that it made his teeth ache. Petra had on blue slacks and a white blouse. He rubbed his hand up and down her back, just below the shoulders. She was not wearing a brassiere.

"I have to leave," he said.

"You have to leave? Are you coming back?"

He started to speak, but she put up her hand. "Never mind," she said. "I don't want you to come back." She sipped her margarita. "Whoever the woman is you just called, I hope the two of you have a splendid evening."

Petra gave him a hard look, and he knew that she really wanted him to go. He stared at her – at the little crust of salt on her bottom lip – and then she turned away from him.

He hesitated for just a second before he left the bar. He went outside and walked about ten steps, and then he was jumped. They got him from behind, and in his shock and confusion he thought that he had been hit by a car. He lost sense of where he was, and although it was a dull blow, he thought that somehow a car had hit him. Looking up from the sidewalk, he saw them – two men, younger than he was, picking at him like vultures, pushing him, rummaging through his jacket and his pockets. The crazy thing was he was on West Tenth Street; there should have been other people on the street, but there were not. His clothes were tearing. His right hand was wet with blood. They had cut his arm, the shirt was bloodstained, he saw his own blood spreading out into a little puddle. He stared at it and was afraid to move his hand out of it. Then the men were gone and he was left half sitting, propped up against a building where they had dragged him. He was able to push himself up, but the man he began telling the story to, a passer-by, kept coming into focus and fading out again. The man had on a sombrero, and he was pulling him up but pulling too hard. His legs didn't have the power to support him – something had happened to his legs – so that when the man loosened his grip he went down on his knees. He kept blinking to stay conscious. He blacked out before he could stand again.

Back in his apartment, later that night with his arm in a cast, he felt confused and ashamed – ashamed for the way he had treated Petra, and ashamed for having been mugged. He wanted to call Karen, but he was too embarrassed. He sat in the chair by the phone, willing her to call him. At midnight the phone rang, and he picked it up at once, sure that his telepathic message had worked. The phone call was from Stephanie, at La Guardia. She had been trying to reach Karen and couldn't. She wanted to know if she could come to his apartment.

"I'm not going through with it," Stephanie said, her voice wavering. "I'm thirty-eight years old, and this was a goddamn accident."

"Calm down," he said. "We can get you an abortion."

"I don't know if I could take a human life," she said, and she began to cry.

"Stephanie?" he said. "You okay? Are you going to get a cab?"

More crying, no answer.

"Because it would be silly for me to get a cab just to come get you. You can make it here okay, can't you, Steph?"

The cabdriver who took him to La Guardia was named Arthur Shales. A small pink baby shoe was glued to the dashboard of the cab. Arthur Shales chainsmoked Picayunes. "Woman I took to Bendel's today, I'm still trying to get over it," he said. "I picked her up at Madison and Seventy-fifth. Took her to Bendel's and pulled up in front and she said, 'Oh, screw Bendel's.' I took her back to Madison and Seventy-fifth."

Going across the bridge, Nick said to Arthur Shales that the woman he was going to pick up was going to be very upset.

"Upset? What do I care? Neither of you are gonna hold a gun to my head, I can take anything. You're my last fares of the night. Take you back where you came from, then I'm heading home myself."

When they were almost at the airport exit, Arthur Shales snorted and said, "Home is a room over an Italian grocery. Guy who runs it woke me up at six this morning, yelling so loud at his supplier. 'You call these tomatoes?' he was saying. 'I could take these out and bat them on the tennis court.' Guy is always griping about tomatoes being so unripe."

Stephanie was standing on the walkway, right where she had said she would be. She looked haggard, and Nick was not sure that he could cope with her. He raised his hand to his shirt pocket for cigarettes, forgetting once again that he had given up smoking. He also forgot that he couldn't grab anything with his right hand because it was in a cast.

"You know who I had in my cab the other day?" Arthur Shales said, coasting to a stop in front of the terminal. "You're not going to believe it. Al Pacino."

For more than a week, Nick and Stephanie tried to reach Karen. Stephanie began to think that Karen was dead. And although Nick chided her for calling Karen's number so often, he began to worry too. Once he went to her apartment on his lunch hour and listened at the door. He heard nothing, but he put his mouth close to the door and asked her to please open the door, if she was there, because there was trouble with Stephanie. As he left the building he had to laugh at what it would have looked like if someone had seen him – a nicely dressed man, with his hands on either side of his mouth, leaning into a door and talking to it. And one of the hands in a cast.

For a week he came straight home from work, to keep Stephanie company. Then he asked Petra if she would have dinner with him. She said no. As he was leaving the office, he passed by her desk without looking at her. She got up and followed him down the hall and said, "I'm having a drink with somebody after work, but I could meet you for a drink around seven o'clock."

He went home to see if Stephanie was all right. She said that she had been sick in the morning, but after the card came in the mail – she held out a postcard to him – she felt much better. The card was addressed to him; it was from Karen, in Bermuda. She said she had spent the afternoon in a sailboat. No explanation. He read the message several times. He felt very relieved. He asked Stephanie if she wanted to go out for a drink with him and Petra. She said no, as he had known she would.

At seven he sat alone at a table in the Blue Bar, with the postcard in his inside pocket. There was a folded newspaper on the little round table where he sat, and his broken right wrist rested on it. He sipped a beer. At 7.30 he opened the paper and looked through the theater section. At quarter to eight he got up and left. He walked over to Fifth Avenue and began to walk downtown. In one of the store windows there was a poster for Bermuda tourism. A woman in a turquoise-blue bathing suit was rising out of blue waves, her mouth in an unnaturally wide smile. She seemed oblivious of the little boy next to her who was tossing a ball into the sky. Standing there, looking at the poster, Nick began a mental game that he had sometimes played in college. He invented a cartoon about Bermuda. It was a split-frame drawing. Half of it showed a beautiful girl, in the arms of her lover, on the pink sandy beach of Bermuda, with the caption: "It's glorious to be here in Bermuda." The other half of the frame showed a tall tired man looking into the window of a travel agency at a picture of the lady and her lover. He would have no lines, but in a balloon above his head he would be wondering if, when he went home, it was the right time to urge an abortion to the friend who had moved into his apartment.

When he got home, Stephanie was not there. She had said that if she felt better, she would go out to eat. He sat down and took off his shoes and socks and hung forward, with his head almost touching his knees, like a droopy doll. Then he went into the bedroom, carrying the shoes and socks, and took off his clothes and put on jeans. The phone rang and he picked it up just as he heard Stephanie's key in the door.

"I'm sorry," Petra said, "I've never stood anybody up before in my life."

"Never mind," he said. "I'm not mad."

"I'm very sorry," she said.

"I drank a beer and read the paper. After what I did to you the other night, I don't blame you."

"I like you," she said. "That was why I didn't come. Because I knew I wouldn't say what I wanted to say. I got as far as Forty-eighth Street and turned around."

"What did you want to say?"

"That I like you. That I like you and that it's a mistake,

because I'm always letting myself in for it, agreeing to see men who treat me badly. I wasn't very flattered the other night."

"I know. I apologize. Look, why don't you meet me at that bar now and let me not walk out on you. Okay?"

"No," she said, her voice changing. "That wasn't why I called. I called to say I was sorry, but I know I did the right thing. I have to hang up now."

He put the phone back and continued to look at the floor. He knew that Stephanie was not even pretending not to have heard. He took a step forward and ripped the phone out of the wall. It was not a very successful dramatic gesture. The phone just popped out of the jack, and he stood there, holding it in his good hand.

"Would you think it was awful if I offered to go to bed with you?" Stephanie asked.

"No," he said. "I think it would be very nice."

Two days later he left work early in the afternoon and went to Kirby's. Dr. Kellogg opened the door and then pointed toward the back of the house and said, "The man you're looking for is reading." He was wearing baggy white pants and a Japanese kimono.

Nick almost had to push through the half-open door because the psychiatrist was so intent on holding the cats back with one foot. In the kitchen Kirby was indeed reading – he was looking at a Bermuda travel brochure and listening to Karen.

She looked sheepish when she saw him. Her face was tan, and her eyes, which were always beautiful, looked startlingly blue now that her face was so dark. She had lavender-tinted sunglasses pushed on top of her head. She and Kirby seemed happy and comfortable in the elegant, air-conditioned house.

"When did you get back?" Nick said.

"A couple of days ago," she said. "The night I last talked to you, I went over to the professor's apartment, and in the morning we went to Bermuda."

Nick had come to Kirby's to get the car keys and borrow the Thunderbird – to go for a ride and be by himself for a while –

and for a moment now he thought of asking her for the keys anyway. He sat down at the table.

"Stephanie is in town," he said. "I think we ought to get a cup of coffee and talk about it."

Her key ring was on the table. If he had the keys, he could be heading for the Lincoln Tunnel. Years ago, they would be walking to the car hand in hand, in love. It would be her birthday. The car's odometer would have 5 miles on it.

One of Kirby's cats jumped up on the table and began to sniff at the butter dish there.

"Would you like to walk over to the Star Thrower and get a cup of coffee?" Nick said.

She got up slowly.

"Don't mind me," Kirby said.

"Would you like to come, Kirby?" she asked.

"Not me. No, no."

She patted Kirby's shoulder, and they went out.

"What happened?" she said, pointing to his hand.

"It's broken."

"How did you break it?"

"Never mind," he said. "I'll tell you when we get there."

When they got there it was not yet four o'clock, and the Star Thrower was closed.

"Well, just tell me what's happening with Stephanie," Karen said impatiently. "I don't really feel like sitting around talking because I haven't even unpacked yet."

"She's at my apartment, and she's pregnant, and she doesn't even talk about Sammy."

She shook her head sadly. "How did you break your hand?" she said.

"I was mugged. After our last pleasant conversation on the phone – the time you told me to come over immediately or not at all. I didn't make it because I was in the emergency room."

"Oh, Christ," she said. "Why didn't you call me?"

"I was embarrassed to call you."

"Why? Why didn't you call?"

"You wouldn't have been there anyway." He took her arm. "Let's find some place to go," he said.

Two young men came up to the door of the Star Thrower. "Isn't this where David had that great Armenian dinner?" one of them said.

"I *told* you it wasn't," the other said, looking at the menu posted to the right of the door.

"I didn't really think this was the place. *You* said it was on this street."

They continued to quarrel as Nick and Karen walked away.

"Why do you think Stephanie came here to the city?" Karen said.

"Because we're her friends," Nick said.

"But she has lots of friends."

"Maybe she thought we were more dependable."

"Why do you say that in that tone of voice? I don't have to tell you every move I'm making. Things went very well in Bermuda. He almost lured me to London."

"Look," he said. "Can't we go somewhere where you can call her?"

He looked at her, shocked because she didn't understand that Stephanie had come to see her, not him. He had seen for a long time that it didn't matter to her how much she meant to him, but he had never realized that she didn't know how much she meant to Stephanie. She didn't understand people. When he found out she had another man, he should have dropped out of her life. She did not deserve her good looks and her fine car and all her money. He turned to face her on the street, ready to tell her what he thought.

"You know what happened there?" she said. "I got sunburned and had a terrible time. He went on to London without me."

He took her arm again and they stood side by side and looked at some sweaters hanging in the window of Countdown.

"So going to Virginia wasn't the answer for them," she said. "Remember when Sammy and Stephanie left town, and we told each other what a stupid idea it was – that it would never work out? Do you think we jinxed them?"

They walked down the street again, saying nothing.

"It would kill me if I had to be a good conversationalist with

you," she said at last. "You're the only person I can rattle on
with." She stopped and leaned into him. "I had a rotten time in
Bermuda," she said. "Nobody should go to a beach but a sand
flea."

"You don't have to make clever conversation with me," he
said.

"I know," she said. "It just happened."

Late in the afternoon of the day that Stephanie had her abortion,
Nick called Sammy from a street phone near his apartment.
Karen and Stephanie were in the apartment, but he had to get
out for a while. Stephanie had seemed pretty cheerful, but
perhaps it was just an act for his benefit. With him gone, she
might talk to Karen about it. All she had told was that it felt like
she had caught an ice pick in the stomach.

"Sammy?" Nick said into the phone. "How are you?" It just
dawned on me that I ought to call and let you know that
Stephanie is all right."

"She has called me herself, several times," Sammy said.
"Collect. From your phone. But thank you for your concern,
Nick." He sounded brusque.

"Oh," Nick said, taken aback. "Just so you know where she
is."

"I could name you as corespondent in the divorce case, you
know?"

"What would you do that for?" Nick said.

"I wouldn't. I just wanted you to know what I could do."

"Sammy – I don't get it. I didn't ask for any of this, you
know."

"Poor Nick. My wife gets pregnant, leaves without a word,
calls from New York with a story about how you had a broken
hand and were having bad luck with women, so she went to bed
with you. Two weeks later I get a phone call from you, all
concern, wanting me to know where Stephanie is."

Nick waited for Sammy to hang up on him.

"You know what happened to you?" Sammy said. "You got
eaten up by New York."

"What kind of dumb thing is that to say?" Nick said. "Are you trying to get even or something?"

"If I wanted to do that, I could tell you that you have bad teeth. Or that Stephanie said you were a lousy lover. What I was trying to do was tell you something important, for a change. Stephanie ran away when I tried to tell it to her, you'll probably hang up on me when I say the same thing to you: you can be happy. For instance, you can get out of New York and get away from Karen. Stephanie could have settled down with a baby."

"This doesn't sound like you, Sammy, to give advice."

He waited for Sammy's answer.

"You think I ought to leave New York?" Nick said.

"Both. Karen *and* New York. Do you know that your normal expression shows pain? Do you know how much Scotch you drank the weekend you visited?"

Nick stared through the grimy plastic window of the phone booth.

"What you just said about my hanging up on you," Nick said. "I was thinking that you were going to hang up on me. When I talk to people, they hang up on me. The conversation just ends that way."

"Why haven't you figured out that you don't know the right kind of people?"

"They're the only people I know."

"Does that seem like any reason for tolerating that sort of rudeness?"

"I guess not."

"Another thing," Sammy went on. "Have you figured out that I'm saying these things to you because when you called I was already drunk? I'm telling you all this because I think you're so numbed out by your lousy life that you probably even don't know I'm not in my right mind."

The operator came on, demanding more money. Nick clattered quarters into the phone. He realized that he was not going to hang up on Sammy, and Sammy was not going to hang up on him. He would have to think of something else to say.

"Give yourself a break," Sammy said. "Boot them out.

Stephanie included. She'll see the light eventually and come back to the farm."

"Should I tell her you'll be there? I don't know if—"

"I told her I'd be here when she called. All the times she called. I just told her that I had no idea of coming to get her. I'll tell you another thing. I'll bet – I'll *bet* – that when she first turned up there she called you from the airport, and she wanted you to come for her, didn't she?"

"Sammy," Nick said, staring around him, wild to get off the phone. "I want to thank you for saying what you think. I'm going to hang up now."

"Forget it," Sammy said. "I'm not in my right mind. Goodbye."

"Goodbye," Nick said.

He hung up and started back to his apartment. He realized that he hadn't told Sammy that Stephanie had had the abortion. On the street he said hello to a little boy – one of the neighborhood children he knew.

He went up the stairs and up to his floor. Some people downstairs were listening to Beethoven. He lingered in the hallway, not wanting to go back to Stephanie and Karen. He took a deep breath and opened the door. Neither of them looked too bad. They said hello silently, each raising one hand.

It had been a hard day. Stephanie's appointment at the abortion clinic had been at eight in the morning. Karen had slept in the apartment with them the night before, on the sofa. Stephanie slept in his bed, and he slept on the floor. None of them had slept much. In the morning they all went to the abortion clinic. Nick had intended to go to work in the afternoon, but when they got back to the apartment he didn't think it was right for him to leave Stephanie. She went back to the bedroom, and he stretched out on the sofa and fell asleep. Before he slept, Karen sat on the sofa with him for a while, and he told her the story of his second mugging. When he woke up, it was four o'clock. He called his office and told them he was sick. Later they all watched the television news together. After that, he offered to go out and get some food, but nobody was hungry. That's when he went out and called Sammy.

Now Stephanie went back into the bedroom. She said she was tired and she was going to work on a crossword puzzle in bed. The phone rang. It was Petra. She and Nick talked a little about a new apartment she was thinking of moving into. "I'm sorry for being so cold-blooded the other night," she said. "The reason I'm calling is to invite myself to your place for a drink, if that's all right with you."

"It's not all right," he said. "I'm sorry. There are some people here now."

"I get it," she said. "Okay. I won't bother you any more."

"You don't understand," he said. He knew he had not explained things well, but the thought of adding Petra to the scene at his apartment was more than he could bear, and he had been too abrupt.

She said goodbye coldly, and he went back to his chair and fell in it, exhausted.

"A girl?" Karen said.

He nodded.

"Not a girl you wanted to hear from."

He shook his head no. He got up and pulled up the blind and looked out to the street. The boy he had said hello to was playing with a hula hoop. The hula hoop was bright blue in the twilight. The kid rotated his hips and kept the hoop spinning perfectly. Karen came to the window and stood next to him. He turned to her, wanting to say that they should go and get the Thunderbird, and as the night air cooled, drive out of the city, smell honeysuckle in the fields, feel the wind blowing.

But the Thunderbird was sold. She had told him the news while they were sitting in the waiting room of the abortion clinic. The car had needed a valve job, and a man she met in Bermuda who knew all about cars had advised her to sell it. Coincidentally, the man – a New York architect – wanted to buy it. Even as Karen told him, he knew she had been set up. If she had been more careful, they could have been in the car now, with the key in the ignition, the radio playing. He stood at the window for a long time. She had been conned, and he was more angry than he could tell her. She had no conception – she had somehow never understood – that Thunderbirds of that year, in good condition, would someday be worth a fortune. She had told him this way: "Don't be upset, because I'm sure I made the right decision. I sold the car as soon as I got back from Bermuda. I'm going to get a new car." He had moved in his chair, there in the clinic. He had had an impulse to get up and hit her. He remembered the scene in New Haven outside the bar, and he understood now that it was as simple as this: he had money that the black man wanted.

Down the street the boy picked up his hula hoop and disappeared around the corner.

"Say you were kidding about selling the car," Nick said.

"When are you going to stop making such a big thing over it?" Karen said.

"That creep cheated you. He talked you into selling it when nothing was wrong with it."

"Stop it," she said. "How come your judgements are always right and my judgements are always wrong?"

"I don't want to fight," he said. "I'm sorry I said anything."

"Okay," she said and leaned her head against him. He draped his right arm over her shoulder. The fingers sticking out of the cast rested a little above her breast.

"I just want to ask one thing," he said, "and then I'll never mention it again. Are you sure the deal is final?"

Karen pushed his hand off her shoulder and walked away. But it was his apartment, and she couldn't go slamming around in it. She sat on the sofa and picked up the newspaper. He watched her. Soon she put it down and stared across the room and into the dark bedroom, where Stephanie had turned off the light. He looked at her sadly for a long time, until she looked up at him with tears in her eyes.

"Do you think maybe we could get it back if I offered him more than he paid me for it?" she said. "You probably don't think that's a sensible suggestion, but at least that way we could get it back."

CAROL BLY

☆ ☆ ☆ ☆

# *Talk of Heroes*

Two women, one with hair gone gray, wearing a woolen dress and carrying a raincoat, and the other only twenty-four, gathering the velvet lapels of her dressing gown around her throat, stood a moment on a low hill overlooking White Bear Lake. A thick evening mist lolled upward from the lake surface itself, so that all the dockside equipment – the polyurethane floats, the white boat lifts, the bobbing milk cartons chained to great weights far below – all the bright playthings of American Midwest lakefronts were hidden. The evening mist suggested much greater, more classic waters than a suburban lake.

Emily Anderson had meant to pause alone for a second before jumping into her car and driving to St. Paul to introduce a speaker, but her daughter, Sandra Anderson-Keefer, had ambled out of the house after her. Sandra began to tell an odd dream she had had when she fell asleep in the late afternoon. It was not exactly to do with Bruce, her husband, but somehow she felt it had to do with a vague semblance of him. Not like a ghost exactly, she told Emily, but something unclear and generalized. Emily shifted the raincoat on her arm and started energetically across the cold grass for the car, with Sandra following, trying to explain the dream sequence.

Emily was feeling the elation of conscientious hosts when they can temporarily escape a ubiquitous houseguest. No matter that Sandra was her daughter, and a humorous and kindly-inclined girl, home to get it, as she put it, all together for a few days – the fact was, Sandra talked a lot and Emily wasn't used to it.

She had not yet given up the silent house on its rise over the lake, the oak trees' dripping, the autumn fogs in the morning and evening. She was used to standing outside for her early morning coffee. She was used to moving about her work, from room to room, without conversation. In the past four days, however, Sandra had followed her from her book-packing in the library to her cleaning of the downstairs closets. Sandra generally left her alone when she made off to her study, saying, "Oh – you're going to work! I won't invade," and wandered into the living room for an afternoon nap. Like many people in personal turmoil, she rose late, didn't dress other than to cloak herself in her dressing gown, and she fell asleep easily throughout the day. For a few hours, later after dinner, she would talk in a jerking, high-pitched voice, about her married life. Her young face gleaming nervously, she would repeat for Emily what Bruce, her husband, had said and then what she had replied. She was trained as a group therapist, so she tended to use phrases like "thinking through her options" – but the griefs of men and women, getting along, not getting along, were there, recognizable despite her sporty jargon.

Emily hid her own relief at escaping for an evening by crying once more as they neared the car, "You're absolutely sure you don't want to come with me to the Tusend Hjem program? Old Mr. Elvekrog – poor dear – would be happy to see you! He'd welcome any member your age – probably with open arms!"

"I bet!" Sandra said.

"And wasn't Chuck Iversen an old friend of yours? He still comes, for his dad's sake no doubt – but he does try to brighten things up."

Sandra said with a laugh, "I made the Tusend Hjem scene with you and Dad for fifteen, sixteen years, and it ruined one evening of every single Christmas vacation, too! Don't you try to talk me into it, Mama! I couldn't hoke up the slightest enthusiasm in Norwegian–American culture now if you gave me a million dollars." Sandra paused. "Seriously, Mama – if you were the speaker you know I wouldn't miss it for anything! But you're introducing – so what we're looking at is a first-quality, four-minute introduction and then a half-hour of horrible speech and a half-hour of horrible slideshow . . ."

"Movie!" said Emily laughing.

"Horrible movie, complete instructions in how to knit Norwegian socks! Then another horrible hour of cookies and coffee with enough caffeine and sugar intake to o.d. Norway itself for a week! And then the awful singing of the Norwegian national anthem, with everyone pretending they still understand the words and care 2 cents for what they mean! No, Mama – sorry! I think *you're* awfully good to do it, but Tusend Hjem is definitely not one of my priorities."

Emily gave her briefcase a cheerful toss into the back seat. "The movie isn't Norwegian knitting," she said. "That's what they were going to have – Mrs. Thorstad talking about Norwegian knitting. But apparently the national office in Brooklyn called up and changed the program. The movie is about World War II."

"Oh my God," Sandra said, smiling in through the open car window. "But I can see why you're interested. You and Dad knew someone, whoever it was, who was in it, didn't you? But it's not my war, Mama. And I know too much about human relationships now to pretend to have feelings I haven't got." She added, with a small lift of chin, "I have kind of a sense of my own war, sort of."

Emily told her, "I will be back as fast as I can leave."

Sandra looked chilled and uncertain; her dressing gown at this late time of day suggested a patient in a hospital rather than a grown woman trying with any bravado to decide whether or not to leave a husband. Emily felt sorry for her, but also at odds: her own mood was public and practical. She was geared simply to do a job. Sandra was thinking of passion only, wandering through her own personal situation all these days. Emily felt the superior edge of administrators who feel superior to expressive talkers – simply because the talkers happen not to be doing any particular work at the moment.

She drove gladly into the gloomy evening. It was only twenty minutes into St. Paul, to West Seventh Street, where Tusend Hjem leased the entire upper story of a very old, well-made brick building. Tusend Hjem was chartered in 1897 as the Minnesota chapter of the national organization of Norwegian–American immigrants. In the old days, there had been tri-weekly gymnastics classes, and everyone had spoke Norwegian, and had known the anthem from which the name, *tusend hjem*, or thousand homes, was taken.

Even now, Mr. Elvekrog's program committee made sure there was a meeting once a month, with some sort of cultural offering. And even when the program content itself left something to be desired (like the films occasionally sent out from the national office), the people could still count on the Norwegian-style boiled coffee, brought up three times with an egg – and the homemade cookies. Mrs. Iversen's committee kept the great gloomy hall absolutely clean; the chipped tiles in the kitchen and bathrooms were scrubbed regularly. Everyone wished they could reach the great west window to wash it.

It was a huge Roman arch, with radiating pie-sections of glass and blackened lead-soldering. It looked like a window meant to light genuinely serious human affairs, like the window of an old science laboratory where honest discoveries were made, or the window of a major embassy where people argued late at night about affairs later described in the papers. In the summertime the sun would just be failing as Tusend Hjem started its meetings, and a smeary, kindly light fell through the dusty glass arch, showing the gym ropes still knotted neatly and the rows of auditorium chairs. Along the high, plastered walls hung photographs of 1920s and 1930s gym classes; the men's knees, jutted out toward the photographer, must by now be full of creaks and aches, if not in many cases put to rest.

Emily closed the heavy street-door of the building, with its clanking nightchains. She started up the clean, wooden stairs. Above her head, she heard the committee members scurrying between kitchen and the great hall. They would be unpacking nine-by-seventeen trays of chocolate bars and paper plates of krullers and fattigmenn, in their little prisons of Saranwrap. The women did not let the men simply stand around, either. "Here – you, Merv!" Mrs. Thorstad cried, just as Emily came to the landing. "Take this!" Then, Mrs. Iversen, hearing Mrs. Thorstad's remark, looked about for her Chuck. He was lounging under a framed illustrated print of the Lord's Prayer in Norwegian, joking with Bernt Nielsen. "You can make yourself useful, too!" his mother cried. "They'll be coming in another fifteen minutes now!" Chuck Iversen was regarded as the clown of Tusend Hjem, so now he made some witty rejoinder and then caught sight of Emily. "Oh boy!" he shouted, laughing, at her. "Good thing you got here!" He began separating dozens of styrofoam coffee cups. "Old Elvekrog is climbing the walls in there worrying – 'Will Emily show up OK?' he asks everyone!"

Emily said with a smile, "He knows perfectly well I'll show up."

Chuck told her, "Yes, but he doesn't know about that so-called famous speaker from Norway that's coming – the one you're supposed to introduce!" Chuck waved his head back to a partitioned corner of the hall. It was an 8-foot-high enclosure, making a little office, something like the little offices put into great factory spaces – islands isolated off from the general noise and work. "You'd better go in there and cheer him up," Chuck said.

Mr. Elvekrog leapt up from his seat the moment she went in the doorway of his office. He came round the desk to give her a brief, limp handshake. "Sometimes I just don't know what to do about National!" he cried.

"What have they done?" Emily asked. She sat down with her raincoat in her lap. Above the flimsy plywood and two-by-four construction of the office, she could see the huge ceiling of the main hall, and part of the steel and glass window. Immediately next to her was a little table covered with thick, artificial velvet of silver-green: on it, in a neat semi-circle, stood propped-up small photographs of Ibsen, Björnstjerne Björnsen, Hamsun, and Haakon VII. There was also a very bright Kodacolor picture of fourteen or fifteen middle-aged American women stuffed into Hardanger national costumes. Their permanents and wing-shaped eyeglasses were heart-breaking, over the blouses of openwork embroidery. Opposite the table stood a file case in which all Tusend Hjem members had file folders. As they died, their folders were moved from the upper drawer to the lower one. Last August, when Emily's husband's file was moved, Mr. Elvekrog had kindly sent her the ribbon awarded her husband for fifty years of Tusend Hjem membership.

Now Mr. Elvekrog, looking very old and nervous, said,

"Well! I wanted to talk to you in here – but of course it doesn't give much privacy!"

Everyone who passed the office looked in. Women went by with Mason jars in which orange sticks bearing tiny Norwegian flags were arranged in a circle, with some Kleenex stuffed in the center to keep them in position. Chuck Iversen and Bernt Nielsen passed, listening to Mrs. Thorstad who was talking loudly about knitting.

"National needn't act so high-handed with me!" said Mr. Elvekrog. "They aren't such fine folk! I was there once, Emily – I wonder if I told you? Right in their office, there, at National. Their office – now – why, it's not even in New York City. It's in Brooklyn and I had a terrible time just to find the place. You have to know to take the BMT subway to the Forty-Sixth Street stop. But Emily – I don't have to tell you – you and your husband must have been there, when you went through on your way to Norway that time, at least! The time I was there, I had called ahead to say I was coming – but do you think anyone met me? Not a soul! All there was was a janitor is all, someone just hired, too – not a genuine Tusend Hjem volunteer – not a real member. And this janitor kept vacuuming around my feet. I kept thinking that the hired coordinator – that's the kind of things they go in for these days – a hired coordinator – would come greet me. Finally, the janitor said, would I move my feet. That did it, Emily! I told him straight out, 'You bet I will! I will just move them right out of here, too!' I have always wondered if the janitor told the rest of them how quick I talked right up to him! Emily, when they call you from National, you would think they were calling from the gates of heaven for the tone they put on! This hired coordinator that called two weeks ago, she made me cancel the evening we had all planned for tonight – all because of this famous Norwegian war hero who was doing a tour across the country anyway!"

"Willi Varig," Emily said.

"Yes, this Willi Varig," Mr. Elvekrog said. He went on in his bitter tone: "I had already asked Mrs. Thorstad would she do her knitting patterns for us. You see, for all these past six weeks we have had an announcement up that Mrs. Thorstad would be showing us the Norwegian knitting patterns which she brought back from Bergen last summer. In the original Norwegian language, too, but with her own translations into English measure. And afterwards, Mrs. Iversen was going to serve her homemade krullers. I try to keep that bulletin board up to date, you know – and then suddenly, National calls up and says we have to have this war hero. Well, Emily – in my book, that war was a long time ago and we all want to forget it. I told them I am sorry we can't accommodate you eking out this so-called war hero's lecture schedule across the United States – which is all they really cared about, I bet. 'We have our own program already planned, thank you,' I told them. They just came back as cool as cats and said, 'Cancel whatever you have and fit this Varig in because he is famous.' Well, Emily, I for one never heard of him! And then they said that this Willi Varig had mentioned to their lecture series manager that he knew you, back in the 1950s, in Oslo, and National asked that you introduce him! I was so surprised! Then they said, well, he would be showing a movie about Norwegian heroes during the war and we were to provide a 16-mm movie projector. Then I saw my way out, Emily! I told them, without mincing any words, that the projector had been lent to the Tomah, Wisconsin, Chapter of Tusend Hjem, and they hadn't returned it yet because it was broken and they wanted to get it fixed before they sent it back. Then National got sassy with me and said there were millions of people in St. Paul and Minneapolis and didn't we know anyone who would trust us with a projector? The upshot of it was, Tomah did finally send our projector back, and you were nice enough to say you *would* introduce this Varig – so we have to just hope it is all fixed up okay. But I can tell you, Emily, without fear of its going any further, that Mrs. Thorstad was really hurt when I had to explain to her that we wouldn't want her knitting program for tonight. But anyway, I am glad it is you doing the introducing, Emily. You two were always such good Tusend Hjem members. And I guess we ought to be grateful to have this famous speaker. Apparently he is talking to all kinds of groups, not just Tusend Hjem chapters, but the American Legion and VFW posts and goodness knows what all else. So finally all I said

was, okay – but you make sure he gets here on time and that he
is sober, too! The last speaker they sent us had had a good deal
to drink. Everyone noticed it. Now they promised this one
would be here no later than 7.30 and it is already twenty to eight
and he isn't here that I can see!" Mr. Elvekrog looked closely
into Emily's eyes. "Emily, does he drink as far as you know?"
he asked in a low voice.

"It is a long time since I knew Willi," Emily told him. "In 1955.
But National is right about at least one thing," she went on in an
encouraging tone. "He really was a very great hero in the war."
She forbore to tell Mr. Elvekrog that she had never once, during
the whole winter when she and her husband had known Willi, seen
the hero sober or even middling-sober. It had always been the
same: They would be eating cod and boiled potatoes in the
smoky, workmen's restaurant above some shops in Drammensveien, while Willi and any one of his various vivid girlfriends
would tell stories. Then Willi would leave them to go out into
the town. He would drink his way down past Karl Johansgate
until he got to the railroad station or the harbor. Much later the
police brought him home, to the flat of whoever the girlfriend of
the moment was. However, Willi, like Emily herself, was much
older now – he might even be sixty. Perhaps he was changed.

"If that speaker doesn't show up, I won't know what to
think!" cried Mr. Elvekrog.

Emily said, "If he doesn't show up, I will tell the group what
he did during the war and then Mrs. Thorstad can show us the
Norwegian knitting patterns if she brought them, or we can ask
her questions at least."

Now it was 8 o'clock. The hall had filled, and Tusend Hjem
members kept turning their heads about from the seats to see if
the speaker had come. Mr. Elvekrog flitted back and forth
between the projector, which he wouldn't trust anyone else with,
and the speaker's microphone on the podium. He pretended to
check the silver-taping of the wires along the aisle. Little slips on
which he had jotted the announcements kept fluttering from his
fingers. Chuck Iversen, the club wit, would rescue them and
make jokes to everyone. "Mr. Elvekrog? Mr. Elvekrog? Did you
drop this?" he would call, waving a slip over people's heads. He

pretended to be making out difficult handwriting. "It says here," he shouted, "that Mrs. Thorstad has promised to send five boxes of fattigmenn to every member of the United States Congress? Can that be right, Mrs. Thorstad?" Everyone laughed and clapped and Mrs. Thorstad grew pink and her eyes got shy as a girl's. People settle to enjoying Chuck's sideshow effects. If their speaker was some big shot too important to bother to show up at their chapter on time, then they darned well, they told each other with grins, had their own people to amuse them, and their own jokes that the speaker wouldn't understand anyway. The older members began passing around the smeary purple-dittoed copies of the Norwegian national anthem, and young people concentrated, biting their lips, some of them trying to think up good jokes to call out, the way Chuck Iversen did.

At last, they all heard the heavy door open on the first floor. It slammed shut with a rattle of nightchains. A male voice made a sharp remark; there was an equally sharp return in a higher, feminine voice, and feet started up the staircase. Definitely, then, two people were coming – very slowly considering how late they were.

It was Willi Varig. At the top of the staircase, he hung onto the handrail newel for a moment, staring round with a red, burly face. Emily recognized him despite the twenty-five years and she went lightly along a side aisle to shake hands with him. At his side stood a woman of thirty or less, who appeared to be supporting him with one arm. She reminded Emily of all of Willi's women in Oslo; it was the same startlingly pretty, rather impatient sort of girl, who would fling herself down to join them at dinner, toss off her SAS jacket and immediately regale them all with a story of what some idiot had done at Fornebu Airport or on an Air France newspaper-delivery flight.

Willi had always had a cynical cast to his nature: he liked a story told with exasperation. He would slam the girl an affection-ate blow on the shoulder blade and cry, "A woman deserves a drink when she has been through what you have been through!"

Now he smiled rather unpleasantly into Emily's face and shook her hand very hard, with a single jerk, in the Norwegian way. He gave a laugh. "All these years! And you have not changed a little!" he said. "I would recognize you anywhere! You do not mind if I shake your hand, I hope?" He introduced the two women, getting their names eventually. In a raucous tone, in loud English, he remarked to the Norwegian girl, "Now this is an American woman that you shake hands with! You do not dare to give her a kiss – not this one! Oh no! No, you do not do that with this one! She would explain to you that she was married already! She would not hit you across the face – she wouldn't do that! She would tell you that she admired you – Oh yes! All that wonderful admiration! But no kisses – not even for old times' sake! So we shake hands!"

The Norwegian woman brought out the bland, stewardess smile which serves a million cold situations. Emily saw Mr. Elvekrog approaching, with his desperate, creased forehead. She introduced him in Norwegian to the two visitors and told him *sotto voce* that she would introduce Willi in two minutes, not four, and that she felt he ought not to try giving the announcements before the anthem. If Willi stayed on his feet another five minutes, she thought, he would just be able to give a three-minute talk. Then he could capsize all he liked, because Mr. Elvekrog could order the lights out and start the film without him.

Supported a little by the girl, Willi began hobbling forward. The two of them tried to pass the projector in the aisle at the same time. Mr. Elvekrog's chair went over and Willi's hip gave the projector itself a smash, but Mr. Elvekrog leapt to the other side and kept it from going over onto the floor. The room was utterly silent. At the podium, waiting until Mr. Elvekrog should have settled the Norwegians in two reserved seats in the center of the first row, Emily decided she would further shorten her introduction, from the look of things – and she would not bet 2 cents on Willi's being able to carry off a discussion period after the film at all.

Then she smiled to the audience and said, "Good evening! I think we will sing the anthem and have the announcements after the speaker tonight, instead of in our usual order. Before I introduce the speaker, though, I *would* like to make one very important announcement. Mrs. Thorstad *will* be showing Tusend Hjem her Norwegian knitting patterns next meeting: we will not get beat out of that!"

Emily then said it was an honor to present a speaker who was a genuine hero. "We haven't a great many real heroes," she told them. "But Willi Varig is one." She told them that Willi had belonged to a group of four Underground agents who sent information back to England from Lofthus, Hardanger, on the west coast of Norway. Willi was caught by the Germans in May of 1944. They questioned him about the names of his colleagues so that they could gather them in as well. Willi's World War II, Emily told them, was fought alone in a cellar which held two other people, both of whom were members of the enemy. They were Gestapo officers who were skilled in making people give them the information they needed. "Now," Emily continued, "the only reason I have told you even this much – when I know that you want to hear the speaker himself – is that I am afraid he won't tell you that he was an extraordinarily brave man. It is an honor to present to you Willi Varig."

Emily took a seat which Mrs. Thorstad, all smiles, energetically pointed out to her, next to herself. Willi made it to the microphone. He turned a belligerent face to Emily and spoke so closely into the mike that his words racketed: "Well then!" he shouted. "I didn't know I was such a hero then! I feel as if I were attending my own funeral sermon!" He gave a rough, very loud laugh, looking about between the rims of his eyelids, expecting the audience to laugh with him. Emily was one of theirs, however, and in any case, they didn't understand his sardonic tone. Most important of all, he was visibly drunk. He looked as if his knees were about to give way.

"It is an honor to address you!" he went on, "since we fought on the same side of the war. I know that the American Legion represents the very bravest of America's veterans!"

Willi's girlfriend leaned forward as if to correct him. But then she sighed, crossed her arms, and leaned back. Mr. Elvekrog half-stood at the projector, and called in his quavering tone, "Herr Varig? This is the Minnesota Chapter of Tusend Hjem!"

Willi pounded his fist on the podium, as if to make a silent point, and then said only, in a kind of snarl: "I think we will now have the film, please, if you will close the lights."

In the sudden, grateful darkness, the people could hear their speaker stumbling back towards his seat. The screen lighted up.

"Norsk Film A/S," the screen told them in white print on black. Then white, typed credits appeared in jerks over clips of a young woman tapping wireless messages under the speckled shade of camouflage; three figures sneaked up under a bridge on which a German-helmeted soldier was slowly walking, occasionally glancing overside; two Norwegian girls smiled widely at two Gestapo officers leaving a wooden hut. But the instant the door was shut, one girl crouched at it, listening, while the other quickly lifted a *dynetrekk* and folded it back, revealing a radio set. She put on a pair of earphones and immediately began sending.

Then, all of a sudden, the projector clattered. Mr. Elvekrog gave an exclamation, the screen whitened with lightning and tortured patterns, the aisle area began to reek of burnt celluloid. In the next instant, Mr. Elvekrog called sharply, "Someone turn the lights on please!" Other, younger, more resonant men's voices added, "Yes – someone get the lights back there!"

People rubbed their eyes in the brightness. They turned to Mr. Elvekrog, who sat beside the projector with curls and curls of movie-tape bunched and falling about his lap and legs. With his bleak expression, he looked like a provincial actor who has just removed an elaborate Louis XVI wig.

Chuck Iversen cried out, "Well, I see that the Tomah Chapter didn't repair the projector too good! So much for lending things to the neighbors is what I say!"

People tittered. They were not a club that relished documentaries anyway. They had been resigned to the film, because they knew that at least coffee and krullers would follow sooner or later. Now it would be sooner, they saw, and they cheered up. With the projector broken, and the fellows beginning to act up, there might be some fun.

Here and there, men stood up and put their hands into their pockets. They wandered back to the cleared area behind all the auditorium seating, away from the women and the others who passively waited in their seats. Meanwhile, Mr. Elvekrog bent over the film feeder. The teeth had somehow shredded some film edge and left celluloid about like auger tailings on the floor. He said in anguish to Emily, who had come back to see if she could help: "National is going to raise a fuss about this! I just know they are!"

Minutes passed. At last, Chuck Iversen shouted to everyone generally, "So what is wrong with singing *Ja, vi elsker dette landet* and have the coffee and cookies? History lessons or cookies, give me cookies every time!"

Someone in the rear, from the knot of men who were changing their weight from foot to foot, shouted, "You don't have any culture, Chuck, is what your trouble is!"

Chuck shouted back, when people stopped laughing: "Oh, to get my hands on the fellow that got off *that* remark!"

The moment was passing into the hands of the people.

"Willi has completely passed out," Emily whispered to Mr. Elvekrog, bending over him while handling film as if she were helping him with the mechanics of repair. "Do you want me to go up and explain very fast exactly what he did during the war and then announce the anthem and you can do the announcements and we will have the lunch?"

"Oh, would you?" cried the program committee chairman.

Up at the podium, Emily waited for silence, glancing over at the Norwegian speaker. He lay oddly twisted on the woman's lap, his left hand hung down between the thighs of her expensive trousers, his face buried in her stomach as her hand patted his shoulder.

Emily said into the PA system, "If we can all somehow get Chuck Iversen to shut up for a second!"

This brought her the laugh she needed.

Then she went on, fast: "Here is what we will do. I am going to tell you very briefly what Willi Varig did. I will keep it down to a few minutes – and then we will do the anthem and announcements and have our coffee. Is that okay with all of you?"

There were nods, almost everywhere in the room, and the scattered muttering directed not to one another in the rows but

directly from individual people to her, which Emily knew meant
the people were relieved – a leader is taking over and it will all
get solved.

Emily told the group about the German invasion of Norway,
in April 1940. She told them how the Norwegian Underground
kept in touch with the RAF and British Intelligence through air
drops, radio, telegraph – and when things were very wrong,
through escape via small boats across the North Sea.

"When I first knew Willi Varig, however," Emily said, "it
was ten years after the war. My husband and I lived in Oslo on a
Fulbright – and German tourists were just beginning to come
into Norway again. Willi used to be drunk nearly every night.
We would have dinner with him, in a small students' dining
room in Drammensveien, which I am sure many of you have
walked in during your summer visits to Norway. Then, after
dinner, Willi would wander down to the Ostbanestasjonen by
himself." Emily paused to let the Norwegian-Americans proudly
whisper back and forth to one another, "Ostbanestasjonen – the
East railway station!"

"Willi would wander along close behind the groups of
tourists getting off the train, deliberately listening to their talk of
getting porters, finding hotels, and so on. He paid no attention
to the younger ones with their rucksacks and knee-socks. They
weren't what he wanted. He followed those of about thirty or
more. When he had determined they were Germans he would
catch up with whichever man appeared to be the father or the
leader and say, in his perfect schoolboy German, 'I beg your
pardon, sir, but is the Herr visiting Norway for the first time?'
The polite German would get over his surprise at being addressed
by a stranger. In the next moment, he would be charmed by this
Norwegian in his good shirt and tie and sports jacket – and
sometimes Willi even went down to the train in his dinner coat –
and the German would smile and say, 'Well – no, actually, it *isn't*
my first time! I have seen Norway before! And I told myself
then, that when I married, the first thing I would do is bring my
wife back to this so beautiful country and I would show her the
wonderful mountains! I especially think the Hardanger plateau is
beautiful! But of course, your city, Oslo, is beautiful as well!'

Then, Willi, smiling, would say, 'Ah, then, the Herr was in
Norway a long time ago and is returning with pleasure? I can
understand that!' and the German, poor chap, would respond,
'Not a *long* time ago – I was stationed here during the War in fact
– and grew very much to love this country!' That, of course, is
what Willi was waiting for, so then he would put a heavy hand
to the German's shoulder, bringing him to a stop. They had been
walking along, with the baggage man and his cart ahead of them.
When Willi stopped the German, the baggage man stopped at
the same moment, before even looking around. Still smiling
now, Willi would say, 'And would the Herr have any idea that
when people love a thing – a person or their country – they do
not like to have it taken away?' and before the German could see
the turn the conversation had taken, Willi would have struck him
as hard as he could manage in the man's face. The German
generally fell down, unless Willi was so drunk he missed his
mark. People stood around waiting for the man to rise. Norwegian railway officials went through the motions of linking
their arms around Willi's elbows. The baggage man turned
forward again and pulled the cart as if nothing had happened.
Soon you would hear the Oslo two-toned police sound. Everyone made a little way for the police. 'Right, Willi!' they said
briskly. 'In you go!' and they popped him into their car. Dozens
of people knew the routine perfectly well. Back at the station,
the policemen would give Willi some coffee and drive him
sedately back up Karl Johansgate, past the castle, up Drammensveien, and deliver him to his woman of the moment."

Emily went on, "That was eleven years after Willi's war was
over. He had been laying a flare path near Stavali, on the
Hardanger plateau, in preparation for an RAF equipment drop.
He was caught by the Germans. Willi noticed, with satisfaction,
that, when the patrol arrested him, his friends, who were two
men and a woman, had vanished. That meant they knew that he
had been taken and that they had not been seen: that was
important. Once anyone was taken prisoner, the others had to
use the pre-planned flight to the sea. Anyone captured would
talk, sooner or later, so you simply had to run either east to
Sweden or west and south to England. Willi's group kept a

shabby fishing boat at Lofthus, with its dinghy shoved under what looked like an abandoned dock. It was arranged that a fisherman take their sailboat out nearly every other day, letting himself be seen on deck, making small repairs, running her sail up and down, trying different engine richnesses. The German coast patrols had trained their glasses on the man for so long they knew his figure by heart – the thick white sweater he wore even on the hottest days when he must have sweltered, and even on the coldest days when he would have been better off with a stormcoat like the other fishermen.

"The Germans took Willi to the nearest office," Emily explained. "A pleasant-spoken young Gestapo officer told Willi that all they really needed were the names of his immediate colleagues and a few practical details. These details would be useful to them, the man explained, with a rueful tone, who had to go on fighting the tiresome war, but not to Willi since he would be able to relax now, in prison. They needed to know his radio frequencies, and the summer's drop plans. At least for now, they told him, that was all they needed. Willi felt he had an hour before he would be made to talk. The German officer would be willing to spend an hour in establishing a trust relationship; beyond that, he would know that Willi was stalling. But up to an hour, he might feel that Willi saw reason and would tell him what he needed for his report. An hour would take Willi's friends from the flare site to Stavali, and another two hours would get them down the steep mountainside to Lofthus. The hour passed as if it were two minutes. The German went out a moment and brought back in with him a colleague whom he politely introduced by name. The colleague knelt by Willi's chair and proceeded to loosen Willi's right kneecap with a screw. Then the colleague, or someone, splashed water on Willi, and when he came to they began again. The second time he came to, he found only the original officer in the room with him. 'You know, Willi, if I may call you by your first name? In a few years' time, perhaps in only one year, the war will be over, and I will go back to Germany, and be married and raise a family. I would like my son to go to Berlin – the University. And the same for you, Willi. You will return to your Oslo and marry and have a

family – you will watch your children waving flags on May 17th
with all the other children – and later, you will watch them
strolling around in their student caps. And we will both get old,
but gradually, easily – in the leisure of time, Willi! You in your
beautiful country, Willi, and I in mine! And there is not a soul
on earth who will remember what was said or done, in this
room, today. What is a single spring day in 1944 when it has
gotten to be 1970, 1980, or perhaps even 1990?' He paused. 'If
you tell me what I have to know simply because it is my job, I
will arrange for you to live, Willi. If you make us *make* you tell
us, you will probably die – but in any case, we would shoot you.
And you know better than to think you won't talk! Everyone
talks! How is your knee now? You know, Willi, when my
colleague comes in again, he will not stick only to the right knee.
Next time it will be the other knee. I can check on it – but I am
pretty sure that is how they do it. They pretty much follow the
same routine each time . . . first the one, then the other. Then
after the war I will go back to Germany and marry and raise my
family – and my wife will never know that I spent today making
a prisoner talk in this room. And of course you will be dead, so
you will never have a wife.' Here the intelligence officer paused,
and then he added, making the only mistake he had made: 'Willi,
everyone talks! . . . *sooner or later.*'"

Emily paused herself and then went on. "The German's
mistake was in saying 'sooner or later.' This reminded Willi that
talking sooner was not at all the same as talking several hours
later. What he had to do was wipe out of his mind's eye the
picture of 1970, 1980, 1990, which the German had kept painting
for him – the picture of the gentle future when all would be
peaceful and wonderful for those still alive to enjoy it. He needed
to put some other picture into his mind's eye – and keep it there
– for one hour, for two hours if he could. He needed to imagine
his friends, the two Underground men and the woman, who
would, if Willi did not talk right away, scramble down the rocky
path behind Lofthus, shove the dinghy out from under its rotten
boarding, and row out to the fishing boat which always stood at
its mooring. He had to force this image into his mind, over and
over – and what helped him to do it was the German's saying

'sooner or later.' So now he said to himself, 'If I last ten minutes more, they have reached the dock. I wonder if dark is coming on now – but I mustn't trust to that, because it is getting on for Sankthansaften and the days are extraordinarily long. If I last,' Willi thought – for now the second German had returned to the cellar room and was kneeling at the other side of Willi's chair, 'if I last another ten minutes, they are all in the dinghy now and they are saying, "Good old Willi! He must not have talked yet!" Now I think I will not last a whole another ten minutes but I could do five, I think, because the fjord is quiet and the motor started right up without any trouble. And now my friend has put on that filthy white sweater which was left right where it was supposed to be and he has the tiller and the others hidden below are sending on the wireless; they are already asking for help now! Thank God then, the motor started up all right for them! And now the Germans are looking at the boat quietly going out the main fjord and saying, "Oh – there's that idiot in the white sweater and that wreck of a boat again!"' Then Willi told himself, 'I do not remember my friends' names anyway. I do not know how many there were of them. I do not remember them. There may have been five, there may have been six. And soon they will be out to sea, and the man in the white sweater will be joined by the people who now can come topside out of hiding. They have sent their wireless call for help, and someone in England or on the Sea and in the Channel has heard, and someone in turn rang up Air/Sea Rescue and they had better have got her mainsail up now – in just this last minute I think they did get their mainsail up all right!' Then when he had passed out again and the enemy had brought him to again Willi said to himself, 'I should say they have picked up a several-force wind out there, but it is from the North so they are running southward to England, south by west, and there is not much difficulty with the waves because they are running with them, but it is rough and the sea is chopped up by the wind.' When Willi woke up the next time he saw in his mind's eye that at last it was night. A submarine rose, shedding a white robing of sea from its bilges, and even after her captain appeared at the conning tower, water slid gently and uniformly off her deck and bilges. The captain was a young Englishman and he shouted at the crew of a Norwegian fishing vessel. The Norwegians brought their boat about so she shuddered now into the wind, and the Englishmen sent over two sailors in a rubber boat. At the submarine, the Norwegian woman handed up a canvas bag and said, 'Will you be so kind as to sink our boat, please, as she may give away information?' The Englishman and his guncrew and the Norwegians watched, their jaws shaking with cold, as the bullets struck the little fishing boat at the waterline. Then the English captain cried, 'Right! Now! Down below with all of you!' The three Underground agents went gingerly below, their feet now gone so cold they felt nothing at the knees and below. They sank gingerly down the rungs and into the oddly motherly, smelly warmth of the sub. Then Willi made the picture in his mind of the submarine's smooth round side frothing and slipping below the huge waves of the North Sea. It moved with its electric ease, far under the tortured waves.

"Then Willi talked. He told the Gestapo officer the names of the two men and the woman. But you see," Emily said heavily to the Tusend Hjem members, "he talked later, not sooner. His partners did make it to England. Then, Germans being Germans, they repaired Willi's knees fairly well. As you all noticed tonight, Willi doesn't walk perfectly, but he does walk.

"And now I am done talking," Emily told them, "but for one thing. If you will please look over to where Willi is now."

Those sitting near Willi and his girlfriend had already been peeping, anyhow. The girl, with Willi's hand still dangling between her legs, glared at no one in particular with her composed, inimical expression. People toward the rear stood up and peered over heads. People whispered. "Now what I am asking of Tusend Hjem is," Emily said, "that we choose. We can keep a kind of mental picture of this Willi here, the one you are looking at right now – or, you can imagine him in your mind's eye, strapped in a chair, with the German intelligence officers. The one who spoke so pleasantly, and the one with the screws. You can remember that scene."

★

Then Mr. Elvekrog came forward, wiping something from the projector off his hands. He gave the announcements, he led them in the Norwegian anthem. Presently, Emily was able to drive the twenty minutes home to White Bear Lake. Mist still rose, more strongly than before, from all the hollows alongside I-35 E. She felt peaceful and absent-minded, and hoped that her daughter would be in bed and the house would be dark and still.

She brought the car very slowly into the drive, so as not to wake Sandra in case she were asleep. Then she crept out and decided to have a look over the lake in the dark. But impressions from the house would creep in, and disturb her mood. She could not help thinking how unhappy her daughter was – how something either major or minor was wrong with Sandra's marriage. She felt, with what she hoped was mistaken intuition, that her daughter was interested in someone other than her husband.

The mist over White Bear Lake was absolutely solid now. The water itself was invisible in the mist and the night, but she felt its presence, so full and rich with rainwater it was nearly rounded upward.

She thought, again, of the Norwegian Underground agents. Neither she nor Willi nor anyone else would ever have the slightest notion what the three people whom Willi had saved had done with their lives. There was nothing to guarantee they had not wasted them. They may never have done anything lovely at all. Emily tried to picture the woman of that Underground team. If she were still alive, she would be old by now. Perhaps she had married for love – but perhaps she had then met someone else, later, who stirred her somehow as she had never imagined possible, but perhaps she did not marry this other person, but stayed with the husband. But then, Emily thought, so many years have passed – likely one or both of the men are dead now. Or perhaps they are utterly dull.

Still, Emily felt herself growing elated, as she stood there staring out over the fog. She did not really have in her mind's eye a picture of aged, paunchy, or lonely old Norwegians. What she really had in mind was the little sailing boat in the North Sea, with its crew young and beautiful; the sea had misted crystal into their hand-knitted caps and sweaters; their hands had chilled

on the sheets and stays and tiller; their knees ably took the sea's
heave – and all the time, the three of them kept looking and
looking, hoping and half-knowing a powerful friend would
emerge from the deep, and come up alongside, and save them.

SCOTT BRADFIELD

☆  ☆  ☆  ☆

# *The Darling*

Afterward Dolores Starr would lie on her bed with a sort of stunned and implicate amazement at the power of things, the power of that vast, soft universe of force contracting gently around her body like a hand. Dolores, she thought. Dolores, dolorous, dolorous star. She didn't feel hurt so much as bewildered and tired, as if she had awoken from a mere dream of struggle in some other, distant room filled with ballooning silence and white, intricate spaces. Usually by now Dad had returned to the kitchen to drink, but sometimes he took his gun from the clothes closet and waved it around for a while. "Maybe we both learned a little lesson today, didn't we, Miss Teen Princess, little Miss Queen of the World." Dad aimed his Walther P-38 at vanity mirror, cheesecloth curtains, Dolores's desktop crucifix. "Ker-*pow*!" Dad said. "Ker-pow, pow, *pow*! *That's* the only lesson most people ever learn, Miss Beautiful, Miss All the Boys Love Her. A bullet in the old brainpan, a crack on the head with a flat rock. Pow, bang. That's just about the only lasting truth *this* goddamn world's got to offer." Dad's gun was very heavy and very solid, and filled the entire apartment with its weight and stress. Dolores liked to hold the gun in her hands too; the entire universe of force seemed to withdraw a little when Dolores took it from the closet; she felt as if she had more air to breathe. Most of all, though, she liked the sudden sound of it, and the way Dad looked at her as if she were someone strange and wholly unfamiliar to him. Then, very slowly, Dad lowered his head on to the kitchen table as Dolores moved his Jim Beam to one side. Dad's brains and blood virtually ruined the checkered tablecloth Dolores had bought at K Mart just that summer, and upstairs Mrs. Morris struck the ceiling three times with her burnished mahogany cane. Mrs. Morris was eighty-seven years old and lived alone. Mrs. Morris lived on a pension, and had bad knees. Mrs. Morris had raised four children of her own and often said she deserved a decent night's sleep every once in a blue moon.

She went to San Francisco and lied about her age, sat at a long Formica table littered with cigarette trays and ashes and solicited marketing surveys. All the operators wore miniature telephone head-sets and resembled the crew of some shoddy spaceship. "Have you graduated college within the last ten years?" Dolores asked people. "Do you ever purchase Hallmark greeting cards? Do you have any children? House pets? Servants? Have you seen the recent television commercial for New Improved Wheatley Wheat Snaps? Have you ever been to Vermont?" She felt like a real adult now, with her own studio apartment on Fulton Street, a super-saver bus pass, a California Federal checking account and even a Versatellar cash card with her own secret card number. She developed a taste for Virginia Slims, piña coladas and Daniel, her Group Module Assistance Coordinator. Daniel was thirty-seven and lived in Brisbane. "The abdominals – that's what goes first. The old midriff section. That's why I either run or swim every morning. That's why I do fifty gut crunchers every night." Daniel had marvelous abdominals, a '67 Karmann Ghia convertible and a bookshelf filled with books. Dolores read Steinbeck's *The Grapes of Wrath*, Durrell's *The Alexandria Quartet* and Tolstoy's *The Death of Ivan Ilych* while Daniel jogged relentlessly down the peninsula, over San Bruno Mountain, around Candlestick Park. Dolores loved the world of books, which were a lot like adulthood, she thought. Both seemed rather smoothly improbable, at once perfectly real and perfectly contrived, like the uniform plaid tweed skirt and red wool sweater she had worn to a Catholic girls' school when she was very small. That was before Grandma died, and Dad started drinking.

Books made people different, she thought. That's why Daniel was different. That's why Dolores felt different every day, after every book. It felt as if every book she read somehow altered her chemical constitution. She thought she would be very happy with Daniel and his books, until the day he hit her. He hit her in the kitchen while she was washing up. He hit her because she hadn't been home when he called. He hit her because she just tried to tell him she was home all night. He hit her because he saw how other men looked at her and how she looked back. He hit her because he couldn't reach into that other part of her where she recognized other men. He hit her because he was just like Dad, he'd been fooling her all the time, he never really read all those books on the shelf. His face was red and damp and he'd been drinking with his friends at the ballpark, and three months later he thought she forgot what he did, thought the entire incident had gone far away when he crashed through the rear screen door, steaming with briny sweat in his Nike tank top and green nylon jogging trunks, and Dolores handed him his tall, cold protein shake. He took it down with one long parched swallow, his Adam's apple bobbing. The protein shake contained nonpasteurized whole milk, two fertile eggs, 8 ounces of liquid protein, wheat germ, vitamin B complex and B12 and three heaped tablespoons of blue crystal Drano. It didn't kill him right away, though. He fell to the floor and pounded it, gurgling deeply in his chest and throat (ironically, Dolores thought, like bad plumbing) and pulled the telephone off the coffee table; it chimed brokenly. His mouth and eyes were pale and dry, and a hard green pellet popped from his throat and ricocheted off the blank, uncomprehending gaze of the Sony Visionstar. In a panic Dolores sought razors in the bathroom, serrated knives in the kitchen, but discovered only Gillette Good News and disposable plastic cutlery. Finally she struck him twice on the back of the head with his simulation ivory and brass league-leading single average bowling trophy, spring 1982. His wallet held almost 300 dollars cash, assorted credit and gas cards. She drove his Karmann Ghia convertible down Highway 5 to Los Angeles, and read Wilde's *The Picture of Dorian Gray* that night in the Van Nuys Motel 6. She liked *The Picture of Dorian Gray* very much.

She made large cash advances on all of Daniel's negotiable cards and opened a money-market liquid-assets account at the Sears Financial Network. She acquired a one-bedroom apartment in Fairfax, a clerical position at TRW and a "new look" from Franklin and Schaeffer in West LA. Men often asked for her number and said complimentary things; men took her to expensive meals, nightclubs, sporting events. In her closet she gradually assembled entire wardrobes of memorabilia from the Dodgers, Raiders, Kings and Angels. Men were easy. They smiled, laughed, offered services, took checks. They were grateful for the smallest attentions. Dolores carried a .380 automatic Beretta in her purse. She liked men, but that didn't mean she was going to take any chances.

Still, she felt vaguely dissatisfied with life. Something important seemed to be missing, or perhaps even beyond her comprehension. It was as if she were always forgetting something. She wanted to be happy. "I guess it's because I never finished high school," she told Michael one day at work. Michael sat with her at the Employee Benefits desk in Personnel. "I guess I never figured out who I wanted to be, like maybe I've gone and wasted some special part of myself somewhere. Maybe because my mother left me when I was very small, I never felt very good about myself as a person. I know I go on lots of dates, but nobody seems to love me for who I really am."

At Michael's suggestion she enrolled in night extension courses at Los Angeles City College. Every Tuesday and Thursday evening after work she attended lectures in abnormal psychology and functional human anatomy. Dr. Peters, who taught functional human anatomy, looked just like Dad before he started drinking. He told her about the jugular, spine, meninges, bile duct. The body was just a delicate bubble, really, which could be broken open very easily; it made her nervous to contemplate twice each week her own physiochemical vulnerability. Infection, hemorrhages, renal failure, metastasis, stroke. Polio, eczema, muscular dystrophy, brain death. Every Friday in lab she dissected large cats and divulged complexes of lymph, nerve and muscle. Dolores much preferred Dr. Deakin in her other class, where she tried to put out of her mind the dead cats with their rictus mouths and smell of formaldehyde. Dr. Deakin was relatively young. He wore pressed and faded Levi's with white, tapered shirts and knit ties. He always punctuated his intense, Socratic monologues with profound, intriguing pauses. "What does it mean . . . this word 'abnormal'? And how do we know

. . . when it truly applies?" He had an overgrown walrus
mustache, and as he paced the lecture floor he gazed up into the
high fluorescents as if entranced by gravid implications only he
could see there, like some spiritual medium. "Don't I think . . .
*I'm* normal? And anytime you contradict me . . . don't I think
*you're* abnormal? Don't we all like to define *ourselves* . . . as the
'normal' ones?" Dolores quickly grew to love him. This was a
man who understood the way the world worked; he could see
far beyond himself into the eyes of other people, other people
who hurt, cared, loved and cried. "I certainly understand the
importance of your class, no kidding," she told him over a shared
turkey-and-sprouts-on-rye at the corner Blimpies. "I have had to
deal with many abnormal people in my life, and I am just
beginning to realize that they were not abnormal at all, but really
were just normal, actually."

Dr. Deakin kept an immaculate duplex in Los Feliz, filled
with lush hanging ferns and gleaming french windows, and
Dolores cut his throat with one of the long steel carving knives
from the immaculate and well-kept Spanish-style kitchen. He
had been perfectly gentle and polite. She hadn't felt angry, or
even perfunctory. There was just something in men which
seemed to demand it now. Something in their eyes. It was like
the look of seduction, really. The blood was suddenly everywhere, and if there was one thing Dolores was firmly resolved
against from that night forward, it was knives. She began making
a few strategic handgun investments. A .38 Special, a 9mm
Parabellum. Dense compact Remington cartridges in a tidy
cardboard box. She joined the National Rifle Association. She
subscribed to *Guns and Ammo*.

Men were easy, but women were different. Women, in fact,
were much more different from Dolores than men. Their glances
click-clicked like the lenses of cameras, their tongues snapped
faintly at you in reproach. They didn't like you talking to any of
their men, and all the men in the world, it seemed, were their
men. Women kept secrets, and liked to pay men special attentions
in private. Dolores didn't even like women, though she hoped it
was a condition which would change with maturity. Women

practiced retributions on grand scales, they wielded sharp blades in profound ritual ceremonies beneath the earth in intricate, vast caverns filled with smoky incense and swelling female voices. Dolores never had a mother, so she never knew. Women shared a secret world of ritual, violence and redemption Dolores could only guess at.

"You know you gotta be careful in LA, don't you, Di?" Michael said, always bringing hot coffee in Styrofoam cups to her desk, candy bars, crackers. "You read the papers, don't you? A single woman's got to be careful in this city; you know why? Because otherwise she'll get murdered, that's why. This city's filled with a lot of very crazy characters, Dolores. For example, just the other day I was reading about a whole club of murderers that lived out in the desert. The women, you see, would go to bars and pick up men. Then they'd take them out to the desert and they'd be murdered by the whole gang. It started out as an Indian cult, but then the white people started getting involved too. Even the white women. They skinned one man completely alive before they murdered him. So, what are you up to later, Di? Feel like a movie, maybe? Or dinner?"

They ate Thai, saw John Wayne in *Red River* and *Rio Bravo*. Dolores particularly liked Angie Dickinson, one of *Rio Bravo*'s costars who would go on later to star in the hit television series *Police Woman*. Angie Dickinson knew a woman could appear feminine and sexy and still know how to take care of herself. Michael sat quietly beside her and didn't even reach for her hand; she could see the movie flickering and inverted in his brown eyes. The movie theater was called the Vista and was located at the corner of Sunset and Hollywood. It was filled with misshapen shadows, stained and thinning velvet draperies, high abandoned balconies and enormous Egyptian-style statues, like some film festival in the Middle Kingdom. "This used to be a gay theater," Michael told her when they first sat down. He shifted uneasily in his seat. "I can still smell them," he said. "Fucking queers."

They bought ice cream next door and then drove to Griffith Park. Michael was silent, and Dolores felt a hard, cool pressure accumulating in her, like the thickness of gravity.

"What are you thinking?" Michael asked.

Every so often they passed the hunched figures of strange
men in the shadows. Usually the strange men wore leather
jackets; they had dark complexions and quick dark hands.

"I don't know. What are *you* thinking?"

Dolores unclasped her purse in her lap. Her right hand slid
through the clutter of checkbooks, wadded Kleenex, random
cosmetics and a dog-eared paperback copy of James M. Cain's
*Mildred Pierce*, sensing the buried and unaltered weight of it there
before she found it. It was always the same, she thought. Men
who really loved you were filled with a sort of emptiness.
Sometimes you wanted to fill that emptiness before it filled you.
They pulled into a secluded parking lot in a grove of drooping
jacarandas. Over the roof of the park the power lines hummed.

"It's not easy living alone in a town like LA," Michael told
her. "I mean, it's not hard for someone like me, since I'm a
highly independent person with a firm commitment to being
exactly who I am. In fact, I can honestly say I have a very firm
commitment to myself, which is not to sound egotistical or
anything. It's just that I'm not one of those people, you know,
who always needs someone telling them, like, this is who you
are." Michael reached under the driver's seat. "Some people
never understand," he said.

Michael withdrew his .357 Magnum Desert Eagle just as
Dolores withdrew her .380 Beretta Model 84, which featured a
thirteen-round staggered magazine and a reversible release. A
crumpled ball of Kleenex, dislodged from the trigger by
Dolores's thumb, tumbled into her lap. It was a full moon
outside that night, making only a dim impression against the
high screen of smog.

Michael looked at Dolores's gun; then he looked at her eyes.
He looked at her gun again. Finally he said, "Don't you have
trouble finding a good clean-burning handload for a piece like
that?"

"I use Blue Dot," Dolores said. "I don't want to stress the
barrel."

They were married in July, bought a condo in the Valley and an
Airedale pup named Bud. "Bud's a pup who's going to have one

solid family unit to depend on," Michael said, dispatched a blizzard of résumés and acquired an administrative position at Lockheed in Burbank. "You've got to believe in yourself if you're going to be happy in this life. Don't you, Bud? Don't you, fellah?" Michael scrubbed the Airedale's addled head between his fingers. The puppy gave a succinct yelp.

"Be careful," Dolores said. "You're hurting him."

They went everywhere and did everything together. Tuesday evenings a self-actualization workshop in Sherman Oaks, Saturday afternoons an advanced gun care and safety program at the Van Nuys Police Academy. They installed a burglar alarm in their home, a doghouse in the blossoming yard and their mutual gun collection behind glass-paneled display cases in the den. "It's like I have all the energy in the world now," Michael said, and decided to build an arboretum in the backyard. "It'll be like our summer home, a home away from home. We'll sit out there and drink iced tea all summer." Michael loved their yard. "Gardening is what I always needed," he told her, returning from the nursery with marigolds, Lincoln roses, peat moss. "It helps me make use of my more positive side, my life-affirming energy. I don't believe in anger anymore. I don't believe in hate. The world's got enough of those negative vibrations already without me making any more of them." He installed floodlights on a high wooden vined terrace, and often worked on the yard alone and late into the evenings.

Dolores, meanwhile, would lie awake in bed at night and imagine the fluttery and somewhat appalled conspiracies of women. "I'm not a thing- or a self-oriented person anymore," Dolores told them. "I'm a goal-oriented person now." Deep in their immaculate caverns, the women murmured; they tried not to listen; they were deeply and mortally offended. "I know you think I've just given in to some man, but that's not true. Michael respects me for being exactly who I am. You can't understand it if you don't know that feeling how wonderful and important that feeling is. It's not something I can just explain." Faint fibrillations, echoes, pulses. The women shared sonorous voices, impossible confidences, their hearts synchronously beating in the black caverns. Dolores didn't trust them; she wanted to get far

away. Someday we'll have our own energy-sufficient cabin in
the Pacific Northwest, she assured herself. We'll have trained
Dobermans, electrified fences, canned goods. We'll have short-
wave, and a proper armory which includes autoloading carbines
and antiballistic missiles. Often she fell asleep before Michael
came to bed, and when she awoke she could hear him already at
work again in the backyard, striking the ground with spades,
shovels, rakes; installing seeds, bulbs, determined little saplings.
"I thought we might have a little vegetable garden right here,"
Michael told her. "Then we don't have to worry so much about
pesticides." Dolores loved to stand at the large picture window
and watch him work. Michael had long, fair-skinned hands
which, finely etched with the brown dirt, resembled beautiful
antique figurines recovered from some archaeological dig. "I'm a
high-energy sort of person," he told her. "I never sleep much."
Bud lay on the sunny grass and contemplated a hovering fly, his
tiny body coiled like the spring of an HK P7. Weekends Dolores
would sit on the faded-green lawn chair, drinking tall ice-cold
drinks and smelling the moist upturned earth. Every few minutes
Michael would look up from his work and smile at her. His tools
lay about casually or leaned against the varnished pine fence like
intimate friends at some large garden party, flaked with dirt like
Michael's hands. There are places outside the world of men and
women, Dolores thought. It's possible to live there safely and
protected, like children with strong, enduring parents.

Then, one Sunday while Michael was pricing planters at
Builders' Emporium, Bud uprooted the foot of a buried postman
among a bed of Michael's blossoming dahlias. His shoelace was
untied, and seemed to signify something, though Dolores was
too shaken to decide exactly what. "I felt impossibly alone," she
told Bud later, cradling him in her arms, dripping his still body
with her tears. "Everything I tried to believe was true about
Michael was really just a lie. His honesty, fidelity, love – all lies.
He never cared about me. He never wanted to share his life with
me. He only wanted his own secret little world." In the basement
she had discovered jars of formaldehyde, handcuffs, ropes and
enormous gray cloth sacks. "He was never going to let me into
that world. I was always going to be completely alone." Bud

was warm and motionless in her arms. It was dark out, and a full moon glowed faintly through the overcast. Then Dolores lay Bud in the trench in Michael's arms. She crossed Michael's arms across Bud, to keep him warm in the long darkness. Michael was wearing his three-piece Bill Blass double-breasted tweed, the same suit he wore the day they were married. Then, gently and with deep regret, Dolores distributed the damp brown earth across them both. It was as if she were burying herself in the tidy garden, placing her own humble body into the deep whispering world of complicit women. The women themselves, though, weren't very happy. Nobody liked her there anymore. They didn't want her with them. Only men liked Dolores. Men and other men.

She drew the curtains on the picture window and every night she slept alone. The loneliness was immense and unsettling. She felt upopulated black continents forming deep inside her body, jagged mossy peninsulas orbited by forlorn craggy islands and glimmering gray water. In the long evenings she sat beside the curtained picture window, motionless within a cone of light from the standing lamp like a display in some anthropological museum, feeling the hard relentless yearning of the planet underneath the yard, the secret articulations of graves and bodies. She never looked at the yard anymore, but only imagined it. Michael's abandoned tools just lay there gathering rust, their wooden handles cracked and splintering. The flower beds and vegetable garden would be overgrown with fast green weeds, the wheelbarrow overturned and covered with a thick gray impasto of cement. And Michael of course, underneath all of it, still telling his lies, still lying to her all night and all day. She couldn't even hear the secret ceremonies of the women anymore. They had gone into deeper caverns where Dolores was no longer privileged. They were teaching her a little lesson. If she wanted to be Miss Little High and Mighty, if she wanted to be independent and on her own, then that's just what she'd have. Just herself; nobody else for her to feel any responsibility toward. Now all she could hear were the power lines buzzing on the high poles, the crickets wheezing, the dark planetary heart beating against the floors of her condo. Sometimes, particularly late at night after she had smoked too much marijuana and too many cigarettes, Michael would appear and attempt to comfort her in her darkest, loneliest hours. He would sit on the beige sofa, absently patting Bud's loose, volitionless head in his lap. "You weren't secure enough in your individuality to allow me to be myself," he told her. "When people love each other, they have to trust each other as well, Di. I think you know that."

Dolores never looked at him directly. She looked instead at the curtained window. She imagined bright spiders spinning their webs in the piles of moldering lumber Michael had purchased for the arboretum. "I don't think I have anything left to say to you anymore," she said.

Sometimes Michael moved to the faded-gray Barcalounger which Dolores had stitched together in places; sometimes the marijuana gave Dolores a vague sense of self-possession, as if she were in complete control of her own lungs, blood, heart. She could will her heart to slow down a bit; she could demand more oxygenation or less. Sometimes she felt as if she were sitting in another, blurred room far away from this one. Usually during these long waking dreams her mind returned to the same questions over and over again. She wondered if her mother was still alive somewhere. Would we recognize one another if we met unexpectedly on the street? she asked herself. Is there something chemical about the bond between a mother and her daughter, or are we just like any two strangers now? Maybe we'll become great friends by sheer chance someday. She will find my naïveté charming; she will teach me all about men. We'll go to movies together and take turns fixing dinner. We'll become devoted room-mates, go to nightclubs, even dancing. In Europe women often go dancing together, and it doesn't necessarily mean they're lesbians or anything.

"You sit cooped up every night smoking grass," Michael told her, the collapsed puppy draped across his knees like a hearth blanket. "I think you've done enough feeling sorry for yourself to last a lifetime. I think it's time you took a little responsibility for your life, and stopped blaming everything on people you love." Michael picked up the container of Herco smokeless shotgun powder from the coffee table. The shotgun, cleaned and loaded, was peering out from underneath Dolores's easy chair. "You don't leave something like this sitting open all day long," he said. "It gets damp." He affixed the aluminum lid with a quick hollow snap. "Also, you better start looking in on the yard. The neighborhood cats have begun digging up Mrs. Winslow again. If I were you, I'd go out there right now and check on Mrs. Winslow."

Dolores took the unfinished joint from the ashtray in her lap and lit it with her Cricket. A seed popped; a fragment of paper sparked and fluttered through the air. Without exhaling, Dolores asked, "Who was Mrs. Winslow?" Her eyes began to water.

Michael shrugged. In his lap, Bud's head rolled to one side, his large eyes dry and vacant like the eyes of some collapsed puppet. "Just some lady worked at the library," he said.

Then, one Friday evening in late summer, Dolores returned home from Von's to discover numerous police cars and ambulances parked in her driveway, their soft red and yellow emergency bulbs pulsing and spinning in the smoggy twilit air. They seemed vaguely sudden and incongruous, like emergency flares designating some roadside picnic. Dolores removed her groceries from the trunk, and a uniformed policeman at the door gazed at her with a sort of official complacency. Loaves of bread, a sack of red Delicious apples, gallons of distilled water in large clear-plastic jugs. Even though she lived alone, she liked to be prepared; if there was one thing life had taught her, you never knew what might happen next. She didn't feel surprised so much as slightly bemused when she was confronted by charges of multiple homicide with Birds Eye frozen vegetables under one arm, nachos and various snack crackers under the other. The arresting officer, Detective Rowlandson, was very kind. He asked her if the cuffs were comfortable. He transferred her frozen foods into the care of one of the random officers who were milling awkwardly about the small living room. The uncurtained window revealed a red, apocalyptic sunset and numerous men in white cloth shirts and trousers digging at the yard. Wearing surgical masks and gloves, they wrapped the moldering figures in white sheets and transferred them to stretchers which were then carried to the open chambers of patient white ambulances. When Detective Rowlandson drove her down the hill in his Eldorado the streets were filled with curious neighbors – housewives in faded terry-cloth robes, children leaning against their Stingray bicycles. "Anything you say can and will be held against you in a court of law," Detective Rowlandson told her, trying to find a classical station on the radio. "I know," Dolores said, "and I think that's perfectly fair." She was turning to look at the young officer in the backseat. The young officer was gazing aimlessly out the window. He seemed a little bored, or even homesick. When they arrived at the station Detective Rowlandson interrogated her in his private office, with another pair of uniformed patrolmen at the door and a cassette tape recorder whirring on the desktop. "Maybe you'd like a little soda or something?" he asked. "Maybe your throat's getting a little parched?" They were all very kind, Dolores thought. Even when they don't really know what's going on, men really do try to do their best. Men really do care about the unapproachable world of women.

She was awarded a private cell and instant, irremediable celebrity. "I can't say I'm proud of what I've done," she told the media, which were assembled around her in a bright fluorescent room of flashing cameras and buzzing tape machines. The journalists sat poised on the edge of their aluminum chairs as if expecting some race to commence without a second's notice. "It's not like I'm stupid either, since I always did well in school whenever I bothered to apply myself, and Dr. Weinstein, who is one of the very kind doctors visiting me while I am incarcerated, says I performed exceptionally well on the Wechsler Adult Intelligence Scale. I guess I can only blame my poor upbringing, being as that my mother left me when I was very little, and as my father beat me when I was little and took advantage of me in many ways which are too delicate to be gotten into at this time and place. But anyway, I can't blame everything on my parents, since I am a grown-up woman who must take responsibility for herself, and so I would like to say that I am solely responsible for all those dead bodies buried in my yard" – which initiated a blizzard of bursting flashblubs – "and of course for my good husband Michael's senseless and untimely demise as well, and if I get sent to the electric chair I will certainly deserve every minute of it since Michael was the kindest, most loving husband the world has ever known, and he was certainly the only man who ever actually tried to understand and care for me in a totally unselfish and caring manner. Thank you very much."

Dolores's private cell was in the women's maximum-security prison in Lancaster. She had a toilet, a washbasin and a prison-issue towel, soap and toothbrush. She had a rough green khaki blanket and bristly sheets. Every afternoon they took her out alone to exercise in the courtyard. She walked calmly around the painted white basketball tableau. She did sit-ups and leg lifts, pausing occasionally to gaze up at the bright California sky. The guards were all women. When she saw the other inmates, they were all women. They all had hard, coarse expressions. Sometimes, far off down the distant cement corridors, Dolores could hear a young woman crying. She sounded very young, almost a child.

Dolores was entering her Russian novel phase. She read *Crime and Punishment*, *Anna Karenina* and *War and Peace*. For the first time in her life, Dolores felt at peace with herself and her innermost being. *It's like I never had a chance before to actually understand what it was like to be totally on my own*, she wrote on her pad of white paper, which was inspected every evening by one of the uniformed guards. *Maybe if I had only had a chance to get to know myself without other people around me all the time making me feel like somebody I wasn't, I wouldn't have killed all those nice people.* She contemplated writing her own autobiography and publishing it under the title *Bad Love*. Her cell was absolutely silent for hours at a time. In fact, Dolores rarely saw any men at all. She felt denser, more compact and more real. It was as if her entire body were filling up with sand. She refused newspapers and magazines. She was a quiet, respectable hermit living alone in a deep cave. She was contemplating convoluted and transcendent things. *Some things you just can't explain*, she told her writing pad. *Sometimes too you can be just happy not explaining them either.*

"They've got you now, baby," Michael said, picking at the celery on her evening meal tray. "As they say in the movies – the jig is up."

"We'll see," Dolores said. She felt a vague glimmer of hope, one which filled her with impossible sadness.

A few days later Dr. Weinstein fell in love with her, and she knew all the peace she had finally grown accustomed to would not last. "Primitive man didn't draw pictures on his walls because he liked pretty *pictures*, for chrissakes," Dr. Weinstein told her during one of his visits, trying to act like he wasn't in love with her, like he was different from other men. "It's not like *Neanderthalus australopithecus* buried his dead out of fucking sympathy and compassion. How much sympathy and compassion do you think you'd get from a *Neanderthalus australopithecus*? Not too damn much, that's how much. Not too damn much at all." He showed her a picture of *Neanderthalus australopithecus* in a large library edition of *The Encylopedia of Human Anthropology*. "You see that guy? You see those teeth, that brow? Why do you think he painted pictures on the wall? For the same reason he ate the still–bloody hearts of the rival tribesmen he killed, that's why. He was appropriating the soul and strength of significant others. Family, beasts, enemies. The sun and the fucking moon, that's what."

He carried a black leather briefcase. He wore a dark suit and glasses. At first he appeared only every few weeks or so and asked her to complete psychological profiles, write personal compositions and analyze photographs of men, women and children in family situations. Then he began arriving every afternoon just as the lunch trays were being collected by a trusty on a wobbly aluminum cart. Sometimes he talked for hours while Dolores sat on her cot, her hands folded between her knees, her blank gaze trained upon the concrete floor which she had scrubbed clean just that morning.

"We do it every day," Dr. Weinstein said. He held the briefcase in his lap with his left hand; his right hand gestured vacantly at the cold and empty air. "We appropriate the souls and strengths of other people. It's just that most of us don't have to kill them, babe. You know what I'm saying at you, Di? You don't mind if I call you Di, do you? I saw it on your Wechsler examination under preferred nicknames. " He offered her cigarettes and she smoked them, inhaling the grainy, desultory smoke, watching it settle across the stone floors like morning mist in a swamp. "Love and aggression are the same thing in human society. They're both responses to the same biochemical hums and pops. You love or hate the other and you want to blast them. You want to break them down into their elements and swallow them. You want to make them one with yourself by devouring, feasting, obliterating. Then they're part of you, aren't they, babe? Then *you're* in complete control. It's a biochemical desire, but when we live in society, see, we learn to develop displacements for those desires. We learn to turn acts into symbolic intentions. You don't *do*, in other words, Di. You learn to seem *not* to do, if you know what I mean. But you really *do* do, secretly, but only in your mind. Only you, babe, you don't know how to do that. You think there's just your mind and the world, that the world's the only object your mind's got to act on. You have to learn to invent other objects. You have to learn to compensate for your desires by instituting certain ritual behaviors in your seriously addled and definitely very sociopathic psyche, Di – and I think I can say that much for certain. Definitely sociopathic. These are things you're supposed to learn – when you're raised properly. But you haven't been raised properly. You've got to be raised all over, right? You see what I'm saying, Di? You've got to be raised all over again. "

Dr. Weinstein testified at her first court appearance, and the charges were dropped on grounds of insanity. "Let's say they were pretty firm grounds, Di. Let's say we had a fucking continent full of firm ground for that one," Dr. Weinstein told her in the government car that took them to a county holding cell after the hearing. Three days later Dolores was remanded to the custody of the state psychiatric clinic in Reseda and, three months after that, quietly transferred to Dr. Weinstein's private facilities in Napa County. It was a different place from prison, and Dolores didn't like it. The grounds were green and unenclosed, with a view of rolling hills patched with vineyards. Dolores was apportioned her own private room, wardrobe, library and lawn chair. The patients here were all very quiet and composed, and didn't look disturbed at all that Dolores could tell. Rachel, an attractive fortyish redhead, told her, "When my husband closed down our savings account and ran off with his secretary to Buenos Aires, I guess I just couldn't cope." Rachel was wearing a polka-dot cotton summer dress and reading *Cosmopolitan*.

Dr. Weinstein was personally committed to raising Dolores all over again. Her diet was strictly regulated. Listlessly, she attended the clinic's mandatory Exercycle workouts. Her blood pressure was intently monitored, her saliva, feces and urine; two interns from UCLA Medical Center received a grant to monitor her endorphins. She was steeped in megavitamins and zinc; she suffered a high colonic. "Symbolic displacement," Dr. Weinstein told her after each morning's "contact therapy" interview in his office. "There are certain amine molecules manufactured in the adrenal gland which generate rage. There's good rage and there's bad rage, and your rage, Di, is very bad. These amines are then conditioned and modified by those massive discharges of the endocrine system concerned with reproduction. Reproduction is something your body anticipates around the clock; your body's always preparing you for reproduction, Di." He took her hand and commented on her long, strong fingers; then he brushed a vein with alcohol and inserted the needle. "It's at the confluences of rage and sex where we're trying to get," he said. "We're trying to draw a line between intentionality and action, pure rage and sudden sex. That's the line that's been eliminated in you, babe. We're going to replace it. We're going to draw it fast and hard." She received the injection three times a day, and Dr. Weinstein began taking her on what he liked to call "field studies." They drove to Marin County and purchased a new Volvo. They went shopping for clothes, curtains, sheets, dishes. Dolores had never really enjoyed shopping that much before, but now she craved it like potato chips; it took her away from herself; she could lose herself in the vast chattering communities of women. Afterward she and Dr. Weinstein would return to his private office at the clinic and watch television; often they attended movies and plays together. He pronounced her fit for the home-based phase of her therapy. They were married in August and set up housekeeping in a beautiful, isolated two-story country house in Sebastopol. Dolores worked mornings at the local day-care center while Dr. Weinstein was at the clinic. Then she had the rest of the day to watch television. She didn't like books anymore. Dr. Weinstein's Literary Guild selections gazed down mutely from the high mahogany bookshelves like zoological specimens cradled in formaldehyde jars.

She still thought of murdering him. Not every day, but periodically. At these times she felt herself inflating with a strange, unidentifiable sensation. Her heart began to pound; the backs of her hands began to itch. Her face grew flushed and hot, and she developed splitting migraines. She had never felt so intensely aware of the flux and convection of her own blood before. "You're learning, Di. You're learning to accept the limitations of your own body, your own mind." Dr. Weinstein sat in the stuffed chair beside the jetting blue flames of the gas fireplace. The latest issue of *The American Journal of Psychiatric Medicine* was propped open against his knee. "Fix us a cup of coffee, babe. Sit down and relax with me." Dolores went into the kitchen and saw the immaculate wooden cooking utensils hanging from the varnished redwood cabinets. Then she went out the back door and made the screen door slam. She drove their second car to the Emporium hall and had a Bloody Mary at Marie Calendar's. She was still filling up with the unidentifiable feelings. She tried to repress them, but she didn't know what she was repressing. Terrible anger and rage, she suspected. That was what Dr. Weinstein told her; that's what the daily injections were investing her with. She was frightened and disoriented. She sat down at a row of plastic stools near a wide mirrored fountain. Blue water streamed from the blowholes of glass dolphins. The fear grew more and more terrible as she watched the pulsing crowds and families. Teenage girls emblazoned with cosmetics. Young couples pushing dazed babies in carriages with tiny stuffed toys dangling from their fabric awnings. Packs of young men with faces flushed with marijuana. It wasn't fear anymore, it was panic. Dolores felt panicked but she couldn't move; she couldn't face the crowds of people; she couldn't face the acres of cars in the vast parking lots. She started to cry and cry. She had never cried in front of strangers before. When someone tried to touch her she pulled away and screamed at them. She didn't know what she screamed, but she knew she didn't want anybody near her. She just wanted to cry and cry, as if the entire world had ended and now only its unaccountable sadness was left, filling her and filling her like the hard colorless rage with which she desperately desired to murder Dr. Weinstein.

After these "episodes" Dolores would be sedated and kept overnight at the clinic. In the morning, Dr. Weinstein would drive her home in the Volvo, usually playing Philip Glass on the car stereo. "It takes a while to adjust," he told her. "We're teaching your entire body how to behave all over again. We're teaching it how to feel and breathe." His right hand reached out and held hers in her lap. She felt enervated and thick with barbiturates. Outside, the entire landscape was blurred and indistinct. "We're teaching you how to love, babe. We're teaching you how to love without hurting anybody." Dolores began to feel extraordinarily lonely and weak. "And you know I love you, Di. You know that, don't you?"

She couldn't even remember the faces of any of her old lovers anymore. Their memory seemed to be draining easily from her like water from a tub. She could remember their names – Daniel, Dr. Deakin, Michael, Dad – but she couldn't remember anything about the quality of their presence, the fabric of their skin or voice or hair, the strength of their muscles or intestines. In the long summer afternoons she would just sit outside in the sculpted front garden, wearing her cashmere robe, black stockings and a silk teddy, beside an ice chest filled with margaritas on the wrought-iron lawn table next to the Valium prescriptions and her strewn cosmetics, and gaze aimlessly at the blue sky, green trees and topiary hedges. There was just a dark inchoate sadness now, formless and buzzing. "It's the recognition that you're alone, babe. It's the human condition, it just means you're sane, that's all. It means you're not swallowing people. It means you know who you are, and who they are, and that line where the twain shall not meet. You're developing a nice clean, bright soul now, like Billy's bright T-shirt in a television detergent commercial. You've got your own world inside now, babe. You're ready to live your own life." Dolores sipped her margarita and thought about *Neanderthal australopithecus*'s cave. Someone had expunged all the pale etchings of bison and mammoth from the rough basalt walls. There was nobody left in the cave at all anymore, not even the flickering fire or the smell of roasting meat. Dolores lit a cigarette and looked at the impossibly blue sky. For a moment she thought she might start crying, but then she didn't.

The following summer Dr. Weinstein pronounced her cured, and exactly one year after that she gave birth to a 9-pound baby boy. The baby had a full head of black matted hair when he was presented to her by the nurse; his eyes were squeezed shut with pain and screaming. She held him against her breasts and listened to his heart beating in her private room while Dr. Weinstein sat beside her, beaming like a streetlamp and holding her hand. After a few days of bloodless discussion, they named the baby Andrew, in honor of Dolores's dad.

☆ ☆ ☆ ☆

# Tall Tales
# from the Mekong Delta

It was in the fifth month of her sobriety. It was after the hospital. It was after her divorce. It was autumn. She had even stopped smoking. She was wearing pink aerobic pants, a pink T-shirt with KAUAI written in lilac across the chest, and tennis shoes. She had just come from the gym. She was walking across a parking lot bordering a city park in West Hollywood. She was carrying cookies for the AA meeting. She was in charge of bringing the food for the meeting. He fell into step with her. He was short, fat, pale. He had bad teeth. His hair was dirty. Later, she would freeze his frame in her mind and study it. She would say he seemed frightened and defeated and trapped, "cagey" was the word she used to describe his eyes, how he measured and evaluated something in the air between them. The way he squinted through hazel eyes, it had nothing to do with the sunlight.

"I'm Lenny," he said, extending his hand. "What's your name?"

She told him. She was holding a bag with packages of cookies in it. After the meeting, she had an appointment with her psychiatrist, then a manicure. She kept walking.

"You a teacher? You look like a teacher," he said.

"I'm a writer," she told him. "I teach creative writing."

"You look like a teacher," Lenny said.

"I'm not just a teacher," she told him. She was annoyed.

"Okay. You're a writer. And you're bad. You're one of those bad girls from Beverly Hills. I've had my eye on you," Lenny said.

She didn't say anything. He was wearing blue jeans, a black

leather jacket zipped to his throat, a long red wool scarf around his neck, and a Dodgers baseball cap. It was too hot a day for the leather jacket and scarf. She didn't find that detail significant. It caught her attention, she touched it briefly and then let it go. She looked but did not see. They were standing on a curb. The meeting was in a community room across the boulevard. She wasn't afraid yet.

"You do drugs? What do you do? Drink too much?" he asked.

"I'm a cocaine addict," she told him.

"Me too. Let's see your tracks. Show me your tracks." Lenny reached out for her arm.

"I don't have any now." She glanced at her arm. She extended her arm into the yellow air between them. The air was already becoming charged and disturbed. "They're gone."

"I see them," Lenny told her, inspecting her arm, turning it over, holding it in the sunlight. He touched the part of her arm behind her elbow where the vein rose. "They're beautiful."

"But there's nothing there," she said.

"Yeah, there is. There always is if you know how to look," Lenny told her. "How many people by the door? How many steps?"

He was talking about the door across the boulevard. His back was turned. She didn't know.

"Four steps," Lenny said. "Nine people. Four women. One odd man. I look. I see."

She was counting the people on the steps in front of the meeting. She didn't say anything.

"Let's get a coffee later. That's what you do, right? You can't get a drink? You go out for coffee?" Lenny was studying her face.

"I don't think so," she said.

"You don't think so? Come on. I'll buy you coffee. You can explain AA to me. You like that Italian shit? That French shit? The little cups?" Lenny was staring at her.

"No, thank you. I'm sorry," she said. He was short and fat and sweating. He looked like he was laughing at her with his eyes.

"You're sorry. I'll show you sorry. Listen. I know what you want. You're one of those smart-ass teachers from Beverly Hills," Lenny said.

"Right," she said. She didn't know why she bothered talking to him.

"You want to get in over your head. You want to see what's on the other side. I'll show you. I'll take you there. It'll be the ride of your life," Lenny said.

"Goodbye," she answered.

Lenny was at her noon meeting the next day. She saw him immediately as she walked through the door. She wondered how he knew that she would be there. As she approached her usual chair, she saw a bouquet of long-stemmed pink roses.

"You look beautiful," Lenny said. "You knew I'd be here. That's why you put that crap on your face. You didn't have that paint on yesterday. Don't do that. You don't need that. Those whores from Beverly Hills need it. Not you. You're a teacher. I like that. Sit down." He picked the roses up. "Sit next to me. You glad to see me?"

"I don't think so." She sat down. Lenny handed the roses to her. She put them on the floor.

"Yeah. You're glad to see me. You were hoping I'd be here. And here I am. You want me to chase you? I'll chase you. Then I'll catch you. Then I'll show you what being in over your head means." Lenny was smiling.

She turned away. When the meeting was over, she stood up quickly and began moving, even before the prayer was finished. "I have to go," she said softly, over her shoulder. She felt she had to apologize. She felt she had to be careful.

"You don't have to go," Lenny said. He caught up with her on the steps. "Yeah. Don't look surprised. Lenny's fast, real fast. And you're lying. Don't ever lie to me. You think I'm stupid? Yeah, you think Lenny's stupid. You think you can get away from me? You can't get away. You got an hour. You don't pick that kid up from the dance school until four. Come on. I'll buy you coffee."

"What are you talking about?" She stopped. Her breath felt

sharp and fierce. It was a warm November. The air felt like glass.

"I know all about you. I know your routine. I been watching you for two weeks. Ever since I got to town. I saw you my first day. You think I'd ask you out on a date and not know your routine?" Lenny stared at her.

She felt her eyes widen. She started to say something but she changed her mind.

"You live at the top of the hill, off of Doheny. You pick up that kid, what's her name, Annie something? You pick her up and take her to dance school. You get coffee next door. Table by the window. You read the paper. Then you go home. Just the two of you. And that Mex cleaning lady. Maria. That her name? Maria? They're all called Maria. And the gardener Friday afternoons. That's it." Lenny lit a cigarette.

"You've been following me?" She was stunned. Her mouth opened.

"Recon," Lenny said.

"I beg your pardon?"

"In Nam. We called it recon. Fly over, get a lay of the land. Or stand behind some trees. Count the personnel. People look but they don't see. I'll tell you about it. Get coffee. You got an hour. Want to hear about Vietnam? I got stories. Choppers? I like choppers. You can take your time, aim. You can hit anything, even dogs. Some days we'd go out just aiming at dogs. Or the black market? Want to hear about that? Profiteering in smack? You're a writer, right? You like stories. I got some tall tales from the Mekong Delta for you, sweetheart. Knock your socks off. Come on." He reached out and touched her arm. "Later you can have your own war stories. I can be one of your tall tales. I can be the tallest."

The sun was strong. The world was washed with white. The day seemed somehow clarified. He was wearing a leather jacket and shaking. It occurred to her that he was sick.

"Excuse me. I must go," she said. "If you follow me, I shall have someone call the police."

"Okay. Okay. Calm down," Lenny was saying behind her. "I'll save you a seat tomorrow, okay?"

She didn't reply. She sat in her car. It was strange how blue the sky seemed, etched with the blue of radium or narcotics. Or China blue, perhaps. Was that a color? The blue of the China Sea? The blue of Vietnam. When he talked about Asia, she could imagine that blue, luminescent with ancient fever, with promises and bridges broken, with the harvest lost in blue flame. Always there were barbarians, shooting the children and dogs.

She locked her car and began driving. It occurred to her, suddenly, that the Chinese took poets as concubines. Their poets slept with warlords. They wrote with gold ink. They ate orchids and smoked opium. They were consecrated by nuance, by birds and silk and the ritual birthdays of gods and nothing changed for a thousand years. And afternoon was absinthe yellow and almond, burnt orange and chrysanthemum. And in the abstract sky, a litany of kites.

She felt herself look for him as she walked into the meeting the next day at noon. The meeting was in the basement of a church. Lenny was standing near the coffeepot with his back to the wall. He was holding two cups of coffee as if he was expecting her. He handed one to her.

"I got seats," he said. He motioned for her to follow. She followed. He pointed to a chair. She sat in it. An older woman was standing at the podium, telling the story of her life. Lenny was wearing a white warm-up suit with a green neon stripe down the sides of the pants and the arms of the jacket. He was wearing a baseball cap. His face seemed younger and tanner than she had remembered.

"Like how I look? I look like a lawyer on his way to tennis, right? I even got a tan. Fit right in. Chameleon Lenny. The best, too." He lit a cigarette. He held the pack out to her.

She shook her head, no. She was staring at the cigarette in his mouth, in his fingers. She could lean her head closer, part her lips, take just one puff.

"I got something to show you," Lenny said.

The meeting was over. They were walking up the stairs from the basement of the church. The sun was strong. She blinked in the light. It was the yellow of a hot autumn, a yellow that seemed amplified and redeemed. She glanced at her watch.

"Don't do that," Lenny said. He was touching the small of her back with his hand. He was helping her walk.

"What?"

"Looking at that fucking watch all the time. Take it off," Lenny said.

"My watch?" She was looking at her wrist as if she had never seen it before.

"Give it here, come on." Lenny put his hand out. He motioned with his fingers. She placed her watch in the palm of his hand.

"That's a good girl," Lenny was saying. "You don't need it. You don't have to know what time it is. You're with me. Don't you get it? You're hungry, I feed you. You're tired, I find a hotel. You're in a structured environment now. You're protected. I protect you. It doesn't matter what time it is." He put her watch in his pocket. "Forget it. I'll buy you a new one. A better one. That was junk. I was embarrassed for you to wear junk like that. Want a Rolex?"

"You can't afford a Rolex," she said. She felt intelligent. She looked into his face.

"I got a drawerful," Lenny told her. "I got all the colors. Red. Black. Gold."

"Where?" She studied his face. They were walking on a side street in Hollywood. The air was a pale blue, bleeding into the horizon, taking the sky.

"In the bank," Lenny said. "In the safety deposit with everything else. All the cash that isn't buried." Lenny smiled.

"What else?" She put her hands on her hips.

"Let's go for a ride," Lenny said.

They were standing at the curb. They were two blocks from the church. A motorcycle was parked there. Lenny took out a key.

"Get on," he said.

"I don't want to get on a motorcycle." She was afraid.

"Yes, you do," Lenny told her. "Sit down on it. Wrap your arms around me. Just lean into me. Nothing else. You'll like it.

You'll be surprised. It's a beautiful day. It looks like Hong Kong today. Want to go to the beach? Want lunch? I know a place in Malibu. You like seafood? Crab? Scampi? Watch the waves?" Lenny was doing something to the motorcycle. He looked at her face.

"No," she said.

"How about Italian? I got a place near the Marina. Owner owes for ten kilos. We'll get a good table. You like linguini?" Lenny sat down on the motorcycle.

She shook her head, no.

"Okay. You're not hungry. You're skinny. You should eat. Come on. We'll go around the block. Get on. Once around the block and I'll bring you back to the church." Lenny reached out his hand through the warm white air.

She looked at his hand and how the air seemed blue near his fingers. It's simply a blue glaze, she was thinking. In Malibu, in Hilo, in the China Sea, forms of blue, confusion and remorse, a dancing dress, a daughter with a mouth precisely your own and it's done, all of it.

Somewhere it was carnival night in the blue wash of a village on the China Sea. On the river, boats passed with low-slung antique masts sliding silently to the blue of the ocean, to the inverted delta where the horizon concluded itself in a rapture of orchid and pewter. That's what she was thinking when she took his hand.

She did not see him for a week. She changed her meeting schedule. She went to women's meetings in the Pacific Palisades and the Valley. She went to meetings she had never been to before. She trembled when she thought about him.

She stopped her car at a red light. It occurred to her that it was an early afternoon autumn in her thirty-eighth year. Then she found herself driving to the community center. The meeting was over. There was no one left on the street. Just one man, sitting alone on the front steps, smoking. Lenny looked up at her and smiled.

"I was expecting you," Lenny said. "I told you. You can't get away from me."

She could feel his eyes on her face, the way when she lived with a painter, she had learned to feel lamplight on her skin. When she had learned to perceive light as an entity. She began to cry.

"Don't cry," Lenny said, his voice soft. "I can't stand you crying. Let's make up. I'll buy you dinner."

"I can't." She didn't look at him.

"Yeah. You can. I'll take you someplace good. Spago? You like those little pizzas with the duck and shit? Lobster? You want the Palm? Then Rangoon Racket Club? Yeah. Don't look surprised. I know the places. I made deals in all those places. What did you think?" He was lighting a cigarette and she could feel his eyes on her skin.

She didn't say anything. They were walking across a parking lot. The autumn made everything ache. Later, it would be worse. At dusk, with the subtle irritation of lamps.

"Yeah. I know what you think. You think Lenny looks like he just crawled out from a rock. This is a disguise. Blue jeans, sneakers. I fit right in. I got a gang of angry Colombians on my ass. Forget it." Lenny stared at her. "You got a boyfriend?"

"What's it to you?"

"What's it to me? That's sharp. I want to date you. I probably want to marry you. You got a boyfriend, I got to hurt him." Lenny smiled.

"I can't believe you said that." She put her hands on her hips.

"You got a boyfriend? I'm going to cut off his arm and beat him with it. Here. Look at this." He was bending over and removing something from his sock. He held it in the palm of his hand.

"Know what this is?" Lenny asked.

She shook her head, no.

"It's a knife, sweetheart," Lenny said.

She could see that now, even before he opened it. A push-button knife. Lenny was reaching behind to his back. He was pulling out something from behind his belt, under his shirt. It was another knife.

"Want to see the guns?"

She felt dizzy. They were standing near her car. It was early in December. The Santa Anas had been blowing. She felt that it had been exceptionally warm for months.

"Don't get in the car," Lenny said. "I can't take it when you leave. Stay near me. Just let me breathe the same air as you. I love you."

"You don't even know me," she said.

"But you know me. You been dreaming me. I'm your ticket to the other side, remember?" Lenny had put his knives away. "Want to hear some more Nam stories? How we ran smack into Honolulu? You'll like this. You like the dope stories. You want to get loaded?"

She shook her head, no.

"You kidding me? You don't want to get high?" Lenny smiled.

"I like being sober," she said.

"Sure," Lenny said. "Let me know when that changes. One phone call. I got the best dope in the world."

They were standing in front of her car. The street beyond the parking lot seemed estranged, the air was tarnished. She hadn't thought about drugs in months. Lenny was handing her something, thin circles of metal. She looked down at her hand. Two dimes seemed to glare in her palm.

"For when you change your mind," Lenny said. He was still smiling.

They were sitting on the grass of a public park after a meeting. Lenny was wearing Bermuda shorts and a green T-shirt that said CANCÚN. They were sitting in a corner of the park with a stucco wall behind them.

"It's our anniversary," Lenny told her. "We been in love four weeks."

"I've lost track of time," she said. She didn't have a watch anymore. The air felt humid, green, stalled. It was December in West Hollywood. She was thinking that the palms were livid with green death. They could be the palms of Vietnam.

"I want to fuck you," Lenny said. "Let's go to your house."

She shook her head, no. She turned away from him. She began to stand up.

"Okay. Okay. You got the kid. I understand that. Let's go to a hotel. You want the Beverly Wilshire? I can't go to the Beverly Hills Hotel. I got a problem there. What about the Four Seasons? You want to fuck in the Four Seasons?"

"You need to get an AIDS test," she said.

"Why?" Lenny looked amused.

"Because you're a heroin addict. Because you've been in jail," she began.

"Who told you that?" Lenny sat up.

"You told me," she said. "Terminal Island. Chino. Folsom? Is is true?"

"Uh-huh," Lenny said. He lit a cigarette. "Five years in Folsom. Consecutive. Sixty months. I topped out."

She stared at him. She thought how easy it would be, to reach and take a cigarette. Just one, once.

"Means I finished my whole sentence. No time off for good behavior. Lenny did the whole sixty." He smiled. "I don't need an AIDS test."

"You're a heroin addict. You shoot cocaine. You're crazy. Who knows what you do or who you do it with?" She was beginning to be afraid.

"You think I'd give you a disease?" Lenny looked hurt.

Silence. She was looking at Lenny's legs, how white the exposed skin was. She was thinking that he brought his sick body to her, that he was bloated enormous with pathology and bad history, with jails and demented resentments.

"Listen. You got nothing to worry about. I don't need a fucking AIDS test. Listen to me. Are you hearing me? You get that disease, I take care of you. I take you to Bangkok. I keep a place there, on the river. Best smack in the world. Fifty cents. I keep you loaded. You'll never suffer. You start hurting, I'll take you out. I'll kill you myself. With my own hands. I promise," Lenny said.

Silence. She was thinking that he must be drawn to her vast emptiness, could he sense that she was aching and hot and always listening? There is always a garish carnival across the boulevard.

We are born, we eat and sleep, conspire and mourn, a birth, a betrayal, an excursion to the harbor, and it's done. All of it, done.

"Come here." Lenny extended his arm. "Come here. You're like a child. Don't be afraid. I want to give you something."

She moved her body closer to his. There are blue enormities, she was thinking, horizons and boulevards. Somewhere, there are blue rocks and they burn.

"Close your eyes," Lenny said. "Open your mouth."

She closed her eyes. She opened her mouth. There was something pressing against her lip. Perhaps it was a flower.

"Close your mouth and breathe," Lenny said.

It was a cigarette. She felt the smoke in her lungs. It had been six months since she smoked. Her hand began to tremble.

"There," Lenny was saying. "You need to smoke. I can tell. It's okay. You can't give up everything at once. Here. Share it. Give me a hit."

They smoked quietly. They passed the cigarette back and forth. She was thinking that she was like a sacked capital. Nothing worked in her plazas. The palm trees were on fire. The air was smoky and blue. No one seemed to notice.

"Sit on my lap. Come on. Sit down. Closer. On my lap," Lenny was saying. "Good. Yeah. Good. I'm not going to bite you. I love you. Want to get married? Want to have a baby? Closer. Let me kiss you. You don't do anything. Let me do it. Now your arms. Yeah. Around my neck. Tighter. Tighter. You worried? You got nothing to worry about. You get sick, I keep you whacked on smack. Then I kill you. So what are you worried? Closer. Yeah. Want to hear about R and R in Bangkok? Want to hear about what you get for a hundred bucks on the river? You'll like this. Lean right up against me. Yeah. Close your eyes."

"Look. It's hot. You want to swim. You like that? Swimming? You know how to swim?" Lenny looked at her. "Yeah? Let's go. I got a place in Bel Air."

"You have a place in Bel Air?" she asked. It was after the

meeting. It was the week before Christmas. It was early afternoon.

"Guy I used to know. I did a little work for him. I introduced him to his wife. He owes me some money. He gave me the keys." Lenny reached in his pocket. He was wearing a white-and-yellow warm-up suit. He produced a key ring. It hung in the hot air between them. "It's got everything there. Food. Booze. Dope. Pool. Tennis court. Computer games. You like that? Pac Man?"

She didn't say anything. She felt she couldn't move. She lit a cigarette. She was buying two packages at a time again. She would be buying cartons soon.

"Look. We'll go for a drive. I'll tell you some more war stories. Come on. I got a nice car today. I got a brand-new red Ferrari. Want to see it? Just take a look. One look. It's at the curb. Give me your hand." Lenny reached out for her hand.

She could remember being a child. It was a child's game in a child's afternoon, before time or distance were factors. When you were told you couldn't move or couldn't see. And for those moments you are paralyzed or blind. You freeze in place. You don't move. You feel that you have been there for years. It does not occur to you that you can move. It does not occur to you that you can break the rules. The world is a collection of absolutes and spells. You know words have a power. You are entranced. The world is a soft blue.

"There. See. I'm not crazy. A red Ferrari. A hundred forty grand. Get in. We'll go around the block. Sit down. Nice interior, huh? Nice stereo. But I got no fucking tapes. Go to the record store with me? You pick out the tapes, okay? Then we'll go to Bel Air. Swim a little. Watch the sunset. Listen to some music. Want to dance? I love to dance. You can't get a disease doing that, right?" Lenny was holding the car door open for her.

She sat down. The ground seemed enormous. It seemed to leap up at her face.

"Yeah. I'm a good driver. Lean back. Relax. I used to drive for a living," Lenny told her.

"What did you drive? A bus?" She smiled.

"A bus? That's sharp. You're one of those sharp little Jewish girls from Beverly Hills with a cocaine problem. Yeah. I know what you're about. All of you. I drove some cars on a few jobs. Couple of jewelry stores, a few banks. Now I fly," Lenny said.

Lenny turned the car onto Sunset Boulevard. In the gardens of the houses behind the gates, everything was in bloom. Patches of color slid past so fast she thought they might be hallucinations. Azaleas and camellias and hibiscus. The green seemed sullen and half asleep. Or perhaps it was opiated, dazed, exhausted from pleasure.

"You fly?" she repeated.

"Planes. You like planes? I'll take you up. I got a plane. Company plane," Lenny told her. "It's in Arizona."

"You're a pilot?" She put out her cigarette and immediately lit another.

"I fly planes for money. Want to fly? I'm going next week. Every second Tuesday. Want to come?" Lenny looked at her.

"Maybe," she said. They had turned on a street north of Sunset. They were winding up a hill. The street was narrow. The bougainvillea was a kind of net near her face. The air smelled of petals and heat.

"Yeah. You'll come with me. I'll show you what I do. I fly over a stretch of desert looks like the moon. There's a small manufacturing business down there. Camouflaged. You'd never see it. I drop some boxes off. I pick some boxes up. Three hours' work. Fifteen grand," Lenny said. "Know what I'm talking about?"

"No."

"Yeah. You don't want to know anything about this. Distribution," Lenny said. "That's federal."

"You do that twice a month?" she asked. They were above Sunset Boulevard. The bougainvillea was a magenta web. There were sounds of birds and insects. They were winding through pine trees. "That's 30,000 dollars a month."

"That's nothing. The real money's the Bogotá run," Lenny said. "Mountains leap up out of the ground, out of nowhere. The Bogotá run drove me crazy. Took me a month to come down. Then the Colombians got mad. You know what I'm talking about?"

"No."

"That's good. You don't want to know anything about the Colombians," Lenny said again.

She was thinking about the Colombians and Bogotá and the town where Lenny said he had a house, Medellín. She was thinking they would have called her *gitana*, with her long black hair and bare feet. She could have fanned herself with handfuls of 100-dollar bills like a green river. She could have borne sons for men crossing borders, searching for the definitive run, the one you don't return from. She would dance in bars in the permanently hot nights. They would say she was intoxicated with grief and dead husbands. Sadness made her dance. When she thought about this, she laughed.

The driveway seemed sudden and steep. They were approaching a walled villa. Lenny pushed numbers on a console. The gate opened.

He parked the red Ferrari. He opened the car door for her. She followed him up a flight of stone steps. The house looked like a Spanish fortress.

A large Christmas wreath with pine cones and a red ribbon hung on the door. The door was unlocked. The floor was tile. They were walking on an Oriental silk carpet, past a piano, a fireplace, a bar. There were ceiling-high glass cabinets in which Chinese artifacts were displayed, vases and bowls and carvings. They were walking through a library, then a room with a huge television, stereo equipment, a pool table. She followed him out a side door.

The pool was built on the edge of the hill. The city below seemed like a sketch for a village, something not quite formed beneath the greenery. Pink and yellow roses had been planted around two sides of the pool. There were beds of azaleas with ferns between them and red camellias, yellow lilies, white daisies, and birds-of-paradise.

"Time to swim," Lenny said.

She was standing near the pool, motionless. "We don't have suits," she said.

"Don't tell nobody, okay?" Lenny was pulling his shirt over his head. He stared at her, a cigarette in his mouth. "It's private. It's walled. Just a cliff out here. And Bernie and Phyllis aren't coming back. Come on. Take off your clothes. What are you? Scared? You're like a child. Come here. I'll help you. Daddy'll help you. Just stand near me. Here. See? Over your head. Over baby's head. Did that hurt? What's that? One of those goddamn French jobs with the hooks in front? You do it. What are you looking at? I put on a few pounds. Okay? I'm a little out of shape. I need some weights. I got to buy some weights. What are you? Skinny? You're so skinny. You one of those vomiters? I'm not going to bite. Come here. Reach down. Take off my necklace. Unlock the chain. Yeah. Good. Now we swim."

The water felt strange and icy. It was nothing like she expected. There were shadows on the far side of the pool. The shadows were hideous. There was nothing ambiguous about them. The water beneath the shadows looked remote and troubled and green. It looked contaminated. The more she swam, the more the infected blue particles clustered on her skin. There would be no way to remove them.

"I have to leave," she said.

The sun was going down. It was an unusual sunset for Los Angeles, red and protracted. Clouds formed islands in the red sky. The sprinklers came on. The air smelled damp and green like a forest. There were pine trees beyond the rose garden. She thought of the smell of camp at nightfall, when she was a child.

"What are you? Crazy? You kidding me? I want to take you out," Lenny said. He got out of the pool. He wrapped a towel around his waist. Then he wrapped a towel around her shoulders. "Don't just stand there. Dry off. Come on. You'll get sick. Dry yourself."

He lit a cigarette for her. "You want to get dressed up, right? I know you skinny broads from Beverly Hills. You want to get dressed up. Look. Let me show you something. You'll like it. I know. Come on." He put out his hand for her. She took it.

They were walking up a marble stairway to the bedroom.

The bedroom windows opened onto a tile balcony. There were sunken tubs in the bathroom. Everything was black marble. The faucets were gold. There were gold chandeliers hanging above them. Every wall had mirrors bordered by bulbs and gold. Lenny was standing in front of a closet.

"Pick something out. Go on. Walk in. Pink. You like pink? No. You like it darker. Yeah. Keep walking. Closet big as a tennis court. They got no taste, right? Looks like Vegas, right? You like red? No. Black. That's you. Here. Black silk." Lenny came out of the closet. He was holding an evening gown. "This your size? All you skinny broads wear the same size."

Lenny handed the dress to her. He stretched out on the bed. "Yeah. Let go of the towel. That's right. Only slower."

He was watching her. He lit a cigarette. His towel had come apart. He was holding something near his lap. It was a jewelry box.

"After you put that crap on your face, the paint, the lipstick, we'll pick out a little something nice for you. Phyllis won't need it. She's not coming back. Yeah." Lenny laughed. "Bernie and Phyllis are entertaining the Colombians by now. Give those boys from the jungle something to chew on. Don't look like that. You like diamonds? I know you like diamonds."

Lenny was stretched out on the bed. The bed belonged to Bernie and Phyllis but they weren't coming back. Lenny was holding a diamond necklace out to her. She wanted it more than she could remember wanting anything.

"I'll put it on you. Come here. Sit down. I won't touch you. Not unless you ask me. I can see you're all dressed up. Just sit near me. I'll do the clasp for you," Lenny offered.

She sat down. She could feel the stones around her throat, cool, individual, like the essence of something that lives in the night. Or something more ancient, part of the fabric of the night itself.

"Now you kiss me. Come on. You want to. I can tell. Kiss me. Know what this costs?" Lenny touched the necklace at her throat with his fingertips. He studied the stones. He left his fingers on her throat. "Sixty, seventy grand maybe. You can kiss me now."

She turned her face toward him. She opened her lips. Outside, the Santa Ana winds were startling, howling as if from a mouth. The air smelled of scorched lemons and oranges, of something delirious and intoxicated. When she closed her eyes, everything was blue.

She didn't see him at her noon meeting the next day or the day after. She thought, Well, that's it. She wasn't sorry. She got a manicure. She went to her psychiatrist. She began taking a steam bath after her aerobics class at the gym. She went Christmas shopping. She bought her daughter a white rabbit coat trimmed with blue fox. She was spending too much money. She didn't care.

It was Christmas Eve when the doorbell rang. There were carols on the radio. She was wearing a silk robe and smoking. She told Maria that she could answer the door.

"You promised never to come here." She was angry. "You promised to respect my life. To recognize my discrete borders."

"Discrete borders?" Lenny repeated. "I'm in serious trouble. Look at me. Can't you see there's something wrong? You look but you don't see."

There was nothing unusual about him. He was wearing blue jeans and a black leather jacket. He was carrying an overnight bag. She could see the motorcycle near the curb. Maybe the Colombians had the red Ferrari. Maybe they were chewing on that now. She didn't ask him in.

"This is it," Lenny was saying. He brushed past her and walked into the living room. He was talking quickly. He was telling her what had happened in the desert, what the Colombians had done. She felt like she was being electrocuted, that her hair was standing on end. It occurred to her that it was a sensation so singular that she might come to enjoy it. There were small blue wounded sounds in the room now. She wondered if they were coming from her.

"I disappear in about five minutes." Lenny looked at her. "You coming?"

She thought about it. "I can't come, no," she said finally. "I have a child."

"We take her," Lenny offered.

She shook her head, no. The room was going dark at the edges, she noticed. Like a field of blue asters, perhaps. Or ice when the sun strikes it. And how curious the blue becomes when clouds cross the sun, when the blue becomes broken, tawdry.

"I had plans for you. I was going to introduce you to some people. I should of met you fifteen years ago. I could have retired. Get me some ice," Lenny said. "Let's have a drink."

"We're in AA. Are you crazy?" She was annoyed.

"I need a drink. I need a fix. I need an automatic weapon. I need a plane," he said. He looked past her to the den. Maria was watching television and wrapping Christmas presents.

"You need a drink, too," Lenny said. "Don't even think about it. The phone. You're an accessory after the fact. You can go to jail. What about your kid then?"

They were standing in her living room. There was a noble pine tree near the fireplace. There were wrapped boxes beneath the branches. Maria asked in Spanish if she needed anything. She said not at the moment. Two glasses with ice, that was all.

"Have a drink," Lenny said. "You can always go back to the meetings. They take you back. They don't mind. I do it all the time. All over the world. I been doing it for ten years."

"I didn't know that," she said. It was almost impossible to talk. It occurred to her that her sanity was becoming intermittent, like a sudden stretch of intact road in an abandoned region. Or radio music, blatant after months of static.

"Give me the bottle. I'll pour you one. Don't look like that. You look like you're going down for the count. Here." Lenny handed the glass to her. She could smell the vodka. "Open your mouth, goddamn it."

She opened her mouth. She took a sip. Then she lit a cigarette.

"Wash the glass when I leave," Lenny said. "They can't prove shit. You don't know me. You were never anywhere. Nothing happened. You listening? You don't look like you're listening. You look like you're on tilt. Come on, baby. Listen to Daddy. That's good. Take another sip."

She took another sip. Lenny was standing near the door.

"You're getting off easy, you know that? I ran out of time. I had plans for you," he was saying.

He was opening the door. "Some ride, huh? Did Daddy do like he said? Get you to the other side? You catch a glimpse? See what's there? I think you're starting to see. Can't say Lenny lied to you, right?"

She took another sip. "Right," she agreed. When this glass was finished she would pour another. When the bottle was empty, she would buy another.

Lenny closed the door. The night stayed outside. She was surprised. She opened her mouth but no sound came out. Instead, blue things flew in, pieces of glass or tin, or necklaces of blue diamonds, perhaps. The air was the blue of a pool when there are shadows, clouds cross the turquoise surface, when you suspect something contagious is leaking, something camouflaged and disrupted. There is only this infected blue enormity elongating defiantly. The blue that knows you and where you live and it's never going to forget.

☆  ☆  ☆  ☆

# Cathedral

This blind man, an old friend of my wife's, he was on his way to spend the night. His wife had died. So he was visiting the dead wife's relatives in Connecticut. He called my wife from his in-laws'. Arrangements were made. He would come by train, a five-hour trip, and my wife would meet him at the station. She hadn't seen him since she worked for him one summer in Seattle ten years ago. But she and the blind man had kept in touch. They made tapes and mailed them back and forth. I wasn't enthusiastic about his visit. He was no one I knew. And his being blind bothered me. My idea of blindness came from the movies. In the movies, the blind moved slowly and never laughed. Sometimes they were led by seeing-eye dogs. A blind man in my house was not something I looked forward to.

That summer in Seattle she had needed a job. She didn't have any money. The man she was going to marry at the end of the summer was in officers' training school. He didn't have any money, either. But she was in love with the guy, and he was in love with her, etc. She'd seen something in the paper: HELP WANTED – *Reading to Blind Man*, and a telephone number. She phoned and went over, was hired on the spot. She'd worked with this blind man all summer. She read stuff to him, case studies, reports, that sort of thing. She helped him organize his little office in the county social-service department. They'd become good friends, my wife and the blind man. How do I know these things? She told me. And she told me something else. On her last day in the office, the blind man asked if he could touch her face. She agreed to this. She told me he touched his fingers to every part of her face, her nose – even her neck! She never forgot it. She even tried to write a poem about it. She was always trying to write a poem. She wrote a poem or two every

year, usually after something really important had happened to
her.

When we first started going out together, she showed me the
poem. In the poem, she recalled his fingers and the way they had
moved around over her face. In the poem, she talked about what
she had felt at the time, about what went through her mind when
the blind man touched her nose and lips. I can remember I didn't
think much of the poem. Of course, I didn't tell her that. Maybe
I just don't understand poetry. I admit it's not the first thing I
reach for when I pick up something to read.

Anyway, this man who'd first enjoyed her favors, the officer-
to-be, he'd been her childhood sweetheart. So okay. I'm saying
that at the end of the summer she let the blind man run his hands
over her face, said goodbye to him, married her childhood, etc.,
who was now a commissioned officer, and she moved away
from Seattle. But they'd kept in touch, she and the blind man.
She made the first contact after a year or so. She called him up
one night from an Air Force base in Alabama. She wanted to
talk. They talked. He asked her to send him a tape and tell him
about her life. She did this. She sent the tape. On the tape, she
told the blind man about her husband and about their life together
in the military. She told the blind man she loved her husband but
she didn't like it where they lived and she didn't like it that he
was a part of the military–industrial thing. She told the blind
man she'd written a poem and he was in it. She told him that she
was writing a poem about what it was like to be an Air Force
officer's wife. The poem wasn't finished yet. She was still writing
it. The blind man made a tape. He sent her the tape. She made a
tape. This went on for years. My wife's officer was posted to
one base and then another. She sent tapes from Moody AFB,
McGuire, McConnell, and finally Travis, near Sacramento,
where one night she got to feeling lonely and cut off from people
she kept losing in that moving-around life. She got to feeling she
couldn't go it another step. She went in and swallowed all the
pills and capsules in the medicine chest and washed them down
with a bottle of gin. Then she got into a hot bath and passed out.

But instead of dying, she got sick. She threw up. Her officer
– why should he have a name? he was the childhood sweetheart,

and what more does he want? – came home from somewhere, found her, and called the ambulance. In time, she put it all on a tape and sent the tape to the blind man. Over the years, she put all kinds of stuff on tapes and sent the tapes off lickety-split. Next to writing a poem every year, I think it was her chief means of recreation. On one tape, she told the blind man she'd decided to live away from her officer for a time. On another tape, she told him about her divorce. She and I began going out, and of course she told her blind man about it. She told him everything, or so it seemed to me. Once she asked me if I'd like to hear the latest tape from the blind man. This was a year ago. I was on the tape, she said. So I said okay, I'd listen to it. I got us drinks and we settled down in the living room. We made ready to listen. First she inserted the tape into the player and adjusted a couple of dials. Then she pushed a lever. The tape squeaked and someone began to talk in this loud voice. She lowered the volume. After a few minutes of harmless chitchat, I heard my own name in the mouth of this stranger, this blind man I didn't even know! And then this: "From all you've said about him, I can only conclude—" But we were interrupted, a knock at the door, something, and we didn't ever get back to the tape. Maybe it was just as well. I'd heard all I wanted to.

Now this same blind man was coming to sleep in my house.

"Maybe I could take him bowling," I said to my wife. She was at the draining board doing scalloped potatoes. She put down the knife she was using and turned around.

"If you love me," she said, "you can do this for me. If you don't love me, okay. But if you had a friend, any friend, and the friend came to visit, I'd make him feel comfortable." She wiped her hands with the dish towel.

"I don't have any blind friends," I said.

"You don't have *any* friends," she said. "Period. Besides," she said, "goddamn it, his wife's just died! Don't you understand that? The man's lost his wife!"

I didn't answer. She'd told me a little about the blind man's wife. Her name was Beulah. Beulah! That's a name for a colored woman.

"Was his wife a Negro?" I asked.

"Are you crazy?" my wife said. "Have you just flipped or something?" She picked up a potato. I saw it hit the floor, then roll under the stove. "What's wrong with you?" she said. "Are you drunk?"

"I'm just asking," I said.

Right then my wife filled me in with more detail than I cared to know. I made a drink and sat at the kitchen table to listen. Pieces of the story began to fall into place.

Beulah had gone to work for the blind man the summer after my wife had stopped working for him. Pretty soon Beulah and the blind man had themselves a church wedding. It was a little wedding – who'd want to go to such a wedding in the first place? – just the two of them, plus the minister and the minister's wife. But it was a church wedding just the same. It was what Beulah had wanted, he'd said. But even then Beulah must have been carrying the cancer in her glands. After they had been inseparable for eight years – my wife's word, *inseparable* – Beulah's health went into a rapid decline. She died in a Seattle hospital room, the blind man sitting beside the bed and holding on to her hand. They'd married, lived and worked together, slept together – had sex, sure – and then the blind man had to bury her. All this without his having ever seen what the goddamned woman looked like. It was beyond my understanding. Hearing this, I felt sorry for the blind man for a little bit. And then I found myself thinking what a pitiful life this woman must have led. Imagine a woman who could never see herself as she was seen in the eyes of her loved one. A woman who could go on day after day and never receive the smallest compliment from her beloved. A woman whose husband could never read the expression on her face, be it misery or something better. Someone who could wear make-up or not – what difference to him? She could, if she wanted, wear green eye-shadow around one eye, a straight pin in her nostril, yellow slacks and purple shoes, no matter. And then to slip off into death, the blind man's hand on her hand, his blind eyes streaming tears – I'm imagining now – her last thought maybe this: that he never even knew what she looked like, and she on an express to the grave. Robert was left with a small insurance policy and half of a 20-peso Mexican coin. The other half of the coin went into the box with her. Pathetic.

So when the time rolled around, my wife went to the depot to pick him up. With nothing to do but wait – sure, I blamed him for that – I was having a drink and watching the TV when I heard the car pull into the drive. I got up from the sofa with my drink and went to the window to have a look.

I saw my wife laughing as she parked the car. I saw her get out of the car and shut the door. She was still wearing a smile. Just amazing. She went around to the other side of the car to where the blind man was already starting to get out. This blind man, feature this, he was wearing a full beard! A beard on a blind man! Too much, I say. The blind man reached into the back seat and dragged out a suitcase. My wife took his arm, shut the car door, and, talking all the way, moved him down the drive and then up the steps to the front porch. I turned off the TV. I finished my drink, rinsed the glass, dried my hands. Then I went to the door.

My wife said, "I want you to meet Robert. Robert, this is my husband. I've told you all about him." She was beaming. She had this blind man by his coat sleeve.

The blind man let go of his suitcase and up came his hand.

I took it. He squeezed hard, held my hand, and then he let it go.

"I feel like we've already met," he boomed.

"Likewise," I said. I didn't know what else to say. Then I said, "Welcome. I've heard a lot about you." We began to move then, a little group, from the porch into the living room, my wife guiding him by the arm. The blind man was carrying his suitcase in his other hand. My wife said things like, "To your left here, Robert. That's right. Now watch it, there's a chair. That's it. Sit down right here. This is the sofa. We just bought this sofa two weeks ago."

I started to say something about the old sofa. I'd liked that old sofa. But I didn't say anything. Then I wanted to say something else, small-talk, about the scenic ride along the Hudson. How going *to* New York, you should sit on the right-hand side of the train, and coming *from* New York, the left-hand side.

"Did you have a good train ride?" I said. "Which side of the train did you sit on, by the way?"

"What a question, which side!" my wife said. "What's it matter which side?" she said.

"I just asked," I said.

"Right side," the blind man said. "I hadn't been on a train in nearly forty years. Not since I was a kid. With my folks. That's been a long time. I'd nearly forgotten the sensation. I have winter in my beard now," he said. "So I've been told, anyway. Do I look distinguished, my dear?" the blind man said to my wife.

"You look distinguished, Robert," she said. "Robert," she said. "Robert, it's just so good to see you."

My wife finally took her eyes off the blind man and looked at me. I had the feeling she didn't like what she saw. I shrugged.

I've never met, or personally known, anyone who was blind. This blind man was late forties, a heavy-set, balding man with stooped shoulders, as if he carried a great weight there. He wore brown slacks, brown shoes, a light-brown shirt, a tie, a sports coat. Spiffy. He also had this full beard. But he didn't use a cane and he didn't wear dark glasses. I'd always thought dark glasses were a must for the blind. Fact was, I wished he had a pair. At first glance, his eyes looked like anyone else's eyes. But if you looked close, there was something different about them. Too much white in the iris, for one thing, and the pupils seemed to move around in the sockets without his knowing it or being able to stop it. Creepy. As I stared at his face, I saw the left pupil turn in toward his nose while the other made an effort to keep in one place. But it was only an effort, for that eye was on the roam without his knowing it or wanting it to be.

I said, "Let me get you a drink. What's your pleasure? We have a little of everything. It's one of our pastimes."

"Bub, I'm a Scotch man myself," he said fast enough in this big voice.

"Right," I said. Bub! "Sure you are. I knew it."

He let his fingers touch his suitcase, which was sitting

alongside the sofa. He was taking his bearings. I didn't blame him for that.

"I'll move that up to your room," my wife said.

"No, that's fine," the blind man said loudly. "It can go up when I go up."

"A little water with the Scotch?" I said.

"Very little," he said.

"I knew it," I said.

He said, "Just a tad. The Irish actor, Barry Fitzgerald? I'm like that fellow. When I drink water, Fitzgerald said, I drink water. When I drink whiskey, I drink whiskey." My wife laughed. The blind man brought his hand up under his beard. He lifted his beard slowly and let it drop.

I did the drinks, three big glasses of Scotch with a splash of water in each. Then we made ourselves comfortable and talked about Robert's travels. First the long flight from the West Coast to Connecticut, we covered that. Then from Connecticut up here by train. We had another drink concerning that leg of the trip.

I remembered having read somewhere that the blind didn't smoke because, as speculation had it, they couldn't see the smoke they exhaled. I thought I knew that much and that much only about blind people. But this blind man smoked his cigarette down to the nubbin and then lit another one. This blind man filled his ashtray and my wife emptied it.

When we sat down at the table for dinner, we had another drink. My wife heaped Robert's plate with cube steak, scalloped potatoes, green beans. I buttered him up two slices of bread. I said, "Here's bread and butter for you." I swallowed some of my drink. "Now let us pray," I said, and the blind man lowered his head. My wife looked at me, her mouth agape. "Pray the phone won't ring and the food doesn't get cold," I said.

We dug in. We ate everything there was to eat on the table. We ate like there was no tomorrow. We didn't talk. We ate. We scarfed. We grazed that table. We were into serious eating. The blind man had right away located his foods, he knew just where everything was on his plate. I watched with admiration as he used his knife and fork on the meat. He'd cut two pieces of meat, fork the meat into his mouth, and then go all out for the scalloped potatoes, the beans next, and then he'd tear off a hunk of buttered bread and eat that. He'd follow this up with a big drink of milk. It didn't seem to bother him to use his fingers once in a while, either.

We finished everything, including half a strawberry pie. For a few moments, we sat as if stunned. Sweat beaded on our faces. Finally, we got up from the table and left the dirty plates. We didn't look back. We took ourselves into the living room and sank into our places again. Robert and my wife sat on the sofa. I took the big chair. We had us two or three more drinks while they talked about the major things that had come to pass for them in the past ten years. For the most part, I just listened. Now and then I joined in. I didn't want him to think I'd left the room, and I didn't want her to think I was feeling left out. They talked of things that had happened to them – to them – these past ten years. I waited in vain to hear my name on my wife's sweet lips: "And then my dear husband came into my life" – something like that. But I heard nothing of the sort. More talk of Robert. Robert had done a little of everything, it seemed, a regular blind jack-of-all-trades. But most recently he and his wife had had an Amway distributorship, from which, I gathered, they'd earned their living, such as it was. The blind man was also a ham radio operator. He talked in his loud voice about conversations he'd had with fellow operators in Guam, in the Philippines, in Alaska, and even in Tahiti. He said he'd have a lot of friends there if he ever wanted to go visit those places. From time to time, he'd turn his blind face toward me, put his hand under his beard, ask me something. How long had I been in my present position? (Three years.) Did I like my work? (I didn't.) Was I going to stay with it? (What were the options?) Finally, when I thought he was beginning to run down, I got up and turned on the TV.

My wife looked at me with irritation. She was heading toward a boil. Then she looked at the blind man and said, "Robert, do you have a TV?"

The blind man said, "My dear, I have two TVs. I have a color set and a black-and-white thing, an old relic. It's funny, but if I turn the TV on, and I'm always turning it on, I turn on the color set. It's funny, don't you think?"

I didn't know what to say to that. I had absolutely nothing to say to that. No opinion. So I watched the news program and tried to listen to what the announcer was saying.

"This is a color TV," the blind man said. "Don't ask me how, but I can tell."

"We traded up a while ago," I said.

The blind man had another taste of his drink. He lifted his beard, sniffed it, and let it fall. He leaned forward on the sofa. He positioned his ashtray on the coffee table, then put the lighter to his cigarette. He leaned back on the sofa and crossed his legs at the ankles.

My wife covered her mouth, and then she yawned. She stretched. She said, "I think I'll go upstairs and put on my robe. I think I'll change into something else. Robert, you make yourself comfortable," she said.

"I'm comfortable," the blind man said.

"I want you to feel comfortable in this house," she said.

"I am comfortable," the blind man said.

After she'd left the room, he and I listened to the weather report and then to the sports roundup. By that time, she'd been gone so long I didn't know if she was going to come back. I thought she might have gone to bed. I wished she'd come back downstairs. I didn't want to be left alone with a blind man. I asked him if he wanted another drink, and he said sure. Then I asked if he wanted to smoke some dope with me. I said I'd just rolled a number. I hadn't, but I planned to do so in about two shakes.

"I'll try some with you," he said.

"Damn right," I said. "That's the stuff."

I got our drinks and sat down on the sofa with him. Then I rolled us two fat numbers. I lit one and passed it. I brought it to his fingers. He took it and inhaled.

"Hold it as long as you can," I said. I could tell he didn't know the first thing.

My wife came back downstairs wearing her pink robe and her pink slippers.

"What do I smell?" she said.

"We thought we'd have us some cannabis," I said.

My wife gave me a savage look. Then she looked at the blind man and said, "Robert, I didn't know you smoked."

He said, "I do now, my dear. There's a first time for everything. But I don't feel anything yet."

"This stuff is pretty mellow," I said. "This stuff is mild. It's dope you can reason with," I said. "It doesn't mess you up."

"Not much it doesn't, bub," he said, and laughed.

My wife sat on the sofa between the blind man and me. I passed her the number. She took it and toked and then passed it back to me. "Which way is this going?" she said. Then she said, "I shouldn't be smoking this. I can hardly keep my eyes open as it is. That dinner did me in. I shouldn't have eaten so much."

"It was the strawberry pie," the blind man said. "That's what did it," he said, and he laughed his big laugh. Then he shook his head.

"There's more strawberry pie," I said.

"Do you want some more, Robert?" my wife said.

"Maybe in a little while," he said.

We gave our attention to the TV. My wife yawned again. She said, "Your bed is made up when you feel like going to bed, Robert. I know you must have had a long day. When you're ready to go to bed, say so." She pulled his arm. "Robert?"

He came to and said, "I've had a real nice time. This beats tapes, doesn't it?"

I said, "Coming at you," and I put the number between his fingers. He inhaled, held the smoke, and then let it go. It was like he'd been doing it since he was nine years old.

"Thanks, bub," he said. "But I think this is all for me. I think I'm beginning to feel it," he said. He held the burning roach out for my wife.

"Same here," she said. "Ditto. Me, too." She took the roach and passed it to me. "I may just sit for a while between you two guys with my eyes closed. But don't let me bother you, okay? Either one of you. If it bothers you, say so. Otherwise, I may just sit here with my eyes closed until you're ready to go to

bed," she said. "Your bed's made up, Robert, when you're
ready. It's right next to our room at the top of the stairs. We'll
show you up when you're ready. You wake me up now, you
guys, if I fall asleep." She said that and then she closed her eyes
and went to sleep.

The news program ended. I got up and changed the channel.
I sat back down on the sofa. I wished my wife hadn't pooped
out. Her head lay across the back of the sofa, her mouth open.
She'd turned so that her robe had slipped away from her legs,
exposing a juicy thigh. I reached to draw her robe back over her,
and it was then that I glanced at the blind man. What the hell! I
flipped the robe open again.

"You say when you want some strawberry pie," I said.

"I will," he said.

I said, "Are you tired? Do you want me to take you up to
your bed? Are you ready to hit the hay?"

"Not yet," he said. "No, I'll stay up with you, bub. If that's
all right. I'll stay up until you're ready to turn in. We haven't had
a chance to talk. Know what I mean? I feel like me and her
monopolized the evening." He lifted his beard and he let it fall.
He picked up his cigarettes and his lighter.

"That's all right," I said. Then I said, "I'm glad for the
company."

And I guess I was. Every night I smoked dope and stayed up
as long as I could before I fell asleep. My wife and I hardly ever
went to bed at the same time. When I did go to sleep, I had these
dreams. Sometimes I'd wake up from one of them, my heart
going crazy.

Something about the church and the Middle Ages was on the
TV. Not your run-of-the-mill TV fare. I wanted to watch
something else. I turned to the other channels. But there was
nothing on them, either. So I turned back to the first channel and
apologized.

"Bub, it's all right," the blind man said. "It's fine with me.
Whatever you want to watch is okay. I'm always learning
something. Learning never ends. It won't hurt me to learn
something tonight. I got ears," he said.

★

We didn't say anything for a time. He was leaning forward with his head turned at me, his right ear aimed in the direction of the set. Very disconcerting. Now and then his eyelids drooped and then they snapped open again. Now and then he put his fingers into his beard and tugged, like he was thinking about something he was hearing on the television.

On the screen, a group of men wearing cowls was being set upon and tormented by men dressed in skeleton costumes and men dressed as devils. The men dressed as devils wore devil masks, horns, and long tails. This pageant was part of a procession. The Englishman who was narrating the thing said it took place in Spain once a year. I tried to explain to the blind man what was happening.

"Skeletons," he said. "I know about skeletons," he said, and he nodded.

The TV showed this one cathedral. Then there was a long, slow look at another one. Finally, the picture switched to the famous one in Paris, with its flying buttresses and its spires reaching up to the clouds. The camera pulled away to show the whole of the cathedral rising above the skyline.

There were times when the Englishman who was telling the thing would shut up, would simply let the camera move around over the cathedrals. Or else the camera would tour the countryside, men in fields walking behind oxen. I waited as long as I could. Then I felt I had to say something. I said, "They're showing the outside of this cathedral now. Gargoyles. Little statues carved to look like monsters. Now I guess they're in Italy. There's paintings on the walls of this one church."

"Are those fresco paintings, bub?" he asked, and he sipped from his drink.

I reached for my glass. But it was empty. I tried to remember what I could remember. "You're asking me are those frescoes?" I said. "That's a good question. I don't know."

The camera moved to a cathedral outside Lisbon. The differences in the Portuguese cathedral compared with the French and Italian were not that great. But they were there. Mostly the interior stuff. Then something occurred to me, and I said, "Something has occurred to me. Do you have any idea what a cathedral is? What they look like, that is? Do you follow me? If somebody says cathedral to you, do you have any notion what they're talking about? Do you know the difference between that and a Baptist church, say?"

He let the smoke dribble from his mouth. "I know they took hundreds of workers fifty or a hundred years to build," he said. "I just heard the man say that, of course. I know generations of the same families worked on a cathedral. I heard him say that, too. The men who began their life's work on them, they never lived to see the completion of their work. In that wise, bub, they're no different from the rest of us, right?" He laughed. Then his eyelids drooped again. His head nodded. He seemed to be snoozing. Maybe he was imagining himself in Portugal. The TV was showing another cathedral now. This one was in Germany. The Englishman's voice droned on. "Cathedrals," the blind man said. He sat up and rolled his head back and forth. "If you want the truth, bub, that's about all I know. What I just said. What I heard him say. But maybe you could describe one to me? I wish you'd do it. I'd like that. If you want to know, I really don't have a good idea."

I stared hard at the shot of the cathedral on the TV. How could I even begin to describe it? But say my life depended on it. Say my life was being threatened by an insane guy who said I had to do it or else.

I stared some more at the cathedral before the picture flipped off into the countryside. There was no use. I turned to the blind man and said, "To begin with, they're very tall." I was looking around the room for clues. "They reach way up. Up and up. Toward the sky. They're so big, some of them, they have to have these supports. To help hold them up, so to speak. These supports are called buttresses. They remind me of viaducts, for some reason. But maybe you don't know viaducts, either? Sometimes the cathedrals have devils and such carved into the front. Sometimes lords and ladies. Don't ask me why this is," I said.

He was nodding. The whole upper part of his body seemed to be moving back and forth.

"I'm not doing so good, am I?" I said.

He stopped nodding and leaned forward on the edge of the sofa. As he listened to me, he was running his fingers through his beard. I wasn't getting through to him, I could see that. But he waited for me to go on just the same. He nodded, like he was trying to encourage me. I tried to think what else to say. "They're really big," I said. "They're massive. They're built of stone. Marble, too, sometimes. In those olden days, when they built cathedrals, men wanted to be close to God. In those olden days, God was an important part of everyone's life. You could tell this from their cathedral-building. I'm sorry," I said, "but it looks like that's the best I can do for you. I'm just no good at it."

"That's all right, bub," the blind man said. "Hey, listen. I hope you don't mind my asking you. Can I ask you something? Let me ask you a simple question, yes or no. I'm just curious and there's no offense. You're my host. But let me ask if you are in any way religious? You don't mind my asking?"

I shook my head. He couldn't see that, though. A wink is the same as a nod to a blind man. "I guess I don't believe in it. In anything. Sometimes it's hard. You know what I'm saying?"

"Sure, I do," he said.

"Right," I said.

The Englishman was still holding forth. My wife sighed in her sleep. She drew a long breath and went on with her sleeping.

"You'll have to forgive me," I said. "But I can't tell you what a cathedral looks like. It just isn't in me to do it. I can't do any more than I've done."

The blind man sat very still, his head down, as he listened to me.

I said, "The truth is, cathedrals don't mean anything special to me. Nothing. Cathedrals. They're something to look at on late-night TV. That's all they are."

It was then that the blind man cleared his throat. He brought something up. He took a handkerchief from his back pocket. Then he said, "I get it, bub. It's okay. It happens. Don't worry about it," he said. "Hey, listen to me. Will you do me a favor? I got an idea. Why don't you find us some heavy paper? And a pen. We'll do something. We'll draw one together. Get us a pen and some heavy paper. Go on, bub, get the stuff," he said.

So I went upstairs. My legs felt like they didn't have any strength in them. They felt like they did after I'd done some running. In my wife's room, I looked around. I found some ballpoints in a little basket on her table. And then I tried to think where to look for the kind of paper he was talking about.

Downstairs, in the kitchen, I found a shopping bag with onion skins in the bottom of the bag. I emptied the bag and shook it. I brought it into the living room and sat down with it near his legs. I moved some things, smoothed the wrinkles from the bag, spread it out on the coffee table.

The blind man got down from the sofa and sat next to me on the carpet.

He ran his fingers over the paper. He went up and down the sides of the paper. The edges, even the edges. He fingered the corners.

"All right," he said. "All right, let's do her."

He found my hand, the hand with the pen. He closed his hand over my hand. "Go ahead, bub, draw," he said. "Draw. You'll see. I'll follow along with you. It'll be okay. Just begin now like I'm telling you. You'll see. Draw," the blind man said.

So I began. First I drew a box that looked like a house. It could have been the house I lived in. Then I put a roof on it. At either end of the roof, I drew spires. Crazy.

"Swell," he said. "Terrific. You're doing fine," he said. "Never thought anything like this could happen in your lifetime, did you, bub? Well, it's a strange life, we all know that. Go on now. Keep it up."

I put in windows with arches. I drew flying buttresses. I hung great doors. I couldn't stop. The TV station went off the air. I put down the pen and closed and opened my fingers. The blind man felt around over the paper. He moved the tips of his fingers over the paper, all over what I had drawn, and he nodded.

"Doing fine," the blind man said.

I took up the pen again, and he found my hand. I kept at it. I'm no artist. But I kept drawing just the same.

My wife opened up her eyes and gazed at us. She sat up on the sofa, her robe hanging open. She said, "What are you doing? Tell me, I want to know."

I didn't answer her.

The blind man said, "We're drawing a cathedral. Me and him are working on it. Press hard," he said to me. "That's right. That's good," he said. "Sure. You got it, bub. I can tell. You didn't think you could. But you can, can't you? You're cooking with gas now. You know what I'm saying? We're going to really have us something here in a minute. How's the old arm?" he said. "Put some people in there now. What's a cathedral without people?"

My wife said, "What's going on? Robert, what are you doing? What's going on?"

"It's all right," he said to her. "Close your eyes now," the blind man said to me.

I did it. I closed them just like he said.

"Are they closed?" he said. "Don't fudge."

"They're closed," I said.

"Keep them that way," he said. He said, "Don't stop now. Draw."

So we kept on with it. His fingers rode my fingers as my hand went over the paper. It was like nothing else in my life up to now.

Then he said, "I think that's it. I think you got it," he said. "Take a look. What do you think?"

But I had my eyes closed. I thought I'd keep them that way for a little longer. I thought it was something I ought to do.

"Well?" he said. "Are you looking?"

My eyes were still closed. I was in my house. I knew that. But I didn't feel like I was inside anything.

"It's really something," I said.

# FRANK CONROY

☆  ☆  ☆  ☆

# *Midair*

A sunny, windy day on the Lower East Side of New York. The year is 1942. Sean, aged six, is being more or less pulled along the sidewalk by his father, who has shown up from nowhere to take him home from school. Sean tries to keep the pace, although he does not remember the last time he has seen this big, exuberant man, nor is he altogether sure that he trusts him. Mary, on the other side, is nine. Her legs are longer, and she seems happy, skipping every now and then, shouting into the wind, calling him Daddy. Sean cannot hear what they're saying except in fragments – the wind tears at the words. His hand, wrist, and part of his forearm are enclosed in his father's fist. The big man strides along, red-faced, chin jutting forward proudly, his whole carriage suggesting the eagerness and confidence of a soldier marching forward to receive some important, hard-won medal.

He is not a soldier, as Sean's mother has recently explained. He is not in the Army (although a war is going on) but in something called a rest home, where people go in order to rest. He does not seem tired, Sean thinks.

"It'll be a different story now, by God," his father says as they turn the corner onto Seventh Street. "A completely different story." Energy seems to radiate from the man like an electrical charge. His body carries a pale-blue corona, and when he speaks his white teeth give off white lightning. "What a day!" He lets go of the children's hands and makes a sweeping gesture. "An absolute pip of a day. Look at that blue sky! The clouds! Seventh Street! Look how vivid the colors are!"

Sean cannot look. He is preoccupied with the unnatural force of his father's enthusiasm. It is as if all that has been pointed out is too far away to be seen. The boy's awareness is focused on the small bubble of space immediately surrounding himself, his

father, and his sister. Within that area he sees clearly – as if his
life depended on it – and there is no part of him left over to see
anything else.

They reach the tenement building and climb the stoop. His
father hesitates at the door.

"The key," he says.

"Mother has it," Mary says.

"You haven't got it?" He rolls his head in exasperation.

"I'm sorry." Mary is afraid she has failed him. "I'm sorry,
Daddy."

Sean is uneasy with her use of the word "Daddy." It sounds
strange, since they never use it. It is not part of their domestic
vocabulary. On those extremely rare occasions when Sean,
Mary, and their mother ever mention the man, the word they
have always used is "Father."

Mrs. Rosenblum, second floor rear, emerges from the house.

"Good morning," his father says, smiling, catching the door.
"In you go, children."

Mrs. Rosenblum has never seen this big man before but
recognizes, from his expensive clothes and confident manner,
that he is a gentleman, and the father of the children. A quick
glance at Mary, smiling as he touches her head, confirms
everything.

"Nice," Mrs. Rosenblum says. "Very nice."

Inside, Sean's father takes the steps two at a time. The
children follow up to the top floor – the fourth – and find him
standing at the door to the apartment, trying the knob.

"No key here, either, I suppose."

"It's the same one," Mary says.

He gives the door a hard push, as if testing. Then he steps
back, looks around, and notices the iron ladder leading up to the
hatch and the roof.

"Aha! More than one way to skin a cat." He strides over to
the ladder and begins to climb. "Follow me, buckos. Up the
mainmast!"

"Daddy, what are you doing?" Mary cries.

"We'll use the fire escape." He pushes up the hatch and
sunlight pours down. "Come on. It's fun!"

Sean can hear the wind whistling up there as his father climbs through. Mary hesitates an instant and then mounts the ladder. As she approaches the top, Sean follows her. He ascends into the sunshine and the wind.

The big man moves rapidly across the tarred roof to the rear of the building and the twin hoops of the fire-escape railing. He shouts back at the children, but his words are lost. He beckons, turns, and grabs the railings. His feet go over the edge and he begins to descend. Then he stops – his head and shoulders visible – and shouts again. Mary moves forward, the big man sinks out of sight, and Sean follows.

The boy steps to the edge and looks over. His father is ten feet below, on the fire-escape landing, red face upturned.

"Come on!" The white teeth flash. "The window's open."

The wind whips Mary's skirt around her knees as she goes over. She has to stop and push the hair out of her eyes. When she reaches the landing below, Sean grabs the hoops. Five floors down, a sheet of newsaper flutters across the cement at the bottom of the airshaft. It seems no bigger than a page from a book. He climbs down. Pigeons rise from the airshaft and scatter. On the landing, he sees his father, already inside, lifting Mary through the kitchen window. He follows quickly on his own.

The kitchen, although entirely familiar in every detail, seems slightly odd in its totality. The abruptness of the entry – without the usual preparation of the other rooms – tinges the scene with unreality. Sean follows his father and sister through the kitchen, into the hall, and to the doorway of his mother's room. His father does not enter but simply stops and looks.

"Have you been here before?" Sean asks.

"Of course he has, silly," Mary says rapidly.

His father turns. "Don't you remember?"

"I don't think so," Sean says.

As they pass the main door to the apartment, toward the front of the hall, his father pauses to slip on the chain lock.

For more than an hour they have been rearranging the books on the living-room shelves, putting them in alphabetical order by author. Sean's father stops every now and then, with some favorite book, to do a dramatic reading. The readings become more and more dramatic. He leans down to the children to emphasize the dialogue, shouting in different voices, gesticulating with his free arm in the air, making faces. But then, abruptly, his mood changes.

"The windows are filthy," he says angrily, striding back and forth from one to another, peering at the glass. The books are forgotten now as he goes to the kitchen. Mary quickly pushes them over to the foot of the bookcase, Sean helps. While doing this, they look very quickly, almost furtively, into each other's eyes. It takes a fraction of a second, but Sean understands. He is aware that his father's unexplained abandonment of an activity in which he had appeared to be so deeply involved has frightened Mary. His own feelings are complex – he is gratified that she is scared, since in his opinion she should have been scared all along, while at the same time his own fear, because of hers, escalates a notch.

"What's going to happen?" Sean asks quietly.

"Nothing. It's okay." She pretends not to be afraid.

"Get Mother." The sound of water running in the kitchen.

Mary considers this. "It's okay. She'll come home from work the way she always does."

"That's a long time. That's too long."

The big man returns with a bucket and some rags. His face seems even more flushed. "We'll do it ourselves. Wait till you see the difference." He moves to the central window, and they are drawn in his wake. Sean recognizes a shift in the atmosphere: before, with the books, there was at least a pretense of the three of them doing something together – a game they might all enjoy – but now his father's attention has narrowed and intensified onto the question of the windows. He seems barely aware of the children.

He washes the panes with rapid, sweeping movements. Then he opens the lower frame, bends through, turns, and sits on the sill to do the outside. Sean can see his father's face, concentrated, frowning, eyes searching the glass for streaks.

Sean begins to move backward.

"No," Mary says quickly. "We have to stay."

The boy stops beside the rocking chair where his mother sits after dinner.

The big man re-enters, and steps back to regard the results of his work. "Much better. Much, much better." He moves on to the next window. "Fresh water, Mary. Take the bucket."

Mary obeys, and goes back to the kitchen.

The big man stares down at the street. Sean stays by the rocking chair.

"You don't remember," the big man says. "Well, that's all right. Time is different for children. In any case, the past is behind us now. What counts is the future." He gives a short, barking laugh. "Another cliché rediscovered! But that's the way it is. You have to penetrate the clichés, you have to live them out to find out how true they are. What a joke!"

Mary brings the bucket of water to his side. Suddenly he moves closer to the window. He has seen something on the street.

"God damn." He moves back rapidly. He turns and runs down the hall to the kitchen. Sean and Mary can see him closing and locking the rear windows. "Bastards!" he shouts.

Mary moves sideways to glance through the window to the street.

"What is it?" Sean asks.

"An ambulance." Her voice is beginning to quaver. "It must be that ambulance."

Now he comes back into the living room and paces. Then he rushes to the newly washed window, opens it, and tears the gauzy curtains from the rod and throws them aside. Sean can see Mary flinch as the curtains are torn. The big man moves from one window to the next, opening them and tearing away the curtains. Wind rushes through the room. Torn curtains rise from the floor and swirl about.

He gathers the children and sits down on the couch, his arms around their shoulders. Sean feels crushed and tries to adjust his position, but his father only tightens his grip. The big man is breathing fast, staring into the hall, at the door.

"Daddy," Mary says. "It hurts."

A slight release of pressure, but Sean is still held so tightly to the man's side he can barely move.

"Oh, the bastards," his father says. "The tricky bastards."

The buzzer sounds. Then, after a moment, a knock on the door. The big man's grip tightens.

Another knock. The sound of a key. Sean watches the door open a few inches until the chain pulls it short. He sees the glint of an eye.

"Mr. Kennedy? This is Dr. Silverman. Would you open the door, please?"

"Alone, are you, Doctor?" An almost lighthearted tone.

A moment's pause. "No. I have Bob and James here with me." A calm voice, reassuring to Sean. "Please let us in."

"The goon squad," his father says.

"Bob in particular is very concerned. And so am I."

"Bob is a Judas."

"Mr. Kennedy. Be reasonable. We've been through this before, after all."

"No, no." As if correcting a slow student. "This is different. I'm through with you people. I'm through with all of that. I've come home, I'm here with my children, and I'm going to stay."

A pause. "Yes. I can see the children."

"We've been having a fine time. We've been washing the windows, Doctor." An almost inaudible chuckle.

"Mr. Kennedy, I implore you to open the door. We simply must come in. We must discuss your plans."

"I'm not going to open the door. And neither are you. What we have here, Doctor, is a Mexican standoff. Do you get my meaning?"

"I'm very sorry to hear you say that." Another pause – longer this time. "Bob would like a word with you."

"Mr. Kennedy? This is Bob." A younger voice.

"I'm not coming back, Bob. Don't try any crap with me. I know why you're here."

"I'm worried about you. You're flying. You know that."

"Got the little white jacket, eh, Bob? The one with the funny sleeves?"

"Look, if you don't come back they'll assign me to Mr. Farnsworth. You wouldn't do that to me. Please."

"Cut the crap, Bob."

"Listen. I'm with you. You know that. I mean, how many times have we talked about your — "

A tremendous crash as the door is kicked in, the frame splintering where the chain has come away. Sean is aware that things are happening very fast now, and yet he can see it all with remarkable clarity. Wood chips drift lazily through the air. Three men rush through the door — two in white uniforms, one in ordinary clothes. He knows they are running toward the couch as fast as they can — their faces frozen masks of strain — but time itself seems to have slowed down.

Still clamped to his father's side, Sean feels himself rise up into the air. He sees his father's other hand make a grab for Mary, who is trying to escape. He gets hold of her hair, but she twists away with a yell. Sean feels betrayed that she has gotten away. She was the one calling him Daddy. The wind roars as the big man rushes to the window and climbs out on the sill.

"Stop where you are!" he shouts back at the men.

Sean cannot see, but he senses that the men have stopped. He can hear Mary crying, hear the wind, and hear the sound of his father's heart racing under the rough tweed of his jacket. He stares down at the street, at the cracks in the sidewalk. With the very limited motion available to his arms, he finds his father's belt and hangs on with both fists.

"You bastards," his father shouts. "What you don't realize is I can do anything. Anything!"

Something akin to sleepiness comes over Sean. As time passes he realizes — a message from a distant outpost — that he has soiled himself. Finally, they are pulled back in, with great speed and strength, and fall to the floor. His father screams as the men cover him.

In college, his father long dead, and all memory of his father's visit in 1942 completely buried, Sean looks for a wife. He is convinced that if he doesn't find someone before he graduates, he will have missed his chance for all time. The idea of living alone terrifies him, although he is not aware that it terrifies him. He lives as if he did not have a past, and so there is a great deal about himself of which he is not aware. He is entirely ignorant of his lack of awareness, and believes himself to be in full control of his existence. He zeroes in on a bright, rather guarded girl he meets in Humanities 301, and devotes himself to winning her hand. It is a long campaign, and the odds are against him – her family disapproves vehemently, for reasons that are never made clear, and she is more intelligent than Sean, and ambitious, in a way he is not, for power in some as yet unnamed career. She is older than he is. She is not afraid of living alone. Yet in the end his tenacity prevails. Graduate school provides no route for her ambition, she drifts for a bit, and finally capitulates over the telephone. Sean is exultant.

They are married by a judge in her parents' midtown brownstone. Sean is 6 feet 2 inches tall, weighs 133 pounds, and appears, with his Irish, slightly acned face, to be all of seventeen. (He is actually twenty-two.) His wife is struck by the irony of the fact that more than half of the relatives watching the event are divorced. Sean is impressed by the activity outside the window during the ceremony. The New York Foundling Hospital is being torn down – the wrecker's ball exploding walls even as the absurdly short judge drones on. For both of them – in a moment of lucidity whose importance they are too young to recognize – the ceremony is anticlimactic, and faintly ridiculous.

Four years pass, and nothing happens. They both have a small monthly income from trust funds. She dabbles in an occasional project or temporary job but always retreats in mysterious frustration to the safety of their apartment. He writes a book, but it contains nothing, since he knows very little about people, or himself. He remains a boy; the marriage that was to launch him into maturity serves instead to extend his boyhood. Husband and wife, they remain children. They live together in good will, oddly sealed off from one another, and from the world. He dreams of people jumping out of windows, holding hands, in eerie accord. He has no idea what the dreams mean, or where they come from. She confesses that she has never believed in romantic love. They are both frightened of the outside, but

they respond differently. She feels that what is out there is too
dangerous to fool with. He feels that, however dangerous, it is
only out there that strength can be found. In some vague,
inchoate way, he knows he needs strength.
Privately, without telling him, she decides to have children.
Philip is born. John is born. Sean is exultant.

A summer night in 1966. Sean drives down from Harlem, where
he has gotten drunk in a jazz club. The bouncer, an old
acquaintance, has sold him an ounce of marijuana. Sean carries it
in a sealed envelope in his back pocket. He turns off the Henry
Hudson Parkway at Ninety-sixth Street, slips along Riverside
Drive for a couple of blocks, turns, and pulls up in front of
Judy's house. It's a strange little building – five floors with a
turret up the side, a dormer window on her top-floor apartment,
bits of crenellation and decoration, like some miniature castle. A
Rapunzel house.
      He had met her on the sidelines during a soccer game.
Kneeling on the grass, he had turned his head to follow the
fullback's kick, and found himself looking instead at the slender,
blue-jeaned thigh of the girl standing next to him. Perhaps it was
the suddenness, the abrupt nearness of the splendid curve of her
backside, the images sinking into him before he had time to
protect himself. The lust he felt was so pure it seemed, for all its
power, magically innocent, and he got to his feet and began
talking to her. (She was eventually to disappear into medical
school, but never, as it turned out, from his memory.)
      He stares up at the dark window. Behind the window is a
room, and in the room a bed, in which for a year he has been
making love to Judy. She is gone now, away for a month,
driving around France in a *deux-chevaux* Citroën leased by him as
a gift. The room is dark and empty, and yet he has to go in. He
does not question the urge. He simply gets out of the car and
approaches the building. Once he is in motion, a kind of heat
suffuses him. He experiences something like tunnel vision.
      Inside, he scans the mailboxes. A few letters are visible
behind the grille in hers. He opens the door with his key and
runs up the stairs – turning at landings, climbing, turning,

climbing, until he is there, at the top floor. It is midnight, and
the building is silent. He slips the key into the lock, turns and
pushes. The door will not open. He has forgotten the police
lock, the iron bar she'd had installed before she left – with a
separate locking mechanism. He doesn't have that key. He leans
against the door for a moment, and the faint scent of the room
inside reaches him. He is dizzy with the scent, and the door
suddenly enrages him. The scent is inside, and he must get inside.

He pounds his shoulder against the glossy black wood in a
steady rhythm, putting all his weight against it. The door shakes
in its hinges, but he can feel the solidity of the iron bar in the
center. There is not an iota of movement in the bar. He moves
back in the hallway – halfway to the rear apartment – runs
forward, raises his right leg, and kicks the central panel of the
door. A terrific crash, but the door does not yield. He continues
to run and kick, in a frenzy, until he starts falling down.

Out of breath, he sits on the stairs to the roof and looks at
Judy's door. He cannot believe there is no way to get it open.
The wood is cracked in several places. Finally, as his breathing
slows, he gives up. The iron bar will never move.

Slowly, swirling like smoke, an idea emerges. He turns and
looks up the stairs, into the darkness. After a moment he stands
up, mounts the stairs, opens the hatch, and climbs out onto the
roof. The air cools him – he is drenched with sweat. Purple sky.
Stars. He crosses the flat part of the roof to the front of the
building, where it suddenly drops off in a steep slope – a
Rapunzel roof, tiled with overlapping slate. There is a masonry
ridge, perhaps an inch high, at the bottom edge, 15 feet down.
He moves sideways until he comes to a place he estimates lies
directly above the dormer window. He gets down on his belly
and carefully slides his legs over onto the tiles, lowering more
and more of himself onto the steep incline, testing to see if he
can control his downward motion. Sufficient control seems
possible, and, very slowly, he releases his grip on the roof and
begins to slide. His face presses against the slate, and he can feel
the sweat from his cheek on the slate. From somewhere off
toward Amsterdam Avenue comes the sound of a siren.

He descends blindly and stops when his toes touch the ridge.

Beyond the ridge, there is empty space and a clear drop to the sidewalk, but he is unafraid. He remains motionless for several moments, and his noisy brain falls still. He is no longer drunk. A profound calm prevails, a sense of peacefulness – as sweet, to him, as water to some traveler in the desert. Carefully, he slides down sideways until his entire body lies along the ridge. He raises his head and looks at the deserted street below – the pools of light under the street lamps, the tops of the parked cars, the square patterns of the cracks in the sidewalk – and there is a cleanness and orderliness to things. He becomes aware that there is a reality that lies behind the appearance of the world, a pure reality he has never sensed before, and the knowledge fills him with gratitude.

He moves his head farther out and looks for the dormer window. There it is. He had thought to hang on to the edge of the roof and swing himself down and into the window. In his mind, he had known he could do anything – anything he was capable of imagining. But now, as he looks at the dormer window – too far away, full of tricky angles – he sees that the plan is impossible. He immediately discards the plan, as if he had been caught up in a story that ended abruptly. He no longer has any interest in getting into the apartment.

Moving slowly and carefully, as calm in his soul as the calmness in the great purple sky above him, he retreats. Using the friction of his arms and legs, of his damp palms and the sides of his shoes, he inches his way up the sloping roof. He reaches the top of the building.

Once inside, he closes the roof door behind him and descends rapidly. He passes the door to the apartment without a glance.

As his children are born, Sean begins to write a book about his past. At first he is ebullient, possessed by gaiety. He doesn't remember much – his childhood all jumbled, without chronology. There are only isolated scenes, places, sights and sounds, moods, in no apparent order. It seems a small thing to write down these floating memories, to play with them at a distance. It seems like fun.

His children, simply by coming into the world, have got

him started. As the work gets difficult, the fact of his children
sustains him in some roundabout fashion. His gaiety changes to
a mood of taut attentiveness, as the past he had trivialized with
his amnesia begins, with tantalizing slowness, to reveal itself. He
knows hard work for the first time in his life, and he is grateful.
Soon he finds himself in a kind of trance; after hours of writing
he will look down at a page or two with a sense of awe, because
the work is better than anything he could reasonably have
expected of himself. He will live this way for four years. In his
mind, his writing, his ability to write at all, is connected to his
children.

He develops a habit of going into their room late at night.
Blue light from the street lamp outside angles through the large
windows to spill on the waxed wooden floor. Philip is three,
sleeping on his side, his small hand holding a rubber frog. Sean
crosses the room and looks at John, aged two. Behind delicate
eyelids, his eyes move in a dream. Sean goes to a spot equidistant
from both beds and sits down on the floor, his legs folded. He
stares at the pale-blue bars of light on the floor and listens. He
hears the children breathe. When they move, he hears them
move. His mind clears. After half an hour he gets up, adjusts
their blankets, and goes to bed.

At a small dinner party with his wife, in Manhattan, he becomes
aware that the host and hostess are tense and abstracted. The
hostess apologizes and explains that she should have cancelled
the dinner. There had been a tragedy that afternoon. The young
couple living directly above, on the eighth floor, had left a
window open, and their baby girl had somehow pulled herself
up and fallen through to her death.

"You're white as a ghost," his wife says as they leave the
table. "Sean, you're trembling."

They forgo coffee, with apologies, and go home immediately. Sean drives fast, parks by a hydrant, and runs up the stoop
into the house.

"It's okay, it's okay," his wife says.

He nods to the sitter in the living room and keeps on going, up the stairs, to the children's room. They are asleep, safe in their beds.

"We have to get guardrails," he says, going to the windows, locking them. "Bars – those things – whatever they are."

"Yes. We will," his wife whispers. "Okay."

"All the windows. Front and back."

"Yes, yes. Don't wake them, now."

That night he must sleep in their room.

Sean lies full length in the oversize bathtub, hot water to his chin. When he comes home from work (he writes in a small office a mile away), he almost always takes a bath. Philip and John push the door open and rush, stark naked, to the tub. They're about to be put to bed, but they've escaped. Sean doesn't move. Philip's head and shoulders are visible, while John, shorter, shows only his head. Their faces are solemn. Sean stares into their clear, intelligent eyes – so near – and waits, showing no expression, so as to draw the moment out. The sight of them is a profound refreshment.

"Do it, Daddy," Philip says.

"Do what?"

"The noise. When you wash your face."

Sean rises to a sitting position. He washes his face, and then rinses by bending forward and lifting cupped handfuls of water. He simultaneously blows and moans into the handfuls of water, making a satisfying noise. The boys smile. The drama of Daddy-in-the-bath fascinates them. They can't get enough of it.

Sean reaches out and lifts first one and then the other over the edge and into the tub. His hands encompass their small chests, and he can feel the life in them. The boys laugh and splash about, slippery as pink seals fresh from the womb. They hang on his neck and slide over his chest.

His wife comes in and pulls them up, into towels. They go off to bed. Later, in the kitchen, she says, "I wish you wouldn't do that."

"What?"

"In the bath like that."

He is nonplussed. "Good heavens. Why not?"

"It could scare them."

"But they love it!"

"It's icky."

"Icky," he repeats. He goes to the refrigerator for some ice. He can feel the anger starting, his face beginning to flush. He makes a drink and goes into the living room. The anger mounts as he hears the sounds of her working in the kitchen, making dinner. Abruptly, he puts down his drink, goes into the hall, down the stairs, and out the front door. He spends the evening in a bar frequented by writers and returns home drunk at three in the morning.

A few years later, Sean drives home from the office. He has worked late, missed dinner. He thinks about his boys, and begins to weep. He pulls off the expressway and parks in the darkness by the docks. It occurs to him that he is in bad trouble. The weeping has come out of nowhere, to overwhelm him, like some exotic physical reflex, and it could as well have happened on the street or in a restaurant. There is more pressure in him than he can control, or even gauge, his pretenses to the contrary notwithstanding. As he calms down, he allows himself to face the fact that his wife has begun to prepare for the end: a whisper of discreet activity – ice-skating with a male friend on weekends, veiled references to an unknown future, a certain coyness around the house. When he goes, he will have to leave the children. He starts the car, and the boys are in his mind; he feels the weight of their souls in his mind.

He unlocks the front door of the house, hangs his coat in the closet, and climbs the stairs. Silence. A fire burns in the fireplace in the empty living room. The kitchen and dining room are empty. He moves along the landing and starts up the second flight of stairs.

"Daddy." Philip is out of sight in his bedroom, but his voice is clear, his tone direct, as if they'd been talking together, as if they were in the middle of a conversation.

"I'm coming." Sean wonders why the house is so quiet. His wife must be up in the attic. John must be asleep.

"Why were you crying?" Philip asks.

Sean stops at the top of the stairs. His first thought is not how the boy knows but if the knowledge has scared him. He goes into the room, and there is Philip, wide awake, kneeling at the foot of his bed, an expectant look on his face.

"Hi." Sean can see the boy is not alarmed. Curious, focused, but not scared.

"Why?" the boy asks. He is six years old.

"Grownups cry sometimes, you know. It's okay."

The boy takes it in, still waiting.

"I'm not sure," Sean says. "It's complicated. Probably a lot of things. But it's okay. I feel better now."

"That's good."

Sean senses the boy's relief. He sits down on the floor. "How did you know I was crying?" He has never felt as close to another human being as he does at this moment. His tone is deliberately casual.

The boy starts to answer, his intelligent face eager, animated. Sean watches the clearly marked stages: First, Philip draws a breath to begin speaking. He is confident. Second, he searches for language to frame what he knows, but, to his puzzlement, it isn't there. Third, he realizes he can't answer the question. He stares into the middle distance for several moments. Sean waits, but he has seen it all in the boy's face.

"I don't know," the boy says. "I just knew."

"I understand."

After a while the boy gives a sudden large yawn, and gets under the covers. Sean goes downstairs.

The time arrives when he must tell the boys he is going away. Philip is eight, and John almost seven. They go up into the attic playroom. Sean masks the storm in his heart and explains that no one in the family is at fault. He has no choice – he must leave, and not live in the house anymore. As he says this, the boys glance quickly at each other – almost furtively – and Sean feels a special sharp, mysterious pang.

★

Twelve years later, Sean stands on line at Gate 6 in Boston's
Logan Airport, waiting to check in for Eastern's 7.45 a.m.
flight to Philadelphia. He is gray-haired, a bit thick around the
middle, wears reading glasses low on his nose, and walks, as he
moves closer to the desk, with a slight limp, from a cartilage
operation on his right knee. He wears a dark suit and a trench-
coat, and carries a soft canvas overnight bag hanging from his
shoulder.

"Morning." The attendant is a black woman with whom he
has checked in every Monday morning for the last two years.
"It's nowhere near full," she says. "I'll upgrade you now." Sean
commutes weekly between the two cities, and the airline has
provided him with a special card. When first class is not full, he
gets a first-class seat at no extra charge. She hands him his
boarding pass, and he nods as he moves away.

He sits down and waits for the boarding call. Businessmen
surround him, two military officers, three stewardesses, a student
carrying a book bag from the university in Boston where Sean
teaches. He doesn't recognize the student but watches him
abstractedly. Philip and John are that age now. Sean recalls that
when his boys entered college, in Washington and Chicago, he
found himself easing up on his own students in Boston, softening
his style despite himself.

The flight is called. He surrenders his ticket and moves down
the enclosed walkway to the open door of the plane. The
stewardess recognizes him and takes his coat. He settles down in
seat 2-A and accepts a cup of coffee. The ritual is familiar and
reassuring. Sean is at ease.

It had not always been thus. When he'd begun commuting,
Sean was tense in the air. It had been difficult for him to look out
the window without a flash of panic. In his fear, he was
abnormally sensitive to the other passengers – controlling his
anger at loud conversations, conscious of any intrusion, however
minute, into the space allotted to him. Expansive people irritated
him the most. He could not abide the way they threw their
elbows about, or thoughtlessly stretched their legs, or clumsily
bumped into his seat. He found himself hating the other passengers, cataloguing their faults like a miser counting money. But

eventually, as he got used to flying, he began to recognize the oddness, the almost pathological oddness of his hatred, and it went away. Only on very rough flights did it recur.

Now he can gaze down through miles of empty space without fear. He wonders why, and concludes that both his former fear of heights and his present lack of fear are inexplicable. The stewardess brings breakfast, and his right knee cracks painfully as he adjusts his position.

The tenth summer of Sunday softball. The game Sean helped to organize had become a tradition in the town of Siasconset. Philip and John began as small boys and grew to young men playing the infield. Sean's second wife had taken pictures from the start, and the effect was that of time-lapse photography – a collapsed history in which the father grew older, the sons grew taller and stronger, and everyone else stayed more or less the same. Sean stood on the mound with a one-run lead, runner at first, and two outs. The batter was Gino, a power hitter. Sean threw an inside pitch and watched Gino's hips come around, watched the bat come around, and heard the snap of solid contact. The ball disappeared in speed toward third base. Sean turned to see John frozen in the air, impossibly high off the ground, feet together, toes pointed down, his legs and torso perfectly aligned in a smooth curve, a continuous brushstroke, his long arm pointing straight up at full extension, and there, nestled deep in the pocket of his glove, the white ball. Sean gave a shout of joy, dimly aware of pain in his knee, shouting all the way down as he fell, twisting, utterly happy, numb with pleasure.

The stewardess clears away his breakfast. Below, New York City slips past. He finds the old neighborhood, even the street, but he can't make out the house where his first wife still lives. They have retained good relations, and talk on the phone every month or so. His second, younger wife approves of the first, and vice versa. Sean is absurdly proud of this.

"Do you ever dream about me?" he had once asked her on the phone. "I mean, do I ever appear in your dreams?"

Slightly taken aback, she had laughed nervously. "No. What an odd question."

"I only ask because you crop up in mine. What is it – eleven years now, twelve? You still show up now and then."

The plane lands smoothly at the Philadelphia airport. Looping his bag over his shoulder, Sean is out the door, through the building, and into a cab.

"Downtown. The Drexler Building."

In his late forties, to his amazement, and through a process he never completely understood, the board of the Drexler Foundation had asked him to direct that part of their organization which gave money to the arts. It is work he enjoys.

He pays the driver and stares up at the Drexler Building – seventy stories of glass reflecting the clouds, the sky. Pushing through the big revolving door, he crosses the lobby, quickening his step as he sees the express elevator ready to leave. He jumps through just as the doors close behind him, pushes the button for the sixty-fifth floor, and turns.

For a split second he is disorientated. Philip, his older son, stands before him on the other side of the elevator, facing front. Sean's heart lurches, and then he sees that it is a young man of Philip's age, size, and general appearance, delivering a large envelope to Glidden & Glidden, on sixty-four. For a moment the two ideas overlap – the idea of Philip and the idea of the young man – and in that moment time seems to slow down. It is as if Sean had seen his son across a supernatural barrier – as if he, Sean, were a ghost haunting the elevator, able to see the real body of his son but unable to be seen by him. An almost unbearable sadness comes over him. As he emerges from this illusion, he knows full well that his son is hundreds of miles away at college, and yet he finds within himself a pressure of love for the young man so great it is all he can do to remain silent. The elevator ascends, and Sean regains control of himself. Now he can see the young man clearly – alert, a little edgy, clear blue eyes, a bit of acne.

"I hate elevators," the young man says, his eyes fixed on the lights above the door indicating the floors.

"I'm not crazy about them, but it beats walking."

The elevator approaches sixty-four, but then the lights go out, the emergency light comes on, and it stops between sixty-three and sixty-four. A slight bump downward. Sean grabs the rail involuntarily. Under the flat white light of the emergency bulb, the young man is pale, gaunt-looking.

"Oh my God," he says.

They fall a few feet more.

The young man presses himself into a corner. His eyes are wild.

Sean is utterly calm.

"Oh God oh God oh God." The young man's voice begins to rise.

"This has happened to me several times," Sean lies. "In Chicago. Once in Baltimore. The elevators have brakes, non-electrical, separate from all the other systems, which automatically engage if the elevator exceeds a certain speed." This, he thinks, is the truth. "Do you understand what I'm saying?"

The young man's mouth is open, as if to scream. He looks in all directions, finally at Sean.

"It can't fall. It can't. Do you understand?"

"Yes." The young man swallows hard.

"We're perfectly safe."

Sean watches the young man as several minutes go by. He remains silent, remembering his own panic in airplanes, his own need for privacy on those occasions, guessing that the boy feels likewise. After another minute, however, he can see the fear rising again in the young man's face. Sean shrugs off his bag and crosses the space between them.

"Listen," he says quietly, "it's going to be okay."

The young man is breathing fast. He stares at Sean without seeing him. Sean reaches out and takes the young man's head in his hands.

"I want you to listen to me now. We are quite safe. Focus on me, now. I know we are safe, and if you focus on me *you* will know we are safe." The young man sees him now. He moves his head slightly in Sean's hands.

"Hypnotism," he whispers.

"No, for Christ's sake, it isn't hypnotism," Sean says. "We're going to stay like this until the lights come on. We're going to stay like this until the door opens, or they come get us, or whatever." Sean can feel the young man begin to calm down. He holds the boy's head gently and stares into his eyes. "Good. That's good."

After a while the lights come on, the elevator rises, and the doors open. The boy jumps out. "Come on, come on!" he cries. Sean smiles. "This is sixty-four. I'm going to sixty-five." The young man moves forward, but the door closes. The elevator goes up one floor, and Sean gets out.

That night, as he lies in bed waiting for sleep, Sean goes over the entire incident in his mind. He laughs aloud, remembering the young man's expression when he realized Sean was going to stay in the elevator.

Then he remembers the day in 1942 when his father showed up unexpectedly, took him home from school, washed the windows, and carried him out on the windowsill. He remembers looking down at the cracks in the sidewalk. Here, in the darkness, he can see the cracks in the sidewalk from more than forty years ago. He feels no fear – only a sense of astonishment.

ANDRE DUBUS

☆　☆　☆　☆

# *The Fat Girl*

Her name was Louise. Once when she was sixteen a boy kissed
her at a barbecue; he was drunk and he jammed his tongue into
her mouth and ran his hands up and down her hips. Her father
kissed her often. He was thin and kind and she could see in his
eyes when he looked at her the lights of love and pity.

It started when Louise was nine. You must start watching
what you eat, her mother would say. I can see you have my
metabolism. Louise also had her mother's pale blond hair. Her
mother was slim and pretty, carried herself erectly, and ate very
little. The two of them would eat bare lunches, while her older
brother ate sandwiches and potato chips, and then her mother
would sit smoking while Louise eyed the bread box, the pantry,
the refrigerator. Wasn't that good, her mother would say. In five
years you'll be in high school and if you're fat the boys won't
like you; they won't ask you out. Boys were as far away as five
years, and she would go to her room and wait for nearly an hour
until she knew her mother was no longer thinking of her, then
she would creep into the kitchen and, listening to her mother
talking on the phone, or her footsteps upstairs, she would open
the bread box, the pantry, the jar of peanut butter. She would
put the sandwich under her shirt and go outside or to the
bathroom to eat it.

Her father was a lawyer and made a lot of money and came
home looking pale and happy. Martinis put color back in his
face, and at dinner he talked to his wife and two children. Oh
give her a potato, he would say to Louise's mother. She's a
growing girl. Her mother's voice then became tense: If she has a
potato she shouldn't have dessert. She should have both, her
father would say, and he would reach over and touch Louise's
cheek or hand or arm.

In high school she had two girlfriends and at night and on weekends they rode in a car or went to movies. In movies she was fascinated by fat actresses. She wondered why they were fat. She knew why she was fat: she was fat because she was Louise. Because God had made her that way. Because she wasn't like her friends Joan and Marjorie, who drank milk shakes after school and were all bones and tight skin. But what about those actresses, with their talents, with their broad and profound faces? Did they eat as heedlessly as Bishop Humphries and his wife who sometimes came to dinner and, as Louise's mother said, gorged between amenities? Or did they try to lose weight, did they go about hungry and angry and thinking of food? She thought of them eating lean meats and salads with friends, and then going home and building strange large sandwiches with French bread. But mostly she believed they did not go through these failures; they were fat because they chose to be. And she was certain of something else too: she could see it in their faces: they did not eat secretly. Which she did: her creeping to the kitchen when she was nine became, in high school, a ritual of deceit and pleasure. She was a furtive eater of sweets. Even her two friends did not know her secret.

Joan was thin, gangling, and flat-chested; she was attractive enough and all she needed was someone to take a second look at her face, but the school was large and there were pretty girls in every classroom and walking all the corridors, so no one ever needed to take a second look at Joan. Marjorie was thin too, an intense, heavy-smoking girl with brittle laughter. She was very intelligent, and with boys she was shy because she knew she made them uncomfortable, and because she was smarter than they were and so could not understand or could not believe the levels they lived on. She was to have a nervous breakdown before earning her Ph.D. in philosophy at the University of California, where she met and married a physicist and discovered within herself an untrammelled passion: she made love with her husband on the couch, the carpet, in the bathtub, and on the washing machine. By that time much had happened to her and she never thought of Louise. Joan would finally stop growing and begin moving with grace and confidence. In college she would have two lovers and then several more during the six years she spent in Boston before marrying a middle-aged editor who had two sons in their early teens, who drank too much, who was tenderly, boyishly grateful for her love, and whose wife had been killed while rock-climbing in New Hampshire with her lover. She would not think of Louise either, except in an earlier time, when lovers were still new to her and she was ecstatically surprised each time one of them loved her and, sometimes at night, lying in a man's arms, she would tell how in high school no one dated her, she had been thin and plain (she would still believe that: that she had been plain; it had never been true) and so had been forced into the weekend and nighttime company of a neurotic smart girl and a shy fat girl. She would say this with self-pity exaggerated by Scotch and her need to be more deeply loved by the man who held her.

She never eats, Joan and Marjorie said of Louise. They ate lunch with her at school, watched her refusing potatoes, ravioli, fried fish. Sometimes she got through the cafeteria line with only a salad. That is how they would remember her: a girl whose hapless body was destined to be fat. No one saw the sandwiches she made and took to her room when she came home from school. No one saw the store of Milky Ways, Butterfingers, Almond Joys, and Hersheys far back on her closet shelf, behind the stuffed animals of her childhood. She was not a hypocrite. When she was out of the house she truly believed she was dieting; she forgot about the candy, as a man speaking into his office dictaphone may forget the lewd photographs hidden in an old shoe in his closet. At other times, away from home, she thought of the waiting candy with near lust. One night driving home from a movie, Marjorie said: "You're lucky you don't smoke; it's incredible what I go through to hide it from my parents." Louise turned to her a smile which was elusive and mysterious; she yearned to be home in bed, eating chocolate in the dark. She did not need to smoke; she already had a vice that was insular and destructive.

She brought it with her to college. She thought she would leave it behind. A move from one place to another, a new room without the haunted closet shelf, would do for her what she could not do for herself. She packed her large dresses and went. For two weeks she was busy with registration, with shyness, with classes; then she began to feel at home. Her room was no longer like a motel. Its walls had stopped watching her, she felt they were her friends, and she gave them her secret. Away from her mother, she did not have to be as elaborate; she kept the candy in her drawer now.

The school was in Massachusetts, a girls' school. When she chose it, when she and her father and mother talked about it in the evenings, everyone so carefully avoided the word boys that sometimes the conversations seemed to be about nothing but boys. There are no boys there, the neuter words said; you will not have to contend with that. In her father's eyes were pity and encouragement; in her mother's was disappointment, and her voice was crisp. They spoke of courses, of small classes where Louise would get more attention. She imagined herself in those small classes; she saw herself as a teacher would see her, as the other girls would; she would get no attention.

The girls at the school were from wealthy families, but most of them wore the uniform of another class: blue jeans and work shirts, and many wore overalls. Louise bought some overalls, washed them until the dark blue faded, and wore them to classes. In the cafeteria she ate as she had in high school, not to lose weight nor even to sustain her lie, but because eating lightly in public had become as habitual as good manners. Everyone had to take gym, and in the locker room with the other girls, and wearing shorts on the volleyball and badminton courts, she hated her body. She liked her body most when she was unaware of it: in bed at night, as sleep gently took her out of her day, out of herself. And she liked parts of her body. She liked her brown eyes and sometimes looked at them in the mirror: they were not shallow eyes, she thought; they were indeed windows of a tender soul, a good heart. She liked her lips and nose, and her chin, finely shaped between her wide and sagging cheeks. Most of all she liked her long pale blond hair, she liked washing and drying it and lying naked on her bed, smelling of shampoo, and feeling the soft hair at her neck and shoulders and back.

Her friend at college was Carrie, who was thin and wore thick glasses and often at night she cried in Louise's room. She did not know why she was crying. She was crying, she said, because she was unhappy. She could say no more. Louise said she was unhappy too, and Carrie moved in with her. One night Carrie talked for hours, sadly and bitterly, about her parents and what they did to each other. When she finished she hugged Louise and they went to bed. Then in the dark Carrie spoke across the room: "Louise? I just wanted to tell you. One night last week I woke up and smelled chocolate. You were eating chocolate, in your bed. I wish you'd eat it in front of me, Louise, whenever you feel like it."

Stiffened in her bed, Louise could think of nothing to say. In the silence she was afraid Carrie would think she was asleep and would tell her again in the morning or tomorrow night. Finally she said okay. Then after a moment she told Carrie if she ever wanted any she could feel free to help herself; the candy was in the top drawer. Then she said thank you.

They were room-mates for four years and in the summers they exchanged letters. Each fall they greeted with embraces, laughter, tears, and moved into their old room, which had been stripped and cleansed of them for the summer. Neither girl enjoyed summer. Carrie did not like being at home because her parents did not love each other. Louise lived in a small city in Louisiana. She did not like the summer because she had lost touch with Joan and Marjorie; they saw each other, but it was not the same. She liked being with her father but with no one else. The flicker of disappointment in her mother's eyes at the airport was a vanguard of the army of relatives and acquaintances who awaited her: they would see her on the streets, in stores, at the country club, in her home, and in theirs; in the first moments of greeting, their eyes would tell her she was still fat Louise, who had been fat as long as they could remember, who had gone to college and returned as fat as ever. Then their eyes dismissed her, and she longed for school and Carrie, and she wrote letters to her friend. But that saddened her too. It wasn't simply that Carrie was her only friend, and when they finished college they might never see each other again. It was that her existence in the

world was so divided; it had begun when she was a child
creeping to the kitchen; now that division was much sharper,
and her friendship with Carrie seemed disproportionate and
perilous. The world she was destined to live in had nothing to
do with the intimate nights in their room at school.

In the summer before their senior year, Carrie fell in love.
She wrote to Louise about him, but she did not write much, and
this hurt Louise more than if Carrie had shown the joy her
writing tried to conceal. That fall they returned to their room;
they were still close and warm, Carrie still needed Louise's ears
and heart at night as she spoke of her parents and her recurring
malaise whose source the two friends never discovered. But on
most weekends Carrie left, and caught a bus to Boston where
her boyfriend studied music. During the week she often spoke
hesitantly of sex; she was not sure if she liked it. But Louise,
eating candy and listening, did not know whether Carrie was
telling the truth or whether, as in her letters of the past summer,
Carrie was keeping from her those delights she may never
experience.

Then one Sunday night when Carrie had just returned from
Boston and was unpacking her overnight bag, she looked at
Louise and said: "I was thinking about you. On the bus coming
home tonight." Looking at Carrie's concerned, determined face,
Louise prepared herself for humiliation. "I was thinking about
when we graduate. What you're going to do. What's to become
of you. I want you to be loved the way I love you. Louise, if I
help you, *really* help you, will you go on a diet?"

Louise entered a period of her life she would remember always,
the way some people remember having endured poverty. Her
diet did not begin the next day. Carrie told her to eat on Monday
as though it were the last day of her life. So for the first time
since grammar school Louise went into a school cafeteria and ate
everything she wanted. At breakfast and lunch and dinner she
glanced around the table to see if the other girls noticed the food
on her tray. They did not. She felt there was a lesson in this, but
it lay beyond her grasp. That night in their room she ate the four
remaining candy bars. During the day Carrie rented a small

refrigerator, bought an electric skillet, an electric broiler, and bathroom scales.

On Tuesday morning Louise stood on the scales, and Carrie wrote in her notebook: *October 14: 184 lbs.* Then she made Louise a cup of black coffee and scrambled one egg and sat with her while she ate. When Carrie went to the dining room for breakfast, Louise walked about the campus for thirty minutes. That was part of the plan. The campus was pretty, on its lawns grew at least one of every tree native to New England, and in the warm morning sun Louise felt a new hope. At noon they met in their room, and Carrie broiled her a piece of hamburger and served it with lettuce. Then while Carrie ate in the dining room Louise walked again. She was weak with hunger and she felt queasy. During her afternoon classes she was nervous and tense, and she chewed her pencil and tapped her heels on the floor and tightened her calves. When she returned to her room late that afternoon, she was so glad to see Carrie that she embraced her; she had felt she could not bear another minute of hunger, but now with Carrie she knew she could make it at least through tonight. Then she would sleep and face tomorrow when it came. Carrie broiled her a steak and served it with lettuce. Louise studied while Carrie ate dinner, then they went for a walk.

That was her ritual and her diet for the rest of the year, Carrie alternating fish and chicken breasts with the steaks for dinner, and every day was nearly as bad as the first. In the evenings she was irritable. In all her life she had never been afflicted by ill temper and she looked upon it now as a demon which, along with hunger, was taking possession of her soul. Often she spoke sharply to Carrie. One night during their after-dinner walk Carrie talked sadly of night, of how darkness made her more aware of herself, and at night she did not know why she was in college, why she studied, why she was walking the earth with other people. They were standing on a wooden footbridge, looking down at a dark pond. Carrie kept talking; perhaps soon she would cry. Suddenly Louise said: "I'm sick of lettuce. I never want to see a piece of lettuce for the rest of my life. I hate it. We shouldn't even buy it, it's immoral."

Carrie was quiet. Louise glanced at her, and the pain and irritation in Carrie's face soothed her. Then she was ashamed. Before she could say she was sorry, Carrie turned to her and said gently: "I know. I know how terrible it is."

Carrie did all the shopping, telling Louise she knew how hard it was to go into a supermarket when you were hungry. And Louise was always hungry. She drank diet soft drinks and started smoking Carrie's cigarettes, learned to enjoy inhaling, thought of cancer and emphysema but they were as far away as those boys her mother had talked about when she was nine. By Thanksgiving she was smoking over a pack a day and her weight in Carrie's notebook was 162 pounds. Carrie was afraid if Louise went home at Thanksgiving she would lapse from the diet, so Louise spent the vacation with Carrie, in Philadelphia. Carrie wrote her family about the diet, and told Louise that she had. On the phone to Philadelphia, Louise said: "I feel like a bedwetter. When I was a little girl I had a friend who used to come spend the night and Mother would put a rubber sheet on the bed and we all pretended there wasn't a rubber sheet and that she hadn't wet the bed. Even me, and I slept with her." At Thanksgiving dinner she lowered her eyes as Carrie's father put two slices of white meat on her plate and passed it to her over the bowls of steaming food.

When she went home at Christmas she weighed 155 pounds; at the airport her mother marveled. Her father laughed and hugged her and said: "But now there's less of you to love." He was troubled by her smoking but only mentioned it once; he told her she was beautiful and, as always, his eyes bathed her with love. During the long vacation her mother cooked for her as Carrie had, and Louise returned to school weighing 146 pounds.

Flying north on the plane she warmly recalled the surprised and congratulatory eyes of her relatives and acquaintances. She had not seen Joan or Marjorie. She thought of returning home in May, weighing the 115 pounds which Carrie had in October set as their goal. Looking toward the stoic days ahead, she felt strong. She thought of those hungry days of fall and early winter (and now: she was hungry now: with almost a frown, almost a brusque shake of the head, she refused peanuts from the steward-

ess): those first weeks of the diet when she was the pawn of an
irascibility which still, conditioned to her ritual as she was, could
at any moment take command of her. She thought of the nights
of trying to sleep while her stomach growled. She thought of her
addiction to cigarettes. She thought of the people at school: not
one teacher, not one girl, had spoken to her about her loss of
weight, not even about her absence from meals. And without
warning her spirit collapsed. She did not feel strong, she did not
feel she was committed to and within reach of achieving a
valuable goal. She felt that somehow she had lost more than
pounds of fat; that some time during her dieting she had lost
herself too. She tried to remember what it had felt like to be
Louise before she had started living on meat and fish, as an
unhappy adult may look sadly in the memory of childhood for
lost virtues and hopes. She looked down at the earth far below,
and it seemed to her that her soul, like her body aboard the
plane, was in some rootless flight. She neither knew its destination nor where it had departed from; it was on some passage
she could not even define.

During the next few weeks she lost weight more slowly and
once for eight days Carrie's daily recording stayed at 136. Louise
woke in the morning thinking of 136 and then she stood on the
scales and they echoed her. She became obsessed with that
number, and there wasn't a day when she didn't say it aloud, and
through the days and nights the number stayed in her mind, and
if a teacher had spoken those digits in a classroom she would
have opened her mouth to speak. What if that's me, she said to
Carrie. I mean what if 136 is my real weight and I just can't lose
anymore. Walking hand-in-hand with her despair was a longing
for this to be true, and that longing angered her and wearied her,
and every day she was gloomy. On the ninth day she weighed
135 pounds. She was not relieved; she thought bitterly of the
months ahead, the shedding of the last 20½ pounds.

On Easter Sunday, which she spent at Carrie's, she weighed
120 pounds, and she ate one slice of glazed pineapple with her
ham and lettuce. She did not enjoy it: she felt she was being
friendly with a recalcitrant enemy who had once tried to destroy
her. Carrie's parents were laudative. She liked them and she

wished they would touch sometimes, and look at each other when they spoke. She guessed they would divorce when Carrie left home, and she vowed that her own marriage would be one of affection and tenderness. She could think about that now: marriage. At school she had read in a Boston paper that this summer the cicadas would come out of their seventeen-year hibernation on Cape Cod, for a month they would mate and then die, leaving their young to burrow into the ground where they would stay for seventeen years. That's me, she had said to Carrie. Only my hibernation lasted twenty-one years.

Often her mother asked in letters and on the phone about the diet, but Louise answered vaguely. When she flew home in late May she weighed 113 pounds, and at the airport her mother cried and hugged her and said again and again: You're so *beau*tiful. Her father blushed and bought her a martini. For days her relatives and acquaintances congratulated her, and the applause in their eyes lasted the entire summer, and she loved their eyes, and swam in the country club pool, the first time she had done this since she was a child.

She lived at home and ate the way her mother did and every morning she weighed herself on the scales in her bathroom. Her mother liked to take her shopping and buy her dresses and they put her old ones in the Goodwill box at the shopping center; Louise thought of them existing on the body of a poor woman whose cheap meals kept her fat. Louise's mother had a photographer come to the house, and Louise posed on the couch and standing beneath a live oak and sitting in a wicker lawn chair next to an azalea bush. The new clothes and the photographer made her feel she was going to another country or becoming a citizen of a new one. In the fall she took a job of no consequence, to give herself something to do.

Also in the fall a young lawyer joined her father's firm, he came one night to dinner, and they started seeing each other. He was the first man outside her family to kiss her since the barbecue when she was sixteen. Louise celebrated Thanksgiving not with rice dressing and candied sweet potatoes and mince meat and pumpkin pies, but by giving Richard her virginity which she

realized, at the very last moment of its existence, she had
embarked on giving him over thirteen months ago, on that
Tuesday in October when Carrie had made her a cup of black
coffee and scrambled one egg. She wrote this to Carrie, who
replied happily by return mail. She also, through glance and
smile and innuendo, tried to tell her mother too. But finally she
controlled that impulse, because Richard felt guilty about making
love with the daughter of his partner and friend. In the spring
they married. The wedding was a large one, in the Episcopal
church, and Carrie flew from Boston to be maid of honor. Her
parents had recently separated and she was living with the
musician and was still victim of her unpredictable malaise. It
overcame her on the night before the wedding, so Louise was up
with her until past three and woke next morning from a sleep so
heavy that she did not want to leave it.

Richard was a lean, tall, energetic man with the metabolism
of a pencil sharpener. Louise fed him everything he wanted. He
liked Italian food and she got recipes from her mother and
watched him eating spaghetti with the sauce she had only tasted,
and ravioli and lasagna, while she ate antipasto with her chianti.
He made a lot of money and borrowed more and they bought a
house whose lawn sloped down to the shore of a lake; they had a
wharf and a boathouse, and Richard bought a boat and they took
friends waterskiing. Richard bought her a car and they spent his
vacations in Mexico, Canada, the Bahamas, and in the fifth year
of their marriage they went to Europe and, according to their
plan, she conceived a child in Paris. On the plane back, as she
looked out the window and beyond the sparkling sea and saw
her country, she felt that it was waiting for her, as her home by
the lake was, and her parents, and her good friends who rode in
the boat and waterskied; she thought of the accumulated warmth
and pelf of her marriage, and how by slimming her body she had
bought into the pleasures of the nation. She felt cunning, and she
smiled to herself, and took Richard's hand.

But these moments of triumph were sparse. On most days
she went about her routine of leisure with a sense of certainty
about herself that came merely from not thinking. But there
were times, with her friends, or with Richard, or alone in the

house, when she was suddenly assaulted by the feeling that she had taken the wrong train and arrived at a place where no one knew her, and where she ought not to be. Often, in bed with Richard, she talked of being fat: "I was the one who started the friendship with Carrie, I chose her, I started the conversations. When I understood that she was my friend I understood something else: I had chosen her for the same reason I'd chosen Joan and Marjorie. They were all thin. I was always thinking about what people saw when they looked at me and I didn't want them to see two fat girls. When I was alone I didn't mind being fat but then I'd have to leave the house again and then I didn't want to look like me. But at home I didn't mind except when I was getting dressed to go out of the house and when Mother looked at me. But I stopped looking at her when she looked at me. And in college I felt good with Carrie; there weren't any boys and I didn't have any other friends and so when I wasn't with Carrie I thought about her and I tried to ignore the other people around me, I tried to make them not exist. A lot of the time I could do that. It was strange, and I felt like a spy."

If Richard was bored by her repetition he pretended not to be. But she knew the story meant very little to him. She could have been telling him of a childhood illness, or wearing braces, or a broken heart at sixteen. He could not see her as she was when she was fat. She felt as though she were trying to tell a foreign lover about her life in the United States, and if only she could command the language he would know and love all of her and she would feel complete. Some of the acquaintances of her childhood were her friends now, and even they did not seem to remember her when she was fat.

Now her body was growing again, and when she put on a maternity dress for the first time she shivered with fear. Richard did not smoke and he asked her, in a voice just short of demand, to stop during her pregnancy. She did. She ate carrots and celery instead of smoking, and at cocktail parties she tried to eat nothing, but after her first drink she ate nuts and cheese and crackers and dips. Always at these parties Richard had talked with his friends and she had rarely spoken to him until they drove home. But now when he noticed her at the hors d'œuvres table he crossed the room and, smiling, led her back to his group. His smile and his hand on her arm told her he was doing his clumsy, husbandly best to help her through a time of female mystery.

She was gaining weight but she told herself it was only the baby, and would leave with its birth. But at other times she knew quite clearly that she was losing the discipline she had fought so hard to gain during her last year with Carrie. She was hungry now as she had been in college, and she ate between meals and after dinner and tried to eat only carrots and celery, but she grew to hate them, and her desire for sweets was as vicious as it had been long ago. At home she ate bread and jam and when she shopped for groceries she bought a candy bar and ate it driving home and put the wrapper in her purse and then in the garbage can under the sink. Her cheeks had filled out, there was loose flesh under her chin, her arms and legs were plump, and her mother was concerned. So was Richard. One night when she brought pie and milk to the living room where they were watching television, he said: "You already had a piece. At dinner."

She did not look at him.

"You're gaining weight. It's not all water, either. It's fat. It'll be summertime. You'll want to get into your bathing suit."

The pie was cherry. She looked at it as her fork cut through it; she speared the piece and rubbed it in the red juice on the plate before lifting it to her mouth.

"You never used to eat pie," he said. "I just think you ought to watch it a bit. It's going to be tough on you this summer."

In her seventh month, with a delight reminiscent of climbing the stairs to Richard's apartment before they were married, she returned to her world of secret gratification. She began hiding candy in her underwear drawer. She ate it during the day and at night while Richard slept, and at breakfast she was distracted, waiting for him to leave.

She gave birth to a son, brought him home, and nursed both him and her appetites. During this time of celibacy she enjoyed her body through her son's mouth; while he suckled she stroked his small head and back. She was hiding candy but she did not conceal her other indulgences: she was smoking again but still she ate between meals, and at dinner she ate what Richard did, and coldly he watched her, he grew petulant, and when the date marking the end of their celibacy came they let it pass. Often in the afternoons her mother visited and scolded her and Louise sat looking at the baby and said nothing until finally, to end it, she promised to diet. When her mother and father came for dinners, her father kissed her and held the baby and her mother said nothing about Louise's body, and her voice was tense. Returning from work in the evenings Richard looked at a soiled plate and glass on the table beside her chair as if detecting traces of infidelity, and at every dinner they fought.

"Look at you," he said. "Lasagna, for God's sake. When are you going to start? It's not simply that you haven't lost any weight. You're gaining. I can see it. I can feel it when you get in bed. Pretty soon you'll weigh more than I do and I'll be sleeping on a trampoline."

"You never touch me anymore."

"I don't want to touch you. Why should I? Have you *looked* at yourself?"

"You're cruel," she said. "I never knew how cruel you were."

She ate, watching him. He did not look at her. Glaring at his plate, he worked with fork and knife like a hurried man at a lunch counter.

"I bet you didn't either," she said.

That night when he was asleep she took a Milky Way to the bathroom. For a while she stood eating in the dark, then she turned on the light. Chewing, she looked at herself in the mirror; she looked at her eyes and hair. Then she stood on the scales and looking at the numbers between her feet, 162, she remembered when she had weighed 136 pounds for eight days. Her memory of those eight days was fond and amusing, as though she were recalling an Easter egg hunt when she was six. She stepped off the scales and pushed them under the lavatory and did not stand on them again.

It was summer and she bought loose dresses and when Richard took friends out on the boat she did not wear a bathing suit or shorts; her friends gave her mischievous glances, and Richard did not look at her. She stopped riding on the boat. She told them she wanted to stay with the baby, and she sat inside holding him until she heard the boat leave the wharf. Then she took him to the front lawn and walked with him in the shade of the trees and talked to him about the blue jays and mockingbirds and cardinals she saw on their branches. Sometimes she stopped and watched the boat out on the lake and the friend skiing behind it.

Every day Richard quarreled, and because his rage went no further than her weight and shape, she felt excluded from it, and she remained calm within layers of flesh and spirit, and watched his frustration, his impotence. He truly believed they were arguing about her weight. She knew better: she knew that beneath the argument lay the question of who Richard was. She thought of him smiling at the wheel of his boat, and long ago courting his slender girl, the daughter of his partner and friend. She thought of Carrie telling her of smelling chocolate in the dark and, after that, watching her eat it night after night. She smiled at Richard, teasing his anger.

He is angry now. He stands in the center of the living room, raging at her, and he wakes the baby. Beneath Richard's voice she hears the soft crying, feels it in her heart, and quietly she rises from her chair and goes upstairs to the child's room and takes him from the crib. She brings him to the living room and sits holding him in her lap, pressing him gently against the folds of fat at her waist. Now Richard is pleading with her. Louise thinks tenderly of Carrie broiling meat and fish in their room, and walking with her in the evenings. She wonders if Carrie still has the malaise. Perhaps she will come for a visit. In Louise's arms now the boy sleeps.

"I'll help you," Richard says. "I'll eat the same things you eat."

But his face does not approach the compassion and determination and love she had seen in Carrie's during what she now recognizes as the worst year of her life. She can remember nothing about that year except hunger, and the meals in her room. She is hungry now. When she puts the boy to bed she will get a candy from her room. She will eat it here, in front of Richard. This room will be hers soon. She considers the possibilities: all these rooms and the lawn where she can do whatever she wishes. She knows he will leave soon. It has been in his eyes all summer. She stands, using one hand to pull herself out of the chair. She carries the boy to his crib, feels him against her large breasts, feels that his sleeping body touches her soul. With a surge of vindication and relief she holds him. Then she kisses his forehead and places him in the crib. She goes to the bedroom and in the dark takes a bar of candy from her drawer. Slowly she descends the stairs. She knows Richard is waiting but she feels his departure so happily that, when she enters the living room, unwrapping the candy, she is surprised to see him standing there.

STUART DYBEK

☆   ☆   ☆   ☆

# *Hot Ice*

## SAINTS

The saint, a virgin, was uncorrupted. She had been frozen in a
block of ice many years ago.
  Her father had found her half-naked body floating facedown
among water lilies, her blond hair fanning at the marshy edge of
the overgrown duck pond people still referred to as the Douglas
Park Lagoon.
  That's how Eddie Kapusta had heard it.
  Douglas Park was a black park now, the lagoon curdled in
milky green scum as if it had soured, and Kapusta didn't doubt
that were he to go there they'd find his body floating in the lily
pads too. But sometimes in winter, riding by on the California
Avenue bus, the park flocked white, deserted, and the lagoon
frozen over, Eddie could almost picture what it had been back
then: swans gliding around the small, wooded island at the
center, and rowboats plying into sunlight from the gaping stone
tunnels of the haunted-looking boathouse.
  The girl had gone rowing with a couple of guys – some said
they were sailors, neighborhood kids going off to the war –
nobody ever said who exactly or why she went with them, as if
it didn't matter. They rowed her around to the blind side of the
little island. Nobody knew what happened there either. It was
necessary for each person to imagine it for himself.
  They were only joking at first was how Kapusta imagined it,
laughing at her broken English, telling her to be friendly or swim
home. One of them stroked her hair, gently, undid her bun, and
as her hair fell cascading over her shoulders surprising them all,
the other reached too suddenly for the buttons on her blouse; she

tore away so hard the boat rocked violently, her slip and bra split, breasts sprung loose, she dove.

Even the suddenness was slow motion the way Kapusta imagined it. But once they were in the water the rest went through his mind in a flash – the boat capsizing, the sailors thrashing for the little island, and the girl struggling alone in that sepia water too warm from summer, just barely deep enough for bullheads, with a mud bottom kids said was quicksand exploding into darkness with each kick. He didn't want to wonder what she remembered as she held her last breath underwater. His mind raced over that to her father wading out into cattails, scooping her half-naked and still limp from the resisting water lilies, and running with her in his arms, across the park crying in Polish or Slovak or Bohemian, whatever they were, and then riding with her on the streetcar he wouldn't let stop until it reached the icehouse he owned, where crazy with grief he sealed her in ice.

"I believe it up to the part about the streetcar," Manny Santora said that summer when they told each other such stories, talking often about things Manny called *weirdness* while pitching quarters in front of Buddy's Bar. "I don't believe he hijacked no streetcar, man."

"What do you think, man, he called a cab?" Pancho, Manny's older brother, asked, winking at Eddie as if he'd scored.

Every time they talked like this Manny and Pancho argued. Pancho believed in everything – ghosts, astrology, legends. His nickname was Padrecito, which went back to his days as an altar boy when he would dress up as a priest and hold mass in the backyard with hosts punched with bottle caps from stale tortillas and real wine he'd collected from bottles the winos had left on door stoops. Eddie's nickname was Eduardo, though the only person who called him that was Manny, who had made it up. Manny wasn't the kind of guy to have a nickname – he was Manny or Santora.

Pancho believed if you played certain rock songs backwards you'd hear secret messages from the devil. He believed in devils and angels. He still believed he had a guardian angel. It was something like being lucky, like making the sign of the cross before you stepped into the batter's box. "It's why I don't get

caught even when I'm caught," he'd say when the cops would
catch him dealing and not take him in. Pancho believed in saints.
For a while he had even belonged to a gang called the Saints.
They'd tried to recruit Manny too, who, though younger, was
tougher than Pancho, but Manny had no use for gangs. "I already
belong to the Loners," he said.

Pancho believed in the girl in ice. In sixth grade, Sister
Joachim, the ancient nun in charge of the altar boys, had told
him the girl should be canonized and that she'd secretly written
to the pope informing him that already there had been miracles
and cures. "All the martyrs didn't die in Rome," she'd told
Pancho. "They're still suffering today in China and Russia and
Korea and even here in your own neighborhood." Like all nuns
she loved Pancho. Dressed in his surplice and cassock he looked
as if he should be beatified himself, a young St. Sebastian or Juan
de la Cruz, the only altar boy in the history of the parish to spend
his money on different-coloured gym shoes so they would match
the priest's vestments – red for martyrs, white for feast days,
black for requiems. The nuns knew he punished himself during
Lent, offering up his pain for the poor souls in purgatory.

Their love for Pancho had made things impossible for Manny
in the Catholic school. He seemed Pancho's opposite in almost
every way and dropped out after they'd held him back in sixth
grade. He switched to public school, but mostly he hung out on
the streets.

"I believe she worked miracles right in this neighborhood,
man," Pancho said.

"Bullshit, man. Like what miracles?" Manny wanted to
know.

"Okay, man, you know Big Antek," Pancho said.

"Big Antek the wino?"

They all knew Big Antek. He bought them beer. He'd been
a butcher in every meat market in the neighborhood, but
drunkenly kept hacking off pieces of his hands, and finally quit
completely to become a full-time alky.

Big Antek had told Pancho about working on Kedzie Avenue
when it was still mostly people from the old country and he had
found a job at a Czech meat market with sawdust on the floor

and skinned rabbits in the window. He wasn't there a week when he got so drunk he passed out in the freezer and when he woke the door was locked and everyone was gone. It was Saturday and he knew they wouldn't open again until Monday and by then he'd be stiff as a two-by-four. He was already shivering so badly he couldn't stand still or he'd fall over. He figured he'd be dead already except that his blood was half alcohol. Parts of him were going numb and he started staggering around, bumping past hanging sides of meat, singing, praying out loud, trying to let the fear out before it became panic. He knew it was hopeless, but he was looking anyway for some place to smash out, some plug to pull, something to stop the cold. At the back of the freezer, behind racks of meat, he found a cooler. It was an old one, the kind that used to stand packed with blocks of ice and bottles of beer in taverns during the war. And seeing it, Big Antek suddenly remembered a moment from his first summer back from the Pacific, discharged from the hospital in Manila and back in Buddy's lounge on Twenty-fourth Street, kitty-corner from a victory garden where a plaque erroneously listed his name among the parish war dead. It was an ordinary moment, nothing dramatic like his life flashing before his eyes, but the memory filled him with such clarity that the freezer became dreamlike beside it. The ball game was on the radio over at Buddy's, DiMaggio in center again, while Bing Crosby crooned from the jukebox, which was playing at the same time. Antek was reaching into Buddy's cooler, up to his elbow in ice water feeling for a beer, while looking out through the open tavern door that framed Twenty-fourth Street as if it were a movie full of girls blurred in brightness, slightly over-exposed blondes, a movie he could step into any time he chose now that he was home; but right at this moment he was taking his time, stretching it out until it encompassed his entire life, the cold bottles bobbing away from his fingertips, clunking against the ice, until finally he grabbed one, hauled it up dripping, wondering what he'd grabbed – a Monarch or Yusay Pilsner or Fox Head 400 – then popped the cork in the opener on the side of the cooler, the foam rising as he tilted his head back and let it pour down his throat, privately celebrating being alive. That moment was what drinking had once been about. It was a good thing to be remembering now when he was dying with nothing else to do about it. He had the funny idea of climbing inside the cooler and going to sleep to continue the memory like a dream. The cooler was thick with frost, so white it seemed to glow. Its lid had been replaced with a slab of dry ice that smoked even within the cold of the freezer, reminding Antek that as kids they'd always called it hot ice. He nudged it aside. Beneath it was a block of ice as clear as if the icemen had just delivered it. There was something frozen inside. He glanced away but knew already, immediately, it was a body. He couldn't move away. He looked again. The longer he stared, the calmer he felt. It was a girl. He could make out her hair, not just blonde but radiating gold like a candle flame behind a window in winter. Her breasts were bare. The ice seemed even clearer. She was beautiful and dreamy looking, not dreamy like sleeping, but the dreamy look DPs sometimes get when they first come to the city. As long as he stayed beside her he didn't shiver. He could feel the blood return; he was warm as if the smoldering dry ice really was hot. He spent the weekend huddled against her, and early Monday morning when the Czech opened the freezer he said to Antek, "Get out . . . you're fired." That's all either one of them said.

"You know what I think," Pancho said. "They moved her body from the icehouse to the butcher shop because the cops checked, man."

"You know what I think," Manny said, "I think you're doing so much shit that even the winos can bullshit you."

They looked hard at one another, Manny especially looking bad because of a beard he was trying to grow that was mostly stubble except for a black knot of hair frizzing from the cleft under his lower lip – a little lip beard like a jazz musician's – and Pancho covered in crosses, a wooden one dangling from a leather thong over his open shirt, a small gold cross on a fine gold chain tight about his throat, and a tiny platinum cross in his right earlobe, and a faded India-ink cross tattooed on his wrist where one would feel for a pulse.

"He's got a cross-shaped dick," Manny said.

"Only when I got a hard-on, man," Pancho said, grinning, and they busted up.

"Hey, Eddie, man," Pancho said, "what you think of all this, man?"

Kapusta just shrugged as he always did. Not that he didn't have any ideas exactly, or that he didn't care. That shrug *was* what Kapusta believed.

"Yeah. Well, man," Pancho said, "I believe there's saints, and miracles happening everywhere only everybody's afraid to admit it. I mean like Ralph's little brother, the blue baby who died when he was eight. He knew he was dying all his life, man, and never complained. He was a saint. Or Big Antek who everybody says is a wino, man. But he treats everybody as human beings. Who you think's more of a saint – him or the president, man? And Mrs. Corillo who everybody thought was crazy because she was praying loud all the time. Remember? She kneeled all day praying for Puerto Rico during that earthquake – the one Roberto Clemente crashed on the way to, going to help. Remember that, man? Mrs. Corillo prayed all day and they thought she was still praying at night, and she was kneeling there dead. She was a saint, man, and so's Roberto Clemente. There should be like a church, St. Roberto Clemente. With a statue of him in his batting stance by the altar. Kids could pray to him at night. That would mean something to them."

"The earthquake wasn't in Puerto Rico, man," Manny told him, "and I don't believe no streetcar'd stop for somebody carrying a dead person."

## AMNESIA

It was hard to believe there ever were streetcars. The city back then, the city of their fathers, which was as far back as a family memory extended, even the city of their childhoods, seemed as remote to Eddie and Manny as the capital of some foreign country.

The past collapsed about them – decayed, bulldozed, obliter-
ated. They walked past block-length gutted factories, past walls
of peeling, multicolored doors hammered up around flooded
excavation pits, hung out in half-boarded storefronts of groceries
that had shut down when they were kids, dusty cans still stacked
on the shelves. Broken glass collected everywhere, mounding
like sand in the little, sunken front yards and gutters. Even the
church's stained-glass windows were patched with plywood.

They could vaguely remember something different before
the cranes and wrecking balls gradually moved in, not order
exactly, but rhythms: five o'clock whistles, air-raid sirens on
Tuesdays, Thursdays when the stockyards blew over like a
brown wind of boiling hooves and bone, at least that's what
people said, screwing up their faces: "Phew! They're making the
glue today!"

Streetcar tracks were long paved over; black webs of trolley
wires vanished. So did the victory gardens that had become weed
beds taking the corroded plaques with the names of neighborhood dead with them.

Things were gone they couldn't remember but missed; and
things were gone they weren't sure ever were there – the pickle
factory by the railroad tracks where a DP with a net worked
scooping rats out of the open vats, troughs for ragmen's horses,
ragmen and their wooden wagons, knife sharpeners pushing
screeching whetstones up alleys hollering "Scissors! Knives!",
hermits living in cardboard shacks behind billboards.

At times, walking past the gaps, they felt as if they were no
longer quite there themselves, half-lost despite familiar street
signs, shadows of themselves superimposed on the present,
except there was no present – everything either rubbled past or
promised future – and they were walking as if floating, getting
nowhere as if they'd smoked too much grass.

That's how it felt those windy nights that fall when Manny
and Eddie circled the county jail. They'd float down California
past the courthouse, Bridwell Correctional, the auto pound,
Communicable Disease Hospital, and then follow the long,
curving concrete wall of the prison back toward Twenty-sixth
Street, sharing a joint, passing it with cupped hands, ready to flip

it if a cop should cruise by, but one place you could count on not to see cops was outside the prison.

Nobody was there; just the wall, railroad tracks, the river, and the factories that lined it – boundaries that remained intact while neighborhoods came and went.

Eddie had never noticed any trees, but swirls of leaves scuffed past their shoes. It was Kapusta's favorite weather, wild, blowing nights that made him feel free, flagpoles knocking in the wind, his clothes flapping like flags. He felt both tight and loose, and totally alive even walking down a street that always made him sad. It was the street that followed the curve of the prison wall, and it didn't have a name. It was hardly a street at all, more a shadow of the wall, potholed, puddled, half-paved, rutted with rusted railroad tracks.

"Trains used to go down this street," Manny said.

"I seen tanks going down this street."

"Tank cars?"

"No, army tanks," Kapusta said.

"Battleships too, Eduardo?" Manny asked seriously. Then the wind ripped a laugh from his mouth that was loud enough to carry over the prison wall.

Kapusta laughed loud too. But he *could* remember tanks, camouflaged with netting, rumbling on flatcars, their cannons outlined by the red lanterns of the dinging crossing gates that were down all along Twenty-sixth Street. It was one of the first things he remembered. He must have been very small. The train seemed endless. He could see the guards in the turrets on the prison wall watching it, the only time he'd ever seen them facing the street. "Still sending them to Korea or someplace," his father had said, and for years after Eddie believed you could get to Korea by train. For years after, he would wake in the middle of the night when it was quiet enough to hear the trains passing blocks away, and lie in bed listening, wondering if the tanks were rumbling past the prison, if not to Korea then to some other war that tanks went to at night; and he would think of the prisoners in their cells locked up for their violence with knives and clubs and cleavers and pistols, and wonder if they were lying awake, listening too as the netted cannons rolled by their barred

windows. Even as a child Eddie knew the names of men inside
there: Milo Hermanski, who had stabbed some guy in the eye in
a fight at Andy's Tap; Billy Gomez, who set the housing project
on fire every time his sister Gina got gang-banged; Ziggy's uncle,
the war hero, who one day blew off the side of Ziggy's mother's
face while she stood ironing her slip during an argument over a
will; and other names of people he didn't know but had heard
about – Benny Bedwell, with his "Elvis" sideburns, who may
have killed the Grimes sister; Mafia hit men; bank robbers;
junkies; perverts; murderers on death row – he could sense them
lying awake listening, could feel the tension of their sleeplessness,
and Pancho lay among them now as Eddie and Manny walked
outside the wall.

They stopped again as they'd been stopping and yelled
together: "Pancho, Panchooooooo," dragging out the last vowel
the way they had as kids standing on the sidewalk calling up at
one another's windows, as if knocking at the door were not
allowed.

"Pancho, we're out here, brother, me and Eddie," Manny
shouted. "Hang tough, man, we ain't forgetting you."

Nobody answered. They kept walking, stopping to shout at
intervals the way they had been doing almost every night.

"If only we knew what building he was in," Eddie said.

They could see the upper stories of the brick buildings rising
over the wall, their grated windows low lit, never dark, floodlights on the roof glaring down.

"Looks like a factory, man," Eddie said. "Looks like the
same guy who planned the Harvester foundry on Western did
the jail."

"You rather be in the army or in there?" Manny asked.

"No way they're getting me in there," Eddie said.

That was when Eddie knew Pancho was crazy, when the
judge had given Pancho a choice at the end of his trial.

"You're a nice-looking kid," the judge had said, "too nice
for prison. What do you want to do with your life?"

"Pose for holy cards," Pancho said, "St. Joseph is my
specialty." Pancho was standing there wearing the tie they had
brought him wound around his head like an Indian headband.

He was wearing a black satin jacket with the signs of the zodiac on the back.

"I'm going to give you a chance to straighten out, to gain some self-respect. The court's attitude would be very sympathetic to any signs of self-direction and patriotism, joining the army, for instance."

"I'm a captain," Pancho told him.

"The army or jail, which is it?"

"I'm a captain, man, *soy capitán, capitán,*" Pancho insisted, humming "La Bamba" under his breath.

"You're a misfit."

Manny was able to visit Pancho every three weeks. Each time it got worse. Sometimes Pancho seemed hardly to recognize him, looking away, refusing to meet Manny's eyes the whole visit. Sometimes he'd cry. For a while at first he wanted to know how things were in the neighborhood. Then he stopped asking, and when Manny tried to tell him the news Pancho would get jumpy, irritable, and lapse into total silence. "I don't wanna talk about out there, man," he told Manny. "I don't wanna remember that world until I'm ready to step into it again. You remember too much in here you go crazy, man. I wanna forget everything, like I never existed."

"His fingernails are gone, man," Manny told Eddie. "He's gnawing on himself like a rat, and when I ask him what's going down all he'll say is 'I'm locked in hell, my angel's gone, I've lost my luck' – bullshit like that, you know? Last time I seen him he says, 'I'm gonna kill myself, man, if they don't stop hitting on me.'"

"I can't fucking believe it. I can't fucking believe he's in there," Eddie said. "He should be in a monastery somewhere; he should've been a priest. He had a vocation."

"He had a vocation to be an altar boy, man," Manny said, spitting it out as if he was disgusted by what he was saying, talking down about his own brother. "It was that nuns-and-priests crap that messed up his head. He was happy being an altar boy, man, if they'd've let him be an altar boy all his life he'd still be happy."

By the time they were halfway down the nameless street it

was drizzling a fine, misty spray, and Manny was yelling in Spanish, "*Estamos contigo, hermano! San Roberto Clemente te ayudará!*"

They broke into "La Bamba," Eddie singing in Spanish too, not sure exactly what he was singing, but it sounded good: "*Yo no soy marinero, soy capitán, capitán, ay, ay, Bamba! ay, ay, Bamba!*" He had lived beside Spanish in the neighborhood all his life, and every so often a word got through, like *juilota*, which was what Manny called pigeons when they used to hunt them with slingshots under the railroad bridges. It seemed a perfect word to Eddie, one in which he could hear both their cooing and the whistling rush of their wings. He didn't remember any words like that in Polish, which his grandma had spoken to him when he was little, and which, Eddie had been told, he could once speak too.

By midnight they were at the end of their circuit, emerging from the unlighted, nameless street, stepping over tracks that continued to curve past blinded switches. Under the streetlights on Twenty-sixth the prison wall appeared rust stained, oozing at the cracks. The wire spooled at the top of the wall looked rusty in the wet light, as did the tracks as if the rain were rusting everything overnight.

They stopped on the corner of Twenty-sixth where the old icehouse stood across the nameless street from the prison. One could still buy ice from a vending machine in front. Without realizing it, Eddie guarded his breathing as if still able to detect the faintest stab of ammonia, although it had been a dozen years since the louvered fans on the icehouse roof had clacked through clouds of vapor.

"Padrecitooooo!" they both hollered.

Their voices bounced back off the wall.

They stood on the corner by the icehouse as if waiting around for someone. From there they could stare down Twenty-sixth – five dark blocks, then an explosion of neon at Kedzie Avenue: taco places, bars, a street plugged in, winking festive as a pinball machine, traffic from it coming toward them in the rain.

The streetlights surged and flickered.

"You see that?" Eddie asked. "They used to say when the streetlights flickered it meant they just fried somebody in the electric chair."

"So much bullshit," Manny said. "*Compadre, no te rajes!*" he yelled at the wall.

"Whatcha tell him?"

"It sounds different in English," Manny said. "'Godfather, do not give up.' It's words from an old song."

Kapusta stepped out into the middle of Twenty-sixth and stood in the misting drizzle squinting at Kedzie through cupped hands, as if he held binoculars. He could make out the traffic light way down there changing to green. He could almost hear the music from the bars that would serve them without asking for IDs so long as Manny was there. "You thirsty by any chance, man?" he asked.

"You buyin' by any chance, man?" Manny said, grinning.

"*Buenas noches*, Pancho," they hollered. "Catch you tomorrow, man."

"Good night, guys," a falsetto voice echoed back from over the wall.

"That ain't Pancho," Manny said.

"Sounds like the singer on old Platters' records," Eddie said. "Ask him if he knows Pancho, man."

"Hey, you know a guy named Pancho Santora?" Manny called.

"Oh, Pancho?" the voice inquired.

"Yeah, Pancho."

"Oh, Cisco!" the voice shouted. They could hear him cackling, "Hey, baby, I don't know no Pancho. Is that rain I smell?"

"It's raining," Eddie hollered.

"Hey, baby, tell me something. What's it like out there tonight?"

Manny and Eddie looked at each other. "Beautiful!" they yelled together.

## GRIEF

There was never a requiem, but by Lent everybody knew that one way or another Pancho was gone. No wreaths, but plenty of rumors: Pancho had hung himself in his cell; his throat had been slashed in the showers; he'd killed another inmate and was under heavy sedation in a psycho ward at Kankakee. And there was talk he'd made a deal and was in the army, shipped off to a war he had sworn he'd never fight; that he had turned snitch and had been secretly relocated with a new identity; or that he had become a trustee and had simply walked away while mowing the grass in front of the courthouse, escaped maybe to Mexico, or maybe just across town to the North Side around Diversey where, if one made the rounds of the leather bars, they might see someone with Pancho's altar-boy eyes staring out from the make-up of a girl.

Some saw him late at night like a ghost haunting the neighborhood, collar up, in the back of the church lighting a vigil candle or veiled in a black mantilla, speeding past, face floating by on a greasy El window.

Rumors were becoming legends, but there was never a wake, never an obituary, and no one knew how to mourn a person who had just disappeared.

For a while Manny disappeared too. He wasn't talking, and Kapusta didn't ask. They had quit walking around the prison wall months before, around Christmas when Pancho refused to let anyone, even Manny, visit. But their night walks had been tapering off before that.

Eddie remembered the very last time they had walked beside the wall together. It was in December, and he was frozen from standing around a burning garbage can on Kedzie, selling Christmas trees. About 10, when the lot closed, Manny came by and they stopped to thaw out at the Carta Blanca. A guy named José kept buying them whiskeys, and they staggered out after midnight into a blizzard.

"Look at this white bullshit," Manny said.

Walking down Twenty-sixth they stopped to fling snowballs

over the wall. Then they decided to stand there singing Christmas carols. Snow was drifting against the wall, erasing the street that had hardly been there. Eddie could tell Manny was starting to go silent. Manny would get the first few words into a carol, singing at the top of his voice, then stop as if choked by the song. His eyes stayed angry when he laughed. Everything was bullshit to him, and finally Eddie couldn't talk to him anymore. Stomping away from the prison through fresh snow, Eddie had said, "If this keeps up, man, I'll need boots."

"It don't *have* to *keep up*, man," Manny snapped. "Nobody's making you come, man. It ain't your brother."

"All I said is I'll need boots, man," Eddie said.

"You said it's hopeless, man; things are always fucking hopeless to you."

"Hey, you're the big realist, man," Eddie told him.

"I never said I was no realist," Manny mumbled.

Kapusta hadn't had a lot of time since then. He had dropped out of school again and was loading trucks at night for UPS. One more semester didn't matter, he figured, and he needed some new clothes, cowboy boots, a green leather jacket. The weather had turned drizzly and mild – a late Easter but an early spring. Eddie had heard Manny was hanging around by himself, still finding bullshit everywhere, only worse. Now he muttered as he walked like some crazy, bitter old man, or one of those black guys reciting the gospel to buildings, telling off posters and billboards, neon signs, stoplights, passing traffic – bullshit, all of it bullshit.

It was Tuesday in Holy Week, the statues inside the church shrouded in violet, when Eddie slipped on his green leather jacket and walked over to Manny's before going to work. He rang the doorbell, then stepped outside in the rain and stood on the sidewalk under Manny's windows, watching cars pass.

After a while Manny came down the stairs and slammed out the door.

"How you doin', man?" Eddie said as if they'd just run into each other by accident.

Manny stared at him. "How far'd you have to chase him for that jacket, man?" he said.

"I knew you'd dig it." Eddie smiled.

They went out for a few beers later that night, after midnight, when Eddie was through working, but instead of going to a bar they ended up just walking. Manny had rolled a couple bombers and they walked down the boulevard along California watching the headlights flash by like a procession of candles. Manny still wasn't saying much, but they were passing the reefer like having a conversation. At Thirty-first, by the Communicable Disease Hospital, Eddie figured they would follow the curve of the boulevard toward the bridge on Western, but Manny turned as if out of habit toward the prison.

They were back walking along the wall. There was still old ice from winter at the base of it.

"The only street in Chicago where it's still winter," Eddie mumbled.

"Remember yelling?" Manny said, almost in a whisper.

"Sure," Eddie nodded.

"Called, joked, prayed, sang Christmas songs, remember that night, how cold we were, man?"

"Yeah."

"What a bunch of stupid bullshit, huh?"

Eddie was afraid Manny was going to start the bullshit stuff again. Manny had stopped and stood looking at the wall.

Then he cupped his hands over his mouth and yelled, "Hey! You dumb fuckers in there! We're back! Can you hear me? Hey, wake up, niggers, hey, spics, hey, honkies, you buncha fuckin' monkeys in cages, hey! We're out here *free*!"

"Hey, Manny, come on, man," Eddie said.

Manny uncupped his hands, shook his head, and smiled. They took a few steps, then Manny whirled back again. "We're out here free, man! We're smokin' reefer, drinking cold beer while you're in there, you assholes! We're on our way to fuck your wives, man, your girlfriends are giving us blow jobs while you jack-offs flog it. Hey, man, I'm pumping your old lady out here right now. She likes it in the ass like you!"

"What are you doing, man?" Eddie was pleading. "Take it easy."

Manny was screaming his lungs out, almost incoherent,

shouting every filthy thing he could think of, and voices, the voices they'd never heard before, had begun shouting back from the other side of the wall.

"Shadup! Shadup! Shadup out there, you crazy fuck!" came the voices.

"She's out here licking my balls, while you're punking each other through the bars of your cage!"

"Shadup!" they were yelling, and then a voice howling over the others, "I'll kill you, motherfucker! When I get out you're dead!"

"Come on out," Manny was yelling. "Come and get me, you pieces of shit, you sleazeballs, you scumbag cocksuckers, you creeps are missing it all, your lives are wasted garbage!"

Now there were too many voices to distinguish, whole tiers, whole buildings yelling and cursing and threatening, *shadup, shadup, shadup*, almost a chant, and then the searchlight from the guardhouse slowly turned and swept the street.

"We gotta get outa here," Eddie said, pulling Manny away. He dragged him to the wall, right up against it where the light couldn't follow, and they started to run, stumbling along the banked strip of filthy ice, dodging stunted trees that grew out at odd angles, running toward Twenty-sixth until Eddie heard the sirens.

"This way, man," he panted, yanking Manny back across the nameless street, jumping puddles and tracks, cutting down a narrow corridor between abandoned truck docks seconds before a squad car, blue dome light revolving, sped past.

They jogged behind the truck docks, not stopping until they came up behind the icehouse. Manny's panting sounded almost like laughing, the way people laugh after they've hurt themselves.

"I hate those motherfuckers," Manny gasped, "all of them, the fucking cops and guards and fucking wall and the bastards behind it. All of them. That must be what makes me a realist, huh, Eddie? I fucking hate them all."

They went back the next night.

Sometimes a thing wasn't a sin – if there was such a thing as

sin – Eddie thought, until it's done a second time. There were
accidents, mistakes that could be forgiven once; it was repeating
them that made them terribly wrong. That was how Eddie felt
about going back the next night.

Manny said he was going whether Eddie came or not, so
Eddie went, afraid to leave Manny on his own, even though he'd
already had trouble trying to get some sleep before going to
work. Eddie could still hear the voices yelling from behind the
wall and dreamed they were all being electrocuted, electrocuted
slowly, by degrees of their crimes, screaming with each surge of
current and flicker of streetlights as if in a hell where electricity
had replaced fire.

Standing on the dark street Wednesday night, outside the
wall again, felt like an extension of his nightmare: Manny raging
almost out of control, shouting curses and insults, baiting them
over the wall the way a child tortures penned watchdogs, until
he had what seemed like the entire west side of the prison
howling back, the guards sweeping the street with searchlights,
sirens wailing toward them from both Thirty-first and Twenty-
sixth.

This time they raced down the tracks that curved toward the
river, picking their way in the dark along the junkyard bank,
flipping rusted cables of moored barges, running through the fire
truck graveyard, following the tracks across the blackened
trestles where they'd once shot pigeons and from which they
could gaze across the industrial prairie that stretched behind
factories all the way to the skyline of downtown. The skyscrapers
glowed like luminiscent peaks in the misty spring night. Manny
and Eddie stopped in the middle of the trestle and leaned over
the railing catching their breath.

"Downtown ain't as far away as I used to think when I was
a kid," Manny panted.

"These tracks'll take you right there," Eddie said quietly, "to
railroad yards under the street, right by the lake."

"How do you know, man?"

"A bunch of us used to hitch rides on the boxcars in seventh
grade." Eddie was talking very quietly, looking away.

"I usually take the bus, you know?" Manny tried joking.

"I ain't goin' back there with you tomorrow," Eddie said. "I ain't goin' back with you ever."

Manny kept staring off toward the light downtown as if he hadn't heard. "Okay," he finally said, more to himself, as if surrendering. "Okay, how about tomorrow we do something else, man?"

## NOSTALGIA

They didn't go back.

The next night, Thursday, Eddie overslept and called in sick for work. He tried to get back to sleep but kept falling into half-dreams in which he could hear the voices shouting behind the prison wall. Finally he got up and opened a window. It was dark out. A day had passed almost unnoticed, and now the night felt as if it were a part of the night before, and the night before a part of the night before that, all connected by his restless dreams, fragments of the same continuous night.

Eddie had said that at some point: "It's like one long night," and later Manny had said the same thing as if it had suddenly occurred to him.

They were strung out almost from the start, drifting stoned under the El tracks before Eddie even realized they weren't still sitting on the stairs in front of Manny's house. That was where Eddie had found him, watching traffic, taking sips out of a bottle of Gallo into which Manny had dropped several hits of speed.

Cars gunned by with their windows rolled down and radios playing loud. It sounded like a summer night.

"Ain't you hot wearin' that jacket, man?" Manny asked him.

"Now that you mention it," Eddie said. He was sweating.

Eddie took his leather jacket off and they knotted a handkerchief around one of the cuffs, then slipped the Gallo bottle down the sleeve. They walked along under the El tracks passing a joint. A train, only two cars long, rattled overhead.

"So what we doing, Eduardo?" Manny kept repeating.

"Walking," Eddie said.

"I feel like doing *something*, you know?"

"We are doing something," Eddie insisted.

Eddie led them over to the Coconut Club on Twenty-second. They couldn't get in, but Eddie wanted to look at the window with its neon-green palm tree and winking blue coconuts.

"That's maybe my favorite window," he said.

"You drag me all the way here to see your favorite window, man?" Manny said.

"It's those blue coconuts," Eddie tried explaining. His mouth was dry, but he couldn't stop talking. He started telling Manny how he had collected windows from the time he was a little kid, even though talking about it made it sound as if windows were more important to him than they actually were. Half the time he was only vaguely aware of collecting them. He would see a window from a bus, like the Greek butcher shop on Halsted with its pyramid of lamb skulls, and make a mental photograph of it. He had special windows all over the city. It was how he held the city together in his mind.

"I'd see all those windows from the El," Eddie said, "when I'd visit my *busha*, my grandma. Like I remember we'd pass this one building where the curtains were all slips hanging by their straps – black ones, white ones, red ones. At night you could see the light bulbs shining through the lace tops. My *busha* said Gypsies lived there." Eddie was walking down the middle of the street, jacket flung over his shoulder, staring up at the windows as if looking for the Gypsies as he talked.

"Someday they're gonna get you as a peeper, man." Manny laughed. "And when they do, don't try explaining to them about this thing of yours for windows, Eduardo."

They were walking down Spaulding back toward Twenty-sixth. The streetlights beamed brighter and brighter, and Manny put his sunglasses on. A breeze was blowing that felt warmer than the air, and they took their shirts off. They saw rats darting along the curb into the sewer on the other side of the street and put their shirts back on.

"The rats get crazy where they start wrecking these old buildings," Manny said.

The cranes and wrecking balls and urban-renewal signs were back with the early spring. They walked around a barricaded site. Water trickled along the gutters from an open hydrant, washing brick dust and debris toward the sewers.

"Can you smell that, man?" Manny asked him, suddenly excited. "I can smell the lake through the hydrant."

"Smells like rust to me," Eddie said.

"I can smell fish! Smelt – the smelt are in! I can smell them right through the hydrant!"

"Smelt?" Eddie said.

"You ain't ever had smelt?" Manny asked. "Little silver fish!"

They caught the Twenty-sixth Street bus – the Polish Zephyr, people called it – going east toward the lake. The back of the bus was empty. They sat in the swaying, long backseat, taking hits out of the bottle in Eddie's sleeve.

"It's usually too early for them yet, but they're out there, Eduardo," Manny kept reassuring him, as if they were actually going fishing.

Eddie nodded. He didn't know anything about smelt. The only fish he ate was canned tuna, but it felt good to be riding somewhere with the windows open and Manny acting more like his old self – sure of himself, laughing easily. Eddie still felt like talking, but his molars were grinding on speed.

The bus jolted down the dark block past Kedzie and was flying when it passed the narrow street between the icehouse and the prison, but Eddie and Manny caught a glimpse out the back window of the railroad tracks that curved down the nameless street. The tracks were lined with fuming red flares that threw a red reflection off the concrete walls. Eddie was sure the flares had been set there for them.

Eddie closed his eyes and sank into the rocking of the bus. Even with his eyes closed he could see the reddish glare of the walls. The glare was ineradicable, at the back of his sockets. The wall had looked the same way it had looked in his dreams. They rode in silence.

"It's like one long night," Eddie said somewhere along the way.

His jaws were really grinding and his legs had forgotten gravity by the time they got to the lakefront. They didn't know the time, but it must have been around 3 or 4 a.m. and the smelt fishers were still out. The lights of their kerosene lanterns reflected along the breakwater over the glossy black lake. Eddie and Manny could hear the water lapping under the pier and the fishermen talking in low voices in different languages.

"My uncle Carlos would talk to the fish," Manny said. "No shit. He'd talk to them in Spanish. He didn't have no choice. Whole time here he couldn't speak English. Said it made his brain stuck. We used to come fishing here all the time – smelt, perch, everything. I'd come instead of going to school. If they weren't hitting, he'd start talking to them, singing them songs."

"Like what?" Eddie said.

"He'd make them up. They were funny, man. It don't come across in English: 'Little silver ones fill up my shoes. My heart is lonesome for the fish of the sea.' It was like very formal how he'd say it. He'd always call this the sea. I'd tell him it's a lake, but he couldn't be talked out of it. He was very stubborn – too stubborn to learn English. I ain't been fishing since he went back to Mexico."

They walked to the end of the pier, then back past the fishermen. A lot of them were old men gently tugging lines between their fingers, lifting nets as if flying underwater kites, plucking the wriggling silver fish from the netting, the yellow light of their lamps glinting off the bright scales.

"I told you they were out here," Manny said.

They sat on a concrete ledge, staring at the dark water, which rocked hypnotically below the soles of their dangling feet.

"Feel like diving in?" Manny asked.

Eddie had just raised the bottle to his lips and paused as if actually considering Manny's question, then shook his head no and took a swallow.

"One time right before my uncle went back to Mexico we

came fishing at night for perch," Manny said. "It was a real hot night, you know? And all these old guys fishing off the pier. No one getting a bite, man, and I started thinking how cool and peaceful it would be to just dive in the water with the fish, and then, like I just did it without even deciding to, clothes and all. Sometimes, man, I still remember that feeling underwater – like I could just keep swimming out, didn't need air, never had to come up. When I couldn't hold my breath no more and came up I could hear my uncle calling my name, and then all the old guys on the pier start calling my name to come back. What I really felt like doing was to keep swimming out until I couldn't hear them, until I couldn't even see their lanterns, man. I wanted to be way the fuck out alone in the middle of the lake when the sun came up. But then I thought about my uncle standing on the pier calling me, so I turned around."

They killed the bottle sitting on a concrete ledge and dropped it into the lake. Then they rode the El back. It was getting lighter without a dawn. The El windows were streaked with rain, the Douglas Avenue station smelled wet. It was a dark morning. They should have ended it then. Instead they sat at Manny's kitchen table drinking instant coffee with canned milk. Eddie kept getting lost in the designs the milk would make, swirls and thunderclouds in his mug of coffee. He was numb and shaky. His jaw ached.

"I'm really crashin'," he told Manny.

"Here," Manny said. "Bring us down easier, man."

"I don't like doing downers, man," Eddie said.

"'Ludes," Manny said, "from Pancho's stash."

They sat across the table from each other for a long time – talking, telling their memories and secrets – only Eddie was too numb to remember exactly what they said. Their voices – his own as well as Manny's – seemed *outside*, removed from the center of his mind.

At one point Manny looked out at the dark morning and said, "It still seems like last night."

"That's right," Eddie agreed. He wanted to say more but couldn't express it. He didn't try. Eddie didn't believe it was what they said that was important. Manny could be talking

Spanish; I could be talking Polish, Eddie thought. It didn't matter. What meant something was sitting at the table together, wrecked together, still awake watching the rainy light spatter the window, walking out again, to the Prague bakery for bismarcks, past people under dripping umbrellas on their way to church.

"Looks like Sunday," Manny said.

"Today's Friday," Eddie said. "It's Good Friday."

"I seen ladies with ashes on their heads waiting for the bus a couple days ago," Manny told him.

They stood in the doorway of the Prague, out of the rain, eating their bismarcks. Just down from the church, the bakery was a place people crowded into after mass. Its windows displayed colored eggs and little frosted Easter lambs.

"One time on Ash Wednesday I was eating a bismarck and Pancho made a cross on my forehead with the powdered sugar like it was ashes. When I went to church the priest wouldn't give me real ashes," Manny said with a grin.

It was one of the few times Eddie had heard Manny mention Pancho. Now that they were outside, Eddie's head felt clearer than it had in the kitchen.

"I used to try and keep my ashes on until Good Friday," he told Manny, "but they'd make me wash."

The church bells were ringing, echoes bouncing off the sidewalks as if deflected by the ceiling of clouds. The neighborhood felt narrower, compressed from above.

"I wonder if it still looks the same in there," Manny said as they passed the church.

They stepped in and stood in the vestibule. The saints of their childhood stood shrouded in purple. The altar was bare, stripped for Good Friday. Old ladies, ignoring the new liturgy, chanted a litany in Polish.

"Same as ever," Eddie whispered as they backed out.

The rain had almost let up. They could hear its accumulated weight in the wing-flaps of pigeons.

"Good Friday was Pancho's favorite holiday, man," Manny said. "Everybody else always picked Christmas or Thanksgiving or Fourth of July. He hadda be different, man. I remember he used to drag me along visiting churches. You ever do that?"

"Hell, yeah," Eddie said. "Every Good Friday we'd go on our bikes. You hadda visit seven of them."

Without agreeing to it they walked from St. Roman's to St. Michael's, a little wooden Franciscan church in an Italian neighborhood; and from there to St. Casimir's, a towering, mournful church with twin copper-green towers. Then, as if following an invisible trail, they walked north up Twenty-second toward St. Anne's, St. Puis's, St. Adalbert's. At first they merely entered and left immediately, as if touching base, but their familiarity with small rituals quickly returned: dipping their fingers in the holy water font by the door, making the automatic sign of the cross as they passed the life-size crucified Christs that hung in the vestibules where old women and school kids clustered to kiss the spikes in the bronze or bloody plaster feet. By St. Anne's, Manny removed his sunglasses, out of respect, the way one removes a hat. Eddie put them on. His eyes felt hard-boiled. The surge of energy he had felt at the bakery had burned out fast. While Manny genuflected to the altar, Eddie slumped in the back pew pretending to pray, drowsing off behind the dark glasses. It never occurred to Eddie to simply go home. His head ached, he could feel his heart racing, and would suddenly jolt awake wondering where Manny was. Manny would be off – jumpy, frazzled, still popping speed on the sly – exploring the church as if searching for something, standing among lines of parishioners waiting to kiss relics the priest wiped repeatedly clean with a rag of silk. Then Manny would be shaking Eddie awake. "How you holding up, man?"

"I'm cool," he'd say, and they would be back on the streets heading for another parish under the overcast sky. Clouds, a shade between slate and lilac, smoked over the spires and roofs; lights flashed on in the bars and *taquerías*. On Eighteenth Street a great blue neon fish leapt in the storefront window of a tiny *ostenaria*. Eddie tried to note the exact location to add to his window collection. They headed along a wall of viaducts to St. Procopius, where, Manny said, both he and Pancho had been baptized. The viaduct walls had been painted by schoolchildren into a mural that seemed to go for miles.

"I don't think we're gonna make seven churches, man,"

Eddie said. He was walking without lifting his feet, his hair plastered by a sweatlike drizzle. It was around 3 p.m. It had been 3 p.m. – Christ's dark hour on the cross – inside the churches all day, but now it was turning 3 p.m. outside too. They could hear the ancient-sounding hymn "*Tantum Ergo*," carrying from down the block.

Eddie sunk into the last pew, kneeling in the red glow of vigil lights that brought back the red flicker of the flares they had seen from the window of the bus as it sped by the prison. Manny had already faded into the procession making the stations of the cross – a shuffling crowd circling the church, kneeling before each station while altar boys censed incense and the priest recited Christ's agony. Old women answered with prayers like moans.

Old women were walking on their knees up the marble aisle to kiss the relics. A few were crying, and Eddie remembered how back in grade school he had heard old women cry sometimes after confession, crying as if their hearts would break, and even as a child he had wondered how such old women could possibly have committed sins terrible enough to demand such bitter weeping. Most everything from that world had changed or disappeared, but the old women had endured – Polish, Bohemian, Spanish, he knew it didn't matter; they were the same, dressed in black coats and babushkas the way holy statues wore violet, in constant mourning. A common pain of loss seemed to burn at the core of their lives, though Eddie had never understood exactly what it was they mourned. Nor how day after day they had sustained the intensity of their grief. He would have given up long ago. In a way he *had* given up, and the ache left behind couldn't be called grief. He had no name for it. He had felt it before Pancho or anyone was lost, almost from the start of memory. If it was grief; it was grief for the living. The hymns, with their ancient, keening melodies and mysterious words, had brought the feeling back, but when he tried to discover the source, to give the feeling a name, it eluded him as always, leaving in its place nostalgia and triggered nerves.

Oh God, he prayed, I'm really crashing.

He was too shaky to kneel, so he stretched out on the pew, lying on his back, eyes shut behind sunglasses, until the church

began to whirl. To control it he tried concentrating on the
stained-glass window overhead. None of the windows that had
ever been special for him were from a church. This one was an
angel, its colors like jewels and coals. Afternoon seemed to be
dying behind it, becoming part of the night, part of the private
history that he and Manny continued between them like a pact.
He could see night shining through the colors of the angel,
dividing into bands as if the angel were a prism for darkness; the
neon and wet streetlights illuminated its wingspread.


# LEGENDS

It started with ice.
   That's how Big Antek sometimes began the story.
   At dusk a gang of little Mexican kids appeared with a few
lumps of dry ice covered in a shoe box, as if they had caught a
bird. *Hot ice*, they called it, though the way they said it sounded
to Antek like *hot eyes*. Kids always have a way of finding stuff
like that. One boy touched his tongue to a piece and screamed
*"Aye!"* when it stuck. They watched the ice boil and fume in a
rain puddle along the curb, and finally they filled a bottle part
way with water, inserted the fragments of ice they had left,
capped the bottle, and set it in the mouth of an alley waiting for
an explosion. When it popped they scattered.
   Manny Santora and Eddie Kapusta came walking up the
alley, wanting Antek to buy them a bottle of rum at Buddy's.
Rum instead of beer. They were celebrating, Kapusta said, but
he didn't say what. Maybe one of them had found a job or had
just been fired, or graduated, or joined the army instead of
waiting around to get drafted. It could be anything. They were
always celebrating. Behind their sunglasses Antek could see they
were high as usual, even before Manny offered him a drag off a
reefer the size of a cigar.
   Probably nobody was hired or fired or had joined anything;
probably it was just so hot they had a good excuse to act crazy.
They each had a bottle of Coke they were fizzing up, squirting.

Eddie had limes stuffed in his pockets and was pretending they were his balls. Manny had a plastic bag of the little ice cubes they sell at gas stations. It was half-melted, and they were scooping handfuls of cubes over each other's heads, stuffing them down their jeans and yowling, rubbing ice on their chests and under their arms as if taking a cold shower. They looked like wild men – shirts hanging from their back pockets, handkerchiefs knotted around their heads, wearing sunglasses, their bodies slick with melted ice water and sweat; two guys in the prime of life going nowhere, both lean, Kapusta almost as tan as Santora, Santora with that frizzy beard under his lip, and Kapusta trying to juggle limes.

They were drinking rum using a method Antek had never seen before, and he had seen his share of drinking – not just in the neighborhood – all over the world when he was in the navy, and not the Bohemian navy either like somebody would always say when he would start telling navy stories.

They claimed they were drinking cuba libres, only they didn't have glasses, so they were mixing the drinks in their mouths, starting with some little cubes, then pouring in rum, coke, a squeeze of lime, and swallowing. Swallowing if one or the other didn't suddenly bust up over some private joke, spraying the whole mouthful out, and both of them choking and coughing and laughing.

"Hey, Antek, lemme build you a drink," Manny kept saying, but Antek shook his head no thanks, and he wasn't known for passing up too many.

This was all going on in front of Buddy's, everyone catching a blast of music and air-conditioning whenever the door opened. It was hot. The moths sizzled as soon as they hit Buddy's buzzing orange sign. A steady beat of moths dropped like cinders on the blinking orange sidewalk where the kids were pitching pennies. Manny passed around what was left in the plastic bag of ice, and the kids stood sucking and crunching the cubes between their teeth.

It reminded Antek of summers when the ice trucks still delivered to Buddy's – flatbeds covered with canvas, the icemen, mainly DPs, wearing leather aprons. Their Popeye forearms, even in August, looked ruddy with cold. They would slide the huge, clear blocks off the tailgate so the whump reverberated through the hollow under the sidewalks, and deep in the ice the clarity shattered. Then with their ice hooks they'd lug the blocks across the sidewalk, trailing a slick, and boot them skidding down the chute into Buddy's beery-smelling cellar. And after the truck pulled away, kids would pick the splinters from the curb and suck them as if they were ice-flavored Popsicles.

Nobody seemed too interested when Antek tried to tell them about the ice trucks, or anything else about how the world had been, for that matter. Antek had been sick and had only recently returned from the VA hospital. Of all his wounds, sickness was the worst. He could examine his hacked butcher's hands almost as kids from the neighborhood did, inspecting the stubs where his fingers had been as if they belonged to someone else, but there were places deep within himself that he couldn't examine, yet where he could feel that something of himself far more essential than fingers was missing. He returned from the VA feeling old and as if the neighborhood had changed in the weeks he had been gone. People had changed. He couldn't be sure, but they treated him differently, colder, as if he were becoming a stranger in the place he had grown up in, now, just when he most needed to belong.

"Hey, Antek," Manny said, "you know what you can tell me? That girl that saved your life in the meat freezer, did she have good tits?"

"I tell you about a miracle and you ask me about tits?" Antek said. "I don't talk about that anymore because now somebody always asks me did she have good tits. Go see."

Kids had been trying for years to sneak into the icehouse to see her. It was what the neighborhood had instead of a haunted house. Each generation had grown up with the story of how her father had ridden with her half-naked body on the streetcar. Even the nuns had heard Antek's story about finding the girl still frozen in the meat freezer. The butcher shop in Kedzie had closed long ago, and the legend was that after the cops had stopped checking, her body had been moved at night back into the icehouse. But the icehouse wasn't easy to break into. It had stood padlocked and heavily boarded for years.

"They're gonna wreck it," Eddie said. "I went by on the bus and they got the crane out in front."

"Uh-oh, last chance, Antek," Manny said. "If you're sure she's in there, maybe we oughta go save her."

"She's in there," Antek said. He noticed the little kids had stopped pitching pennies and were listening.

"Well, you owe her something after what she done for you – don't he, Eduardo?"

The kids who were listening chuckled, then started to go back to their pennies.

"You wanna go, I'll go!" Antek said loudly.

"All right, let's go."

Antek got up unsteadily. He stared at Eddie and Manny. "You guys couldn't loan me enough for a taste of wine just until I get my disability check?"

The little kids tagged after them to the end of the block, then turned back bored. Manny and Eddie kept going, picking the pace up a step or two ahead of Antek, exchanging looks and grinning. But Antek knew that no matter how much they joked or what excuses they gave, they were going, like him, for one last look. They were just old enough to have seen the icehouse before it shut down. It was a special building, the kind a child couldn't help but notice and remember – there, on the corner across the street from the prison, a factory that made ice, humming with fans, its louvered roof dripping and clacking, lost in acrid clouds of its own escaping vapor.

The automatic ice machine in front had already been carted away. The doors were still padlocked, but the way the crane was parked it was possible for Manny and Eddie to climb the boom onto the roof.

Antek waited below. He gazed up at the new Plexiglas guard turrets on the prison wall. From his angle all he could see was the bluish fluorescence of their lighting. He watched Manny and Eddie jump from the boom to the roof, high enough to stare across at the turrets like snipers, to draw a level bead on the backs of the guards, high enough to gaze over the wall at the dim, barred windows of the buildings that resembled foundries more than ever in the sweltering heat.

Below, Antek stood swallowing wine, expecting more from the night than a condemned building. He didn't know exactly what else he expected. Perhaps only a scent, like the stab of remembered ammonia he might have detected if he were still young enough to climb the boom. Perhaps the secret isolation he imagined Manny and Eddie feeling now, alone on the roof, as if lost in clouds of vapor. At street level, passing traffic drowned out the tick of a single cricket keeping time on the roof – a cricket so loud and insistent that Manny didn't stop to worry about the noise when he kicked in the louvers. And Antek, though he had once awakened in a freezer, couldn't imagine the shock of cold that Manny and Eddie felt as they dropped out of the summer night to the floor below.

Earlier, on their way down Twenty-sixth, Manny had stopped to pick up an unused flare from along the tracks, and Antek pictured them inside now, Manny, his hand wrapped in a handkerchief, holding the flare away from him like a Roman candle, its red glare sputtering off the beams and walls.

There wasn't much to see – empty corners, insulated pipes. Their breaths steamed. They tugged on their shirts. Instinctively, they traced the cold down a metal staircase. Cold was rising from the ground floor through the soles of their gym shoes.

The ground floor was stacked to the ceiling with junked ice machines. A wind as from an enormous air conditioner was blowing down a narrow aisle between the machines. At the end of the aisle a concrete ramp slanted down to the basement.

That was where Antek suspected they would end up, the basement, a cavernous space extending under the nameless street, slowly collapsing as if the thick, melting pillars of ice along its walls had served as its foundation. The floor was spongy with waterlogged sawdust. An echoing rain plipped from the ceiling. The air smelled thawed, and ached clammy in the lungs.

"It's fuckin' freezing," Eddie whispered.

Manny swung the flare in a slow arc, its reflections glancing as if they stood among cracked mirrors. Blocks of ice, framed in defrosted freezer coils, glowed back faintly, like aquarium windows, from niches along the walls. They were melting unevenly and leaned at precarious angles. Several had already tottered to the sawdust, where they lay like quarry stones from a wrecked cathedral. Manny and Eddie picked their way among them, pausing to wipe the slick of water from their surfaces and peer into the ice, but deep networks of cracks refracted the light. They could see only frozen shadows and had to guess at the forms: fish, birds, shanks of meat, a dog, a cat, a chair, what appeared to be a bicycle.

But Antek knew they would recognize her when they found her. There would be no mistaking the light. In the smoky, phosphorous glare her hair would reflect gold like a candle behind a frosted pane. He was waiting for them to bring her out. He had finished the wine and flung the pint bottle onto the street so that it shattered. The streets were empty. He was waiting patiently, and though he had nowhere else to be it was still a long wait. He would wait as long as it might take, but even so he wondered if there was time enough left to him for another miracle in his life. He could hear the cricket now, composing time instead of music, working its way headfirst from the roof down the brick wall. Listening to it, Antek became acutely aware of the silence of the prison across the street. He thought of all the men on the other side of the wall and wondered how many were still awake, listening to the cricket, waiting patiently as they sweated in the heavy night.

Manny and Eddie, shivering, their hands burning numb from grappling with ice, unbarred the rear door that opened onto the loading platform behind the icehouse. They pushed out an old handcar and rolled it onto the tracks that came right up to the dock. They had already slid the block of ice onto the handcar and draped it with a canvas tarp. Even gently inching it on they had heard the ice cracking. The block of ice had felt too light for its size, fragile, ready to break apart.

"It feels like we're kidnapping somebody," Eddie whispered.

"Just think of it as ice."

"I can't."

"We can't just leave her here, Eduardo."

"What'll we do with her?"
"We'll think of something."
"What about Antek?"
"Forget him."

They pushed off. Rust slowed them at first, but as the tracks inclined toward the river they gained momentum. It was like learning to row. By the trestle they hit their rhythm. Speed became wind – hair blowing, shirts flapping open, the tarp billowing up off the ice. The skyline gleamed ahead, and though Manny couldn't see the lake, he could feel it stretching beyond the skyscrapers; he could recall the sudden lightness of freedom he'd felt once when he had speared out underwater and glided effortlessly away, one moment expanding into another, while the flow of water cleansed him of memory, and not even the sound of his own breath disrupted the silence. The smelt would have disappeared to wherever they disappeared to, but the fishermen would still be sitting at the edge of the breakwater, their backs to the city, dreaming up fish. And if the fishermen still remembered his name, they might call it repeatedly in a chorus of voices echoing out over the dark surface of the water, but this time, Manny knew, there would be no turning back. He knew now where they were taking her, where she would finally be released. They were rushing through waist-deep weeds, crossing the vast tracts of prairie behind the factories, clattering over bridges and viaducts. Below, streetlights shimmered watery in the old industrial neighborhoods. Shiny with sweat, the girl already melting free between them, they forced themselves faster, rowing like a couple of sailors.

# LOUISE ERDRICH

☆ ☆ ☆ ☆

# *Scales*

## ALBERTINE JOHNSON

I was sitting before my third or fourth Jellybean, which is anisette, grain alcohol, a lit match, and small wet explosion in the brain. On my left sat Gerry Nanapush of the Chippewa Tribe. On my right sat Dot Adare of the has-been, of the never-was, of the what's-in-front-of-me people. Still in her belly and tensed in its fluids coiled the child of their union, the child we were waiting for, the child whose name we were making a strenuous and lengthy search for in a cramped and littered bar at the very edge of that Dakota town.

Gerry had been on the wagon for thirteen years. He was drinking a tall glass of tonic water in which a crescent of soiled lemon bobbed, along with a Maraschino cherry or two. He was thirty-five years old and had been in prison, or out of prison and on the run, for almost half of those years. He was not in the clear yet nor would he ever be, that is why the yellow tennis player's visor was pulled down to the rim of his eyeglass frames. The bar was dimly lit and smoky; his glasses were very dark. Poor visibility must have been the reason Officer Lovchik saw him first.

Lovchik started toward us with his hand on his hip, but Gerry was over the backside of the booth and out the door before Lovchik got close enough to make a positive identification.

"Siddown with us," said Dot to Lovchik, when he neared our booth. "I'll buy you a drink. It's so dead here. No one's been through all night."

Lovchik sighed, sat, and ordered a blackberry brandy.

"Now tell me," she said, staring at him, "honestly. What do you think of the name Ketchup Face?"

★

It was through Gerry that I first met Dot, in a bar like that one only denser with striving drinkers, construction crews who had come into town because a new interstate highway was passing near it. I was stuck there, having run out of money and ideas of where to go next. I was twenty-two and knew I'd soon have to do something different with my life. But no matter what that would be, I had to make some money first.

I had heard Gerry Nanapush was around, and because he was famous for leading a hunger strike at the state pen, as well as having been Henry Lamartine's brother and some kind of boyfriend to Aunt June, I went to look for him. He was not hard to find, being large. I sat down next to him and we struck up a conversation, during the long course of which we became friendly enough for Gerry to put his arm around me.

Dot entered at exactly the wrong moment. She was quick-tempered anyway, and being pregnant (Gerry had gotten her that way on a prison visit six months previous) increased her irritability. It was only natural then, I guess, that she would pull the barstool out from under me and threaten my life. Only I didn't believe she was threatening my life at the time. I had a false view of pregnant women. I thought of them as wearing invisible halos, not committing mayhem.

"I'm gonna bend you out of shape," she said, flexing her hands over me. Her hands were small, broad, capable, with pointed nails. I used to do the wrong thing sometimes when I was drinking, and that time I did the wrong thing, even though I was stretched out on the floor beneath her. I started laughing at her because her hands were so small (though strong and determined looking – I should have been more conscious of that). She was about to dive on top of me, six-month belly and all, but Gerry caught her in midair and carried her, yelling, out the door. The next morning I reported for work. It was my first day on the job, and the only other woman on the construction site besides me was Dot Adare.

That day Dot just glared toward me from a distance. She worked in the weigh shack, and I was hired to press buttons on the conveyor belt. All I had to do was adjust the speeds on the belt for sand, rocks, or gravel and make sure it was aimed toward the right pile. There was a pyramid for each type of material, which was used to make hot-mix and cement. Across the wide yard, I saw Dot emerge from the little weigh shack from time to time. I couldn't tell whether she recognized me, but I thought, by the end of the day, that she probably didn't. I found out differently the next morning when I went to the company truck for coffee.

She got me alongside of the truck somehow, away from the men. She didn't say a word, just held the buck knife out where I could see it, blade toward me. She jiggled the handle, and the tip waved like the pointy head of a pit viper. Blind. Heat seeking. I was completely astonished. I had just put the plastic cover on my coffee and it steamed between my hands.

"Well, I'm sorry I laughed," I said. She stepped back. I peeled the lid off my coffee, took a sip, and then I said the wrong thing again.

"And I wasn't going after your boyfriend."

"Why not?" she said at once. "What's wrong with him?"

I saw that I was going to lose this argument no matter what I said, so for once I did the right thing. I threw my coffee in her face and ran. Later on that day, Dot came out of the weigh shack and yelled, "Okay then!" I was close enough to see that she even grinned. I waved. From then on things were better between us, which was lucky, because I turned out to be such a good button presser that within two weeks I was promoted to the weigh shack, to help Dot.

It wasn't that Dot needed help weighing trucks, it was just a formality for the state highway department. I never quite understood, but it seems Dot had been both the truck weigher and the truck-weight inspector for a while, until someone caught wind of this. The company hired me to actually weigh the trucks, and Dot was hired by the state to make sure I recorded accurate weights. What she really did was sleep, knit, or eat all day. Between truckloads I did the same. I didn't even have to get off my stool to weigh the trucks, because the arm of the scale projected through a rectangular hole and the weights appeared right in front of me. The standard back dumps, bellydumps, and yellow company trucks eased onto a platform built over the arm next to the shack. I wrote their weight on a little pink slip, clipped the paper in a clothespin attached to a broom handle, and handed it up to the driver. I kept a copy of the pink slip on a yellow slip that I put in a metal filebox. No one ever picked up the filebox, so I never knew what the yellow slips were for. The company paid me very well.

It was early July when Dot and I started working together. At first I sat as far away from her as possible and never took my eyes off her knitting needles, although it made me a little dizzy to watch her work. It wasn't long before we came to an understanding, though, and after this I felt perfectly comfortable with Dot. She was nothing but direct, you see, and told me right off that only three things made her angry. Number one was someone flirting with Gerry. Number two was a cigarette leech, someone who was always quitting but smoking yours. Number three was a piss-ant. I asked her what that was. "A piss-ant," she said, "is a man with fat buns who tries to sell you things. A Jaycee, an Elk, a Kiwanis." I always knew where I stood with Dot, so I trusted her. I knew that if I fell out of her favor she would threaten me and give me time to run before she tried anything physical.

By mid-July our shack was unbearable, for it drew heat in from the bare yard and held it. We sat outside most of the time, moving around the shack to catch what shade fell, letting the raw hot wind off the beetfields suck the sweat from our armpits and legs. But the seasons change fast in North Dakota. We spent the last day of August jumping from foot to numb foot before Hadji, the foreman, dragged a little column of bottled gas into the shack. He lit the spoked wheel on its head, it bloomed, and from then on we huddled close to the heater, eating, dozing, or sitting mindless in its small radius of dry warmth.

By that time Dot weighed over 200 pounds, most of it peanut-butter cups and egg-salad sandwiches. She was a short, broad-beamed woman with long yellow eyes and spaces between each of her strong teeth. When we began working together, her hair was cropped close. By the cold months it had grown out in thick quills – brown at the shank, orange at the tip. The orange dye job had not suited her coloring. By that time, too, Dot's belly was round and full, for she was due in October. The child rode high, and she often rested her forearms on it while she knitted. One of Dot's most peculiar feats was transforming that gentle task into something perverse. She knit viciously, jerking the yarn around her thumb until the tip whitened, pulling each stitch so tightly that the little garments she finished stood up by themselves like miniature suits of mail.

I thought that the child would need those tight stitches when it was born. Although Dot as expecting mother lived a fairly calm life, it was clear that she had also moved loosely among the dangerous elements. The child, for example, had been conceived in a visiting room at the state prison. Dot had straddled Gerry's lap in a corner the closed-circuit TV did not quite scan. Through a hole ripped in her pantyhose and a hole ripped in Gerry's jeans they somehow managed to join and, miraculously, to conceive. Not long after my conversation with Gerry in the bar, he was caught. That time he went back peacefully, and didn't put up a fight. He was mainly in the penitentiary for breaking out of it, anyway, since for his crime of assault and battery he had received three years and time off for good behavior. He just never managed to serve those three years or behave well. He broke out time after time, and was caught each time he did it, regular as clockwork.

Gerry was talented at getting out, that's a fact. He boasted that no steel or concrete shitbarn could hold a Chippewa, and he had eellike properties in spite of his enormous size. Greased with lard once, he squirmed into a 6-foot-thick prison wall and vanished. Some thought he had stuck there, immured forever, and that he would bring luck, like the bones of slaves sealed in the wall of China. But Gerry rubbed his own belly for luck and brought luck to no one else, for he appeared, suddenly, at Dot's door, and she was hard-pressed to hide him.

She managed for nearly a month. Hiding a 6-foot-plus, 250-pound Indian in the middle of a town that doesn't like Indians in the first place isn't easy. A month was quite an accomplishment, when you know what she was up against. She spent most of her time walking to and from the grocery store, padding along on her swollen feet, astonishing the neighbors with the size of what they thought was her appetite. Stacks of pork chops, whole fryers, thick steaks disappeared overnight, and since Gerry couldn't take the garbage out by day, sometimes he threw the bones out the windows, where they collected, where dogs soon learned to wait for a handout and fought and squabbled over whatever there was.

The neighbors finally complained, and one day, while Dot was at work, Lovchik knocked on the door of the trailer house. Gerry answered, sighed, and walked over to their car. He was so good at getting out of the joint and so terrible at getting caught. It was as if he couldn't stay out of their hands. Dot knew his problem and told him that he was crazy to think he could walk out of prison and then live like a normal person. Dot told him that didn't work. She told him to get lost for a while on the reservation or to let his mother, Lulu, who had a long successful history of hiding men, keep him under cover. She told him to change his name, to let the straggly hairs above his lip grow, disguising his face. But Gerry wouldn't do any of that. He simply knew he did not belong in prison, although he admitted it had done him some good when he was younger, hadn't known how to be a criminal, and so had taken lessons from professionals. Now that he knew all there was to know, however, he couldn't see the point of staying in a prison and taking the same lessons over and over. "A hate factory," he called it once, and said it manufactured black poisons in his stomach that he couldn't get rid of although he poked a finger down his throat and retched and tried to be a clean and normal person in spite of everything.

Gerry's problem, you see, was he believed in justice, not laws. He felt he had paid for his crime, which was done in a drunk heat and to settle the question with a cowboy of whether a Chippewa was also a nigger. Gerry said that the two had never settled it between them, but that the cowboy at least knew that if a Chippewa was a nigger he was sure also a hell of a mean and low-down fighter. For Gerry did not believe in fighting by any rules but reservation rules, which is to say the first thing Gerry did to the cowboy, after they squared off, was kick his balls.

It hadn't been much of a fight after that, and since there were

both white and Indian witnesses, Gerry thought it would blow
over if it ever reached court. But there is nothing more vengeful
and determined in this world than a cowboy with sore balls, and
Gerry soon found this out. He also found that white people are
good witnesses to have on your side, because they have names,
addresses, social security numbers, and work phones. But they
are terrible witnesses to have against you, almost as bad as having
Indians witness for you.

Not only did Gerry's friends lack all forms of identification
except their band cards, not only did they disappear (out of no
malice but simply because Gerry was tried during powwow
time), but the few he did manage to get were not interested in
looking judge or jury in the eyes. They mumbled into their laps.
Gerry's friends, you see, had no confidence in the United States
judicial system. They did not seem comfortable in the court-
room, and this increased their unreliability in the eyes of judge
and jury. If you trust the authorities, they trust you better back,
it seems. It looked that way to Gerry, anyhow.

A local doctor testified on behalf of the cowboy's testicles,
and said his fertility might be impaired. Gerry got a little angry
at that, and said right out in court that he could hardly believe he
had done that much damage since the cowboy's balls were very
small targets, it had been dark, and his aim was off anyway
because of two, or maybe it was three, beers. That made matters
worse, of course, and Gerry was socked with a sentence that was
heavy for a first offense, but not bad for an Indian. Some said he
got off lucky.

Only one good thing came from the whole experience, said
Gerry, and that was that maybe the cowboy would not have any
little cowboys, although, Gerry also said, he had nightmares
sometimes that the cowboy did manage to have little cowboys,
all born with full sets of grinning teeth, Stetson hats, and little
balls hard as plum pits.

So you see, it was difficult for Gerry, as an Indian, to retain the
natural good humor of his ancestors in these modern circumstances. He tried though, and since he believed in justice, not
laws, Gerry knew where he belonged – out of prison, in the

bosom of his new family. And in spite of the fact that he was untrained in the honest life, he wanted it. He was even interested in getting a job. It didn't matter what kind of job. "Anything for a change," Gerry said. He wanted to go right out and apply for one, in fact, the moment he was free. But of course Dot wouldn't let him. And so, because he wanted to be with Dot, he stayed hidden in her trailer house even though they both realized, or must have, that it wouldn't be long before the police came asking around or the neighbors wised up and Gerry Nanapush would be back at square one again. So it happened. Lovchik came for him. And Dot now believed she would have to go through the end of her pregnancy and the delivery all by herself.

Dot was angry about having to go through it alone, and besides that, she loved Gerry with a deep and true love – that was clear. She knit his absences into thick little suits for the child, suits that would have stopped a truck on a dark road with their colors – Bazooka pink, bruise blue, the screaming orange flaggers wore.

The child was as restless a prisoner as its father, and grew more anxious and unruly as the time of release neared. As a place to spend a nine-month sentence in, Dot wasn't much. Her body was inhospitable. Her skin was loose, sallow, and draped like upholstery fabric over her short, boardlike bones. Like the shack we spent our days in, she seemed jerry-built, thrown into the world with loosely nailed limbs and lightly puttied joints. Some pregnant women's bellies look like they always have been there. But Dot's stomach was an odd shape, almost square, and had the tacked-on air of a new and unpainted bay window. The child was clearly ready for a break and not interested in earning its parole, for it kept her awake all night by pounding reasonlessly at her inner walls or beating against her bladder until she swore. "Kid wants out, bad," poor Dot would groan. "You think it might be premature?" From the outside, anyway, the child looked big enough to stand and walk and maybe even run straight out of the maternity ward the moment it was born.

The sun, at the time, rose around seven, and we got to the weigh shack while the frost was still thick on the gravel. Each morning

I started the gas heater, turning the nozzle and standing back, flipping the match at it the way you would feed a fanged animal. Then one morning I saw the red bud through the window, lit already. But when I opened the door the shack was empty. There was, however, evidence of an overnight visitor – cigarette stubs, a few beer cans crushed to flat disks. I swept these things out and didn't say a word about them to Dot when she arrived.

She seemed to know something was in the air, however; her face lifted from time to time all that morning. She sniffed, and even I could smell the lingering odor of sweat like sour wheat, the faint reek of slept-in clothes and gasoline. Once, that morning, Dot looked at me and narrowed her long, hooded eyes. "I got pains," she said, "every so often. Like it's going to come sometime soon. Well, all I can say is he better drag ass to get here, that Gerry." She closed her eyes then, and went to sleep.

Ed Rafferty, one of the drivers, pulled in with a load. It was overweight, and when I handed him the pink slip he grinned. There were two scales, you see, on the way to the cement plant, and if a driver got past the state-run scale early, before the state officials were there, the company would pay for whatever he got away with. But it was not illicit gravel that tipped the wedge past the red mark on the balance. When I walked back inside I saw the weight had gone down to just under the red. Ed drove off, still laughing, and I assumed that he had leaned on the arm of the scale, increasing the weight.

"That Ed," I said, "got me again."

But Dot stared past me, needles poised in her fist like a picador's lances. It gave me a start, to see her frozen in such a menacing pose. It was not the sort of pose to turn your back on, but I did turn, following her gaze to the door, which a man's body filled suddenly.

Gerry, of course it was Gerry. He'd tipped the weight up past the red and leapt down, cat-quick for all his mass, and silent. I hadn't heard his step. Gravel crushed, evidently, but did not roll beneath his tight, thin boots.

He was bigger than I remembered from the bar, or perhaps it was just that we'd been living in that dollhouse of a weigh shack so long that everything else looked huge. He was so big that he had to hunker one shoulder beneath the lintel and back his belly in, pushing the doorframe wider with his long, soft hands. It was the hands I watched as Gerry filled the shack. His plump fingers looked so graceful and artistic against his smooth mass. He used them prettily. Revolving agile wrists he reached across the few inches left between himself and Dot. Then his littlest fingers curled like a woman's at tea, and he disarmed his wife. He drew the needles out of Dot's fists, and examined the little garment that hung like a queer fruit beneath.

"S'very, very nice," he said, scrutinizing the tiny, even stitches. "S'for the kid?"

Dot nodded solemnly and dropped her eyes to her lap. It was an almost tender moment. The silence lasted so long that I got embarrassed and would have left had I not been wedged firmly behind his hip in one corner.

Gerry stood there, smoothing black hair behind his ears. Again, there was a queer delicacy about the way he did this. So many things Gerry did might remind you of the way that a beautiful courtesan, standing naked before a mirror, would touch herself – lovingly, conscious of her attractions. He nodded encouragingly. "Let's go then," said Dot.

Suave, grand, gigantic, they moved across the construction site and then, by mysterious means, slipped their bodies into Dot's compact car. I expected the car to belly down, thought the muffler would scrape the ground behind them. But instead they flew, raising a great spume of dust that hung in the air a long time after they were out of sight.

I went back into the weigh shack when the air behind them had settled. I was bored, dead bored. And since one thing meant about as much to me as another, I picked up her needles and began knitting, as well as I could anyway, jerking the yarn back after each stitch, becoming more and more absorbed in my work until, as it happened, I came suddenly to the end of the garment, snipped the yarn, and worked the loose ends back into the collar of the thick little suit.

★

I missed Dot in the days that followed, days so alike they welded seamlessly to one another and took your mind away. I seemed to exist in a suspension and spent my time sitting at the window watching nothing until the sun went down, bruising the whole sky as it dropped, clotting my heart. I couldn't name anything I felt anymore, although I knew it was a kind of boredom. I had been living the same life too long. I did jumping jacks and pushups and stood on my head in the little shack to break the tedium, but too much solitude rots the brain. I wondered how Gerry had stood it. Sometimes I grabbed drivers out of their trucks and talked loudly and quickly and inconsequentially as a madwoman. There were other times I couldn't talk at all because my tongue had rusted to the roof of my mouth.

Sometimes I daydreamed about Dot and Gerry. I had many choice daydreams, but theirs was my favorite. I pictured them in Dot's long tan trailer house, both hungry. Heads swaying, clasped hands swinging between them like hooked trunks, they moved through the kitchen feeding casually from boxes and bags on the counters, like ponderous animals alone in a forest. When they had fed, they moved on to the bedroom and settled themselves upon Dot's king-size and sateen-quilted spread. They rubbed together, locked and unlocked their parts. They set the trailer rocking on its cement-block-and-plywood foundation and the tremors spread, causing cups to fall, plates to shatter in the china hutches of their more established neighbors.

But what of the child there, suspended between them? Did it know how to weather such tropical storms? It was a week past the week it was due, and I expected the good news to come any moment. I was anxious to hear the outcome, but still, I was surprised when Gerry rumbled to the weigh-shack door on a huge and ancient, rust-pocked, untrustworthy-looking machine that was like no motorcycle I'd ever seen before.

"She asst for you," he hissed. "Quick, get on!"

I hoisted myself up behind him, although there wasn't room on the seat. I clawed his smooth back for a handhold and finally perched, or so it seemed, on the rim of his heavy belt. Flylike, glued to him by suction, we rode as one person, whipping a great wind around us. Cars scattered, the lights blinked and flickered on the main street. Pedestrians swiveled to catch a glimpse of us – a mountain tearing by balanced on a toy, and clinging to the sheer northwest face, a scrawny half-breed howling something that Dopplered across the bridge and faded out, finally, in the parking lot of Saint Adalbert's Hospital.

In the waiting room we settled on chairs molded of orange plastic. The spike legs splayed beneath Gerry's mass but managed to support him the four hours we waited. Nurses passed, settling like field gulls among reports and prescriptions, eyeing us with reserved hostility. Gerry hardly spoke. He didn't have to. I watched his ribs and the small of his back darken with sweat. For that well-lighted tunnel, the waiting room, the tin rack of magazines, all were the props and inevitable features of insti-tutions. From time to time Gerry paced in the time-honored manner of the prisoner or expectant father. He made lengthy trips to the bathroom. All the quickness and delicacy of his movements had disappeared, and he was only a poor tired fat man in those hours, a husband worried about his wife, menaced, tired of getting caught.

At last the gulls emerged and drew Gerry in among them. He visited Dot for perhaps half an hour, and then came out of her room. Again he settled, the plastic chair twitched beneath him. He looked bewildered and silly and a little addled with what he had seen. The shaded lenses of his glasses kept slipping down his nose. Beside him, I felt the aftermath of the shock wave traveling from the epicenter deep in his flesh outward from part of him that had shifted along a crevice. The tremors moved in widening rings. When they reached the very surface of him, and when he began trembling, Gerry stood suddenly. "I'm going after cigars," he said, and walked quickly away.

His steps quickened to a near run as he moved down the corridor. Waiting for the elevator, he flexed his nimble fingers. Dot told me she had once sent him to the store for a roll of toilet paper. It was eight months before she saw him again, for he'd met the local constabulary on the way. So I knew, when he flexed his fingers, that he was thinking of pulling the biker's gloves over his knuckles, of running. It was perhaps the very first time in his life he had something to run for.

It seemed to me, at that moment, that I should at least let Gerry know it was all right for him to leave, to run as far and fast as he had to now. Although I felt heavy – my body had gone slack, and my lungs ached with smoke – I jumped up. I signaled him from the end of the corridor. Gerry turned, unwillingly turned. He looked my way just as two of our local police – Officers Lovchik and Harriss – pushed open the fire door that sealed off the staircase behind me. I didn't see them and was shocked at first that my wave caused such an extreme reaction in Gerry.

His hair stiffened. His body lifted like a hot-air balloon filling suddenly. Behind him there was a wide, tall window. Gerry opened it and sent the screen into thin air with an elegant chorus-girl kick. Then he followed the screen, squeezing himself unbelievably through the frame like a fat rabbit disappearing down a hole. It was three stories down to the cement and asphalt parking lot.

Officers Lovchik and Harriss gained the window. The nurses followed. I slipped through the fire exit and took the back stairs down into the parking lot, believing I would find him stunned and broken there.

But Gerry had chosen his window with exceptional luck, for the officers had parked their car directly underneath. Gerry landed just over the driver's seat, caving the roof into the steering wheel. He bounced off the hood of the car and then, limping, a bit dazed perhaps, straddled his bike. Out of duty, Lovchik released several rounds into the still trees below him. The reports were still echoing when I reached the front of the building.

I was just in time to see Gerry Nanapush, emboldened by his godlike leap and recovery, pop a wheelie and disappear between the neat shrubs that marked the entrance to the hospital.

Two weeks later Dot and her girl, who was finally named Shawn, like most girls born that year, came back to work at the scales. Things went on as they had before, except that Shawn kept us occupied during the long hours. She was large, of course, and had a sturdy pair of lungs she used often. When she cried, she screwed her face into fierce baby wrinkles and would not be placated with sugar tits or pacifiers. Dot unzipped her parka halfway, pulled her blouse up, and let her nurse for what seemed like hours. We could scarcely believe her appetite. Dot was a diligent producer of milk, however. Her breasts, like overfilled inner tubes, strained at her nylon blouses. Sometimes when she thought no one was looking, Dot rose and carried them in the crooks of her arms, for her shoulders were growing bowed beneath their weight.

The trucks came in on the hour, or half hour. I heard the rush of air brakes, gears grinding only inches from my head. It occurred to me that although I measured many tons every day, I would never know how heavy a ton was unless it fell on me. I wasn't lonely now that Dot had returned. The season would end soon, and we wondered what had happened to Gerry.

There were only a few weeks left of work when we heard that Gerry was caught again. He'd picked the wrong reservation to hide on – Pine Ridge. As always, it was overrun with federal agents and armored vehicles. Weapons were stashed everywhere and easy to acquire. Gerry got himself a weapon. Two men tried to arrest him. Gerry would not go along, and when he started to run and the shooting started, Gerry shot and killed a clean-shaven man with dark hair and light eyes, a state trooper, a man whose picture was printed in all the papers.

They sent Gerry to prison in Marion, Illinois. He was placed in the control unit. He receives visitors in a room where no touching is allowed, where the voice is carried by phone, glances meet through sheets of Plexiglas, and no children will ever be engendered.

Dot and I continued to work the last weeks together. Once we weighed baby Shawn. We unlatched her little knit suit, heavy as armor, and bundled her in a light, crocheted blanket. Dot went into the shack to adjust the weights. I stood there with Shawn. She was such a solid child, she seemed heavy as lead in my arms.

I placed her on the ramp between the wheel sights and held her steady for a moment, then took my hands slowly away. She stared calmly into the rough distant sky. She did not flinch when the wind came from every direction, wrapping us tight enough to squeeze the very breath from a stone. She was so dense with life, such a powerful distillation of Dot and Gerry, it seemed she might weigh about as much as any load. But that was only a thought, of course. For as it turned out, she was too light and did not register at all.

RICHARD FORD

☆ ☆ ☆ ☆

# *Rock Springs*

Edna and I had started down from Kalispell heading for Tampa–St. Pete where I still had some friends from the old glory days who wouldn't put the police on me. I had managed to scrape with the law in Kalispell over several bad checks – which is a prison crime in Montana. And I knew Edna was already looking at her cards and thinking about a move, since it wasn't the first time I'd been in law scrapes in my life. She herself had already had troubles aplenty, losing her kids, and keeping her ex-husband Danny from breaking in her house and stealing her things while she was at work, which was really why I had moved in in the first place, that and needing to give my daughter Cheryl a better shake in things.

I don't know what was between Edna and me. Just beached by the same tides when you got down to it. But love has been built on frailer ground than that, as I well know. And when I came in the house that afternoon I just asked her if she wanted to go to Florida with me and she said, "Why not."

Edna and I had been a pair eight months, more or less man and wife, some of which time I had been out of work, and some when I'd worked at the dog track as a hot handler and could help with the rent and talk sense to Danny when he came around. Danny was afraid of me because Edna had told him I'd been in prison in Florida for killing a man once, though that wasn't true. I had once been in jail in Tallahassee for stealing tires and had gotten into a fight on the county farm where a man had lost his eye. But I hadn't done the hurting, and Edna just wanted the story worse than it was so Danny wouldn't act crazy and make her have to take her kids back, since she had made a good adjustment to not having them, and I already had Cheryl with me. I'm not a violent person and would never put a man's eye out, much less kill someone. My former wife Helen would come all the way from Waikiki Beach to testify to that. We never had violence, and I believe in crossing the street to stay out of trouble's way. Though Danny didn't know that.

But we were half down through Wyoming going toward I–80 and feeling good about things, when the oil light flashed on in the car I'd stolen, a sign I knew to be a bad one.

I'd gotten us a good car, a cranberry Mercedes I'd stolen out of an opthalmologist's lot in Whitefish, Montana. I stole it because I thought it would be comfortable over a long haul, because I thought it got good mileage, which it didn't, and because I'd never had a good car in my life, just old Chevy junkers and used trucks back from when I was a kid swamping citrus with Cubans.

The car made us all high that day. I ran the windows up and down and Edna told us some jokes and made faces. She could be lively. Her features would light up like a beacon and you could see her beauty, which wasn't ordinary. It all made me giddy, and I drove clear down to Bozeman, then straight on through the park to Jackson Hole. I rented us the bridal suite in the Quality Court in Jackson, and left Cheryl and Little Duke sleeping while Edna and I drove to a rib barn and drank beer and laughed till after midnight.

It felt like a whole new beginning for us, bad memories left behind and a new horizon to build on. I got so worked up I had a tattoo done on my arm that said, FAMOUS TIMES, and Edna bought a Bailey hat with an Indian feather band and a little turquoise and silver bracelet for Cheryl, and we made love on the seat of the car in the Quality Court parking lot just as the sun was burning up in the Snake River, and everything seemed then like the end of the rainbow.

It was that very enthusiasm in fact that made me keep the car one day longer instead of driving it in the river and stealing another one like I should have done and *had* done before.

Where the car went bad there wasn't a town in sight or even a house, just some low mountains maybe 50 miles away, or maybe 100, a barbed wire fence in both directions, hardpan prairie, and some hawks sailing through the evening air seizing insects.

I got out to look at the motor and Edna got out with Cheryl and the dog to let them have a pee by the car. I checked the water and checked the oil stick and both of them said perfect.

"What's that light mean, Earl?" Edna said. She had come and stood by the car with her hat on. She was just sizing things up for herself.

"We shouldn't run it," I said. "Something's not right in the oil."

She looked around at Cheryl and Little Duke who were peeing on the hardtop side-by-side like two little dolls, then out at the mountains which were becoming purple and lost in the distance. "What're we going to do?" she said. She wasn't worried yet, but she wanted to know what I was thinking about.

"Let me try it again," I said.

"That's a good idea," she said, and we all got back in the car.

When I tried the motor it turned over right away and the red light stayed off and there weren't any noises to make you think something was wrong. I let it idle a minute, then pushed the accelerator down and watched the red bulb, but there wasn't any light on, and I started wondering if maybe I hadn't dreamed I saw it, or that it had been the sun catching an angle off the window chrome, or maybe I was scared of something and didn't know it.

"What's the matter with it, Daddy?" Cheryl said from the back seat. I looked back at her and she had on her turquoise bracelet and Edna's hat set back on the back of her head. She looked like a little cowgirl in the movies.

"Nothing honey, everything's fine now," I said.

"Little Duke tinkled where I tinkled," Cheryl said and laughed.

"You're two of a kind," Edna said, not looking back. Edna was usually good with Cheryl, but I knew she was tired now. We hadn't had much sleep, and she had a tendency to get cranky when she didn't sleep. "We oughta ditch this damn car first chance we get," she said.

"What's the first chance we've got?" I said. I knew she'd been at the map.

"Rock Springs, Wyoming," Edna said with conviction. "Thirty miles down this road." She pointed out ahead. I had wanted all along to drive the car into Florida like a big success story. But I knew Edna was right about it, that we shouldn't take crazy chances. I had kept thinking of it as my car and not the opthalmologist's, and that was how you got caught in these things.

"Then my belief is we ought to go to Rock Springs and negotiate ourselves a new car," I said. I wanted to stay up-beat, like everything was panning out right.

"Great idea," Edna said, and leaned over and kissed me hard on the mouth.

"Now you're talking," Cheryl said. "Let's get on out of here right now."

The sunset that day I remember as being the prettiest I'd ever seen. Just as it touched the rim of the horizon it all at once fired the air into jewels and red sequins the precise likes of which I had never seen before and haven't seen since. The west has it all over everywhere for sunsets, even Florida where it's supposedly flat but where half the time trees block your view.

"It's cocktail hour," Edna said after we'd driven a while. "We ought to have a drink and celebrate something." She felt a lot better thinking we were going to get rid of the car. It certainly had dark troubles and was something you'd want to put behind you.

Edna had out a whiskey bottle and some plastic cups and was measuring levels on the glove box lid. She liked drinking, and she liked drinking in the car, which was something you got used to in Montana where it wasn't against the law, though strangely enough where a bad check would land you in Deer Lodge Prison for a year.

"Did I ever tell you I once had a monkey?" Edna said, setting my drink on the dashboard where I could reach it when I was ready. Her spirits were already picked up. She was like that, up one minute and down the next.

"I don't think you ever did tell me that," I said. "Where were you then?"

"Missoula," she said. She put her bare feet on the dash and rested the cup on her breasts. "I was waitressing at the Am-Vets. It was before I met you. Some guy came in one day with a monkey. A spider monkey. And I said, just to be joking, 'I'll roll you for that monkey.' And the guy said, 'Just one roll?' And I said sure. He put the monkey down on the bar, picked up the cup and rolled out box cars. I picked it up and rolled out three fives. And I just stood there looking at the guy. He was just some guy passing through, a vet. He got a strange look on his face – I'm sure not as strange as the one I had – but he looked kind of sad and surprised and satisfied all at once. I said, 'We can roll again.' But he said, 'No, I never roll twice for anything.' And he sat and drank a beer and talked about one thing and another for a while, about Nuclear War and building a strong-hold somewhere up in the Bitterroot, whatever it was, while I just watched the monkey, wondering what I was going to do with it when the guy left. And pretty soon he got up and said, 'Well good-bye, Chipper,' that was this monkey's name, of course. And then he left before I could say anything. And the monkey just sat on the bar all that night. I don't know what made me think of that, Earl. Just something weird. I'm letting my mind wander."

"That's perfectly fine," I said. I took a drink of my drink. "I'd never own a monkey," I said after a minute. "They're too nasty. I'm sure Cheryl would like a monkey though, wouldn't you honey?" Cheryl was down on the seat playing with Little Duke. She used to talk about monkeys all the time then, which was when she was ten. "What'd you ever do with that monkey?" I said, watching the speedometer. We were having to go slower now because the red light kept fluttering on. And all I could do to keep it off was go slower. We were maybe going thirty-five and it was an hour before dark, and I was hoping Rock Springs wasn't far away.

"You really want to know?" she said. She gave me a quick sharp glance, then looked back at the empty desert as if she was brooding over it.

"Sure," I said. I was still up-beat. I figured *I* could worry about breaking down and let other people be happy for a change.

"I kept it a week," she said. She seemed gloomy all of a sudden, as if she saw some aspect of the story she had never seen before. "I took it home and back and forth to the Am-Vets on my shifts. And it didn't cause any trouble. I fixed a chair up for it to sit on back of the bar, and people liked it. It made a nice little clicking noise. We changed its name to Mary because Oscar figured out it was a girl. Though I was never really comfortable with it at home. I felt like it watched me too much. Then one day a guy came in, some guy who'd been in Viet Nam, still wore a fatigue coat. And he said to me, 'Don't you know that a monkey'll kill you? It's got more strength in its fingers than you got in your whole body.' He said people had been killed in Viet Nam by monkeys, bunches of them marauding while you were asleep and killing you and covering you with leaves. I didn't believe a word of it, except that when I got home and got undressed I started looking over across the room at Mary on her chair in the dark watching me. And I got the creeps. And after a while I got up and went out to the car, got a length of clothesline wire, and came back in and wired her to the door knob through her little silver collar, and went back and tried to sleep. And I guess I must've slept the sleep of the dead – though I don't remember it – because when I got up I found Mary had tipped off her chair back and hanged herself on the wire line. I'd made it too short."

Edna seemed badly affected by that story and slid low in the seat so she couldn't see out over the dash. "Isn't that a shameful story, Earl, what happened to that poor little monkey?"

"I see a town! I see a town!" Cheryl started yelling from the back seat, and right up Little Duke started yapping and the whole car fell into a racket. And sure enough she had seen something I hadn't, which was Rock Springs, Wyoming, at the bottom of a long hill, a little glowing jewel in the desert with I–80 running on the north side, and the black desert spread out behind.

"That's it, honey," I said. "That's where we're going. You saw it first."

"We're hungry," Cheryl said. "Little Duke wants some fish,

and I want spaghetti." She put her arms around my neck and hugged me.

"Then you'll just get it," I said. "You can have anything you want. And so can Edna and so can Little Duke." I looked over at Edna smiling, but she was staring at me with eyes that were fierce with anger. "What's wrong?" I said.

"Don't you care anything about that awful thing that happened to me?" she said. Her mouth was drawn tight and her eyes kept cutting back at Cheryl and Little Duke, as if they had been tormenting her.

"Of course I do," I said. "I thought that was an awful thing." I didn't want her to be unhappy. We were almost there and pretty soon we could sit down and have a real meal without thinking somebody might be hunting us.

"You want to know what I did with that monkey?" Edna said.

"Sure I do," I said.

She said, "I put him in a green garbage bag, put it in the trunk of my car, drove to the dump and threw him in the trash." She was staring at me darkly, as if the story meant something to her that was real important but that only she could see and that the rest of the world was a fool for.

"Well that's horrible," I said. "But I don't see what else you could do. You didn't mean to kill it. You'd have done it differently if you had. And then you had to get rid of it, and I don't know what else you could do. Throwing it away seems unsympathetic to somebody, probably, but not to me. Sometimes that's all you can do, and you can't worry about what somebody else thinks." I tried to smile at her, but the red light was staying on if I pushed the accelerator at all, and I was trying to gauge if we could coast to the Interstate before the car gave out completely. I looked at Edna again. "What else can I say?" I said.

"Nothing," she said and stared back at the dark highway. "I should've known that's what you'd think. You've got a character that leaves something out, Earl. I've known that a long time."

"And yet here you are," I said. "And you're not doing so bad. Things could be a lot worse. At least we're all together."

"Things could always be worse," Edna said. "You could go to the electric chair tomorrow."

"That's right," I said. "And somewhere somebody probably will. Only it won't be you."

"I'm hungry," said Cheryl. "When're we gonna eat? Let's find a motel. I'm tired of this, Little Duke's tired of it too."

Where the car stopped rolling was some distance from the Interstate, though you could see the clear outline of it in the dark with Rock Springs lighting up the sky behind. You could hear the big tractors hitting the spacers in the overpass, revving up for the climb to the mountains.

I shut off the lights.

"What're we going to do now?" Edna said irritably, giving me a bitter look.

"I'm figuring it," I said. "It won't be hard, whatever it is. You won't have to do anything."

"I'd hope not," she said and looked the other way.

Across the road and across a dry wash 100 yards, was what looked like a huge mobile home town with a factory or a refinery of some kind lit up behind it, and in full swing. There were lights on in a lot of the mobile homes, and there were cars moving along an access road that ended near the freeway overpass a mile the other way. The lights in the mobile homes seemed friendly to me, and I knew right then what I should do.

"Get out," I said and opened the door.

"Are we walking?" Edna said.

"We're pushing," I said.

"I'm not pushing," Edna said and reached up and locked her door.

"All right," I said. "Then you just steer."

"You pushing us to Rock Springs, are you, Earl? It doesn't look like it's more than about 3 miles," Edna said.

"I'll push," Cheryl said from the back.

"No, hon. Daddy'll push. You just get out with Little Duke and move out of the way."

Edna gave me a threatening look just as if I'd tried to hit her. But when I got out she slid into my seat and took the wheel, staring angrily ahead straight into the cottonwood scrub.

"Edna can't drive that car," Cheryl said from out in the dark. "She'll run it in the ditch."

"Yes she can, hon. Edna can drive it as good as I can. Probably better."

"No she can't," Cheryl said. "No she can't, either." And I thought she was about to cry but she didn't.

I told Edna to keep the ignition on so it wouldn't lock up, and to steer into the cottonwoods with the parking lights on so she could see. And when I started, she steered it straight off into the trees and I kept pushing until we were twenty yards into the cover and the tires sank in the soft sand, and nothing at all could be seen from the road.

"Now where are we?" she said, sitting at the wheel. Her voice was tired and hard, and I knew she would put a meal to use. She had a sweet nature, and I recognized this wasn't her fault, but mine. Only I wished she could be more hopeful like I was.

"You stay right here and I'll go over to that trailer park and call us a cab," I said.

"What cab?" Edna said, her mouth wrinkled as if she'd never heard anything like that in her life.

"There'll be cabs," I said and tried to smile at her. "There's cabs everywhere."

"What're you going to tell him when he gets here? Our stolen car broke down and we need a ride to where we can steal another one? That'll be a big hit, Earl."

"I'll talk," I said. "You just listen to the radio ten minutes then walk out to the shoulder. And you and Cheryl act nice. I don't want her making suspicions."

"Like we're not suspicious enough already, right?" Edna looked up at me out of the lighted car. "You don't think right, did you know that, Earl? You think the world's stupid and you're smart. But that's not how it is. I feel sorry for you. You might've *been* something, but things just went crazy someplace."

I had thought about poor Danny. He was a vet, and crazy as a shithouse mouse, and I was glad he wasn't in for all this. "Just get the baby in the car," I said, trying to be patient. "I'm hungry like you are."

"I'm tired of this," Edna said. "I wish I'd stayed in Montana."

"Then you can go back in the morning," I said. "I'll buy the ticket and put you on the bus. But not till then."

"Just get on with it, Earl," she said, slumping down in the seat, turning off the parking lights with one foot and the radio on with the other.

The mobile home community was as big as any I'd ever seen. It was attached in some way to the plant that was lighted up behind it, because I could see a car once in a while leave one of the trailer streets, turn in the direction of the plant, then go slowly into it. Everything in the plant was white, and you could see that all the trailers were painted white and looked exactly alike. A deep hum came out of the plant, and I thought as I got closer that it wouldn't be a location I'd ever want to work in.

I went right to the first trailer where there was a light and knocked on the metal door. Kids' toys were lying in the gravel around the little wood steps, and I could hear talking on TV that suddenly went off. I heard a woman's voice talking and then the door opened wide.

A large Negro woman with a wide friendly face stood in the doorway. She smiled at me and moved forward as if she was going to come out, but stopped at the top step. There was a little Negro boy behind her peeping out from behind her legs, watching me with his eyes half closed. The trailer had that feeling that no one else was inside, which was a feeling I knew something about.

"I'm sorry to intrude," I said. "But I've run up on a little bad luck tonight. My name's Earl Middleton."

The woman looked at me, then out into the night toward the freeway as if what I had said was something she was going to be able to see. "What kind of bad luck?" she said, looking down at me again.

"My car broke down out on the highway," I said. "I can't fix it myself, and I wondered if I could use your phone to call for help."

The woman smiled down at me knowingly. "We can't live without cars, can we?"

"That's the honest truth," I said.

"They're like our hearts," she said firmly, her face shining in the little bulb light that burned beside the door. "Where's your car situated?"

I turned and looked over into the dark, but I couldn't see anything because of where we'd put it. "It's over there," I said. "You can't see it in the dark."

"Who all's with you now?" the woman said. "Have you got your wife with you?"

"She's with my little girl and our dog in the car," I said. "My daughter's asleep or I would have brought them."

"They shouldn't be left in that dark by themselves," the woman said and frowned. "There's too much unsavoriness out there."

"The best I can do is hurry back," I said. I tried to look sincere, since everything except Cheryl being asleep and Edna being my wife was the truth. The truth is meant to serve you if you'll let it, and I wanted it to serve me. "I'll pay for the phone call," I said. "If you'll bring the phone to the door I'll call from right here."

The woman looked at me again as if she was searching for a truth of her own, then back out into the night. She was maybe in her sixties but I couldn't say for sure. "You're not going to rob me, are you, Mr. Middleton?" she said, and smiled like it was a joke between us.

"Not tonight," I said and smiled a genuine smile. "I'm not up to it tonight. Maybe another time."

"Then I guess Terrel and I can let you use our phone with Daddy not here, can't we, Terrel? This is my grandson, Terrel Junior, Mr. Middleton." She put her hand on the boy's head and looked down at him. "Terrel won't talk. Though if he did he'd tell you to use our phone. He's a sweet boy." She opened the screen for me to come in.

The trailer was a big one with a new rug and a new couch and a living room that expanded to give the space of a real house. Something good and sweet was cooking in the kitchen and the trailer felt like it was somebody's comfortable new home instead of just temporary. I've lived in trailers, but they were just snailbacks with one room and no toilet, and they always felt cramped and unhappy – though I've thought maybe it might've been me that was unhappy in them.

There was a big Sony TV and a lot of kid's toys scattered on the floor. I recognized a Greyound Bus I'd gotten for Cheryl. The phone was beside a new leather recliner, and the Negro woman pointed for me to sit down and call, and gave me the phone book. Terrel began fingering his toys and the woman sat on the couch while I called, watching me and smiling.

There were three listings for cab companies, all with one number different. I called the numbers in order and didn't get an answer until the last one which answered with the name of the second company. I said I was on the highway beyond the Interstate and that my wife and family needed to be taken to town and I would arrange for a tow later. While I was giving the location, I looked up the name of a tow service to tell the driver in case he asked.

When I hung up the Negro woman was sitting looking at me with the same look she had been staring with into the dark, a look that seemed to want truth. She was smiling though, something pleased her and I reminded her of it.

"This is a very nice home," I said, resting in the recliner which felt like the driver's seat of the Mercedes, and where I'd have been happy to stay.

"This isn't *our* house, Mr. Middleton," the Negro woman said. "The company owns these. They give them to us for nothing. We have our own home in Rockford, Illinois."

"That's wonderful," I said.

"It's never wonderful when you have to be away from home, Mr. Middleton, though we're only here three months, and it'll be easier when Terrel Junior begins his special school. You see, our son was killed in the war, and his wife ran off without Terrel Junior. Though you shouldn't worry. He can't understand us. His little feelings can't be hurt." The woman folded her hands in her lap and smiled in a satisfied way. She was an attractive woman and had on a blue and pink floral dress that made her seem bigger than she could've been, just the right woman to sit on the couch she was sitting on. She was good nature's picture, and I was glad she could be, with her little brain-damaged boy,

living in a place where no one in his right mind would want to
live a minute. "Where do you live, Mr. Middleton?" she said
politely, smiling in the same sympathetic way.

"My family and I are in transit," I said. "I'm an opthalmologist, and we're moving back to Florida where I'm from. I'm
setting up practice in some little town where it's warm year
round. I haven't decided where."

"Florida's a wonderful place," the woman said. "I think
Terrel would like it there."

"Could I ask you something?" I said.

"You certainly may," the woman said. Terrel had begun
pushing his Greyound across the front of the TV screen, making
a scratch that no one watching the set could miss. "Stop that,
Terrel Junior," the woman said quietly. But Terrel kept pushing
his bus on the glass, and she smiled at me again as if we both
understood something sad. Except I knew Cheryl would never
damage a television set. She had respect for nice things, and I
was sorry for the lady that Terrel didn't. "What did you want to
ask?" the woman said.

"What goes on in that plant or whatever it is back there
beyond these trailers, where all the lights are on?"

"Gold," the woman said and smiled.

"It's what?" I said.

"Gold," the Negro woman said, smiling as she had for
almost all the time I'd been there. "It's a gold mine."

"They're mining gold back there?" I said, pointing.

"Every night and every day," she said, smiling in a pleased
way.

"Does your husband work there?" I said.

"He's the assayer," she said. "He controls the quality. He
works three months a year, and we live the rest of the time at
home in Rockford. We've waited a long time for this. We've
been happy to have our grandson, but I won't say I'll be sorry to
have him go. We're ready to start our lives over." She smiled
broadly at me and then at Terrel who was giving her a spiteful
look from the floor. "You said you had a daughter," the Negro
woman said. "And what's her name?"

"Irma Cheryl," I said. "She's named for my mother."

"That's nice," she said. "And she's healthy, too. I can see it in your face." She looked over at Terrel Junior.

"I guess I'm lucky," I said.

"So far you are," she said. "But children bring you grief, the same way they bring you joy. We were unhappy for a long time before my husband got his job in the gold mine. Now, when Terrel starts to school, we'll be kids again." She stood up. "You might miss your cab, Mr. Middleton," she said, walking toward the door, though not to be forcing me out. She was too polite. "If *we* can't see your car, the cab surely won't be able to."

"That's true," I said, and got up off the recliner where I'd been so comfortable. "None of us have eaten yet, and your food makes me know how hungry we probably all are."

"There are fine restaurants in town, and you'll find them," the Negro woman said. "I'm sorry you didn't meet my husband. He's a wonderful man. He's everything to me."

"Tell him I appreciate the phone," I said. "You saved me."

"You weren't hard to save," the woman said. "Saving people is what we were all put on earth to do. I just passed you on to whatever's coming to you."

"Let's hope it's good," I said, stepping back into the dark.

"I'll be hoping, Mr. Middleton. Terrel and I will both be hoping."

I waved to her as I walked out into the darkness toward the car where it was hidden in the night.

The cab had already arrived when I got there. I could see its little red and green roof lights all the way across the dry wash, and it made me worry that Edna was already saying something to get us in trouble, something about the car or where we'd come from, something that would create suspicion on us. I thought, then, how I never planned things well enough. There was always a gap between my plan and what happened, and that I only responded to things as they came along, and hoped I wouldn't get in trouble. I was an offender in the law's eyes. But I always *thought* differently, as if I weren't an offender and had no intention of being one, which was the truth. But as I read on a napkin once, between the idea and the act a whole kingdom lies. And I had a hard time with my acts, which were oftentimes offender's acts, and my ideas, which were as good as the gold they mined there where the bright lights were blazing.

"We're waiting for you, Daddy," Cheryl said when I crossed the road. "The taxicab's already here."

"I see, hon," I said and gave Cheryl a big hug. The cab driver was sitting in the driver's seat having a smoke with the lights on inside. Edna was leaning against the back of the cab between the tail lights, wearing her Bailey hat. "What'd you tell him?" I said when I got close.

"Nothin'," she said. "What's there to tell?"

"Did he see the car?"

She glanced over in the direction of the trees where we had hid the Mercedes. Nothing was visible in the darkness, though I could hear Little Duke combing around in the underbrush tracking something, his little collar tinkling. "Where're we going?" she said. "I'm so hungry I could pass out."

"Edna's in a terrible mood," Cheryl said. "She already snapped at me."

"We're tired, honey," I said. "So try to be nicer."

"She's never nice," Cheryl said.

"Run go get Little Duke," I said. "And hurry back."

"I guess *my* questions come last here, right?" Edna said.

I put my arm around her. "That's not true," I said.

"Did you find somebody over there in the trailers you'd rather stay with? You were gone long enough."

"That's not a thing to say," I said. "I was just trying to make things look right, so we don't get put in jail."

"So *you* don't, you mean," Edna said and laughed a little laugh I didn't like hearing.

"That's right. So I won't," I said. "I'd be the one in Dutch." I stared out at the big lighted assemblage of white buildings and white lights beyond the trailer community, plumes of white smokes escaping up into the heartless Wyoming sky, the whole company of buildings looking like some unbelievable castle, humming away in a distorted dream. "You know what all those buildings are there?" I said to Edna, who hadn't moved, and who didn't really seem to care if she ever moved anymore ever.

"No. But I can't say it matters, 'cause it isn't a motel and it isn't a restaurant," she said.

"It's a gold mine," I said, staring at the gold mine, which I knew now from walking to the trailer was a greater distance from us than it seemed, though it seemed huge and near up against the cold sky. I thought there should've been a wall around it with guards, instead of just the lights and no fence. It seemed as if anyone could go in and take what they wanted, just the way I had gone up to that woman's trailer and used the telephone, though that obviously wasn't true.

Edna began to laugh then. Not the mean laugh I didn't like, but a laugh that had something caring behind it, a full laugh that enjoyed a joke, a laugh she was laughing the first time I laid eyes on her in Missoula in the East Gate Bar in 1979, a laugh we used to laugh together when Cheryl was still with her mother, and I was working steady at the track and not stealing cars or passing bogus checks to merchants. A better time all around. And for some reason it made me laugh just hearing her, and we both stood there behind the cab in the dark laughing at the gold mine in the desert, me with my arm around her and Cheryl out rustling up Little Duke and the cab driver smoking in the cab, and our stolen Mercedes Benz that I had such hopes for in Florida, stuck up to its axle in sand where I'd never get to see it again.

"I always wondered what a gold mine would look like when I saw it," Edna said, still laughing, wiping a tear from her eye.

"Me too," I said. "I was always curious about it."

"We're a couple of fools, ain't we, Earl?" she said, unable to quit laughing completely. "We're two of a kind."

"It might be a good sign, though," I said.

"How could it be?" she said. "It's not our gold mine. There aren't any drive-up windows." She was still laughing.

"We've seen it," I said, pointing. "That's it right there. It may mean we're getting closer. Some people never see it at all."

"In a pig's eye, Earl," she said. "You and me see it in a pig's eye."

And she turned and got in the cab to go.

★

The cab driver didn't ask anything about our car or where it was, to mean he'd noticed something queer. All of which made me feel like we had made a clean break from the car and couldn't be connected with it until it was too late, if ever. The driver told us a lot about Rock Springs while he drove, that because of the gold mine a lot of people had moved there in just six months, people from all over including New York, and that most of them lived out in the trailers. Prostitutes from New York City who he called "B-girls" had come into town, he said, on the prosperity tide and Cadillacs with New York plates cruised the little streets every night full of Negroes with big hats who ran the women. He told us everybody who got in his cab now wanted to know where the women were, and that when he got our call he almost didn't come because some of the trailers were brothels operated by the mine for engineers and computer people away from home. He said he got tired of running back and forth out there just for vile business. He said that *Sixty Minutes* had even done a program about Rock Springs and that a blow-up had resulted in Cheyenne, though nothing could be done unless the prosperity left town. "It's prosperity's fruit," the driver said. "I'd rather be poor, which is lucky for me."

He said all the motels were sky high, but since we were a family he could show us a nice one that was affordable. But I told him we wanted a first-rate place where they took animals and the money didn't matter because we had had a hard day and wanted to finish on a high note. I also knew that it was in the little nowhere places that the police look for you and find you. People I'd known were always being arrested in cheap hotels and tourist courts with names you'd never heard of before. Never in Holiday Inns or Travel-Lodges.

I asked him to drive us to the middle of town and back out again so Cheryl could see the train station, and while we were there I saw a pink Cadillac with New York licenses and a TV aerial, being driven slowly by a Negro in a big hat, down a narrow street where there were just bars and a Chinese res-taurant. It was an odd sight, nothing you could ever expect.

"There's your pure criminal element," the cab driver said, and seemed sad. "I'm sorry for people like you to see a thing like that. We've got a nice town here, but there're some that wants to ruin it for everybody. There used to be a way to deal with trash and criminals, but those days are gone forever."

"You said it," Edna said.

"You shouldn't let it get *you* down," I said to the cab driver. "There's more of you than them. And there always will be. You're the best advertisement this town has. I know Cheryl will remember you and not *that* man, won't you honey?" But Cheryl was asleep by then, holding Little Duke in her arms on the taxi seat.

The driver took us to the Ramada Inn on the Interstate, not far from where we'd broken down. I had a small pain of regret as we drove under the Ramada awning, that we hadn't driven up in a cranberry-colored Mercedes, but instead in a beat-up old Chrysler taxi driven by an old man full of complaints. Though I knew it was for the best. We were better off without that car, better really in any other car but that one, where the signs had turned bad.

I registered in under another name and paid for the room in cash so there wouldn't be any questions. On the line where it said *representing* I wrote opthalmologist and put MD after the name. It had a nice look to it, even though it wasn't my name.

When we got to the room, which was on the back where I'd asked for it, I put Cheryl on one of the beds and Little Duke beside her so they'd sleep. She'd missed dinner, but it only meant she'd be hungry in the morning, when she could have anything she wanted. A few missed meals don't make a kid bad. I'd missed a lot of them myself and haven't turned out completely bad.

"Let's have some fried chicken," I said to Edna when she came out of the bathroom. "They have good fried chicken at the Ramadas, and I noticed the buffet was still up. Cheryl can stay right here, where it's safe, till we're back."

"I guess I'm not hungry anymore," Edna said. She stood at the window staring out into the dark. I could see out the window past her some yellowish foggy glow in the sky. For a moment I thought it was the gold mine out in the distance lighting the night, though it was only the Interstate.

"We could order up," I said. "Whatever you want. There's a menu on the phone book. You could just have a salad."

"You go ahead," she said. "I've lost my hungry spirit." She sat on the bed beside Cheryl and Little Duke, and looked at them in a sweet way and put her hand on Cheryl's cheek just as if she'd had a fever. "Sweet little girl," she said. "Everybody loves you."

"What do you want to do?" I said. "I'd like to eat. Maybe *I'll* order up some chicken."

"Why don't you do that?" she said. "It's your favorite." And she smiled at me from the bed.

I sat on the other bed and dialed room service. I asked for chicken, garden salad, potato and a roll, plus a piece of hot apple pie and iced tea. I realized I hadn't eaten all day. When I put down the phone I saw that Edna was watching me from the other bed, not in a hateful way or a loving way, just in a way that seemed to say she didn't understand something and was going to ask me about it.

"How did watching me get so entertaining?" I said, and smiled at her. I was trying to be friendly. I knew how tired she must be. It was after 9 o'clock.

"I was just thinking how much I hated being in a motel without a car that was mine to drive. Isn't that funny? I started feeling like that last night when that purple car wasn't mine. That purple car just gave me the willies, I guess, Earl."

"One of those cars *outside* is yours," I said. "Just stand right there and pick it out."

"I know," she said. "But that's different, isn't it?" She reached and got her blue Bailey hat, put it on her head, and set it way back like Dale Evans. She looked sweet. "I used to like to go to motels, you know," she said. "There's something secret about them and free – I was never paying, of course. But you felt safe from everything and free to do what you wanted because you'd made the decision to be here and paid that price, and all the rest was the good part. Fucking and everything, you know." She smiled at me in a good-natured way.

"Isn't that the way this is?" I said. I was sitting on the bed watching her, not knowing what to expect her to say next.

"I don't guess it is, Earl," she said and stared out the window. "I'm thirty-two and I'm going to have to give up on motels. I can't keep that fantasy going anymore."

"Don't you like this place?" I said and looked around at the room. I appreciated the modern paintings and the low-boy bureau and the big TV. It seemed like a plenty nice enough place to me, considering where we'd been already.

"No, I don't," Edna said with real conviction. "There's no use in my getting mad at you about it. It isn't your fault. You do the best you can for everybody. But every trip teaches you something. And I've learned I need to give up on motels before some bad thing happens to me. I'm sorry."

"What does that mean?" I said, because I really didn't know what she had in mind to do, though I should've guessed.

"I guess I'll take that ticket you mentioned," she said, and got up and faced the window. "Tomorrow's soon enough. We haven't got a car to take me anyhow."

"Well, that's a fine thing," I said, sitting on the bed, feeling like I was in a shock. I wanted to say something to her, to argue with her, but I couldn't think what to say that seemed right. I didn't want to be mad at her, but it made me mad.

"You've got a right to be mad at me, Earl," she said, "but I don't think you can really blame me." She turned around and faced me and sat on the window ledge, her hands on her knees. Someone knocked on the door. I just yelled for them to set the tray down and put it on the bill.

"I guess I *do* blame you," I said. I was angry. I thought about how I could have disappeared into the trailer community and hadn't, had come back to keep things going, had tried to take control of things for everybody when they looked bad.

"Don't. I wish you wouldn't," Edna said, and smiled at me like she wanted me to hug her. "Anybody ought to have their choice in things if they can. Don't you believe that, Earl? Here I am out here in the desert where I don't know anything, in a stolen car, in a motel room under an assumed name, with no money of my own, a kid that's not mine, and the law after me. And I have a choice to get out of all of it by getting on a bus. What would you do? I know exactly what you'd do."

"You think you do," I said. But I didn't want to get into an argument about it and tell her all I could've done and didn't do. Because it wouldn't have done any good. When you get to the point of arguing, you're past the point of changing anybody's mind, even though it's supposed to be the other way, and maybe for some classes of people it is, just never mine.

Edna smiled at me and came across the room and put her arms around me where I was sitting on the bed. Cheryl rolled over and looked at us and smiled, then closed her eyes, and the room was quiet. I was beginning to think of Rock Springs in the way I knew I would always think of it, a low-down city full of crimes and whores and disappointments, a place where a woman left me, instead of a place where I got things on the straight track once and for all, a place I saw a gold mine.

"Eat your chicken, Earl," Edna said. "Then we can go to bed. I'm tired, but I'd like to make love to you, anyway. None of this is a matter of not loving you, you know that."

Sometime late in the night after Edna was asleep, I got up and walked outside into the parking lot. It could've been any time because there was still the light from the Interstate frosting the low sky, and the big red Ramada sign humming motionlessly in the night and no light at all in the east to indicate it might be morning. The lot was full of cars all nosed-in, most of them with suitcases strapped to their roofs and their trunks weighed down with belongings the people were taking someplace, to a new home or a vacation resort in the mountains. I had laid in bed a long time after Edna was asleep, watching the Atlanta Braves on cable television, trying to get my mind off how I'd feel when I saw that bus pull away the next day, and how I'd feel when I turned around and there stood Cheryl and Little Duke and no one to see about them but me all alone, and that the first thing I had to do was get hold of some automobile and get the plates switched, then get them some breakfast and get us all on the road to Florida, all in the space of probably two hours, since that Mercedes would certainly look less hid in the daytime than the night, and word travels fast. I've always taken care of Cheryl myself, as long as I've had her with me. None of the women ever did, most of them didn't even seem to like her, though they took care of me in a way so that I could care for her. And I knew that once Edna left all that was going to get harder. Though what I wanted most to do was not think about it just for a little while, try to let my mind go limp so it could be strong for the rest of what there was. I thought that the difference between a successful life and an unsuccessful one, between me at that moment and all the people who owned the cars that were nosed-in to their proper places in the lot, maybe between me and that woman out in the trailers by the gold mine, was how well you were able to put things like this out of your mind and not be bothered by them, and maybe too, by how many troubles like this one you had to face in a lifetime. Through luck or design they had all faced fewer troubles, and by their own characters, they forgot them faster. And that's what I wanted for me. Fewer troubles, fewer memories of trouble.

I walked over to a car, a Pontiac with Ohio tags, one of the ones with bundles and suitcases strapped to the top and a lot more in the trunk, by the way it was riding. I looked inside the driver's window. There were maps and paperback books and sunglasses and the little plastic holders for cans that hang on the window wells. And in the back there were kid's toys and some pillows and a cat box with a cat sitting in it staring up at me like I was the face of the moon. It all looked familiar to me, the very same things I would have in my car if I had a car. Nothing seemed surprising, nothing different. Though I had a funny sensation at that moment and turned and looked up at the windows along the back of the Ramada Inn. All were dark except two. Mine and another one. And I wondered, because it seemed funny, what would you think a man was doing if you saw him in the middle of the night, looking in the windows of cars in the parking lot of the Ramada Inn? Would you think he was trying to get his head cleared? Would you think he was trying to get ready for a day when trouble would come to him? Would you think his girlfriend was leaving him? Would you think he had a daughter? Would you think he was anybody like you?

☆   ☆   ☆   ☆

# A Romantic Weekend

She was meeting a man she had recently and abruptly fallen in love with. She was in a state of ghastly anxiety. He was married, for one thing, to a Korean woman whom he described as the embodiment of all that was feminine and elegant. Not only that, but a psychic had told her that a relationship with him could cripple her emotionally for the rest of her life. On top of this, she was tormented by the feeling that she looked inadequate. Perhaps her body tilted too far forward as she walked, perhaps her jacket made her torso look bulky in contrast to her calves and ankles, which were probably skinny. She felt like an object unraveling in every direction. In anticipation of their meeting, she had not been able to sleep the night before; she had therefore eaten some amphetamines and these had heightened her feeling of disintegration.

When she arrived at the corner he wasn't there. She stood against a building, trying to arrange her body in the least repulsive configuration possible. Her discomfort mounted. She crossed the street and stood on the other corner. It seemed as though everyone who walked by was eating. A large, distracted businessman went by holding a half-eaten hot dog. Two girls passed, sharing cashews from a white bag. The eating added to her sense that the world was disorderly and unbeautiful. She became acutely aware of the garbage on the street. The wind stirred it; a candy wrapper waved forlornly from its trapped position in the mesh of a jammed public wastebasket. This was all wrong, all horrible. Her meeting with him should be perfect and scrap-free. She couldn't bear the thought of flapping trash. Why wasn't he there to meet her? Minutes passed. Her shoulders drew together.

She stepped into a flower store. The store was clean and

white, except for a few smudges on the linoleum floor. Homo-
sexuals with low voices stood behind the counter. Arranged
stalks bearing absurd blossoms protruded from sedate round
vases and bristled in the aisles. She had a paroxysm of fantasy.
He held her, helpless and swooning, in his arms. They were
supported by a soft ball of puffy blue stuff. Thornless roses
surrounded their heads. His gaze penetrated her so thoroughly,
it was as though he had thrust his hand into her chest and begun
feeling her ribs one by one. This was all right with her. "I have
never met anyone I felt this way about," he said. "I love you."
He made her do things she'd never done before, and then they
went for a walk and looked at the new tulips that were bound to
have grown up somewhere. None of this felt stupid or corny,
but she knew that it was. Miserably, she tried to gain a sense of
proportion. She stared at the flowers. They were an agony of
bright, organized beauty. She couldn't help it. She wanted to
give him flowers. She wanted to be with him in a room full of
flowers. She visualized herself standing in front of him, bearing
a handful of blameless flowers trapped in the ugly pastel paper
the florist would staple around them. The vision was brutally
embarrassing, too much so to stay in her mind for more than
seconds.

She stepped out of the flower store. He was not there. Her
anxiety approached despair. They were supposed to spend the
weekend together.

He stood in a cheap pizza stand across the street, eating a
greasy slice and watching her as she stood on the corner. Her
anxiety was visible to him. It was at once disconcerting and
weirdly attractive. Her appearance otherwise was not pleasing.
He couldn't quite put his finger on why this was. Perhaps it was
the suggestion of meekness in her dress, of a desire to be
inconspicuous, or worse, of plain thoughtlessness about how
clothes looked on her.

He had met her at a party during the previous week. She
immediately reminded him of a girl he had known years before,
Sharon, a painfully serious girl with a pale, gentle face whom he
had tormented off and on for two years before leaving for his
wife. Although it had gratified him enormously to leave her, he

had missed hurting her for years, and had been half-consciously looking for another woman with a similarly fatal combination of pride, weakness and a foolish lust for something resembling passion. On meeting Beth, he was astonished at how much she looked, talked and moved like his former victim. She was delicately morbid in all her gestures, sensitive, arrogant, vulnerable to flattery. She veered between extravagant outbursts of opinion and sudden, uncertain halts, during which she seemed to look to him for approval. She was in love with the idea of intelligence, and she overestimated her own. Her sense of the world, though she presented it aggressively, could be, he sensed, snatched out from under her with little or no trouble. She said, "I hope you are a savage."

He went home with her that night. He lay with her on her sagging, lumpy single mattress, tipping his head to blow smoke into the room. She butted her forehead against his chest. The mattress squeaked with every movement. He told her about Sharon. "I had a relationship like that when I was in college," she said. "Somebody opened me up in a way that I had no control over. He hurt me. He changed me completely. Now I can't have sex normally."

The room was pathetically decorated with postcards, pictures of huge-eyed Japanese cartoon characters, and tiny, maddening toys that she had obviously gone out of her way to find, displayed in a tightly arranged tumble on her dresser. A frail model airplane dangled from the light above her dresser. Next to it was a pasted-up cartoon of a pink-haired girl cringing open-mouthed before a spike-haired boy-villain in shorts and glasses. Her short skirt was blown up by the force of his threatening expression, and her panties showed. What kind of person would put crap like this up on her wall?

"I'm afraid of you," she murmured.

"Why?"

"Because I just am."

"Don't worry. I won't give you any more pain than you can handle."

She curled against him and squeezed her feet together like a stretching cat. Her socks were thick and ugly, and her feet were large for her size. Details like this could repel him, but he felt tenderly toward the long, grubby, squeezed-together feet. He said, "I want a slave."

She said, "I don't know. We'll see."

He asked her to spend the weekend with him three days later.

It had seemed like a good idea at the time, but now he felt an irritating combination of guilt and anxiety. He thought of his wife, making breakfast with her delicate, methodical movements, or in the bathroom, painstakingly applying kohl under her huge eyes, flicking away the excess with pretty, birdlike finger gestures, her thin elbows raised, her eyes blank with concentration. He thought of Beth, naked and bound, blindfolded and spread-eagled on the floor of her cluttered apartment. Her cartoon characters grinned as he beat her with a whip. Welts rose on her breasts, thighs, stomach and arms. She screamed and twisted, wrenching her neck from side to side. She was going to be scarred for life. He had another picture of her sitting across from him at a restaurant, very erect, one arm on the table, her face serious and intent. Her large glasses drew her face down, made it look somber and elegant. She was smoking a cigarette with slow, mournful intakes of breath. These images lay on top of one another, forming a hideously confusing grid. How was he going to sort them out? He managed to separate the picture of his wife and the original picture of blindfolded Beth and hold them apart. He imagined himself traveling happily between the two. Perhaps, as time went on, he could bring Beth home and have his wife beat her too. She would do the dishes and serve them dinner. The grid closed up again and his stomach went into a moil. The thing was complicated and potentially exhausting. He looked at the anxious girl on the corner. She had said that she wanted to be hurt, but he suspected that she didn't understand what that meant.

He should probably just stay in the pizza place and watch her until she went away. It might be entertaining to see how long she waited. He felt a certain pity for her. He also felt, from his glassed-in vantage point, as though he were torturing an insect. He gloated as he ate his pizza.

At the height of her anxiety she saw him through the glass wall of the pizza stand. She immediately noticed his gloating countenance. She recognized the coldly scornful element in his watching and waiting as opposed to greeting her. She suffered, but only for an instant; she was then smitten by love. She smiled and crossed the street with a senseless confidence in the power of her smile.

"I was about to come over," he said. "I had to eat first. I was starving." He folded the last of his pizza in half and stuck it in his mouth.

She noticed a piece of bright orange pizza stuck between his teeth, and it endeared him to her.

They left the pizza stand. He walked with wide steps, and his heavy black overcoat swung rakishly, she thought, above his boots. He was a slight, slender boy with a pale, narrow face and blond hair that wisped across one brow. In the big coat he looked like the young pet of a budding secret police force. She thought he was beautiful.

He hailed a cab and directed the driver to the airport. He looked at her sitting beside him. "This is going to be a disaster," he said. "I'll probably wind up leaving you there and coming back alone."

"I hope not," she said. "I don't have any money. If you left me there, I wouldn't be able to get back by myself."

"That's too bad. Because I might." He watched her face for a reaction. It showed discomfort and excitement and something that he could only qualify as foolishness, as if she had just dropped a tray full of glasses in public. "Don't worry, I wouldn't do that," he said. "But I like the idea that I could."

"So do I." She was terribly distressed. She wanted to throw her arms around him.

He thought: There is something wrong. Her passivity was pleasing, as was her silence and her willingness to place herself in his hands. But he sensed another element present in her that he could not define and did not like. Her tightly folded hands were nervous and repulsive. Her public posture was brittle, not pliant. There was a rigidity that if cracked would yield nothing. He was disconcerted to realize that he didn't know if he could crack it anyway. He began to feel uncomfortable. Perhaps the weekend would be a disaster.

They arrived at the airport an hour early. They went to a bar and drank. The bar was an open-ended cube with a red neon sign that said "Cocktails." There was no sense of shelter in it. The furniture was spindly and exposed, and there were no doors to protect you from the sight of dazed, unattractive passengers wandering through the airport with their luggage. She ordered a Bloody Mary.

"I can't believe you ordered that," he said.

"Why not?"

"Because I want a bloody Beth." He gave her a look that made her think of a neurotic dog with its tongue hanging out, waiting to bite someone.

"Oh," she said.

He offered her a cigarette.

"I don't smoke," she said. "I told you twice."

"Well, you should start."

They sat quietly and drank for several minutes.

"Do you like to look at people?" she asked.

She was clearly struggling to talk to him. He saw that her face had become very tense. He could've increased her discomfort, but for the moment he had lost the energy to do so. "Yes," he said. "I do."

They spent some moments regarding the people around them. They were short on material. There were only a few customers in the bar; most of them were men in suits who sat there seemingly enmeshed in a web of habit and accumulated rancor that they called their personalities, so utterly unaware of their entanglement that they clearly considered themselves men of the world, even though they had long ago stopped noticing it. Then a couple walked through the door, carrying luggage. The woman's bright skirt flashed with each step. The man walked ahead of her. He walked too fast for her to keep up. She looked harried. Her eyes were wide and dark and clotted with make-up; there was a mole on her chin. He paused, as though considering whether he would stop for a drink. He decided not to and strode again. Her earrings jiggled as she followed. They left a faint trail of sex and disappointment behind them.

Beth watched the woman's hips move under her skirt. "There was something unpleasant about them," she said.

"Yes, there was."

It cheered her to find this point of contact. "I'm sorry I'm not more talkative," she said.

"That's all right." His narrow eyes became feral once again. "Women should be quiet." It suddenly struck her that it would seem completely natural if he lunged forward and bit her face.

"I agree," she said sharply. "There aren't many men around worth talking to."

He was nonplussed by her peevish tone. Perhaps, he thought, he'd imagined it.

He hadn't.

They had more drinks on the plane. They were served a hunk of white-frosted raisin pastry in a red paper bag. He wasn't hungry, but the vulgar cake appealed to him so he stuck it in his baggage.

They had a brief discussion about shoes, from the point of view of expense and aesthetics. They talked about intelligence and art. There were large gaps of silence that were disheartening to both of them. She began talking about old people, and how nice they should be. He had a picture of her kneeling on the floor in black stockings and handcuffs. This picture became blurred, static-ridden, and then obscured by their conversation. He felt a ghastly sense of longing. He called back the picture, which no longer gave him any pleasure. He superimposed it upon a picture of himself standing in a nightclub the week before, holding a drink and talking to a rather combative girl who wanted his number.

"Some old people are beautiful in an unearthly way," she continued. "I saw this old lady in the drugstore the other day who must've been in her nineties. She was so fragile and pretty, she was like a little elf."

He looked at her and said, "Are you going to start being fun to be around or are you going to be a big drag?"

She didn't answer right away. She didn't see how this followed her comment about the old lady. "I don't know."

"I don't think you're very sexual," he said. "You're not the way I thought you were when I first met you."

She was so hurt by this that she had difficulty answering. Finally, she said, "I can be very sexual or very unsexual depending on who I'm with and in what situation. It has to be the right kind of thing. I'm sort of a cerebral person. I think I respond to things in a cerebral way, mostly."

"That's what I mean."

She was struck dumb with frustration. She had obviously disappointed him in some fundamental way, which she felt was completely due to misunderstanding. If only she could think of the correct thing to say, she was sure she could clear it up. The blue puffball thing unfurled itself before her with sickening power. It was the same image of him holding her and gazing into her eyes with bone-dislodging intent, thinly veiling the many shattering events that she anticipated between them. The prospect made her disoriented with pleasure. The only problem was, this image seemed to have no connection with what was happening now. She tried to think back to the time they had spent in her apartment, when he had held her and said, "You're cute." What had happened between then and now to so disappoint him?

She hadn't yet noticed how much he had disappointed her.

He couldn't tell if he was disappointing her or not. She completely mystified him, especially after her abrupt speech on cerebralism. It was now impossible to even have a clear picture of what he wanted to do to this unglamorous creature, who looked as though she bit her nails and read books at night. Dim, half-formed pictures of his wife, Sharon, Beth and a sixteen-year-old Chinese hooker he'd seen a month before crawled aimlessly over each other. He sat and brooded in a bad-natured and slightly drunken way.

She sat next to him, diminished and fretful, with idiot radio songs about sex in her head.

★

They were staying in his grandmother's deserted apartment in Washington, DC. The complex was a series of building blocks seemingly arranged at random, stuck together and painted the least attractive colors available. It was surrounded by bright green grass and a circular driveway, and placed on a quiet highway that led into the city. There was a drive-in bank and an insurance office next to it. It was enveloped in the steady, continuous noise of cars driving by at roughly the same speed.

"This is a horrible building," she said as they traveled up in the elevator.

The door slid open and they walked down a hall carpeted with dense brown nylon. The grandmother's apartment opened before them. Beth found the refrigerator and opened it. There was a crumpled package of French bread, a jar of hot peppers, several lumps covered with aluminum foil, two bottles of wine and a six-pack. "Is your grandmother an alcoholic?" she asked.

"I don't know." He dropped his heavy leather bag and her white canvas one in the living room, took off his coat and threw it on the bags. She watched him standing there, pale and gaunt in a black leather shirt tied at his waist with a leather belt. That image of him would stay with her for years for no good reason and with no emotional significance. He dropped into a chair, his thin arms flopping lightly on its arms. He nodded at the tray of whiskey, Scotch and liqueurs on the coffee table before him. "Why don't you make yourself a drink?"

She dropped to her knees beside the table and nervously played with the bottles. He was watching her quietly, his expression hooded. She plucked a bottle of thick chocolate liqueur from the cluster, poured herself a glass and sat in the chair across from his with both hands around it. She could no longer ignore the character of the apartment. It was brutally ridiculous, almost sadistic in its absurdity. The couch and chairs were covered with a floral print. A thin maize carpet zipped across the floor. There were throw rugs. There were artificial flowers. There was an abundance of small tables and shelves housing a legion of figures; grinning glass maidens in sumptuous gowns bore baskets of glass roses, ceramic birds warbled from the ceramic stumps they clung to, glass horses galloped across teakwood pastures. A ceramic weather poodle and his diamond-eyed kitty-cat companions silently watched the silent scene in the room.

"Are you all right?" he asked.

"I hate this apartment. It's really awful."

"What were you expecting? Jesus Christ. It's a lot like yours, you know."

"Yes. That's true, I have to admit." She drank her liqueur.

"Do you think you could improve your attitude about this whole thing? You might try being a little more positive."

Coming from him, this question was preposterous. He must be so pathologically insecure that his perception of his own behavior was thoroughly distorted. He saw rejection everywhere, she decided; she must reassure him. "But I do feel positive about being here," she said. She paused, searching for the best way to express the extremity of her positive feelings. She invisibly implored him to see and mount their blue puffball bed. "It would be impossible for you to disappoint me. The whole idea of you makes me happy. Anything you do will be all right."

Her generosity unnerved him. He wondered if she realized what she was saying. "Does anybody know you're here?" he asked. "Did you tell anyone where you were going?"

"No." She had in fact told several people.

"That wasn't very smart."

"Why not?"

"You don't know me at all. Anything could happen to you."

She put her glass on the coffee table, crossed the floor and dropped to her knees between his legs. She threw her arms around his thighs. She nuzzled his groin with her nose. He tightened. She unzipped his pants. "Stop," he said. "Wait." She took his shoulders — she had a surprisingly strong grip — and pulled him to the carpet. His hovering brood of images and plans was suddenly upended, as though it had been sitting on a table that a rampaging crazy person had flipped over. He felt assaulted and invaded. This was not what he had in mind, but to refuse would make him seem somehow less virile than she. Queasily, he stripped off her clothes and put their bodies in a viable position. He fastened his teeth on her breast and bit her. She made a surprised noise and her body stiffened. He bit her again, harder. She screamed. He wanted to draw blood. Her screams were short and stifled. He could tell that she was trying to like being bitten, but that she did not. He gnawed her breast. She screamed sharply. They screwed. They broke apart and regarded each other warily. She put her hand on his tentatively. He realized what had been disturbing him about her. With other women whom he had been with in similar situations, he had experienced a relaxing sense of emptiness within them that had made it easy for him to get inside them and, once there, smear himself all over their innermost territory until it was no longer theirs but his. His wife did not have this empty quality, yet the gracious way in which she emptied herself for him made her submission, as far as it went, all the more poignant. This exasperating girl, on the other hand, contained a tangible some-thingness that she not only refused to expunge, but that seemed to willfully expand itself so that he banged into it with every attempt to invade her. He didn't mind the somethingness; he rather liked it, in fact, and had looked forward to seeing it demolished. But she refused to let him do it. Why had she told him she was a masochist? He looked at her body. Her limbs were muscular and alert. He considered taking her by the neck and bashing her head against the floor.

He stood abruptly. "I want to get something to eat. I'm starving."

She put her hand on his ankle. Her desire to abase herself had been completely frustrated. She had pulled him to the rug certain that if only they could fuck, he would enter her with overwhelming force and take complete control of her. Instead she had barely felt him, and what she had felt was remote and cold. Somewhere on her exterior he'd been doing some biting thing that meant nothing to her and was quite unpleasant. Despairing, she held his ankle tighter and put her forehead on the carpet. At least she could stay at his feet, worshipping. He twisted free and walked away. "Come on," he said.

The car was in the parking lot. It was because of the car that this weekend had come about. It was his wife's car, an expensive thing that her ex-husband had given her. It had been in Washington for over a year; he was here to retrieve it and drive it back to New York.

Beth was appalled by the car. It was a loud yellow monster with a narrow, vicious shape and absurd doors that snapped up from the roof and out like wings. In another setting it might have seemed glamorous, but here, behind this equally monstrous building, in her unsatisfactory clothing, the idea of sitting in it with him struck her as comparable to putting on a clown nose and wearing it to dinner.

They drove down a suburban highway lined with small businesses, malls and restaurants. It was twilight; several neon signs blinked consolingly.

"Do you think you could make some effort to change your mood?" he said.

"I'm not in a bad mood," she said wearily. "I just feel blank."

Not blank enough, he thought.

He pulled into a Roy Rogers fast food cafeteria. She thought: He is not even going to take me to a nice place. She was insulted. It seemed as though he was insulting her on purpose. The idea was incredible to her.

She walked through the line with him, but did not take any of the shiny dishes of food displayed on the fluorescent-lit aluminum shelves. He felt a pang of worry. He was no longer angry, and her drawn white face disturbed him.

"Why aren't you eating?"

"I'm not hungry."

They sat down. He picked at his food, eyeing her with veiled alarm. It occurred to her that it might embarrass him to eat in front of her while she ate nothing. She asked if she could have some of his salad. He eagerly passed her the entire bowl of pale leaves strewn with orange dressing. "Have it all."

He huddled his shoulders orphanlike as he ate; his blond hair stood tangled like pensive weeds. "I don't know why you're not eating," he said fretfully. "You're going to be hungry later on."

Her predisposition to adore him was provoked. She smiled.

"Why are you staring at me like that?" he asked.

"I'm just enjoying the way you look. You're very airy."

Again, his eyes showed alarm.

"Sometimes when I look at you, I feel like I'm seeing a tank of small, quick fish, the bright darting kind that go every which way."

He paused, stunned and dangle-forked over his pinched, curled-up steak. "I'm beginning to think you're out of your fucking mind."

Her happy expression collapsed.

"Why can't you talk to me in a half-normal fucking way?" he continued. "Like the way we talked on the plane. I liked that. That was a conversation." In fact, he hadn't liked the conversation on the plane either, but compared to this one, it seemed quite all right.

When they got back to the apartment, they sat on the floor and drank more alcohol. "I want you to drink a lot," he said. "I want to make you do things you don't want to do."

"But I won't do anything I don't want to do. You have to make me want it."

He lay on his back in silent frustration.

"What are your parents like?" she asked.

"What?"

"Your parents. What are they like?"

"I don't know. I don't have that much to do with them. My mother is nice. My father's a prick. That's what they're like." He put one hand over his face; a square-shaped album-style view of his family presented itself. They were all at the breakfast table, talking and reaching for things. His mother moved in the background, a slim, worried shadow in her pink robe. His sister sat next to him, tall, blond and arrogant, talking and flicking at toast crumbs in the corners of her mouth. His father sat at the head of the table, his big arms spread over everything, leaning over his plate as if he had to defend it, gnawing his breakfast. He felt unhappy and then angry. He thought of a little Italian girl he had met in a go-go bar a while back, and comforted himself with the memory of her slim haunches and pretty high-heeled feet on either side of his head as she squatted over him.

"It seems that way with my parents when you first look at them. But in fact my mother is much more aggressive and, I would say, more cruel than my father, even though she's more passive and soft on the surface."

She began a lengthy and, in his view, incredible and unnecessary history of her family life, including descriptions of her brother and sister. Her entire family seemed to have a collectively disturbed personality characterized by long brooding silences, unpleasing compulsive sloppiness (unflushed toilets, used Kleenex abandoned everywhere, dirty underwear on the floor) and outbursts of irrational, violent anger. It was horrible. He wanted to go home.

He poked himself up on his elbows. "Are you a liar?" he asked. "Do you lie often?"

She stopped in midsentence and looked at him. She seemed to consider the question earnestly. "No," she said. "Not really. I mean, I can lie, but I usually don't about important things. Why do you ask?"

"Why did you tell me you were a masochist?"

"What makes you think I'm not?"

"You don't act like one."

"Well, I don't know how you can say that. You hardly know me. We've hardly done anything yet."

"What do you want to do?"

"I can't just come out and tell you. It would ruin it."

He picked up his cigarette lighter and flicked it, picked up her shirt and stuck the lighter underneath. She didn't move fast enough. She screamed and leapt to her feet.

"Don't do that! That's awful!"

He rolled over on his stomach. "See. I told you. You're not a masochist."

"Shit! That wasn't erotic in the least. I don't come when I stub my toe either."

In the ensuing silence it occurred to her that she was angry, and had been for some time.

"I'm tired," she said. "I want to go to bed." She walked out of the room.

He sat up. "Well, we're making decisions, aren't we?"

She re-entered the room. "Where are we supposed to sleep, anyway?"

He showed her the guest room and the fold-out couch. She immediately began dismantling the couch with stiff, angry movements. Her body seemed full of unnatural energy and purpose. She had, he decided, ruined the weekend, not only for him but for herself. Her willfull, masculine, stupid something-ness had obstructed their mutual pleasure and satisfaction. The only course of action left was hostility. He opened his grand-mother's writing desk and took out a piece of paper and a Magic Marker. He wrote the word "stupid" in thick black letters. He held it first near her chest, like a placard, and then above her crotch. She ignored him.

"Where are the sheets?" she asked.

"How'd you get so tough all of a sudden?" He threw the paper on the desk and took a sheet from a dresser drawer.

"We'll need a blanket too, if we open the window. And I want to open the window."

He regarded her sarcastically. "You're just keeping yourself from getting what you want by acting like this."

"You obviously don't know what I want."

They got undressed. He contemptuously took in the muscu-lar, energetic look of her body. She looked more like a boy than a girl, in spite of her pronounced hips and round breasts. Her short, spiky red hair was more than enough to render her masculine. Even the dark bruise he had inflicted on her breast and the slight burn from his lighter failed to lend her a more feminine quality.

She opened the window. They got under the blanket on the fold-out couch and lay there, not touching, as though they really were about to sleep. Of course, neither one of them could.

"Why is this happening?" she asked.

"You tell me."

"I don't know. I really don't know." Her voice was small and pathetic.

"Part of it is that you don't talk when you should, and then you talk too much when you shouldn't be saying anything at all."

In confusion, she reviewed the various moments they had spent together, trying to classify them in terms of whether or not it had been appropriate to speak, and to rate her performance accordingly. Her confusion increased. Tears floated on her eyes. She curled her body against his.

"You're hurting my feelings," she said, "but I don't think you're doing it on purpose."

He was briefly touched. "Accidental pain," he said musingly. He took her head in both hands and pushed it between his legs. She opened her mouth compliantly. He had hurt her after all, he reflected. She was confused and exhausted, and at this instant, anyway, she was doing what he wanted her to do. Still, it wasn't enough. He released her and she moved upward to lie on top of him, resting her head on his shoulder. She spoke dreamily. "I would do anything with you."

"You would not. You would be disgusted."

"Disgusted by what?"

"You would be disgusted if I even told you."

She rolled away from him. "It's probably nothing."

"Have you ever been pissed on?"

He gloated as he felt her body tighten.

"No."

"Well, that's what I want to do to you."

"On your grandmother's rug?"

"I want you to drink it. If any got on the rug, you'd clean it up."

"Oh."

"I knew you'd be shocked."

"I'm not. I just never wanted to do it."

"So? That isn't any good to me."

In fact, she was shocked. Then she was humiliated, and not in the way she had planned. Her seductive puffball cloud deflated with a flaccid hiss, leaving two drunken, bad-tempered, incompetent, malodorous people blinking and uncomfortable on its remains. She stared at the ugly roses with their heads collapsed in a dead wilt and slowly saw what a jerk she'd been. Then she got mad.

"Do you like people to piss on you?" she asked.

"Yeah. Last month I met this great girl at Billy's Topless. She pissed in my face for only 20 bucks."

His voice was high-pitched and stupidly aggressive, like some weird kid who would walk up to you on the street and offer to take care of your sexual needs. How, she thought miserably, could she have mistaken this hostile moron for the dark, brooding hero who would crush her like an insect and then talk about life and art?

"There's a lot of other things I'd like to do too," he said with odd self-righteousness. "But I don't think you could handle it."

"It's not a question of handling it." She said these last two words very sarcastically. "So far everything you've said to me has been incredibly banal. You haven't presented anything in a way that's even remotely attractive." She sounded like a prim, prematurely adult child complaining to her teacher about someone putting a worm down her back.

He felt like an idiot. How had he gotten stuck with this prissy, reedy-voiced thing with a huge forehead who poked and picked over everything that came out of his mouth? He longed for a dim-eyed little slut with a big, bright mouth and black vinyl underwear. What had he had in mind when he brought this girl here, anyway? Her serious, desperate face, panicked and tear-stained. Her ridiculous air of sacrifice and abandonment as he spread-eagled and bound her. White skin that marked easily. Frightened eyes. An exposed personality that could be yanked from her and held out of reach like . . . oh, he could see it only in scraps; his imagination fumbled and lost its grip. He looked at her hatefully self-possessed, compact little form. He pushed her roughly. "Oh, I'd do anything with you," he mimicked. "You would not."

She rolled away on her side, her body curled tightly. He felt her trembling. She sniffed.

"Don't tell me I've broken your heart."

She continued crying.

"This isn't bothering me at all," he said. "In fact, I'm rather enjoying it."

The trembling stopped. She sniffed once, turned on her back and looked at him with puzzled eyes. She blinked. He suddenly felt tired. I shouldn't be doing this, he thought. She is actually a nice person. For a moment he had an impulse to embrace her. He had a stronger impulse to beat her. He looked around the room until he saw a light wood stick that his grandmother had for some reason left standing in the corner. He pointed at it.

"Get me that stick. I want to beat you with it."

"I don't want to."

"Get it. I want to humiliate you even more."

She shook her head, her eyes wide with alarm. She held the blanket up to her chin.

"Come on," he coaxed. "Let me beat you. I'd be much nicer after I beat you."

"I don't think you're capable of being as nice as you'd have to be to interest me at this point."

"All right. I'll get it myself." He got the stick and snatched the blanket from her body.

She sat, her legs curled in a kneeling position. "Don't," she said. "I'm scared."

"You should be scared," he said. "I'm going to torture you." He brandished the stick, which actually felt as though it would break on the second or third blow. They froze in their positions, staring at each other.

She was the first to drop her eyes. She regarded the torn-off blanket meditatively. "You have really disappointed me," she said. "This whole thing has been a complete waste of time."

He sat on the bed, stick in lap. "You don't care about my feelings."

"I think I want to sleep in the next room."

They couldn't sleep separately any better than they could sleep together. She lay curled up on the couch pondering what seemed to be the ugly nature of her life. He lay wound in a blanket, blinking in the dark, as a dislocated, manic and unpleasing revue of his sexual experiences stumbled through his memory in a queasy scramble.

In the morning they agreed that they would return to Manhattan immediately. Despite their mutual ill humor, they fornicated again, mostly because they could more easily ignore each other while doing so.

They packed quickly and silently.

"It's going to be a long drive back," he said. "Try not to make me feel like too much of a prick, okay?"

"I don't care what you feel like."

He would have liked to dump her at the side of the road somewhere, but he wasn't indifferent enough to societal rules to do that. Besides, he felt vaguely sorry that he had made her cry, and while this made him view her grudgingly, he felt obliged not to worsen the situation. Ideally she would disappear, taking her stupid canvas bag with her. In reality, she sat beside him in the car with more solidity and presence than she had displayed since they met on the corner in Manhattan. She seemed fully prepared to sit in silence for the entire six-hour drive. He turned on the radio.

"Would you mind turning that down a little?"

"Anything for you."

She rolled her eyes.

Without much hope, he employed a tactic he used to pacify his wife when they argued. He would give her a choice and let her make it. "Would you like something to eat?" he asked. "You must be starving."

She was. They spent almost an hour driving up and down the available streets trying to find a restaurant she wanted to be in. She finally chose a small, clean egg-and toast place. Her humor visibly improved as they sat before their breakfast. "I like eggs," she said. "They are so comforting."

He began to talk to her out of sheer curiosity. They talked about music, college, people they knew in common and drugs they used to take as teenagers. She said that when she had taken LSD, she had often lost her sense of identity so completely that she didn't recognize herself in the mirror. This pathetic statement brought back her attractiveness in a terrific rush. She noted the quick dark gleam in his eyes.

"You should've let me beat you," he said. "I wouldn't have hurt you too much."

"That's not the point. The moment was wrong. It wouldn't have meant anything."

"It would've meant something to me." He paused. "But you probably would've spoilt it. You would've started screaming right away and made me stop."

The construction workers at the next table stared at them quizzically. She smiled pleasantly at them and returned her gaze to him. "You don't know that."

He was so relieved at the ease between them that he put his arm around her as they left the restaurant. She stretched up and kissed his neck.

"We just had the wrong idea about each other," she said. "It's nobody's fault that we're incompatible."

"Well, soon we'll be in Manhattan, and it'll be all over. You'll never have to see me again." He hoped she would dispute this, but she didn't.

They continued to talk in the car, about the nature of time, their parents and the injustice of racism.

She was too exhausted to extract much from the pedestrian conversation, but the sound of his voice, the position of his body and his sudden receptivity were intoxicating. Time took on a grainy, dreamy aspect that made impossible conversations and unlikely gestures feasible, like a space capsule that enables its inhabitants to happily walk up the wall. The peculiar little car became a warm, humming cocoon, like a miniature house she had, as a little girl, assembled out of odds and ends for invented characters. She felt as if she were a very young child, when every notion that appeared in her head was new and naked of association and thus needed to be expressed carefully so it didn't become malformed. She wanted to set every one of them before him in a row, as she had once presented crayon drawings to her father in a neat many-colored sequence. Then he would shift his posture slightly or make a gesture that suddenly made him seem so helpless and frail that she longed to protect him and cosset him away, like a delicate pet in a matchbox filled with cotton. She rested her head on his shoulder and lovingly regarded the legs that bent at the knee and tapered to the booted feet resting on the brakes or the accelerator. This was as good as her original fantasy, possibly even better.

"Can I abuse you some more now?" he asked sweetly. "In the car?"

"What do you want to do?"

"Gag you? That's all, I'd just like to gag you."

"But I want to talk to you."

He sighed. "You're really not a masochist, you know."

She shrugged. "Maybe not. It always seemed like I was."

"You might have fantasies, but I don't think you have any concept of a real slave mentality. You have too much ego to be part of another person."

"I don't know, I've never had the chance to try it. I've never met anyone I wanted to do that with."

"If you were a slave, you wouldn't make the choice."

"All right, I'm not a slave. With me it's more a matter of love." She was just barely aware that she was pitching her voice higher and softer than it was naturally, so that she sounded like a cartoon girl. "It's like the highest form of love."

He thought this was really cute. Sure it was nauseating, but it was feminine in a radio-song kind of way.

"You don't seem interested in love. It's not about that for you."

"That's not true. That's not true at all. Why do you think I was so rough back there? Deep down, I'm afraid I'll fall in love with you, that I'll need to be with you and fuck you . . . forever." He was enjoying himself now. He was beginning to see her as a locked garden that he could sneak into and sit in for days, tearing the heads off the flowers.

On one hand, she was beside herself with bliss. On the other, she was scrutinizing him carefully from behind an opaque façade as he entered her pasteboard scene of flora and fauna. Could he function as a character in this landscape? She imagined sitting across from him in a Japanese restaurant, talking about anything. He would look intently into her eyes . . .

He saw her apartment and then his. He saw them existing a nice distance apart, each of them blocked off by cleanly cut boundaries. Her apartment bloomed with scenes that spiraled toward him in colorful circular motions and then froze suddenly and clearly in place. She was crawling blindfolded across the floor. She was bound and naked in an S&M bar. She was sitting next to him in a taxi, her skirt pulled up, his fingers in her vagina.

. . . and then they would go back to her apartment. He would beat her and fuck her mouth.

Then he would go home to his wife, and she would make dinner for him. It was so well balanced, the mere contemplation of it gave him pleasure.

The next day he would send her flowers.

He let go of the wheel with one hand and patted her head. She gripped his shirt frantically.

He thought: This could work out fine.

ALLAN GURGANUS

☆　☆　☆　☆

# *Minor Heroism*

## Something About My Father

*For William Maxwell*

## 1. AT WAR, AT HOME

Imagine him in his prime. A fairly rich and large-eared farm boy newly cured of being a farm boy by what he called Th' War, meaning the second one. He'd signed up in Charlottesville when most of his fraternity had done it as a group, and up till then he had been somewhat humorlessly typical. He had been hung up with the rest of them in the fraternity of the university that Jefferson designed, and he was as lean and carefully prepared as all the very best Virginia hams. And it would seem to follow that, in 1942, my father began being made more valuable by several years of smoke. But this smoke was not the curative Virginia kind; it was the high-flying smoke of German cities burning. My father was a bombardier. He became a minor hero in the Second World War and a major hero in Virginia/Carolina. He was photographed as Betty Grable stood on tiptoe to kiss him. He was tall. He still is. But his height meant most when he was dressed as an officer in our Army Air Corps. Today, in civvies, he is just another mildly handsome businessman. It was in uniform that Father looked most like himself.

Heroes should have looks. His were better than most, better than wholesome. It was one of those faces that fit handsomely into photographs and under a brimmed cap. It seemed to know in every pose that captions would be under it eventually. His profile, nearly as good as a Barrymore's, was better for being blunted slightly by boarding-school boxing. With very combed

blond hair waving back in the way hair did then, his was a face
that even from the front told much about itself in silhouette.
Many of the photos still exist.

When I was a child in the years just after that war, people
cornered me with accounts of my father's valor. They told me in
front of other children how, though everybody's father had
certainly helped with it, mine had done more than most to insure
that the Nazi plot to rule the world – to rule the very ground on
which this birthday party was now taking place – had been
crushed by the Americans. They mentioned the Freedoms, four
in all, and promised that the whole white world was now capable
of worshiping in whichever ways it chose. They said to me, "Do
you know what your father did?" I was told how people had
printed "Welcome Richard!" on broad banners made of sheets
that stretched all the way across Main Street.

But before the war was won and he came home, there was
the business about what they made my grandmother do. Though
bossy when alone with family, she was a remarkably shy woman,
even for then. In North Carolina, in 1942, shyness was less
unusual than it is today. Both parents' families had been equally
distinguished and austere, and, as if to commemorate this, she
parted her hair impartially down the middle and most always
wore the same rare brooch at the exact center of her collar and
throat. I once saw her hiding in the dark back hallway of her
house; eyes opened very wide, she stood against a wall, as
unwanted guests on the front porch repeatedly rang the door
chimes.

She had been reared at home with her three sisters, on a
Raleigh side street in a house cool most of the year with the
amount of marble in it: veined tabletops, hearths arched and
white as tombs, classical statuary, athletic and luminous in dark
corners. The marble hearths and statues floated upright in the
house's murk. Tabletops rode the gloom like oval rafts. It seemed
the marble objects were the rooms' true residents, directing every
household current into eddies split around themselves and cool-
ing off whatever drifted past them.

But Grandmother's wish for the stillness of 1909 was inap-
propriate in 1942. There was a war going on and her son, they

told her, was crucial to the local view of it. They put much unnecessary pressure on a lady so easily swayed. All it took was one unscrupulous question about how much patriotism she really felt as, after all, a longtime member of the DAR. At this, she said that yes, yes, she would do it, but only if they did not ask her to speak. Of course, those present assured her, she wouldn't have to utter one syllable she didn't rightly feel she could or should utter. But no one believed she would stay silent once she got up there and got the feel of it from all the bunting hung around. They forced her, in this way, to sit on public platforms. When the speaker selling war bonds acknowledged her, seated there as formal as her central brooch, she winced in recognition of her name and nodded back to him and tried to smile out at the audience like a mother, but she looked like a potentially bereaved one.

Mrs. Roosevelt herself came through on a decorated train and got off and walked over to the platform they'd set up outside the station, and not even then would my grandmother speak a public sentence to those gathered on the street and hanging out the windows of the Bank and those who dangled legs like extra letters over the sign usually spelling Ekstein's Finer Men's Apparel. Suspended from four lampposts were giant photos of my father in uniform, in profile. When Mrs. Roosevelt came over as the ceremony ended and said how handsome my father must be, to judge from his pictures over there, my grandmother finally spoke. She was nodding and thanking Eleanor Roosevelt as an equal when she noticed Mrs. Roosevelt wore no hat, which seemed odd in one of her station. What she was wearing, its weight tugging at the fabric of one shoulder, was a huge pale, wide-mouthed orchid which, some suggested afterwards, had looked much like her.

But Mrs. Roosevelt had won them over nonetheless, and it was lucky that others overheard what she said to Grandmother about my father's good looks. Grandmother would never have repeated it to anyone. Though she acknowledged things graciously, she never started them. In this way, she had become an adult and then a wife and, quite soon after that, a mother. Some were annoyed by this belief of hers that silence was always

in good taste, but most people felt it was probably fine the way
she was; that somehow it was more patriotic for a wife and
mother not to say too much – except, of course, for Mrs.
Roosevelt, and some people even felt that way about Mrs.
Roosevelt.

The photograph of Betty Grable kissing my father's flat cheek
seemed to hold the house up. I was born in 1947 and, as far as I
knew, it had always been there. People who did not come often
to the house would sometimes ask to see it. They were led back
to the den, where it was hung with the medals. Smiling, they
stooped to get the picture window's reflection off of it, and
they'd shake their heads and nod appreciatively. I remember
someone's saying that when you were young during a war it is
hard to know later if you liked being young during a war or
liked just being young or maybe even the war itself, who knows?
     In the picture, he does not return her kiss but stands there; a
statuesque soldier, newly decorated for minor heroism, accepts
the homage of a distant voluptuous country. He is enjoying it
probably, but he does not smile, for at that moment the fate of
the Western world as we now know it still hung in the balance.
But Betty Grable could smile. It was all right if she did, and the
official Army photographer, whose job it was to photograph the
wake of morale she left behind, snapped an Army camera, and
there it was – on most front pages in either Carolina and with
practically the whole page to itself in our local *Falls Herald
Traveler*. And though manliness and the national moment for-
bade he show it, yes, certainly my father was enjoying the kiss
synchronized with flashbulbs, just as local boys too young to go
themselves were not too young to go at themselves several times
a day upon finding this hometown representative in a favorite
national fantasy with a Grable whose legs were here not even
photographed to advantage, though the boys knew them well
enough from other pictures. The local boys looked over at the
grainy photograph they'd cut out and pinned up to the wallpaper
beside their beds, and for a while there, several times a day, any
number of them were replacing my father in his uniform, with
Grable breathing right there beside them in her WAC's outfit

shortened way beyond regulations. And after the ceremony, as the dots of flashbulbs were still dying out of their vision, there the boys were, there he was, the local high-school valedictorian, in the south of England, wearing my father's uniform and medals and walking across a muddy camp with Grable on his arm. He was looking down at her little WAC's cap pinned to the blond hair swept up on top. Pulling back the tent flap, she goes in first; he waits, takes a few more drags from the Camel he is smoking, then flips it smoothly into a nearby puddle and goes in himself. She is right there, patriotically spread-eagled on the tent floor, waiting for more minor heroism. In the flexed nostrils of the class valedictorian, the stink of weatherproofed canvas combines with the scent of Betty Grable's own perfume, a perfume that all the factories at home are working overtime to make available for her to bolster soldiers' morale, perfume that all the smokestacks smoke for hours to make one ounce of, perfume that all the factory girls at home helped make with skilled fingers, factory girls waiting up in their little rooms for men, disheveled healthy girls with their own skilled factory hands working up themselves with thoughts of soldierhood and regulation bayoneting and, oh, how crucial my own father was to local high-school boys behind closed doors in the early spring of 1945.

But when I was eight years old, some adult would take me aside and say, "Bryan, do you know what your father did before you were even born? Has he told you about what he did?" I said I didn't know for sure but that they used to paint little German planes on their bombers every time they shot a real one down, and my daddy's score was very high. They said no, not that. Not exactly. It was Dresden, the terrible and decisive firebombing of Dresden, that had been his real moment.

I nodded and always imagined a city of plate and saucer monuments and crockery apartments and wartime's smoking smokestacks made of stacked white bottomless coffee cups. And in the center of the shining city was an oil depot, looking very like a soup tureen of Mother's – a white one too large for just us to use but brought out for dinner parties and reunions and once, I remembered, filled with vegetable alphabet soup. I'd stood, amazed to see the very spindly alphabet I was then learning to draw between blue lines fattened up and floating on the top of something I and all my family, even my illiterate younger brother, could drink down like reading. But the tureen I imagined there in Dresden was a million gallons high and filled to the top with the crudest, blackest German oil that fueled the deadly U-boats. A remarkable target for my father in his clear air over the heart of gleaming Dresden. In my conception, the black bomb wobbles toward the very shadow of it growing on the glossy upper disc of all those gallons. The life-sized shadow meets the real bomb falling in and going off down at the very bottom. Such beautiful war-movie slow motion now allows a perfect view of all the damage as the tank pops jaggedly open and out the gallons gush into the tranquil city. Black oil gluts the sewers of the sanitation system. The overflow is fingering up and out into the gutters and makes a black street map of the white municipality. Borne alone in the dark gloss are clusters of diced carrots and chopped celery from my mother's kitchen, and there come the fat paste letters of the alphabet, movable type sucked down with the black into the gasping manholes. The level rises – filling, incidentally, the holes, which are the handles of the chaste white coffee cups. Darkness crawls about and then above the town and finally defines a surface that a cup or saucer may float along on briefly, till tilting, then filling viscously, they sink in, one by one, until they all are underneath. Now everything is underneath. All the quaintness of Germany, all the cuckoo clocks are under, all the perfect German sheet music played by countless amateurs on Sundays, and, worst for me, all the inedible lost letters of my mother's English alphabet have become one glossy black deluge which now shows just the tiny moving shadow of my father's bomber, speeding back to England, back to the USO show, which will not begin till he is there in a seat being saved for him.

The photographers are smoking at the airport now; they are awaiting him. They are men also in the Army. Their job is to photograph the bombardiers like my handsome father, crawling from the cockpit, less exerted than excited by the damage he has done, looking clean and highly combed as when he left some hours ago.

But by the time I was imagining the bombing of Dresden, my father was done with all that. The war had been won. Dresden's place setting was being sorted out. With Germany having an Occupation forced upon it, it was time my father settled into a job himself. His fading local glamor at least proved useful in helping him choose a career. Cashing in on people's memories of him, he became an insurance salesman. It was not hard, selling insurance, and with his law degree, with the certificates Grandfather had given him, with the smattering of rents collected from the colored-tenant houses – the only remnants of Grandmother's "fortune" – Father felt he could more than make do. He married a clever girl he'd met at a deb party before the war. He brought her south from Richmond and carried her into a 30,000-dollar house already paid for in advance by his cashing in certificates in companies making aluminum and small-screened televisions – all companies on the brink of booming when he sold their stocks. But though he was without much business sense, still there was the 30,000-dollar house, much larger than what one could buy oneself today for that amount of money. So my father and my mother moved into a house that echoed slightly because it had more rooms than furniture. Sometimes the guest room was occupied by a recurrent itinerant aunt; but when she was gone the doors were closed, the heating ducts turned off, and three bedrooms, now accommodating only boxes full of unused wedding gifts, again stood very vacant.

My father still wrote to war buddies. They often passed through town en route to Florida, howling in through the front door to hug him. A lot of them were dark men, hairy in a way my father and his fair Carolina friends were not. It seemed that all New Yorkers were brown-eyed and sooty from the city; they looked odd here in the clear to amber light of our Tidewater. Mentioning their wives waiting out in the car, they lifted eyebrows suggestively, as in the old days – as if that were some notorious and easy girl out there. Mother never liked their wives much, and when they'd left, Father told her she was a snob.

"War buddies' wives are not necessarily war buddies themselves," she quipped. Once, when he insisted, after hanging up
the phone, that they drive two hundred miles to a motel where
someone from his squadron was staying on the way to Miami,
Mother mentioned a bridge tournament; she said, "Show him
my picture," and settled luxuriously back onto the couch with
the latest novel by Daphne du Maurier. "He already saw your
picture and he's heard more about you than you'd ever guess!"
my father shouted as he stormed out with the car keys and an
unopened bottle of Jack Daniel's and, slamming the door, rattled
the china cabinet. Very early the next morning, he came in drunk
and in a loud voice over the telephone canceled an afternoon
appointment to sell Group Life. My mother wandered down to
breakfast in her quilted yellow housecoat, and noticed a broken
headlight on the Packard parked at the wrong angle outside.
When they'd settled at the table, coffee poured, she offered him
the usual tirade about his egotism, her suffering, and their
marriage, which she liked to say was "crumbling, Richard,
crumbling!" I sat eating scrambled eggs with a big round training
spoon, and my younger brother dropped his baby bottle on the
floor, then looked down at it till I picked it up. "Oh yeah?" my
father said. And then she said, "Don't you use that trashy New
York slang around your children." "Oh yeah?" he said.

But when you are definitely home from the European Theater,
which is dead now, and war buddies you'd have given your life
for now phone less and less, are more and more just Christmas
cards with photos of new children, cards signed in a woman's
hand, when insurance (fire, burglary, auto, and life) is now what
people think of when they think of you, when Marilyn Monroe
is filling the shoes of Betty Grable, who's retired, what do you
do then?
    You find that the headaches are because you suddenly need
reading glasses. You resign yourself to buying bourbon by the
case because it is cheaper and you now have room to store that
much, and you have no doubt that it will somehow get drunk
up. You call your two sons soldiers when they submit stiff-
faced, thin-armed, to Jonas Salk's discovery. You pay someone

to keep the yard worthy of your wartime aerial-photo vision of its symmetry and shape from overhead. You take your wife to the occasions you count on the country club to invent, and there, with friends who have become clients and friends who have not become clients and with clients who want to become your friends, the two of you get more than genteelly drunk, even by Eastern Carolina's lubricated standards. And afterward, after the baby-sitter has been overpaid to cover your tardiness and the fact that the front of your jacket is dark from some accidental spillage and to cover the expense of the cab that must be called to get her home, in the silence after that, of the house becoming increasingly more valuable as the boxwoods expand themselves outside, with the hint of dawn coming on, you both manage to know what a prime moment in the history of your physiques this is.

Otherwise, you learn to make do, and when some threat arises you are soldierly in disposing of it. Almost, there are not enough threats anymore. Here you are, among the most successful of the bombardiers, now grounded, in the awful safety of this decade, in its suburbs. You do what you can around the house and grounds to re-create some of that drama you remember from the forties. All the events that made one's life eventful: The Axis. Roosevelt Dead. Hiroshima.

The furnace explodes early one morning. You carry Helen outside, dump her onto a lawn chair, rush back for the sleeping boys, dash across the street and pull the fire alarm. Later the fire chief emerges from the basement of the house and ambles around the engine and out toward your family group, huddled in pajamas among the neighbors, who have brought blankets, coffee, garden hoses. "Nothing serious," he says. "The furnace sort of exploded. A little soot, but nothing serious."

"What do you mean, 'nothing serious'? You should have heard it. I thought we were being attacked or something."

"Noisy," the fire chief admits, scratching his head, trying to be both tactful and professional, "but nothing serious."

The next day, you order a fire-alarm system for the house. While the children grumble, while a siren howls and neighbors watch over fences, you stage your first weekly firedrill. After two of these, the drills are discontinued.

It is a personal affront when tent caterpillars invade four of the yard's eleven trees. A neighbor says you'll have to burn them out; only thing they understand. The yardman prepares to do it, till you curtly give him the day off. This job, worthy of you, will require a little strategy. There are moments when a father and his boys must work together. Standing in the back door, you shout, "Now is the time for all good boys to come to the aid of their father and their yard!" "*What?*" Helen asks.

You put a torch together – a broom handle, rags, some kerosene. You ignite it with your wartime Zippo. Up into the infested tree nearest the house you crawl. This is a mission; for once, in peacetime, you know exactly what you're going to do. The boys watch idly from the ground as you sear the first lumps of worms out of the plum tree. Smoke suddenly everywhere and such a smell. "You two down there, don't just stand around. Stomp on the ones getting away." Clusters of black caterpillars, pounds of them, are toppling from their webs, falling to the ground and steaming.

Making girlish noises, your sons start hopping on the smoldering worms. Bradley jogs about, eyes straight ahead; he lifts his knees and makes a calisthenic game of it. Feeling dizzy, Bryan shuts his eyes, holds out his arms for balance, and earnestly pretends he's dancing, though his tennis shoes keep slipping out from under him.

In the tree, you find you've started muttering almost forgotten, complicated curses from the war as, one by one, you solemnly eradicate these black colonies of pests. Your sons' whimpering infuriates you suddenly. "Shut up down there, you two. You'll do your job and keep your mouths closed. These things are going to get to other trees. They'll get over into the Bennetts' yard if we don't kill them now. This is no game here, this is an emergency, so quit squealing like sissies and stomp on them. That clear?"

Your two children look up at the orange glow inside the tree, at a single wing-tip shoe visible among the leaves. In unison, they say, "Yes sir."

## 2. MY ELDER SON

I'm not as young as I used to be and it follows that my sons aren't either. Bradley, our baby, is twenty-five now and makes 120,000 dollars a year. He graduated third in his class from the law school of the University of Virginia. He's now with a fine corporation-law firm working out of Georgetown. Brad married Elaine last May at a garden wedding that was rained out but that was nice anyway. The bridesmaids' dresses were made of some thin material that got transparent when wet. Elaine is from a fine old Maryland family. Her father served as attorney general of the state a few administrations back. Now Brad and Elaine are renovating a town house in Washington, doing most of the work themselves. What with Elaine's small private income and her looks and taste, and with Brad's salary, my wife and I feel good about their progress in life. Elaine always remembers us with little cards and gifts on birthdays and anniversaries. It's a comfort.

Bryan is our elder son. He's twenty-seven and a mystery to me. Two years ago he gave up a fairly good job as a designer of furniture. He decided to become a writer. When he was home last Christmas, we heard him typing a few times, but he never offered to show us anything he'd written. I have no doubt that it's good. He has always had a real flair for the arts. But if you've never read a word your son has written and if you understand the kind of money a writer can expect to make, it's hard to work up any real enthusiasm for this occupation.

To support himself, Bryan does articles for a magazine called *Dance World*. When people ask me what he's doing, I tell them he writes for a magazine in New York. If they ask me which one, then I'm forced to level with them. I'd have to be a writer myself to describe the sinking feeling I get when I tell this about my elder son. Helen says that my attitude in the matter is unreasonable. All I know is, the first year he worked for the magazine he sent us a free subscription, and it got so I couldn't even stand to see copies on the coffee table. I could hardly believe some of the pictures of the men. Looking at them, you didn't know whether to laugh or cry or get angry or what.

My wife also informs me that there are two kinds of dance, ballet and modern, and that Bryan's specialty is modern. Helen says, with lots of enthusiam, that modern is less costumed but just as athletic as ballet. Somehow, knowing this doesn't help.

You might say Bryan and I have never really seen eye to eye. He has always had certain mannerisms and his talents are unlike my own. When he was younger he stayed pale from spending too much time indoors. I kept telling Helen that one day he'd discover the world outside. I said, "Now he keeps a diary, he paints still lifes, he reads French like a Frenchman, but believe you me, one day he'll come around. You watch."

I see I might have been wrong. He's twenty-seven years old and I think the only women he ever talks to are waitresses. He lives with some actor-model room-mate. We had lunch with them in New York. The roommate met us at the restaurant. I was expecting somebody thin who looked pretty much like Bryan. In walks this big, broad-shouldered kid, taller than me and with a suntan and a jaw like a lifeguard's. For a second, I was ashamed of myself for having jumped to certain conclusions. Then the first thing I noticed was his handshake. One of those dead fish. Second thing I noticed was, he'd smashed his thumb-nail in something; it was black. Third thing was that all his fingernails were black. Nail polish. I could hardly understand what this meant. I thought it must be for medicinal purposes, because how could anybody do that for decoration? Helen was staring so hard I had to nudge her under the table. Usually she's the one nudging me. Afterwards she said she wouldn't have been so startled if it had been red polish, but black?

Now that we've met Jacques, he seems to be everywhere we look. Helen never forgets a face, and she keeps finding his picture in magazine ads – mostly for whiskey and shirts, once for soap. In these ads his nails are never black. I won't get over that. The kid looked like he should be on the US Olympic team carrying a torch – and then the handshake, the nails, and his trying to talk all during lunch about the music of the forties. He kept asking

Helen and me about Kay Kayser and his Kollege of Musical
Knowledge, and about the Andrews Sisters. Helen surprised me
by remembering the name of each Andrews Sister and knowing
the order in which some'd died. She entered right into the
discussion. He asked her how it felt to have heard "Tangerine"
when it was new, and Helen was sitting right there telling him.
Jacques kept saying over and over again, "What a period, what a
period!" For a person like myself, who loved the forties, the
silliness of this kind of conversation made me sick. As if anybody like that could ever understand what it meant to be alive
then.

You send your sons to the best schools possible, and you
hope that their friends will be bright kids from similar back-
grounds. Sometimes I wonder what my son and this type of
person have in common. Then I take a guess, and right away I'm
wishing I could forget my own conclusions.

I was not going to mention it, but as long as I've built up
this much steam I might as well. Last spring, Bryan came down
to his brother's wedding in Baltimore. We were glad he came. It
was right that he should be there, but I won't even begin to
describe the person, the creature, he brought along with him.
Everyone who saw this particular person immediately got very
disturbed. This particular person somehow managed to get into
and spoil about half of Bradley and Elaine's wedding pictures.
Elaine's parents were obliged to find a place for Bryan and his
guest to stay during the weekend of the wedding. They were
certainly very gracious about it and never said one word about
this person's appearance. But Helen was so upset and embarrassed she cried most of the nights we were there. Because of the
strain, she looked terrible at the wedding.

Of course, it was Helen who was always telling Bryan he
was gifted. She was enrolling him in adult art classes with nude
models when he was twelve damn years old, buying him 30-
dollar picture books full of abstract paintings, driving him 15
miles to the next town because our local barbers couldn't "cut
with the curl." I told her she was spoiling him, but beyond that
what could I do? I'd always said that the boys should have
nothing but the best. No, I'm definitely not blaming Helen.

After all, that's one reason you make your money, so you can spoil your kids in ways you weren't.

You start off with a child, a son, and for the first six years he's on your side. It's clear there's nothing wrong with him. He's healthy, and you're relieved. He's pretty much like all the others. Not quite as noisy, maybe not quite as tough, but that might be a good sign, too. Then things somehow get off the track. He's coming in with a bloodied nose once a week, and you know damned well that nothing happened to the kid that did it. He's inside listening to records when he ought to be outside playing with the others. His face starts looking unlike yours and hers. You come home from a hard day's work and find him sitting in a high-backed chair cutting shapes out of colored paper and spreading them on the rug. You wonder for a moment if this white-skinned kid can be fourteen years old; can he be half your responsibility, half your fault? Of course, there are times when everything seems well enough. He takes out girls. He learns to drive. His tenor comes and goes, then comes to stay. One day you see he's nicked himself while shaving, and all the time you feel you should be grooming an heir he grows paler, taller, and more peculiar. He locks doors behind himself and startles you in the dark hallways of your own house. You're afraid of his next phase – afraid how the finished product will compare with the block's other boys, with his own kid brother who plays on the junior varsity and mows other people's lawns for money.

At the PTA open house a teacher pulls you aside and tells you, all excited, "Bryan can do anything he likes in the world. How few of us can do absolutely anything we like. He's among the chosen few, and I thought you both should know." His mother beams all evening, but afterwards you find him in the kitchen, at the table, dripping candle wax on black paper. "An experiment," he mumbles as you walk into the room toward the refrigerator. You feel clumsy and you try with your expression to apologize for having barged in like this through the swinging door. But, after all, you tell yourself, it *is* your kitchen and your table, that is your son. The "anything" his sad teacher promised gives you more distress than comfort.

He drops calling you just Dad and changes you to Father. One night you turn on the television and hear him say, "Television is for fools," and dash out of the room, offended by your need to see the news. You expect more from him as he gets older, but the distance grows. He reminds you of a thin, peculiar fellow you knew slightly in the Army, a bookworm nobody spoke to.

Till last New Year's Eve, I felt I'd had a pretty good track record as a father. I mean, I knew I'd made some mistakes, but somehow, over the years, you forget specifically what they've been. Bryan had come south for Christmas for the first time in two years. Helen and I got home from a party at the Club. We were slightly drunk. Bryan was sitting up reading when we got in. He was curled on the living-room couch in a floor-length maroon bathrobe he'd worn most of his visit. He was reading something he'd brought down from New York. He laughs at our books and magazines, picks up Helen's novels and giggles at them and puts them down again.

Charlie Fentress had announced his daughter's engagement at the New Year's Eve party. The band played a few bars of the Wedding March. Bradley and Elaine weren't married yet and Brad had decided to spend Christmas with his college roommate on St. Thomas. Only Bryan was home. Edward and Mildred Fox took Helen and me aside at the party to say they just wanted to let us know they were going to be grandparents. They were hugging each other and they both had tears in their eyes. The band played "Auld Lang Syne." It seemed everyone was being honored and rewarded by their children but us. Bryan had laughed at our suggestion that he come to the party and see his old friends. "What would I talk to them about?" he asked. "The pill, kindergarten car pools?" His quickness with words has made him all the more upsetting. But we got home and there was our son on the couch. There he was. His hair cut in a shaggy expensive way, and wearing a silk bathrobe. He looked over his shoulder at us as we stood in the foyer taking off our coats and rubbers with a little drunken difficulty.

"How was the prom, kids?" he asked and turned back to his book. I walked into the living room. On the coffee table before the couch I saw a bottle of cognac I'd paid forty bucks for, three years earlier. A snifter was beside it and a lot of wet rings, some of the cognac spilled on the tabletop.

"Who told you you could open that bottle?" I asked him.

"Father, it's New Year's Eve. Let up a little." The back of his head was still toward me.

"Look what you've done to that table. Your mother breaks her back keeping this place decent and you act like you're at the goddamned Holiday Inn."

It's easy enough now to say I shouldn't have cuffed him. But I felt like doing it, and I was just drunk enough to do what I felt like doing. He hadn't even bothered to turn around while I was talking. I took a backswing while he was reading. Helen said, "Richard!" in a warning tone of voice, but, like me, she really didn't think I'd do it. I smacked him with my best golfer's swing right across his fashionable haircut, and knocked him off the couch onto the floor. It scared me as much as it seemed to scare him. For a minute he lay blinking up at me, mouth open, on the carpet. We were like that for a second. His mouth open, mine open, and Helen with both hands pressed over hers. Then she was all over me, trying to hold my arms like I was going to kill him. He got up, straightened his robe, and marched upstairs. The whole thing was so sloppy it made me sick. Even with all I'd drunk I couldn't sleep.

The next morning there was to be a New Year's Day church service at Trinity Episcopal. Helen had asked Bryan to come with us, but we didn't think he'd get up, since it was before his usual rising time, which was anywhere from noon till three. Helen and I were eating breakfast. We were dressed for church, eating without talking, trying not to think about the night before, but thinking about it anyway.

We were both staring at our eggs and coffee when Bryan came downstairs, all dressed for church. His head was bound up in a professional-looking gauze-and-tape bandage that covered most of his hair and forehead. The tanned ears stuck up over the white cap. He looked like someone recovering from brain surgery. Helen was drinking her coffee as he came in. In the middle of swallowing, she went into a genteel coughing fit.

Bryan poured himself a cup. As he was adding cream and sugar, he said cheerfully, "Father, when people at church ask what happened to me – and inevitably they will ask – I intend to tell them exactly who's responsible for this."

I sat staring down the table at him. We were squared off, me at my usual place, he at his. I started chewing on my back molars in a way I hadn't done since the war. He went on drinking his coffee. Once in a while, he'd glance up at me over his cup. He seemed pleased with himself. Helen was staring at him with her mouth half open. She would look from him to me, her face all strained, as if she wanted me to explain him to her. So this is it, I thought. That one over there with the bandages, that's my elder son and heir. I had to decide then whether I would really break his head or if I'd let things go. At some point, you have to decide with children whether you're going to kill them or let them go.

I thought of those foreign-exchange students we sometimes had to dinner when they passed through our town. Odd-looking kids with funny-shaped glasses, sometimes bad teeth, and accents half the time Helen and I couldn't understand. But we always pretended we did. You could tell when they had asked a question, and even though you hadn't really caught it, you still nodded and said, "Yes." And when it turned out that the question couldn't be answered with a simple Yes, when they stared at us, at least we'd shown that we had wanted to agree. In the long run, that was all Helen and myself could do for International Good Will.

So at this breakfast I decided to give Bryan the benefit of the doubt. I told myself I'd treat him at least as well as we treated these nonwhite foreign students who come to dinner for just one night. You didn't even expect thank-you notes from them. These kids' customs were so different, their homes so far from us here. But we were always kind to them, thinking of American kids who'd be in their country someday. So I told myself there at the table, if not as a father then at least as a host and an American, I should treat Bryan at least as well as one of them. After all, a foreigner is mostly what he's been to us.

Helen didn't want him to go out bandaged like that, but you

have to take your own kid to church. Besides, if we hadn't taken
him he'd have called a cab and how would that have looked? I'm
sure he told whoever asked about his head whatever it was he'd
decided to tell.

He left for New York that very afternoon, still wrapped up
like somebody with amnesia. Except for Bradley's wedding, we
haven't seen him since. I suspect that he's in secret correspondence
with his mother, and that's fine and natural, I suppose. Some
days she's more tearful than others. In the middle of a meal,
she'll fold her napkin, place it on the table, leave the room.

Someday he'll probably publish a story or a whole book
about what a tyrant I've been. I can imagine a chapter listing all
the times I ever raised my voice or hit him. Of course, people
always believe what's down in black and white before they'll
listen to just one man's word about what happened. I have made
some mistakes, I know. But I won't accept his verdict of me.
I'm not a villain. If anything, I've wanted too much for him,
and, considering all the ways you can go wrong with a son, it
seems the one he would be quickest to forgive.

## 3. ADDENDUM

In this drawing I am doing, a tall red man holds the hand of a
small white boy. The man wears a decorative uniform: policeman, soldier, milkman. He is much taller than the child, but his
right arm has been conveniently elongated, elasticized like a sling
or bandage so it easily supports the boy's white hand.

My art teacher called me out into the hallway on the last day
of school and whispered, "You mustn't tell the other children,
but you're the best drawer I have ever taught in eighteen years.
The most imaginative. Of your age group, I mean." Now,
deciding to place the man and boy before a doorway just like
that one there, with a similar selection of Mother's houseplants
sprouting all around them, I recall Miss Whipple's compliment.
I feel fully capable of adding exactly what I intend. When I'm

done, people will say, "Look. He's drawn a man, a boy, a doorway, and some plants in pots." There is a comfort in knowing you can make things recognizable.

I have lots of room on this table we inherited early from my farmer grandfather and his shy-in-public wife. It was built to seat a family of ten, plus guests. I am alone here at my usual end. Mother, Daddy, Bradley, and I each have a whole side to ourselves and must speak up to be heard by everyone. Venetian blinds cross the dining-room window, and sunshine throws a laddered shadow straight across the walnut surface of the table. The round-ended bars of light rest there in a row, like giant versions of my own crayons.

My brother and his friends are playing baseball in the front yard. They chant their jeers to various Episcopalian cadences. A few minutes back, a foul ball rattled off the roof. The grandfather clock in the foyer musically commemorates each and every fifteen minutes, however uneventful, and my crayon seems responsible for every drowsy sound.

The surface of the table gives a sudden jerk, and the crayoned frond of the potted palm I'm drawing takes an unexpected twist. I look up and watch my handsome father seat himself at the far end of the table and spread his mail like a game of solitaire. Crosshatched with sunlight, his white shirt is dazzling and reflected in the tabletop. From his favorite coffee cup, steam climbs. It twists and plaits itself up through the alternating stripes of sun and slatted shadow. He holds an envelope to the light and rips into it with one finger. With that same hand, he slapped me two days ago. It burned across my face and swiveled my whole head in that direction. I go back to my control of crayons. Maybe he'll take his bills into the study and leave me here to excel privately at drawing.

His voice startles me. "Why don't you go outside and play with the others? It would do you some good." I continue drawing. Indoor clouds rain blue and purple pellets on the houseplants. "Did you hear me down there?" "Yes sir." "What don't you like about baseball? Are you afraid you'll get hurt or what?" I know I must say something. "I like drawing." A pause. Still watching me, he drinks from his coffee cup. "But it's summer, Bryan. It's a beautiful summer morning and you're seven years old and when—" "Eight," I say, not looking up. "What?" "Eight years old." "All right, then, eight, all the more reason. If you've got to draw on a day like this, what's in here that you can't draw just as well outside?" All the floating clumps of leaves have sprouted pots. "I asked you a question. What do you find to draw, sitting in here like this?" A challenge. He thinks I don't know. Most Imaginative of My Age, and he thinks I don't even know what I'm drawing. Tell him an airplane, tell him an airplane. "You," I say, despite myself. "Drawing me?" Why did I tell? Now he'll want to see it. Casually, he glances again through his mail. "So, you're drawing your dad, huh? Well, let's have a look." I note that he's forgotten all about the baseball game. After slapping me two times in one week, he's crazy if he thinks I'll spend all morning drawing him and then get up and walk to the far end of the table and deliver it. He only notices my drawing when he wants to show that it's a waste of time. I won't let him see this. Absolutely not. Unless it's that or getting slapped again.

"It's really not any good," I assure him.

"Let me see it."

"You won't think it's any good. You'll get mad 'cause it's not the way you really look."

"Bring it here."

"Well, I drew in the door and plants behind you, and I think you really have to see it from down here at this end, because this is where I drew it from."

"I can't turn around and see those," he says, peeved at conceding this. "Bring it here, Bryan."

I concentrate on the black crayon in my damp right fist. I study the picture itself. "Daddy," I begin, definite. "I just don't feel like you would . . . I don't want you . . . to see it . . . yet. I'll show you later, in a minute, later on."

"This is getting ridiculous, young man. I'm asking you to bring that to me. Are you going to bring it or aren't you? It's that simple."

I have included him here, but that makes the drawing even more mine, less his. It's the one thing in this house of his that's really mine right now. The man's mouth is a single horizontal line. The boy's a silly U-shape. "It's mine," I say quietly.

"You said it was a picture of me."

"It is, but I'm the one that did it. Please Daddy, don't make me this time."

A long silence from the far end of the table. "I'm waiting, Bryan. Bring that down here right this second."

Almost before I think of it, the crayon is scribbling. In tight black loops it traps and then eclipses half the page. I choose one figure. The face and hands are lost forever underneath an oily whorl. There is the chanting from the front yard, the scratchy circling of my crayon, less loud as black wax accumulates. My exertion delicately clinks his coffee cup against its saucer. As I scrawl, feeling sick and elated at this solution, I grind my teeth and stare straight at my enormous father, smaller than usual at the far end of the table. He seems to be sitting for a portrait as I furiously describe a neat black cyclone on the page. His jaw is set. I can hear his breathing. I know the signs. Any second he will lunge down here, grab me by the shirt, lift and shake me, slap me once with a hand the full size of my head; he'll shove me, stumbling, toward my room, shrieking in my own defense. Now, just as he places both palms on the table to come for me, I stand. I lift the drawing by its upper corners and carry the page as if wet.

I move toward his chair, the only chair with arms. He is waiting there to punish me for drawing during summer, for drawing anything but him all day, for then un-drawing him without permission. I stare between his eyes at the faint inch making two eyebrows one grim horizontal line.

I warily approach him in my acolyte's gait. I hold up the drawing, a white flag, between his body and mine. I am now beside his chair. Seated, he is just as tall as I am standing. On his forehead there are rows of pores, and over that the teeth marks where the comb passed through his hair. His back is pressed straight against the chair, hands still tense on the table's edge. Over his business mail I place my artwork. One flimsy piece of white paper with some colored markings on it. His eyes move from my face down to my drawing. He sees the figure there. I hear him quietly exhale. His solid hands reach out and pick the paper up. I am very conscious of the hands. There I am, that's me, I feel him thinking. He has recognized himself. I release my breath and gratefully inhale some of Miss Whipple's wonder at my own imagination. Good for something, it has just spared me a whipping. I've sketched an image of him for himself, while I am permanently off the page, and saved. He is not asking why the uniformed gentleman's longer arm is weighed with this bristling black cancellation. He is now responding to the easy magic of a drawing of a uniform on a tall figure, the horizontal mouth, the buttons and braid.

"So, there I am . . ." he says, relaxing. "Why'd you do this crossing out? What was that under there?"

I have lost interest in the drawing. I stare out the window at the summer lawn where my brother and six neighbor kids are climbing a young evergreen, tilting it almost to the ground. "Nothing," I say.

"So, there I am. Those are sure some ears you gave me. What are these round things here on front? Are those medals? Medals for what?" He hesitates to risk a guess. I look back from the venetian blinds and stare at him. He sits studying the drawing, his face rosy, jovial now. More than anything, I want suddenly to hug him, to move forward and throw my arms around his neck. I want to cry and have him hold me. Lift me off the floor and up into the air and hold me. Instead, there seems to be a layer of electricity around him. I know I will be shocked for touching him with no reason. Somewhere in the house an alarm will sound, the grandfather clock will gong all out of sequence, the door chimes will go wild, sirens will howl out of the heating ducts, and foul balls will crash through every window in the place. I look at him and, in answer to his question, shrug.

He holds the drawing out for me to take. He's done with it. Slipping past his chair, I saunter to the back door and, on my way outside, turn around. I see him seated in stripes of light at the vacant family table. Sad, he holds my own drawing out to me as if offering a gift or an apology or some artwork of his own. Something changes in me, seeing him like this, but as I pass into the sunlight I fight to keep my voice quite cool and formal and call back, "I'm finished, Daddy. You may keep it now. It's yours."

BARRY HANNAH

✫  ✫  ✫  ✫

# *Testimony of Pilot*

When I was ten, eleven and twelve, I did a good bit of my play
in the backyard of a three-story wooden house my father had
bought and rented out, his first venture into real estate. We lived
right across the street from it, but over here was the place to do
your real play. Here there was a harrowed but overgrown
garden, a vine-swallowed fence at the back end, and beyond the
fence a cornfield which belonged to someone else. This was not
the country. This was the town, Clinton, Mississippi, between
Jackson on the east and Vicksburg on the west. On this lot stood
a few water oaks, a few plum bushes, and much overgrowth of
honeysuckle vine. At the very back end, at the fence, stood three
strong nude chinaberry trees.

In Mississippi it is difficult to achieve a vista. But my friends
and I had one here at the back corner of the garden. We could
see across the cornfield, see the one lone tin-roofed house this
side of the railroad tracks, then on across the tracks many other
bleaker houses with rustier tin roofs, smoke coming out of the
chimneys in the late fall. This was niggertown. We had binoculars and could see the colored children hustling about and perhaps
a hopeless sow or two with her brood enclosed in a tiny boarded-
up area. Through the binoculars one afternoon in October we
watched some men corner and beat a large hog on the brain.
They used an ax and the thing kept running around, head leaning
toward the ground, for several minutes before it lay down. I
thought I saw the men laughing when it finally did. One of them
was staggering, plainly drunk to my sight from 300 yards away.
He had the long knife. Because of that scene I considered Negroes
savage cowards for a good five more years of my life. Our maid
brought some sausage to my mother and when it was put in the
pan to fry, I made a point of running out of the house.

I went directly across the street and to the back end of the garden behind the apartment house we owned, without my breakfast. That was Saturday. Eventually, Radcleve saw me. His parents had him mowing the yard that ran alongside my dad's property. He clicked off the power mower and I went over to his fence, which was storm wire. His mother maintained handsome flowery grounds at all costs; she had a leaf-mold bin and St. Augustine grass as solid as a rug.

Radcleve himself was a violent experimental chemist. When Radcleve was eight, he threw a whole package of .22 shells against the sidewalk in front of his house until one of them went off, driving lead fragments into his calf, most of them still deep in there where the surgeons never dared tamper. Radcleve knew about the sulfur, potassium nitrate and charcoal mixture for gunpowder when he was ten. He bought things through the mail when he ran out of ingredients in his chemistry sets. When he was an infant, his father, a quiet man who owned the Chevrolet agency in town, bought an entire bankrupt sporting-goods store, and in the middle of their backyard he built a house, plain-painted and neat, one room and a heater, where Radcleve's redundant toys forevermore were kept – all the possible toys he would need for boyhood. There were things in there that Radcleve and I were not mature enough for and did not know the real use of. When we were eleven, we uncrated the new Dunlop golf balls and went on up on a shelf for the tennis rackets, went out in the middle of his yard, and served new golf ball after new golf ball with blasts of the rackets over into the cornfield, out of sight. When the strings busted we just went in and got another racket. We were absorbed by how a good smack would set the heavy little pills on an endless flight. Then Radcleve's father came down. He simply dismissed me. He took Radcleve into the house and covered his whole body with a belt. But within the week Radcleve had invented the mortar. It was a steel pipe into which a flashlight battery fit perfectly, like a bullet into a muzzle. He had drilled a hole for the fuse of an M–80 firecracker at the base, for the charge. It was a grand cannon, set up on a stack of bricks at the back of my dad's property, which was the free place to play. When it shot, it would back up

violently with thick smoke and you could hear the flashlight
battery whistling off. So that morning when I ran out of the
house protesting the hog sausage, I told Radcleve to bring over
the mortar. His ma and dad were in Jackson for the day, and he
came right over with the pipe, the batteries and the M–80
explosives. He had two gross of them.

Before, we'd shot off toward the woods to the right of
niggertown. I turned the bricks to the left; I made us a very fine
cannon carriage pointing toward niggertown. When Radcleve
appeared, he had two pairs of binoculars around his neck, one
pair a newly plundered German unit as big as a brace of whiskey
bottles. I told him I wanted to shoot for that house where we
saw them killing the pig. Radcleve loved the idea. We singled
out the house with heavy use of the binoculars.

There were children in the yard. Then they all went in. Two
men came out of the back door. I thought I recognized the
drunkard from the other afternoon. I helped Radcleve fix the
direction of the cannon. We estimated the altitude we needed to
get down there. Radcleve put the M–80 in the breech with its
fuse standing out of the hole. I dropped the flashlight battery in.
I lit the fuse. We backed off. The M–80 blasted off deafeningly,
smoke rose, but my concentration was on that particular house
over there. I brought the binoculars. We waited six or seven
seconds. I heard a great joyful wallop on tin. "We've hit him on
the first try, the first try!" I yelled. Radcleve was ecstatic. "Right
on his roof!" We bolstered up the brick carriage. Radcleve
remembered the correct height of the cannon exactly. So we
fixed it, loaded it, lit it and backed off. The battery landed on the
roof, blat, again, louder. I looked to see if there wasn't a great
dent or hole in the roof. I could not understand why niggers
weren't pouring out distraught from that house. We shot the
mortar again and again, and always our battery hit the tin roof.
Sometimes there was only a dull thud, but other times there was
a wild distress of tin. I was still looking through the binoculars,
amazed that the niggers wouldn't even come out of their house
to see what was hitting their roof. Radcleve was on to it better
than me. I looked over at him and he had the huge German
binocs much lower than I did. He was looking straight through

the cornfield, which was all bare and open, with nothing left but rotten stalks. "What we've been hitting is the roof of that house just this side of the tracks. White people live in there," he said.

I took up my binoculars again. I looked around the yard of that white wooden house on this side of the tracks, almost next to the railroad. When I found the tin roof, I saw four significant dents in it. I saw one of our batteries lying in the middle of a sort of crater. I took the binoculars down into the yard and saw a blond middle-aged woman looking our way.

"Somebody's coming up toward us. He's from that house and he's got, I think, some sort of fancy gun with him. It might be an automatic weapon."

I ran my binoculars all over the cornfield. Then, in a line with the house, I saw him. He was coming our way but having some trouble with the rows and dead stalks of the cornfield.

"That is just a boy like us. All he's got is a saxophone with him," I told Radcleve. I had recently got in the school band, playing drums, and had seen all the weird horns that made up a band.

I watched this boy with the saxophone through the binoculars until he was 10 feet from us. This was Quadberry. His name was Ard, short for Arden. His shoes were foot-square wads of mud from the cornfield. When he saw us across the fence and above him, he stuck out his arm in my direction.

"My dad says stop it!"

"We weren't doing anything," says Radcleve.

"Mother saw the smoke puff up from here. Dad has a hangover."

"A what?"

"It's a headache from indiscretion. You're lucky he does. He's picked up the poker to rap on you, but he can't move further the way his head is."

"What's your name? You're not in the band," I said, focusing on the saxophone.

"It's Ard Quadberry. Why do you keep looking at me through the binoculars?"

It was because he was odd, with his hair and its white ends, and his Arab nose, and now his name. Add to that the saxophone.

"My dad's a doctor at the college. Mother's a musician. You better quit what you're doing. . . . I was out practicing in the garage. I saw one of those flashlight batteries roll off the roof. Could I see what you shoot 'em with?"

"No," said Radcleve. Then he said: "If you'll play that horn."

Quadberry stood out there ten feet below us in the field, skinny, feet and pants booted with black mud, and at his chest the slung-on, very complex, radiant horn.

Quadberry began sucking and licking the reed. I didn't care much for this act, and there was too much desperate oralness in his face when he began playing. That was why I chose the drums. One had to engage himself like suck's revenge with a horn. But what Quadberry was playing was pleasant and intricate. I was sure it was advanced, and there was no squawking, as from the other eleven-year-olds on sax in the band room. He made the end with a clean upward riff, holding the final note high, pure and unwavering.

"Good!" I called to him.

Quadberry was trying to move out of the sunken row toward us, but his heavy shoes were impeding him.

"Sounded like a duck. Sounded like a girl duck," said Radcleve, who was kneeling down and packing a mudball around one of the M–80s. I saw and I was an accomplice, because I did nothing. Radcleve lit the fuse and heaved the mudball over the fence. An M–80 is a very serious firecracker; it is like the charge they use to shoot up those sprays 600 feet on July Fourth at country clubs. It went off, this one, even bigger than most M–80s.

When we looked over the fence, we saw Quadberry all muck specks and fragments of stalks. He was covering the mouthpiece of his horn with both hands. Then I saw there was blood pouring out of, it seemed, his right eye. I thought he was bleeding directly out of his eye.

"Quadberry?" I called.

He turned around and never said a word to me until I was eighteen. He walked back holding his eye and staggering through the cornstalks. Radcleve had him in the binoculars. Radcleve was trembling . . . but intrigued.

"His mother just screamed. She's running out in the field to get him."

I thought we'd blinded him, but we hadn't. I thought the Quadberrys would get the police or call my father, but they didn't. The upshot of this is that Quadberry had a permanent white space next to his right eye, a spot that looked like a tiny upset crown.

I went from sixth through half of twelfth grade ignoring him and that wound. I was coming on as a drummer and a lover, but if Quadberry happened to appear within 50 feet of me and my most tender, intimate sweetheart, I would duck out. Quadberry grew up just like the rest of us. His father was still a doctor – professor of history – at the town college; his mother was still blond, and a musician. She was organist at an Episcopalian church in Jackson, the big capital city 10 miles east of us.

As for Radcleve, he still had no ear for music, but he was there, my buddy. He was repentant about Quadberry, although not so much as I. He'd thrown the mud grenade over the fence only to see what would happen. He had not really wanted to maim. Quadberry had played his tune on the sax, Radcleve had played his tune on the mud grenade. It was just a shame they happened to cross talents.

Radcleve went into a long period of nearly nothing after he gave up violent explosives. Then he trained himself to copy the comic strips, *Steve Canyon* to *Major Hoople*, until he became quite a versatile cartoonist with some very provocative new faces and bodies that were gesturing intriguingly. He could never fill in the speech balloons with the smart words they needed. Sometimes he would pencil in "Err" or "What?" in the empty speech places. I saw him a great deal. Radcleve was not spooked by Quadberry. He even once asked Quadberry what his opinion was of his future as a cartoonist. Quadberry told Radcleve that if he took all his cartoons and stuffed himself with them, he would make an interesting dead man. After that, Radcleve was shy of him too.

When I was a senior we had an extraordinary band. Word was we had outplayed all the big AAA division bands last April in the state contest. Then came news that a new blazing saxophone player was coming into the band as first chair. This person had spent summers in Vermont in music camps, and he was coming in with us for the concert season. Our director, a lovable aesthete named Richard Prender, announced to us in a proud silent moment that the boy was joining us tomorrow night. The effect was that everybody should push over a seat or two and make room for this boy and his talent. I was annoyed. Here I'd been with the band and had kept hold of the taste among the whole percussion section. I could play rock and jazz drum and didn't even really need to be here. I could be in Vermont too, give me a piano and a bass. I looked at the kid on first sax, who was going to be supplanted tomorrow. For two years he had thought he was the star, then suddenly enters this boy who's three times better.

The new boy was Quadberry. He came in, but he was meek, and when he tuned up he put his head almost on the floor, bending over trying to be inconspicuous. The girls in the band had wanted him to be handsome, but Quadberry refused and kept himself in such hiding among the sax section that he was neither handsome, ugly, cute or anything. What he was was pretty near invisible, except for the bell of his horn, the all-but-closed eyes, the Arabian nose, the brown hair with its halo of white ends, the desperate oralness, the giant reed punched into his face, and hazy Quadberry, loving the sound in a private dignified ecstasy.

I say dignified because of what came out of the end of his horn. He was more than what Prender had told us he would be. Because of Quadberry, we could take the band arrangement of Ravel's *Bolero* with us to the state contest. Quadberry would do the saxophone solo. He would switch to alto sax, he would do the sly Moorish ride. When he played, I heard the sweetness, I heard the horn which finally brought human *talk* into the realm of music. It could sound like the mutterings of a field nigger, and then it could get up into inhumanly careless beauty, it could get among mutinous helium bursts around Saturn. I already loved *Bolero* for the constant drum part. The percussion was always there, driving along with the subtly increasing triplets, insistent,

insistent, at last outraged and trying to steal the whole show from the horns and the others. I knew a large boy with dirty blond hair, name of Wyatt, who played viola in the Jackson Symphony and sousaphone in our band – one of the rare closet transmutations of my time – who was forever claiming to have discovered the central *Bolero* one Sunday afternoon over FM radio as he had seven distinct sexual moments with a certain B., girl flutist with black bangs and skin like mayonnaise, while the drums of Ravel carried them on and on in a ceremony of Spanish sex. It was agreed by all the canny in the band that *Bolero* was exactly the piece to make the band soar – now especially as we had Quadberry, who made his walk into the piece like an actual lean Spanish bandit. This boy could blow his horn. He was, as I had suspected, a genius. His solo was not quite the same as the New York Phil's saxophonist's, but it was better. It came in and was with us. It entered my spine and, I am sure, went up the skirts of the girls. I had almost deafened myself playing drums in the most famous rock and jazz band in the state, but I could hear the voice that went through and out that horn. It sounded like a very troubled forty-year-old man, a man who had had his brow in his hands a long time.

The next time I saw Quadberry up close, in fact the first time I had seen him up close since we were eleven and he was bleeding in the cornfield, was in late February. I had only three classes this last semester, and went up to the band room often, to loaf and complain and keep up my touch on the drums. Prender let me keep my set in one of the instrument rooms, with a tarpaulin thrown over it, and I would drag it out to the practice room and whale away. Sometimes a group of sophomores would come up and I would make them marvel, whaling away as if not only deaf but blind to them, although I wasn't at all. If I saw a sophomore girl with exceptional bod or face, I would do miracles of technique I never knew were in me. I would amaze myself. I would be threatening Buddy Rich and Sam Morello. But this time when I went into the instrument room, there was Quadberry on one side, and, back in a dark corner, a small ninth-grade euphonium player whose face was all red. The little boy was weeping and grinning at the same time.

"Queerberry," the boy said softly.

Quadberry flew upon him like a demon. He grabbed the boy's collar, slapped his face, and yanked his arms behind him in a merciless wrestler's grip, the one that made them bawl on TV. Then the boy broke it and slugged Quadberry in the lips and ran across to my side of the room. He said "Queerberry" softly again and jumped for the door. Quadberry plunged across the room and tackled him on the threshold. Now that the boy was under him, Quadberry pounded the top of his head with his fist made like a mallet. The boy kept calling him "Queerberry" throughout this. He had not learned his lesson. The boy seemed to be going into concussion, so I stepped over and touched Quadberry, telling him to quit. Quadberry obeyed and stood up off the boy, who crawled with a bruised grin, saying "Queerberry." Quadberry made a move toward him, but I blocked it.

"Why are you beating up on this little guy?" I said. Quadberry was sweating and his eyes were wild with hate; he was a big fellow now, though lean. He was, at six feet tall, bigger than me.

"He kept calling me Queerberry."

"What do you care?" I asked.

"I care," Quadberry said, and left me standing there.

We were to play at Millsaps College Auditorium for the concert. It was April. We got on the buses, a few took their cars, and were a big tense crowd getting over there. To Jackson was only a twenty-minute trip. The director, Prender, followed the bus in his Volkswagen. There was a thick fog. A flashing ambulance, snaking the lanes, piled into him head on. Prender, who I would imagine was thinking of *Bolero* and hearing the young horn voices in his band – perhaps he was dwelling on Quadberry's spectacular gypsy entrance, or perhaps he was meditating on the percussion section, of which I was the king – passed into the airs of band-director heaven. We were told by the student director as we set up on the stage. The student director was a senior from the town college, very much afflicted, almost to the point of drooling, by a love and respect for Dick Prender, and now afflicted by a heartbreaking esteem for his ghost. As were we all.

I loved the tough and tender director awesomely and never knew it until I found myself bawling along with all the rest of the boys of the percussion. I told them to keep setting up, keep tuning, keep screwing the stands together, keep hauling in the kettledrums. To just quit and bawl seemed a betrayal to Prender. I caught some girl clarinetists trying to flee the stage and go have their cry. I told them to get the hell back to their section. They obeyed me. Then I found the student director. I had to have my say.

"Look. I say we just play *Bolero* and junk the rest. That's our horse. We can't play *Brighton Beach* and *Neptune's Daughter*. We'll never make it through them. And they're too happy."

"We aren't going to play anything," he said. "Man, to play is filthy. Did you ever hear Prender play piano? Do you know what a cool man he was in all things?"

"We play. He got us ready, and we play."

"Man, you can't play any more than I can direct. You're bawling your face off. Look out there at the rest of them. Man, it's a herd, it's a weeping herd."

"What's wrong? Why aren't you pulling this crowd together?" This was Quadberry, who had come up urgently. "I got those little brats in my section sitting down, but we've got people abandoning the stage, tearful little finks throwing their horns on the floor."

"I'm not directing," said the mustached college man.

"Then get out of here. You're weak, weak!"

"Man, we've got teenagers in ruin here, we got sorrowville. Nobody can—"

"Go ahead. Do your number. Weak out on us."

"Man, I—"

Quadberry was already up on the podium, shaking his arms.

"We're right here! The band is right here! Tell your friends to get back in their seats. We're doing *Bolero*. Just put *Bolero* up and start tuning. *I'm* directing. I'll be right here in front of you. You look at *me*! Don't you dare quit on Prender. Don't you dare quit on me. You've got to be heard. *I've* got to be heard. Prender wanted me to be heard. I am the star, and I say we sit down and blow."

And so we did. We all tuned and were burning low for the
advent into *Bolero*, though we couldn't believe that Quadberry
was going to remain with his saxophone strapped to him and
conduct us as well as play his solo. The judges, who apparently
hadn't heard about Prender's death, walked down to their
balcony desks.

One of them called out "Ready" and Quadberry's hand was
instantly up in the air, his fingers hard as if around the stem of
something like a torch. This was not Prender's way, but it had
to do. We went into the number cleanly and Quadberry one-
armed it in the conducting. He kept his face, this look of hostility,
at the reeds and the trumpets. I was glad he did not look toward
me and the percussion boys like that. But he must have known
we would be constant and tasteful because I was the king there. As
for the others, the soloists especially, he was scaring them into
excellence. Prender had never got quite this from them. Boys
became men and girls became women as Quadberry directed us
through *Bolero*. I even became a bit better of a man myself,
though Quadberry did not look my way. When he turned around
toward the people in the auditorium to enter on his solo, I knew
it was my baby. I and the drums were the metronome. That was
no trouble. It was talent to keep the metronome ticking amidst
any given chaos of sound.

But this keeps one's mind occupied and I have no idea what
Quadberry sounded like on his sax ride. All I know is that he
looked grief-stricken and pale, and small. Sweat had popped out
on his forehead. He bent over extremely. He was wearing the
red brass button jacket and black pants, black bow tie at the
throat, just like the rest of us. In this outfit he bent over his horn
almost out of sight. For a moment, before I caught the glint of
his horn through the music stands, I thought he had pitched
forward off the stage. He went down so far to do his deep oral
thing, his conducting arm had disappeared so quickly, I didn't
know but what he was having a seizure.

When *Bolero* was over, the audience stood up and made meat
out of their hands applauding. The judges themselves applauded.
The band stood up, bawling again, for Prender and because we
had done so well. The student director rushed out crying to

embrace Quadberry, who eluded him with his dipping shoulders. The crowd was still clapping insanely. I wanted to see Quadberry myself. I waded through the red backs, through the bow ties, over the white bucks. Here was the first-chair clarinetist, who had done his bit like an angel; he sat close to the podium and could hear Quadberry.

"Was Quadberry good?" I asked him.

"Are you kidding? These tears in my eyes, they're for how good he was. He was too good. I'll never touch my clarinet again." The clarinetist slung the pieces of his horn into their case like underwear and a toothbrush.

I found Quadberry fitting the sections of his alto in the velvet holds of his case.

"Hooray," I said. "Hip damn hooray for you."

Arden was smiling too, showing a lot of teeth I had never seen. His smile was sly. He knew he had pulled off a monster unlikelihood.

"Hip hip hooray for me," he said. "Look at her. I had the bell of the horn almost smack in her face."

There was a woman of about thirty sitting in the front row of the auditorium. She wore a sundress with a drastic cleavage up front; looked like something that hung around New Orleans and kneaded your heart to death with her feet. She was still mesmerized by Quadberry. She bore on him with a stare and there was moisture in her cleavage.

"You played well."

"Well? Play well? Yes."

He was trying not to look at her directly. Look at *me*, I beckoned to her with full face: I was the *drums*. She arose and left.

"I was walking downhill in a valley, is all I was doing," said Quadberry. "Another man, a wizard, was playing my horn." He locked his sax case. "I feel nasty for not being able to cry like the rest of them. Look at them. Look at them crying."

True, the children of the band were still weeping, standing around the stage. Several moms and dads had come up among them, and they were misty-eyed too. The mixture of grief and superb music had been unbearable.

A girl in tears appeared next to Quadberry. She was a majorette in football season and played third-chair sax during the concert season. Not even her violent sorrow could take the beauty out of the face of this girl. I had watched her for a number of years – her alertness to her own beauty, the pride of her legs in the majorette outfit – and had taken out her younger sister, a second-rate version of her and a wayward overcompensating nymphomaniac whom several of us made a hobby out of pitying. Well, here was Lilian herself crying in Quadberry's face. She told him that she'd run off the stage when she heard about Prender, dropped her horn and everything, and had thrown herself into a tavern across the street and drunk two beers quickly for some kind of relief. But she had come back through the front doors of the auditorium and sat down, dizzy with beer, and seen Quadberry, the miraculous way he had gone on with *Bolero*. And now she was eaten up by feelings of guilt, weakness, cowardice.

"We didn't miss you," said Quadberry.

"Please forgive me. Tell me to do something to make up for it."

"Don't breathe my way, then. You've got beer all over your breath."

"I want to talk to you."

"Take my horn case and go out, get in my car, and wait for me. It's the ugly Plymouth in front of the school bus."

"I know," she said.

Lilian Field, this lovely teary thing, with the rather pious grace of her carriage, with the voice full of imminent swoon, picked up Quadberry's horn case and her own and walked off the stage.

I told the percussion boys to wrap up the packing. Into my suitcase I put my own gear and also managed to steal drum keys, two pairs of brushes, a 20-inch Turkish cymbal, a Gretsch snare drum that I desired for my collection, a wood block, kettle-drum mallets, a tuning harp and a score sheet of *Bolero* full of marginal notes I'd written down straight from the mouth of Dick Prender, thinking I might want to look at the score sheet sometime in the future when I was having a fit of nostalgia such as I am having right now as I write this. I had never done any serious stealing before, and I was stealing for my art. Prender was dead, the band had done its last thing of the year, I was a senior. Things were finished at the high school. I was just looting a sinking ship. I could hardly lift the suitcase. As I was pushing it across the stage, Quadberry was there again.

"You can ride back with me if you want to."

"But you've got Lilian."

"Please ride back with me . . . us. Please."

"Why?"

"To help me get rid of her. Her breath is full of beer. My father always had that breath. Every time he was friendly, he had that breath. And she looks a great deal like my mother." We were interrupted by the Tupelo band director. He put his baton against Quadberry's arm.

"You were big with *Bolero*, son, but that doesn't mean you own the stage."

Quadberry caught the end of the suitcase and helped me with it out to the steps behind the auditorium. The buses were gone. There sat his ugly ocher Plymouth; it was a failed, gay, experimental shade from the Chrysler people. Lilian was sitting in the front seat wearing her shirt and bow tie, her coat off.

"Are you going to ride back with me?" Quadberry said to me.

"I think I would spoil something. You never saw her when she was a majorette. She's not stupid, either. She likes to show off a little, but she's not stupid. She's in the History Club."

"My father has a doctorate in history. She smells of beer."

I said, "She drank two cans of beer when she heard about Prender."

"There are a lot of other things to do when you hear about death. What I did for example. She ran away. She fell to pieces."

"She's waiting for us," I said.

"One damned thing I am never going to do is drink."

"I've never seen your mother up close, but Lilian doesn't look like your mother. She doesn't look like anybody's mother."

I rode with them silently to Clinton. Lilian made no bones about being disappointed I was in the car, though she said nothing. I knew it would be like this and I hated it. Other girls in town would not be so unhappy that I was in the car with them. I looked for flaws in Lilian's face and neck and hair, but there weren't any. Couldn't there be a mole, an enlarged pore, too much gum on a tooth, a single awkward hair around the ear? No. Memory, the whole lying opera of it, is killing me now. Lilian was faultless beauty, even sweating, even and especially in the white man's shirt and the bow tie clamping together her collar, when one knew her uncomfortable bosoms, her poor nipples. . . .

"Don't take me back to the band room. Turn off here and let me off at my house," I said to Quadberry. He didn't turn off.

"Don't tell Arden what to do. He can do what he wants to," said Lilian, ignoring me and speaking to me at the same time. I couldn't bear her hatred. I asked Quadberry to please just stop the car and let me out here, wherever he was: this front yard of the mobile home would do. I was so earnest that he stopped the car. He handed back the keys and I dragged my suitcase out of the trunk, then flung the keys back to him and kicked the car to get it going again.

My band came together in the summer. We were the Bop Fiends . . . that was our name. Two of them were from Ole Miss, our bass player was from Memphis State, but when we got together this time, I didn't call the tenor sax, who went to Mississippi Southern, because Quadberry wanted to play with us. During the school year the college boys and I fell into minor groups to pick up 20 dollars on a weekend, playing dances for the Moose Lodge, medical-student fraternities in Jackson, teenage recreation centers in Greenwood, and such as that. But come summer we were the Bop Fiends again, and the price for us went up to 1,200 dollars a gig. Where they wanted the best rock and bop and they had some bread, we were called. The summer after I was a senior, we played in Alabama, Louisiana and Arkansas. Our fame was getting out there on the interstate route.

This was the summer that I made myself deaf.

Years ago Prender had invited down an old friend from a high school in Michigan. He asked me over to meet the friend, who had been a drummer with Stan Kenton at one time and was now a band director just like Prender. This fellow was almost totally deaf and he warned me very sincerely about deafing myself. He said there would come a point when you had to lean over and concentrate all your hearing on what the band was doing and that was the time to quit for a while, because if you didn't you would be irrevocably deaf like him in a month or two. I listened to him but could not take him seriously. Here was an oldish man who had his problems. My ears had ages of hearing left. Not so. I played the drums so loud the summer after I graduated from high school that I made myself, eventually, stone deaf.

We were at, say, the National Guard Armory in Lake Village, Arkansas, Quadberry out in front of us on the stage they'd built. Down on the floor were hundreds of sweaty teenagers. Four girls in sundresses, showing what they could, were leaning on the stage with broad ignorant lust on their minds. I'd play so loud for one particular chick, I'd get absolutely out of control. The guitar boys would have to turn the volume up full blast to compensate. Thus I went deaf. Anyhow, the dramatic idea was to release Quadberry on a very soft sweet ballad right in the middle of a long ear-piercing run of rock-and-roll tunes. I'd get out the brushes and we would astonish the crowd with our tenderness. By August, I was so deaf I had to watch Quadberry's fingers changing notes on the saxophone, had to use my eyes to keep time. The other members of the Bop Fiends told me I was hitting out of time. I pretended I was trying to do experimental things with rhythm when the truth was I simply could no longer hear. I was no longer a tasteful drummer, either, I had become deaf through lack of taste.

Which was – taste – exactly the quality that made Quadberry wicked on the saxophone. During the howling, during the churning, Quadberry had taste. The noise did not affect his personality; he was solid as a brick. He could blend. Oh, he could hoot through his horn when the right time came, but he could do supporting roles for an hour. Then, when we brought him out front for his solo on something like "Take Five," he would play with such light blissful technique that he even

eclipsed Paul Desmond. The girls around the stage did not cause
him to enter into excessive loudness or vibrato.

Quadberry had his own girlfriend now, Lilian back at
Clinton, who put all the sundressed things around the stage in
the shade. In my mind I had congratulated him for getting up
next to this beauty, but in June and July, when I was still hearing
things a little, he never said a word about her. It was one night
in August, when I could hear nothing and was driving him to his
house, that he asked me to turn off the inside light and spoke in
a retarded deliberate way. He knew I was deaf and counted on
my being able to read lips.

"Don't . . . make . . . fun . . . of her . . . or me . . . We . . .
think . . . she . . . is . . . in trouble."

I wagged my head. Never would I make fun of him or her.
She detested me because I had taken out her helpless little sister
for a few weeks, but I would never think there was anything
funny about Lilian, for all her haughtiness. I only thought of this
event as monumentally curious.

"No one except you knows," he said.

"Why did you tell me?"

"Because I'm going away and you have to take care of her. I
wouldn't trust her with anybody but you."

"She hates the sight of my face. Where are you going?"

"Annapolis."

"You aren't going to any damned Annapolis."

"That was the only school that wanted me."

"You're going to play your saxophone on a boat?"

"I don't know what I'm going to do."

"How . . . how can you just leave her?"

"She wants me to. She's very excited about me at Annapolis.
William [this is my name], there is no girl I could imagine who
has more inner sweetness than Lilian."

I entered the town college, as did Lilian. She was in the same
chemistry class I was. But she was rows away. It was difficult to
learn anything, being deaf. The professor wasn't a pantomimer –
but finally he went to the blackboard with the formulas and the

algebra of problems, to my happiness. I hung in and made a B.
At the end of the semester I was swaggering around the grade
sheet he'd posted. I happened to see Lilian's grade. She'd only
made a C. Beautiful Lilian got only a C while I, with my
handicap, had made a B.

It had been a very difficult chemistry class. I had watched
Lilian's stomach the whole way through. It was not growing. I
wanted to see her look like a watermelon, make herself an
amazing mother shape.

When I made the B and Lilian made the C, I got up my
courage and finally went to see her. She answered the door. Her
parents weren't home. I'd never wanted this office of watching
over her as Quadberry wanted me to, and this is what I told her.
She asked me into the house. The rooms smelled of nail polish
and pipe smoke. I was hoping her little sister wasn't in the house,
and my wish came true. We were alone.

"You can quit watching over me."

"Are you pregnant?"

"No." Then she started crying. "I wanted to be. But I'm
not."

"What do you hear from Quadberry?"

She said something, but she had her back to me. She looked
to me for an answer, but I had nothing to say. I knew she'd said
something, but I hadn't heard it.

"He doesn't play the saxophone anymore," she said.

This made me angry.

"Why not?"

"Too much math and science and navigation. He wants to
fly. That's what his dream is now. He wants to get into an F-
something jet."

I asked her to say this over and she did. Lilian really was full
of inner sweetness, as Quadberry had said. She understood that I
was deaf. Perhaps Quadberry had told her.

The rest of the time in her house I simply witnessed her
beauty and her mouth moving.

I went through college. To me it is interesting that I kept a B
average and did it all deaf, though I know this isn't interesting to

people who aren't deaf. I loved music, and never heard it. I loved poetry, and never heard a word that came out of the mouths of the visiting poets who read at the campus. I loved my mother and dad, but never heard a sound they made. One Christmas Eve, Radcleve was back from Ole Miss and threw an M–80 out in the street for old times' sake. I saw it explode, but there was only a pressure in my ears. I was at parties when lusts were raging and I went home with two girls (I am medium handsome) who lived in apartments of the old two-story 1920 vintage, and I took my shirt off and made love to them. But I have no real idea what their reaction was. They were stunned and all smiles when I got up, but I have no idea whether I gave them the last pleasure or not. I hope I did. I've always been partial to women and have always wanted to see them satisfied till their eyes popped out.

Through Lilian I got the word that Quadberry was out of Annapolis and now flying jets off the *Bonhomme Richard*, an aircraft carrier headed for Vietnam. He telegrammed her that he would set down at the Jackson airport at 10 o'clock one night. So Lilian and I were out there waiting. It was a familiar place to her. She was a stewardess and her loops were mainly in the South. She wore a beige raincoat, had red sandals on her feet; I was in a black turtleneck and corduroy jacket, feeling significant, so significant I could barely stand it. I'd already made myself the lead writer at Gordon-Marx Advertising in Jackson. I hadn't seen Lilian in a year. Her eyes were strained, no longer the bright blue things they were when she was a pious beauty. We drank coffee together. I loved her. As far as I knew, she'd been faithful to Quadberry.

He came down in an F–something Navy jet right on the dot of ten. She ran out on the airport pavement to meet him. I saw her crawl up the ladder. Quadberry never got out of the plane. I could see him in his blue helmet. Lilian backed down the ladder. Then Quadberry had the cockpit cover him again. He turned the plane around so its flaming red end was at us. He took it down the runway. We saw him leap out into the night at the middle of the runway going west, toward San Diego and the *Bonhomme Richard*. Lilian was crying.

"What did he say?" I asked.

"He said, 'I am a dragon. America the beautiful, like you will never know.' He wanted to give you a message. He was glad you were here."

"What was the message?"

"The same thing. 'I am a dragon. America the beautiful, like you will never know.'"

"Did he say anything else?"

"Not a thing."

"Did he express any love toward you?"

"He wasn't Ard. He was somebody with a sneer in a helmet."

"He's going to war, Lilian."

"I asked him to kiss me and he told me to get off the plane, he was firing up and it was dangerous."

"Arden is going to war. He's just on his way to Vietnam and he wanted us to know that. It wasn't just him he wanted us to see. It was him in the jet he wanted us to see. He *is* that black jet. You can't kiss an airplane."

"And what are we supposed to do?" cried sweet Lilian.

"We've just got to hang around. He didn't have to lift off and disappear straight up like that. That was to tell us how he isn't with us anymore."

Lilian asked me what she was supposed to do now. I told her she was supposed to come with me to my apartment in the old 1920 Clinton place where I was. I was supposed to take care of her. Quadberry had said so. His six-year-old directive was still working.

She slept on the fold-out bed of the sofa for a while. This was the only bed in my place. I stood in the dark in the kitchen and drank a quarter bottle of gin on ice. I would not turn on the light and spoil her sleep. The prospect of Lilian asleep in my apartment made me feel like a chaplain on a visit to the Holy Land; I stood there getting drunk, biting my tongue when dreams of lust burst on me. That black jet Quadberry wanted us to see him in, its flaming rear end, his blasting straight up into the night at mid-runway – what precisely was he wanting to say in this stunt? Was he saying remember him forever or forget him forever? But I had my own life and was neither going to mother-hen it over his memory nor his old sweetheart. What did he mean, *America the beautiful, like you will never know*? I, William Howly, knew a goddamn good bit about America the beautiful, even as a deaf man. Being deaf had brought me up closer to people. There were only about five I knew, but I knew their mouth movements, the perspiration under their noses, their tongues moving over the crowns of their teeth, their fingers on their lips. Quadberry, I said, you don't have to get up next to the stars in your black jet to see America the beautiful.

I was deciding to lie down on the kitchen floor and sleep the night, when Lilian turned on the light and appeared in her panties and bra. Her body was perfect except for a tiny bit of fat on her upper thighs. She'd sunbathed herself so her limbs were brown, and her stomach, and the instinct was to rip off the white underneath and lick, suck, say something terrific into the flesh that you discovered.

She was moving her mouth.

"Say it again slowly."

"I'm lonely. When he took off in his jet, I think it meant he wasn't ever going to see me again. I think it meant he was laughing at both of us. He's an astronaut and he spits on us."

"You want me on the bed with you?" I asked.

"I know you're an intellectual. We could keep on the lights so you'd know what I said."

"You want to say things? This isn't going to be just sex?"

"It could never be just sex."

"I agree. Go to sleep. Let me make up my mind whether to come in there. Turn out the lights."

Again the dark, and I thought I would cheat not only Quadberry but the entire Quadberry family if I did what was natural.

I fell asleep.

Quadberry escorted B–52s on bombing missions into North Vietnam. He was catapulted off the *Bonhomme Richard* in his suit at 100 degrees temperature, often at night, and put the F–8 on all it could get – the tiny cockpit, the immense long 2-million-dollar fuselage, wings, tail and jet engine, Quadberry, the genius master of his dragon, going up to 20,000 feet to be cool. He'd meet with the big B–52 turtle of the air and get in a position, his cockpit glowing with green and orange lights, and turn on his transistor radio. There was only one really good band, never mind the old American rock-and-roll from Cambodia, and that was Red Chinese opera. Quadberry loved it. He loved the nasal horde in the finale, when the peasants won over the old fat dilettante mayor. Then he'd turn the jet around when he saw the squatty abrupt little fires way down there after the B–52s had dropped their diet. It was a seven-hour trip. Sometimes he slept, but his body knew when to wake up. Another thirty minutes and there was his ship waiting for him out in the waves.

All his trips weren't this easy. He'd have to blast out in daytime and get with the B–52s, and a SAM missile would come up among them. Two of his mates were taken down by these missiles. But Quadberry, as on saxophone, had endless learned technique. He'd put his jet perpendicular in the air and make the SAMs look silly. He even shot down two of them. Then, one day in daylight, a MIG came floating up level with him and his squadron. Quadberry couldn't believe it. Others in the squadron were shy, but Quadberry knew where and how the MIG could shoot. He flew below the cannons and then came in behind it. He knew the MIG wanted one of the B–52s and not mainly him. The MIG was so concentrated on the fat B–52 that he forgot about Quadberry. It was really an amateur suicide pilot in the MIG. Quadberry got on top of him and let down a missile, rising out of the way of it. The missile blew off the tail of the MIG. But then Quadberry wanted to see if the man got safely out of the cockpit. He thought it would be pleasant if the fellow got out with his parachute working. Then Quadberry saw that the fellow wanted to collide his wreckage with the B–52, so Quadberry turned himself over and cannoned, evaporated the pilot and cockpit. It was the first man he'd killed.

The next trip out, Quadberry was hit by a ground missile. But his jet kept flying. He flew it 100 miles and got to the sea. There was the *Bonhomme Richard*, so he ejected. His back was snapped but, by God, he landed right on the deck. His mates caught him in their arms and cut the parachute off him. His back hurt for weeks, but he was all right. He rested and recuperated in Hawaii for a month.

Then he went off the front of the ship. Just like that, his F-6 plopped in the ocean and sank like a rock. Quadberry saw the ship go over him. He knew he shouldn't eject just yet. If he ejected now he'd knock his head on the bottom and get chewed up in the motor blades. So Quadberry waited. His plane was sinking in the green and he could see the hull of the aircraft carrier getting smaller, but he had oxygen through his mask and it didn't seem that urgent a decision. Just let the big ship get over. Down what later proved to be 60 feet, he pushed the ejection button. It fired him away, bless it, and he woke up 10 feet under the surface swimming against an almost overwhelming body of underwater parachute. But two of his mates were in a helicopter, one of them on the ladder to lift him out.

Now Quadberry's back was really hurt. He was out of this war and all wars for good.

Lilian, the stewardess, was killed in a crash. Her jet exploded with a hijacker's bomb, an inept bomb which wasn't supposed to go off, 15 miles out of Havana; the poor pilot, the poor passengers, the poor stewardesses were all splattered like flesh sparklers over the water just out of Cuba. A fisherman found one seat of the airplane. Castro expressed regrets.

Quadberry came back to Clinton two weeks after Lilian and the others bound for Tampa were dead. He hadn't heard about her. So I told him Lilian was dead when I met him at the airport. Quadberry was thin and rather meek in his civvies – a gray suit and an out-of-style tie. The white ends of his hair were not there – the halo had disappeared – because his hair was cut short. The Arab nose seemed a pitiable defect in an ash-whiskered face that was beyond anemic now. He looked shorter, stooped. The truth was he was sick, his back was killing him. His breath was heavy-laden with airplane martinis and in his limp right hand he held a wet cigar. I told him about Lilian. He mumbled something sideways that I could not possibly make out.

"You've got to speak right at me, remember? Remember me, Quadberry?"

"Mom and Dad of course aren't here."

"No. Why aren't they?"

"He wrote me a letter after we bombed Hué. Said he hadn't sent me to Annapolis to bomb the architecture of Hué. He had been there once and had some important experience – French-kissed the queen of Hué or the like. Anyway, he said I'd have to do a hell of a lot of repentance for that. But he and Mom are separate people. Why isn't *she* here?"

"I don't know."

"I'm not asking you the question. The question is to God."

He shook his head. Then he sat down on the floor of the terminal. People had to walk around. I asked him to get up.

"No. How is old Clinton?"

"Horrible. Aluminum subdivisions, cigar boxes with four thin columns in front, thick as a hive. We got a turquoise water tank; got a shopping center, a monster Jitney Jungle, fifth-rate teeny-boppers covering the place like ants." Why was I being so frank just now, as Quadberry sat on the floor downcast, drooped over like a long weak candle? "It's not our town anymore, Ard. It's going to hurt to drive back into it. Hurts me every day. Please get up."

"And Lilian's not even over there now."

"No. She's a cloud over the Gulf of Mexico. You flew out of Pensacola once. You know what beauty those pink and blue clouds are. That's how I think of her."

"Was there a funeral?"

"Oh, yes. Her Methodist preacher and a big crowd over at Wright Ferguson funeral home. Your mother and father were there. Your father shouldn't have come. He could barely walk. Please get up."

"Why? What am I going to do, where am I going?"

"You've got your saxophone."

"Was there a coffin? Did you all go by and see the pink or blue cloud in it?" He was sneering now as he had done when he was eleven and fourteen and seventeen.

"Yes, they had a very ornate coffin."

"Lilian was the Unknown Stewardess. I'm not getting up."

"I said you still have your saxophone."

"No, I don't. I tried to play it on the ship after the last time I hurt my back. No go. I can't bend my neck or spine to play it. The pain kills me."

"Well, *don't* get up, then. Why am I asking you to get up? I'm just a deaf drummer, too vain to buy a hearing aid. Can't stand to write the ad copy I do. Wasn't I a good drummer?"

"Superb."

"But we can't be in this condition forever. The police are going to come and make you get up if we do it much longer."

The police didn't come. It was Quadberry's mother who came. She looked me in the face and grabbed my shoulders before she saw Ard on the floor. When she saw him she yanked him off the floor, hugging him passionately. She was shaking with sobs. Quadberry was gathered to her as if he were a rope she was trying to wrap around herself. Her mouth was all over him. Quadberry's mother was a good-looking woman of fifty. I simply held her purse. He cried out that his back was hurting. At last she let him go.

'So now we walk," I said.

"Dad's in the car trying to quit crying," said his mother.

"This is nice," Quadberry said. "I thought everything and everybody was dead around here." He put his arms around his mother. "Let's all go off and kill some time together." His mother's hair was on his lips. "You?" he asked me.

"Murder the devil out of it," I said.

I pretended to follow their car back to their house in Clinton. But when we were going through Jackson, I took the North 55 exit and disappeared from them, exhibiting a great amount of taste, I thought. I would get in their way in this reunion. I had an unimprovable apartment on Old Canton Road in a huge plaster house, Spanish style, with a terrace and ferns and yucca plants, and a green door where I went in. When I woke up I didn't have to make my coffee or fry my egg. The girl who slept in my bed did that. She was Lilian's little sister, Esther Field. Esther was pretty in a minor way and I was proud how I had tamed her to clean and cook around the place. The Field family would appreciate how I lived with her. I showed her the broom and the skillet, and she loved them. She also learned to speak very slowly when she had to say something.

Esther answered the phone when Quadberry called me seven months later. She gave me his message. He wanted to know my opinion on a decision he had to make. There was this Dr. Gordon, a surgeon at Emory Hospital in Atlanta, who said he could cure Quadberry's back problem. Quadberry's back was killing him. He was in torture even holding up the phone to say this. The surgeon said there was a seventy-five/twenty-five chance. Seventy-five that it would be successful, twenty-five that it would be fatal. Esther waited for my opinion. I told her to tell Quadberry to go over to Emory. He'd got through with luck in Vietnam, and now he should ride it out in this petty back operation.

Esther delivered the message and hung up.

"He said the surgeon's just his age; he's some genius from Johns Hopkins Hospital. He said this Gordon guy has published a lot of articles on spinal operations," said Esther.

"Fine and good. All is happy. Come to bed."

I felt her mouth and her voice on my ears, but I could hear only a sort of loud pulse from the girl. All I could do was move toward moisture and nipples and hair.

Quadberry lost his gamble at Emory Hospital in Atlanta. The brilliant surgeon his age lost him. Quadberry died. He died with his Arabian nose up in the air.

That is why I told this story and will never tell another.

RON HANSEN

☆  ☆  ☆  ☆

# *Wickedness*

At the end of the nineteenth century a girl from Delaware got on
a milk train in Omaha and took a green wool seat in the second-
class car. August was outside the window, and sunlight was a
yellow glare on the trees. Up front, a railway conductor in a
navy-blue uniform was gingerly backing down the aisle with a
heavy package in a gunnysack that a boy was helping him with.
They were talking about an agreeable seat away from the hot
Nebraska day that was persistent outside, and then they were
setting their cargo across the runnered aisle from the girl and
tilting it against the shellacked wooden wall of the railway car
before walking back up the aisle and elsewhere into August.
   She was sixteen years old and an Easterner just recently hired
as a county schoolteacher, but she knew enough about prairie
farming to think the heavy package was a crank-and-piston
washing machine or a boxed plowshare and coulter, something
no higher than the bloody stump where the poultry were
chopped with a hatchet and then wildly high-stepped around the
yard. Soon, however, there was a juggling movement and the
gunnysack slipped aside, and she saw an old man sitting there,
his limbs hacked away, and dark holes where his ears ought to
have been, the skin pursed at his jaw hinge like pink lips in a
kiss. The milk train jerked into a roll through the railway yard,
and the old man was jounced so that his gray cheek pressed
against the hot window glass. Although he didn't complain, it
seemed an uneasy position, and the girl wished she had the
courage to get up from her seat and tug the jolting body upright.
She instead got to her page in *Quo Vadis* and pretended to be so
rapt by the book that she didn't look up again until Columbus,
where a doctor with liquorice on his breath sat heavily beside her
and openly stared over his newspaper before whispering that the

poor man was a carpenter in Genoa who'd been caught out in the great blizzard of 1888. Had she heard of that one?

The girl shook her head.

She ought to look out for their winters, the doctor said. Weather in Nebraska could be the wickedest thing she ever saw.

She didn't know what to say, so she said nothing. And at Genoa a young teamster got on in order to carry out the old man, whose half body was heavy enough that the boy had to yank the gunnysack up the aisle like 60 pounds of mail.

In the year 1888, on the twelfth day of January, a pink sun was up just after seven and southeastern zephyrs of such soft temperature were sailing over the Great Plains that squatters walked their properties in high rubber boots and April jackets and some farmhands took off their Civil War greatcoats to rake silage into the cattle troughs. However, sheep that ate whatever they could the night before raised their heads away from food and sniffed the salt tang in the air. And all that morning streetcar mules were reported to be acting up, nipping each other, jingling the hitch rings, foolishly waggling their dark manes and necks as though beset by gnats and horseflies.

A Danish cattleman named Axel Hansen later said he was near the Snake River and tipping a teaspoon of saleratus into a yearling's mouth when he heard a faint groaning in the north that was like the noise of a high waterfall at a fair distance. Axel looked toward Dakota, and there half the sky was suddenly gray and black and indigo blue with great storm clouds that were seething up as high as the sun and wrangling toward him at horse speed. Weeds were being uprooted, sapling trees were bullwhipping, and the top inches of snow and prairie soil were being sucked up and stirred like the dirty flour that was called red dog. And then the onslaught hit him hard as furniture, flying him onto his back so that when Axel looked up, he seemed to be deep undersea and in icehouse cold. Eddying snow made it hard to breathe any way but sideways, and getting up to just his knees and hands seemed a great attainment. Although his sod house was but a quarter-mile away, it took Axel four hours to get there. Half his face was frozen gray and hard as weatherboarding so the cattleman was speechless until nightfall, and then Axel Hansen simply told his wife, That was not pleasant.

Cow tails stuck out sideways when the wind caught them. Sparrows and crows whumped hard against the windowpanes, their eyes seeking out an escape, their wings fanned out and flattened as though pinned up in an ornithologist's display. Cats died, dogs died, pigeons died. Entire farms of cattle and pigs and geese and chickens were wiped out in a single night. Horizontal snow that was hard and dry as salt dashed and seethed over everything, sloped up like rooftops, tricked its way across creek beds and ditches, milkily purled down city streets, stole shanties and coops and pens from a bleak landscape that was even then called the Great American Desert. Everything about the blizzard seemed to have personality and hateful intention. Especially the cold. At 6 a.m., the temperature at Valentine, Nebraska, was 30 degrees above zero. Half a day later the temperature was 14 below, a drop of 44 degrees and the difference between having toes and not, between staying alive overnight and not, between ordinary concerns and one overriding idea.

Ainslie Classen was hopelessly lost in the whiteness and tilting low under the jamming gale when his right elbow jarred against a joist of his pigsty. He walked around the sty by skating his sore red hands along the upright shiplap and then squeezed inside through the slops trough. The pigs scampered over to him, seeking his protection, and Ainslie put himself among them, getting down in their stink and their body heat, socking them away only when they ganged up or when two or three presumed he was food. Hurt was nailing into his finger joints until he thought to work his hands into the pigs' hot wastes, and smeared some onto his skin. The pigs grunted around him and intelligently snuffled at his body with their pink and tender noses, and Ainslie thought, *You are not me but I am you*, and Ainslie Classen got through the night without shame or injury.

Whereas a Hartington woman took two steps out her door and disappeared until the snow sank away in April and raised her body up from her garden patch.

An Omaha cigar maker got off the Leavenworth Street

trolley that night, 50 yards from his own home and 5 yards from another's. The completeness of the blizzard so puzzled him that the cigar maker tramped up and down the block more than 20 times and then slept against a lamp-post and died.

A cattle inspector froze to death getting up on his quarter horse. The next morning he was still tilting the saddle with his upright weight, one cowboy boot just inside the iced stirrup, one bear-paw mitten over the horn and reins. His quarter horse apparently kept waiting for him to complete his mount, and then the quarter horse died too.

A Chicago boy visiting his brother for the holidays was going to a neighbor's farm to borrow a scoop shovel when the night train of blizzard raged in and overwhelmed him. His tracks showed the boy mistakenly slanted past the sod house he'd just come from, and then tilted foward with perhaps the vain hope of running into some shop or shed or railway depot. His body was found four days later and 27 miles from home.

A forty-year-old wife sought out her husband in the open range land near O'Neill and days later was found standing up in her muskrat coat and black bandanna, her scarf-wrapped hands tightly clenching the top strand of rabbit wire that was keeping her upright, her blue eyes still open but cloudily bottled by a half inch of ice, her jaw unhinged as though she'd died yelling out a name.

The 1 a.m. report from the Chief Signal Officer in Washington, DC, had said Kansas and Nebraska could expect "fair weather, followed by snow, brisk to high southerly winds gradually diminishing in force, becoming westerly and warmer, followed by colder."

Sin Thomas undertook the job of taking Emily Flint home from their Holt County schoolhouse just before noon. Sin's age was sixteen, and Emily was not only six years younger but also practically kin to him, since her stepfather was Sin's older brother. Sin took the girl's hand and they haltingly tilted against the uprighting gale on their walk to a dark horse, gray-maned and gray-tailed with ice. Sin cracked the reins loose of the crowbar tie-up and helped Emily up onto his horse, jumping up onto the croup from a soapbox and clinging the girl to him as though she were groceries he couldn't let spill.

Everything she knew was no longer there. She was in a book without descriptions. She could put her hand out and her hand would disappear. Although Sin knew the general direction to Emily's house, the geography was so duned and drunk with snow that Sin gave up trying to nudge his horse one way or another and permitted its slight adjustments away from the wind. Hours passed and the horse strayed southeast into Wheeler County, and then in misery and pneumonia it stopped, planting its overworked legs like four parts of an argument and slinging its head away from Sin's yanks and then hanging its nose in anguish. Emily hopped down into the snow and held on to the boy's coat as Sin uncinched the saddle and jerked off a green horse blanket and slapped it against his iron leggings in order to crack the ice from it. And then Sin scooped out a deep nook in a snow slope that was as high and steep as the roof of a New Hampshire house. Emily tightly wrapped herself in the green horse blanket and slumped inside the nook in the snow, and the boy crept on top of her and stayed like that, trying not to press into her.

Emily would never say what was said or was cautiously not said that night. She may have been hysterical. In spite of the fact that Emily was out of the wind, she later said that the January night's temperature was like wire-cutting pliers that snipped at her ears and toes and fingertips until the horrible pain became only a nettling and then a kind of sleep and her feet seemed as dead as her shoes. Emily wept, but her tears froze cold as penny nails and her upper lip seemed candlewaxed by her nose and she couldn't stop herself from feeling the difference in the body on top of her. She thought Sin Thomas was responsible, that the night suited his secret purpose, and she so complained of the bitter cold that Sin finally took off his Newmarket overcoat and tailored it around the girl; but sixty years later, when Emily wrote her own account of the ordeal, she forgot to say anything about him giving her his overcoat and only said in an ordinary way that they spent the night inside a snowdrift and that "by morning the storm had subsided."

With daybreak Sin told Emily to stay there and, with or without his Newmarket overcoat, the boy walked away with the forlorn hope of chancing upon his horse. Winds were still high, the temperature was 35 degrees below zero, and the snow was deep enough that Sin pulled lopsidedly with every step and then toppled over just a few yards away. And then it was impossible for him to get to his knees, and Sin only sank deeper when he attempted to swim up into the high wave of snow hanging over him. Sin told himself that he would try again to get out, but first he'd build up his strength by napping for just a little while. He arranged his body in the snow gully so that the sunlight angled onto it, and then Sin Thomas gave in to sleep and within twenty minutes died.

His body was discovered at noon by a Wheeler County search party, and shortly after that they came upon Emily. She was carried to a nearby house where she slumped in a kitchen chair while girls her own age dipped Emily's hands and feet into pans of ice water. She could look up over a windowsill and see Sin Thomas's body standing upright on the porch, his hands woodenly crossed at his chest, so Emily kept her brown eyes on the pinewood floor and slept that night with jars of hot water against her skin. She could not walk for two months. Even scissoring tired her hands. She took a cashier's job with the Nebraska Farm Implements Company and kept it for forty-five years, staying all her life in Holt County. She died in a wheelchair on a hospital porch in the month of April. She was wearing a glamorous sable coat. She never married.

The T. E. D. Schusters' only child was a seven-year-old boy named Cleo who rode his Shetland pony to the Westpoint school that day and had not shown up on the doorstep by 2 p.m., when Mr. Schuster went down into the root cellar, dumped purple sugar beets onto the earthen floor, and upended the bushel basket over his head as he slung himself against the onslaught in his second try for Westpoint. Hours later Mrs. Schuster was tapping powdered salt onto the night candles in order to preserve the wax when the door abruptly blew open and Mr. Schuster stood there without Cleo and utterly white and petrified with cold. She warmed him up with okra soup and tenderly wrapped his frozen feet and hands in strips of gauze that she'd dipped in kerosene, and they were sitting on milking stools by a red-hot stove, their ankles just touching, only the usual sentiments being expressed, when they heard a clopping on the wooden stoop and looked out to see the dark Shetland pony turned gray and shaggy-bearded with ice, his legs as wobbly as if he'd just been born. Jammed under the saddle skirt was a damp, rolled-up note from the Scottish schoolteacher that said, Cleo is safe. The Schusters invited the pony into the house and bewildered him with praises as Cleo's mother scraped ice from the pony's shag with her own ivory comb, and Cleo's father gave him sugar from the Dresden bowl as steam rose up from the pony's back.

Even at 6 o'clock that evening, there was no heat in Mathias Aachen's house, and the seven Aachen children were in whatever stockings and clothing they owned as they put their hands on a Hay-burner stove that was no warmer than soap. When a jar of apricots burst open that night and the iced orange syrup did not ooze out, Aachen's wife told the children, You ought now to get under your covers. While the seven were crying and crowding onto their dirty floor mattresses, she ran the green tent cloth along the iron wire dividing the house and slid underneath horse blankets in Mathias Aachen's gray wool trousers and her own gray dress and a ghastly muskrat coat that in hot weather gave birth to insects.

Aachen said, Every one of us will be dying of cold before morning. Freezing here. In Nebraska.

His wife just lay there, saying nothing.

Aachen later said he sat up bodingly until shortly after 1 p.m., when the house temperature was so exceedingly cold that a gray suede of ice was on the teapot and his pretty girls were whimpering in their sleep. You are not meant to stay here, Aachen thought, and tilted hot candle wax into his right ear and then his left, until he could only hear his body drumming blood. And then Aachen got his Navy Colt and kissed his wife and killed her. And then walked under the green tent cloth and killed his seven children, stopping twice to capture a scuttling boy and stopping once more to reload.

Hattie Benedict was in her Antelope County schoolyard overseeing the noon recess in a black cardigan sweater and gray wool dress when the January blizzard caught her unaware. She had been impatiently watching four girls in flying coats playing Ante I Over by tossing a spindle of chartreuse yarn over the one-room schoolhouse, and then a sharp cold petted her neck and Hattie turned toward the open fields of hoarfrosted scraggle and yellow grass. Just a half mile away was a gray blur of snow underneath a dark sky that was all hurry and calamity, like a nighttime city of sin-black buildings and havoc in the streets. Wind tortured a creekside cottonwood until it cracked apart. A tin water pail rang in a skipping roll to the horse path. One quarter of the tar-paper roof was torn from the schoolhouse and sailed southeast 40 feet. And only then did Hattie yell for the older boys with their cigarettes and clay pipes to hurry in from the prairie 20 rods away, and she was hustling a dallying girl inside just as the snowstorm socked into her Antelope County schoolhouse, shipping the building awry off its timber skids so that the southwest side heavily dropped 6 inches and the oak-plank floor became a slope that Hattie ascended unsteadily while ordering the children to open their *Webster Franklin Fourth Reader* to the Lord's Prayer in verse and to say it aloud. And then Hattie stood by her desk with her pink hands held theatrically to her cheeks as she looked up at the walking noise of bricks being jarred from the chimney and down the roof. Every window view was as white as if butchers' paper had been tacked up. Winds pounded into the windowpanes and dry window putty trickled onto the unpainted sills. Even the slough grass fire in the Hay-burner stove was sucked high into the tin stack pipe so that the soot on it reddened and snapped. Hattie could only stare. Four of the boys were just about Hattie's age, so she didn't say anything when they ignored the reading assignment and earnestly got up from the wooden benches in order to argue *oughts* and *ought nots* in the cloakroom. She heard the girls saying Amen and then she saw Janusz Vasko, who was fifteen years old and had grown up in Nebraska weather, gravely exiting the cloakroom with a cigarette behind one ear and his right hand raised high overhead. Hattie called on him, and Janusz said the older boys agreed that they could get the little ones home, but only if they went out right away. And before she could even give it thought, Janusz tied his red handkerchief over his nose and mouth and jabbed his orange corduroy trousers inside his antelope boots with a pencil.

Yes, Hattie said, please go, and Janusz got the boys and girls to link themselves together with jump ropes and twine and piano wire, and twelve of Hattie Benedict's pupils walked out into a nothingness that the boys knew from their shoes up and dully worked their way across as though each crooked stump and tilted fence post was a word they could spell in a plain-spoken sentence in a book of practical knowledge. Hours later the children showed up at their homes, aching and crying in raw pain. Each was given cocoa or the green tea of the elder flower and hot bricks were put next to their feet while they napped and newspapers printed their names incorrectly. And then, one by one, the children disappeared from history.

Except for Johan and Alma Lindquist, aged nine and six, who stayed behind in the schoolhouse, owing to the greater distance to their ranch. Hattie opened a week-old Omaha news-paper on her desktop and with caution peeled a spotted yellow apple on it, eating tan slices from her scissor blade as she peered out at children who seemed irritatingly sad and pathetic. She said, You wish you were home.

The Lindquists stared.

Me too, she said. She dropped the apple core onto the newspaper page and watched it ripple with the juice stain. Have you any idea where Pennysylvania is?

East, the boy said. Johan was eating pepper cheese and day-old rye bread from a tin lunch box that sparked with electricity whenever he touched it. And his sister nudged him to show how her yellow hair was beguiled toward her green rubber comb whenever she brought it near.

Hattie was talking in such quick English that she could tell the Lindquists couldn't quite understand it. She kept hearing the

snow pinging and pattering against the windowpanes, and the
storm howling like clarinets down the stack pipe, but she
perceived the increasing cold in the room only when she looked
to the Lindquists and saw their Danish sentences grayly blossoming as they spoke. Hattie went into the cloakroom and skidded
out the poorhouse box, rummaging from it a Scotch plaid scarf
that she wrapped twice around her skull and ears just as a squaw
would, and snipping off the fingertips of some red knitted gloves
that were only slightly too small. She put them on and then she
got into her secondhand coat and Alma whispered to her brother
but Hattie said she'd have no whispering, she hated that, she
couldn't wait for their kin to show up for them, she had too
many responsibilities, and nothing interesting ever happened in
the country. Everything was stupid. Everything was work. She
didn't even have a girlfriend. She said she'd once been sick for
four days, and two by two practically every woman in Neligh
mistrustfully visited her rooming house to squint at Hattie and
palm her forehead and talk about her symptoms. And then they'd
snail out into the hallway and prattle and whisper in the hawk
and spit of the German language.

Alma looked at Johan with misunderstanding and terror, and
Hattie told them to get out paper and pencils; she was going to
say some necessary things and the children were going to write
them down. She slowly paced as she constructed a paragraph,
one knuckle darkly striping the blackboard, but she couldn't
properly express herself. She had forgotten herself so absolutely
that she thought forgetting was a yeast in the air; or that the
onslaught's only point was to say over and over again that she
was next to nothing. Easily bewildered. Easily dismayed. The
Lindquists were shying from the crazy woman and concentrating
their shame on a nickel pad of Wisconsin paper. And Hattie
thought, *You'll give me an ugly name and there will be cartoons and
snickering and the older girls will idly slay me with jokes and imitations.*

She explained she was taking them to her rooming house,
and she strode purposefully out into the great blizzard as if she
were going out to a garden to fetch some strawberries, and Johan
dutifully followed, but Alma stayed inside the schoolhouse with

her purple scarf up over her mouth and nose and her own dark sandwich of pepper cheese and rye bread clutched to her breast like a prayer book. And then Johan stepped out of the utter whiteness to say Alma had to hurry up, that Miss Benedict was angrily asking him if his sister had forgotten how to use her legs. So Alma stepped out of the one-room schoolhouse, sinking deep in the snow and sloshing ahead in it as she would in a pond until she caught up with Hattie Benedict, who took the Lindquists' hands in her own and walked them into the utter whiteness and night of the afternoon. Seeking to blindly go north to her rooming house, Hattie put her high button shoes in the deep tracks that Janusz and the schoolchildren had made, but she misstepped twice, and that was enough to get her on a screw-tape path over snow humps and hillocks that took her south and west and very nearly into a great wilderness that was like a sea in high gale.

Hattie imagined herself reaching the Elkhorn River and discovering her rooming house standing high and honorable under the sky's insanity. And then she and the Lindquist children would duck over their teaspoons of tomato soup and soda crackers as the town's brooms and scarecrows teetered over them, hooking their green hands on the boy and girl and saying, Tell us about it. She therefore created a heroine's part for herself and tried to keep to it as she floundered through drifts as high as a four-poster bed in a white room of piety and weeping. Hattie pretended gaiety by saying once, See how it swirls! but she saw that the Lindquists were tucking deep inside themselves as they trudged forward and fell and got up again, the wind drawing tears from their squinting eyes, the hard, dry snow hitting their skin like wildly flying pencils. Hours passed as Hattie tipped away from the press of the wind into country that was a puzzle to her, but she kept saying, Just a little farther, until she saw Alma playing Gretel by secretly trailing her right hand along a high wave of snow in order to secretly let go yet another crumb of her rye bread. And then, just ahead of her, she saw some pepper cheese that the girl dropped some time ago. Hissing spindrifts tore away from the snow swells and spiked her face like sharp pins, but then a door seemed to inch ajar and Hattie saw the slight, dark change of a haystack and she cut toward it, announcing that they'd stay there for the night.

She slashed away an access into the haystack and ordered Alma to crawl inside, but the girl hesitated as if she were still thinking of the gingerbread house and the witch's oven, and Hattie acidly whispered, You'll be a dainty mouthful. She meant it as a joke but her green eyes must have seemed crazy, because the little girl was crying when Hattie got inside the haystack next to her, and then Johan was crying, too, and Hattie hugged the Lindquists to her body and tried to shush them with a hymn by Dr. Watts, gently singing, Hush, my dears, lie still and slumber. She couldn't get her feet inside the haystack, but she couldn't feel them anyway just then, and the haystack was making everything else seem right and possible. She talked to the children about hot pastries and taffy and Christmas presents, and that night she made up a story about the horrible storm being a wicked old man whose only thought was to eat them up, but he couldn't find them in the haystack even though he looked and looked. The old man was howling, she said, because he was so hungry.

At daybreak a party of farmers from Neligh rode out on their high plowhorses to the Antelope County schoolhouse in order to get Hattie and the Lindquist children, but the room was empty and the bluetick hound that was with them kept scratching up rye bread until the party walked along behind it on footpaths that wreathed around the schoolyard and into a haystack 20 rods away where the older boys smoked and spit tobacco juice at recess. The Lindquist girl and the boy were killed by the cold, but Hattie Benedict had stayed alive inside the hay, and she wouldn't come out again until the party of men yanked her by the ankles. Even then she kept the girl's body hugged against one side and the boy's body hugged to the other, and when she was put up on one horse, she stared down at them with green eyes that were empty of thought or understanding and inquired if they'd be okay. Yes, one man said. You took good care of them.

Bent Lindquist ripped down his kitchen cupboards and carpentered his own triangular caskets, blacking them with shoe polish, and then swaddled Alma and Johan in black alpaca that

was kindly provided by an elder in the Church of Jesus Christ of
Latter-Day Saints. And all that night Danish women sat up with
the bodies, sopping the Lindquists' skin with vinegar so as to
impede putrefaction.

Hattie Benedict woke up in a Lincoln hospital with sweet oil
of spermaceti on her hands and lips, and weeks later a Kansas
City surgeon amputated her feet with a polished silver hacksaw
in the presence of his anatomy class. She was walking again by
June, but she was attached to cork-and-iron shoes and she sighed
and grunted with every step. Within a year she grew so overweight that she gave up her crutches for a wicker-backed
wheelchair and stayed in Antelope County on a pension of 40
dollars per month, letting her dark hair grow dirty and leafy,
reading one popular romance per day. And yet she complained
so much about her helplessness, especially in winter, that the
Protestant churches took up a collection and Hattie Benedict was
shipped by train to Oakland, California, whence she sent postcards saying she'd married a trolley repairman and she hated
Nebraska, hated their horrible weather, hated their petty lives.

On Friday the thirteenth some pioneers went to the upper stories
of their houses to jack up the windows and crawl out onto snow
that was like a jeweled ceiling over their properties. Everything
was sloped and planed and caped and whitely furbeloved. One
man couldn't get over his boyish delight in tramping about on
deer-hide snowshoes at the height of his roof gutters, or that his
dogwood tree was forgotten but for twigs sticking out of the
snow like a skeleton's fingers. His name was Eldad Alderman,
and he jabbed a bamboo fishing pole in four likely spots a couple
of feet below his snowshoes before the bamboo finally thumped
against the plank roof of his chicken coop. He spent two hours
spading down to the coop and then squeezed in through the one
window in order to walk among the fowl and count up. Half his
sixty hens were alive; the other half were still nesting, their
orange beaks lying against their white hackles, sitting there like a
dress shop's hats, their pure white eggs not yet cold underneath
them. In gratitude to those thirty chickens that withstood the
ordeal, Eldad gave them Dutch whey and curds and eventually

wrote a letter praising their constitutions in the *American Poultry Yard*.

Anna Shevschenko managed to get oxen inside a shelter sturdily constructed of oak scantling and a high stack of barley straw, but the snow powder was so fine and fiercely penetrating that it sifted through and slowly accumulated on the floor. The oxen tamped it down and inchingly rose toward the oak scantling rafters, where they were stopped as the snow flooded up, and by daybreak were overcome and finally asphyxiated. Widow Schevschenko decided then that an old woman could not keep a Nebraska farm alone, and she left for the East in February.

One man lost 300 Rhode Island Red chickens; another lost 26 Hereford cattle and sold their hides for 2 dollars apiece. Hours after the Hubenka boy permitted 21 hogs to get out of the snowstorm and join their 40 Holsteins in the upper barn, the planked floor in the cattle linter collapsed under the extra weight and the livestock perished. Since even coal picks could no more than chip the earth, the iron-hard bodies were hauled aside until they could be put underground in April, and just about then some Pawnee Indians showed up outside David City. Knowing their manner of living, Mr. Hubenka told them where the carcasses were rotting in the sea wrack of weed tangles and thaw-water jetsam, and the Pawnee rode their ponies onto the property one night and hauled the carrion away.

And there were stories about a Union Pacific train being arrested by snow on a railway siding near Lincoln, and the merchandizers in the smoking car playing euchre, high five, and flinch until sunup; about cowboys staying inside a Hazard bunkhouse for three days and getting bellyaches from eating so many tins of anchovies and saltine crackers; about the Omaha YMCA where shop clerks paged through inspirational pamphlets or played checkers and cribbage or napped in green leather Chesterfield chairs until the great blizzard petered out.

Half a century later, in Atkinson, there was a cranky talker named Bates, who maintained he was the fellow who first thought of attaching the word *blizzard* to the onslaught of high winds and slashing dry snow and ought to be given credit for it. And later, too, a Lincoln woman remembered herself as a little

girl peering out through yellowed window paper at a yard and
countryside that were as white as the first day of God's creation.
And then a great white Brahma bull with street-wide horns
trotted up to the house, the night's snow puffing up from his
heavy footsteps like soap flakes, gray funnels of air flaring from
his nostrils and wisping away in the horrible cold. With a tilt of
his head the great bull sought out the hiding girl under a
Chesterfield table and, having seen her, sighed and trotted back
toward Oklahoma.

Wild turkey were sighted over the next few weeks, their
wattled heads and necks just above the snow like dark sticks,
some of them petrified that way but others simply waiting for
happier times to come. The onslaught also killed prairie dogs,
jackrabbits, and crows, and the coyotes that relied upon them for
food got so hungry that skulks of them would loiter like juveniles
in the yards at night and yearn for scraps and castaways in old
songs of agony that were always misunderstood.

Addie Dillingham was seventeen and irresistible that January day
of the great blizzard, a beautiful English girl in an hourglass dress
and an ankle-length otter-skin coat that was sculpted brazenly to
display a womanly bosom and bustle. She had gently agreed to
join an upperclassman at the Nebraska School of Medicine on a
journey across the green ice of the Missouri River to Iowa, where
there was a party at the Masonic Temple in order to celebrate the
final linking of Omaha and Council Bluffs. The medical student
was Repler Hitchcock of Council Bluffs – a good companion, a
Republican, and an Episcopalian – who yearned to practice
electro-therapeutics in Cuernavaca, Mexico. He paid for their
three-course luncheon at the Paxton Hotel and then the couple
strolled down Douglas Street with 400 other partygoers, who
got into cutters and one-horse open sleighs just underneath the
iron legs and girders of what would eventually be called the Ak-
Sar-Ben Bridge. At a cap-pistol shot the party jerked away from
Nebraska and there were champagne toasts and cheers and
yahooing, but gradually the party scattered and Addie could only
hear the iron shoes of the plowhorse and the racing sleigh hushing
across the shaded window glass of river, like those tropical

flowers shaped like saucers and cups that slide across the green silk of a pond of their own accord.

At the Masonic Temple there were coconut macaroons and hot syllabub made with cider and brandy, and quadrille dancing on a puncheon floor to songs like the "Butterfly Whirl" and "Cheater Swing" and "The Girl I Left Behind Me." Although the day was getting dark and there was talk about a great snowstorm roistering outside, Addie insisted on staying out on the dance floor until only twenty people remained and the quadrille caller had put away his violin and his sister's cello. Addie smiled and said, Oh what fun! as Repler tidily helped her into her mother's otter-skin coat and then escorted her out into a grand empire of snow that Addie thought was thrilling. And then, although the world by then was wrathfully meaning everything it said, she walked alone to the railroad depot at Ninth and Broadway so she could take the one-stop train called The Dummy across to Omaha.

Addie sipped hot cocoa as she passed sixty minutes up close to the railroad depot's coal stoker oven and some other party-goers sang of Good King Wenceslaus over a parlor organ. And then an old yardman who was sheeped in snow trudged through the high drifts by the door and announced that no more trains would be going out until morning.

Half the couples stranded there had family in Council Bluffs and decided to stay overnight, but the idea of traipsing back to Repler's house and sleeping in his sister's trundle bed seemed squalid to Addie, and she decided to walk the iron railway trestle across to Omaha.

Addie was a half hour away from the Iowa railway yard and up on the tracks over the great Missouri before she had second thoughts. White hatchings and tracings of snow flew at her horizontally. Wind had rippled snow up against the southern girders so that the high white skin was pleated and patterned like oyster shell. Every creosote tie was tented with snow that angled down into dark troughs that Addie could fit a leg through. Everything else was night sky and mystery, and the world she knew had disappeared. And yet she walked out onto the trestle, teetering over to a catwalk and sidestepping along it in high-button shoes, 40 feet above the ice, her left hand taking the yield from one guy wire as her right hand sought out another. Yelling winds were yanking at her, and the iron trestle was swaying enough to tilt her over into nothingness, as though Addie Dillingham were a playground game it was just inventing. Halfway across, her gray tam-o'shanter was snagged out just far enough into space that she could follow its spider-drop into the night, but she only stared at the great river that was lying there moon-white with snow and intractable. Wishing for her to jump.

Years later Addie thought that she got to Nebraska and did not give up and was not overfrightened because she was seventeen and could do no wrong, and accidents and dying seemed a government you could vote against, a mother you could ignore. She said she panicked at one jolt of wind and sank down to her knees up there and briefly touched her forehead to iron that hurt her skin like teeth, but when she got up again, she could see the ink-black stitching of the woods just east of Omaha and the shanties on timber piers just above the Missouri River's jagged stacks of ice. And she grinned as she thought how she would look to a vagrant down there plying his way along a rope in order to assay his trotlines for gar and catfish and then, perhaps, appraising the night as if he'd heard a crazy woman screaming in a faraway hospital room. And she'd be jauntily up there on the iron trestle like a new star you could wish on, and as joyous as the last high notes of "The Girl I Left Behind Me."

AMY HEMPEL

☆ ☆ ☆ ☆

# In the Cemetery
# Where Al Jolson is Buried

*For Jessica*

"Tell me things I won't mind forgetting," she said. "Make it useless stuff or skip it."

I began. I told her insects fly through rain, missing every drop, never getting wet. I told her no one in America owned a tape-recorder before Bing Crosby did. I told her the shape of the moon is like a banana – you see it looking full, you're seeing it end-on.

The camera made me self-conscious and I stopped. It was trained on us from a ceiling mount – the kind of camera banks use to photograph robbers. It played our image to the nurses down the hall in Intensive Care.

"Go on, girl," she said, "you get used to it."

I had my audience. I went on. Did she know that Tammy Wynette had changed her tune? Really. That now she sings "Stand By Your *Friends*"? Paul Anka did it too, I said. Does "You're Having *Our* Baby." He got sick of all that feminist bitching.

"What else?" she said. "Have you got something else?"

Oh yes. For her I would always have something else.

"Did you know when they taught the first chimp to talk, it lied? When they asked her who did it on the desk, she signed back Max, the janitor. And when they pressed her, she said she was sorry, that it was really the project director. But she was a mother, so I guess she had her reasons."

"Oh, that's good," she said. "A parable."

"There's more about the chimp," I said. "But it will break your heart."

"No thanks," she says, and scratches at her mask.

We look like good-guy outlaws. Good or bad, I am not used to the mask yet. I keep touching the warm spot where my breath, thank God, comes out. She is used to hers. She only ties the strings on top. The other ones – a pro by now – she lets hang loose.

We call this place the Marcus Welby Hospital. It's the white one with the palm trees under the opening credits of all those shows. A Hollywood hospital, though in fact it is several miles west. Off camera, there is a beach across the street.

She introduces me to a nurse as "the Best Friend." The impersonal article is more intimate. It tells me that *they* are intimate, my friend and her nurse.

"I was telling her we used to drink Canada Dry Ginger Ale and pretend we were in Canada."

"That's how dumb *we* were," I say.

"You could be sisters," the nurse says.

So how come, I'll bet they are wondering, it took me so long to get to such a glamorous place? But do they ask?

They do not ask.

Two months, and how long is the drive?

The best I can explain it is this – I have a friend who worked one summer in a mortuary. He used to tell me stories. The one that really got me was not the grisliest, but it's the one that did. A man wrecked his car on 101 going south. He did not lose consciousness. But his arm was taken down to the wet bone – and when he looked at it – it scared him to death. I mean, he died.

So I didn't dare look any closer. But now I'm doing it – and hoping I won't be scared to death.

She shakes out a summer-weight blanket, showing a leg you did not want to see. Except for that, you look at her and understand the law that requires two people to be with the body at all times.

"I thought of something," she says. "I thought of it last night. I think there is a real and present need here. You know," she says, "like for someone to do it for you when you can't do it yourself. You call them up whenever you want – like when push comes to shove."

She grabs the bedside phone and loops the cord around her neck.

"Hey," she says, "the End o' the Line."

She keeps on, giddy with something. But I don't know with what.

"The giveaway was the solarium," she says. "That's where Marcus Welby broke the news to his patients. Then here's the real doctor suggesting we talk in the solarium. So I knew I was going to die.

"I can't remember," she says, "what does Kübler-Ross* say comes after Denial?"

It seems to me Anger must be next. Then Bargaining, Depression, and so on and so forth. But I keep my guesses to myself.

"The only thing is," she says, "is where's Resurrection? God knows I want to do it by the book. But she left out Resurrection."

She laughs, and I cling to the sound the way someone dangling above a ravine holds fast to the thrown rope.

We could have cried then, but when we didn't, we couldn't.

"Tell me," she says, "about that chimp with the talking hands. What do they do when the thing ends and the chimp says, 'I don't want to go back to the zoo?'"

When I don't say anything, she says, "Okay – then tell me another animal story. I like animal stories. But not a sick one – I don't want to know about all the Seeing Eye dogs going blind."

No, I would not tell her a sick one.

"How about the hearing-ear dogs?" I say. "They're not going deaf, but they are getting very judgmental. For instance, there's this golden retriever in Jersey, he wakes up the deaf

* Elisabeth Kübler-Ross (1926–   ), author of popular books on death and dying.

mother, and drags her into the daughter's room because the kid has got a flashlight and is reading under the covers."

"Oh, you're killing me," she says. "Yes, you're definitely killing me."

"They say the smart dog obeys, but the smarter dog knows when to *diso*bey."

"Yes," she says, "the smarter *anything* knows when to disobey. Now, for example."

She is flirting with the Good Doctor, who has just appeared. Unlike the Bad Doctor, who checks the IV drip before saying good morning, the Good Doctor says things like "God didn't give epileptics a fair shake." He awards himself points for the cripples he could have hit in the parking lot. Because the Good Doctor is a little in love with her he says maybe a year. He pulls a chair up to her bed and suggests I might like to spend an hour on the beach.

"Bring me something back," she says. "Anything from the beach. Or the gift shop. Taste is no object."

The doctor slowly draws the curtain around her bed.

"Wait!" she cries.

I look in at her.

"Anything," she says, "except a magazine subscription."

The doctor turns away.

I watch her mouth laugh.

What seems dangerous often is not – black snakes, for example, or clear-air turbulence. While things that just lie there, like this beach, are loaded with jeopardy. A yellow dust rising from the ground, the heat that ripens melons overnight – this is earthquake weather. You can sit here braiding the fringe on your towel and the sand will all of a sudden suck down like an hourglass. The air roars. In the cheap apartments onshore, bathtubs fill themselves and gardens roll up and over like green waves. If nothing happens, the dust will drift and the heat deepen till fear turns to desire. Nerves like that are only bought off by catastrophe.

"It never happens when you're thinking about it," she observed once.

"Earthquake, earthquake, earthquake," she said.

"Earthquake, earthquake, earthquake," I said.

Like the aviaphobe who keeps the plane aloft with prayer, we kept it up till an aftershock cracked the ceiling.

That was after the big one in '72. We were in college; our dormitory was 5 miles from the epicenter. When the ride was over and my jabbering pulse began to slow, she served five parts champagne to one part orange juice and joked about living in Ocean View, Kansas. I offered to drive her to Hawaii on the new world psychics predicted would surface the next time, or the next.

I could not say that now – next. *Whose* next? she could ask.

Was I the only one who noticed that the experts had stopped saying *if* and now spoke of *when*? Of course not; the fearful ran to thousands. We watched the traffic of Japanese beetles for deviation. Deviation might mean more natural violence.

I wanted her to be afraid with me, but she said, "I don't know. I'm just not."

She was afraid of nothing, not even of flying.

I have this dream before a flight where we buckle in and the plane moves down the runway. It takes off at 35 miles an hour, and then we're airborne, skimming the tree tops. Still, we arrive in New York on time. It is so pleasant. One night I flew to Moscow this way.

She flew with me once. That time she flew with me she ate macadamia nuts while the wings bounced. She knows the wing tips can bend 30 feet up and 30 feet down without coming off. She believes it. She trusts the laws of aerodynamics. My mind stampedes. I can almost accept that a battleship floats, and everybody knows steel sinks.

I see fear in her now and I am not going to try to talk her out of it. She is right to be afraid.

After a quake, the 6 o'clock news airs a film clip of first-graders yelling at the broken playground per their teacher's instructions.

"*Bad* earth!" they shout, because anger is stronger than fear.

★

But the beach is standing still today. Everyone on it is tranquil-
ized, numb or asleep. Teenaged girls rub coconut oil on each
other's hard-to-reach places. They smell like macaroons. They
pry open compacts like clamshells; mirrors catch the sun and
throw a spray of white rays across glazed shoulders. The girls
arrange their wet hair with silk flowers the way they learned in
*Seventeen*. They pose.

A formation of low-riders★ pulls over to watch with a six-
pack. They get vocal when the girls check their tan lines. When
the beer is gone, so are they – flexing their cars on up the
boulevard.

Above this aggressive health are the twin wrought-iron
terraces, painted flamingo pink, of the Palm Royale. Someone
dies there every time the sheets are changed. There's an ambulance in the driveway, so the remaining residents line the
balconies, rocking and not talking, one-upped.

The ocean they stare at is dangerous, and not just the
undertow. You can almost see the slapping tails of sand sharks
keeping cruising bodies alive.

If she looked, she could see this, some of it, from her
window. She would be the first to say how little it takes to make
a thing all wrong.

There was a second bed in the room when I returned. For two
beats I didn't get it. Then it hit me like an open coffin.

She wants every minute, I thought. She wants my life.

"You missed Gussie," she said.

Gussie is her parents' 300-pound narcoleptic maid. Her
attacks often come at the ironing board. The pillowcases in that
family are all bordered with scorch.

"It's a hard trip for her," I said. "How is she?"

"Well, she didn't fall asleep, if that's what you mean. Gussie's
great – you know what she said? She said, 'Darlin' just keep
prayin', down on your knees.'"

She shrugged. "See anybody good?"

★ Drivers of rebuilt, underslung cars.

"No," I said, "just the new Charlie's Angel. And I saw Cher's car down near the Arcade."

"Cher's car is worth *three* Charlie's Angels," she said. "What else am I missing?"

"It's earthquake weather," I told her.

"The best thing to do about earthquakes," she said, "is not to live in California."

"That's useful," I said. "You sound like Reverend Ike: 'The best thing to do for the poor is not to be one of them.'"

We're crazy about Reverend Ike.

I noticed her face was bloated.

"You know," she said, "I feel like hell. I'm about to stop having fun."

"The ancients have a saying," I said. "There are times when the wolves are silent; there are times when the moon howls.'"

"What's that, Navajo?"

"Palm Royale lobby graffiti," I said. "I bought a paper there. I'll read to you."

"Even though I care about nothing?" she said.

I turned to page three, to a UPI filler datelined Mexico City. I read her "Man Robs Bank with Chicken," about a man who bought a barbecued chicken at a stand down the block from a bank. Passing the bank, he got the idea. He walked in and approached a teller. He pointed the brown paper bag at her and she handed over the day's receipts. It was the smell of barbecue sauce that eventually led to his capture.

The story made her hungry, she said, so I took the elevator down six floors to the cafeteria and brought back all the ice cream she wanted. We lay side by side, adjustable beds cranked up for optimal TV viewing, littering the sheets with Good Humor wrappers, picking toasted almonds out of the gauze. We were Lucy and Ethel, Mary and Rhoda in extremis. The blinds were closed to keep light off the screen.

We watched a movie starring men we used to think we wanted to sleep with. Hers was a tough cop out to stop mine, a vicious rapist who went after cocktail waitresses.

"This is a good movie," she said, when snipers felled them both.

I missed her already; my straight man, my diary.

A Filipino nurse tiptoed in and gave her an injection. She removed the pile of Popsicle sticks from the nightstand – enough to splint a small animal.

The injection made us sleepy – me in the way I picked up her inflection till her mother couldn't tell us apart on the phone. We slept.

I dreamed she was a decorator, come to furnish my house. She worked in secret, singing to herself. When she finished, she guided me proudly to the door. "How do you like it?" she asked, easing me inside.

Every beam and sill and shelf and knob was draped in black bunting, with streamers of black crepe looped around darkened mirrors.

"I have to go home," I said when she woke up.

She thought I meant home to her house in the Canyon, and I had to say No, *home* home. I twisted my hands in the hackneyed fashion of people in pain. I was supposed to offer something. The Best Friend. I could not even offer to come back.

I felt weak and small and failed. Also exhilarated. I had a convertible in the parking lot. Once out of that room, I would drive it too fast down the coast highway through the crab-smelling air. A stop in Malibu for sangria. The music in the place would be sexy and loud. They would serve papaya and shrimp and watermelon ice. After dinner I would pick up beach boys. I would shimmer with life, buzz with heat, vibrate with health, stay up all night with one and then the other.

Without a word, she yanked off her mask and threw it on the floor. She kicked at the blanket and moved to the door. She must have hated having to pause for breath and balance before slamming out of Isolation, and out of the second room, the one where you scrub and tie on the white masks.

A voice shouted her name in alarm, and people ran down the corridor. The Good Doctor was paged over the intercom. I opened the door and the nurses at the station stared hard, as if this flight had been my idea.

"Where is she?" I asked, and they nodded to the supply closet.

I looked in. Two nurses were kneeling beside her on the floor, talking to her in low voices. One held a mask over her nose and mouth, the other rubbed her back in slow circles. The nurses glanced up to see if I was the doctor, and when they saw I wasn't, they went back to what they were doing.

"There, there, honey," they cooed.

On the morning she was moved to the cemetery, the one where Al Jolson is buried, I enrolled in a Fear of Flying class. "What is your worst fear?" the instructor asked, and I answered, "That I will finish this course and still be afraid."

I sleep with a glass of water on the nightstand so I can see by its level if the coastal earth is trembling or if the shaking is still me.

What do I remember? I remember only the useless things I hear – that Bob Dylan's mother invented Wite-out, that twenty-three people must be in a room before there is a fifty-fifty chance two will have the same birthdate. Who cares whether or not it's true? In my head there are bath towels swaddling this stuff. Nothing else seeps through.

I review those things that will figure in the retelling: a kiss through surgical gauze, the pale hand correcting the position of the wig. I noted these gestures as they happened, not in any retrospect. Though I don't know why looking *back* should show us more than looking *at*. It is just possible I will say I stayed the night. And who is there that can say I did not?

Nothing else gets through until I think of the chimp, the one with the talking hands.

In the course of the experiment, that chimp had a baby. Imagine how her trainers must have thrilled when the mother, without prompting, began to sign to the newborn. Baby, drink milk. Baby, play ball. And when the baby died, the mother stood over the body, her wrinkled hands moving with animal grace, forming again and again the words, Baby, come hug, Baby, come hug, fluent now in the language of grief.

☆  ☆  ☆  ☆

# Nobody's Fool

Floyd headed up the hill to feed the dogs. They had been hoping for him, pacing the length of the near fence, for an hour. He was that much later than usual; it was his day to shave. A man with the shakes would be a fool to shave fast. When Floyd opened the door to the shed to get the food, Goldie padded down to the gate and poked her muzzle through the gap by the latch, sniffing, her blind eyes blue as the sky. Cinder, the puppy, tromped over the empty pans, dumping the water basin in his clumsy hunger. The bald patch on his hip was hairing over and he no longer limped. He looked as if he had been rolling in ashes. He always could find trouble.

"Now, listen," Floyd said, pleased as he always was by their boiling-over welcome. He staggered a little under the weight of the chow sack. It was hard to open. He tugged at the string, then took out his knife and cut it. He should have done what Ida said, put some food in a bucket and not carried the whole bag, but how could he, after she said it? The bag only weighed 25 pounds. That wasn't too much for a man. She was at work. She'd never know it if he didn't do what she said, and why should he? Just because she said?

"It'll weigh even less going back downhill," he told the dogs. They were busy eating. He stood in the open gate, watching them. They weren't doing anything but eat. They ate loud.

"All you think about's your belly," he said.

It was nice weather. Floyd liked spring. He thought he'd get the rake and sweep up those last oak leaves. Ida said for him not to get up on the ladder and do the gutters, but he could still rake. He'd rake.

Then – before he could say more than "Whoa" – the dogs got out, got past him, escaped, tore away across the yard as if they'd been planning it for weeks. Cinder was leading, Goldie at his heels. For a blind dog, Goldie was keeping up.

"Y'all don't," Floyd said.

But they did. Straight down across Ida's rye grass, under the cedar fence, and free, barking out of sight as if they were closing on a coon. Floyd listened for the squeal of brakes – nothing – so that was all right, they made it across the highway, heading for the woods behind the shopping plaza. He could imagine them pelting on like that for hours, till their dinner gave out and they circled back for supper.

"They'll be back before you get home," Floyd said aloud. He hoped so. He didn't want to hear from Ida about it. She'd say he couldn't even manage that, to leave it to her to do from now on.

"I was just trying to save you from walking up here in the mud and ruining your shoes," Floyd said.

He'd remember to mention that, if the subject came up. Let her think about *that* for a while. "The world ain't all me-me-me," he said.

He stopped to scrabble up the dog chow that had spilled from the sack while the dogs had his attention. He toed the rest over onto their pans and left the gate open.

"They'll be back," he said.

He started down to the house, the sack of chow in his arms like a baby. Ida had been a difficult child, sure of her ways and disapproving of everybody else's, from day one. Things had to be nice and they had to be all her way. Or she'd kick sand. Or do without. Or starve. She was proud. Nice about things, always wanting better. "Like her mama," he said.

Once Ida had gone without her lunch. Refused to eat it. Opened her brown sack at school and announced, "This isn't mine. Someone stole my lunch," in that flash and fury against all things wrong and second best that carried her through high school, chin high, and on past college too, to tell the world, for her living, how it was doing things wrong too. That day, she said, "My mama don't make black banana sandwiches." The teacher sent home a note. Floyd remembered it like yesterday. He laughed.

He set the chow sack against the shed door and sighed. It had been easier on the downhill. "A sight easier," he said. The pain in his shoulder eased in a minute, but he thought he would rest some more before he started raking. He sat on the patio and chewed. It was pouch tobacco, not his usual plug. Ida had bought it for him. She didn't approve and didn't see any difference. Besides, Piggly Wiggly didn't carry Bull of the Woods, and Piggly Wiggly was where she got double coupons.

"No use in telling you," Floyd told her.

All day long he'd talk to her like that, till she came home from work. They'd eat in silence, or else she'd talk, talk, talk at him. It wasn't always quarreling, but it wore him out, so he'd go to his room and listen to the radio till bedtime. Ida liked her TV in the evenings. She laughed along. Sometimes she talked on the phone at the same time.

It was ringing now.

Floyd spit into his soup can and had a sip of Coca-Cola before he answered.

"Hay-lo," he said. "This here's Floyd."

"I'm Bob, the computer," the voice said. Floyd listened. He didn't know Bob.

"Did you say computer?" Floyd asked.

The voice talked on without pause. It didn't matter if you were listening or not, Floyd thought. He hung up. "Bad as you," he told Ida. He had better to do.

Ida said, "All you had to do was shut that gate."

"I was just trying to save you from some trouble," he said.

"Then why didn't you shut the gate?"

They were driving slowly along. All the yards they passed were empty. Everyone was at work, or indoors, watching TV. There was only one dog in sight – a Doberman.

Floyd said, "Those'll kill you soon as look at you."

Ida stopped the car and got out. The Doberman danced as he barked, his clipped ears, healing in their splints, white as horns.

"Somebody's bad news," Floyd said.

Ida got in and drove them on. They turned left. Her window

was rolled down so she could whistle. She beat on the side of the
car with her hand. Cinder and Goldie were nowhere to be seen.

"They'll come home when they get hungry," Floyd told her.

"You're the one who's hungry," Ida said. "That's why you
want to give up looking." Whatever Floyd knew, she knew
better.

Floyd took some tobacco and packed his cheek.

"And don't you spit from that window," Ida said. "I ran this
car through the Bubble Wash this afternoon."

"I'd swaller it first," Floyd said.

They went past the shopping center. At the mud lane into the
pines where the dirt bikers roared on weekends, Ida slowed.

"You reckon my babies got this far?" she said.

"I hope they'd have more sense," Floyd said. "Why do they
dock them dogs like that? Ears and tail too. Didn't leave him
more than a nub."

Ida said, turning onto the mud, "It's dry enough. We won't
get stuck." She rocked them slowly along the ruts, trying not to
splatter her clean car. Floyd sat up straight, his fist on the door
handle. They ran over a piece of chrome from a junked car.
There was a mattress sagging against a dinette chair. Ida edged
past. Then they came to the scrap roofing and old tires, blocking
the way.

"Trash is all they are who'd do a thing like that," Ida said.
She had to saw the car, back and forth, back and forth, to get
them turned around and headed back to the road. When she got
to the highway, she blew out her breath and just sat there.

"Ain't nothing come," Floyd said. "Either way."

"You-can-give-me-a-minute," Ida said, like she was counting out change, each coin clicking down to pay a righteous debt.

"Just trying to help," Floyd said, folding his hands.

"Help like yours I need like a hole in the ground," Ida said.
"All you had to do was *shut that gate!*"

Floyd opened the door and got out. He had to spit. He
worked on that.

She leaned across the seat and yelled, "You going to run off
too?"

He swiveled around. "Better for both of us if I did."

"Wipe your chin," she said. She handed him a Kleenex. She was always right there with her Kleenex, her coasters, her spray wax, her dictionary, her Lysol, her vitamin tablets, her salt substitute.

He turned his back on her. "Ain't good for nothing no more," he said, just loud enough if she cared to deny it. He could set off, walking, if he knew which way was north. He could find friends. He checked the sun, held his hand forth, counting the hours between it and the horizon. He still wore his watch on his grandpa's chain, but it was broken.

"Get in this car, Daddy," she said, gunning it. Next thing she'd be blowing the horn.

"Maybe I'll walk," he said. "I've walked further'n that."

"*Right now, Mister,*" Ida said.

"Many a day," Floyd said. But he was already trembling, like he'd gone miles. That lint cough, the one the mill had retired him for, bent him over, blind. He didn't even notice it any more. He stood up, wiped his eyes, and eased back into the car.

"Pore as a snake," he said, catching his breath.

She just stared at him. "Why do you do this? Behave like a child? I've had students no worse than you. They don't waste *my* time, not a minute. I send them out."

She drove toward home, fast. The tire made a flap-flapping sound on the asphalt. Floyd heard it, but didn't mention it. Maybe they'd wreck.

She heard it too.

She slowed, eased over onto the shoulder, past the sign that said: BOILD P'NUT AHEAD FRESH HOT GOOD. Closed till summer.

"Well, check and *see*," she said. "Can't you even do that?"

Floyd got out and looked. There was a piece of board stuck to the right rear tire. The tire went on down to flat as soon as he had kicked the board loose. The long nails left holes like snakebite.

Ida got out and looked, too.

"I don't suppose anyone'll stop," she said. "Why should they?"

Floyd said, "I can fix it."

She didn't count on that, he could see. "I'll trouble you for them keys," he said.

When he got the trunk open and was fiddling with the jack – it had to fit in those holes in the bumper and he couldn't get it right – a truck pulled up behind them and a man in a camouflage jumpsuit offered to help.

It didn't take him long.

Floyd unbuttoned his front pocket and unwadded three bills from his snap purse. He handed them to the man. "Many thanks," he said. "If there's ever anything I can do for you some day . . ."

The man pushed the money back. He laughed. "Keep it, old-timer. Buy yourself some Red Man." He swung up into his truck and drove away.

Floyd stood there for a minute. Ida was already back in the car, washing her hands on a little towelette. Floyd flung the dollars into the sedge. He kicked at one of the bills that fluttered by.

Ida started the engine. "Daddy?"

When he shut his door, it hung up.

"*Slam* it!" Ida said. "Can you?"

Floyd said, "Don't worry about *me.*"

They rode along not talking.

Just before they turned onto the street where Ida's house was, Floyd said, "If you was to need a transplant, I'd be who to ask. You can have anything I've got that'd do you any good."

Ida aimed the car up the drive, braked sharp, rammed the lever into park, then jerked out the keys. "I don't need anything presently," she said. She laughed.

Floyd just sat there, thinking. Ida went on into the house. She didn't look back out, or wonder.

The dogs came home on their own. Ida was out at the fence welcoming them, pouring red-eye gravy on their chow, talking to them like children past 9 o'clock that night. Floyd watched from the kitchen door. He couldn't have gravy. Ida read where it was bad for his heart.

Floyd went to his room and packed.

He didn't know whether to tell her or just leave a note, but if he told her, she'd have something to say.

"Nothing I ain't heard," he decided.

He stayed in his room till she had left for work the next morning. As she left, she tapped on his door.

"Daddy? Daddy?"

When he didn't answer, she went on to school. He could hear her muttering, "Like a rock . . . whole place could burn down around him . . . thank Jesus he doesn't smoke . . ." She had to be at school by 7.30.

Floyd waited till her taillights were good and gone. Then he tied up the pillowcase with his extra overalls and Sunday shirt. Ida hated his overalls, hated the very sight and color of denim, but Floyd didn't mind it. He'd spent his life making it, so why should he mind? He was drawing 75 cents a day – "A *day*," Floyd said – at the sawmill when he got hired on at the cotton mill for 3 dollars a day. It made a difference in their life right from the first paycheck. Ida didn't know how to be grateful, that was what it was. Floyd had his Bible in the sack, too, and the photograph of all of them, that summer day at the river when he got himself baptized and stopped drinking for all time. A man could change for the better, Floyd knew. He liked to keep the evidence at hand. He put his knife in his pocket and counted what was left of his pension. He had enough.

He reached down his hat from the closet shelf, and put it on, by touch, from long experience. Floyd knew who he was. He could shave in the dark. His hat had that trademark billiard–rack block to the crown. Ida hated that hat. Said a sock cap, like babies wear, was warmer. She bought him one, and a muffler to match. Floyd left it in the box, saying, "Where's my mittens, Mama?" and wouldn't even wear it to feed the dogs.

Floyd dug out his pencil and licked it twice.

*Now Ida*, he wrote, *dont bother. I done it before and I no how to live. A man has to pull his own weight at least. I done fed the dogs. When I am settled I will let you no.*

*Yore dad, Floyd.*

He added at the bottom: *no usen caling me*
*it'll be long distance.*

*No usen hunting me.*
*I don't like it hear.*
*All you do is fuss.*
In fairness, he marked that out so she'd read: *All we do is fuss.*

He set out, walking strong. If a man offered him a ride, he'd consider it. But he felt strong enough for miles, if no one did. When he saw just the right sapling he carved it down some and kept it in hand.

"To scare off varmints," Floyd said, nobody's fool. He read the papers.

He was meeting all the traffic on its way to town jobs. He wasn't going that way. Nobody even slowed. Some of them had on their headlights. The wisps of fog off the river blew into pieces as they drove through it. Even without the traffic, there was a wind. He stopped to put on his extra shirt. As he bent to retie the pillowsack – caught between his legs as if he were shoeing a horse – his hat blew off, skipping along, teasing him into chasing it with his stick.

Then the wind played a trick. Lifted the hat over the railing of the bridge and tossed it up, sailing it out on a curve, into the water below. Floyd watched it settle into its reflection, sinking slow. It was considerably oiled after years, randomly waterproofed by Wildroot. A little fishing skiff putted up to the rocks below the bridge and their mere trolling wake sent it under.

"Adios, hat," Floyd said.

He walked on across the bridge, then, bare-headed, clear-headed, undizzy. There was more to think about than a lost hat.

"I played here as a boy," he told the fishermen at the other end of the bridge. "Used to jump right off the mill into the deep over yonder."

The man looked where Floyd pointed.

The lake covered it now. And the fields he'd run. "Prettiest cotton," Floyd said. He saw the fisherman didn't remember.

"It's this new road," Floyd said, irritated. "It don't go where it used to, just to town and back. Look over *yonder*," he said. "That hill?"

The man looked again.

"Me and this old boy hauled Book Gravely up it with ropes and mules to be buried close by. Drownded himself in the mill. Nowhere else to swim, but you had to be strong against the tow. Dry summer."

The man said, "Drought, huh?" He was busy with his fishing. He took out a little red and white lure from his box and hooked it on his line. Floyd watched it swing out and down, and the ripples spread wide, from such a little thing.

"Grass growed in the riverbeds so cows could graze," Floyd said. "Only green left in the county." He got thirsty remembering. He wiped his face.

"Things was different then," Floyd said. "Book didn't have no kin and it being hot, we couldn't ship him. We did it as decent as we could."

"Back then, folks was different," the fisherman said. "Cared for each other, you know."

"It's so," Floyd said. He studied the man for likeness. "You from around here?"

"My mama was from over at Rose Creek."

"Maybe she knowed her," Floyd said.

"Who?"

"The lady who come on toward nightfall and laid weeds on Book's grave. We rolled a rock on it to mark it but nobody knowed who she was, never did."

"Weeds?" He was pulling at his fish, a little one, not worth keeping.

"Weeds was all he got, and a fieldstone, but that was more than he might've, considering."

"Mama never said nothing about that," the man said.

"We always wondered," Floyd said.

The man went back to his fishing. Floyd looked out at the lake.

"Nah, mama never said nothing about that," the fisherman said again.

Floyd checked his dead watch. It was a habit, marking time. He always had to be doing something useful, or he felt he was slacking. He said, "I could talk all day," and the man said, "Yeah, I know what you mean. I could fish for a living."

"Same thing," Floyd said. "Back to work, then, son." He took up his sack and headed on up the hill. He told the man, as he went on, "Take it easy on them crappie, son, save some for the rest of us."

Floyd struck off up the hill strong, past the Marina, not looking back. He had to rest his breath, though, at the top. He stood poking at the crumbly shale on the bank by Spain's old place, honeysuckled over now, boarded up.

"Dead now," Floyd said. "I knowed him good as a brother. His little sick wife. All them flowers he growed for her to look at."

Floyd blew his nose.

When the chicken truck stopped, Floyd told the man, "I won't say no," and got up in the cab. He had to leave his hickory stick behind. He glanced back, to memorize *where*, in case he got back by there. "I hope not," he said. They were rolling. The radio was on, and the heater. Floyd sank asleep almost at once.

The lady at welfare said Floyd *had* to tell her his name. He didn't see his way clear to do that. He said he'd manage, then, without her help. Could she recommend a rooming house? She wrote the directions on a scrap of paper and he took that – and his pillowcase – and stepped off toward town, steady as he could in case she was watching from the window. "I'm no hobo," Floyd said.

At the rooming house it turned out he had enough money for one week, if he ate lean. Floyd knew how to manage that, too.

He couldn't change his Social Security till the next week. The agent only came to the courthouse on Tuesdays. Even so, it meant the next check would go on to Ida's, too late to stop it now.

"If I was to die, mid-month, she'd have to pay it all back," Floyd said. He thought that through, how she'd look when she got the letter saying IMPORTANT and she read how she'd have to miss work to get it straightened out.

"Ida, she hates paperwork," Floyd said.

Every day he walked the streets, looking for work. He got a

few little jobs – mainly handyman chores – mainly for widows who couldn't even change the light bulb in their ovens. Floyd had a little problem with that, too, till the man at Otasco told him to buy the heat-resistant bulb. That woman told him, when he came back with the right bulb and explained he wouldn't charge her for his mistake, "You're not too handy but you're sure a man."

He did better on raking. Hammermill had a lot of oaks.

"They bad to hold their leaves till spring," Floyd said, door to door. He had all the work like that he needed. He piled the leaves up and burned them if they didn't want them turned into their gardens. He didn't know anything about that ordinance against burning.

"I ain't from around here," he told the police. They didn't hold him. He wasn't a vagrant. He didn't have any money to pay a fine. They could see that. They didn't shame him into crying or telling Ida's name. He didn't even feel bad about it till he got to his room to rest. He lay on his cot, weak. He couldn't even go out the next day, to straighten out about Social Security. He kept a fever, and his cough was worse.

He thought Ida had found him. He thought Ida was spying on him. He told Mrs. Sloane, when she came around to get the rent. "Look." He showed her the markings, their code, the way they numbered his room when they came checking up. She laughed.

She said, "Ridiculous!" just like Ida.

"It's where the cash register tape got in some water," she told him. "The ink's left a stain on your table, that's all."

He knew by the way she laughed it off that she was one of them. He couldn't stay any longer. But he paid her what he could, so she'd think he was going to.

That night he took his Bible and extra clothes and left by the back door, while Mrs. Sloane and the others were in the front room, watching TV. He could hear them laughing.

It was twelve steps down to the back yard. Floyd took them in one. He landed hard on his arm. He crawled back up to the house and into bed before he called for help.

"I heard it snap," he told the doctor.

They didn't know to look for his things. They lay out in the rain all night. His Bible was ruined.

Floyd had paid Mrs. Sloane all the extra he had, and the hospital wanted more. If he gave them his real name for Medicare, he was as good as back with Ida again. They'd call her before the plaster dried.

He wasn't going to be handed back. He had legs.

Floyd walked out of the hospital. It was easy.

"They weren't expecting *that*," he said, getting clean away. He headed back by Mrs. Sloane's, and when she was talking to the milkman, he slipped around and got his things. He took the alleys and lanes, walking like he had business. He had his sleeve pulled down over the cast. He fit in. No one noticed. He staggered, bummed up from the fall, but he kept on going. He loosened up as he pressed on. He could feel the heartbeat in his broken bone. He didn't dwell on it.

It was raining now. That was a good thing. He sat on one of the benches in the park by the post office. He needed to think. He needed his tobacco. His head was clearer than it had been. Day was just getting going. The sparrows and starlings were awake, drifting down from the eaves and clock tower. From the courthouse roof the pigeons rose with a sound like worn-out cards being shuffled. Floyd watched them wheel. He always did like first light best. He felt young. Like he was on his way to school. Or to the mill. And none of the things that went wrong had yet come to him.

Then he thought, But they're behind me, at least, if they had to happen. The *pastness* was something. If he was young, it'd all be ahead, even if he didn't know to dread it. What was ahead now? He didn't know that, either. So it was like being young.

"If ignorance is peace," Floyd said, "I oughta be getting more out of it."

He felt for his Bible. It was swollen and damp, its pages sealed to each other around the photograph of his baptizing.

"Never mind," he said. He knew by heart what was in there. He knew what he had to do before sundown that very night. He stood. After he got moving, he was warmer. His feet woke. He picked up speed heading down the sidewalk toward the railroad.

He didn't even feel hungry any more. At the depot he turned south.

It was a Saturday. Plenty of traffic going both ways. He got a ride in the first mile that carried him as far as the river. After that, he rode, wind-whipped, with the sun in his eyes, in a plumber's truck that got him down to the four-way stop. There were three in the cab already. He didn't mind riding in back. "Take it easy," they told him.

"Or any way I can get it," Floyd said. He felt good. As if it were home he was nearing, not just Ida's. He walked up the drive fast.

Ida was still in her housecoat and slippers. She answered the door with half a biscuit in her hand. She just stood and stared, without swallowing. She looked hollowed out, like she could use that biscuit and some sleep too, Floyd thought. He saw, in that light, she looked way past grown, on the downhill side, like him.

"Daddy?" She reached for his hurt arm.

"I just have this one thing to say," Floyd said. "Let me say it."

She turned him loose.

"I think I made a mistake about that dog gate," he said. "That's what I think."

She kept staring.

"Next time I won't," he told her.

She still didn't say anything.

"What do *you* think?" he wondered. She had about gripped a hole all the way through the biscuit. She took another bite and leaned against the door.

"You still mad?" Why didn't she say something?

"Talk at me," he said.

If he could just get her started, it'd be all right again. He didn't have to listen.

"Ida," he said, priming the pump, "I throwed away my hat."

☆   ☆   ☆   ☆

# *Exchange Value*

Me and my brother Loftis came in by the old lady's window. There was some kinda boobytrap – boxes of broken glass – that shoulda warned us Miss Bailey wasn't the easy mark we made her to be. She had been living alone for twenty years in 4-B down the hall from Loftis and me, long before our folks died – a hincty, half-bald West Indian woman with a craglike face, who kept her door barricaded, shutters closed, and wore the same sorrylooking outfit – black wingtip shoes, cropfingered gloves in winter, and a man's floppy hat – like maybe she dressed half-asleep or in a dark attic. Loftis, he figured Miss Bailey had some grandtheft dough stashed inside, jim, or leastways a shoebox full of money, 'cause she never spent a nickel on herself, not even for food, and only left her place at night.

Anyway, we figured Miss Bailey was gone. Her mailbox be full, and Pookie White, who run the Thirty-ninth Street Creole restaurant, he say she ain't dropped by in days to collect the handouts he give her so she can get by. So here's me and Loftis, tipping around Miss Bailey's blackdark kitchen. The floor be littered with fruitrinds, roaches, old food furred with blue mold. Her dirty dishes be stacked in a sink spidered with cracks, and it looks like the old lady been living, lately, on Ritz crackers and Department of Agriculture (Welfare Office) peanut butter. Her toilet be stopped up, too, and, on the bathroom floor, there's five Maxwell House coffee cans full of shit. Me, I was closing her bathroom door when I whiffed this evil smell so bad, so thick, I could hardly breathe, and what breath I drew horrible, like a solid thing in my throatpipes, like soup. "Cooter," Loftis whisper, low, across the room, "you smell that?" He went right on sniffing it, like people do for some reason when something be smelling stanky, then took out his headrag and held it over his mouth. "That's the awfulest stink I *ever* smelled!" Then, head low, he slipped his long self into the living room. Me, I stayed by the window, gulping air, and do you know why?

You oughta know, up front, that I ain't too good at this gangster stuff, and I had a real bad feeling about Miss Bailey from the get-go. Mama used to say it was Loftis, not me, who'd go places – I see her standing at the sideboard by the sink now, big as a Frigidaire, white with flour to her elbows, a washtowel over her shoulder, while we ate a breakfast of cornbread and syrup. He graduated fifth at DuSable High School, had two gigs, and, like Papa, he be always wanting the things white people had out in Hyde Park, where Mama did daywork. Loftis, he the kinda brother who buys *Esquire*, sews Hart, Schnaffner and Marx labels in Robert Hall suits, talks properlike, packs his hair with Murrays, and took classes in politics and stuff at the Black People's Topographical Library in the late 1960s; who, at thirty, makes his bed military style, reads *Black Scholar* on the bus he takes to the plant, and, come hell or high water, plans to make a Big Score. Loftis, he say I'm 'bout as useful on a hustle – or when it comes to getting ahead – as a headcold, and he say he has to count my legs sometimes to be sure I ain't a mule, seeing how, for all my eighteen years, I can't keep no job and sorta stay close to home, watching TV or reading *World's Finest* comic books, or maybe just laying dead, listening to music, imagining I see faces or foreign places in water stains on the wallpaper, 'cause somedays when I remember Papa, then Mama killing theyselves for chump change – a pitiful li'l bowl of porridge – I get to thinking that even if I ain't had all I wanted, maybe I've had, you know, all I'm ever gonna get.

"Cooter," Loftis say from the living room. "You best get in here quick."

Loftis, he'd switched on Miss Bailey's sulfur-colored living room lights, so for a second I couldn't see and started coughing – the smell be so powerful it hit my nostrils like coke – and when my eyes cleared, shapes evolved from the light, and I thought for an instant like I'd slipped in space. I seen why Loftis called me, and went back two steps. See, 4-B is so small, if you ring

Miss Bailey's doorbell the toilet'd flush. But her living room, webbed in dust, be filled to the max with dollars of all denominations, stacks of stock in General Motors, Gulf Oil, and 3M Corporation in old White Owl cigar boxes, battered purses, or bound in pink rubber bands. It be like the kind of cubby-hole kids play in, but filled with . . . *things* – everything – like a world within a world, you take it from me, so like picturebook scenes of plentifulness you could seal yourself off in here and settle forever. Loftis and me both drew breath suddenly. There be unopened cases of Jack Daniel's, three safes cemented to the floor, hundreds of matchbooks, unworn clothes, a zinc laundry tub, dozens of wedding rings, rubbish, World War II magazines, a carton of one hundred canned sardines, mink stoles, old rags, a birdcage, a bucket of silver dollars, thousands of books, paintings, quarters in tobacco cans, two pianos, glass jars of pennies, a set of bagpipes, an almost complete Model A Ford dappled with rust, and, I swear, three sections of a dead tree.

"Godamighty damn!" My head be light; I sat on an upended peachcrate and picked me up a bottle of Jack Daniel's.

"Don't you touch *anything*!" Loftis, he panting a little; he slap both hands on a table. "Not until we inventory this stuff."

"Inventory? Aw Lord, Loftis," I say, "something ain't *right* about this stash. There could be a curse on it . . ."

"Boy, sometimes you act weakminded."

"For real, Loftis, I got a feeling . . ."

Loftis, he shucked off his shoes and sat down heavily on the lumpy arm of a stuffed chair. "Don't say *anything*." He chewed his knuckles, and for the first time Loftis looked like he didn't know his next move. "Let me think, okay?" He squeezed his nose in a way he has when thinking hard, sighed, then stood up, and say, "There's something you better see in that bedroom yonder. Cover up your mouth."

"Loftis, I ain't going in there."

He look at me right funny then. "She's a miser, that's all. She saves things."

"But a tree?" I say. "Loftis, a *tree* ain't normal!"

"Cooter, I ain't gonna tell you twice."

Like always, I followed Loftis, who swung his flashlight

from the plant – he a nightwatchman – into Miss Bailey's
bedroom, but me, I'm thinking how trippy this thing is getting,
remembering how, last year, when I had a paper route, the old
lady, with her queer crablike walk, pulled my coat for some
change in the hallway, and when I give her a handful of dimes,
she say in her old Inner Sanctum voice, 'Thank you, Co-o-oter,'
then gulped the coins down like aspirin, no lie, and scurried off
like a hunchback. Me, I wanted no parts of this squirrelly old
broad, but Loftis, he holding my wrist now, beaming his light
onto a low bed. The room had a funny, museumlike smell. Real
sour. It was full of dirty laundry. And I be sure the old lady's
stuff had a terrible string attached when Loftis, looking away,
lifted her bedsheets and a knot of flies rose. I stepped back and
held my breath. Miss Bailey be in her long-sleeved flannel
nightgown, bloated, like she'd been inflated by a tire pump, her
crazy putty face bald with rot, flyblown, her fingers big as
bananas. Her wristwatch be ticking softly beside a stump of half-
eaten bread. Above the bed, her wall had roaches squashed in
little circles of bloodstain. Maggots clustered in her eyes, her
ears, and one fistsized rat rattled in her flesh. My eyes snapped
shut. My knees failed, then I did a Hollywood faint. When I
surfaced, Loftis, he be sitting beside me in the living room,
where he'd drug me, reading a wrinkled, yellow article from the
Chicago *Daily Defender.*

"Listen to this," Loftis say. "'Elnora Bailey, forty-five, a
Negro housemaid in the Highland Park home of Henry Conners,
is the beneficiary of her employer's will. An old American
family, the Connerses arrived in this country on the *Providence,*
shortly after the voyage of the *Mayflower.* The family flourished
in the early days of the 1900s'. . . !" He went on, getting
breath. "'A distinguished and wealthy industrialist, without
heirs or a wife, Conners willed his entire estate to Miss Bailey
of 3347 N. Clark Street for her twenty years of service to his
family' . . ." Loftis, he give that Geoffrey Holder laugh of his,
low and deep, then it eased up his throat until it hit a high note
and tipped his head back onto his shoulders. "Cooter, that was
before we was born! Miss Bailey kept this in the Bible next to
her bed."

Standing, I braced myself with one hand against the wall. "She didn't earn it?"

"Naw." Loftis, he folded the paper – "Not one penny" – and stuffed it in his shirt pocket. His jaw looked tight as a horseshoe. "Way *I* see it," he say, "this was her one shot in a lifetime to be rich, but, being country, she had backward ways and blew it." Rubbing his hands, he stood up to survey the living room. "Somebody's gonna find Miss Bailey soon, but if we stay on the case – Cooter, don't you square up on me now – we can tote everything to our place before daybreak. Best we start with the big stuff."

"But why didn't she *use* it, huh? Tell me that?"

Loftis, he don't pay me no mind. When he gets an idea in his head, you can't dig it out with a chisel. How long it took me and Loftis to inventory, then haul Miss Bailey's queer old stuff to our crib, I can't say, but that decrepit old ninnyhammer's hoard come to 879,543 dollars in cash money, thirty-two bank books (some deposits be only 5 dollars), and me, I wasn't sure I was dreaming or what, but I suddenly flashed on this feeling, once we left her flat, that all the fears Loftis and me had about the future be gone, 'cause Miss Bailey's property was the past – the power of that fellah Henry Conners trapped like a bottle spirit, which we could live off, so it was the future, too, pure potential: can *do*. Loftis got to talking on about how that piano we pushed home be equal to a thousand bills, jim, which equals, say, a bad TEAC A-3340 tape deck, or a down payment on a deuce-and-a-quarter. Its value be (Loftis say) that of a universal standard of measure, relational, unreal as number, so that tape deck could turn, magically, into two gold lamé suits, a trip to Tijuana, or twenty-five rimjobs from a ho – we had 879,543 dollars' worth of wishes, if you can deal with that. Be like Miss Bailey's stuff is raw energy, and Loftis and me, like wizards, can transform her stuff into anything else at will. All we had to do, it seemed to me, was decide exactly what to exchange it for.

While Loftis studied this over (he looked funny, like a potato trying to say something, after the inventory, and sat, real quiet, in the kitchen), I filled my pockets with fifties, grabbed me a cab downtown to grease, yum, at one of them high-hat restaurants in the Loop. . . . But then I thought better of it, you know, like I'd be out of place – just another jig putting on airs – and scarfed instead at a ribjoint till both my eyes bubbled. This fat lady making fishburgers in the back favored an old hardleg babysitter I once had, a Mrs. Paine who made me eat ochre, and I wanted so bad to say, "Loftis and me Got Ovuh," but I couldn't put that in the wind, could I, so I hatted up. Then I copped a boss silk necktie, cashmere socks, and a whistle-slick maxie leather jacket on State Street, took cabs *every*where, but when I got home that evening a funny, Pandoralike feeling hit me. I took off the jacket, boxed it – it looked so trifling in the hallway's weak light – and, tired, turned my key in the door. I couldn't get in. Loftis, he'd changed the lock and, when he finally let me in, looking vaguer, crabby, like something out of the Book of Revelations, I seen this elaborate boobytrapped tunnel of cardboard and razor blades behind him, with a 2-foot space just big enough for him or me to crawl through. That wasn't all. Two bags of trash from the furnace room be sitting inside the door. Loftis, he give my leather jacket this evil look, hauled me inside, and hit me upside the head.

"How much this thing set us back?"

"Two fifty." My jaws be tight; I toss him my receipt. "You want me to take it back? Maybe I can get something else . . ."

Loftis, he say, not to me, but to the receipt, "Remember the time Mama gave me that ring we had in the family for fifty years? And I took it to Merchandise Mart and sold it for a few pieces of candy?" He hitched his chair forward, and sat with his elbows on his knees. "That's what you did, Cooter. You crawled into a Clark bar." He commence to rip up my receipt, then picked up his flashlight and keys. "The instant you buy something you *lose* the power to buy something." He button up his coat with holes in the elbows, showing his blue shirt, then turned round at the tunnel to say: "Don't touch Miss Bailey's money, or drink her splo, or do *any*thing until I get back."

"Where you going?"

"To work. It's Wednesday, ain't it?"

"You going to work?"

"Yeah."

"You got to go *really*? Loftis," I say, "what you brang them bags of trash in here for?"

"It ain't trash!" He cut his eyes at me. "There's good clothes in there. Mr. Peterson tossed them out, he don't care, but I saw some use in them, that's all."

"Loftis . . ."

"Yeah?"

"What we gonna do with all this money?"

Loftis pressed his fingers to his eyelids, and for a second he look caged, or like somebody'd kicked him in his stomach. Then he cut me some slack: "Let me think on it tonight – it don't pay to rush – then we can TCB, okay?"

Five hours after Loftis leave for work, that old blister Mr. Peterson, our landlord, he come collecting rent, find Miss Bailey's body in apartment 4-B, and phoned the Fire Department. Me, I be folding my new jacket in tissue paper to keep it fresh, adding the box to Miss Bailey's unsunned treasures, when two paramedics squeezed her on a long stretcher through a crowd in the hallway. See, I had to pin her from the stairhead, looking down one last time at this dizzy old lady, and I seen something in her face, like maybe she'd been poor as Job's turkey for thirty years, suffering that special Negro fear of using up what little we get in this life – Loftis, he call that entropy – believing in her belly, and for all her faith, jim, there just ain't no more coming tomorrow from grace, or the Lord, or from her own labor, like she can't kill nothing, and won't nothing die . . . so when Conners will her his wealth, it put her through changes, she be spellbound, possessed by the promise of life, panicky about depletion, and locked now in the past 'cause *every* purchase, you know, has to be a poor buy: a loss of life. Me, I wasn't worried none. Loftis, he got a brain trained by years of talking trash with people in Frog Hudson's Barber Shop on Thirty-fifth Street. By morning, I knew, he'd have some kinda wheeze worked out.

But Loftis, he don't come home. Me, I got plenty worried. I listen to the hi-fi all day Thursday, only pawing outside to peep down the stairs, like that'd make Loftis come sooner. So Thursday go by: and come Friday the head's out of kilter – first there's

an ogrelike belch from the toilet-bowl, then water bursts from
the bathroom into the kitchen – and me, I can't call the super
(how do I explain the tunnel?), so I gave up and quit bailing. But
on Sat'day, I could smell greens cooking next door. Twice I
almost opened Miss Bailey's sardines, even though starving be
less an evil than eating up our stash, but I waited till it was dark
and, lightheaded with hunger, I stepped outside to Pookie
White's, lay a hardluck story on him, and Pookie, he give me
some jambalaya and gumbo. Back home in the living room,
fingerfeeding myself, barricaded in by all that hope made
material, the Kid felt like a king in his counting room, or God in
February, the month before He made the world (Mama's saying),
and I copped some z's in an armchair till I heard the door move
on its hinges, then bumping in the tunnel, and a heavy-footed
walk thumped into the bedroom.

   "Loftis?" I rubbed my eyes. "You back?" It be Sunday
morning. Six-thirty sharp. Darkness dissolved slowly into the
strangeness of twilight, with the rays of sunlight flaring at exactly
the same angle they fall each night, as if the hour be an island, a
moment, outside time. Me, I'm afraid Loftis gonna fuss 'bout
my not straightening up, letting things go. I went into the
bathroom, poured water in the one-spigot washstand – brown
rust come bursting out in flakes – and rinsed my face. "Loftis,
you supposed to be home four days ago. Hey," I say, toweling
my face, "you okay, brah?" How come he don't answer me?
Wiping my hands on the seat of my trousers, I tipped into
Loftis's room. He sleeping with his mouth open. His legs be
drawn up, both fists clenched between his knees. He'd kicked his
blanket on the floor. In his sleep, Loftis laughed, or moaned, it
be hard to tell. His eyelids, not quite shut, show slits of white. I
decided to wait till Loftis wake up for his decision, but turning,
I seen his watch, keys, and what looked in the first stain of
sunlight to be a carefully wrapped piece of newspaper on his
nightstand. The sun surged up in a bright shimmer, focusing the
bedroom slowly like solution do a photographic image in the
developer. And then something so freakish went down I ain't
sure it took place. Fumblefingered, I unfolded the paper and
inside be a blemished penny. It be like somebody hit me hard

between the shoulderblades. Taped on the penny be a slip of paper, and on the paper be the note, "Found while walking down Devon Avenue." I hear Loftis mumble like he trapped in a nightmare. "Hold tight," I whisper, "it's all right." Me, I wanted to tell Loftis how Miss Bailey looked four days ago, that maybe it didn't have to be like that for us – did it? – because we could change. Couldn't we? Me, I pull his packed sheets over him, wrap up the penny, and, when I locate Miss Bailey's glass jar in the living room, put it away carefully, for now, with the rest of our things.

# DENIS JOHNSON

☆  ☆  ☆  ☆

# *Emergency*

I'd been working in the emergency room for about three weeks,
I guess. This was in 1973, before the summer ended. With
nothing to do on the overnight shift but batch the insurance
reports from the daytime shifts, I just started wandering around,
over to the coronary-care unit, down to the cafeteria, et cetera,
looking for Georgie, the orderly, a pretty good friend of mine.
He often stole pills from the cabinets.

He was running over the tiled floor of the operating room
with a mop. "Are you still doing that?" I said.

"Jesus, there's a lot of blood here," he complained.

"Where?" The floor looked clean enough to me.

"What the hell were they doing in here?" he asked me.

"They were performing surgery, Georgie," I told him.

"There's so much goop inside of us, man," he said, "and it
all wants to get out." He leaned his mop against a cabinet.

"What are you crying for?" I didn't understand.

He stood still, raised both arms slowly behind his head, and
tightened his ponytail. Then he grabbed the mop and started
making broad random arcs with it, trembling and weeping and
moving all around the place really fast. "What am I *crying* for?"
he said. "Jesus. Wow, oh boy, perfect."

I was hanging out in the ER with fat, quivering Nurse. One of
the Family Service doctors that nobody liked came in looking for
Georgie to wipe up after him. "Where's Georgie?" this guy
asked.

"Georgie's in OR," Nurse said.

"Again?"

"No," Nurse said. "Still."

"Still? Doing what?"

"Cleaning the floor."

"Again?"

"No," Nurse said again. "Still."

Back in OR, Georgie dropped his mop and bent over in the posture of a child soiling its diapers. He stared down with his mouth open in terror.

He said, "What am I going to do about these fucking *shoes*, man?"

"Whatever you stole," I said, "I guess you already ate it all, right?"

"Listen to how they squish," he said, walking around carefully on his heels.

"Let me check your pockets, man."

He stood still a minute, and I found his stash. I left him two of each, whatever they were. "Shift is about half over," I told him.

"Good. Because I really, really, really need a drink," he said. "Will you please help me get this blood mopped *up*?"

Around 3.30 a.m. a guy with a knife in his eye came in, led by Georgie.

"I hope *you* didn't do that to him," Nurse said.

"Me?" Georgie said. "No. He was like this."

"My wife did it," the man said. The blade was buried to the hilt in the outside corner of his left eye. It was a hunting knife kind of thing.

"Who brought you in?" Nurse said.

"Nobody. I just walked down. It's only three blocks," the man said.

Nurse peered at him. "We'd better get you lying down."

"Okay, I'm certainly ready for something like that," the man said.

She peered a bit longer into his face. "Is your other eye," she said, "a glass eye?"

"It's plastic, or something artificial like that," he said.

"And you can see out of *this* eye?" she asked, meaning the wounded one.

"I can see. But I can't make a fist out of my left hand because this knife is doing something to my brain."

"My God," Nurse said.

"I guess I'd better get the doctor," I said.

"There you go," Nurse agreed.

They got him lying down, and Georgie says to the patient, "Name?"

"Terrence Weber."

"Your face is dark. I can't see what you're saying."

"Georgie," I said.

"What are you saying, man? I can't see."

Nurse came over, and Georgie said to her, "His face is dark."

She leaned over the patient. "How long ago did this happen, Terry?" she shouted down into his face.

"Just a while ago. My wife did it. I was asleep," the patient said.

"Do you want the police?"

He thought about it and finally said, "Not unless I die."

Nurse went to the wall intercom and buzzed the doctor on duty, the Family Service person. "Got a surprise for you," she said over the intercom. He took his time getting down the hall to her, because he knew she hated Family Service and her happy tone of voice could only mean something beyond his competence and potentially humiliating.

He peeked into the trauma room and saw the situation: the clerk – that is, me – standing next to the orderly, Georgie, both of us on drugs, looking down at a patient with a knife sticking up out of his face.

"What seems to be the trouble?" he said.

The doctor gathered the three of us around him in the office and said, "Here's the situation. We've got to get a team here, an entire team. I want a good eye man. A great eye man. The best eye man. I want a brain surgeon. And I want a really good gas man, get me a genius. I'm not touching that head. I'm just going to watch this one. I know my limits. We'll just get him prepped and sit tight. Orderly!"

"Do you mean me?" Georgie said. "Should I get him prepped?"

"Is this a hospital?" the doctor asked. "Is this the emergency room? Is that a patient? Are you the orderly?"

I dialed the hospital operator and told her to get me the eye man and the brain man and the gas man.

Georgie could be heard across the hall, washing his hands and singing a Neil Young song that went "Hello cowgirl in the sand. Is this place at your command?"

"That person is not right, not at all, not one bit," the doctor said.

"As long as my instructions are audible to him it doesn't concern me," Nurse insisted, spooning stuff up out of a little Dixie cup. "I've got my own life and the protection of my family to think of."

"Well, okay, okay. Don't chew my head off," the doctor said.

The eye man was on vacation or something. While the hospital's operator called around to find someone else just as good, the other specialists were hurrying through the night to join us. I stood around looking at charts and chewing up more of Georgie's pills. Some of them tasted the way urine smells, some of them burned, some of them tasted like chalk. Various nurses, and two physicians who'd been tending somebody in ICU, were hanging out down here with us now.

Everybody had a different idea about exactly how to approach the problem of removing the knife from Terrence Weber's brain. But when Georgie came in from prepping the patient – from shaving the patient's eyebrow and disinfecting the area around the wound, and so on – he seemed to be holding the hunting knife in his left hand.

The talk just dropped off a cliff.

"Where," the doctor asked finally, "did you get that?"

Nobody said one thing more, not for quite a long time.

After a while, one of the ICU nurses said, "Your shoelace is untied." Georgie laid the knife on a chart and bent down to fix his shoe.

★

There were twenty more minutes left to get through.

"How's the guy doing?" I asked.

"Who?" Georgie said.

It turned out that Terrence Weber still had excellent vision in the one good eye, and acceptable motor and reflex, despite his earlier motor complaint. "His vitals are normal," Nurse said. "There's nothing wrong with the guy. It's one of those things."

After a while you forget it's summer. You don't remember what the morning is. I'd worked two doubles with eight hours off in between, which I'd spent sleeping on a gurney in the nurses' station. Georgie's pills were making me feel like a giant helium-filled balloon, but I was wide awake. Georgie and I went out to the lot, to his orange pickup.

We lay down on a stretch of dusty plywood in the back of the truck with the daylight knocking against our eyelids and the fragrance of alfalfa thickening on our tongues.

"I want to go to church," Georgie said.

"Let's go to the county fair."

"I'd like to worship. I would."

"They have these injured hawks and eagles there. From the Humane Society," I said.

"I need a quiet chapel about now."

Georgie and I had a terrific time driving around. For a while the day was clear and peaceful. It was one of the moments you stay in, to hell with all the troubles of before and after. The sky is blue, and the dead are coming back. Later in the afternoon, with sad resignation, the county fair bares its breasts. A champion of the drug LSD, a very famous guru of the love generation, is being interviewed amid a TV crew off to the left of the poultry cages. His eyeballs look like he bought them in a joke shop. It doesn't occur to me, as I pity this extraterrestrial, that in my life I've taken as much acid as he has.

After that, we got lost. We drove for hours, literally hours, but we couldn't find the road back to town.

Georgie started to complain. "That was the worst fair I've been to. Where were the rides?"

"They had rides," I said.

"I didn't see one ride."

A jackrabbit scurried out in front of us, and we hit it.

"There was a merry-go-round, a Ferris wheel, and a thing called the Hammer that people were bent over vomiting from after they got off," I said. "Are you completely blind?"

"What was that?"

"A rabbit."

"Something thumped."

"You hit him. *He* thumped."

Georgie stood on the brake pedal. "Rabbit stew."

He threw the truck in reverse and zigzagged back toward the rabbit. "Where's my hunting knife?" He almost ran over the poor animal a second time.

"We'll camp in the wilderness," he said. "In the morning we'll breakfast on its haunches." He was waving Terrence Weber's hunting knife around in what I was sure was a dangerous way.

In a minute he was standing at the edge of the fields, cutting the scrawny little thing up, tossing away its organs. "I should have been a doctor," he cried.

A family in a big Dodge, the only car we'd seen for a long time, slowed down and gawked out the windows as they passed by. The father said, "What is it, a snake?"

"No, it's not a snake," Georgie said. "It's a rabbit with babies inside it."

"Babies!" the mother said, and the father sped the car forward, over the protests of several little kids in the back.

Georgie came back to my side of the truck with his shirtfront stretched out in front of him as if he were carrying apples in it, or some such, but they were, in fact, slimy miniature bunnies. "No way I'm eating those things," I told him.

"Take them, take them, I gotta drive, take them," he said, dumping them in my lap and getting in on his side of the truck. He started driving along faster and faster, with a look of glory on his face. "We killed the mother and saved the children," he said.

"It's getting late," I said. "Let's get back to town."

"You bet." Sixty, seventy, eighty-five, just topping ninety.

"These rabbits better be kept warm." One at a time I slid the little things in between my shirt buttons and nestled them against my belly. "They're hardly moving," I told Georgie.

"We'll get some milk and sugar and all that, and we'll raise them up ourselves. They'll get as big as gorillas."

The road we were lost on cut straight through the middle of the world. It was still daytime, but the sun had no more power than an ornament or a sponge. In this light the truck's hood, which had been bright orange, had turned a deep blue.

Georgie let us drift to the shoulder of the road, slowly, slowly, as if he'd fallen asleep or given up trying to find his way.

"What is it?"

"We can't go on. I don't have any headlights," Georgie said.

We parked under a strange sky with a faint image of a quarter-moon superimposed on it.

There was a little wood beside us. This day had been dry and hot, the buck pines and what all simmering patiently, but as we sat there smoking cigarettes it started to get very cold.

"The summer's over," I said.

That was the year when arctic clouds moved down over the Midwest, and we had two weeks of winter in September.

"Do you realize it's going to snow?" Georgie asked me.

He was right, a gun-blue storm was shaping up. We got out and walked around idiotically. The beautiful chill! That sudden crispness, and the tang of evergreen stabbing us!

The gusts of snow twisted themselves around our heads while the night fell. I couldn't find the truck. We just kept getting more and more lost. I kept calling, "Georgie, can you see?" and he kept saying, "See what? See what?"

The only light visible was a streak of sunset flickering below the hem of the clouds. We headed that way.

We bumped softly down a hill toward an open field that seemed to be a military graveyard, filled with rows and rows of austere, identical markers over soldiers' graves. I'd never before come across this cemetery. On the farther side of the field, just beyond the curtains of snow, the sky was torn away and the angels were descending out of a brilliant blue summer, their huge faces streaked with light and full of pity. The sight of them cut through my heart and down the knuckles of my spine, and if there'd been anything in my bowels I would have messed my pants from fear.

Georgie opened his arms and cried out, "It's the drive-in, man!"

"The drive-in . . ." I wasn't sure what these words meant.

"They're showing movies in a fucking blizzard!" Georgie screamed.

"I see. I thought it was something else," I said.

We walked carefully down there and climbed through the busted fence and stood in the very back. The speakers, which I'd mistaken for grave markers, muttered in unison. Then there was tinkly music, of which I could very nearly make out the tune. Famous movie stars rode bicycles beside a river, laughing out of their gigantic lovely mouths. If anybody had come to see this show, they'd left when the weather started. Not one car remained, not even a broken-down one from last week, or one left here because it was out of gas. In a couple of minutes, in the middle of a whirling square dance, the screen turned black, the cinematic summer ended, the snow went dark, there was nothing but my breath.

"I'm starting to get my eyes back," Georgie said in another minute.

A general grayness was giving birth to various shapes, it was true. "But which ones are close and which ones are far off?" I begged him to tell me.

By trial and error, with a lot of walking back and forth in wet shoes, we found the truck and sat inside it, shivering.

"Let's get out of here," I said.

"We can't go anywhere without headlights."

"We've gotta get back. We're a long way from home."

"No, we're not."

"We must have come 300 miles."

"We're right outside town, Fuckhead. We've just been driving around and around."

"This is no place to camp. I hear the interstate over there."

"We'll just stay here till it gets late. We can drive home late. We'll be invisible."

We listened to the big rigs going from San Francisco to Pennsylvania along the interstate, like shudders down a long hacksaw blade, while the snow buried us.

Eventually Georgie said, "We better get some milk for those bunnies."

"We don't have *milk*," I said.

"We'll mix sugar up with it."

"Will you forget about this milk all of a sudden?"

"They're mammals, man."

"Forget about those rabbits."

"Where are they, anyway?"

"You're not listening to me. I said, 'Forget the rabbits.'"

"Where are they?"

The truth was I'd forgotten all about them, and they were dead.

"They slid around behind me and got squashed," I said tearfully.

"They slid around *behind*?"

He watched while I pried them out from behind my back.

I picked them out one at a time and held them in my hands and we looked at them. There were eight. They weren't any bigger than my fingers, but everything was there.

Little feet! Eyelids! Even whiskers! "Deceased," I said.

Georgie asked, "Does everything you touch turn to shit? Does this happen to you every time?"

"No wonder they call me Fuckhead."

"It's a name that's going to stick."

"I realize that."

"'Fuckhead' is gonna ride you to your grave."

"I just said so. I agreed with you in advance," I said.

Or maybe that wasn't the time it snowed. Maybe it was the time we slept in the truck and I rolled over on the bunnies and flattened them. It doesn't matter. What's important for me to remember now is that early the next morning the snow was melted off the windshield and the daylight woke me up. A mist covered everything, and with the sunshine, was beginning to grow sharp and strange. The bunnies weren't a problem yet, or they'd already been a problem and were already forgotten, and there was nothing on my mind. I felt the beauty of the morning. I could understand how a drowning man might suddenly feel a deep thirst being quenched. Or how the slave might become a friend to his master. Georgie slept with his face right on the steering wheel.

I saw bits of snow resembling an abundance of blossoms on the stems of the drive-in speakers – no, revealing the blossoms that were always there. A bull elk stood still in the pasture beyond the fence giving off an air of authority and stupidity. And a coyote jogged across the pasture and faded away among the saplings.

That afternoon we got back to work in time to resume everything as if it had never stopped happening and we'd never been anywhere else.

"The Lord," the intercom said, "is my shepherd." It did that each evening because this was a Catholic hospital. "Our Father who art in Heaven," and so on.

"Yeah, yeah," Nurse said.

The man with the knife in his head, Terrence Weber, was released around suppertime. They'd kept him overnight and given him an eyepatch – all for no reason, really.

He stopped off at ER to say good-bye. "Well, those pills they gave me make everything taste terrible," he said.

"It could have been worse," Nurse said.

"Even my tongue."

"It's just a miracle you didn't end up sightless or at least dead," she reminded him.

The patient recognized me. He acknowledged me with a smile. "I was peeping on the lady next door while she was out there sunbathing," he said. "My wife decided to blind me."

He shook Georgie's hand. Georgie didn't know him. "Who are you supposed to be?" he asked Terrence Weber.

★

Some hours before that, Georgie had said something that had suddenly and completely explained the difference between us. We'd been driving back toward town, along the Old Highway, through the flatness. We picked up a hitchhiker, a boy I knew. We stopped the truck and the boy climbed slowly up out of the fields as out of the mouth of a volcano. His name was Hardee. He looked even worse than we probably did.

"We got messed up and slept in the truck all night," I told Hardee.

"I had a feeling," Hardee said. "Either that or, you know, driving 1,000 miles."

"That, too," I said.

"Or you're sick or diseased or something."

"Who's this guy?" Georgie asked.

"This is Hardee. He lived with me last summer. I found him on the doorstep. What happened to your dog?" I asked Hardee.

"He's still down there."

"Yeah, I heard you went to Texas."

"I was working on a bee farm," Hardee said.

"Wow. Do those things sting you?"

"Not like you'd think," Hardee said. "You're part of their daily drill. It's all part of a harmony."

Outside, the same identical stretch of ground repeatedly rolled past our faces. The day was cloudless, blinding. But Georgie said, "Look at that," pointing straight ahead of us.

One star was so hot it showed, bright and blue, in the empty sky.

"I recognized you right away," I told Hardee. "But what happened to your hair? Who chopped it off?"

"I hate to say."

"Don't tell me."

"They drafted me."

"Oh no."

"Oh yeah. I'm AWOL. I'm bad AWOL. I got to get to Canada."

"Oh, that's terrible," I said to Hardee.

"Don't worry," Georgie said. "We'll get you there."

"How?"

"Somehow. I think I know some people. Don't worry. You're on your way to Canada."

That world! These days it's all been erased and they've rolled it up like a scroll and put it away somewhere. Yes, I can touch it with my fingers. But where is it?

After a while Hardee asked Georgie, "What do you do for a job?" and Georgie said, "I save lives."

THOM JONES

☆  ☆  ☆  ☆

# The Pugilist at Rest

Hey Baby got caught writing a letter to his girl when he was supposed to be taking notes on the specs of the M-14 rifle. We were sitting in a stifling hot Quonset hut during the first weeks of boot camp, August 1966, at the Marine Corps Recruit Depot in San Diego. Sergeant Wright snatched the letter out of Hey Baby's hand, and later that night in the squad bay he read the letter to the Marine recruits of Platoon 263, his voice laden with sarcasm. "*Hey Baby!*" he began, and then as he went into the body of the letter he worked himself into a state of outrage and disgust. It was a letter to *Rosie Rottencrotch*, he said at the end, and what really mattered, what was really at issue and what was of utter importance was not *Rosie Rottencrotch* and her steaming-hot panties but rather the muzzle velocity of the M-14 rifle.

Hey Baby paid for the letter by doing a hundred squat thrusts on the concrete floor of the squad bay, but the main prize he won that night was that he became forever known as Hey Baby to the recruits of Platoon 263 – in addition to being a shitbird, a faggot, a turd, a maggot, and other such standard appellations. To top it all off, shortly after the incident, Hey Baby got a Dear John from his girl back in Chicago, of whom Sergeant Wright, myself, and seventy-eight other Marine recruits had come to know just a little.

Hey Baby was not in the Marine Corps for very long. The reason for this was that he started in on my buddy, Jorgeson. Jorgeson was my main man, and Hey Baby started calling him Jorgepussy and began harassing him and pushing him around. He was down on Jorgeson because whenever we were taught some sort of combat maneuver or tactic, Jorgeson would say, under his breath, "You could get *killed* if you try that." Or, "Your ass is *had*, if you do that." You got the feeling that

Jorgeson didn't think loving the American flag and defending
democratic ideals in Southeast Asia were all that important. He
told me that what he really wanted to do was have an artist's loft
in the SoHo district of New York City, wear a beret, eat liver-
sausage sandwiches made with stale baguettes, drink tokay wine,
smoke dope, paint pictures, and listen to the wailing, sorrowful
songs of that French singer Edith Piaf, otherwise known as "The
Little Sparrow."

After the first half hour of boot camp most of the other recruits
wanted to get out, too, but they nourished dreams of surfboards,
Corvettes, and blonde babes. Jorgeson wanted to be a beatnik
and hang out with Jack Kerouac and Neal Cassady, slam down
burning shots of amber whiskey, and hear Charles Mingus play
real cool jazz on the bass fiddle. He wanted to practice Zen
Buddhism, throw the I Ching, eat couscous, and study astrology
charts. All of this was foreign territory to me. I had grown up in
Aurora, Illinois, and had never heard of such things. Jorgeson
had a sharp tongue and was so supercilious in his remarks that I
didn't know quite how seriously I should take this talk, but I
enjoyed his humor and I did believe he had the sensibilities of an
artist. It was not some vague yearning. I believed very much that
he could become a painter of pictures. At that point he wasn't
putting his heart and soul into becoming a Marine. He wasn't a
true believer like me.

Some weeks after Hey Baby began hassling Jorgeson, Sergeant
Wright gave us his best speech: "You men are going off to war,
and it's not a pretty thing," etc. & etc., "and if Luke the Gook
knocks down one of your buddies, a fellow-Marine, you are
going to risk your life and go in and get that Marine and you are
going to bring him out. Not because I said so. No! You are
going after that Marine because *you* are a Marine, a member of
the most elite fighting force in the world, and that man out there
who's gone down is a Marine, and he's your *buddy*. He is your
brother! Once you are a Marine, you are *always* a Marine and
you will never let another Marine down." Etc. & etc. "You can
take a Marine out of the Corps but you can't take the Corps out
of a Marine." Etc. & etc. At the time it seemed to me a very
good speech, and it stirred me deeply. Sergeant Wright was no

candy ass. He was one squared-away dude, and he could call cadence. Man, it puts a lump in my throat when I remember how that man could sing cadence. Apart from Jorgeson, I think all of the recruits in Platoon 263 were proud of Sergeant Wright. He was the real thing, the genuine article. He was a crackerjack Marine.

In the course of training, lots of the recruits dropped out of the original platoon. Some couldn't pass the physical-fitness tests and had to go to a special camp for pussies. This was a particularly shameful shortcoming, the most humiliating apart from bed-wetting. Other recruits would get pneumonia, strep throat, infected foot blisters, or whatever, and lose time that way. Some didn't qualify at the rifle range. One would break a leg. Another would have a nervous breakdown (and this was also deplorable). People dropped out right and left. When the recruit corrected whatever deficiency he had, or when he got better, he would be picked up by another platoon that was in the stage of basic training that he had been in when his training was interrupted. Platoon 263 picked up dozens of recruits in this fashion. If everything went well, however, you got through with the whole business in twelve weeks. That's not a long time, but it seemed like a long time. You did not see a female in all that time. You did not see a newspaper or a television set. You did not eat a candy bar. Another thing was the fact that you had someone on top of you, watching every move you made. When it was time to "shit, shower, and shave," you were given just ten minutes, and had to confront lines and so on to complete the entire affair. Head calls were so infrequent that I spent a lot of time that might otherwise have been neutral or painless in the eye-watering anxiety that I was going to piss my pants. We *ran* to chow, where we were faced with enormous steam vents that spewed out a sickening smell of rancid, super-heated grease. Still, we entered the mess hall with ravenous appetites, ate a huge tray of food in just a few minutes, and then *ran* back to our company area in formation, choking back the burning bile of a meal too big to be eaten so fast. God forbid that you would lose control and vomit.

If all had gone well in the preceding hours, Sergeant Wright would permit us to smoke one cigarette after each meal. Jorgeson had shown me the wisdom of switching from Camels to Pall Malls – they were much longer, packed a pretty good jolt, and when we snapped open our brushed-chrome Zippos, torched up, and inhaled the first few drags, we shared the overmastering pleasure that tobacco can bring if you use it seldom and judiciously. These were always the best moments of the day – brief respites from the tyrannical repression of recruit training. As we got close to the end of it all Jorgeson liked to play a little game. He used to say to me (with fragrant blue smoke curling out of his nostrils), "If someone said, 'I'll give you ten thousand dollars to do all of this again,' what would you say?" "No way, Jack!" He would keep on upping it until he had John Beresford Tipton, the guy from "The Millionaire," offering me a check for a million bucks. "Not for any money," I'd say.

While they were all smoldering under various pressures, the recruits were also getting pretty "salty" – they were beginning to believe. They were beginning to think of themselves as Marines. If you could make it through this, the reasoning went, you wouldn't crack in combat. So I remember that I had tears in my eyes when Sergeant Wright gave us the spiel about how a Marine would charge a machine-gun nest to save his buddies, dive on a hand grenade, do whatever it takes – and yet I was ashamed when Jorgeson caught me wiping them away. All of the recruits were teary except Jorgeson. He had those very clear cobalt-blue eyes. They were so remarkable that they caused you to notice Jorgeson in a crowd. There was unusual beauty in these eyes, and there was an extraordinary power in them. Apart from having a pleasant enough face, Jorgeson was small and unassuming except for these eyes. Anyhow, when he caught me getting sentimental he gave me this look that penetrated to the core of my being. It was the icy look of absolute contempt, and it caused me to doubt myself. I said, "Man! Can't you get into it? For Christ's sake!"

"I'm not like you," he said. "But I am into it, more than you could ever know. I never told you this before, but I am Kal-El, born on the planet Krypton and rocketed to Earth as an infant, moments before my world exploded. Disguised as a mild-mannered Marine, I have resolved to use my powers for the good of mankind. Whenever danger appears on the scene, truth and justice will be served as I slip into the green U.S.M.C. utility uniform and become Earth's greatest hero."

I got highly pissed and didn't talk to him for a couple of days after this. Then, about two weeks before boot camp was over, when we were running out to the parade field for drill with our rifles at port arms, all assholes and elbows, I saw Hey Baby give Jorgeson a nasty shove with his M-14. Hey Baby was a large and fairly tough young man who liked to displace his aggressive impulses on Jorgeson, but he wasn't as big or as tough as I.

Jorgeson nearly fell down as the other recruits scrambled out to the parade field, and Hey Baby gave a short, malicious laugh. I ran past Jorgeson and caught up to Hey Baby; he picked me up in his peripheral vision, but by then it was too late. I set my body so that I could put everything into it, and with one deft stroke I hammered him in the temple with the sharp edge of the steel butt plate of my M-14. It was not exactly a premeditated crime, although I had been laying to get him. My idea before this had simply been to lay my hands on him, but now I had blood in my eye. I was a skilled boxer, and I knew the temple was a vulnerable spot; the human skull is otherwise hard and durable, except at its base. There was a sickening crunch, and Hey Baby dropped into the ice plants along the side of the company street.

The entire platoon was out on the parade field when the house mouse screamed at the assistant D.I., who rushed back to the scene of the crime to find Hey Baby crumpled in a fetal position in the ice plants with blood all over the place. There was blood from the scalp wound as well as a froth of blood emitting from his nostrils and his mouth. Blood was leaking from his right ear. Did I see skull fragments and a brain tissue? It seemed that I did. To tell you the truth, I wouldn't have cared in the least if I had killed him, but like most criminals I was very much afraid of getting caught. It suddenly occurred to me that I could be headed for the brig for a long time. My heart was pounding out of my chest. Yet the larger part of me didn't care. Jorgeson was my

buddy, and I wasn't going to stand still and let someone fuck
him over.

The platoon waited at parade rest while Sergeant Wright came
out of the duty hut and took command of the situation. An
ambulance was called, and it came almost immediately. A
number of corpsmen squatted down alongside the fallen man for
what seemed an eternity. Eventually they took Hey Baby off
with a fractured skull. It would be the last we ever saw of him.
Three evenings later, in the squad bay, the assistant D.I. told us
rather ominously that Hey Baby had recovered consciousness.
That's all he said. What did *that* mean? I was worried, because
Hey Baby had seen me make my move, but, as it turned out,
when he came to he had forgotten the incident and all events of
the preceding two weeks. Retrograde amnesia. Lucky for me. I
also knew that at least three other recruits had seen what I did,
but none of them reported me. Every member of the platoon
was called in and grilled by a team of hard-ass captains and a
light colonel from the Criminal Investigation Detachment. It
took a certain amount of balls to lie to them, yet none of my
fellow-jarheads reported me. I was well liked and Hey Baby was
not. Indeed, many felt that he got exactly what was coming to
him.

The other day – Memorial Day, as it happened – I was cleaning
some stuff out of the attic when I came upon my old dress-blue
uniform. It's a beautiful uniform, easily the most handsome
worn by any of the U.S. armed forces. The rich color recalled
Jorgeson's eyes for me – not that the color matched, but in the
sense that the color of each was so startling. The tunic does not
have lapels, of course, but a high collar with red piping and the
traditional golden eagle, globe, and anchor insignia on either side
of the neck clasp. The tunic buttons are not brassy – although
they are in fact made of brass – but are a delicate gold in color,
like Florentine gold. On the sleeves of the tunic my staff
sergeant's chevrons are gold on red. High on the left breast is a
rainbow display of fruit salad representing my various combat
citations. Just below these are my marksmanship badges; I shot
Expert in rifle as well as pistol.

I opened a sandalwood box and took my various medals out of the large plastic bag I had packed them in to prevent them from tarnishing. The Navy Cross and the two Silver Stars are the best; they are such pretty things they dazzle you. I found a couple of Thai sticks in the sandalwood box as well. I took a whiff of the box and smelled the smells of Saigon – the whores, the dope, the saffron, cloves, jasmine, and patchouli oil. I put the Thai sticks back, recalling the three-day hangover that particular batch of dope had given me more than twenty-three years before. Again I looked at my dress-blue tunic. My most distinctive badge, the crowning glory, and the one of which I am most proud, is the set of Airborne wings. I remember how it was, walking around Oceanside, California – the Airborne wings and the high-and-tight haircut were recognized by all the Marines; they meant you were the crème de la crème, you were a recon Marine.

Recon was all Jorgeson's idea. We had lost touch with each other after boot camp. I was sent to com school in San Diego, where I had to sit in a hot Class A wool uniform all day and learn the Morse code. I deliberately flunked out, and when I was given the perfunctory option for a second shot, I told the colonel, "Hell no, sir. I want to go 003 – infantry. I want to be a ground-pounder. I didn't join the service to sit at a desk all day."

I was on a bus to Camp Pendleton three days later, and when I got there I ran into Jorgeson. I had been thinking of him a lot. He was a clerk in headquarters company. Much to my astonishment, he was fifteen pounds heavier, and had grown two inches, and he told me he was hitting the weight pile every night after running seven miles up and down the foothills of Pendleton in combat boots, carrying a rifle and a full field pack. After the usual what's-been-happening? b.s., he got down to business and said, "They need people in Force Recon, what do you think? Headquarters is one boring motherfucker."

I said, "Recon? Paratrooper? You got to be shittin' me! When did you get so gung-ho, man?"

He said, "Hey, you were the one who *bought* the program. Don't fade on me now, goddamn it! Look, we pass the physical fitness test and then they send us to jump school at Benning. If we pass that, we're in. And we'll pass. Those doggies ain't got jack. Semper fi, motherfucker! Let's do it."

There was no more talk of Neal Cassady, Edith Piaf, or the artist's loft in SoHo. I said, "If Sergeant Wright could only see you now!"

We were just three days in country when we got dropped in somewhere up north near the DMZ. It was a routine reconnaissance patrol. It was not supposed to be any kind of big deal at all – just acclimation. The morning after our drop we approached a clear field. I recall that it gave me a funny feeling, but I was too new to fully trust my instincts. *Everything* was spooky; I was fresh meat, F.N.G. – A Fucking New Guy.

Before moving into the field, our team leader sent Hanes – a lance corporal, a short-timer, with only twelve days left before his rotation was over – across the field as a point man. This was a bad omen and everyone knew it. Hanes had two Purple Hearts. He followed the order with no hesitation and crossed the field without drawing fire. The team leader signaled for us to fan out and told me to circumvent the field and hump through the jungle to investigate a small mound of loose red dirt that I had missed completely but that he had picked up with his trained eye. I remember I kept saying, "Where?" He pointed to a heap of earth about thirty yards along the tree line and about ten feet back in the bushes. Most likely it was an anthill, but you never knew – it could have been an NVA tunnel. "Over there," he hissed. "Goddamn it, do I have to draw pictures for you?"

I moved smartly in the direction of the mound while the rest of the team reconverged to discuss something. As I approached the mound I saw that it was in fact an anthill, and I looked back at the team and saw they were already halfway across the field, moving very fast.

Suddenly there were several loud hollow pops and the cry "Incoming!" Seconds later the first of a half-dozen mortar rounds landed in the loose earth surrounding the anthill. For a millisecond, everything went black. I was blown back and lifted up on a cushion of warm air. At first it was like the thrill of a carnival ride, but it was quickly followed by that stunned, jangly, electric feeling you get when you hit your crazy bone. Like that, but not confined to a small area like the elbow. I felt it shoot through my spine and into all four limbs. A thick plaster of sand and red clay plugged up my nostrils and ears. Grit was blown in between my teeth. If I hadn't been wearing a pair of Ray-Ban aviator shades, I would certainly have been blinded permanently – as it was, my eyes were loaded with grit. (I later discovered that fine red earth was somehow blown in behind the crystal of my pressure-tested Rolex Submariner, underneath my fingernails and toenails, and deep into the pores of my skin.) When I was able to, I pulled out a canteen filled with lemon-lime Kool-Aid and tried to flood my eyes clean. This helped a little, but my eyes still felt like they were on fire. I rinsed them again and blinked furiously.

I rolled over on my stomach in the prone position and leveled my field-issue M-16. A company of screaming NVA soldiers ran into the field, firing as they came – I saw their green tracer rounds blanket the position where the team had quickly congregated to lay out a perimeter, but none of our own red tracers were going out. Several of the Marines had been killed outright by the mortar rounds. Jorgeson was all right, and I saw him cast a nervous glance in my direction. Then he turned to the enemy and began to fire his M-16. I clicked my rifle on to automatic and pulled the trigger, but the gun was loaded with dirt and it wouldn't fire.

Apart from Jorgeson, the only other American putting out any fire was Second Lieutenant Milton, also a fairly new guy, a "cherry," who was down on one knee firing his .45, an exercise in almost complete futility. I assumed that Milton's 16 had jammed, like mine, and watched as AK-47 rounds, having penetrated his flak jacket and then his chest, ripped through the back of his field pack and buzzed into the jungle beyond like a deadly swarm of bees. A few seconds later, I heard the swoosh of an RPG rocket, a dud round that dinged the lieutenant's left shoulder before it flew off in the bush behind him. It took off his whole arm, and for an instant I could see the white bone and ligaments of his shoulder, and then red flesh of muscle tissue, looking very much like fresh prime beef, well marbled and encased in a thin layer of yellowish-white adipose tissue that quickly became saturated with dark-red blood. What a lot of blood there was. Still, Milton continued to fire his .45. When he emptied his clip, I watched him remove a fresh one from his web gear and attempt to load the pistol with one hand. He seemed to fumble with the fresh clip for a long time, until at last he dropped it, along with his .45. The lieutenant's head slowly sagged forward, but he stayed up on one knee with his remaining arm extended out to the enemy, palm upward in the soulful, heart-rending gesture of Al Jolson doing a rendition of "Mammy."

A hail of green tracer rounds buzzed past Jorgeson, but he cooly returned fire in short, controlled bursts. The light, tinny pops from his M-16 did not sound very reassuring, but I saw several NVA go down. AK-47 fire kicked up red dust all around Jorgeson's feet. He was basically out in the open, and if ever a man was totally alone it was Jorgeson. He was dead meat and he had to know it. It was very strange that he wasn't hit immediately.

Jorgeson zigged his way over to the body of a large black Marine who carried an M-60 machine gun. Most of the recon Marines carried grease guns or Swedish Ks; an M-60 was too heavy for traveling light and fast, but this Marine had been big and he had been paranoid. I had known him least of anyone in the squad. In three days he had said nothing to me, I suppose because I was F.N.G., and had spooked him. Indeed, now he was dead. That august seeker of truth, Schopenhauer, was correct: *We are like lambs in a field, disporting themselves under the eye of the butcher, who chooses out first one and then another for his prey. So it is that in our good days we are all unconscious of the evil Fates may have presently in store for us – sickness, poverty, mutilation, loss of sight or reason.*

It was difficult to judge how quickly time was moving. Although my senses had been stunned by the concussion of the mortar rounds, they were, however paradoxical this may seem, more acute than ever before. I watched Jorgeson pick up the machine gun and begin to spread an impressive field of fire back at the enemy. *Thuk thuk thuk, thuk thuk thuk, thuk thuk thuk!* I saw several more bodies fall, and began to think that things might turn out all right after all. The NVA dropped for cover, and many of them turned back and headed for the tree line. Jorgeson fired off a couple of bandoliers, and after he stopped to load another, he turned back and looked at me with those blue eyes and a smile like "How am I doing?" Then I heard the steel-cork pop of an M-79 launcher and saw a rocket grenade explode through Jorgeson's upper abdomen, causing him to do something like a back flip. His M-60 machine gun flew straight up into the air. The barrel was glowing red like a hot poker, and continued to fire in a "cook off" until the entire bandolier had run through.

In the meantime I had pulled a cleaning rod out of my pack and worked it through the barrel of my M-16. When I next tried to shoot, the Tonka-toy son of a bitch remained jammed, and at last I frantically broke it down to find the source of the problem. I had a dirty bolt. Fucking dirt everywhere. With numbed fingers I removed the firing pin and worked it over with a toothbrush, dropping it in the red dirt, picking it up, cleaning it, and dropping it again. My fingers felt like Novocain, and while I could see far away, I was unable to see up close. I poured some more Kool-Aid over my eyes. It was impossible for me to get my weapon clean. Lucky for me, ultimately.

Suddenly NVA soldiers were running through the field shoving bayonets into the bodies of the downed Marines. It was not until an NVA trooper kicked Lieutenant Milton out of his tripod position that he finally fell to the ground. Then the soldiers started going through the dead Marines' gear. I was still frantically struggling with my weapon when it began to dawn on me that the enemy had forgotten me in the excitement of the firefight. I wondered what had happened to Hanes and if he had gotten clear. I doubted it, and hopped on my survival radio to call in an air strike when finally a canny NVA trooper did remember me and headed in my direction most ricky-tick.

With a tight grip on the spoon, I pulled the pin on a fragmentation grenade and then unsheathed my K-bar. About this time, Jorgeson let off a horrendous shriek – a gut shot is worse than anything. Or did Jorgeson scream to save my life? The NVA moving in my direction turned back to him, studied him for a moment, and then thrust a bayonet into his heart. As badly as my own eyes hurt, I was able to see Jorgeson's eyes – a final flash of glorious azure before they faded into the unfocused and glazed gray of death. I repinned the grenade, got up on my knees, and scrambled away until finally I was on my feet with a useless and incomplete handful of M-16 parts, and I was running as fast and as hard as I have ever run in my life. A pair of Phantom F-4s came in very low with delayed-action high-explosive rounds and napalm. I could feel the almost unbearable heat waves of the latter, volley after volley. I can still feel it and smell it to this day.

Concerning Lance Corporal Hanes: they found him later, fried to a crisp by the napalm, but it was nonetheless ascertained that he had been mutilated while alive. He was like the rest of us – eighteen, nineteen, twenty years old. What did we know of life? Before Vietnam, Hanes didn't think he would ever die. I mean, yes, he knew that in theory he would die, but he *felt* like he was going to live forever. I know that I felt that way. Hanes was down to twelve days and a wake-up. When other Marines saw a short-timer get greased, it devastated their morale. However, when I saw them zip up the body bag on Hanes I became incensed. Why hadn't Milton sent him back to the rear to burn shit or something when he got so short? Twelve days to go and then mutilated. Fucking Milton! Fucking second lieutenant!

Theogenes was the greatest of gladiators. He was a boxer who served under the patronage of a cruel nobleman, a prince who took great delight in bloody spectacles. Although this was several hundred years before the times of those most enlightened of men, Socrates, Plato, and Aristotle, and well after the Minoans of Crete, it still remains a high point in the history of Western civilization and culture. It was the approximate time of Homer, the greatest poet who ever lived. Then, as now, violence, suffering and the cheapness of life were the rule.

The sort of boxing Theogenes practiced was not like modern-day boxing with those kindergarten Queensberry Rules. The two contestants were not permitted the freedom of a ring. Instead, they were strapped to flat stones, facing each other nose-to-nose. When the signal was given, they would begin hammering each other with fists encased in heavy leather thongs. It was a fight to the death. Fourteen hundred and twenty-five times Theogenes was strapped to the stone and fourteen hundred and twenty-five times he emerged a victor.

Perhaps it is Theogenes who is depicted in the famous Roman statue (based on the earlier Greek original) of "The Pugilist at Rest." I keep a grainy black-and-white photograph of it in my room. The statue depicts a muscular athlete approaching his middle age. He has a thick beard and a full head of curly hair. In addition to the telltale broken nose and cauliflower ears of a boxer, the pugilist has the slanted, drooping brows that bespeak torn nerves. Also, the forehead is piled with scar tissue. As may be expected, the pugilist has the musculature of a fighter. His neck and trapezius muscles are well developed. His shoulders are enormous; his chest is thick and flat, without the bulging pectorals of the bodybuilder. His back, oblique, and abdominal muscles are highly pronounced, and he has that greatest asset of the modern boxer – sturdy legs. The arms are large, particularly the forearms, which are reinforced with the leather wrappings of the cestus. It is the body of a small heavyweight – lithe rather than bulky, but by no means lacking in power: a Jack Johnson or a Dempsey, say. If you see the authentic statue at the Terme Museum, in Rome, you will see that the seated boxer is really not much more than a light-heavyweight. People were small in those days. The important thing was that he was perfectly proportioned.

The pugilist is sitting on a rock with his forearms balanced on his thighs. That he is seated and not pacing implies that he has been through all this many times before. It appears that he is conserving his strength. His head is turned as if he were looking over his shoulder – as if someone had just whispered something to him. It is in this that the "art" of the sculpture is conveyed to the viewer. Could it be that someone has just summoned him to the arena? There is a slight look of befuddlement on his face, but there is no trace of fear. There is an air about him that suggests that he is eager to proceed and does not wish to cause anyone any trouble or to create a delay, even though his life will soon be on the line. Besides the deformities on his noble face, there is also the suggestion of weariness and philosophical resignation. *All the world's a stage, and all the men and women merely players.* Exactly! He knew this more than two thousand years before Shakespeare penned the line. How did he come to be at this place in space and time? Would he rather be safely removed to the countryside – an obscure, stinking peasant shoving a plow behind a mule? Would that be better? Or does he revel in his role? Perhaps he once did, but surely not now. Is this the great Theogenes or merely a journeyman fighter, a former slave or criminal bought by one of the many contractors who for months trained the condemned for their brief moment in the arena? I wonder if Marcus Aurelius loved the "Pugilist" as I do, and came to study it and to meditate before it.

I cut and ran from that field in Southeast Asia. I've read that Davy Crockett, hero of the American frontier, was cowering under a bed when Santa Anna and his soldiers stormed into the Alamo. What is the truth? Jack Dempsey used to get so scared before his fights that he sometimes wet his pants. But look what he did to Willard and to Luis Firpo, the Wild Bull of the Pampas! It was something close to homicide. What is courage? What is cowardice? The magnificent Roberto Duran gave us *"No más,"* but who had a greater fighting heart than Duran?

I got over that first scare and saw that I was something quite other than that which I had known myself to be. Hey Baby proved only my warm-up act. There was a reservoir of malice, poison, and vicious sadism in my soul, and it poured forth freely in the jungles and rice paddies of Vietnam. I pulled three tours. I wanted some payback for Jorgeson. I grieved for Lance Corporal Hanes. I grieved for myself and what I had lost. I committed unspeakable crimes and got medals for it.

It was only fair that I got a head injury myself. I never got a scratch in Vietnam, but I got tagged in a boxing smoker at Pendleton. Fought a bad-ass light-heavyweight from artillery. Nobody would fight this guy. He could box. He had all the moves. But mainly he was a puncher – it was said that he could punch with either hand. It was said that his hand speed was superb. I had finished off at least a half rack of Hamm's before I

went in with him and started getting hit with head shots I didn't
even see coming. They were right. His hand speed *was* superb.

I was twenty-seven years old, smoked two packs a day, was a
borderline alcoholic. I shouldn't have fought him – I knew that –
but he had been making noise. A very long time before, I had
been the middleweight champion of the 1st Marine Division. I
had been a so-called war hero. I had been a recon Marine. But
now I was a garrison Marine and in no kind of shape.

He put me down almost immediately, and when I got up I
was terribly afraid. I was tight and I could not breathe. It felt like
he was hitting me in the face with a ball-peen hammer. It felt like
he was busting light bulbs in my face. Rather than one opponent,
I saw three. I was convinced his gloves were loaded, and a wave
of self-pity ran through me.

I began to move. He made a mistake by expending a lot of
energy trying to put me away quickly. I had no intention of
going down again, and I knew I wouldn't. My buddies were
watching, and I had to give them a good show. While I was
afraid, I was also exhilarated; I had not felt this alive since
Vietnam. I began to score with my left jab, and because of this I
was able to withstand his bull charges and divert them. I thought
he would throw his bolt, but in the beginning he was tireless. I
must have hit him with four hundred left jabs. It got so that I
could score at will, with either hand, but he would counter, trap
me on the ropes, and pound. He was the better puncher and was
truly hurting me, but I was scoring, and as the fight went on the
momentum shifted and I took over. I staggered him again and
again. The Marines at ringside were screaming for me to put him
away, but however much I tried, I could not. Although I could
barely stand by the end, I was sorry that the fight was over. Who
had won? The referee raised my arm in victory, but I think it
was pretty much a draw. Judging a prizefight is a very subjective
thing.

About an hour after the bout, when the adrenaline had
subsided, I realized I had a terrible headache. It kept getting
worse, and I rushed out of the NCO Club, where I had gone
with my buddies to get loaded.

I stumbled outside, struggling to breathe, and I headed away

from the company area toward Sheepshit Hill, one of the many
low brown foothills in the vicinity. Like a dog who wants to die
alone, so it was with me. Everything got swirly, and I dropped
in the bushes.

I was unconscious for nearly an hour, and for the next two
weeks I walked around like I was drunk, with double vision. I
had constant headaches and seemed to have grown old overnight.
My health was gone.

I became a very timid individual. I became introspective. I
wondered what had made me act the way I had acted. Why had
I killed my fellowmen in war, without any feeling, remorse, or
regret? And when the war was over, why did I continue to drink
and swagger around and get into fistfights? Why did I like to
dish out pain, and why did I take positive delight in the suffering
of others? Was I insane? Was it too much testosterone? Women
don't do things like that. The rapacious Will to Power lost its
hold on me. Suddenly I began to feel sympathetic to the cares
and sufferings of all living creatures. You lose your health and
you start thinking this way.

Has man become any better since the times of Theogenes? The
world is replete with badness. I'm not talking about that old
routine where you drag out the Spanish Inquisition, the Holocaust, Joseph Stalin, the Khmer Rouge, etc. It happens in our
own backyard. Twentieth-century America is one of the most
materially prosperous nations in history. But take a walk through
an American prison, a nursing home, the slums where the
homeless live in cardboard boxes, a cancer ward. Go to a
Vietnam vets' meeting, or an A.A. meeting, or an Overeaters
Anonymous meeting. *How hollow and unreal a thing is life, how
deceitful are its pleasures, what horrible aspects it possesses.* Is the
world not rather like a hell, as Schopenhauer, that clearheaded
seer – who has helped me transform my suffering into an object
of understanding – was so quick to point out? They called him a
pessimist and dismissed him with a word, but it is peace and self-
renewal that I have found in his pages.

About a year after my fight with the guy from artillery I started
having seizures. I suffered from a form of left-temporal-lobe

seizure which is sometimes called Dostoyevski's epilepsy. It's so rare as to be almost unknown. Freud, himself a neurologist, speculated that Dostoyevski was a hysterical epileptic, and that his fits were unrelated to brain damage – psychogenic in origin. Dostoyevski did not have his first attack until the age of twenty-five, when he was imprisoned in Siberia and received fifty lashes after complaining about the food. Freud figured that after Dostoyevski's mock execution, the four years' imprisonment in Siberia, the tormented childhood, the murder of his tyrannical father, etc. & etc. – he had all the earmarks of hysteria, of grave psychological trauma. And Dostoyevski had displayed the trademark features of the psychomotor epileptic long before his first attack. These days physicians insist there is no such thing as the "epileptic personality." I think they say this because they do not want to add to the burden of the epileptic's suffering with an extra stigma. Privately they do believe in these traits. Dostoyevski was nervous and depressed, a tormented hypochondriac, a compulsive writer obsessed with religious and philosophic themes. He was hyperloquacious, raving, etc. & etc. His gambling addiction is well known. By most accounts he was a sick soul.

The peculiar and most distinctive thing about his epilepsy was that in the split second before his fit – in the aura, which is in fact officially a part of the attack – Dostoyevski experienced a sense of felicity, of ecstatic well-being unlike anything an ordinary mortal could hope to imagine. It was the experience of satori. Not the nickel-and-dime satori of Abraham Maslow, but the Supreme. He said that he wouldn't trade ten years of life for this feeling, and I, who have had it, too, would have to agree. I can't explain it, I don't understand it – it becomes slippery and elusive when it gets any distance on you – but I have felt this down to the core of my being. Yes, God exists! But then it slides away and I lose it. I become a doubter. Even Dostoyevski, the fervent Christian, makes an almost airtight case against the possibility of the existence of God in the Grand Inquisitor digression in *The Brothers Karamazov*. It is probably the greatest passage in all of world literature, and it tilts you to the court of the atheist. This is what happens when you approach Him with the intellect.

It is thought that St. Paul had a temporal-lobe fit on the road to Damascus. Paul warns us in First Corinthians that God will confound the intellectuals. It is known that Muhammad composed the Koran after attacks of epilepsy. Black Elk experienced fits before his grand "buffalo" vision. Joan of Arc is thought to have been a left-temporal-lobe epileptic. Each of these in a terrible flash of brain lightning was able to pierce the murky veil of illusion which is spread over all things. Just so did the scales fall from my eyes. It is called the "sacred disease."

But what a price. I rarely leave the house anymore. To avoid falling injuries, I always wear my old boxer's headgear, and I always carry my mouthpiece. Rather more often than the aura where "every common bush is afire with God," I have the typical epileptic aura, which is that of terror and impending doom. If I can keep my head and think of it, and if there is time, I slip the mouthpiece in and thus avoid biting my tongue. I bit it in half once, and when they sewed it back together it swelled enormously, like a huge red-and-black sausage. I was unable to close my mouth for more than two weeks.

The fits are coming more and more. I'm loaded on Depakene, phenobarbital, Tegretol, Dilantin – the whole shit load. A nurse from the V.A. bought a pair of Staffordshire terriers for me and trained them to watch me as I sleep, in case I have a fit and smother facedown in my bedding. What delightful companions these dogs are! One of them, Gloria, is especially intrepid and clever. Inevitably, when I come to I find that the dogs have dragged me into the kitchen, away from blankets and pillows, rugs, and objects that might suffocate me; and that they have turned me on my back. There's Gloria, barking in my face. Isn't this incredible?

My sister brought a neurosurgeon over to my place around Christmas – not some V.A. butcher but a guy from the university hospital. He was a slick dude in a nine-hundred-dollar suit. He came down on me hard, like a used-car salesman. He wants to cauterize a small spot in a nerve bundle in my brain. "It's not a lobotomy, it's a *cingulotomy*," he said.

Reckless, desperate, last-ditch psychosurgery is still pretty much unthinkable in the conservative medical establishment. That's why he made a personal visit to my place. A house call. Drumming up some action to make himself a name. "See that bottle of Thorazine?" he said. "You can throw that poison away," he said. "All that amitriptyline. That's garbage, you can toss that, too." He said, "Tell me something. How can you take all of that shit and still walk?" He said, "You take enough drugs to drop an elephant."

He wants to cut me. He said that the feelings of guilt and worthlessness, and the heaviness of a heart blackened by sin, will go away. "It is *not* a lobotomy," he said.

I don't like the guy. I don't trust him. I'm not convinced, but I can't go on like this. If I am not having a panic attack I am engulfed in tedious, unrelenting depression. I am overcome with a deadening sense of languor; I can't *do* anything. I wanted to give my buddies a good show! What a goddamn fool. I am a goddamn fool!

It has taken me six months to put my thoughts in order, but I wanted to do it in case I am a vegetable after the operation. I know that my buddy Jorgeson was a real American hero. I wish that he had lived to be something else, if not a painter of pictures then even some kind of fuckup with a factory job and four divorces, bankruptcy petitions, in and out of jail. I wish he had been that. I wish he had been *anything* rather than a real American hero. So, then, if I am to feel somewhat *indifferent* to life after the operation, all the better. If not, not.

If I had a more conventional sense of morality I would shitcan those dress blues, and I'd send that Navy Cross to Jorgeson's brother. Jorgeson was the one who won it, who pulled the John Wayne number up there near Khe Sanh and saved my life, although I lied and took the credit for all of those dead NVA. He had created a stunning body count – nothing like Theogenes, but Jorgeson only had something like twelve minutes total in the theater of war.

The high command almost awarded me the Medal of Honor, but of course there were no witnesses to what I claimed I had done, and I had saved no one's life. When I think back on it, my tale probably did not sound as credible as I thought it had at the time. I was only nineteen years old and not all that practiced a liar. I figure if they *had* given me the Medal of Honor, I would have stood in the ring up at Camp Las Pulgas in Pendleton and let that light-heavyweight from artillery fucking kill me.

Now I'm thinking I might call Hey Baby and ask how he's doing. No shit, a couple of neuropsychs – we probably have a lot in common. I could apologize to him. But I learned from my fits that you don't have to do that. Good and evil are only illusions. Still, I cannot help but wonder sometimes if my vision of the Supreme Reality was any more real than the demons visited upon schizophrenics and madmen. Has it all been just a stupid neurochemical event? Is there no God at all? The human heart rebels against this.

If they fuck up the operation, I hope I get to keep my dogs somehow – maybe stay at my sister's place. If they send me to the nuthouse I lose the dogs for sure.

☆ ☆ ☆ ☆

# *Departures*

The priest is arriving on the train. He is not really a priest, because he is only twenty-five and is still a seminarian, but he wears a Roman collar, and everyone thinks he is a priest, and he thinks of himself as a priest. It is six years since he has visited his parents in their home. They have visited him at the seminary, of course, but this is his first visit to them, and he is very anxious about it.

There is a crazy couple across the aisle, and as the train pulls into the station their anger and excitement come near to hysteria; they have just had — as they keep saying — a scrape with death. "We could have been killed," she says, her voice sharp, abused. "We've had a terrible scrape with death." She only pretends to speak to her husband; actually she is addressing the priest and the couple in front of him and the whole car. Her eyes are glassy and wild and she goes on talking with small gasps and shrieks while her husband — glassy-eyed, too, and in shock — says, "You're right, you're right," and wrestles a red plastic suitcase from the rack overhead. They are still exclaiming as they forge down the aisle, important and proud at being almost dead.

The priest waits. He does not want to be near those crazy people when he greets his parents. This will be a special moment and he wants it to be perfect. These six years have made him ill at ease in public. He cannot stand the noise, the rudeness, the urgency in voices. Emotions spill out of people, they shout in public; anger bristles everywhere, in everyone, in the street, the train station, the train. People chew gum. They belch. They push. He is revolted by the vulgarity, the nakedness of it all. In the seminary there is no emotion, no anger, no urgency — at least not visibly. Everyone keeps inside himself whatever it is he feels.

So the priest stays in his seat until the crazy people have

disappeared from the car. Then he gets up, sets his face in a smile
– a half-smile – and prepares to meet his parents. As he climbs
down the steep iron steps, he is conscious of people on the
platform looking. At him? Or just for somebody they are here
to meet? Suddenly a woman shrieks and the priest turns to help
her, thinking she must be hurt, thinking of Anna Karenina
beneath the train wheels. But no. The woman is merely excited
and the scream is only delight at seeing a boy, her son probably.
"Billy," she says, "Billy baby." She hugs him, kisses him,
screams again. The boy is embarrassed and the priest, embarrassed too, turns away. Mother and son, he thinks, a travesty.
He has told his parents he will meet them in the waiting room,
on the east side, and he joins the crowd moving toward the
stairs. Ahead of him he sees another priest, about his own age,
red-haired and stout. Sanity, he thinks, an oasis. But as they
reach the bottom of the stairs a woman lunges at the red-haired
priest, hugging him once and then again, while a man – his
father, with the same red hair and fat – slaps him on the back
over and over. "Father Joe," they call him, though, by their ages,
he has to be their son. The woman puts her arm under Father
Joe's and leans into him, her possession.
    There is a disturbance now; somebody is shouting, some-
body touches his arm. It is the crazy couple, even more hysterical
than before, asking him something, insisting he explain to
another couple what happened on the train. A little crowd is
gathering and the priest, confused, turns from person to person.
He is not listening, he merely wants to get away. And then
suddenly he sees his mother smiling from beyond the crowd and
his father behind her, his hands on her shoulders, smiling. They
are a picture of order in all this chaos. The crazy woman tugs at
his arm, but he pulls away from her and, moving blindly through
the crowd, walks toward his mother and father. Yes, the priest
thinks, I will bring order out of chaos.
    His mother is beautiful, radiant, and she will not be dead for
another fifteen years. She smiles and comes to meet him and he
will remember her this way, always. He will wake in the night
remembering how she is now, what he does to her. Because as
she goes to put her arms around him, as she lifts her face to kiss

him, he says to her, with a smile made icy by his self-control, "I'll just kiss you on the cheek – don't touch me – and I'll shake hands with Dad, and then we'll turn and walk out of here." And he bends to kiss her on the cheek, but stops because she has pulled slightly away; she has gone white, and the look of panic on her face is not nearly so terrible as the look of drowning in her eyes.

The priest's father has been dead for five years and now the priest sits by his mother's bedside waiting for her to die. Fifteen years have passed since his train came in and he did not kiss her and she turned her face away. His mother has Parkinson's disease and the benign effects of L-Dopa have worn off, so that she is bent now and trembles violently whenever she tries to do anything for herself. She drools sometimes and sometimes she cannot control her bowels. But the priest has been told it is not Parkinson's which is killing her; it is cancer. The priest thinks a great deal about death and about the things that kill us. He is not surprised, being forty and having seen many people to their deaths, that dying is not only an agony, it is boredom. He has been waiting by her bedside for months now, an hour or two each day, and still she has not died.

His mother is unconscious much of the time. Or barely conscious; it is hard for him to tell. On the occasions when she turns to him and says something, he is astonished that very often it is something he has been thinking himself. A month before he had been remembering his father's quick death, a quick and merciful heart attack – how it had been the death his father would have chosen if he were given choices. "Your father died well," she said, and the priest leaned forward in surprise. He thought she had been unconscious. "Father?" he asked. "He died the way he would have wanted," she said. "Yes," he said, "I was thinking that." She sighed and shook her head, and a tear showed in the corner of her eye. "What?" he asked. "This is not the way I would have chosen," she said. And though he did not say them he thought the words he hated most: "self-pity." So he bit the inside of his lip and said, "Try to sleep, Mother."

Again, a week or so later, he was thinking how he had

always taken from them, his mother and father; he had never given them anything. He looked at her lying there, her eyes closed, sweating, and he thought, I'll wet the washcloth and put it on her forehead. But before he could reach the washcloth she said to him, "You've always given to us. You've given us everything." And she looked at him with the drowning look.

This sort of thing has happened several times. He has begun to wonder if he causes her to think of what he is thinking: the exercise of the stronger mind on the weaker. No, it can't be that. And so he sits by her bed reading his Shakespeare – he is completing his Ph.D. in English – and sometimes he adjusts her pillows or wipes her forehead, and when she is able he talks to her. But more and more now it is a matter of waiting for the end. Her medication has been increased; even when she is not unconscious she is so heavily doped against the pain that conversation is impossible. He waits.

The priest's mother is living and the priest is waiting for her to die. He is wanting her to die now that the pain is so bad, now that he cannot bear any longer the suffering, the boredom. But she does not die.

And then finally she does die. But before she dies she wakes and talks to him one last time. He has been thinking of the train, that terrible day when he destroyed everything, when he tried to bring some order out of chaos and said, "Don't touch me" and she turned away from him. He has been thinking of that all day and now she wakes and drugged, confused, looks at him and says, "You're not to worry. When the train comes in, I won't kiss you. I won't touch you." "No!" the priest cries out sharply. "Mother, no." He leans over the bed to kiss her, but as he does she turns from him, saying, "I'll be good. I promise. I'll be good." And with her dying breath, her face still turned from him, she says, "I will."

It is the same day. It is always the same day, except that now he remembers it differently. The priest is leaving on the train, Boston to Springfield, a three-hour trip. He is not really a priest, because he is only twenty-five and is still a seminarian, but he thinks of himself as a priest and so do his parents. His father will not die for another ten years, his mother for fifteen. They will both live to see him ordained.

The train pulls out of the station and the priest begins to read his book, Sartre's *L'existentialisme est un humanisme*. It is boring but good for him. Existentialism is good and humanism is good, and he feels that boredom is just something that goes along with the package. He reads half a page before he realizes he has no idea what he is reading. He is upset about something. What? He doesn't know. Was it getting on the train? Seeing all those people elbowing one another to get ahead, that old woman chewing gum, the man who belched? Partly that. He felt so alien, so removed from them – inhuman. All that pushing and shoving, and there are plenty of empty seats. It makes no sense.

The door between the cars opens and a middle-aged couple come in. She is carrying two shopping bags, one full of presents, wrapped in metallic papers, the other full of something the priest cannot see, because there is a sweater over the top. The man drags an enormous red suitcase, which bumps his leg at every step. It is a warm day and they are both perspiring.

"How about here?" she says, pointing to the seat directly in front of the priest, but then she sees him and says, "No, over here instead," and she backs up, bumping into her husband, who drops the suitcase and curses. "Here," she says. "Yes, this is nice. This side is better. This is fine. Sit down, Freddie. No, let me get next to the window." The man groans and says nothing, giving all his attention to getting the suitcase up into the luggage rack. "This, too," she says, giving him the bag with the presents. "No, I'll keep it at my feet," she says, and takes the bag back. Finally they are settled. The priest has watched them from where he sits, on the other side of the aisle, one seat back, and he continues to watch them. He is surprised to find the taste of acid in his mouth. He wants to spit; he doesn't know why.

Where he has felt uneasy before, he now feels anger. At himself, perhaps. He returns to his book. He is more than a seminarian, he is a Jesuit seminarian, and so he has an obligation to theology and to culture. But after another two pages he decides he does not have an obligation to Sartre and he puts the book in his briefcase. He decides to meditate. Jesuits meditate for at least an hour each day, usually on some incident, some moment, in the life of Christ, and he has never missed meditation once, not even when he lay for a week in the infirmary with a temperature of 103.

In fact, the infirmary meditation is the nearest he has come to a kind of mystical experience. He had been meditating on the Crucifixion, lying in bed with his scalding temperature, watching what was happening. He saw them drive the nails through the wrists, through the bent feet, saw them lift the heavy cross to the correct angle, until the base thudded into the stone notch that would hold it upright. There was a groan and some blood splattered onto the seamless white tunic they had stripped from him and which now lay at the base of the cross. And then there was blackness. He fell asleep, he supposed, and when he woke, his body soaked with sweat from the fever, he tried to see that white tunic beneath the cross. But he could not see it, he could see only the broad back of a soldier and he could hear the rattle of dice. Then the soldier moved and he could see the others, three of them, taking their turns with the dice, gambling for the tunic and the sandals. And when the last had thrown, one of the soldiers scooped up the dice and held them out to the priest. His hand hung there, offering the dice in his open palm, and while they all stared the priest put out his own hand and slowly, tentatively, took the dice. And then, with the small strength he could muster, he closed his fist around them.

The priest was fevered for three days more, and what he remembered after was that for those three days he held the dice in his hands. It is a meditation the priest can call back at will. He can and he does now, though he does not know why. Not because of the way it makes him feel – because feeling, he knows, has nothing to do with anything. No, he calls it back because it has something to do with *not* feeling, with the reason he is a priest in the first place.

At college his room-mate had said to him one day, "Seeing as how you're a Catholic, and the best thing a Catholic can do with his life is be a priest, don't you feel obliged to be a priest?" He laughed, seeing he had struck deep. "I mean, you're smart enough, and you're moral enough – you don't screw or anything

– so why not? I mean, aren't you obliged to?" The words were insignificant; it was what they did to him at that particular moment that mattered. Because he had been thinking of the priesthood and wanting, but fearing to ask for, a sign. His roommate's words seemed some kind of sign – no miraculous intervention, just the intervention of pure reason. Not a lightning bolt from heaven, he said to himself, just a slammed door. And the meditation of the dice seemed somehow a confirmation of this sign.

The priest opens his eyes. The train has been stopped for some time, new people have got on, and now it is pulling slowly away from the platform. They are near Worcester somewhere. The priest looks out the window opposite him and can see up ahead a grassy hill where three small boys are waving to the train. On the other side of the aisle the woman is rummaging through her shopping bag, totally absorbed with whatever she has in there. The man is gone – he is at the far end of the car getting a drink of water. The train pulls alongside the little boys and the priest waves to them, but they do not wave back. They throw stones, which fall short of the train – all except one, which strikes the window next to the woman with the shopping bag. It makes a sharp sound and at once there appears on the window a white spot the size of a nickel and, radiating from it, a sunburst of silver cracks. The priest sits forward prepared to do something, but there is nothing to be done. Despite the noise, like a door slamming, the woman does not seem to hear; she continues plunging her hand into the bag and bringing out things he cannot see. The other people around are either sleeping or absorbed in their reading. No one has noticed except him.

The man returns with a cup of water for his wife. She drinks it and they sit in silence looking out the window. "Was that window like that before?" he asks. "Of course," she says. And then she looks at it. "Well, I'm not sure," she says. She puts her finger on the spot of white and traces one of the cracks that radiate from it. "It looks like it's been broken," she says. "Somebody must have thrown a stone," he says, and settles back in his seat. "Well, if it happened while I was sitting here, I could have been hurt – if the glass broke," she says. "It was probably

just a stone," he says. "It could have broken. I could have been
hurt," she says, "if it was a bullet. I could have been . . ."

She is excited now and leans forward to the couple in front
of her. "Did you see this happen? Did you see this window get
broken? Right by my head?" But they have seen nothing. She
turns to the man across the aisle, to the couple in front of him,
to the empty seats behind her. Nobody has seen. The conductor
appears and she waves at him, calling, "Look at this, there's been
an accident. Somebody broke this window right while I was
sitting here."

The conductor looks at the window and at the woman and
at the window again. "What?" he says. He looks at the people in
front of the couple and across the aisle from them; he looks at
the priest. The priest says, "A little boy threw a stone and it hit
the window." "Do you see? Do you hear?" the woman says.
And she turns to the priest. "Was it a stone? Was I sitting here?
Right by the window?" "Yes," the priest says. "I could have
been killed," the woman says to the conductor. "Do you hear
what the priest said? Would a priest lie? It could have been a
bullet." "Damned kids," the conductor says and moves down
the aisle. "We've had a narrow escape from death, Freddie," she
says, and from here to Springfield her anger and her enthusiasm
grow.

The priest is sick. The chaos of life, the chaos of mind. It is
all hopeless. Look at that crazy couple. The boredom of lives
lived so purposelessly depresses him, sickens him. The emotion,
the anger, the public displays.

The train is in Springfield but he waits until the crazy couple
get off. He does not want to be near them when he meets his
parents. Getting off the train, he hears a woman shriek as she
descends upon her son; he sees a fat priest with red hair; he is
overwhelmed by the noise, the vulgarity. And then there is a
disturbance of some sort. It is the crazy couple. Her husband is
tugging at the priest's arm, the woman is trying to draw him
into a group that has gathered around her. "The priest saw it
all," she is saying. "See that priest? He's living proof. If it weren't
for that priest, we wouldn't be here now." But the priest does
not hear what she says, because suddenly beyond the crowd he

sees his mother, looking beautiful and composed, smiling, and behind her his father. She will not be dead for fifteen years. They will live to see him ordained, his life fulfilled.

He goes to meet them, conscious that he is in public, conscious of a small circle of order in this chaos. And as his mother opens her arms to him, he says, "I'll just kiss you on the cheek – don't touch me – then . . ." But already she has begun to turn away.

The priest is arriving on the train – New York to Boston, a five-hour trip. He has been a priest for many years and, he sometimes thinks, he is a good priest. But what is "good," he thinks. He thinks he does not know that. Sometimes he thinks he does not care. Thinking is his life now and that seems enough. Thinking and seeming. He is fifty-five and will not be dead for another fifteen years. But dying is a moment he does not care to think about.

The priest is coming back from New York, where he attended the wake of his last living relative. There is a peculiar satisfaction in that, a finality he does not fully understand but which he recognizes all the same. He would have said the burial Mass for his aunt but she died on Good Friday, which means the burial cannot take place until Monday, and so the priest is coming back to Boston, where he can be used at midnight tonight in the Easter Vigil services. And then tomorrow the Mass of the Resurrection – whoopee. He is irreverent, sometimes, in the way he thinks; it is his psyche's accommodation to absurdity, or perhaps pain, or bitterness. Anyway, he will be back in Boston in no time, and then he will go to his room and have a good belt of Scotch, and then a couple of hours in bed to recover for the Easter Vigil.

Trains mean nothing to him anymore. He does not see the people who chew gum, who push, who carry on angrily over nothing. He does not care. That is simply how they are, that is how life is, and what can anyone do about it?

His drinking is not a problem, he thinks. It might have become one if he had not, at forty, gone for his Ph.D. in English. That has stabilized him somehow; teaching English is more human than teaching theology. He is grateful for the diversions provided by his Ph.D. He has seen too many priests hit forty and realize nothing else is ever going to happen to them, and he has seen the dodges they take – running off with the school nurse, having affairs with their students' mothers, hitting the bottle. His dodge would have been – would be – hitting the bottle. But it will not happen to him. He is careful, for now. He drinks a fifth of Scotch each week, and if he runs out before the week is over, then he goes without. Of course, he does, on occasion, stop by somebody else's room and have a drink from his Scotch. But that is social drinking. That is different. He is handling his after-forty problem very well. He has no regrets, he thinks.

The train pulls into the station and he pushes his way to the front of the car. He is eager to get off and get home. He does not hear the woman who shrieks with pleasure as she descends upon her teenage son. He does not notice the demonstrations of anger and frustration and delight. He does not even smell the rank odor of cigarette butts and urine. He just keeps his eyes cast down and makes his way through the waiting room to the cab stand. Leave the dead to bury the dead, he used to think as he left these depressing public places, but now he does not think about them at all. He is a priest who has left the world to itself, truly.

He is home in his little room and he pours himself a Scotch and drinks it. He showers and stands in front of the long mirror examining the evidence of too much food, too much drink. He will have to cut down. He puts on his yellow pajamas and sets the clock. He has four hours before he must put on vestments for the Easter liturgy; and so he stretches out on the bed and closes his eyes, ready for sleep. But the trip to New York and the aunt's wake and the trip back to Boston swim through his mind and he cannot sleep. He feels good, and he feels guilty for feeling good. The boredom is over, those long hours on trains, the unpleasantness of all those strangers at the wake. Over is good, he thinks. Finality is good. But what is good? Well, he *feels* good and that's something.

The priest wakes from a nightmare. His head aches and he has trouble getting his breath. He is shivering. What was he dreaming? He cannot remember. He is late. He hurries through his shower, shaves, dresses, his mind going back and back to the dream. But always it eludes him. Perhaps it was the soldier dream again. He no longer meditates, but often in his sleep he sees the soldier's back and hears the rattle of dice. The soldier shifts position and the priest sees the others, three of them, taking their turns with the dice. Finally, as always, the last one scoops up the dice and hands them to the priest, who takes them and closes his fist on them and when he looks down – this is the new part, the awful part – he sees that blood is oozing from between his fingers. And then he wakes up. The old meditation, which for years gave him some kind of abstract comfort, has turned to dream and to nightmare. But it was not the soldier dream tonight, it was . . . And again the dream eludes him.

The priest is vested now, saying a brief prayer before leading the procession to the rear of the chapel. The vigil is a long and complicated ritual and in his mind he ticks off the major sections. There is the striking of the new fire – a tricky business, because all the lights are out and you have to fumble around with the flint device. Then the blessing of the new fire, the blessing of the Easter candle, the solemn procession. The singing will be tough, because he has a weak voice. The readings. Then the blessing of the baptismal water . . . Death by drowning, he thinks, and for a second his mind veers to *The Waste Land*, but then he comes back to the vigil. The baptism of the baby – he must check the baby's name before that part of the ceremony – and then the litany and finally, at midnight, Mass. Fire and water. Burning and drowning. Light in the darkness. The water that gives rebirth. It is a symbolism so ancient, so basic, that it must guarantee a reality, he thinks.

And so the ceremony has begun and the priest stands in the vestibule surrounded by the entire community. The lights have been extinguished in the chapel and now the light over the door goes out and they are plunged into complete blackness. They are waiting, all of them, for him to strike flint against flint and start that spark which will be the light shining in the darkness. The flint grates and grates again, and just as he has begun to think he

will never get it to work right, there is a flicker and a dot of light
and then a flame. The flame catches in the little pot of wax and
by its light the priest begins the blessing of the new fire.

"The Lord be with you," he says. And the community
responds, "And with your spirit." He breathes easy, because the
rest of the prayer he knows by heart. He stares into the fire,
reciting the blessing. "Let us pray. O God, through Your Son
Jesus Christ, You bestowed the light of Your glory upon the
faithful. Sanctify . . ."

But then, in the fire, he recognizes his nightmare. He sees
the soldier's back and hears the rattle of dice; the soldier moves
and the priest sees not the three other soldiers but his mother;
her drowning face is turned away from him and her hand is held
out. In her hand are those dice – bloody, eyeless.

"Sanctify . . ." the priest says once more, and now it is time
to raise his hand in blessing, but for the moment he cannot, and
he continues to stare into the fire. "Sanctify . . ." he says again,
staring and staring, still unable to bless, unable to go on or turn
away.

"Sanctify . . ."

The word echoes in the darkness and the light flickers until
with his bare hands the priest reaches forward and puts the
fire out.

# RALPH LOMBREGLIA

☆　☆　☆　☆

# *Men under Water*

The Peter Pan Diner, 10.30 a.m. Breakfast with Gunther.

"You're depressed again," Gunther says to me. "I can tell."
He has the catsup bottle in one fist like a chisel or a caulking gun,
and with the heel of his other hand he's hammering catsup over
his hash browns and scrambled eggs. He's getting some on the
bacon and toast, too.

"I'm not depressed," I say.

"You're not eating."

"Gunther, I eat at home, remember? At breakfast time. I
never eat here."

He slips into his pouting voice. "You used to," he says.

This is a bad sign. It means that Gunther is especially needy
and delusional today. I haven't ordered anything but coffee in
the Peter Pan since the first week I worked for him, more than
six months ago.

I look at him, busying himself with breakfast on the other
side of the booth. Lately I've spent more hours of each week
with Gunther than I've spent with my wife, and still there are
times – this moment is one of them – when I see him as I saw
him the day we met, times when I cannot get beyond the
amazing epidermal surface of the man. Gunther is one of the
largest people I've ever known, but it's more than that, more
than his general enormousness, the smooth expanse of his
completely bald head, the perfect beardlessness of his broad face.
Gunther has no eyebrows, no body hair whatsoever as far as I
know; even the large nostrils of his great, wide nose are pink
hairless tunnels running up into his skull. His velour pullover is
open to his sternum, and the exposed chest is precisely the
complexion of all the rest of him – the shrimplike color of new
Play-Doh, the substance from which Gunther sometimes seems

to be made. Under the movie lights he likes to muck around with, his skin goes translucent and you can watch the blood vessels keeping him alive.

"If you're not depressed," he says around a mouthful of catsup and eggs, "what are you?"

"Subdued," I say.

"Oh," he says. "Well, would you mind knocking off being subdued? You're not putting out any energy. I can't do it all by myself."

"Do what?"

"Write this goddam screenplay," he says.

"Oh. Which screenplay is this?"

"You know perfectly well which screenplay. The sci-fi one with the giant radioactive crayfish and the girl scientist who understands them, and who's also the love interest for the guy scientist. The one we've been working on all week."

"Oh, that one," I say. "I forgot. I thought maybe you meant the Kung Fu screenplay. I guess that was last week."

"You want to work on that one? Hey, we could even do a hybrid of the two. Say these huge radioactive crayfish attack mankind with a sort of lobster version of Kung Fu, bopping people with their big claws. The guy scientist also happens to be a martial-arts master. In the end, he conquers the lobsters by building robots programmed to hit them in their pressure points. But before that there's a scene where the lobsters grab the girl and he has to take a couple of them down with his bare hands."

"No, Gunther." I sip my coffee and stare out the window above the personal jukebox mounted on the wall of our booth. The jukebox is playing Roy Orbison's "Pretty Woman," Gunther's favorite song. He put it on to cheer me up.

Outside, a light gray ash is falling from the sky like rain. Cleveland has a lot of smokestack industry, and the Peter Pan is one of the venerable old smokestack-area diners. That's why we come here to eat. Not because we work in the plants ourselves – our work, like God, is everywhere and nowhere – but because this is where reality is, the life and labor of the folk, the source of all art. Someday, after he's made the two or three commercial pictures that will establish him as one of the major film forces of our time, Gunther wants to celebrate his native city in a cinematic tone poem about the ballet of heavy manufacture, the romance of rubber and steel.

I show him my wristwatch. "What about the Puerto Rican couple on Liberty Place with the gas leak in their stove? Or the nursing students on Meadow with no hot water? You told them today for sure. And your answering service. I'll bet you didn't call your answering service. You'll call it at three this afternoon, and then we'll have to work until nine tonight."

Gunther throws his fork onto his plate. People at the counter turn on their stools to look at us. "This is your whole problem," he says. He clangs his coffee cup with his spoon to get the attention of our waitress. It's Alice today, a good woman. If Gunther gets too abusive, she'll pour coffee in his lap. She's done it before. She comes over now and fills our cups.

"I try to foster a creative spirit," Gunther says to me. Alice flashes him a look, the coffeepot poised in the air. He stops talking and stares at the table until she's gone on her way. "I try to pay you for your imagination," he says, "not just for dumb monkey work I could get anybody to do. I try to treat you like an artist. And all you want to do is fix toilets." He picks up the cream and sugar and pours long streams of each into his cup. Then he starts the singsongy voice. "Yes, for a certain number of hours each week we have to do some essentially noncreative work, things that are not really what artists like us should be doing – painting apartments, replacing water heaters, fixing toilets. But it keeps us humble, I say. I try to be philosophical about it. I don't go into a mood just because I can't work on my movies every minute of every day."

"I left my house three hours ago, Gunther."

"Here we go again," he says.

He doesn't start paying my hourly wages until we leave the diner. But if I don't go over to Gunther's house each morning and wake him up and, while he takes a shower, watch parts of movies he's videotaped, and then listen to him rant about screenplays over breakfast at the Peter Pan, we won't go to work at all and I won't be paid anything.

He turns to the jukebox and speaks to Roy Orbison. "Roy,"

he says, "what am I going to do with this guy? Sensitive and
gifted, yes, but he has real limitations. He actually wants to work
for wages." He turns back to me. "You're not being flexible," he
says. "That's a major character flaw; you should watch that.
How many times have I explained this to you? You're working
for – and will soon be the partner of – an important motion
picture producer who happens at the moment to be trapped
inside a landlord's body."

"That's not how it was advertised," I say. "It was advertised:
'Handyman and general helper, no experience necessary.' That's
the ad I responded to. You changed it to scriptwriter after I was
hired."

"After I discovered the talent I can't let you throw away,
even if you want to. A good part of each week is ours to be
talented together, you and me. We toss some ideas back and
forth" – he slaps my shoulder – "and in a couple of weeks we
have a screenplay. I round up some investors, we start shooting
the movie, we're on our way. We could have made some
progress on this movie right here at breakfast, but no, you're
subdued. You think that just because we have to go fix a toilet
today, that's all we are, two guys who have to fix a toilet, and
you let it get you down."

"What toilet?" I say. "You're keeping something from me."

"Weren't you the one who wanted me to call my answering
service?"

He stands up and tosses his wadded napkin onto his plate,
smiling and bobbing his head from side to side like Hardy to
Laurel. He leans toward me over the table as if to confide a great
truth, a truth that will be true long after everything else is dust.
"Rock band," he says, and strides away from the booth. Then he
comes back, doing his wicked leer. "The horror, the horror," he
adds.

We pay our bill and stroll out of the Peter Pan into the
sunlight and ashes, me in my paint-spattered carpenter's pants
and sweatshirt, Gunther swaggering in his red-and-yellow-striped
velour pullover and racing shades. It's 11.30 a.m., almost time
for lunch. The rest of the world has already accomplished much
since waking, and laid down foundations for the accomplishment

of much more. We have accomplished nothing. But neither have
we yet lost everything, I remind myself. We still have much of
what we had when the day began. I have my job with Gunther –
twenty dollars an hour under the table, starting now – and
Gunther has his small real estate empire, his Ford Bronco, the
ability to pay me 20 dollars for each hour I ride around in it with
him, and an unflagging, magical belief in the rightness of his life
and methods despite all evidence to the contrary.

And he has me. We have each other.

Tina, my wife, cannot believe I continue to hold this job. We
need the money, but Tina has had enough. She can't take any
more stories about Gunther. She can't take what working for
Gunther is doing to me. I'm no longer the man she married,
Tina says. My inability to leave Gunther has raised serious
questions about the deep structure of my personality, and now
Tina wants us both to go in for counseling. She says she's
become a kind of co-alcoholic, living through my experiences
with this man. She's had to go through it all with me, even
though it's not her life, and now in some perverse way she feels
that she works for Gunther too.

Every night when I get home I must drink for one full hour
and rail to Tina about Gunther. I tell her what Gunther has done
to me that day, what he's done to his tenants, the lies he's made
me tell the tenants about those things, the movie-script ideas he's
forced me to invent. After an hour I'm usually able to take a
shower and have dinner. But it's growing longer now, up to two
hours sometimes. At first it was exotic and Tina enjoyed it. Every
night I would bring home amazing new stories. Tina would listen
and shake her head in wonder, marveling over the character of
Gunther, the shamelessness of the business world, the length and
breadth of the illusions men can entertain about themselves.

But then late last winter I came home one night with the
Pakistani-baby story. Tina teaches in a day-care center, and the
Pakistani-baby story pushed her over the edge. I'd been shoveling
snow at Gunther's garden-apartment buildings when a Pakistani
woman came out into the parking lot in her flowing ocher robes,
weeping and screaming because there was no heat and her baby

was freezing. I went inside to have a look, something I'm not supposed to do on my own. I'm supposed to refer tenants to Gunther's answering service, nothing more. In the apartment I could see my breath more clearly than I could outside. The woman's baby was swaddled in many blankets; only its nose and lips were sticking out, and they were blue. Sitting at the dinette table in his overcoat was the woman's husband, a little brown man with mournful eyes, eating a bowl of curry and shivering. Something big snapped inside me when I saw their lives. I showed them how to call the tenants'-rights division of Legal Aid, and then I gave them Gunther's unlisted home number, the most forbidden thing there is. Gunther and I had our biggest fight over the Pakistani family. When I got home, Tina spent the whole evening trying to calm me down. I quit for two entire weeks that time, finally going back for 3 dollars more an hour.

But now I must quit this job forever, Tina says – really quit, not just quit the way I do every week.

Every Friday when Gunther pays me what I'm owed, I put the cash in my pocket and say Sayonara. After a full week of Gunther, I can't envision one more day. He shakes his head, looks at the ground, asks me what he's done wrong. Nothing, Gunther, I always say, not a thing, you're a prince. I just can't take the real estate life anymore.

You lack vision, he always says. You're turning your back on a brilliant future. The real estate is only a stop along the way, Reggie. Next stop, Hollywood!

No can do, Gunther, I say. We shake hands and go our separate ways forever. Sunday morning I buy the paper and read the ads. Again each week, in return for two-thirds of a person's waking life, the free market offers enough money to rent a shed and eat a can of beans every day. "I'm presently holding the best job in Cleveland," I tell Tina. She puts her hands over her ears. Then Sunday afternoon Gunther calls to offer me an hourly increase of 50 cents over what I made the previous week. I accept his new offer. I started at 4 dollars an hour. I'm up to twenty now. In his big house on a hill above town, Gunther has shown me where he hides his gun. When I reach 50 dollars an hour, he wants me to kill him.

Gunther's real estate holdings consist of two three-story brick garden-apartment buildings down near the Projects, eight or nine rambling wooden Victorians scattered all over the rest of town, and miscellaneous. Miscellaneous includes some garages Gunther rents to people for their cars, and a couple of apartments he has the nerve to rent over the garages. Of the enormous Victorians, three are divided vertically into two-families, and another five or six – the ones in the better areas – have been partitioned into warrens of small studios and one-bedrooms for which Gunther charges outrageous rents. The massage parlor is in one of those; when Gunther's feeling uninspired, we go there and pretend we have to check on things. Only one of the Victorians – the biggest one, in the worst neighborhood – has its original structure and gets rented as one place, to one party.

Acid Rain, the rock band, lives there.

Now Gunther hits the gravel of Acid Rain's horseshoe drive going fast, and then jumps on the brake so we slide sideways the last 30 feet to the house. Three old Chevy vans are parked around the drive, all painted with the band's name and logo – a thundercloud with a skull and crossbones in it – and seven huge Harley-Davidsons. In the backyard is a big Doberman and an ever bigger shepherd, both on frail-looking chains. They start howling at us. The washing machine and dryer are still out there, their doors torn off, birds and squirrels living in them, and enough old hibachi grills to build a rusty bridge to Barbecueland. Here and there stray concrete blocks and bricks are making dead rectangular voids in the 2-foot-high crabgrass.

Gunther loads my arms with equipment from the back of the Bronco – coils of pipe, rolls of solder, garnet paper, a plumber's snake, a portable light, extension cords, a large toolbox. He leads the way with the propane torch, me following him to the house like a pack mule. Luke, the leader of Acid Rain, greets us.

"Why the fuck don't you call your answering service?" Luke says.

"Now, Luke," says Gunther, "I don't think you should be the one to start casting stones. I could say hurtful things to you too. I could say, for instance, why don't you stop trying to flush each other down the toilets? It clogs them up."

"Ha, ha," Luke says. Then he doesn't say anything else, because he doesn't know where Gunther's breaking point is. Luke is not dumb, but you can see in his face that he can't figure Gunther out. He understands that Gunther did not go from being a poor, snot-nosed son of a drunked-up electrician to owning a small real estate empire by taking unlimited abuse from people like him. But then sometimes Gunther seems a jolly fellow who doesn't always act in his own best interests. It's confusing for Luke. I sympathize.

And then there's the way Gunther looks, the massive pink presence of him.

Luke reports that all three toilets in the house are broken. I look at Gunther and narrow my eyes. He looks away, sheepish. On the ride over here, Gunther let slip that Acid Rain first called about their toilet a week ago. It was just the first-floor toilet then.

We make our way through the house. Acid Rain's place was an opulent Cleveland mansion once, and there are still great cut-glass chandeliers hanging in the downstairs rooms above the drums and amplifiers and dismantled motorcycles. The glass pendants are gray blobs now, coated with greasy dust. The residents have decorated the chandeliers with panty hose, pictures from motorcycle magazines, tennis balls, guitar strings. We head upstairs to begin with the topmost toilet. The law of gravity. Various tattooed men are wandering around with women in black leather. Catastrophic metal music is playing in all the rooms on the second floor.

I'd like to mention here that I'm a great lover of music, and so is Tina. We believe that music transcends all the differences between people, and we like to get out when we can to hear a band and dance and have fun. Even after all the things I had witnessed here, we still had perfectly open minds the night we went to see Acid Rain play at the Glo-Worm, over on the other side of the beltway. That's all I can say. When Tina finds out I was here again today, she'll go crazy. Maybe I won't even go home tonight.

Otis, the keyboard player, appears in a doorway on the second floor. Otis is completely blind, and two of Acid Rain's roadies – all the roadies and many other people live in the house with the band – are blind in one eye apiece. People can be blind for many reasons, and you don't ordinarily think of blindness as caused by the blind person, the result of something he did to himself. But with Acid Rain, the thought leaps to mind. Over the months, I've watched to see if other ones become blind too – from drinking rubbing alcohol, say, or fighting among themselves over food or females, the way squirrels do. So far, it's only the same three.

"Is that my landlord?" Otis says. "Do I hear my landlord's voice?"

"My man Otis," says Gunther. "How you doing, Otis?"

"How am I doing? I'm going to the bathroom in the backyard, motherfucker. That's how I'm doing."

"It's under control now, Otis," Gunther says, sidestepping quietly around him and motioning for me to follow. But I'm draped with the coils of pipe, extension cords, the plumber's snake, and I clank when I move.

Otis grabs me. "The dude who mows the lawn, right?" he says. "The landlord's sidekick?"

"I just work for the guy, Otis," I say. "You think it's a picnic? You think he doesn't do the same to me? Every day's a nightmare with this bozo, Otis."

Otis smiles and holds out his palm. "Hey," he says.

I slap his hand. "Renters of the world unite. Death to landlords."

"Right on!" Otis says, slapping me back. "Let's do it now!"

"No, Otis," I say. "Let him fix the toilets first."

"Good point," Otis says. "Okay. I'll be waiting right here."

We head up the last flight of stairs. "You overdid it a little," Gunther says, "but I was still impressed. You were convincing, and I liked the way you improvised under pressure. I thought you were just a writer. Now I find out you have natural acting ability. I'm giving you a screen test when we get back home."

On the third floor, Gunther sees the toilet from the hallway.
His face becomes an image of the human capacity for sadness. "I
think I just got a blown mind gasket," he says. He lights up the
propane torch and shoots little bursts of blue flame into the bathroom. "Firing retro rockets," he says. "Leaving doomed planet."

"Two words, Gunther," I say. "Just two little words."

"I know," he says. "You quit."

"No," I say. "Roto-Rooter."

"That's one word," he says. We back away from the bathroom. Gunther grips the banister and looks down into the
spacious stairwell as though he might plunge himself into it.
Then his head snaps up and he slaps me in the belly. "I just had
an incredible idea," he says.

"No, Gunther," I say. "Whatever it is. Please, no."

"Everything just fell together for me," he says. "Oh, man,
this is good."

Back down on the landing, Otis is waiting. "Otis," Gunther
says. "It's bigger than we thought. We have to call Roto-
Rooter."

"You lie," Otis says, producing a length of chain from his
leather vest.

"No, Otis," I say. "He's telling the truth this one time. It
was my idea to call Roto-Rooter. There's no way this clown can
fix these toilets."

"Okay," Otis says. "I believe you, brother. But if you lie, I
kill you too."

"Don't worry, Otis," I say.

We head downstairs. In the kitchen we find Luke and some
of the women swigging on bottles of Colt 45.

"Luke," Gunther says. "My man. I want to ask you a
question. You like movies, Luke?"

"I like going to the bathroom," Luke says, slamming his
bottle on the table.

"We're calling Roto-Rooter on that, Luke, okay? Roto-
Rooter, like on TV? The guys in the big yellow truck with the
little sissy uniforms? You'll be able to make poo-poo right here
tonight. Now sit down. I want you to answer my question. You
like movies?"

"Yeah, sure."

"Okay. When was the last time you saw a really great movie about an American rock-and-roll band? I mean a movie that had it all – bar scenes, motorcycle scenes, dressing room scenes, rehearsal scenes, groupie love scenes, and the monster victory-concert scene at the end when the band comes back to its hometown after making it big. A movie that captured all the suffering and the glory, the whole incredible life of a great, semi-famous cult rock band in a medium-sized American city, Luke, when was the last time you saw a movie like that?"

"I never saw no such movie," Luke says.

"That's right!" Gunther says.

The Peter Pan Diner, 2.00 p.m. Alice comes over with the menus. "You guys really making a big day of it, huh?" she says.

"We're celebrating, Alice," Gunther says. "Two meat-loaf specials, one for me and one for my lucky charm here. Gravy on everything. That's the password today, Alice. Gravy."

Alice flashes me a look – can I handle him by myself? I nod and she takes the menus away.

Gunther is on an inspirational roll. "This is it!" he says, gripping my shoulder. "My movie! Plot, characters, myth, fantasy! Commercial potential! It was right under my nose! But that's the way it always is in the art game, eh, Roscoe?" He pulls a legal pad out of his briefcase. "So what do you think? I say we start with the Luke character – let's call him Luke – we start with him as an inner-city kid, you know, getting his first guitar, getting beat on by his alcoholic father because he practices guitar instead of getting a job. Plays good pool and B-ball, but he's better on guitar. Everybody's against him. His fellow gang members think guitar is for queers. And we need the bad father, right? We've got to give Luke something big to rebel against. I mean, he can't *like* his father."

"Cliché, Gunther. Cliché, cliché, cliché."

"You always say that. Well, I say life's a cliché! I'm not letting that stop me!"

"Scratch the childhood," I say. "It begins with music, the

band rehearsing in this tenement while the titles roll up the screen. Helicopter shot of the building, close in on the window of their apartment, music getting louder and louder until we're right in there with them. Then the landlord bursts in, demanding the rent. They don't have any money, so they beat the landlord to death with their guitars."

"Sounds like a cliché to me!" Gunther says, chortling and writing it all down. "But it's not bad! We might be able to use that! Okay, no childhood. Maybe we can put it back later. Or maybe – how about this? – Luke can go back and see his old dad in the hospital after he's famous. The old dad has the big C in his liver now, but together they watch Luke in concert on the tube in his hospital room. Just before he dies he recognizes how wrong he always was."

"And he apologizes for the way things were. And it straightens Luke's head out about his life."

"Right!"

"Perfect."

"And the record biz, hey? We need a big scene with these parasitic record-producer types who want to tell Luke how to play, what kinds of clothes to wear. They want to make Luke like everybody else so they can use him to get all this money to put up their own noses. But Luke has a dream. He tells everybody to screw themselves. In the end they all want to kiss his ass."

"That's good," I say. "That's original." The meat-loaf specials arrive. We dive into gravy. "Gunther," I say after a few bites, "it takes millions of dollars to make a real movie. You realize that, right? Millions."

"I have a little surprise for you," he says in the nursery-rhyme voice.

"No, Gunther, please, whatever it is, no."

"We're going to my place after lunch," he says. "Hollywood's paying your salary for the rest of the day. Before, I was going to leave you with the toilets and do the heavy business on my own. And I was worried, I admit it, because I didn't have the killer idea to show the big boys. But it came to me when I needed it. We're partners now, Ricardo. I always said you wouldn't be sorry if you stuck with me."

"Big boys?" I say. "What big boys?"

At Gunther's house, a silver Mercedes with vanity plates is parked at the top of the drive. Gunther downshifts the Bronco and creeps toward the silver car as though he can't believe it's actually there. "This is really happening," he says.

For a year now he's been running an ad in the paper to attract investors to his film-production company. Every month a few cranks respond; that's all, nobody with money. But yesterday when he called his answering service he found a message from these guys. They've invested in movies before. He told me about it on the way over here.

He parks the Bronco and gets out. The two men getting out of the Mercedes look like they want to get back in when they see him. The driver is a thin young guy with a spiky haircut, blue–green iridescent jacket, Hawaiian shirt, black jeans, red shoes. The passenger is a small man in his early sixties, salt-and-pepper hair brushed back, business suit. Gunther introduces himself and shakes hands. He motions for me to come over. "Gentlemen," he says, "this is my associate, Flip. Flip is the co-author of my new screenplay."

I shake hands too. The driver's name is Willie. He's into the whole sullen James Dean thing. The passenger is Joseph, kindly and soft-spoken, with an Eastern European accent. His voice makes me see scenes for a movie version of our horrible century – bombings and occupations, pogroms, refugee camps, a boy in shabby knickers calling out the prices of fruit on the streets of the New World.

Both men are looking at my clothes. I brush the front of myself, but none of the paint spatters come off. "We like to be comfortable," I say.

Willie licks his lips, dubious, but Joseph smiles and nods. We go inside. Willie and Joseph look around. Gunther's place looks good. It's a big old house that didn't look so good when I first saw it, but often, while his tenants suffer, Gunther has me work around here. I've painted every room, sanded and finished the floors. One week in the winter we tore out the whole kitchen and put in a new one. Sometimes Gunther even has me clean the bathrooms for MaryLou, his wife, while he sits on a hassock in the hall telling me about screenplay ideas.

"You're prospering, Gunther," Joseph says.

"I guess I'm doing all right," Gunther says. He's more nervous than I thought he was. He tries to wink at me but botches it and looks like he's just been poked in the eye. "Flip, would you show Joseph and Willie into the living room? Gin and tonics, gentlemen?"

"Very good," Joseph says.

"Flip? Or would you prefer one of those nice English ales?"

"Gin and tonic is fine, Gunther," I say. I take the men into the living room. The furnishings are trim and tasteful, vaguely Scandinavian. They were chosen by MaryLou. Gunther would have chosen a lot of chrome bars and Naugahyde. The living room makes me realize in a sudden sweet way just how completely MaryLou holds Gunther's life together for him, what an impossible piece of luck or inspiration it was that he married her. If she ever left him he'd have to die, but she never will. She's a loving soul, from people even poorer than his, her head not easily turned from grateful devotion. Gunther put her through college while he worked, and never made it to college himself. She teaches grammar school now and thinks his carryings-on are what you put up with when you're married to a genius.

We sit down. French doors open from the living room into the dining room, now the office of the production company, where the big, useless 16-mm Movieola is poised like an old burro grazing among the bundles of screenplay drafts stacked everywhere. I've written whole scenes of them while Gunther's tenants acted out their martyrdom. Joseph and Willie are peering in there from the sofa. They don't know what to make of it all. I hear Gunther clinking glassware in the distant kitchen.

In a voice as soft as Joseph's I say, "Gunther is an unusual person." It's hardly an outlandish statement. They nod, meaning that they'd noticed, and wait for me to go on. "He's actually rather amazing. Four, five years ago he had nothing. Now he owns properties all over town. Everything he has he built up for himself, with no help from anyone. His drive to succeed is unstoppable. All his life he's dreamed of making movies. He works on screenplays in his sleep." I lean forward and lower my voice even further. "His father was an electrician who drank himself to death, beat the kids, and smashed up the house all the time when Gunther was growing up. Now Gunther supports his old mother, bought a nice little house for her to live in across town. He put his wife through college. You'll see him come in here with a Coke for himself. He never touches a drink, straight as an arrow. You understand what I'm saying. I'm talking about character, what motivates a man."

Everything I'm telling Willie and Joseph is true. Yes, I'm casting it in a certain light, even perceiving it as I say it, but I'm not telling a single lie.

"A lot of people have had it tough," Willie says.

But Joseph waves his hand. "I appreciate what you say," he says.

Gunther comes in with the drinks on a tray, three gin-and-tonics and a Coke for himself. He sits down in a big chair. "Well," he says. Then he's about to say something else, but nothing comes out. We sip our drinks, waiting.

"So, Gunther," Joseph says, "you want to make a movie."

Gunther nods without expression. To the untrained eye, he looks as enigmatic as Buddha, full of secret knowledge. But I've learned to read the fantastic face. He wants to speak, but his body has locked up on him. He never really believed that a man like Joseph would come to his house someday. His stage fright is as immense and immovable as himself.

"Joseph," I say. "Willie. Have you ever noticed that beyond the basic animal requirements there are very few things that all human beings must have, and that these few things are not physical but rather metaphysical, things of the spirit? Faith of some kind is the obvious example. Can you think of another?"

Willie looks at Joseph. "This is kind of a weird thing to be talking about," Willie says.

But Joseph thinks it over and says, "Love, of course."

"Oh, good," I say. "Right. The big one. And how about learning, some systematic acquisition of knowledge?"

"Yes," Joseph says, nodding his head.

"Now I'm thinking of one more," I say. "One more non-physical thing that all people must have, a thing that is always present whenever human beings gather together in grief or in joy."

Willie looks at his watch. Part of his job is to protect Joseph's precious time. "This is kind of like Twenty Questions," he says. "This might be fun at a party."

"Party is a clue," I say.

Joseph straightens up on the sofa. "Music!" he says.

I nod my head and smile. "Yes, Joseph, music."

"The nonphysical part fooled me," Willie says.

"Now, friends," I say, "the movie we're going to make is about music. Joseph, I'll bet there's a tape machine in your car out there. I'm going to guess what's on it at this very moment. Mozart."

"Wrong!" Joseph says, clapping his hands. "Mozart is in the glove compartment, I'll grant you that! But on the machine is Prokofiev. We listened to it on the way over here." He wags his finger at me. "You were wrong, smart boy!"

"Ha-ha!" I say. "But still I've made my point. You take your favorite music with you wherever you go. *And*," I say, "the second part of my point – it's music that Willie doesn't like."

"Right!" Joseph says. "He complains every day. But that part was easy, smart boy. Look at Willie's clothes, look at his hair."

"Sure," I say. "But look further, Joseph. Look at Willie and see the American moviegoer. We practically have Mr. Entertainment sitting right here. And that, Joseph, is why – for the crucial question – we must now defer to Willie."

I sip my drink.

"Willie," I say. "I have a question for you. When was the last time you saw a really great movie about an American rock-and-roll band? I mean a movie that had it all – bar scenes, motorcycle scenes, dressing room scenes, rehearsal scenes, groupie love scenes, and the monster victory-concert scene at the end when the band comes back to its hometown after making it big. A movie that captured all the suffering and the glory, the whole incredible life of a great, semi-famous cult rock band in a medium-sized American city. Willie, when was the last time you saw a movie like that?"

"I never saw any such movie," Willie says.

"That's right," I say.

Gunther's kitchen, 5.00 p.m. Gunther on the floor on his hands and knees.

"Gunther, get up," I say, looking in the refrigerator for those good English ales he was talking about. "Stop doing that. Show some self-respect. Where are those ales, you charlatan, you complete fraud? What if I'd decided to have one?"

"There wouldn't have been any left," he says, continuing to do what he's been doing – crawling on all fours, nudging MaryLou's silver serving tray around the floor with his nose the way a dog nudges its bowl. Periodically he howls like a dog too, and when he does, tears spring from his eyes – which he takes care not to let drip upon the small slip of blue paper resting on the silver tray.

"I'm making a movie!" he keeps bawling between howls.

The slip of blue paper is the check Joseph wrote to Gunther before driving away in the silver Mercedes ten minutes ago. It's for an amount so large I can't bring myself to say it. When he wrote it, Joseph called it good-faith money. He has more, and he knows other investors.

I finish making another gin-and-tonic. "Gunther," I say. "I have to tell you something, and I want you to brace yourself. I'm not doing this movie with you."

He clambers up from the floor, Joseph's check in his hand. "Flip," he says. "Don't even joke about things like that, Flip."

"I'm not joking. Where did you get 'Flip', by the way?"

"It just came to me," Gunther says. "But I like it. That's you from now on. Flip, my man Flip."

"It's not bad," I say. "But you'll have to find somebody else."

"There is nobody else! Nobody like you! Nobody with your talent! Hey! A third of this money's yours! Half of it's yours! It's all yours, Flip!"

"I already have to go to a marriage counselor on account of you," I say. "If I throw in on this movie, Tina divorces me."

"She won't!" Gunther says. "Not when she hears about the money! I'll talk to her. Call her right now, I'll talk to her. No! We'll bring her in! Can she write? Can she act? Can she sing?"

"No, Gunther. She can't do anything. She's a vegetable now. The only thing she can do is say the word *quit*, over and over. If you ask me again I'm leaving, and I still have most of a drink here." I raise my glass. "Congratulations, pal."

"Thanks, Flip. Flip! We have to celebrate somehow! We have to do something fun together!"

"I can't think of anything, Gunther."

"It's hot out. It's muggy. Flip! You've never been in my pool!"

"I didn't bring my suit today, Gunther."

"You can use one of my suits."

"Really, Gunther."

He pounds upstairs. When he comes back down, he's in his trunks, a total embodiment of what it is to be flesh. He tosses me an extra pair. They're like a hot-air balloon or a parachute. I put them on in the bathroom and come out holding a yard of excess suit behind me. Gunther has the stapler from his desk. He staples the trunks until they stay up by themselves.

We go out the back door and into the yard. Gunther's pool is a big one, with all the fixtures: three ladders, two diving boards, ropes with colorful floats. The blue water sparkles with points of early evening light. "Just a quick dip in the low end here, Gunther," I say. "I have to get home for dinner."

"Flip," he says. "Did I tell you I started taking real scuba-diving lessons? From a registered diving teacher at the Y? He's been showing the class all this neat stuff, special things you have to do in case of emergencies. I have to show you a couple of these things. I can teach you the basics of diving in about two minutes."

"Gunther, no, really. I've always had a slight fear of the

water, to tell you the truth. I was swept out into the ocean once when I was a kid, and lifeguards had to save me with a motorboat."

"You never told me that," he says. "That would make a great scene. You should be a little more forthcoming with your experiences. It would help you rise above them." He starts getting the scuba stuff out of the equipment shed. "Now look, these are what we call weight belts. They keep you from floating to the top." He hands me one and starts putting one on himself.

I drop it on the grass. "See you, Gunther. It's been, you know, nice."

He grabs my shoulder. "MaryLou goes diving with me, Flip, and she can't even drive a stick shift. Are you telling me you're afraid to do this? I know, you have to go home. Hey, it's been a special day. I'm asking you to take a little dive with me to celebrate. Ten lousy minutes for a little fun, and then you can go home."

I pick up the weight belt and put it on. Gunther is tying a heavy rope around his waist. About 20 feet of rope is left when he's finished, and he proceeds to tie the other end around me. "Like mountain climbers," he says.

"Divers don't do that, Gunther. No diver ties himself to another diver."

"Yes, they do, Flip. In certain kinds of salvage operations they do. It's a special knot that comes undone when you pull on it." He pulls on the knot and the rope drops off my waist onto the grass. "Okay?" He reties the rope for me. "I have this neat maneuver I want to show you – what divers do when one diver for some reason loses his tank or runs out of air. We have to do this particular maneuver if we want to have some fun here today, because I only have one tank with air in it."

"Oh, Christ."

"Put on your flippers, Flip," he says, putting on the only tank with air in it.

I put on the flippers and we slap across the lawn to the concrete apron along the edge of the pool. Gunther explains that we're going to fall into the deep end on our backs, get ourselves oriented under water, and then start sharing the one mouthpiece.

I'm going to love it, he says. It'll be much more interesting than simply having my own tank. He shows me how to put the mouthpiece in and out without swallowing water. "Granted, it's a little different up here on land," he says. "Ready? Lower your mask."

I lower my mask. Then, without even giving me a signal, Gunther topples backward like a bomb leaving a plane. The splash he makes comes right over my head like an ocean wave and then the rope runs out and snaps me into the vortex behind him.

Under the water it's white and opaque, with millions of tiny bubbles, and I can't see anything. Then I make out Gunther, his legs and arms wafting gently like seaweed fronds. I watch him swim for a few seconds, fascinated by how graceful he is under water, the way whales are said to be. I can see him smiling around the mouthpiece. He waves goodbye to me as I sink. The weight belt is doing much more to me than to Gunther; soon I'm directly beneath him and panicking. I try to swim upward, but I don't know how to use the flippers and can't kick with them on. I pull on the special knot, but it doesn't work now that it's wet. I try to undo the weight belt, but it's jammed by the rope. I'm about to start crying, despite the unexpected thought that crying under water would be absurd.

Then I feel myself rising toward the surface. Arm over arm, Gunther is hauling me up by the umbilical rope. When he gets me to his level, he pushes the mouthpiece into my face. I'm afraid to breathe through it. *Breathe!* he says with his hands. I breathe. The air from the tank is the most wonderful thing I've ever known, physical ecstasy and my life to do over again. After a few breaths of it I'm all calmed down.

Gunther points to me and moves his arms and legs. *You're supposed to hold yourself up*, he's saying. I point to myself and make some gestures: *I can't*. He gestures, *Try*, takes the mouthpiece away, and lets go of the rope. I try again and sink stupidly, all the way down. He hauls me back up, collects the excess rope, and ties it all into one big bow between us, so that I can't sink too far away.

We fall into a rhythm with the tank, two breaths each time,

passing the hose back and forth peace-pipe fashion. Peace is what it is, an amazing, liquid peace. Each sharing of the air is the deepest cooperation between comrades, something solid and good that would never be withheld. We hear nothing but the gurgling of the tank and somewhere, very distant, the persistent *om* of the pool filter. Random thoughts and memories bubble through me like Aqualung air, one notion after another in bubbly succession, each considered for a globular instant and then allowed to bubble away forever. I've never envied anything Gunther has, but maybe I've misunderstood it all, because I envy this. If I had a lot of money, a swimming pool and a scuba tank would be the first things I'd buy, so that I could leave the earth this way for an hour or two every evening.

A small kick or motion of the arm sends us orbiting slowly around each other in the water like space walkers. Behind Gunther's face mask his eyes are closed. He might almost be sleeping. I see that this is the essential Gunther – who he really is and who he'd be on land, too, if he didn't have to do what he does up there because of what his father did to him.

He opens his eyes and sees me staring at him. He smiles and gestures to the blueness around us as if to say, *Aren't you glad you stayed to check this out?* I nod and give him the okay sign. He points to the surface of the water, shrugs his shoulders, and flops his arms. He actually laughs and a bubble floats out of his mouth with the message, *You really saved me up there.*

I tap my chest, meaning, *I know I did, you huge oaf.*

*But the rock-and-roll movie was my idea!* he adds, slapping his own chest defiantly. *And I'm not a bad man!* he adds, kicking his feet. *Not as bad as you make out, that's for sure. You're such a judgmental person. My tenants don't need to talk to me about every goddam leaky faucet.*

*What about that Pakistani baby?* I signal, imitating the mother's flowing robes and jutting out my chin self-righteously.

*Okay,* he nods, *that was wrong, I admit it.*

I make a signal to my heart, meaning, *That really upset my wife. You almost destroyed my marriage.*

He shakes his head with great irritation and lashes his pink fists through the blue water. *Me destroy your marriage! Did you ever think that maybe you shouldn't complain to your wife so much? I'll bet she doesn't bring home every single stupid thing that happens to her every day and inflict it on you. You're such a baby!*

I nod sadly. *Okay, you have a point*

He rolls onto his back and starts paddling both of us around the depths of the pool. I let myself be towed along, staring up at the silvery surface of the water, taking my turns on the scuba tank. The water's surface reminds me of the silver screen of a movie theater, and as a game I try to see a movie in it. At first I don't see anything, and then after a while I begin to see the rock-and-roll movie. I see precisely how it ought to go, what scenes it ought to have, all the things about life that you could make people understand while you had their attention with the music. I see that the world really needs this great, honest, full-of-heart movie about an American band, and that if I don't do it with Gunther he'll screw it up and it won't be the movie I'm seeing. Or Joseph will bring in somebody else to take my place. Somebody else will get to give the world all the pleasure and instruction of the great rock-and-roll movie, and then the world will give that person the swimming pool and scuba tank in return. Why shouldn't it be me?

# D. R. MACDONALD

☆ ☆ ☆ ☆

# *The Flowers of Bermuda*

Bilkie Sutherland took the postcard from behind his rubber bib and slowly read the message one more time: "I'm going here soon. I hope your lobsters are plentiful. My best to Bella. God bless you. Yours, Gordon MacLean." Bilkie flipped it over: a washed out photograph in black and white. *The Holy Isle. Iona. Inner Hebrides.* On the land stood stone ruins, no man or woman anywhere, and grim fences of cloud shadowed a dark sea. So this was Iona.

"You want that engine looked at?" Angus Carmichael, in his deepwater boots, was standing on the wharf above Bilkie's boat.

"Not now. I heard from the minister."

"MacLean?"

"He's almost to Iona now."

Angus laughed, working a toothpick around in his teeth. "Man dear, *I've* been to Iona, was there last Sunday." Angus meant where his wife was from, a Cape Breton village with a Highland museum open in the summer, and a St. Columba Church.

"It's a very religious place," Bilkie said, ignoring him. "Very ancient, in that way."

"Like you, Bilkie."

"I'm the same as the rest of you."

"No, Bilkie. Sometimes you're not. And neither is your Reverend MacLean."

Angus's discarded toothpick fluttered down to the deck. Bilkie picked it up and dropped it over the side. Angus never cared whether his own deck was flecked with gurry and flies. Nor was he keen on Gordon MacLean. Said the man was after putting in a good word for the Catholics. But that wasn't the minister's point at all. "We're all one faith, if we go back to Iona," is what he'd said. And nothing much more than that.

As Bilkie laid out his gear for the next day's work, he heard singing. No one sang around here anymore. Radios took care of that. He stood up to listen. Ah! It was Johnny, Angus's only boy, home from Dalhousie for the summer. He had a good strong voice, that boy, one they could use over at the church. But you didn't see him there, not since college. No singer himself, Bilkie could appreciate a good tune. His grandfather had worked the schooners in the West Indies trade, and Johnny's song had the flavor of that, of those rolling vessels . . . "'He could smell the flowers of Bermuda in the gale, when he died on the North Rock Shoal . . .'" Bilkie stared into the wet darkness underneath the wharf where pilings were studded with snails. Algae hung like slicked hair on the rocks. He had saved Gordon MacLean under that wharf, when the man was just a tyke. While hunting for eels, Gordon had slipped and fallen, and Bilkie heard his cries and came down along the rocks on the other side to pull him out, a desperate boy clutching for his hand.

Bilkie's car, a big salt-eaten Ford, was parked at the end of the wharf, and whenever he saw it he wished again for horses who could shuck salt like rain. At home the well pump had quit this morning and made him grumpy. He'd had to use the woods, squat out there under a fir, the birds barely stirring overhead, him staring at shoots of Indian Pipe wondering what in hell they lived on, leafless, white as wax, hardly a flower at all. Up by the roadside blue lupines were a little past their prime. What flowers, he wondered, grew on Iona?

The car swayed through rain ruts, past clumps of St. Johnswort (*Allas colmcille* his grandfather had called them) that gave a wild yellow border to the driveway. His house appeared slowly behind a corridor of tall maples. In their long shade red cows rested. Sometimes everything seemed fixed, for good. His animals, his life. But God had taken away his only boy, and Bilkie could not fathom that even yet. For a time he had kept sheep, but quit because killing the lambs bothered him.

Bella was waiting at the front door, not the back, her palm

pressed to her face. He stopped shy of the porch, hoping it wasn't a new well-pump they needed:

"What's wrong?"

"Rev. MacLean's been stabbed in Oban," his wife said, her voice thin.

Bilkie repeated the words to himself. There was a swallows' nest above the door. The birds swooped and clamored. "Not there?" he said. "Not in Scotland?" A mist of respect, almost reverence, hovered over the old country. You didn't get stabbed there.

"Jessie told me on the phone, not a minute ago. Oh, he'll live all right. He's living."

Over supper Bella related what she knew. Gordon MacLean had been walking in Oban, in the evening it was, a woman friend with him. Two young thugs up from Glasgow went for her handbag, right rough about it too. Gordon collared one but the other shoved a knife in his back.

"He's not a big man either," Bilkie said, returning a forkful of boiled potato to his plate. He had known Gordon as a child around the wharf, a little boy who asked hard questions. He had pulled him from the water. He'd seen him go off to seminary, thinking he would never come back to Cape Breton, not to this corner of it, but after a while he did. To think of him lying in blood, on a sidewalk in Oban. "Did they catch the devils?"

"They did. He'll have to testify."

"What, go back there?"

"When he's able. Be a long time until the trial."

Bilkie felt betrayed. A big stone had slipped somehow out of place. Certain things did not go wrong there, not in the Islands where his people came from. Here, crime was up, too few caring about a day's work, kids scorning church. Greedier now, more for themselves, people were. But knives, what the hell. There in the Hebrides they'd worked things out, hadn't they, over a long span of time? It had seemed to him a place of hard wisdom, hard won. Not a definite place, for he had never been there, but something like stone about it: sea-washed, nicely worn, and high cliffs where waves whitened against the rocks.

He knew about the Clearances, yes, about the bad laws that drove his grandfather out of Lewis where he'd lived in a turf house. But even then they weren't knifing people. Gordon MacLean, a minister of God, couldn't return there and come to no harm? To Mull first he'd been headed, to MacLean country. And then to Iona, across a strait not much wider than this one. But a knife stopped him in Oban, a nice sort of town by the sea.

From his parlor window Bilkie could see a bit of the church in the east, the dull white shingles of its steeple above the dark spruce. *We all have Iona inside us*, the man had said. *Our faith was lighted there.* Why then did this happen?

Bilkie had asked such a question before and found no answer. They'd had a son, he and Bella, so he knew about shock, and about grief. Even now, thinking of his son and the schoolhouse could suck the wind right out of him. The boy was born late in their lives anyway, and maybe Bilkie's hopes had come too much to rest in him. Was that the sin? Torquil they called him, an old name out of the Hebrides, after Bella's dad. But one October afternoon when the boy was nine, he left the schoolhouse and forgot his coat, a pea coat, new, with a big collar turned up like a sailor's. So he went back to get it, back to the old white schoolhouse where he was learning about the world. It was just a summer house now, owned by strangers. But that day it was locked tight, and the teacher gone home. A young woman. No blame to her. His boy jimmied open the window with his knife. They were big, double-hung windows, and you could see them open yet on a warm weekend, hear people drunk behind the screens. But Torquil had tried to hoist himself over the sill, and the upper half of the window unjammed then and came down on his neck. Late in the day it was they found him, searching last the grounds of the school. A time of day about now. The sash lay along his small shoulders like a yoke, that cruel piece of wood, blood in his nose like someone had punched him. . . .

Bilkie barely slept. He was chased by a misty street, black and wet, and harrowing cries that seemed one moment a man's, the next a beast's. He was not given to getting up in the night but he dressed and went outside to walk off the dreariness he'd woke to. A cold and brilliant moon brightened the ground fog which layered the pasture like a fallen cloud. The high ridge of hill behind his fields was ragged with wormshot spruce, wicks of branch against the sky. As a boy he'd walked those high woods with his grandfather who offered him the Gaelic names of things, most of them forgotten now, gone with the good trees. One day he'd told Bilkie about the words for heaven and hell, how they, Druid words, went far back before the time of Christ. *Ifrinn*, the Isle of the Cold Clime, was a dark and frigid region of venomous reptiles and savage wolves. There the wicked were doomed to wander, chilled to their very bones and bereft even of the company of their fellow sinners. And the old heaven, though the Christians kept that name too, was also different: *Flathinnis*, the Isle of the Brave, a paradise full of light which lay far distant, somewhere in the Western Ocean. "I like that some better," His grandfather had said. "Just the going there would be good. As for hell, nothing's worse than cold and loneliness."

As he moved through the fog, it thinned like steam, but gathered again and closed in behind him. Suddenly he heard hoofbeats. Faintly at first, then louder. He turned in a circle, listening. Not a cow of his. They were well-fenced. Maybe the Dunlops' next door. But cow or horse it was coming toward him at a good clip and yet he couldn't make it out, strain as he might. Soon his heart picked up the quick, even thud of the hooves, and when in the pale fog a shape grew and darkened and then burst forth, a head shaggy as seaweed and cruelly horned, he raised his arms wildly in a shout of fear and confusion as the bull shied past him, a dark rush of heat and breath, staggering him like a blow. Aw, that goddamn Highland bull, that ugly bugger. Trembling with anger and surprise, he listened to it crash through thickets off up the hill, the fog eddying in its wake, until Bella called him and he turned back to the house.

On the porch of the manse Bilkie waited for Mrs. MacQueen to answer the door. The porch Rev. MacLean had built, but the white paint and black trim were Bilkie's work, donated last summer when his lobstering was done. He'd enjoyed those few days around the minister. One afternoon when Bilkie was on the ladder he thought he heard Gordon talking to himself, but no, he was looking up, shading his eyes. "It's only a mile from Mull, Iona," Gordon said to him. "Just across the Sound. So it's part of going home, really." Bilkie had said yes, he could see that. But he wasn't sure, even now, that he and the minister meant home in the same way. "Monks lived there, Bilkie. For a long, long time. They had a different view of the world, a different feel for it altogether. God was still *new*, there, you see. Their faith was . . . robust."

Mrs. MacQueen, the housekeeper, filled the doorway and Bilkie told her what he would like.

"A book about Iona?" She was looking him up and down. She smelled of Joy, lemon-scented, the same stuff he used on his decks. "I don't read the man's books, dear, I dust them."

"He wouldn't mind me looking. Me and himself are friends." He rapped the trim of the door. "My paint."

"Well, he could have used some friends in Oban."

Mrs. MacQueen showed him into the minister's study, making it clear she would not leave. She turned the television on low, as if this were a sickroom, and sat down on a hassock, craning her ear to the screen.

Wine-colored drapes, half-drawn, gave the room a warm light. Bookshelves lined one wall, floor to ceiling, and Bilkie touched their bindings as he passed. He hadn't a clue where to begin or how to search in this hush: he only wanted to know more about that place, and maybe when the man returned they could talk about what went wrong there. But he felt shy with Mrs. MacQueen in the room. A map of Scotland was thumb-tacked to the wall. The old clan territories were done in bright colors. Lewis he spotted easily, and Mull. And tiny Iona. On the desktop, under sprigs of lilac in a small vase, he saw a slim red book. In it were notes in Gordon's hand. With a quick glance at the housekeeper, he took it to the leather chair close by the north window, a good bright spot where Gordon must have sat many a time, binoculars propped on the sill. Bilkie put them to his eyes instinctively. Behind the manse a long meadow ran down to the shore. Across the half mile of water his boat rocked gently in the light swells. Strange to see his yellow slicker hanging by the wheel, emptied of him. Moving the glasses slightly he made out Angus standing over his boy, Johnny, hunched down into some work or other. Good with engines, was Johnny. Suddenly Angus looked toward Bilkie. Of course his eyes would take in only the white manse on the hill, and the church beside it. Yet Bilkie felt seen in a peculiar way and he put down the binoculars.

Aware of the time, he turned pages, reading what he could grasp. That Iona's founder, St. Columba, had sailed there from Ireland to serve his kinsmen, the Scots of Dalriada. That he and his monks labored with their own hands, tilling and building, and that in their tiny boats they spread the faith into the remote and lesser isles, converting even the heathen Picts. That even before he was born, Columba's glory had been foretold to his mother in a dream: "An angel of the Lord appeared to her, and brought her a beautiful robe – a robe which had all the colors of all the flowers of the world. Immediately it was rapt away from her, and she saw it spread across the heavens, stretched out over plains and woods and mountains. . . ." He read testaments to St. Columba's powers and example, how once in a great storm his ship met swelling waves that rose like mountains, but at his prayer they were stilled. He was a poet and loved singing, and songs praising Columba could keep you from harm. His bed was bare rock and his pillow a stone. During the three days and three nights of his funeral, a great wind blew, without rain, and no boat could reach or leave the island.

Bilkie was deep in the book when Mrs. MacQueen, exclaiming, "That's desperate, just desperate!", turned off the soap opera and came over to him.

"You'll have to go now," she said. "This isn't the public library, dear, and I have cleaning to do."

He would never talk himself past her again, not with Gordon away. He returned the book to the desk and followed her to the front door.

"Did you ever pray to a saint, Mrs. MacQueen?"

She crossed her arms. "I'm no RC, Mr. Sutherland."

"I don't think that matters, Mrs. MacQueen. The minister has a terrible wound. Say a word to St. Columba."

"He's healing. He's getting better and soon might be coming home, is what I heard."

The next morning the sun glared up from a smooth sea as Bilkie hauled his traps, moving from one swing to another over the grounds his grandfather had claimed. By the time Bilkie was old enough to fish, there was a little money in it. But you had to work. Nobody ever gave it to you, and the season was short. He had started out young hauling by hand, setting out his swings in the old method, the backlines anchored with kellicks, and when he wasn't hauling he was rowing, and damned hard if a wind was on or the tide against you. He had always worked alone, rowed alone. Except when his boy was with him, and that seemed as brief now as a passing bird. He preferred it out here by himself, free of the land for awhile, the ocean at his back.

This season the water was so clear he could see ten fathoms, see the yellow backline snaking down, the traps rising. His grandfather told him about the waters of the West Indies, the clear blue seas with the sun so far down in them it wouldn't seem like drowning at all, for the light there.

He graffed a buoy and passed the line over the hauler, drawing the trap up to the washboard where he quickly culled the dripping, scurrying collection. He measured the lobsters, threw a berried one back. But after he dropped the trap and moved on, he knew he'd forgotten, for the second time that morning, to put in fresh bait. To hell with it. On the bleak rocks of the Bird Islands shags spread their dark wings to dry. A school of mackerel shimmered near the boat, an expanding and contracting disturbance just beneath the surface as they fed. He cut the engine, letting the boat drift like his mind. He hummed the song of Johnny Carmichael but stopped. Couldn't get the damn tune out of his head. Sick of it. He picked a mackerel out of the bait box and turned it over in his hands, stroking the luminous flow of stripes a kind of sky was named for: a beautiful fish, if you looked at it – the smooth skin, dark yet silvery. Gordon MacLean said from the pulpit that a man should find beauty in what's around him, for that too was God. But for Bilkie everything had been so familiar, everything he knew and saw and felt, until

Torquil died. He took out his knife and slid it slowly into the dead fish: now, what might that be like, a piece of steel like that inside you? A feeling you'd carry a long while, there, under the scar.

Astern, the head of the cape rose behind buff-colored cliffs, up into the deep green nap of the mountain. He had no fears here, never in weather like this when the sea was barely breathing. Still, he missed the man, the sound of his voice on Sunday. The last service before he left for Iona, the minister had read Psalm 44, the one, he said, that St. Columba sang to win the Picts away from their magi, the Druids . . . *O God, our fathers have told us, what work thou didst in their days, in the times of old . . .*

After Bilkie lost his son, he'd stayed away from church, from the mournful looks and explanations, why he should accept God's taking an innocent boy in such a way. His heart was sore, he told Bella, and had to heal up, and nothing in the church then could help it. But a few weeks after Rev. MacLean arrived, Bilkie went to hear him. Damn it, the man could preach. Not like those TV preachers who couldn't put out anything much but their palms and a phone number. A slender string it was that Gordon MacLean couldn't take a tune from. And only once had he mentioned Torquil in a roundabout way, to show he was aware there'd been a boy, that he knew what a son could mean.

As Bilkie turned in toward the wharf that afternoon, he saw three boats in ahead of him. Above Angus's blue and white Cape Islander the men had gathered in a close circle, talking and nodding. Only Johnny Carmichael was still down below, sitting on the gunnels with his guitar. Bilkie approached the wharf in a wide arc, trying to discern what he saw in the huddled men and the boy off alone bent into his instrument. He brought his boat up into the lee and flung a line to Angus who was waving for it.

"Bilkie, you're late, boy!" he shouted.

"Aw, I was feeling slow today!"

When the lines were secured, Angus called down to him. "Did you hear about it?"

"About what?"

"The minister, Bilkie, for God's sake! He's passed away! It was sudden, you know. Complications. Not expected at all."

Bilkie's hands were pressed against a crate he'd been about to shift. He could feel the lobsters stirring under the wood. He looked up at Angus. "I knew that already," he said.

Instead of going home, Bilkie drove to a tavern 15 miles away. He sat near a window at one of the many small tables. Complications. Lord. The sun felt warm on his hands and he watched bubbles rise in his glass of beer. The tavern was quiet but tonight it would be roaring. Peering into the dim interior he made out Jimmy Carey alone at a table. Jimmy was Irish and had acted cranky here more than once. But he seemed old and mild now, back there in the afternoon dark, not the hell-raiser he used to be. And wasn't St. Columba an Irishman, after all? Bilkie raised his glass and held it there until Jimmy, who looked as if he'd been hailed from across the world, noticed it and raised his own in return. Bilkie beckoned him over. They drank until well past supper, leaning over the little table and knocking glasses from time to time. Bilkie told him about St. Columba, about the monks in their frail vessels.

"You know about St. Brendan, of course," Jimmy said, his eyes fixing on Bilkie but looking nowhere. "They say he got as far as here even, and clear to Bermuda before he was done."

"Bermuda I know about." Bilkie tried to sing what he remembered. "'Oh there be flowers in Bermuda, beauty lies on every hand . . . and there be laughter, ease and drink for every man . . .'" He leaned close to Jimmy's face: "'. . . but there not be joy for *me*.'"

On the highway Bilkie focused hard on the center line, thinking that Jimmy Carey might have bought one round at least, St. Brendan be damned. To the west the strait ran deep and dark, the sun just gone from it as he turned away towards home. Bad time to meet the mounties. He lurched to a stop by the roadside where a small waterfall lay hidden. He plunged through a line of alders into air immediately cool. The falls stepped gently through mossed granite, down to a wide, clear pool, and he remembered Bella bending her head into it years ago, her hair fanning out red there as she washed the salt away after swimming. He knelt and cupped the water, so cold he groaned, over his face again and again.

As he drove the curves the white church appeared and disappeared above the trees. When he came upon it, it seemed aloof, unattended. Cars were parked carelessly along the drive-way to the manse, and Bilkie slowed down long enough to see a man and woman climbing the front steps, Mrs. MacQueen, in her flowered apron, waiting at the door. Oh, there'd be some coming and going today, the sharing of the hard news. When he felt the schoolhouse approaching, he vowed again not to look, not to bother what went on there. But he couldn't miss the blue tent in the front yard, and the life raft filled with water for a wading pool. This time he did not slow down. Too often he had wondered about the blow on the neck, about what his son had felt, and who, in that instant, he had blamed . . . something so simple as a window coming down on his bones. There. In a schoolhouse.

Bella had not seen Bilkie drunk like this in years, but she knew why and said nothing, not even about Rev. MacLean. She could not get him to come inside for supper. He reeled around angrily in the lower pasture, hieing cows away when they trotted toward the fence for handouts of fresh hay. He shouted up at the ridge. Finally he stalked to the back door.

"Gordon was going to Iona," he said to his wife. "He could check the fury of wild animals, that saint they had there. Did Gordon no damn good, eh?"

"You've had some drink, Bilkie, and I've had none. I'm tired now."

He stepped up close to her and took her face in his hands. "Ah, Bella. Your hair was so pretty."

She made him go to bed, but after dark he woke. He smelled of the boat and wanted to wash. Hearing a car, he went over to the window. Near his neighbor's upper pasture headlights bounced and staggered over the rough ground. They halted, backed up, then swept suddenly in another direction until the shaggy bull galloped across the beams. Loose again. A smallish, wild-looking beast they'd imported from Scotland. Could live out on its own in the dead of winter, that animal. You might see it way off in a clearing, quiet, shouldering snow like a monument. The headlights, off again in pursuit, captured the bull briefly but it careened away into the darkness, and the car – a Dunlop boy at the wheel no doubt – raked the field blindly. Complications. A stone for a pillow. His own boy would be a man now. Passed away, like a wave.

It was difficult for Bilkie to get up that day. He had always opened his eyes on the dark side of 4 a.m. but now Bella had to push and coax him. He sat on the edge of the bed for a long time staring at the half-model of a schooner mounted on the wall. His grandfather had worked her, the *Ocean Rose*, lost on Hogsty Reef in the Bahamas with his Uncle Bill aboard.

"You don't get up anymore. What's the matter with you?" Bella said. He took the cup of coffee she held out to him, nodding vaguely. Squalls had lashed the house all night and now a thick drizzle whispered over the roof. "You know Rev. MacLean is coming home this day, and tonight they'll wake him."

"I can't go," Bilkie said.

"What would he think, you not there at his wake with the others who loved him?"

"He's not thinking at all anymore. That's just a body there, coming back."

"Don't be terrible. Don't be the way you were after Torquil."

"They could have buried him over there. Couldn't they have? Near where he wanted to go?"

"He was born *here*, Bilkie. Nobody asked, I don't suppose, one way or the other."

He could see that she'd been crying. He put the coffee down carefully on the window sill and took her hands in his, still warm from the cup. "Bella, dear," he said. "You washed your hair in that water. It must have hurt, eh? Water so cold as that?"

Gusts rocked the car as Bilkie crossed the bridge that joined the other island. He was determined to take himself out of the fuss, some of it from people who would never bestir themselves were Gordon MacLean here and breathing. Above him the weather moved fast. The sky would whiten in patches but all the while churn with clouds black as the cliffs by the lighthouse. There was a good lop on the water, looking east from the bridge, and when the strait opened out a few miles away the Atlantic flashed white against an ebbing tide.

In the lee of the wharf the lobster boats were surging like tethered horses. No one was around. The waves broke among the pilings beneath him and the timbers creaked. He walked to the seaward end where Angus had stacked his broken traps. Across the roughening water the manse looked small, the cars tiny around it. Every morning his grandfather would say, old as he was, *Dh'iarr am muir a thadhal.* The sea wants to be visited.

He threw off his lines and headed out into the strait, rounding up into the wind, battering the waves until he checked back on the throttle. In the turns of wind he smelled the mackerel in the bait box, the fumes of the engine. But as he drew abreast of Campbell Point, a gust of fragrance came off the land and he strained to see its source in the long, blowing grass of the point. It was quickly gone and there was nothing to account for it but what had been there all along – the thin line of beach, the grass thick as hay all the way back to the woods. To the west, on the New Skye Road, he glimpsed St. David's Church, a small white building behind a veil of rain, set in the dense spruce, no one there now but Bible Camp kids in the summer.

The sea was lively at the mouth of the strait where wind and tide met head to head. He bucked into the whitecaps, slashes of spray cracking over the bow. The waves deepened as the sea widened out but he'd ride better when he reached the deeper water where the breaking crests would cease. He had a notion of the West Indies, of his grandfather under sails, out there over the curve of the world and rolling along in worse weather than this. Hadn't the Irish monks set out in their currachs of wickerwork and hide, just for the love of God? They had survived. They reached those islands they sailed for, only dimly sure where they were. But maybe you could come by miracles easier then, when all of life was harder, and God closer to the sea than he was now.

Now with no saints around, saints who could sow a field and sail a boat, you had to find your own miracles. You couldn't travel to them, could you, Gordon, boy?

He would have to go back. He would have to stand at the wake holding his hat like the rest of them, looking at Gordon who'd come dead such a distance. Bilkie watched the rhythm of the waves. He needed a break in them to bring his boat around and run with the sea. But then he wasn't hearing the engine anymore, and the boat was falling away, coming around slowly with no more sound than a sail would make. Columba. A dove. Strange name for a man. *Colmcille. Caoir gheal*, his grandfather called waves like these. A bright flaming of white. The sea had turned darker than the sky, and over the land the boat was swinging toward, clouds lay heavy and thick, eased along like stones, dark as dolmens. "Ah!" was all Bilkie said when the wave rose under him, lifting the boat high like an offering.

CHRISTOPHER McILROY

☆ ☆ ☆ ☆

# *All My Relations*

When Jack Oldenburg first spoke to him, Milton Enos leaned over his paper plate, scooping beans into his mouth as if he didn't hear. Breaking through the murmur of *o'otham* conversation, the white man's speech was sharp and harsh. But Oldenburg stood over him, waiting.

Oldenburg had just lost his ranch hand, sick. If Milton reported to the Box-J sober in the morning, he could work for a couple of weeks until the cowboy returned or Oldenburg found a permanent hand.

"Okay," Milton said, knowing he wouldn't go. Earlier in the day his wife and son had left for California, so he had several days' drinking to do. Following his meal at the convenience mart he would hitch to the Sundowner Lounge at the edge of the reservation.

After a sleepless night Milton saddled his horse for the ride to Oldenburg's, unable to bear his empty house. As Milton crossed the wide, dry bed of the Gila River, leaving the outskirts of Hashan, the house ceased to exist for him and he thought he would never go back. Milton's stomach jogged over the pommel with the horse's easy gait. Two hours from Hashan, Oldenburg's Box-J was the only ranch in an area either left desert or irrigated for cotton and sorghum. Its 20 square miles included hills, arroyos, and the eastern tip of a mountain range – gray-pink granite knobs split by ravines. The sun burned the top of the mountains red.

Oldenburg stood beside his corral, tall and thin as one of its mesquite logs. First, he said, sections of the barbed-wire fence had broken down, which meant chopping and trimming new posts.

Milton's first swings of the ax made him dizzy and sick. He flailed wildly, waiting with horror for the bite of the ax into his foot. But soon he gained control over his stroke. Though soft, his big arms were strong. Sweat and alcohol poured out of him until he stank.

In the afternoon Milton and Oldenburg rode the fence line.

"Hasn't been repaired in years," Oldenburg said. "My hand Jenkins is old." Oldenburg himself was well over sixty, his crew cut white and his face dried up like a dead man's. He had bright eyes, though, and fine white teeth. Where the fence was flattened to the ground, Milton saw a swatch of red and white cowhide snagged on the barbed wire. He'd lost a few head in the mountains, Oldenburg said, and after the fence was secure they'd round them up.

"One thing I'll tell you," Oldenburg said. "You can't drink while you work for me. Alcohol is poison in a business."

Milton nodded. By reputation he knew Oldenburg had a tree stump up his ass. Milton's wife C.C. had said she'd bring their son Allen back when Milton stopped drinking. For good? he'd asked. How would she know when was for good? For all anybody knew tomorrow might be the first day of for good, or 25,500 days later he might get drunk again. For a moment Milton remembered playing Monopoly with C.C. and Allen several weekends before. As usual, Milton and Allen were winning. Pretending not to be furious, C.C. smiled her big, sweet grin. Milton and the boy imitated her, stretching their mouths, until she couldn't help laughing. Milton clicked them off like a TV set and saw only mesquite, and rocky sand, sky, and the line of fence. After his two weeks, Milton thought, he'd throw a drunk like World War Ten.

At the end of the day Milton accepted Oldenburg's offer: 75 dollars a week plus room and board, weekend off. Oldenburg winced apologetically proposing the wage; the ranch didn't make money, he explained.

They ate at a metal table in the dining room. Milton, whose pleasure in food went beyond filling his stomach, appreciated Oldenburg's meat loaf – diced with onion, the center concealing three hard-boiled eggs. Milton couldn't identify the seasonings except for chili. "What's in this?" he asked.

"Sage, chili, cumin and Worcestershire sauce."

"*Heyyy.*"

Inside his two-room adobe, Milton was so tired he couldn't feel his body, and lying down felt the same as standing up. He slept without dreaming until Oldenburg rattled the door at daybreak.

Milton dug holes and planted posts. By noon his sweat had lost its salt and tasted like pure spring water. Then he didn't sweat at all. Chilled and shaking at the end of the day, his body felt as if he'd been thrown by a horse. The pain gave him a secret exultation which he hoarded from Oldenburg, saying nothing. Yet he felt he was offering the man part of the ache as a secret gift. Slyly, he thumped his cup on the table and screeched his chair back with exaggerated vigor. Milton was afraid of liking Oldenburg too much. He liked people easily, even those who were not *o'otham* – especially those, perhaps, because he wanted them to prove he needn't hate them.

Milton worked ten-, eleven-hour days. The soreness left his muscles, though he was as tired the fourth evening as he had been the first. Thursday night Oldenburg baked a chicken.

"You're steady," Oldenburg said. "I've seen you Pimas work hard before. What's your regular job?"

"I've worked for the government." Milton had ridden rodeo, sold wild horses he captured in the mountains, broken horses. Most often there was welfare. Recently he had completed two CETA training programs, one as a hospital orderly and the other baking cakes. But the reservation hospital wasn't hiring, and the town of Hashan had no bakeries. For centuries, Milton had heard, when the Gila flowed, the *o'otham* had been farmers. Settlements and overgrazing upstream had choked off the river only a few generations past. Sometimes Milton tried to envision green plots of squash, beans, and ripening grains, watered by earthen ditches, spreading from the banks. He imagined his back flexing easily in the heat as he bent to the rows, foliage swishing his legs, finally the villagers diving into the cool river, splashing delightedly.

"I don't think Jenkins is coming out of the hospital," Oldenburg said. "This job is yours if you want it." Milton was stunned. He had never held a permanent position.

In just a week of hard work, good eating, and no drinking, Milton had lost weight. Waking Friday morning, he pounded his belly with his hand; it answered him like a drum. He danced in front of the bathroom mirror, swiveling his hips, urging himself against the sink as if it were a partner. At lunch he told Oldenburg he would spend the weekend with friends in Hashan.

When he tossed the post-hole digger into the shed, Milton felt light and strong, as if instead of sinking fence posts he'd spent the afternoon in a deep, satisfying nap. On the way to the guest house, his bowels turned over and a sharp pain set into his head. He saw the battered station wagon rolling down the drive, C.C. at the wheel, Allen's tight face in the window.

Milton threw his work clothes against the wall. After a stinging shower, he changed and mounted his horse for the ride to Vigiliano Lopez's.

Five hours later, the Sundowner was closing. Instead of his customary beer, Milton had been drinking highball glasses of straight vodka. He felt paler and paler, like water, until he was water. His image peeled off him like a wet decal and he was only water in the shape of a man. He flowed onto the bar, hooking his water elbows onto the wooden ridge for support. Then he was lifted from the stool, tilted backward, floating on the pickup bed like vapor.

Milton woke feeling the *pong*, *pong* of a basketball bouncing outside. The vibration traveled along the dirt floor of Lopez's living room, up the couch Milton lay on. The sun was dazzling. Looking out the window, Milton saw 6-foot-5, 300-pound Bosque dribbling the ball with both hands, knocking the other players aside. As he jammed the ball into the low hoop, it hit the back of the rim, bouncing high over the makeshift plywood backboard. A boy and two dogs chased it.

Seeing beer cans in the dirt, Milton went outside. He took his shirt off and sat against the house with a warm Bud. The lean young boys fired in jump shots, or when they missed, their fathers and older brothers pushed and wrestled for the rebound. Lopez grabbed a loose ball and ran with it, whirling for a turnaround fadeaway that traveled 3 feet. He laughed, and said to Milton, "When we took you home you started fighting us.

Bosque had to pick you up and squeeze you, and when he did, everything came out like toothpaste."

"Try our new puke-flavored toothpaste," someone said, laughing.

"Looks like pizza."

"So we brought you here."

Milton said nothing. He watched the arms and broad backs collide. The young boys on the sidelines practiced lassoing the players' feet, the dogs, the ball. When he finished a beer, Milton started another. Later in the afternoon he sent boys to his house for the rest of his clothes and important belongings.

When the game broke up, some of the men joined the women in the shade of a mesquite. Saddling a half-broke wild colt, the boys took turns careening across the field. Lopez drove a truckload to the rodeo arena, where a bronc rider from Bapchule was practicing. Compact and muscular, with silver spurs and collar tabs, he rode out the horse's bucks, smoothing the animal to a canter. Two of Milton's drunk friends tried and were thrown immediately. For a third, the horse didn't buck but instead circled the arena at a dead run, dodging the lassos and open gates. From the announcer's booth Lopez called an imaginary race as horse and rider passed the grandstand again and again – "coming down the backstretch now, whoops, there he goes for another lap, this horse is not a quitter, ladies and gentlemen."

"Go ahead, Milton," Lopez said. "You used to ride."

Milton shook his head. Allen, thirteen, recently had graduated from steers to bulls. In both classes he had finished first or second in every start, earning as much money in the past months as his father and mother combined. Would there be rodeo in California? Milton wondered. In school, too, Allen was a prodigy, learning high school geometry in eighth grade. If he studied hard, the school counselor said, he could finish high school in three years and win a college scholarship. Milton didn't know where the boy's talent came from.

Tears filled Milton's eyes.

"Aaaah," Bosque said. His big hand gripped Milton's arm. They walked back to Lopez's house and split a couple of sixes under the mesquite until the men returned. Audrey Lopez and the other wives prepared chili and chimuth dough while the men played horseshoes and drank in the dusk.

By the end of dinner everyone was drunk. Milton, face sweating, was explaining to Audrey Lopez, "Just a few weeks ago, Allen wins some kind of puzzle contest for the whole state, okay? And he's on TV. And C.C. and I have got our faces up to the screen so we can hear every word he's saying. And we can't believe it. He's talking on TV, and his hair's sticking up on the side, just like it always does.

"I see them so real. When C.C. plays volleyball she's like a rubber ball, she's so little and round. She *dives* for those spikes, and her hair goes flying back."

Lopez slid his leg along Audrey's shoulder. "Good song," he said. "Let's dance." The radio was playing Top Forty.

"Wait. I'm listening to this man."

"Milton talks you into tomorrow afternoon. Come on." Lopez pulled her shoulder.

Audrey shrugged him off and laid her hand on Milton's arm. "His wife and son are gone."

"Dried-up old bitch," Lopez said. "C.C.'s too old for you, man, she's way older than he is. You lost nothing."

Grabbing a barbecue fork, ramming Lopez against the wall, Milton chopped the fork into Lopez's shoulder. A woman screamed, Milton heard his own grunts as the glistening tines rose and stabbed. Lopez ducked and his knife came up. Milton deflected the lunge with his fork, the knife blade springing down its long shank. Milton shouted as the knife thudded into the wall. His little finger had bounded into the air and lay on the floor, looking like a brown pebble.

Bosque drove both men to the hospital. The doctor cauterized, stitched, and bandaged the wound, and gave Milton a tetanus shot. If Milton had brought the severed finger – the top two joints – the doctor said, he might have sewn it on. The men refused to stay overnight. When they returned to the party, couples were dancing the choti and bolero to a Mexican radio station. Gulps of vodka deadened the pain in Milton's finger. He and Lopez kept opposite corners of the living room until dawn, when Lopez pushed Audrey into Milton's arms and said, "Get some dancing, man."

Sunday Milton slept under the mesquite until evening, when he rode to the Box-J.

"That's your mistake, Milton," Oldenburg said. "Everyone's entitled to one mistake. Next time you drink you're gone. You believe me?"

Milton did. He felt like weeping. The next day he roamed the fence line, his chest and neck clotted with the frustration of being unable to work. The horse's jouncing spurted blood through the white bandage on his finger. Finally he rode out a back gate and into the midst of the granite mountains. Past a sparkling dome broken by a slump of shattered rock, Milton trotted into a narrow cut choked with mesquite. As a boy, he would hunt wild horses, for days in these ravines, alone, with only a canvas food bag tied to the saddle. He remembered sleeping on the ground without a blanket, beneath a lone sycamore that had survived years of drought. Waking as dawn lit the mountain crests, he would force through the brush, gnawing a medallion of jerked beef. Most often when he startled a horse, the animal would clatter into a side gully, boxing itself in. Then roping was easy. Once when Milton flushed a stringy gray mustang, the horse charged him instead; Milton had no time to uncoil his rope before the gray was past. Milton wheeled, pursuing at a full gallop out the canyon and onto the *bajada*. Twig-matted tail streaming behind, the mustang was outrunning him, and Milton had one chance with the rope. He dropped the loop around the gray's neck, jarring the animal to its haunches. It was so long ago. Today, Milton reflected, the headlong chase would have pinned him and the horse to Oldenburg's barbed-wire fence.

The sycamore held its place, older and larger. Though encountering no horses, Milton returned three stray cattle to Oldenburg's ranch. For a month, while the slightest jolt could rupture the wound, he hunted down mavericks in the miles of ravine, painted the ranch buildings, and repaired the roofs, one-handed. Even as the finger healed, the missing segment unbalanced his grip. Swinging the pick or ax, shoveling, he would clench his right hand so tightly the entire arm would tremble. By the second month a new hand had evolved, with the musculature of the other fingers, the palm, and the wrist more pronounced. The pinky stub acted as a stabilizer against pickshaft or rope. Milton had rebuilt the fence and combed the granite mountain, rounding up another two dozen head. Oldenburg's herd had increased to 120.

In late August Milton rode beyond the granite range to the Ka kai Mountains, a low, twisted ridge of volcanic rock that he had avoided because he once saw the Devil there. Needing to piss, he had stumbled away from a beer party and followed a trail rising between the boulders. Watching the ground for snakes, Milton had almost collided with a man standing in the path. The stranger was a very big, ugly Indian, but Milton knew it was the Devil because his eyes were black, not human, and he spoke in a booming voice that rolled echoes off the cliffs. Milton shuddered uncontrollably and shriveled to the size of a spider. Afterwards he found he had fallen and cut himself. Cholla segments were embedded in his leg. The Devil had said only: "Beware of Satan within you."

The meeting enhanced Milton's prestige, and Allen was impressed, though not C.C. "You see?" she said. "What did I always tell you?"

In daylight the mountains looked like no more than a pile of cinders. Milton chose an arroyo that cut through the scorched black rubble into red slabs, canyon walls which rose over Milton's head, then above the mesquite. Chasing a calf until it disappeared in a side draw, Milton left the animal for later. The canyon twisted deeper into the mountains, the red cliffs now 300 feet high. The polished rock glowed. Milton was twelve years old, and his brothers were fighting.

"You took my car," Steven said.

"So what," Lee said. Milton's favorite brother, he was slim and handsome, with small ears and thick, glossy hair that fell almost into his eyes. Weekends he took Milton into Phoenix to play pool and pinball, sometimes to the shopping mall for Cokes. He always had girls, even Mexicans and whites.

"I told you if you took my car I was going to kill you." Steven always said crazy things. At breakfast, if Milton didn't pass him the milk right away – "How'd you like this knife in your eye?" About their mother – "Bitch wouldn't give me a dime. I'm going to shit on her bed." He wore a white rag around his head and hung out with gangs. Now they would call him a cholo.

"So what," Lee said. "Kill me." Cocking his leg, he wiped the dusty boot heel carefully against the couch. Milton was sitting on the couch.

Steven ran down the hall and came back with a .22. He pointed it at Lee's head, there was a shocking noise, a red spot appeared in Lee's forehead, and he collapsed on the rug.

"Oh my GOD," Steven said. Fingers clawed against his temples, he rushed out the door. Milton snatched the gun and chased him, firing on the run. Steven, bigger and faster, out-distanced him in the desert. Milton didn't come home for three days. Steven wasn't prosecuted and he moved to Denver. If he returned, Milton would kill him, even twenty years later.

Milton's horse ambled down the white sand, the dry bed curving around a red outcropping. Trapped by the canyon walls, the late summer air was hot and close. The weight of Milton's family fell on his back like a landslide – his father, driving home drunk from Casa Grande, slewing across the divider, head-on into another pickup. The four children had flown like crickets from the back, landing unhurt in the dirt bank. The driver of the other truck died, and Milton's mother lost the shape of her face.

Milton felt himself turning to water. He circled his horse, routed the calf from the slit in the wall, and drove it miles to the ranch. At dinner he told Oldenburg he needed a trip to town.

"You'll lose your job," Oldenburg said.

Milton ate with his water fingers, spilling food and the orange juice that Oldenburg always served. "The lives of *o'otham* is a soap opera," he cried, trying to dispel his shame by insulting himself. "I love my boy, okay? But it's him who has to hold me when I go for C.C. He doesn't hold me with his strength. He holds me because I see him, and I stop. Sometimes I don't stop."

Oldenburg served Milton cake for dessert and told him to take the next day off, if he wanted.

The following morning Milton lay on his bed, sweating. In his mind were no thought or images save the swirls of chill, unpleasant water that washed over him. He could transform the water, making it a cold lake that pumped his heart loudly and shrank his genitals, or a clear stream immersing him in swift currents and veins of sunlight, but he could not change the water into thoughts. The green carpeting and blue-striped drapes in his room sickened him. He could have finished a pint of vodka before he knew he was drinking.

He could not imagine losing his work.

Abruptly Milton rose. In the corral he fitted a rope bridle over the horse's head. As he rode past Oldenburg, the man looked up from a bench of tack he was fussing with, then quickly lowered his head.

"I'm going to the mountains," Milton said.

He let the horse carry him into the charred crust of the canyon. The scarlet walls rose high and sheer, closing off the black peaks beyond. Tethering the horse to a mesquite, Milton sat in the sand. The cliffs seemed almost to meet above him. Heat gathered over his head and forced down on him. A lizard skittered by his ear, up the wall. A tortoise lumbered across the wash. The water rippling through Milton became a shimmering on the far wall, scenes of his life. Milton racing after Steven, aiming at the zigzagging blue shirt, the crack of the gun, a palo verde trunk catching the rifle barrel and spinning Milton to his knees. His father's empty boots beside the couch, where he slept. His mother in baggy gray slacks, growing fatter. C.C.'s head snapping back from Milton's open palm. The pictures flickered over the cliff. Milton sat while shadow climbed the rock, and a cool breeze funneled through the canyon, and night fell. Scooping a hole in the sand, Milton lay face to the stone while the canyon rustled and sighed. The wind rushed around a stone spur, scattering sand grains on his face. Several times in the night footsteps passed so near that the ground yielded beneath Milton's head. Huddled, shivering, he thought his heart had stopped and fell asleep from terror. He dreamed of the cliffs, an unbroken glassy red.

Early in the morning, Milton woke and stretched, refreshed by the cool air. The only prints beside him were his own. That evening he wrote to C.C. in care of her California aunt, telling her he'd quit drinking.

When C.C. didn't respond, Milton wrote again asking at least for word of Allen, who would have entered high school. C.C. replied, "When I got here the doctor said I had a broken nose. Allen says he has no father."

Milton knew he must hide to avoid drinking. When he asked Oldenburg's permission to spend a day in the granite mountains, Oldenburg said he would go, too. They camped against a rock turret. The light in the sky faded and the fire leaped up. In the weeks since the former hand Jenkins's death, Oldenburg had become, if possible, more silent. Milton, meanwhile, admitted he had been a "chatterbox," recalling high school field trips to Phoenix fifteen years before, and rodeos in Tucson, Prescott, Sells, and White River. Oldenburg, fingertips joined at his chin, occasionally nodded or smiled. Tonight Milton squatted, arms around his knees, staring into the fire. About to share his most insistent emotions with Oldenburg, Milton felt a giddy excitement, as if he were showing himself naked to a woman for the first time. Intimacy with a white man evoked stepping off the school bus in Phoenix, where buildings like great stone crystals, blanketed in dreamy snow, spilled thousands of white people into the street.

Milton told Oldenburg what C.C. had said.

"Your drinking has scarred them like acid. It will be time before they heal," Oldenburg said.

"There shouldn't be *o'otham* families," Milton exclaimed. "We should stop having children."

Oldenburg shook his head. After a while he said, "Milton, I hope you're not bitter because I won't let you drink. Drawing the line helps you. It's not easy living right. I've tried all my life and gained nothing – I lost both my sons in war and my wife divorced me to marry a piece of human trash. And still, in my own poor way, I try to live right." Oldenburg relaxed his shoulders and settled on his haunches.

Milton laid another mesquite limb across the fire. As the black of the sky intensified, the stars appeared as a glinting powder. Milton sipped two cups of coffee against the chill. Oldenburg, firelight sparkling off his silver tooth, wool cap pulled low over his stretched face, looked like an old grand-mother. Laughing, Milton told him so. Oldenburg laughed too rocking on his heels.

Soon after Oldenburg went to bed, Milton's mood changed. He hated the embers of the fire, the wind sweeping the rock knoll, the whirring of bats. He hated each stone and twig littering the campsite. His own fingers, spread across his knees, were like dumb, sleeping snakes. Poisonous things. He was glad one of them had been chopped off. Unrolling his blanket, he lay on his back, fists clenched. He dug his hands and heels into the ground as if staked to it. After lying stiffly, eyes open, for an hour, he got up, slung his coiled rope over his shoulder, and walked down the hillside.

Brush and cactus were lit by a rising moon. Reaching a sheer drop, Milton jammed boot toes into rock fissures, seized tufts of saltbush, to let himself down. In the stream bed he walked quickly until he joined the main river course. After a few miles' meandering through arroyos and over ridges, he arrived at the big sycamore and went to sleep.

Waking before dawn, Milton padded along the wash, hug-ging the granite. The cold morning silence was audible, a high, pure ringing. Milton heard the horse's snort before he saw it tearing clumps of grass from the gully bank, head tossing, lips drawn back over its yellow teeth. Rope at his hip, Milton stalked from boulder to boulder. When he stepped forward, whirling the lariat once, the horse reared, but quieted instantly as the noose tightened around its neck. Milton tugged the rope; the animal neighed and skipped backward, but followed.

During the next two days, Milton and Oldenburg captured three more spindly, wiry horses. Oldenburg would flush the mustangs toward Milton, who missed only once with the lasso.

The stallions Milton kept in separate pens and later sold as rodeo broncs. Within a couple of weeks he had broken the mares.

Milton consumed himself in chores. Though the Box-J was a small ranch, labor was unremitting. In the fall, summer calves were rounded up and "worked" – branded with the Box-J, castrated, and dehorned. The previous winter's calves, now some 400–500 pounds each, were held in side pens for weighing and loading onto the packer's shipping trucks. The pens were so dilapidated that Milton tore them down and built new ones. Winter, Milton drove daily pickup loads of sorghum hay, a supplement for the withered winter grasses, to drop spots at the water holes. Oldenburg hired extra help for the spring roundup, working the new winter calves. Summer, Milton roved on horseback, troubleshooting. The fence line would need repair. Oldenburg taught Milton to recognize cancer eye, which could destroy a cow's market value. A low water tank meant Oldenburg must overhaul the windmill. Throughout the year Milton inspected the herd, groomed the horses, maintained the buildings, kept tools and equipment in working order.

Certain moments, standing high in the stirrups, surveying the herd and the land which stretched from horizon to horizon as if mirroring the sky, Milton could believe all belonged to him.

Every two weeks, when Oldenburg drove into Casa Grande for supplies, Milton deposited half his wages – his first savings account – and mailed the rest to C.C. These checks were like money thrown blindly over the shoulder. So thoroughly had Milton driven his family from his mind that he couldn't summon them back, even if he wished to. When, just before sleep, spent from the day's work, he glimpsed C.C. and Allen, the faces seemed unreal. They were like people he had met and loved profoundly one night at a party, then forgotten.

The night of the first November frost, soon after the wild-horse roundup, Oldenburg had asked Milton if he played cards. Milton didn't.

"Too bad," Oldenburg said. "It gets dull evenings. Jenkins and I played gin rummy. We'd go to 5,000, take us a couple of weeks, and then start again."

"We could cook," Milton said.

On Sunday he and Oldenburg baked cakes. Milton missed the pressurized frosting cans with which he'd squirted flowers and desert scenes at the CETA bakery, but Oldenburg's cherry-chocolate layer cake was so good he ate a third of it. Oldenburg complimented him on his angel food.

Oldenburg bought a paperback *Joy of Cooking* in Casa Grande. Though he and Milton had been satisfied with their main dishes, they tried Carbonnade Flamande, Chicken Paprika, Quick Spaghetti Meat Pie. Milton liked New England Boiled Dinner. Mostly they made desserts. After experimenting with mousses and custard, they settled on cakes – banana, golden, seed, sponge, four-egg, Lady Baltimore, the Rombauer Special. Stacks of foil-wrapped cakes accumulated in the freezer. The men contributed cakes to charitable bake sales. Milton found that after his nightly slab of cake sleep came more easily and gently.

The men were serious in the kitchen. Standing side by side in white aprons tacked together from sheets, Milton whisking egg whites, Oldenburg drizzling chocolate over pound cake, they would say little. Milton might ask the whereabouts of a spice; Oldenburg's refusal to label the jars irritated him. Then they sat by the warm stove, feet propped on crates, and steamed themselves in the moist smells.

As they relaxed on a Sunday afternoon, eating fresh, hot cake, Oldenburg startled Milton by wondering aloud if his own wife were still alive. She had left him in 1963, and they'd had no contact since their second son was killed in 1969, more than ten years before.

"She wanted a Nevada divorce," Oldenburg said, "but I served papers on her first, and I got custody of the boys. I prevented a great injustice." He had sold his business in Colorado and bought the ranch. "The boys hated it," he said. "They couldn't wait to join the Army."

In Hashan, Milton said, she and her lover would have been killed.

Oldenburg shook his head impatiently. "He's deserted her, certainly. He was a basketball coach and much younger than she was."

A Pima phrase – he knew little Pima – occurred to Milton. *Ne ha: jun* – all my relations. "Here is the opposite," Milton said. "We should call this the No Relations Ranch."

Oldenburg sputtered with laughter. "Yes! And we'd need a new brand. Little round faces with big X's over them."

"You'd better be careful. People would start calling it the Tick-tack-toe Ranch."

"Or a manual, you know, a sex manual, for fornication. The X's doing it to the O's."

Lightheaded from the rich, heavily frosted cake, they sprayed crumbs from their mouths, laughing.

At the Pinal Country Fair in May, Oldenburg entered a walnut pie and goaded Milton into baking his specialty, a jelly roll. It received honorable mention, while Oldenburg won second prize.

Milton wrote C.C., "I'm better than a restaurant."

C.C. didn't answer. When Valley Bank opened a Hashan branch in June, Milton transferred his account and began meeting his friends for the first time in a year. They needled him, "Milton, you sleeping with that old man?" His second Friday in town, Milton was writing out a deposit slip when he heard Bosque say, "Milton Oldenburg."

"Yes, Daddy just gave him his allowance," said Helene Mashad, the teller.

Bosque punched him on the shoulder and put out his hand. Milton shook it, self-conscious about his missing finger.

Bosque was cashing his unemployment check. The factory where he'd manufactured plastic tote bags for the past six months had closed. "Doesn't matter," Bosque said. "I'm living good." Before leaving, he said to come on by.

"You know what Oldenburg's doing, don't you?" Helene said, smoothing the wrinkles from Milton's check. She still wore her long, lavender Phoenix nails and a frothy perm. After years in Phoenix, she'd relocated at the new branch, closer to her home in Black Butte. "Oldenburg wants to marry you. Then he'll get some kind of government project money for his Indian wife. Or he'll adopt you. Same deal."

"It's not me who's the wife or child, I run that place."
Nervous speaking to a woman again, Milton rambled, boasting
of his authority over hired crews, what Oldenburg called his
"quick mind and fast hands" cutting calves or constructing a
corner brace, his skill with new tools. Even his baking. "He has
to be the wife," Milton said. "He's a better cook." Milton leaned
his hip against the counter. "Older woman. He's so old he turned
white. And he lost his shape." Milton's hands made breasts.
"Nothing left."

They both laughed. Elated by the success of his joke, Milton
asked her to dinner. Helene said yes, pick her up at six.

Milton was uneasy in Hashan. The dusty buildings – adobes,
sandwich houses of mud and board, slump-block tract homes –
seemed part of the unreal life that included his family. To kill
time, he rode to the trading post in Black Butte, a few miles in
the direction of Oldenburg's ranch, and read magazines. When
he arrived at the bank, Helene slapped her forehead: she hadn't
known he was on horseback. Phew, she said, she didn't want to
go out with a horse. Milton should follow her home and take a
bath first.

They never left her house. She was eager for him, and Milton
realized that as a man he'd been dead for a year. They made love
until early morning. Milton lay propped against the headboard,
his arm encircling her, her cheek resting on his chest. She briskly
stroked his hand.

"Your poor finger," she said. "I hear Lopez has little circles
in his shoulders like where worms have gone into a tomato."

"It was bad," Milton said, closing his hand.

"I can't stand the men in this town, the drunken pigs,"
Helene said. "I don't know why I came back."

Helene wasn't what Milton wanted, but he liked her well
enough to visit once or twice a month. Because she lived outside
Hashan, few people knew of the affair. They would eat dinner
and see a movie in Casa Grande or Phoenix, and go to bed.
Sometimes they simply watched TV in bed, or drove Helene's
Toyota through the desert, for miles without seeing another
light.

★

When Milton returned from his second weekend with Helene, Oldenburg was peevish. "You drink with that woman?" he said. "You going to send her picture to your wife?" Emergencies arose that kept Milton on the ranch weekends. After selling two wild colts to a stable, Milton took Helene to Phoenix overnight. Oldenburg berated him, "The cows don't calve on Saturday and Sunday? They don't get sick? A shed doesn't blow down on Sunday?" Still the men baked together. At the beginning of the school year they entered a fund-raising bake-off sponsored by the PTO. Oldenburg won first with a Boston cream pie, and Milton's apple ring took second.

Helene transferred to Casa Grande, and Milton brought his account with her, relieved to avoid Hashan. Conversations with his friends were strained and dead. He worked; they didn't. They drank; he didn't. They had families. Milton nodded when he saw them but no longer stopped to talk.

Fridays after Helene punched out, they might browse in the Casa Grande shopping center. Milton was drawn to the camera displays, neat lumps of technology embedded in towers of colorful film boxes. The Lerners Shop manikins fascinated him – bony stick figures like the bleached branches of felled cotton-wood, a beautiful still arrangement. "Imagine Pimas in those," Helene said, pointing to the squares and triangles of glittering cloth. She puffed out her cheeks and spread her arms. Milton squeezed her small buttocks. Helene's legs were the slimmest of any o'otham woman he'd known.

During the second week of October, when Milton and a hired crew had set up shipping pens and begun culling the calves, a rare fall downpour, tail end of a Gulf hurricane, struck. For six hours thunder exploded and snarls of lightning webbed the sky. The deluge turned the ground to slop, sprang leaks in the roof, and washed out the floodgates at the edge of the granite moun-tains. Cattle stampeded through the openings; one died, en-tangled in the barbed wire. When the skies cleared, Oldenburg estimated that a quarter of the cash animals, some 300 dollars apiece, had escaped. The shipping trucks were due in two days.

The next morning, a new hired man brought further news: over the weekend, a fight had broken out at the Sundowner. The fat end of a pool cue had caught Audrey Lopez across the throat, crushing her windpipe. Her funeral was to be at two in the afternoon.

Milton stood helplessly before Oldenburg. In the aftermath of the storm, the sky was piercingly blue, and a bracing wind stung his cheeks. Oldenburg's collar fluttered.

"You have to go," Oldenburg said. "There's no question."

"You'll lose too much money," Milton said stubbornly. "The cattle are in the mountains and I know every little canyon where they run."

"There's no question," Oldenburg repeated. "The right way is always plain, though we do our best to obscure it."

The service took place in a small, white, Spanish-style church. At the cemetery the mourners stood bareheaded, the sun glinting off their hair. The cemetery was on a knoll, and in the broad afternoon light the surrounding plains, spotted by occasional cloud shadow, seemed immensely distant, like valleys at the foot of a solitary butte. Milton imagined the people at the tip of a rock spire miles in the clouds. The overcast dimmed them, and shreds of cumulus drifted past their backs and bowed heads.

Afterwards the men adjourned to the Lopez House, where Vigiliano Lopez rushed about the living room, flinging chairs aside to clear a center space. A ring of some twenty men sat on chairs or against the wall. Bosque arrived carrying three cold cases and two quarts of Crown Russe. More bottles appeared. Lopez started one Crown Russe in each direction and stalked back and forth from the kitchen, delivering beer and slapping bags of potato chips at the men's feet.

At his turn, Milton passed the bottle along.

"Drink, you goddamn Milton Oldenburg," Lopez said.

Milton said, "I'll lose my job."

"So?" Lopez shrugged distractedly. "I haven't had a job in a year. I don't need a job." Lopez had been the only Pima miner at the nearby Loma Linda pit until Anaconda shut it down. He pushed his hair repeatedly off his forehead, as if trying to remember something, then turned up the radio.

Milton sat erect in the chair, hands planted on his knees. He gobbled the potato chips. No one avoided him, nor he anyone else, yet talk was impossible. Grief surged through the party like a wave. Milton felt it in over-loud conversation, silences, the restlessness – no one able to stay in one place for long. Laughter came in fits. Over the radio, the wailing tremolos of the Mexican ballads were oppressive and nerve-racking. The power of feeling in the room moved Milton and frightened him, but he was outside it.

Joining the others would be as simple as claiming the vodka bottle on its next round, Milton knew. But he remembered standing tall in the stirrups, as if he could see over the edge of the yellow horizon, the end of Oldenburg's land, and he kept his hands spread on his knees. At the thought of vodka's sickly tastelessness, bile rose in his throat. Pretending to drink, tipping the bottle and plugging it with his tongue, would be foolish and shameful. Out of friendship and respect for Lopez, he could not leave. Their wounding each other, Milton realized, had bound him more closely to Lopez.

As night fell the men became drunker and louder. Bosque went out for more liquor. When he returned, he danced with the oil-drum cookstove, blackening his hands and shirt.

"Hey, not with my wife," Lopez said, grabbing the drum and humping it against the wall. "Need somebody to do you right, baby," he said. The drum clanged to the floor. The men cheered. Lopez, knees bent and hands outstretched as if waiting for something to drop into them, lurched to the middle of the room. A smile was glazed over his face. He saw Milton.

"Drink with me, you son of a bitch," he shouted.

Milton motioned for the Crown Russe, a third full. "Half for you, half for me," he said. Marking a spot on the label with his finger, Milton took two long swallows and held out the bottle for Lopez. Lopez drank and flipped the empty bottle over his shoulder. Side by side, arms around each other, Milton and Lopez danced the *cumbia*. Lopez's weight sagged until Milton practically carried him. The man's trailing feet hooked an extension cord, sending a lamp and the radio crashing to the floor. Lopez collapsed.

Milton ran outside and retched. Immediately he was

refreshed and lucid. The stars burned like drill-points of light. Patting the horse into an easy walk, Milton sat back in the saddle, reins loose in his lap, and gave himself to the brilliant stillness. As his eyes adjusted to the night, he could distinguish the black silhouettes of mountains against the lesser dark of the sky. Faint stars emerged over the ranges, bringing the peaks closer. The mountains were calm and friendly, even the jagged line of the Ka kai.

That night Milton dreamed that a chocolate-colored flood swept through Hashan. The *o'otham* bobbed on the foam; from the shore others drove backward into the torrent, arms raised symmetrically by their heads. Receding, the flood left bodies swollen in the mud – Milton's brother Lee, their mother, belly down, rising in a mound. Milton, long hair fixed in the mud, stared upward. His hands were so full of fingers they had become agaves, clusters of fleshy, spiny leaves. Peering down at him, C.C. and Allen were black against the sun, arms crooked as if for flight. Milton was glad they had escaped.

Milton woke serene and energetic, the dream forgotten. Over breakfast Oldenburg studied him intently – clear gray eyes, a slight frown – but said nothing. The penned calves were weighed and loaded onto the shipping trucks. Many remained free, and the year would be a loss.

Milton wrote C.C. of Audrey Lopez's death. "I had a big drink to keep Lopez company," he added, "but I threw it up. It was the first booze in more than a year. I don't like it anymore."

Lying beside Milton the following weekend, Helene said, "Poor finger. I'll give you another one." She laid her pinky against the stub so a new finger seemed to grow. Her lavender nail looked like the fancy gem of a ring. She lifted, lowered the finger. "And Lopez with the purple spots on his shoulder like the eyes of a potato," she said. She shifted, and her small, hard nipple brushed Milton's side. "It's a wonder you two didn't fight."

"Shut up," Milton said. "His wife is dead."

"I know. It's terrible." She had worried for him, Helene said, knowing he would be at the funeral with Lopez. He should have brought her.

"I didn't want you there," Milton said. "You don't have the

right feelings." He left before dawn and hadn't returned to
Helene when C.C. replied.

"I was shocked to hear about Audrey," C.C. wrote. "I feel
sad about it every day. Hashan is such a bad place. But it isn't
any better here. At Allen's school there are gangs and not just
Mexicans but black and white too."

She wrote again: "I miss you. I've been thinking about
coming back. Allen says he won't but he'll come with me in the
end. The money has helped. Thank you."

Milton threw up his arms and danced on the corral dirt, still
moist and reddened from fluke autumn rains. Shouting, he
danced on one leg and the other, dipping from side to side as if
soaring, his head whirling. Oldenburg's nagging – where will
they live? – worried him little. Over dinner Oldenburg suggested, "They'll live in your old place, and you can visit them on
weekends. We'll have to move our baking to the middle of the
week."

Milton knew he must be with the *o'otham*. Announcing a
ride into the mountains, he saddled up and galloped toward
Hashan. Because he couldn't see the faces of his family his joy
felt weirdly rootless. The past year he had killed them inside.
The sudden aches for Allen, the sensation of carrying C.C.'s
weight in his arms from the adobe to the ranch house, were like
the twinges of heat, cold and pain from his missing finger. As if
straining after their elusive faces, Milton rode faster. His straw
hat, blown back and held by its cord, flapped at his ear. The
horse's neck was soaked with sweat.

Bosque's fat wife said he wasn't home. Milton made a plan
for the Sundowner: after one draft for sociability, he would play
the shuffleboard game. Tying up at a light pole, Milton hesitated
in the lounge doorway. The familiarity of the raw wood beams
crisscrossing the bare Sheetrock walls frightened him. But
Bosque, sliding his rear off a barstool, called, "Milton
Oldenburg."

"C.C's hauling her little tail home," Milton announced,
"And the boy."

"All *riiight*." Bosque pumped his hand up and down. Milton's
embarrassment at his missing finger disappeared in the vastness

of Bosque's grip. Friends he hadn't spoken to in months surrounded him. "When's she coming? They going to live on the
ranch? Oldenburg will have a whole Indian family now."
Warmed by their celebration of his good luck, Milton ordered
pitchers. His glass of draft was deep gold and sweeter than he
had remembered, though flat. Others treated him in return.
Someone told a story of Bosque building a scrap wood raft to
sail the shallow lake left by the rains. Halfway across, the raft
had broken apart and sunk. "Bosque was all mud up to his eyes,"
the storyteller said. "He looked like a bull rolling in cow flop."
Everyone laughed.

Fuzzy after a half-dozen beers, Milton felt his heart pound,
and his blood. He saw them then – C.C., wings of hair, white
teeth, dimpled round cheeks. Allen's straight bangs and small,
unsmiling mouth. Their eyes were black with ripples of light,
reflections on a pool. Milton was drawn into that pool, lost.
Terror washed over him like a cold liquid, and he ordered a
vodka.

"I'm drunk," he told the neighbor on his right.

"Could be. Let's check that out, Milton," the man said.

"I never worked."

"No way," the man said, shaking his head.

"I didn't make a living for them."

"Not even a little bitty bit," the man agreed.

"Not even this much," Milton said, holding his thumb and
forefinger almost closed, momentarily diverted by the game. "I
hurt them."

Holding up his hands, the man yelled, "Not me."

"I tortured them. They don't belong to me. I don't have a
family," Milton mumbled. Quickly he drank three double
vodkas. The jukebox streamed colors, and he floated on its
garbled music.

Shoving against the men's room door, Milton splashed into
the urinal, wavering against the stall. He groped for the sundowner's rear exit. The cold bit through his jacket. Milton
pitched against a stack of bricks.

Waking in the dark, Milton jumped to his feet. C.C. was
coming, and his job was in danger. He was foreman of a white

man's ranch. Allen and C.C. would be amazed at his spread. With a bigger bank account than three-quarters of Hashan, Milton could support them for a year on savings alone. The night before was an ugly blur. But his tongue was bitter, his head thudded, he had the shakes. Cursing, Milton mounted and kicked the horse into a canter. To deceive Oldenburg he must work like a crazy man and sweat out his hangover. The fits of nausea made him moan with frustration. He kicked the horse and struck his own head.

Milton arrived an hour after sunup. Shooing the horse into the corral with a smack to the rump, he stood foggily at the gate, unable to remember his chore from the previous day. A ladder leaning against the barn reminded him: patching. He lugged a roll of asphalt roofing up the ladder. Scrambling over the steep pitch didn't frighten him, even when he slipped and tore his hands. He smeared tar, pressed the material into place, drove the nails. Every stroke was true, two per nail. Milton had laid half a new roof when Oldenburg called him.

"Come down." Oldenburg was pointing to the corral. The gate was still ajar. Milton's horse, head drooping, dozed against the wall, but the other three were gone.

Milton stood before him, wobbly from exertion, blood draining from his head.

"You lied," Oldenburg said. "You abandoned your job. The week is *my* time. You've been drunk. I'm going to have to let you go, Milton."

Milton couldn't speak.

"You understand, don't you?" Oldenburg said more rapidly. His eyes flicked down, back to Milton. "Do you see what happens?" His arms extended toward the empty corral.

"So I lose a day running them down."

Smiling slightly, Oldenburg shook his head. "You miss the point. It would be wrong for me to break my word. You'd have no cause to believe me again and our agreement would be meaningless."

"Once a year I get drunk," Milton burst out. "We'll put a name on it, November Something Milton's Holiday."

Oldenburg smiled again. "Once a month . . . once a week

. . . I'm sorry. I'll give you two weeks' pay but you can leave any time." He turned.

"I've worked hard for you!" Milton's throat felt as if it were closing up.

Oldenburg stopped, brow furrowed. "It's sad," he said. "You've managed the Box-J better than I could. I'm going to miss our baking." He paused. "But we have to go on, Milton, don't you see? My family leaves me, Jenkins leaves me, you leave me. But *I* go on." He walked away.

Two long steps, a knee in the back, arms around the neck, and he could break the man in half – Milton's arms dropped. He had lost his urge for violence. Long after Oldenburg had disappeared into the open green range where the horses were, Milton stood by the corral. Then, arms over his head as if escaping a cloudburst, he ran into the adobe, packed his belongings in a sheet, and that afternoon rode the exhausted horse back to his old home.

To C.C. Milton wrote, "I don't have my job anymore but there's plenty of money in the bank." Weeks later she replied, "Milton, I know what's going on. I can't come home to this." But she would continue to write him, she said. Milton saw no one. Pacing the house, he talked to the portraits over the TV – Allen's eighth-grade class picture, a computer-drawn black-dot composition of C.C. from the O'otham Tash carnival. He disturbed nothing, not even the year-and-a-half-old pile of dishes in the sink.

For several weeks he laid fence for a Highway Maintenance heavy equipment yard. Working with a new type of fence, chain link topped with barbed wire, cheered him. The foreman was lax, married to one of Milton's cousins, so when Milton requested the leftover spools of barbed wire, he said, "Sure. It's paid for."

Milton dug holes around his house and cut posts from the warped, gnarled mesquite growing in the vacant land. As he worked, the blue sky poured through chinks in the posts, reminding Milton pleasantly of the timeless first days repairing the line at Oldenburg's range. When he had finished stringing the wire, Milton's house was enclosed in a neat box – two thorned strands, glinting silver. Sunlight jumped off the metal in zigzag bolts. In Hashan, where fences were unknown and the beige ground was broken only by houses, cactus, and drab shrubs, the effect was as startling as if Milton had wrapped his home in Christmas lights.

Milton sat on the back doorstep, drinking beer. Discouraged by the fence, no one visited at first. But dogs still ran through the yard, as did children, who preferred scaling the fence to slithering under it. Their legs waggled precariously on the stiffly swaying wire; then they hopped down, dashed to the opposite side, and climbed out, awkward as spiders. Milton's fence became a community joke, which made him popular. Instead of walking through the gap behind the house, friends would crawl between the strands or try to vault them. Or they would lean on the posts, passing a beer back and forth while they chatted.

Keeping her promise, C.C. wrote that Allen had shot up tall. Even running track he wore his Walkman, she said. But he smoked, and she had to yell at him. Last term he'd made nearly all A's.

Milton grew extremely fat, seldom leaving the house except to shop or work the odd jobs his new skills brought him. Through spring and summer he drowsed on the doorstep. In November, almost a year after he'd left Oldenburg's, he fell asleep on the concrete slab and spent the night without jacket or blanket. The next day he was very sick, and Bosque and Lopez drove him to the hospital. The doctor said he had pneumonia.

Milton's first day in ICU, Bosque and Lopez shot craps with him during visiting hours. But as Milton's lungs continued to fill with fluids, his heart, invaded by fatty tissues from his years of drinking, weakened. Four days after entering the hospital, he suffered a heart attack.

In the coronary ward, restricted to ten-minute visits, Milton dreamed, feeling as if the fluids had leaked into his skull and his brain was sodden. In one dream the agaves again sprouted from his wrists, their stalks reaching into the sky. Milton gave the name *ne ha: jun* – all my relations – to his agave hands.

The next morning C.C. and Allen appeared in the doorway. Huge, billowing, formless as smoke, they approached the bed in a peculiar rolling motion. Milton was afraid. From the dreams he realized his deepest love was drawn from a great lake far beneath him, and that lake was death. But understanding, he lost his fear. He held out his arms to them.

JAMES ALAN McPHERSEN

☆　☆　☆　☆

# *The Story of a Dead Man*

It is not true that Billy Renfro was killed during that trouble in
Houston. The man is an accomplished liar and likes to keep his
enemies nervous. It was he who spread this madness. The truth
of what happened, he told me in Chicago, was this: After
tracking the debtor to a rented room, Billy Renfro's common
sense was overwhelmed by the romantic aspects of the adventure.
That was why he kicked open the door, charged boldly into the
room, and shouted, "Monroe Ellis, give *up* Mr. Floyd's Cadillac
that you done miss nine payments on!" Unhappily for Billy,
neither Monroe Ellis nor the woman with him was in the giving-
up mood. The woman fired first, aiming from underneath Ellis
on the bed. Contrary to most reports, that bullet only wounded
Billy's arm. It was one of the subsequent blasts from Monroe's
.38 that entered Billy's side. But this wound did not slow Billy's
retreat from the room, the rooming house, or the city of
Houston. He was alive and fully recovered when I saw him in
Chicago, on his way back from Harvey after reclaiming a
defaulted Chevy.

　　Neither is it true, as certain of his enemies have maintained,
that Billy's left eye was lost during a rumble with that red-neck
storekeep outside Limehouse, South Carolina. That eye, I now
have reason to believe, was lost during domestic troubles. That
is quite another story. But I have his full account of the
Limehouse difficulty: Billy had stopped off there en route to
Charleston to repossess another defaulting car for this same Mr.
Floyd Dillingham. He entered the general store with the sole
intention of buying a big orange soda. However, the owner of
the joint, a die-hard white supremacist, refused to execute the
transaction. Being naturally suspicious of governmental intervention, Billy fell back on his own resources: He reached for the .22

he carried under his shirt for just such dalliances. But the storekeep was too swift. While Billy's right hand was still moving cloth, the red-neck was caressing the trigger of his Springfield and looking joyous. "Private club, *Mr.* Nigger!" the red-neck sang. Though he is a liar and a madman, my cousin Billy Renfro is no fool. He allowed himself to be two-stepped and back-backed out of the place, the storekeep, of course, making all the leading moves. As Billy sped off, the red-neck fired several rounds into the air and gave a hungry rebel yell. Billy did not respond.

On his return from Charleston, however, the defaulted car reclaimed, he experienced an overpowering thirst for a big orange soda. This thirst became obsessive as he neared Limehouse. It was a hot, sleepy day, nearing sunset, and his arrival at the general store went unnoticed. Billy was at the counter blowing gently on his .22 before the storekeep could resurface from the reveries he enjoyed, dozing in his wicker rocking chair. "*Two* big orange sodas and a dill pickle!" my cousin ordered. Liar that he is, he told me in Chicago that he belched nonchalantly before departing from the store. I do not believe this, but I believe him when he said he shot off five rounds, and gave a swamp cry, when he was in his car and pointed toward Atlanta. Ah, Billy! It is part of his style to add such touches.

I bother to refute these rumors because the man is my cousin, and I am honor-bound to love him as I know he really is. He and I are one with the same ancestors, and whatever fires rage in him I must look to find smolderings of within myself. Recognizing this obligation, I here attempt to deflate mean rumors circulated by his enemies, cut through the fat of Billy's own lies, and lay bare the muscle of his life. From youth onward, he has possessed a warm heart and a certain tolerance of misfortune; and he is as likely, for a friend, to strip the shirt from his own back as he is to murder. That he contains such broad extremes speaks favorably of his eventual reform.

I myself have contributed considerable energy toward this goal. In Chicago, when we drank together in that dive on Halstead, I offered my best advice for whatever it was worth to him. "We are no longer young men," I said. "The foam has settled down into the beer. I, myself, no longer chase women, speak hotly, challenge opinions too far different from my own. I have learned it is to my advantage to get along. Chelseia, the woman I plan to marry, you will meet in a few hours. She is steady and refined, and will bear me sturdy children. In short, Billy, in my manhood I have become aware of complexity. You owe it to the family, and to the memory of your mother, to do the same."

Billy swished his Scotch and drank it down, then rapped the glass on the table to alert the barmaid. When she looked, he pointed two fingers downward toward our glasses and kissed at her. Then, turning to focus his single, red-rimmed eye on my face, he said, "Bullshit!"

He was dressed in the black gabardine suit of an undertaker. Dried purple-black blood streaked his coat sleeves, his black string tie, and the collars of the dirty white shirt he wore.

"People change, Billy," I said.

"Bullshit!" Billy Renfro said.

I looked closely at him and saw a gangster. He was not the kind of man I wanted to meet my family. I glanced at my watch and sipped my drink. I listened to his stories.

Billy spun his usual lies.

This meeting in Chicago took place three years after he began work for this Mr. Dillingham, seven years after his mother's death, and thirteen years after Billy, at seventeen, went to prison for life. But I will speak here of his life before he went to prison, for insights into what he might have become. His mother was my father's sister, and both gave their first-born males the same treasured family name. Both my cousin and I were named "William" after our paternal grandfather, Willie Joe Warner, a jackleg Baptist preacher. But because her child was somewhat older, Billy's mother claimed for him the more affectionate nickname "Billy." I will not speak here of the grandfather in whose shadow we both lived, but I have heard it mentioned in the family that he favored, in his old age, the name "William" over the more secular "Billy." I would not swear to this, however, because my father winked when he told it to me. And

Billy's mother, whom we nicknamed "Mama Love," laughed loudly when I asked her confirmation. I accepted my name. Billy gloried in his, draining from it as much territory as the world would concede.

He outgrew me from the start, perhaps because his father succumbed to alcohol before Billy was ten. And his mother, soon afterward made invalid by a stroke, let her son roam freely. Evenings at his house, playing in his room, Billy taught me the dozens, chanted bawdy songs, drilled me on how to eyeball a girl with maximum style. I followed as much of his advice, given the stricter circumstances of my home, as was discreet. I loved him, but I loved his mother more. Billy loved only the streets. And since Mama Love could not contain his wanderings, she gave up finally and developed a defensive sense of humor. While Billy gallivanted, I would go and sit with her and listen to her spin raucous anecdotes about her wayward son. She loved him deeply. This was witnessed in the contrast between her merry, mysterious eyes and her unhappy face whenever she shook her head and sighed, and said, "Ah, Billy! He just won't *do*!"

I suffered with Mama Love when Billy, at sixteen, threw away his youth. Here, as I recall, is how it happened: Always one to embrace completely any adventure, Billy ran wild with a crowd of older boys whose imaginations lacked the brakes of self-restraint. Following their tottering lead, Billy was dared to test the first full wetness of his manhood in the arms of a much experienced girl. This girl, I have reason to believe, knew better than he how unerringly passion can boomerang, especially when heated by the trusting flame of innocence. I believe that Billy was unaware. At least this was his defense to the girl's father, and also to the female judge notorious in our city for curbing wayward boys, and protecting the coffers of the state, with one stiff dose of justice.

"You feed that baby," Judge Gladys Moon told him.

I was with him in court that day and heard Billy's plea. He said, "Judge, that baby don't even *look* like me."

Judge Moon sat stone-faced and sober. "You feed it anyway," she told Billy, "and it might look like you. Feed it for twenty-one years, and if it don't look like you after twenty-one years, you don't have to feed it no more."

While I completed school, he worked as the relay man on a garbage truck. While I attended church and learned social graces, he became more a loner, grew sullen, worked a tentative cynicism into his voice. The whites of his eyes reddened. He cultivated a process, dressed flashily, began socializing on a certain street corner sanctified by a tree that had once stood there. These developments cracked his mother's heart. She believed with Judge Gladys Moon that it was Billy's baby. He protested this violently, expressing bitterness that of all the boys who had known the girl, he alone had had to pay. And because Mama Love could not bear to fight him, she ordered him finally out of her home. Yet she still loved her son, and often sent messages and food to him by me. But during this time I began avoiding most social contacts with Billy, because I too believed that he was guilty. Besides, our vocabularies were growing rapidly apart. He moved into a rented room with his common-law wife and child, a room in a section of the city I dreaded to enter. The year I finished high school and won a church scholarship to college, Billy stabbed during a dice game a man who had questioned the honor of Billy's common-law wife. But to Billy's credit it must be said that he waited until the man, who was winning, had lost back to the others in the game as much as they had lost to him. The code required such graciousness, even before a deadly act. This man died, and Billy's life was finished.

As a favor to his mother, who could not go herself, I took off from college and went by bus to Harper's Farm, where, in those days, black men were stocked for the road gangs. I waited for Billy in the moist, chicken-wired reception room. Around me sat weeping mothers, sportily dressed sweethearts, somber wives. The pungent smells of overripe peaches, sweat, potato salad, toilet water and fried chicken assaulted my nose. Over in a corner, on a wooden bench, a sun-whipped trustee, with his eyes closed and his face turned upward toward the ceiling, was singing:

>      *They 'cuse me of* mur-der,
>         *Never harm a man*
>         *Never harm a man.*
>      *I say, "Wake up, old* Dead Man
>         *Help me ca'ry my load*
>         *Help me ca'ry my load! . . ."*

I did not want to be in such a place.

When Billy came out and took his seat, I studied him through the chicken wire. This was long before he lost the eye, and there was the beginning of a rough handsomeness about his face. His hair, processed heavily now in the style of Nat King Cole, was protected from the flies and red dust by a blue and yellow cloth bandanna. He wore prison-issue blues, the worn paleness of which contrasted favorably with his sun-glossed skin. He chewed gum rapidly. Behind him, coming in the door from the prison section, I could see gelded young men walking with legs jangling loosely. Caged, they seemed bent on proving, to watching wives and sweethearts, that their manhood was still intact.

"Billy," I said through the dirty wire, "why do you insist on breaking your mama's heart? She suffers because she cannot be here. Yet she would suffer even more if she could see you here in this death-infected place. Look around you at these wasted men," I urged him, "then look me in the eye and tell me you like the future you have set for yourself."

But he would not look me in the eye. Nor would he respond to my pleadings. Instead, he chewed arrogantly. Then he smiled. In that smile was a mysterious humor that I had not, before this meeting, observed in his manner. Billy looked past me, perhaps at the waiting women seated on the benches against the walls, perhaps at the humming trustee. He tossed his head and said, "Me, I'm a dead man."

I drew my chair up closer to the wire. "It does not have to end that way," I told him.

"What you doin' with you life?" he asked me.

"Making something of it," I answered.

"That's good," Billy said.

Over in the corner, the trustee stopped humming and sang:

*Well, the load so* hea-vy
*I can* hardly *go*
*I can* hardly *go* . . .

I talked a while about college. Billy chewed in a relaxed way and listened. I tried my best to communicate to him some sense of the broader options available to the man in possession of salable knowledge. I mapped out my future in blocks of years, stepladders of subgoals, ending with an affirmation of my ultimate ambition to settle into the good life in Los Angeles.

Billy smiled and gave several agreeable nods. But when my conversation came to dwell on the wonders of Los Angeles, he interrupted suddenly. "Looka here," he said. "How 'bout runnin' cross the road and get me a hot sausage sandwich, heavy on the mustard, and a big orange soda."

I looked hard at him and wanted to weep. "Is that *all* you want?" I asked.

Billy chewed steadily. "No," he answered, looking out over the crowded room. "Bring me a side of fries, hold the salt."

Then he laughed, a strange, uncaring demon laughter. The sound bragged of his urge to self-destruct. Ah, Billy! He just would not *do*! He listened only to the beating of his own heart.

The last time I saw him, before we drank together in Chicago, was when he was furloughed from Harper's Farm to attend Mama Love's funeral. She died, I believe, from a broken heart and loneliness, although the doctor claimed it was the predictable second stroke. I returned home from college to gather with the family. And after the burial, while the others ate, Billy and I drank heavily together in the back room of his mother's rented house. All day he had smiled broadly at the grief and embarrassment of the family. Now he sat on his old bed, drinking with absolute detachment. I sat near him on a hard-back chair, talking aimlessly of college, of the admirable habits of girls met there, of my ambition to find, in a year or so, permanent employment in Los Angeles. Billy said nothing. But toward midnight, after the other members of the family had left and I grew tearful in recollecting the martyred life of Mama Love, Billy turned to face me. "What *you* cryin' for, *motherfucker*?" he said. "It's *my* mama!" Just then the prison guard, who had escorted him home, came in the room and touched Billy on the shoulder. My cousin rose slowly from the bed, and laughing with that same clucking sound in his chest, he sang:

*I'm Wild Nigger Bill*
*From Red Pepper Hill;*
*I never did die, and I never will . . .*

He chanted this song with such complete absorption, and laughed so menacingly, that I shuddered, and covered my face, and knew with his mother that Billy was doomed.

Seven years later, following his parole, Billy Renfro began work for Mr. Floyd Dillingham of Atlanta's Dillingham Automotives, Inc. A liberal man, Mr. Dillingham had negotiated with the state for Billy's release. The job was to track down Negroes who had defaulted on their car payments. No white man would even consider such employment. I do believe that Dillingham wanted a Negro with a reputation for ruthlessness sufficient to strike fear into the hearts of the deadbeats. In the inevitable tug between desire and justice, some of Dillingham's clients had been known to kill. Paid agents do not grow old in such an enterprise. Had I seen Billy Renfro I would have advised him of this, but I did not see him after the funeral for almost ten years. However, word-of-mouth reports from members of the family, bits of gossip from home folk passing through, placed him now in New York, now in California, one month wounded in a Detroit hospital, another month married to a woman romanced during a repossession mission outside Baton Rouge.

In contrast to him, I moved westward, but only as far as Chicago, and settled in against this city's soul-killing winter winds. I purged from my speech all traces of the South and warmed myself by the fire of my thirty-year plan. Employment was available in the credit reference section of the Melrose Department Store, and there I established, though slowly, a reputation for efficiency and tact. Because I got along, I began moving up. In my second year in Chicago, I found and courted

Chelseia Raymond, a family-backed, efficiency-minded girl. She was the kind of woman I needed to make my children safe. Her family loved me, and had the grace to overlook the fact that I had once been a poor migrant from the South. Third-generation Chicagoans, they nonetheless opened their hearts and home to me as if I had been native to their city. With their backing, I settled into this rough-and-tumble city and learned to dodge all events detracting attention from the direction in which I had determined to move. From time to time, trudging through the winter slush on Michigan, I would pause to explore a reflection of myself in a store window. By my fifth year in Chicago, I became satisfied that no one could have mistaken me for a refugee from the South.

This was my situation when Billy Renfro came to visit.

But it is certainly not true, as Billy has gossiped among the family, that when he arrived I refused to see him at my office. I do not call the man a liar, but I do say his imagination is sometimes a stranger to the truth. For the sake of accuracy, here is the truth of what happened: It was not my fault that Billy got only as far into our office as the receptionist's desk. It may be he was not dressed properly for the occasion. I know that I received his card from Mrs. Mohr only *after* he had left the building, when I was going out to lunch. She told me, with a nervousness I could not at first understand, "The gentleman said he's related to you." On my honor as a member of the family, I did not deny the bond. I accepted his card. Its face was embossed in elegant script:

RED PEPPER COLLECTION AGENCY
*"We Bring Back the Goods"*
B. J. Renfro, Pres.

On the back of the card Billy had scribbled: "Got me a turkee over in Harvey. Call soon. Yours truly, Billy Joe."

We met, as I have said, in the late afternoon of the following day at a bar over on Halstead. At first I did not recognize Billy. The years had treated him so unkindly. A single red eye inspected me as I approached the booth where he sat drinking. His left eye socket was hollow, no more than a shriveled piece of flesh pressed grimly against skull. His outfit – the black gabardine suit, the dirty white shirt, the black string tie – brought to my mind the image of an undertaker. Dried blood and dirt smeared the fabric of his sleeve, looking eerily green in the blue-smoked light. We shook hands awkwardly, and I slid into the booth across from him. I looked closely at his face and saw death walking.

Billy grinned foolishly.

"I have heard," I began with much politeness, "that at the point of death your whole life passes in review before your eyes. Knowing this, I wonder about the agony you will suffer with only one eye in service. Won't it take twice as long, and prolong your pains, before your full life passes and goes away?"

Billy looked hurt. He insisted the eye had been lost during domestic troubles with a woman. I did not believe this, and he began embellishing the statement with extravagant lies. He drained his glass, leaned forward across the table, and said, "It was a hard-hearted woman down in Eufaula, Alabama, that done it, a widow-woman name of Miss Ruby Watson. I was laid up at her place, tired of runnin' the road for Mr. Floyd. She done root work, said she was gonna make me smart and set me up in business, if I done right by her. It didn't make no nevermind to me. I just laid on in the cut and took these white pills she give me. But I didn't feel no smarter. Mr. Floyd, he sent a telegram over there. He said, 'Billy Joe, *son*, come on *home*, these niggers just *a-stealin'* my cars!'" Billy laughed loudly, using the sound to catch the attention of the barmaid. When she looked, he held up two rough brown fingers. She brought the drinks over and Billy tried to feel her rump. The woman jostled playfully against his arm. He rinsed his mouth with the Scotch and continued.

"I said, '*Motherfuck a Mr. Floyd!* I'm livin' my life *right here!*' I kept takin' them pills, layin' steady in the cut, but I didn't feel no smarter. Then one day I seed her go out to the fields. I seed her pickin' up *jackrabbit* shit. I didn't say nothin'. I just snuck on back to the house and got in bed with my .22. She come in and go to give me the stuff. I sit up and say, 'Miss Ruby, all this time I been wastin' round here, and all you been givin' me is jackrabbit shit.' She was a old widow-woman, Ruby, and I guess they just crafty that way. She just laugh at me and stood over the bed and say, '*Now* you gettin' *smart.*' Well, that's when I whip my .22 under her nose. But she just keep laughin' and say, 'Them bullets *dead* by now. Don't you know them bullets dead?' She had me. She knowed it. I knowed it. She sat down on the bed and commence to stroke my chest. She say, 'Now ain't *you* a sight? Don't even know whichaway is up. But you *my* sweetmeat now, and there ain't a damn thing you can do about it.'"

Billy looked calmly around the bar-room, like a priest about to say Mass. And yet beneath his cool exterior I thought I sensed, in the broad sweep of his red eye, the hint of a certain rough pride. "When she said that," he went on, "I *knowed* what I had to do. I gived the gun to her. I made her point it at my head. I told Miss Ruby, 'Me, I'm just dumb enough to believe it ain't even loaded. And if it is, it won't be the first time I been dead.' Then I ram my fist in her jaw."

I waited. The clink of glasses and the noisy blend of bar-room voices teased my anticipating ear. Billy was a master of suspense. Finally, I said, "So you called her bluff, got your eye shot out, but proved you were a man."

Billy laughed, his demon thumbing triumphantly in his chest. "Naw," he said. "She pulled the trigger and *killed* me. That's how come I'm back on the road for Mr. Floyd today."

Such were his lies that evening in that bar on Halstead.

While the purple and red jukebox belted accommodating rhythms, and while a couple slow-dragged, Billy spun yarns about his adventures. He told magnificent lies. He spoke of the chain gang, of buddies still anchored there, and hummed snatches of songs, remembered from that time, which still sustained him. He assessed his errors in the Houston incident, and as an aside contrasted the pungency of Mexican cuisine in joints as far apart as Brownsville, Oakland, Tempe, Arizona. Billy pantomimed, while standing, his one eye fixed on the barmaid, the body movements of black men in Savannah and San Francisco, and speculated how the spirit of a region informed the rhythms of a man's fucking. From this he moved to assessments of women in

Buffalo, Cleveland, Hartford, Newark, and East Saint Louis, offering details about liaisons in these cities that convinced him, should he ever marry, that Southern women provide the safest, strongest havens. He spoke of Limehouse, South Carolina, but only in passing on his way to recollections of a Newark house-rent party, the highlights of a fish fry in Baltimore, the economics of picking beans in New Jersey if one is ever stranded there, in August, without cash. Billy recited his contributions to bus-depot graffiti inscribed on stalls in Memphis, Little Rock, Phoenix, and Los Angeles, and observed that practitioners of this art became more assertive, sexually and politically, the farther west one went. I heard his accounts of fights, poker games, epic bouts of wrestling, with recalcitrant claimers of defaulted cars. Billy conveyed the flow of his emotions while contracting an assignation, on a lonely highway driving southward from Denver, when he and the woman driver of a car licensed in Maine sped sexual brags for three hundred miles before ending, in silent completion, in a wet cornfield just west of Kansas City.

While he was still reciting, I went quickly to the telephone and called Chelseia.

It is certainly not true, though Billy maintains otherwise, that my in-laws and Chelseia ordered him out of their home. What happened that evening with the Raymonds is still fresh in my mind. They were civil to Billy, though a little bit wary about why he wore blue sunshades. I had advised him to take this precaution while at my apartment, where Billy had bathed and shaved and changed into one of my better suits. Before visiting the Raymonds he had been completely transformed. His muscles rippled in the close embrace of my gray pinstripe; his face, clean shaven now, was set off favorably by one of my sky-blue shirts; my very best red and white polka-dot tie swept deftly into the V of my chest-hugging vest. Even Billy's scuffed shoes had been spit-polished and shone like hot tar. This outfit, together with my blue sunshades shielding his eyesocket from inspection, gave Billy the appearance of a publicity-shy banker.

Mr. and Mrs. Raymond were enormously impressed.

"What business are you in, Mr. Renfro?" Mrs. Raymond asked, while her husband passed around the cheese board.

Conforming to my warnings, Billy spoke briefly. "Automotives," he answered.

Chelseia, seated next to me on the sofa, said nothing. But she watched Billy very closely.

"Selling?" Mrs. Raymond asked. She was a round, self-possessed woman who called me "darling" and winked reassuringly whenever we drank more than two glasses of sherry. She had already given me the understanding that Chelseia was mine. "You have a dealership, then?" she asked Billy.

He sat on a purple settee, his legs crossed elegantly, a glass of sherry posed in his hand. He pretended he had not heard Mrs. Raymond.

I had not anticipated that Chelseia's parents would be at home. Usually on Thursday evenings they played canasta with a church group. But, being selfless people, they had canceled their engagement when they heard from Chelseia that my cousin was in town. Mr. Raymond himself had prepared the dinner. I wanted things to go smoothly. "Billy is more a traveling salesman," I answered for my cousin. "His business takes him around the country."

Mr. Raymond sighed and stroked the top of his head. He was completely bald. He said, "It does my heart good to see the younger generation getting a few breaks. Why, in my day, with two degrees, all I could get was being a redcap down at the Union Station."

"Of course you've been out to California?" Mrs. Raymond said quickly. Both she and her husband had worked very hard to achieve the good life, and she did not like to hear him reminisce.

"Yes, m'am," Billy answered.

"We've got relatives out in Culver City," Chelseia volunteered. She had sensed my tension, and had not asked why Billy was wearing a suit she had selected for me at Marshall Fields, but she stared long and hard at the blue-tinted sunshades, familiar to her from our long summer walks along the lakeshore.

"Is it true what they say about those movie stars?" Mr. Raymond asked Billy.

Such was the flow of conversation during dinner.

For well over an hour, Billy successfully maintained his cloud of mystery. And at such moments when it seemed about to break apart in the breeze of chitchat, I puffed it back into place with a swift retort. We were relaxed until after dinner, when Mr. Raymond, still rummaging in the storehouses of his youth, lit up a cigar and became expansive. He loosened his tie and began telling anecdotes about his escapades as a redcap. Chelseia, her eyes flitting nervously, kept saying, "Please, don't get naughty now, Daddy." But her words were of no avail. Billy, puffing fiercely on a cigar, laughed and egged him on. Mrs. Raymond smiled painfully. Several times Chelseia knocked her knee against my leg beneath the table. Toward 10.30 Mr. Raymond brought out a bottle of bourbon. He said, "How about a little snort, Mr. Renfro?" and winked at Billy. My cousin willfully ignored the suggestion in my stare. "Call me Billy," he said to Mr. Raymond, draining his water glass.

In less than half an hour, drunk now, Billy was offering tales about his own exploits on the Coast. Mr. Raymond kept laughing, shaking his head wistfully, and saying, "I *knew* it was true what they say about them stars." And while Billy dived for more details on this point, Mr. Raymond regaled us with anecdotes drawn from his days as a bellhop at the Palmer House. When he mentioned the adventures of a hustling bellhop named "Swifty," Billy leaned forward, pounded the table, and shouted, "Damn if I don't *know* that nigger. He in *Dee*troit now, still *just as crazy as a bedbug!*"

Mrs. Raymond coughed violently and left the room.

From this point onward the evening deteriorated. Chelseia sat with a cold and distant expression on her face. From time to time she kicked my foot beneath the table. I flashed signals to Billy, tried to head off his speech when I perceived where it was leading, suggested many times that we should go. But none of it was of any use. Billy seemed to have induced some unhealthy chemical reaction in Mr. Raymond. He and Billy seemed locked in some unholy union. He laughed, giggled, and hooted as he talked. Even when Mrs. Raymond returned to the room in a housecoat, her husband did not lower his voice. When Mr.

Raymond, on his fourth bourbon, started to recite a salacious jingle, Billy jumped up and overruled it with a more earthy variant. But in the rush of excitement while reciting the punch line, he laughed lustily, screeched, and tore off his glasses. This one gesture destroyed all his mystery. His single eye, red-rimmed and watery, flashed horribly in the soft glow of the green and red Tiffany lamp.

Chelseia gasped.

"Why, Mr. Renfro," said Mrs. Raymond, the back of her hand drawn to her mouth, "whatever happened to your eye?"

"Nothing but a knife fight," Chelseia muttered.

"Let it go," called Mr. Raymond across the littered dining table. "It's not our business." He was drunk, but there was an extreme soberness in his voice. He said to all of us, "Let it go."

Mrs. Raymond acted on this cue. "When you get back South," she said to Billy, "tell the family that William is a very nice young man." She rounded the table with her right arm outstretched. She grasped and wagged Billy's limp right hand. "What did you say your business was?"

Billy looked confused. "Automotives, m'am," he told her.

"Washing or pumping gas?" Chelseia said. It was not a question, and the tone of her voice I had heard before in the chill of the winter winds off Lake Michigan. When I looked at Chelseia I saw in her face a vengeful twist I had not before then, and have never since, seen in her store of expressions. Mrs. Raymond had this very same look.

Billy stiffened. He jerked his hand away from Mrs. Raymond. He looked enraged.

The rest of the evening has been clouded by his lies.

But it is certainly true that I tried hard to save the situation, although Billy has maintained that I turned on him. The man is a notorious liar, and likes to keep the family jumpy. Here is the truth of what happened: I moved quickly to Billy's side. I put my hand on his shoulder. I faced the Raymonds for the two of us. I said, "Thank you for a splendid evening." But all my tact was introduced too late. With a purposeful shrug, Billy separated his shoulder from my hand. All our eyes were on him. Only Mr.

Raymond, sitting drooped and still in his chair, seemed distracted by thoughts of other matters.

Someone had to take control. I took it as best I could. "A red-neck down in South Carolina shot out Billy's eye," I said. "Billy is too proud to speak of it."

"*Bull*shit!" Billy said.

By this one word, and through his subsequent actions, Billy himself completely severed what was left of our family bond.

He stripped off my coat, my vest, my polka-dot tie. These he flung on the purple settee. My sky-blue shirt he let fall to the floor. Billy stood broad-shouldered and brown in a ragged, yellowed undershirt. He directed all our eyes to weltlike scars on his arms and neck. "These here come from runnin' round the country," he grinned. "And I'm *keep* runnin' till the pork chops get thicker and they give me 2 dollars more."

"Please, Billy," I pleaded. "Please, Billy, tell the truth now."

He laughed wickedly, his teeth clamped tight. His eyes darted from me, to Chelseia, to Mrs. Raymond standing by the table with her right hand clutching her chest.

But Billy did not tell the truth. His story to me in the bar on Halstead vanished like a summer cloud. He pointed to his empty eye socket and said, "I lost this over in Harvey several years ago. Mr. Floyd Dillingham, my boss, was the one that sent me up here. He had this here turkey that flew the coop with a fistful of notes due on his Impala. Nigger's name was Wilfred 'Inner City' Jones, and he had balls enough to cruise pass Mr. Floyd's lot and honk when he was leavin' town. People on the corner saw him frontin' off Mr. Floyd. It looked bad. Mr. Floyd called me in and gived me my runnin' orders. He say, '*Fuck the money*, Billy. What he done is bad for *business*! Now bring me back my *car* or that nigger's *ass*!'" He pounded the table twice, with great seriousness in his face, as if still hearing the beat of his boss's voice. Mrs. Raymond and Chelseia jumped each time he pounded. But Mr. Raymond remained seated in his chair, his head bowed, his eyes closed. Billy smiled slightly. "I put out word I was lookin' for Inner City. He put out word he was lookin' for me to come lookin' for him. Said I would find him waitin' for me over in Birmingham, if I came lookin' that far. But I knowed that

Earline, his old lady, was up here in Harvey and he only felt safe with his head up under her dress. So I bought me a one-way bus ticket." Billy moved to the table, swished the last of the bourbon in his glass and drank it down. Then he set the glass on the white tablecloth and arranged soiled knives and forks around it, setting the scene. "He must have been layin' for me," he went on, "'cause when I knock on the door people commence to scuffle round inside. Then Earline sing out, 'What you want?' I holler back, 'Them keys to that Impala park outside or a piece of Inner City's ass, it don't matter to me which one!' They was quiet for a minute, then Inner City holler, 'Come on in, *motherfucker*, and take your choice!' I went on in."

His single eye, though red-rimmed and watery, sparkled dimly with pride. I sensed that he was enjoying himself, though Mrs. Raymond was almost in a swoon. She was dabbing excitedly at her forehead with a dinner napkin. I saw Billy watching her. I saw him smile. I thought I saw him lick his lips. "Inner City was shootin' wild from behind the bed," he continued. "Though he is in bad with Mr. Floyd, I won't bad-talk his reputation by sayin' where them bullets hit. But I stood in the middle of room and shout, 'Missed me, *sap-sucker!*' Then I opened up with my .38, whistlin' whilst I worked. My habit is to aim high when ladies is present, 'cause a scared woman can talk quick sense to a hard-headed man. Pretty soon Inner City yell out, 'Hey Billy, let's be *gentlemens* and do this without no heat!' He slide his gun out from under the bed. I throwed mine on the sheets and wait. Then Earline yell, 'Hey Billy, what about that .22 you keeps strap to your spine?' They was quiet for a minute. Me, I didn't move. Then I heard Inner City pop Earline in the jaw. While she was still hollerin' he rise up from under the bed, limber as a bear. His eyes was steamin' and his jaws was tight. He wolf, 'I'ma *keep* that Impala, Billy, but first I'ma do me some business on your *ass!*'"

By now Billy had moved the gravy-stained knife closer to the glass. He leaned over the table like a magician about to pluck a pigeon from thin air. But suddenly his body relaxed. He straightened and reached one hand into his pocket. "Now I ain't sayin' it was *easy*," he said, looking directly at Chelseia, "but I *do* say I just ain't *use* to buyin' no bus ticket and ridin' with a sore ass and a bleedin' eye all the way home." He tossed a set of car keys onto the table. Tiny flecks of dried blood flew from the keys as they clinked against the glass. Then Billy laughed loud and confidently. It was an even, bass-filled laughter that sounded the image of a persistent demon pounding happily against a friendly door. "One of us knowed he had to die," he announced calmly. "Next time, it might be *me*."

"You common *street nigger!*" Chelseia shouted.

Billy held his naked arm toward me as if he were a ringmaster introducing an act. "And this here's my cousin William," he told Chelseia.

Mrs. Raymond shuddered and rushed from the room.

And then there came a burst of wild, almost hysterical laughter. But this was not Billy. I turned and saw Mr. Raymond. His bald head was bent almost into his empty plate. He seemed to be shedding tears.

"Billy!" I pleaded. "Tell the truth. Sometimes, Billy, please tell the *truth!*"

But he ignored me. Instead, he joined with Mr. Raymond in this wild, uncaring laughter.

"Gangster!" Chelseia shouted.

"God bless Mr. Floyd!" Billy yelled.

Someone had to keep order. I assumed that responsibility. I was the one who asked Billy out.

But it is not true, contrary to rumors circulating in my family, that Billy Renfro is unwelcome in my home. His own lying stories spread this madness, and both he and I know the truth of where I stand. As far as I am concerned, he is welcome here at any time. Chelseia is another matter, but even she has said she would not interfere if Billy chose to come again. She would even let me prepare dinner for him. Whenever I am confronted by members of the family with one of his lies, I say this in response. For whatever it is worth to them, or to Billy. The man is, after all, my cousin. It is a point of family pride. Chelseia agrees, and says our family unit will likely be the place where Billy finds ultimate reconstruction, once he has put aside his wanderings. I say it is just a matter of time. We are, after all, the same age. Yet I have already charted my course. I have settled into Chicago, against the winter whippings of this city's winds. He can do the same. But as things stand now, he is still someplace out there, with a single eye flickering over open roadways, in his careless search for an exciting death. Ah, *Billy!*

# *Murderers*

When my uncle Moe dropped dead of a heart attack I became expert in the subway system. With a nickel I'd get to Queens, twist and zoom to Coney Island, twist again toward the George Washington Bridge – beyond which was darkness. I wanted proximity to darkness, strangeness. Who doesn't? The poor in spirit, the ignorant and frightened. My family came from Poland, then never went any place until they had heart attacks. The consummation of years in one neighborhood: a black Cadillac, corpse inside. We should have buried Uncle Moe where he shuffled away his life, in the kitchen or toilet, under the linoleum, near the coffeepot. Anyhow, they were dropping on Henry Street and Cherry Street. Blue lips. The previous winter it was cousin Charlie, forty-five years old. Moe, Charlie, Sam, Adele – family meant a punch in the chest, fire in the arm. I didn't want to wait for it. I went to Harlem, the Polo Grounds, Far Rockaway, thousands of miles on nickels, mainly underground. Tenements watched me go, day after day, fingering nickels. One afternoon I stopped to grind my heel against the curb. Melvin and Arnold Bloom appeared, then Harold Cohen, Melvin said, "You step in dog shit?" Grinding was my answer. Harold Cohen said, "The rabbi is home. I saw him on Market Street. He was walking fast." Oily Arnold, eleven years old, began to urge: "Let's go up to our roof." The decision waited for me. I considered the roof, the view of industrial Brooklyn, the Battery, ships in the river, bridges, towers, and the rabbi's apartment. "All right," I said. We didn't giggle or look to one another for moral signals. We were running.

The blinds were up and curtains pulled, giving sunlight, wind, birds to the rabbi's apartment – a magnificent metropolitan view. The rabbi and his wife never took it, but in the light and air of summer afternoons, in the eye of gull and pigeon, they were joyous. A bearded young man, and his young pink wife, sacramentally bald. Beard and Baldy, with everything to see, looked at each other. From a water tank on the opposite roof, higher than their windows, we looked at them. In psychoanalysis this is "The Primal Scene." To achieve the primal scene we crossed a ledge 6 inches wide. A half-inch indentation in the brick gave us fingerholds. We dragged bellies and groins against the brick face to a steel ladder. It went up the side of the building, bolted into brick, and up the side of the water tank to a slanted tin roof which caught the afternoon sun. We sat on that roof like angels, shot through with light, derealized in brilliance. Our sneakers sucked hot slanted metal. Palms and fingers pressed to bone on nailheads.

The Brooklyn Navy Yard with destroyers and aircraft carriers, the Statue of Liberty putting the sky to the torch, the dull remote skyscrapers of Wall Street, and the Empire State Building were among the wonders we dominated. Our view of the holy man and his wife, on their living-room couch and floor, on the bed in their bedroom, could not be improved. Unless we got closer. But 50 feet across the air was right. We heard their phonograph and watched them dancing. We couldn't hear the gratifications or see pimples. We smelled nothing. We didn't want to touch.

For a while I watched them. Then I gazed beyond into shimmering nullity, gray, blue, and green murmuring over rooftops and towers. I had watched them before. I could tantalize myself with this brief ocular perversion, the general cleansing nihil of a view. This was the beginning of philosophy. I indulged in ambience, in space like eons. So what if my uncle Moe was dead? I was philosophical and luxurious. I didn't even have to look at the rabbi and his wife. After all, how many times had we dissolved stickball games when the rabbi came home? How many times had we risked shameful discovery, scrambling up the ladder, exposed to their windows – if they looked. We risked life itself to achieve this eminence. I looked at the rabbi and his wife.

Today she was a blonde. Bald didn't mean no wigs. She had

ten wigs, ten colors, fifty styles. She looked different, the same, and very good. A human theme in which nothing begat anything and was gorgeous. To me she was the world's lesson. Aryan yellow slipped through pins about her ears. An olive complexion mediated yellow hair and Arabic black eyes. Could one care what she really looked like? What was *really*? The minute you wondered, she looked like something else, in another wig, another style. Without the wigs she was a baldy-bean lady. Today she was a blonde. Not blonde. *A* blonde. The phonograph blared and her deep loops flowed Tommy Dorsey, Benny Goodman, and then the thing itself, Choo-Choo Lopez. Rumba! One, two-three. One, two-three. The rabbi stepped away to delight in blonde imagination. Twirling and individual, he stepped away snapping fingers, going high and light on his toes. A short bearded man, balls afling, cock shuddering like a springboard. Rumba! One, two-three. *Ole! Vaya*, Choo-Choo!

> *I was on my way to spend some time in Cuba.*
> *Stopped off at Miami Beach, la-la.*
> *Oh, what rumba they teach, la-la.*
> *Way down in Miami Beach,*
> *Oh, what a chroombah they teach, la-la.*
> *Way-down-in-Miami-Beach.*

She, on the other hand, was somewhat reserved. A shift in one lush hip was total rumba. He was Mr. Life. She was dancing. He was a naked man. She was what she was in the garment of her soft, essential self. He was snapping, clapping, hopping to the beat. The beat lived in her visible music, her lovely self. Except for the wig. Also a watchband that desecrated her wrist. But it gave her a bit of the whorish. She never took it off.

Harold Cohen began a cocktail-mixer motion, masturbating with two fists. Seeing him at such hard futile work, braced only by sneakers, was terrifying. But I grinned. Out of terror, I twisted an encouraging face. Melvin Bloom kept one hand on the tin. The other knuckled the rumba numbers into the back of my head. Nodding like a defective, little Arnold Bloom chewed his lip and squealed as the rabbi and his wife smacked together. The rabbi clapped her buttocks, fingers buried in the cleft. They stood only on his legs. His back arched, knees bent, thighs thick with thrust, up, up, up. Her legs wrapped his hips, ankles crossed, hooked for constriction. "Oi, oi, oi," she cried, wig flashing left, right, tossing the Brooklyn Navy Yard, the Statue of Liberty, and the Empire State Building to hell. Arnold squealed oi, squealing rubber. His sneaker heels stabbed tin to stop his slide. Melvin said, "Idiot." Arnold's ring hooked a nailhead and the ring and ring finger remained. The hand, the arm, the rest of him, were gone.

We rumbled down the ladder. "Oi, oi, oi," she yelled. In a freak of ecstasy her eyes had rolled and caught us. The rabbi drilled to her quick and she had us. "OI, OI," she yelled above congas going clop, doom-doom, clop, doom-doom on the way to Cuba. The rabbi flew to the window, a red mouth opening in his beard: "Murderers." He couldn't know what he said. Melvin Bloom was crying. My fingers were tearing, bleeding into brick. Harold Cohen, like an adding machine, gibbered the name of God. We moved down the ledge quickly as we dared. Bongos went tocka-ti-tocka, tocka-ti-tocka. The rabbi screamed, "MELVIN BLOOM, PHILLIP LIEBOWITZ, HAROLD COHEN, MELVIN BLOOM," as if our names, screamed this way, naming us where we hung, smashed us into brick.

Nothing was discussed.

The rabbi used his connections, arrangements were made. We were sent to a camp in New Jersey. We hiked and played volleyball. One day, apropos of nothing, Melvin came to me and said little Arnold had been made of gold and he, Melvin, of shit. I appreciated the sentiment, but to my mind they were both made of shit. Harold Cohen never again spoke to either of us. The counselors in the camp were World War II veterans, introspective men. Some carried shrapnel in their bodies. One had a metal plate in his head. Whatever you said to them they seemed to be thinking of something else, even when they answered. But step out of line and a plastic lanyard whistled burning notice across your ass.

At night, lying in the bunkhouse, I listened to owls. I'd never before heard that sound, the sound of darkness, blooming, opening inside you like a mouth.

# SUSAN MINOT

☆  ☆  ☆  ☆

# *Accident*

Caitlin and Delilah are blabbing away in the kitchen. Sherman, who's in the TV room next to a screen window, can hear them, down at the end of the porch, where they've got the back door open. The girls never stop talking, worrying about their boy-friends, worrying about Dad, always having fits – especially since their mother died. Sherman behaves like his father and ignores them. Mr. Vincent is in there with him, sitting on the other couch in the dim light, with his book and his drink. They both watch when the sports comes on. Sherman has the cat in his lap, not thinking much, sixteen years old.

The smell from the kitchen fills the whole downstairs. "We're having roast beef," says Sherman, looking at the cat's paw and pressing it so the claws come out. Mr. Vincent turns his face and registers this information with a nod. Then he goes back to his book.

The girls take turns running the house. Of the seven kids in the family, only five are at home now. Gus, who's nineteen, is in Kennebunkport for the summer, mapping and injecting trees for a forestry service. Sophie, who comes between Caitlin and Delilah, took off for Colorado with some friends when Delilah moved home. Sophie had been there since the winter, when their mother was killed. Caitlin, who is twenty-three, lives in Cambridge and works for a woman who collects art. She comes out to Marshport on the weekends to go to the beach and also, she says, to be with Dad.

The girls yell for Sherman to come set the table. If his younger brother were there, Sherman would make him do it, but Chicky is out at his friend Richard's house. Sherman drops the cat on the rug and traipses down the hall, past all the coat hooks and into the bright-yellow kitchen.

"Set it for seven," says Delilah. She's the dark one, the smallest, with a chunky waist but the rest of her like bird bones. "Hal's coming out after work." She used to live in Somerville with Hal, who's a carpenter. They met in college. When Hal comes out for the weekends, he slips off to Sherman and Chicky's room and smokes pot with them. Delilah usually gets high, too – only later, after Mr. Vincent has gone to bed and they bring the bong into the TV room.

Sherman takes down some plates.

"Not those," says Caitlin. She's flipping the roast potatoes in the oven but looks over her shoulder to see what he's doing. "Use the Harvard plates."

He puts the blue and white plates around the table that they've been eating at all their lives – white with a yellow trim. Underneath are metal things that jab into your knees. When they were young, they came down for breakfast and their mother would have set it the night before – six bowls, one at each place. Only six, because Minnie wasn't born yet – she came later.

"Yah," says Delilah, supervising. "Those are good." Mr. Vincent doesn't like to eat in the big dining room, so they squeeze in here. With everyone sitting, you can barely get between the counter and the table.

Then the girls start in. First Delilah says, "Have you thought about what you're going to do this summer?"

Sherman opens a drawer. "Get a job," he says.

"Do you have any idea what?" Caitlin leans against the icebox, arms folded, waiting.

"Nope." He puts the forks on the left, the knives on the right.

Delilah lights a cigarette from a burner. "Have you even started looking?" she asks.

"Not yet."

"Chicky has a job with Mr. Lewis," says Caitlin.

"Yup," Sherman says. Mr. Lewis's son, Richard, happens to be Chicky's best friend.

"Dad's not going to let you stay at home if you don't have a job."

"I know." His sisters watch while he folds the napkins into triangles.

"So what are you going to do?" Caitlin asks.

"Get a job," he says, to shut her up.

"Sherman," she says. Her forehead wrinkles. "What do you expect? That a job's going to come find you?"

He turns a plate so the building on it is right-side up.

"Leave him alone, Caity," says Delilah, and puts her cigarette out under the faucet. "He'll get a job. Won't you, Sherman?"

"Hope so." He steps back from the table, finished.

"Thanks," says Delilah. "Is Chicky back yet?"

"Dunno." He turns to walk out.

"Wait," she says. "Are you going to that party tonight?"

"What party?" asks Caitlin, lightening up.

Delilah makes it sound like a big deal. "Chicky's friends are having a party at Richard's by Jingle Beach."

"Fun," says Caitlin encouragingly. The girls have parties at the house – huge ones. Some kids from town crashed the last one and refused to leave. Mr. Vincent was next door at the Drapers', spending the night, away from the blaring music. Gus picked a fight and made a dent in the plaster. Caitlin called the cops.

"You should go," Delilah tells Sherman. "Why not?"

Sherman retreats to his room to get a quick buzz before dinner. He and Chicky share the maid's room downstairs, at the back of the house. It's where they spend most of their time, away from everybody, playing Bob Marley nonstop. On the walls are some of Sherman's drawings – abstract ones that look like shattered panes of glass. One charcoal sketch, on Chicky's side of the room, is of Mum. The smile looks flat, because Sherman did it from a photograph. She has her sunglasses on and is wearing pigtails.

Sherman sips his joint in front of the window. The kitchen bell rings, calling Minnie home. Then Sherman hears, down at the marsh, the familiar rattle of the train going by, the train that hit Mum's car and killed her. Sherman has certain theories about the accident, and about the family, and gives them to Chicky late at night, each in his bed – brothers. Sherman can tell his brother things he knows won't get repeated, especially to the girls.

The other night, with the reggae going, Sherman said, "As soon as I get enough money, I'm going to the West Indies. To live."

"You are?" said Chicky. Sherman always had these schemes.

"Yup," said Sherman, wide awake.

There was silence on the other side of the room, and Sherman could practically hear his brother thinking. Finally, Chicky said, "Okay. I'll meet you there."

Out the window Sherman sees Minnie at the end of the driveway pushing her bike up the hill. She gets back on and rides fast, her seven-year-old legs pedaling furiously, her pigtails out like stiff brushes. She abandons her bike on the slope of the lawn, then runs around to the porch. Sherman smirks, feeling the pot. From listening all his life, he can tell that a car down on the avenue is turning up their driveway, and, sure enough, Hal's heap turns toward the house, rumbling and ticking, about to stall.

Delilah calls, "Hello, honey," from the porch. Hal gets out, grabbing cigarettes off the dashboard. Minnie's voice goes, "Hi, Hal," and then Sherman sees her hanging over the porch railing. Delilah says, "You have time for a quick shower," and Sherman snickers, hearing that.

When the bell rings again, it means it's suppertime. Going into the kitchen. Sherman answers the phone.

"That better be Chicky," says Delilah, making gravy at the stove. "Where is he? Tell him we're eating this second."

Keeping the receiver close, Sherman turns away. Chicky's still at Richard's, staying for dinner. "Wanna come to this party later?" he asks Sherman. "Then you can give me a ride home." Chicky is at the age when his voice sounds like water gurgling – first loud, then soft and far away.

"All right," Sherman says. They'll probably have pot. Chicky's friend Bruce usually has good pot.

Delilah is still blabbing away. "Typical Chicky. Where is he? Why didn't he call before?"

Sherman hangs up.

"Well?" Caitlin asks.

"He's staying there for supper."

"Thanks a lot for telling us," says Delilah. Minnie is already at her place, the table up to her neck.

Mr. Vincent strides in, patting his chest pockets. "Another culinary delight? What have we here?" He pushes in some chairs and peers into the bowls on the counter.

"Chicky just called," Delilah tells him. "He's eating at Richard's." She waits for his reaction.

"Splendid, splendid," says Mr. Vincent. He parks himself by the sink and waits to go last, his wrists tucked under his armpits. Caitlin starts Minnie's plate, and Sherman goes next. "Don't take so many onions," she says, and he drops a couple back with his fingers. Chicky always gets out of it – being at home.

Hal comes in with his hair slicked back after his shower. He's wearing a purple shirt that Delilah gave him. "Hello, Mr. Vincent," he says, before doing anything. Delilah waves his plate for him to take.

"Good evening to you, Hal." Mr. Vincent keeps his heels tightly together.

"Come on, Dad," says Caitlin. "Come get some food."

He nods at her back; he'll go when he's ready. Delilah puts Chicky's milk at Hal's place and removes the extra setting.

The last one to sit down is Mr. Vincent, at the head. Delilah says, "I got a letter from Gus." She looks down at her father's plate. "Is that all you're having? Aren't you taking any broccoli?"

He says, "We'll have broccoli from my garden in late July. Please pass the gravy, Minnie my love."

Minnie doesn't move, so Sherman pokes her.

"What did Gus say?" Caitlin always puts huge chunks of butter on her potatoes.

"He and Bub are living in a tent."

Mr. Vincent rolls his eyes. "Good ol' Gus," he says wearily.

"He is?" asks Minnie. She holds on to her fork with a tiny fist. "Where?"

"In the woods," says Delilah, talking with her mouth full. "They have Dinty Moore every night."

"Yuck," says Caitlin.

"What's dinty more?" asks Minnie.

Delilah points her knife in the air, like a teacher. "From a can."

Sherman feels a paw bat his calf, and slips a piece of meat to the cat under the table. His father notices this and frowns, but doesn't say anything.

"And they hear bears roaming around at night," Delilah says.

"Really?" Minnie believes everything.

"You'll be pleased to know the lettuce is coming along superbly," says Mr. Vincent. "We should have some next week."

"Good," says Caitlin. Everyone eats.

The back door is open behind Mr. Vincent, and with no one talking they can hear clearly the train rattling by down through the woods, along the marsh. Then it clatters off faintly. Sherman glances at Hal and can tell by his slow chewing that the noise makes him nervous. Everyone else keeps on with the meal, ignoring it, acting as if they're used to it by now.

When they left the party, Sherman walked smack into a privet hedge on his way to the car. Chicky stopped on the gravel, his long arms hanging down. "I don't think you better drive," he said.

"Well, I am," said Sherman. He cast a glance back at his brother, his face almost cross-eyed from drinking. "Come if you want."

Chicky watched him get in the little Volkswagen. Inside at Richard's, music was playing, and a softened bass thumped in the night. Chicky thought for a moment, but he didn't know how else to get home.

Sherman drove fast down the side streets, under the leafy shadows of the streetlights. When they came into town, which was lit up and empty, he accelerated to fifty. Chicky kept quiet in his seat. At the fork, the car headed straight for the Wayward Dog Tavern.

"Sherman!" Chicky grabbed the wheel to make the corner.

Sherman jerked his elbow up and knocked his hand away. "Cut it out," he said. He was flooring it.

Chicky braced himself on the dashboard and thought, This is it, we're going to die, whipping past the houses at one o'clock in the morning. They saw no other cars, luckily, since Sherman was straddling the line the whole time. On the straightaway, Chicky sat back slightly. Then, at the Lighthouse Inn, the car made the turn at a tilt, just missing the center island. They bounded over the roller-coaster hills on Sea Street, and turned onto Chatham Avenue, nearly sideswiping a stone pillar.

Then Chicky said, "Let me out." They had come to the top of the hill before the road curved around the beach. Sherman jammed on the brakes. "You're too drunk," Chicky pleaded, on the verge of tears. He felt better now, though, with the car stopped.

Sherman didn't move. His round shoulders were hunched. "So get out," he said finally. For a moment, Chicky thought about trying to push him out of the car, but he knew how strong Sherman was, and when drunk he was even stronger. Chicky opened the door and got out.

The second it clipped shut, Sherman took off, tires screeching, and careened around the bend of the beach wall. Chicky stood there, shaky, the streetlight above him like a stooped bird, neck curved, stupid. He started down the hill, his sneakers slapping on the soft tar. The car's hum grew fainter as it rounded the cove, its noise carrying across the still, black water. Then, when the sound reached a certain pitch, he heard the crash, and a quick engine rev, then a faraway tinkling of glass.

Chicky bolted. He ran over the dark road, past the streetlights on one side, the beach wall on the other. In his ears was a whirring as he flew along. The car was a dark hump, jacked up on the fire hydrant. Panting, he went to the window. Sherman's head was motionless on the steering wheel.

"Sherman." He reached through the window to touch his brother's shoulder. Slowly, like a ghost, Sherman lifted his head, dazed. There was dark blood striped down his face, and a mess at his mouth. He started groping, like a sleepwalker, for the inside door handle. "Wait," Chicky said. "Are you okay? Are you all right? Wait. Let me go get help."

He started up the hill. "Stay there," he called back. He heard the door open.

"I'm coming," said Sherman.

"No." It was as if Sherman were rising from the dead. "Just wait there."

"Don't tell Dad," Sherman warned. Chicky made out his dark figure stumbling out of the car, then propping himself against it with one arm.

Chicky tore up the hill, up the driveway, around its curves. The porch light was on and the lights in the TV room. When he burst through the front door everything seemed small. The TV was going quietly.

Delilah and Hal were still up. "There you are," said Delilah. She had her sewing basket out. When she looked a moment longer at him, her expression changed. "What is it?" Hal was bent over the low table, gluing something together, holding Delilah's feet in his lap.

"Sherman crashed the car."

"Oh my God." She jumped up. "Are you okay? Where is he?"

"I wasn't in it. I got out before Booth Cove. He hit the hydrant near the Singers'. I told him to stay there, but he—"

They all rushed out, but stopped on the porch. Down on the driveway, coming out of the darkness, was Sherman, like a phantom. Delilah took quick steps down the stairs. "My God, Sherman, are you all right?" She put her hand up near his face but wouldn't touch it. "We better get you to a hospital."

Sherman looked distractedly into the darkness. "I gotta go get the car," he said, squinting toward the house. Then he started peering around in the bushes.

"Are you crazy?" said Delilah. "Leave it. Just come inside." She seized his arm, but he shoved her off.

Above them, the window in Caitlin's room opened. "What's going on down there?" she said, her voice creaky with sleep.

No one answered her. Delilah said, "Come on, Sherman, please!"

Caitlin called, more sharply, "What happened?"

Delilah looked up and whispered, "Sherman cracked up the car. I'm trying to get him to come inside."

Caitlin yelled, "Sherman!"

"Ssshhh!" Delilah went. "You'll wake Dad."

Caitlin whispered back, "Well, Dad should be woken."

Delilah turned, frowning, into the shadows. "Sherman, what are you doing?"

He had gotten on Minnie's bike and started to pedal away, weaving across the driveway, his knees jammed against the handlebars. "Gotta go get the car," he said.

"I'm waking Dad," said Caitlin from above. Then the window went rattling down.

"Hal," Delilah pleaded. Hal and Chicky were still on the porch. "Will you come help?"

Hal went down onto the driveway. From the edge of the light came the clatter of the bike falling over. In one motion, Sherman righted it and got back on. Hal strode over and grabbed the handlebars. "Come on, buddy," he said. "We'll get the car later."

Sherman took a look at him and shoved the bike out from under himself. It wheeled away and toppled over. He headed off blindly in the opposite direction. Hal took him by the shoulder and led him up to the porch.

Caitlin came out in her bathrobe. "Dad's coming," she said, moving to let Sherman and Hal pass.

In the hall, Sherman broke away. "Lemme go," he said. He bowled off toward his room. Hal and Delilah rushed after him; he went faster. Right by the steps leading down to the playroom, they caught up with him and tried to drag him back to the kitchen. He tripped and fell.

Caitlin and Chicky, still back in the hall, couldn't see what happened, but they heard Sherman thudding down the steps.

"Oh my God," Delilah said. "He's going to kill himself."

Caitlin touched Chicky gently. "Are you all right?"

He nodded.

Mr. Vincent appeared at the upstairs banister, a blue towel wrapped around his waist.

"Quick, Dad," cried Caitlin. "He needs help."

Mr. Vincent descended the stairs, not saying anything, frowning. They followed him down the hallway. Delilah said, "He won't listen. He's all cut up." Everyone crowded onto the landing. Down on the playroom floor, Sherman was floundering to his knees.

"Can you get up here?" asked Mr. Vincent, staying at the top.

Sherman peered upward with measuring eyes and gripped the banister. "I want to talk to you," he said, enunciating each word carefully.

"Come up here, then," said Mr. Vincent. Sherman hauled himself along the banister, which was an old oar. His father said, "Are you drunk?"

"Yup," said Sherman.

Mr. Vincent turned to Chicky. "Where's the car?"

"Down by the Singers'. He hit a hydrant."

"You okay," Mr. Vincent said, not as a question. His chest was the color of a pale crab shell, yellowish and soft.

Chicky's eyes welled up. "Uh-huh."

Sherman said, "I want ta talk ta you." When Sherman got drunk, he'd get his thug voice.

"Let's take a look at that cut," said Mr. Vincent, heading for the kitchen. "You might need stitches."

Mr. Vincent snapped on the light and went around the table. Delilah tried leading Sherman to the sink, but he brushed her aside, looking only at his father. He leaned heavily against the counter.

Delilah stamped her foot. "Will you *let* me?"

Sherman kept glaring at Mr. Vincent. "You're my faddah," he said, oblivious of everyone else. Caitlin and Chicky hung back by the calendar.

Delilah said, "Dad, will you tell him to let me wash it off?"

Caitlin hugged herself. The bathrobe she had on was an old one of Mum's. "I think we should take him to the hospital," she said.

Sherman's voice was eerie and low. "Are you my faddah or not?"

Mr. Vincent sat down at the head of the table. "Of course I

am," he said in his nervous deep voice. He rested his elbows on
the table, locked his hands, and rubbed his thumbs together
earnestly.

They all waited, staying very still. "Then you should act like
a faddah," Sherman said.

Everybody looked at him and then at Mr. Vincent. He
pushed back his chair and sat up as straight as a rod, the way he
did when he was demonstrating posture, and firmly planted his
hands on his bare knees. He looked at Sherman and waited.

The thug voice was thick. "Then why don't you never act
like it?"

Mr. Vincent stayed stiff. "Like what?"

Sherman stared at him, his head set. Delilah touched his arm
and whispered, "Sherman," but he wasn't hearing a thing.

Mr. Vincent stood up. "You're drunk," he said. "I'm not
going to talk to someone who's drunk." He tried to go between
the table and the counter to leave, but Sherman grabbed his arm,
pinching it, making white marks.

"I want ta talk ta you," he said through clenched teeth.

Mr. Vincent yanked his arm away. "Now, cut this out – I'll
talk to you when you're sober," he said, disgusted. He hurried
out of the room, bumping into stray chairs on the way. All the
children turned in the direction of his diminishing footsteps.

Then from Sherman came a kind of wail, a hollow cry like
something heard on a marsh, and he looped around at the waist.
Delilah tried to calm him, her hands fluttering around as if she
were chasing after a bird that had gotten in the house. Caitlin let
out a sob and clapped her palm over her mouth, staring at
Sherman.

Chicky looked at her. It was like when their mother died.
When you first heard the news, when it first hit you, it was like
that – you couldn't breathe. It was as if the Devil had appeared
for an instant, and you couldn't breathe.

Sherman kept up his wail, his shoulders swaying. As she
watched him, Delilah's eyes got wider and wider, and then she
began to cry softly. She touched him, saying, "Oh, Shermy.
Oh, honey." Then she got taken over by her own crying and

turned to Hal and put her face into his chest and her shoulders shook up and down and her neck showed where the hair parted.

Chicky stepped past them and went to the back door and opened it and stood there. The crickets outside, a million of them, were ticking *reek reek reek* in the dark. He turned back around.

Then it wasn't the same anymore as when their mother had died. It wasn't as if you had seen the Devil only in a flash. It wasn't as if he had appeared for an instant and then was gone again. Now the feeling was this: that the Devil had swooped down and had landed and was lingering with them all, hulking in the middle of the kitchen table, settling down to stay.

# LORRIE MOORE

☆  ☆  ☆  ☆

# *Like Life*

*Everybody likes the circus.*
*Clowns! elephants! trained horses! peanuts!*
*Everybody likes the circus.*
*Acrobats! tight-rope walkers! camels! band music!*
*Suppose you had a choice of going to the circus*
*or painting a picture. Which would you choose?*
*You'd choose the circus.*
*Everybody likes the circus.*

V. M. Hillyer and E. G. Huey,
*A Child's History of Art*

All the movies that year were about people with plates in their heads: Spirits from another galaxy gather in a resort town at night, taking over the townspeople – all but the man with the plate in his head. Or: A girl with a plate in her head wanders a city beach, believing she is someone else. Evidence washes up on shore. There are sailors. Or: A woman dreams of a beautiful house in which no one lives, and one day she passes the actual house – a cupola, gables, and a porch. She walks up to it, knocks on the door, and it is opened slowly by her! a woman who is a twin of herself, grinning. She has a plate in her head.

Life seemed to have become like that. It had burst out of itself, like a bug.

In February a thaw gave the city the weepy ooze of a wound. There were many colds, people coughing in the subways. The sidewalks foamed to a cheese of spit, and the stoops, doorways, bus shelters were hedged with Rosies – that is what they were called – the jobless men, women, children with gourd lumps of fevers, imploring, hating eyes, and puffed lavender mouths, stark as paintings of mouths. The Rosies sold flowers: a prim tulip, an overflowing iris. Mostly no one bought any. Mostly it was just other Rosies, trading bloom for bloom, until one of them, a woman or a child, died in the street, the others gathering around in a wail, in the tiny, dark morning hours, which weren't morning at all but night.

That year was the first that it became illegal – for those who lived in apartments or houses – not to have a television. The government claimed that important information, information necessary for survival, might need to be broadcast automatically, might need simply to burst on, which it could do. Civilization was at stake, it was said. "Already at the stake," said others, who had come to suspect that they were being spied on, controlled, that what they had thought when they were little – that the people on the television could also see you – now was true. You were supposed to leave it plugged in at all times, the plastic antenna raised in a V – for victory or peace, no one could say.

Mamie lost sleep. She began to distrust things, even her own words; too much had moved in. Objects implanted in your body – fillings, earrings, contraceptives – like satellite dishes, could be picking up messages, substituting their words for yours, feeding you lines. You never knew. Open your mouth, it might betray you with lies, with lackadaise, with moods and speak not your own. The things you were saying might be old radio programs bounced off the foil of your molars, or taxi calls fielded by the mussely glove of your ear. What you described as real might be only a picture, something from *Life* magazine you were forced to live out, after the photography, in imitation. Whole bodies, perhaps, could be ventriloquized. Approximated. You could sit on the lap of a thing and just move your lips. You could become afraid. You could become afraid someone was making you afraid: a new fear, like a gourmet's, a paranoid's paranoia.

This was not the future. This was what was with you now in the house.

Mamie lived in a converted beauty parlor storefront – a tin ceiling, a stench of turpentine, and extra sinks. At night her husband, a struggling painter, moody and beer-breathed, lay sleeping next to her, curled against her, an indifferent whistle in his nose. She closed her eyes. *What all to love in the world*, went a prayer from her childhood. What all to love?

The lumber of his bones piled close.

The radiator racked and spitting. Heat flapping like birds up the pipes.

She remained awake. On nights when she did sleep, her dreams were about the end of life. They involved getting somewhere, getting to the place where she was supposed to die, where it was okay. She was always in a group, like a fire drill or a class trip. Can we die here? Are we there yet? Which way can it possibly be?

Or else there was the house dream. Always the house dream, like the movie of the dream of the house. She would find a house, knock on the door, and it would open slowly, a wedge of dark, and then stop, her own profile greeting her, hanging there midair like a chandelier.

*Death*, said her husband, Rudy. He kept a small hatchet under the mattress, in case of intruders. *Death*. Last year she had gone to a doctor, who had looked at her throat and a mole on her back, studying them like Rorschachs for whatever he might see in them. He removed the mole and put it floating in a pathologist's vial, a tiny marine animal. Peering in at her throat, he said, "Precancer" – like a secret or a zodiac sign.

"*Pre*cancer?" she had repeated quietly, for she was a quiet woman. "Isn't that . . . like *life*?" She was sitting, and he was standing. He fumbled with some alcohol and cotton balls, which he kept on the counter in kitcheny-looking jars, the flour and sugar of the medical world.

He took her wrist and briefly squeezed. "It's *like* life, but it's not *necessarily* life."

There was a wrought-iron fence all around and a locked gate, but it was the bird feeder she remarked first, the wooden arms, the open mouth of boards stuck up there on a single leg. It was nearing Valentine's Day, an angry slosh of a morning, and she was on her way to a realtor, a different one this time, not far from the Fourth and Smith stop of the F train – from where you could see the Statue of Liberty. On her way, she had come upon a house with a bird feeder. A bird feeder! And a tree in front, a towering oak, over 150 years old. A grade school teacher had brought her class to it and now stood in front of it, pointing and saying, "A hundred and fifty years ago. Can anyone tell me when that was?"

But it was the bird feeder, initially: a cross with an angle-roofed shelter at the head – a naked scarecrow bedecked with horizontals like a Frank Lloyd Wright house, or an alpine motel, its wooden ledges strewn with millet seed. In the freckled snow below lay tiny condiment cups of peanut butter, knocked to the ground. A flibberty squirrel, hopping and pausing in spasms, lifted each cup to his nose and nibbled. On the feeder itself was a pair of pigeons – lidless, thick-necked, municipal gargoyles; but there, wasn't that also a sparrow? And a grosbeak?

The house was a real house, one of the few left in New York. A falling-down Edwardian Gothic with a cupola, once painted a silvery gray and now chipping. There was a porch and latticework of carpenter's lace – a house one would go to for piano lessons, if people still took piano lessons, a house invariably seized for a funeral home. It was squeezed between two store-fronts – the realtor's and a laundromat.

"You're looking for a one-bedroom?" said the realtor.

"Yes," said Mamie, though it suddenly seemed both too little and too much to ask for. The realtor had the confident hair and make-up of a woman who had lived forever in New York, a woman who knew ever so wearily how to tie a scarf. Mamie studied the realtor's scarf, guessing the exact geometry of the folds, the location of the knot. If Mamie ever had surgery, scars in a crisscross up her throat, she would have to know such things. A hat, a scarf, a dot of rouge, mints in the mouth: Everyone in New York was hiding something, eventually.

The real estate agent took out an application form. She picked up a pen. "Your name?"

"Mamie Cournand."

"*What?* Here. You fill this out."

It was pretty much the same form she'd filled out previously

at other agencies. What sort of apartment are you looking for;
how much do you make; how do you make it . . .?

"What is children's historical illustrator?" deadpanned the
realtor. "If you don't mind me asking."

"I, uh, work on a series of history publications, picture books
actually, for chil — "

"Freelance?" She looked at Mamie with doubt, suspicion,
and then with sympathy to encourage candor.

"It's for the McWilliams Company." She began to lie. "I've
got an office there that I use. The address is written here." She
rose slightly from her seat, to point it out.

The realtor pulled away. "I'm oriented," she said.

"Oriented?"

"You don't need to reach and point. This your home and
work phone? This your age . . .? You forgot to put in your age."

"Thirty-five."

"Thirty-five," she repeated, writing it in. "You look
younger." She looked at Mamie. "What are you willing to pay?"

"Um, up to nine hundred or so."

"Good luck," she snorted, and still seated in her caster-
wheeled chair, she trundled over to the file cabinet, lifted out a
manila folder, flipped it open. She placed Mamie's application on
top. "This isn't the eighties anymore, you know."

Mamie cleared her throat. Deep in the back she could feel the
wound sticking there, unhealed. "It hasn't not been for very
long. I mean, just a few years." The awkward, frightened look
had leaped to her eyes again, she knew. Fear making a child of
her face – she hated this in herself. As a girl, she had always
listened in a slightly stricken way and never spoke unless she was
asked a question. When she was in college she was the kind of
student sometimes too anxious to enter the cafeteria. Often she
just stayed in her room and drank warm iced tea from a mix and
a Hot Pot. "You live right over here?" The realtor motioned
behind her. "Why are you moving?"

"I'm leaving my husband."

The corner of her mouth curled. "*In this day and age?* Good
luck." She shrugged and spun around to dig through files again.
There was a long silence, the realtor shaking her head.

Mamie craned her neck. "I'd like to see what you have, at any rate."

"We've got nothing." The realtor slammed the file drawer and twisted back around. "But keep trying us. We might have something tomorrow. We're expecting some listings then."

They had been married for fourteen years, living on Brooklyn's south slope for almost ten. It was a neighborhood once so Irish that even as late as the fifties, kids had played soccer in the street and shouted in Gaelic. When she and Rudy first moved in, the area was full of Italian men who barely knew Italian and leaned out of the windows of private clubs, shouting "How aw ya?" Now Hispanic girls in bright leotards gathered on the corner after school, smoking cigarettes and *scoming* the streets. *Scoming*, said the boys. Artists had taken up residence, as well as struggling actors, junkies, desperate Rosies in the street. *Watch out*, went the joke, *for the struggling actors.*

Mamie and Rudy's former beauty parlor now had a padlocked door and boarded front windows. Inside remained the original lavender walls, the gold metallic trim. They had built a loft at one end of the place, and at the other were bookcases, easels, canvases, and a drawing table. Stacked against the wall by the door were Rudy's huge paintings of snarling dogs and Virgin Marys. He had a series of each, and hoped, before he died, *before I shoot myself in the head on my fortieth birthday*, to have a gallery. Until then he painted apartments or borrowed money from Mamie. He was responsible for only one bill – utilities – and on several occasions had had to rush out to intercept Con Ed men arriving with helmets and boots to disconnect the electricity. "Never a dull moment," Rudy would say, thrusting cash into their hands. Once he had tried to pay the bill with two small still lifes.

"You don't think about the real world, Rudy. There's a real world out there." There was in him, she felt, only a fine line between insanity and charm. "A real world about to explode."

"You don't think I worry about the world *exploding*?" His expression darkened. "You don't think I get tears in my eyes

every fucking day thinking about those Rembrandts at the Met
and what's going to happen to them when it does?"

"Rudy, I went to a realtor today."

Probably in their marriage she had been too dreamy and
inconsistent. For love to last, you had to have illusions or have
no illusions at all. But you had to stick to one or the other. It
was the switching back and forth that endangered things.

"Again?" Rudy sighed, ironic but hurt. Once love had
seemed like magic. Now it seemed like tricks. You had to learn
the sleight-of-hand, the snarling dog, the Hail Marys and hoops
of it! Through all the muck of themselves, the times they had
unobligated each other, the anger, the permitted absences, the
loneliness grown dangerous, she had always returned to him.
He'd had faith in that – abracadabra! But eventually the deadliness
set in again. Could you live in the dead excellence of a thing –
the stupid mortar of a body, the stubborn husk love had crawled
from? Yes, he thought.

The television flashed on automatically, one of the government ads: pretty couples testifying to their undying devotion,
undying bodies. "We are the Undying," they said, and they
cuddled their children, who had freckles that bled together on
the cheeks, and toys with glassy button eyes. *Undying*, the
commercials said. *Be undying*. "I can't bear it," Mamie said. "I
can't bear the brother and sister of us. I can't bear the mother and
son of us. I can't bear the Undying commercials. I can't bear
washing my hair in dishwashing liquid, or doing the dishes in
cheap shampoo, because we're too broke or disorganized or
depressed to have both at the same time." Always, they'd made
do. For toilet paper they used holiday-imprinted napkins –
cocktail napkins with poinsettias on them. A big box of them,
with a tray, had been sent to Rudy by mistake. For towels they
used bath mats. For bath mats more poinsettia napkins. They
bought discount soaps with sayings on the label like *Be gentle and
you need not be strong*. "We're camping out here, Rudy. This is
camping!" She tried to appeal to something he would understand.
"My work. It's affecting my work. Look at this!" and she went
over to a small drawing table and held up her half-finished sketch
of Squanto planting corn. She'd been attempting a nuclear

metaphor: white man learning to plant things in the ground, which would later burst forth; how the white man had gotten carried away with planting. "He looks like a toad."

"He looks like a catcher for the Boston Red Sox." Rudy smiled. Would she smile? He grew mock-serious: "The faculties of discernment and generosity are always at war. You must decide whether you will be muse or artist. A woman cannot be both."

"I can't believe you," she said, staring accusingly around their apartment. "This is not life. This is something else," and the whole ill-lit place stared back at her, hurt, a ditzy old beauty parlor flunking someone else's math.

"Forget this Squanto thing," he said, looking compassionate. "I've got an idea for you. I've thought about it all day: a children's book called *Too Many Lesbians.*" He began motioning with his arms. "Lesbians in bushes, lesbians in trees . . . *Find the lesbians . . .*"

"I'm going out for some air," she said, and she grabbed her coat and flew out the door. It was evening already, zinc gray and chill, the puddles freezing on the walks in a thin glaze. She hurried past the shivering Rosies at the corner, hurried six blocks in a zigzag to look at the bird feeder again. Visit a place at night, she knew, and it was yours.

When she reached it, the house was dark, holding its breath, soundless so as not to be discovered. She pressed her face against the gate, the hard cilia of its ironwork, and sighed, longing for another existence, one that belonged to a woman who lived in a house like this, the lovely brow of its mansard roof, thoughtful with rooms. She felt a distrust of her own life, like those aerospace engineers reluctant to fly in planes of their own design, fearing death by their own claptrappery.

The bird feeder stood tall as a constable. There were no birds.

"You should never leave. You just always come back," whispered Rudy. *A tourist in your own despair,* he had once said. It was the title of one of his paintings. One of a snarling dog leaping over a sofa.

She stared through the small window by their bed, a strip of
sky and one dim star, an asterisk to take her away briefly to an
explanation – the night bragging a footnote. He held her, kissed
her. Here in bed was when he seemed to her not to be doing
imitations of other people. After fifteen years, she had seen all
the imitations – friends, parents, movie actors – until it was a
little scary, as if he were many different people at once, people to
turn to, not in distress, but like a channel on television, a mind
gone crazy with cable. He was Jimmy Stewart. He was Elvis
Presley. "When you were growing up, were your parents
funny?" she asked him once.

"*My parents?* You've got to be kidding," he said. "I mean,
once in a while they *memorized* something." He was Dylan on
the harmonica. Lifelike; absolutely lifelike. He was James
Cagney. He was some musical blend he called Smokey Robinson
Caruso.

"Don't you think we'd have beautiful children?" Rudy now
pleaded, sleepily, his hand smoothing the bangs off her brow.

"They'd be nervous and insane," she murmured.

"You're strung out about your health."

"But maybe they'd also be able to do imitations."

Rudy kissed her throat, her ears, her throat again. She had to
spit daily into a jar she kept in the bathroom, and to visit the
clinic regularly, bringing the jar.

"You think we don't love each other anymore," he said. He
was capable of tenderness. Though sometimes he was rough,
pressing himself upon her with a force that startled her, wanting
to make love and kissing her meanly against the wall: *come on,
come on*; though his paintings had grown more violent, feverish
swirls of men in business suits sodomizing animals: *this is my
statement about yuppies, okay?*; though in coffee shops he often
lorded over her spells of sorrowful boredom by looking disgusted while she blinked soggily into her lunch – here without
his clothes on, with her face open to him, he could be a tender
husband. "You think that, but it's not true." Years ago she had
come to know his little lies, harmless for the most part and born
of vanity and doubts, and sometimes fueled merely by a desire
to hide from things whose truth took too much effort to figure

out. She knew the way he would tell the same anecdotes from his life, over and over again, each time a little differently, the exaggerations and contradictions sometimes having a particular purpose – his self-portrait as Undiscovered Genius – and sometimes not seeming to have one at all. "Six inches from the door was an empty shopping cart jammed up against the door," he told her once, and she said, "Rudy, how can it be 6 inches from the door but also jammed up against it?"

"It was full of newspapers and tin cans, stuff like that. I don't know."

She couldn't even say when the love between them had begun to sicken, how long it had been gasping drearily over its own grave of rage and obligation. They had spent over a third of their lives together – a third, like sleep. He was the only man who had ever, even once, claimed to find her beautiful. And he had stuck with her, loved her, even when she was twenty and in terrified thrall to sex, not daring to move, out of politeness or was it timidity. He had helped her. Later she learned to crave the drugged heart of sex, the drugs at the core of it: All the necessary kissing and fussing seemed only that – necessary – to get to the drugs. But it had all been with Rudy, always with him. "Now we are truly in cahoots," she exulted, the day they were married at the county clerk's.

"I don't look good in cahoots," he said, his arm swung loosely around. "Let's go get tattoos."

What kisses there were in disappointment: sorrow fueled them, pushed them to a place. The city writhed, and the world shut down all around. Rudy gave pouting mouths to his Virgin Marys, popped open cans of beer, watched old movies on TV. *"You are happy until you say you are happy. Then you are no longer happy*. Bonnard. The great painter of happiness articulating itself to death."

Maybe she'd thought life would provide her with something more lasting, more flattering than sexual love, but it never had, not really. For a while, she'd felt like one of the girls on the street corner: a world of leotards and drugs – drugs you hungered for and got to fast.

"Don't you think we have a very special love?" asked Rudy.

But she wasn't believing in special love. Even when everyone was being practical, she believed – like a yearning for wind in winter – in only one kind of love, the kind in art: where you die for it. She had read too many books, said Rudy, Victorian novels where the children spoke in the subjunctive. *You take too much to heart*, he wrote her once, when she was away, living in Boston with an aging aunt and a sketch pad.

"I would never die for you," she said softly.

"Sure you would," said Rudy. He sighed, lay back. "Do you want a glass of water? I'll get down and get it."

At times her marriage seemed like a saint, guillotined and still walking for miles through the city, carrying its head. She often thought of the whole apartment going up in flames. What would she take with her? What few things would she grab for her new life? The thought exhilarated her. *You take too much to heart.*

In the house dream, she walks in past the gate and the bird feeder and knocks on the door. It opens slowly and she steps in, in and around, until it is she herself who is opening it, from the other side, wondering who has knocked.

"*Death*," said Rudy again. "Death by nuclear holocaust. Everyone's having those dreams. Except for me. I'm having these completely embarrassing nightmares about bad haircuts and not knowing anyone at a party."

In the morning, sun spilled in through the window by the bed. There was more light in the apartment in winter when there was snow on their overhang and it reflected sunlight inward, making garnet of the rug and striping the bed. A stray tomcat they had befriended, taken in, and fed lounged on the sill. They called him Food Man or Bill of the Baskervilles, and occasionally Rudy was kind to him, lifting the cat up high so that it could check out the bookcases, sniff the ceiling, which it liked to do. Mamie put birdseed out in the snow to attract pigeons, who would amuse the cat through the glass when he was inside. Cat TV. Rudy, she knew, hated pigeons, their lizard feet and pea brains, their strangely bovine meanress. He admired his friend

Marco, who had put metal stakes outside on his air conditioner to keep pigeons from landing there.

Ordinarily Mamie was the first one up, the one to make coffee, the one to head cautiously down the makeshift rungs hammered in the side post, the one to pad out to the kitchen area, heat up water, rinse out mugs, brew coffee, get juice, and bring it all back to bed. This was how they had breakfast, the bedclothes a calico of spills.

But today, as on the other days he feared she would leave him, Rudy wormed naked out of the covers before her, jack-knifed at the loft's edge, descended to the floor with a thump. Mamie watched his body: lanky, big-eared; his back, his arms, his hips. No one ever talked about a man's hips, the hard twin saddles of them. He put on a pair of boxer shorts. "I like these underwear," he said. "They make me feel like David Niven."

He made coffee from water they stored in a plastic garbage barrel. They had it delivered this way, weekly, like seltzer, and they paid twenty dollars for it. They washed dishes in the water that came through the faucets, and they even took quick showers in it, though they risked rashes, said the government doctors. Once Mamie hadn't heard a special radio warning and had taken a shower, scrubbing hard with an old biscuit of loofah, only to step out with burning welts on her arms and shoulders: There had been a chemical pumped into the water, she learned later, one thought to impede the growth of viruses from river-rat fleas. She had soothed her skin with mayonnaise, which was all they had, and the blisters peeled open to a pink ham flesh beneath.

Except for the pleasure of Rudy bringing her coffee – the gift of it – she hated this place. But you could live with a hate. She had. It was so powerful, it had manners; it moved to one side most of the time to let you pass. It was mere dislike that clouded and nagged and stepped in front of your spirit, like a child wanting something.

Rudy returned with the coffee. Mamie rolled to the bed's edge and took the poinsettia tray from him, as he climbed back up and over her. "It's the Coffee Man," she said, trying to sound cheerful, perhaps even to chirp. Shouldn't she try? She placed the tray between them, picked up her coffee, and sipped. It was funny: With each swallow she could recast this fetid place, resee it with a caffeinated heart's eye, make it beautiful even. But it would be the drizzle of affection felt for a hated place before you left it. And she would leave. Again. She would turn the walls and sinks and the turpentined dust to a memory, make it the scene of mild crimes, and think of it with a false, willowy love.

But then you could get to calling everything false and willowy and never know anymore what was true and from the heart.

The cat came and curled up next to her. She massaged the cool, leathery wafer of its ear and plucked dust from its whiskers. He cocked his head and closed his eyes sleepily, content. How sad, she thought, how awful, how fortunate to be an animal and mistake grooming for love.

She placed a hand on Rudy's arm. He bent his head to kiss it, but then couldn't bend that far without spilling his coffee, and so straightened up again.

"Are you ever lonely?" Mamie asked him. Every moment of a morning seemed battled for, the past and future both seeking custody. She laid her cheek against his arm.

"Mamie," he said softly, and that was all.

In the last five years almost all of their friends had died.

*The Indians weren't used to the illnesses that the English brought with them to the new world. Many Indians got sick. When they got chicken pox or mumps, they sometimes died. A very proud Indian might happen to wake up one morning and look in the mirror he'd gotten from an English trader and see red spots polka-dotting his face! The proud Indian would be very upset. He might hurl himself against a tree to maim himself. Or he might throw himself over a cliff or into a fire (picture).*

The agent had on a different scarf today – a turquoise jacquard, twisted into a long coil that she wore wrapped around her neck like a collar. "A room," she said quickly. "Would you settle for a room?"

"I'm not sure," said Mamie. When she spoke with someone snappy and high-powered like that, she felt depressed and under siege.

"Well, come back when you are," said the agent, in her chair, trundling toward the files.

Mamie took the train into Manhattan. She would walk around the art galleries in SoHo, after she dropped off a manuscript at the McWilliams Company. Then she would come back home via the clinic. She had her glass jar in her purse.

In the McWilliams bathroom was a secretary named Goz, whom Mamie had spoken to a few times. Goz was standing in front of the mirror, applying eye make-up. "Hey, how ya doin'?" she said, when she saw Mamie.

Mamie stood next to her, washed her face off from the subway, and dug through her purse for a hairbrush. "I'm okay. How are you?"

"All right." Goz sighed. She had two wax perfume wands, mascara, and several colors of eye shadow spread out on the mirror ledge. She scrutinized her own reflection and sucked in her cheeks. "You know, it's taken me years to get my eye make-up to look like this."

Mamie smiled sympathetically. "A lot of practice, huh."

"No – years of *eye make-up*. I let it build up."

Mamie leaned over and brushed her hair upside down.

"Hmmm," said Goz a little irritably. "What have you been doing these days?"

"Oh, a children's thing again. It's the first time I've done the pictures *and* the text." Mamie straightened and threw her head back. "I'm, um, dropping off a chapter for Seth today." Her hair fell around her face in a penumbra. She looked insane.

"Oh. Hmm," said Goz. She was watching Mamie's hair with interest. "I like *neat* hair. I don't think a woman should look as if sex has already happened."

Mamie smiled at her. "How about you? You going out a lot, having fun?"

"Yeah," said Goz a little defensively. Everyone these days was defensive about their lives. Everyone had settled. "I'm going out. I'm going out with this *man*. And my friends are going out with these *men*. And sometimes we all go out together. The trouble is we're all about thirty years younger than these guys. We'll go to a restaurant or something and I'll look around the table and like every man at our table is thirty years older than his date."

"A father–daughter banquet," said Mamie, trying to joke. "We used to have those at our church."

Goz stared at her. "Yeah," she said, finally turning to put away all her make-up. "You still with that guy who lives in a beauty parlor?"

"Rudy. My husband."

"Whatever," said Goz, and she went into a stall and closed the door.

*None of the English seemed to be getting sick. This caused much whispering in the Indian villages. "We are dying," they said. "But they are not. How come?"*

*And so the chief, weak and ailing, would put on English clothes and go to the Englishmen* (picture).

"This is for Seth Billets," Mamie said, handing the receptionist a large manila envelope. "If he has any questions, he can just phone me. Thanks." She turned and fled the building, taking the stairs rather than the elevator. She never liked to meet with Seth. He tended to be harried and abstracted, and they worked just as well together on the phone. "Mamie? Great stuff," he liked to say. "I'm sending the manuscript back with my suggestions. But ignore them." And always the manuscript arrived three weeks later with comments in the margin like *Oh please* and *No shit.*

She bought a paper and walked downtown toward some galleries she knew on Grand Street, stopping at a coffee shop on Lafayette. Usually she ordered a cup of coffee *and* a cup of tea, as well as a brownie, propping up her sadness with chocolate and caffeine so that it became an anxiety.

"You want something or nothing?" the waitress asked her.

"What?" Startled, Mamie ordered the Slenderella.

"Good choice," said the waitress, as if it had been a test, and then hurried to the kitchen in a palsied jog.

Mamie spread the paper out at a diagonal and read, the pages stoically full of news of the war in India and, locally, of the women's bodies dredged up weekly from the Gowanus Canal.

Disappeared women, with contusions. Beaten and drowned. Secretaries, students, a Rosie or two.

The Slenderella came with egg salad, and she ate it slowly, dissolving it in her mouth, its moist, mothering yellow. On the obituary page there were different deaths, young men, as in a war, and always the ending: *He is survived by his parents.*

Leaving the paper on the table as a tip, she spent the rest of the morning wandering in and out of galleries, looking at paintings that seemed much worse to her than Rudy's. Why these and not her husband's? Painting pictures was the only thing he had ever wanted to do, but no one was helping him. Age had already grabbed him in the face: His cheeks sagged houndishly, his beard was shot with white. Bristly hairs sprouted like wheat from his ears. She used to go with him to art openings, listening to people say bewildering things like "Syntax? Don't you just love *syntax*?" or "Now you know why people are starving in India – we had to wait an hour for our biriyani!" She began to leave early – while he lingered there, dressed in a secondhand pair of black leather pants he looked terrible in, chatting up the dealers, the famous, the successful. He would offer to show them his slides. Or he would go into his rap about Theoretical Disaster Art, how if you can depict atrocities, you can prevent them. "Anticipate, and imitate," he said. "You can preclude and dispirit a holocaust by depriving it of its originality; enough books and plays and paintings, you can change history by getting there first."

One East Village dealer looked him heavily in the eye and said, "You know, in a hive, when a bee has something to communicate, it does a dance. But if the bee does not stop dancing, the others sting it to death," and the dealer then turned and started talking to someone else.

Rudy always walked home alone, slow across the bridge, his life exactly the same as it was. His heart, she knew, was full of that ghetto desire to leap from poor to rich with a single, simple act, that yearning that exhausted the poor – something the city required: an exhausted poor. He would comb the dumpsters for clothes, for artbooks, for pieces of wood to build into frames and stretchers, and in the early hours of the morning he would arrive

home with some huge dried flower he had scavenged, a wobbly
plant stand, or a small, beveled mirror. At noon, without an
apartment to paint, he might go into the city, to the corner of
Broadway and Wall, to play his harmonica for coins. Sea
chanteys and Dylan. Sometimes passersby would slow down on
"Shenandoah," which he played so mournfully that even what
he called "some plagiarist of living," in a beige all-weather coat,
"some guy who wears his asshole on his sleeve," might stop on
his lunch hour to let a part of himself leap up in the hearing, in
communion, in reminder of times left behind. But mostly,
everyone just sailed past, tense with errands, stubbing their feet
on the shoe box Rudy'd placed on the sidewalk for contributions.
He did not play badly. And he could look as handsome as an
actor. But mad – something there in the eyes. Madmen, in fact,
were attracted to him, came bounding up to him like buddies,
shouting psychotically, shaking his hand and putting their arms
around him while he played.

But people with money wouldn't give it to a guy with a
harmonica. A guy with a harmonica had to be a drinker. To say
nothing of a guy with a harmonica wearing a T-shirt that read:
*Wino Cogito: I Think Therefore I Drink.* "I forget sometimes,"
said Rudy, unconvincingly. "I forget and wear that shirt." People
with money would spend 6 dollars on a cocktail for themselves,
but not 80 cents toward a draft beer for a guy with a shirt like
that. Rudy would return home with enough cash for one new
brush, and with that new brush would paint a picture of a bunch
of businessmen sodomizing farm animals. "The best thing about
figure painting," he liked to say, "is deciding what everyone will
wear."

On days when he and his friend Marco got apartment-
painting work, they would make real money, tax free, and treat
themselves to Chinese food. They called their housepainting
partnership We Aim for the Wall, and as a gimmick they gave
out balloons. On these occasions rich people liked them – "Hey,
where's my balloon, guys?" – until they discovered liquor
missing or unfamiliar long-distance calls on their phone bills. As
a result, referrals were rare.

And now something was happening to him. At night, even

more than before, he would push her, force her, and she was growing afraid of him. *I love you*, he would murmur. *If only you knew how much.* He'd grip her painfully at the shoulders, his mouth tight on hers, his body hurting her. In museums and galleries he quietly mocked her opinions. "You don't know anything about art," he would say, scornfully shaking his head, if she liked something by someone who wasn't Rembrandt, someone he felt competitive with, someone his own age, someone who was a woman.

She began going alone, as now, whizzing around the gallery partitions and then stopping, long, in front of a piece she liked, one that pulled her in and danced a little before letting her go. She liked scenes, something with water and a boat, but she rarely found any. Mostly there was only what she called Warning Label art: *Like Man*, said one. *Love Hates*, said another.

Or she would go to a movie. A boy with a plate in his head falls in love with a girl who spurns him. He kidnaps her, feeds her, then kills her by opening up her skull to put a plate in there, too. He props her up in a chair and paints watercolors of her in the nude.

On the subway back, in the afternoon, every beggar seemed to her to have Rudy's face, turning, leering. They would come upon her suddenly, sit next to her and belch, take out a harmonica and play an old folk tune. Or sit far away and just look. She would glance up, and every bum in the car would have his stare, persistent as pain.

She got off at Fourth Avenue and dropped her jar off at the clinic.

"We'll telemail you the results," said a young man in a silvery suit, a technician who eyed her warily.

"All right," she said.

To console herself she went to a shop around the corner and tried on clothes. She and Rudy used to do this sometimes, two young poor people, posing in expensive outfits, just to show the other what they would look like *if only*. They would step out of the dressing rooms and curtsy and bow, exasperating the salesperson. Then they would return all the clothes to the racks, go home, make love. Once, before he left the store, Rudy pulled a formal suit off the rack and screamed, "I don't go to these places!" That same night, in the throes of a nightmare, he had groped for the hatchet beneath him and raised it above her, his mouth open, his eyes gone. "Wake up," she'd pleaded, and squeezed his arm until he lowered it, staring emptily at her, confusion smashed against recognition, a surface broken for air.

"Come here," Rudy said, when she got home. He had made a dinner of fruit and spinach salad, plus large turkey drumsticks that had been on sale – a Caveman Special. He was a little drunk. The painting he had been working on, Mamie could see now, was of a snarling dog *leaping upon* a Virgin Mary, tearing at her lederhosen – not a good sign. Next to the canvas, cockroaches were smashed on the floor like maple creams.

"I'm tired, Rudy," she said.

"Come on." The cabbagey rot of his one bad molar drifted toward her like a cloud. She moved away from him. "After dinner I want you to go for a walk with me, then. At least." He belched.

"All right." She sat down at the table and he joined her. The television was on, a rerun of *Lust for Life*, Rudy's favorite movie.

"What a madman, van Gogh," he drawled. "Shooting himself in the stomach. Any sane person would shoot themselves in the head."

"Of course," said Mamie, staring into the spinach leaves; orange sections lay dead on the top like goldfish. She chewed on the turkey leg, which was gamy and dry. "This is delicious, Rudy." *Any sane person would shoot themselves in the head.* For dessert there was a candy bar, split in two.

They went out. It was dusk, the sun not setting as quickly as in January, when it descended fast as a window shade, but now slowing a little, a lingering, hesitant light. A black eye yellowing. They walked together down the slope toward South Brooklyn, into the streak of orange that would soon be night. They seemed somehow to be racing one another, first one of them slightly ahead, then the other. They passed the old brick row homes, the St. Thomas Aquinas Church, the station stop for the F train and the G, that train that went nowhere, it was said, because it went from Brooklyn to Queens, never to Manhattan; no one was ever on it.

They continued walking beneath the el. A train roared deafeningly above them. The streetlights grew sparse, the houses smaller, fenced and slightly collapsed, like the residents of an old folks' home, waiting to die and staring. What stores there were were closed and dark. A skinny black Labrador in front of one of them sniffed at some bags of garbage, nuzzled them as if they were dead bodies that required turning to reveal the murder weapon, the ice pick in the back. Rudy took Mamie's hand. Mamie could feel it – hard, scaly, chapped from turpentine, the nails ridged as seashells, the thumbs blackened by accidents on the job, dark blood underneath, growing out. "Look at your hands," said Mamie, stopping and holding his hand under a streetlight. There was melted chocolate still on his palm, and he pulled it away self-consciously, wiped it on his coat. "You should use some lotion or something, Rudy. Your hands are going to fall off and land on the sidewalk with a big clank."

"So don't hold them."

The Gowanus Canal lay ahead of them. Already the cold sour smell of it, milky with chemicals, blew onto their faces. "Where are we going, anyway?" she asked. A man in a buttonless coat approached them from the bridge, then crossed and kept walking. "This is a little weird, isn't it, being out here at this hour?" They had come to the drawbridge over the canal and stopped. It was strange, this toxic little vein, strange to stand above it, looking down at night, in a dangerous neighborhood, as if they were in love and entitled to such adventures. Sometimes it seemed she and Rudy were two people attempting to tango, sweating and trying, long after the orchestra had grown tired, long after everyone else had gone home.

Rudy leaned his arms on the railing of the bridge, and another train roared over them, an F train, with its raspberry-pink square. "This is the highest elevated in the city," he said, though the train was drowning him out.

Once the train had passed, Mamie murmured, "I know." When Rudy started giving tours of Brooklyn like this, she knew something was the matter.

"Don't you bet there are bodies in this water? Ones the papers haven't notified us of yet? Don't you bet that there are mobsters, and molls, and just the bodies of women that men never learned to love?"

"Rudy, what are you saying?"

"I'll bet there are more bodies here," he said, and for a moment Mamie could see the old familiar rage in his face, though it flew off again, like a bird, and in that moment there seemed nothing on his face at all, a station between trains, until his features pitched suddenly inward, and he began to cry into the sleeves of his coat, into his hard, gravelly hands.

"Rudy, what is it?" She stood behind him and held him, put her arms around his waist, her cheek against his back. There had been times he had consoled her this way, times when he had simply rubbed her back and connected her again to something: Those times when it seemed she'd floated off and was living far away, he had been like a medium calling her from the dead. "Here we are in the Backrub Cave," he'd said, hovering above her, the quilt spread over them both in a small, warm hut, all the ages of childhood returning to her with his hands. Life was long enough so that you could keep relearning things, think and feel and realize again what you used to know.

He coughed and didn't turn around. "I want to prove to my parents I'm not a fuck-up." Once, when he was twelve, his father had offered to drive him to Andrew Wyeth's house. "You wanna be an artist, dontcha, son? Well, I found out where he lives!"

"It's a little late to be worrying about what our parents think of us," she said. Rudy tended to cling to things that were beside the point – the point was always too frightening. Another train roared by, and the water beneath them wafted up sour and sulfuric. "What is it, really, Rudy? What is it you fear?"

"The Three Stooges," he said. "Poverty, Obscurity, Masturbation. Also the three E's. Ennui. Anomie. Misery. Give me one good reason why we should go on living." He was shouting.

"Sorry," she sighed. She pulled away from him, brushed something from his coat. "You've caught me on a bad day." She searched his profile for an emotion, one that had found dress but not weapons. "I mean, it's life or nothing, right? You don't have to love it, you only have to—" She couldn't think of what.

"We live in a terrible world," he said, and he turned to look at her, wistful and in pain. She could smell that acrid, animal smell hot under his arms. He could smell like that sometimes, like a crazy person. One time she mentioned it, and he went immediately to perfume himself with her bath powder, coming to bed smelling like her. Another time, mistaking the container, he sprinkled himself all over with Ajax.

"Happy Valentine's Day."

"Yes," she said, fear thick in her voice. "Can we go back now?"

*He would sit among them with great dignity and courtesy. "You must pray to this god of yours that keeps you so well. You must pray to him to let us live. Or, if we are to die, let us then go live with your god so that we too may know him." There was silence among the Englishmen. "You see," added the chief, "we pray to our god, but he does not listen. We have done something to offend." Then the chief would stand, go home, remove his English clothes, and die* (picture).

Goz was in the ladies' room again, and she smiled as Mamie entered. "Going to ask me about my love life?" she said, flossing her teeth in front of the mirror. "You always do."

"All right," said Mamie. "How's your love life?"

Goz sawed back and forth with the floss, then tugged it out. "I don't have a love life. I have a *like* life."

Mamie smiled. She thought how nice that might be, to be peacefully free from love – love and its desire for itself – a husband and wife like two army buddies with stories and World Series bets.

"It's pure, it's stripped, it's friendly. Coffee and dispassion. You should try it." She ducked into one of the stalls and locked it. "Nothing is safe anymore," she called out from inside.

Mamie left, went to a record store, and bought records. No one had been buying them for years now, and you could get them for 75 cents. She bought only albums that had a song with the word *heart* in the title: *The Vernacular Heart*, *Hectic Heart*, *A Heart Is Just a Bicycle Behind Your Ribs*. Then she had to leave. Outside the dizzying heat of the store, she clutched them to her chest and walked, down through the decaying restaurant smells of China-town toward the Brooklyn Bridge. The sidewalks were fetid and wet, and the day was warm, as if spring had already come. Everyone was out walking. She would stop at the clinic on the way home and drop off her jar.

She thought of a dream she had had the night before. In the dream a door in the apartment opened up and suddenly there were more rooms, rooms she hadn't known existed, a whole house beneath, which was hers. There were birds living inside, and everything was very dark but beautiful, room after room, with windows open for the birds. On the walls were needlepoint samplers that read: *Die Here*. The real estate agent with the scarf kept saying, "In this day and age" and "It's a steal." Goz was there, her blond hair tipped in red and growing dark roots. Tricolor like candy corn. "Just us girls," she kept saying. It was the end of the world, and they were supposed to live there together, as long as it took to die, until their gums felt strange and they got colds and lost their hair, the television all dots and snow. She remembered some sort of movement – bunched and panicky, through stairwells, corridors, dark tunnels hidden behind paintings – and then, in the dream, it untangled to a fluttering stasis.

When she reached the bridge, she noticed some commotion, a disturbance up ahead, halfway across. Two helicopters were circling in the sky, and there was a small crowd at the center of the pedestrian walk. A fire truck and a police car whizzed by beneath her on the right, lights flashing. She walked to the edge of the crowd. "What is it?" she asked a man.

"Look." He pointed toward another man, who had climbed out over the iron mesh and crossbeams, out to the far railing of the bridge. His wrists were banded in black, and his hands held on to the suspension cables. His back arched and his body swayed out over the water below, as if caught in a web of steel parallelograms. His head dangled like someone crucified, and the wind tore through his hair. In the obscured profile, she thought she could make out the features.

"Oh, my God," she said.

"The woman in front of us says he's the guy wanted for the Gowanus Canal murders. See the police boats circling down there?" Two red-and-white speedboats were churning up water. One of the helicopters hovered noisily above.

"Oh, my God," Mamie said again, and pushed her way through the crowd. A white heat burst in her brain. A police motorbike pulled up on the walkway behind her. A policeman with pistols got off. "It's someone I know," Mamie repeated to people, and elbowed them aside. "It's someone I know." She held her purse and bag in front of her and pushed. The policeman was following close behind, so she pressed hard. When she came to the place directly across from the man, she put down her things and lifted her knee up onto the rail, swung her leg over, and began to crawl, metal to skin, toward the outer reaches of the bridge. "Hey!" someone shouted. The policeman. "Hey!" Cars sped beneath her, and an oceany wind rushed into her mouth. She tried not to look down. "Rudy!" she called out, but it seemed feeble in the roar, her throat a half throat. "It's me!" She felt surrounded by sky, moving toward it, getting closer. Her nails broke against metal. She *was* getting closer, close enough, soon, to grab him, to talk to him, to take his face in her hands and say something about *let's go home*. But then suddenly, too far from her, he relinquished his grip on the cables and fell, turning, his limbs like a windmill, vanishing into the East River below.

She froze. *Rudy.* Two people screamed. There was a whirring noise from the crowd behind her, people pressed to the railings. *No, not this.* "Excuse me, m'am," shouted a voice. "Did you say you knew this man?"

She inched backward on her knees, lowered herself to the walkway. Her legs were scraped and bleeding, but she didn't feel them. Someone was touching her, clamping hands around her arms. Her purse and bag were still where she'd left them, leaning against the cement, and she jerked free, grabbed them, and began to run.

She ran the rest of the way across the bridge, down into the ammonia dank of a passageway, then up again to an old ruined park, zigzagging through the fruit streets of the Heights – Cranberry, Pineapple – along the hexagonal cobbles of the promenade, along the water, and then up left, in a ricochet against the DON'T WALK lights. She did not stop running even when she found herself in Carroll Gardens, heading toward the Gowanus Canal. *No, not this.* She ran up the slope of South Brooklyn for twenty minutes, through traffic, through red lights and sirens, beneath the scary whoop of helicopters and a bellowing plane, until she reached the house with the bird feeder, and when she got there, scarcely able to breathe, she sank down on the concrete lip of its fence and let out a cry, solitary and strangled, into her bag of songs.

The afternoon darkened. Two Rosies shuffled by, ignoring her, but slowing down, winded. They, too, decided to sit on the low wall of the fence, but chose to do so at some distance. She had already slid into the underclass of the sick, she knew, but they didn't recognize her yet. "Are you okay?" she heard one Rosie say to the other, putting her box of flowers down on the sidewalk.

"I'm okay," said her friend.

"You look worse."

"Maybe," she sighed. "The thing is you never know why you're any particular place. You get up, you move. You keep thinking there's some other way than this."

"Look at *her*," snorted the friend, motioning toward Mamie.

"What?" said the other, and then they fell silent.

A fire truck clanged by. Sirens wailed in outrage. After some time Mamie got up, slow as an arthritic, clutching only her purse – her jar still in it – leaving the records behind. She began to walk, stumbling on a raised crack in the pavement. And she noticed something: The house with the bird feeder didn't have a cupola at all. It didn't even have a bird feeder. It simply had a sign that said RESTAURANT, and there was a pigeon on it.

She walked by the Rosies and gave them a dollar for an iris. "My," said the one handing it to her.

At the apartment, the lights were on and the padlock hung open like a hook. She stood for a moment, then kicked at the door with her foot, banging the inside knob against the wall. There was no other sound, and she hesitated there in the doorway, a form of desire, a hovering thing that cannot enter a room. But slowly she took a step, the heel of her hand pressed to the doorjamb to steady her.

He was there, hair dry, wearing different clothes. His arms were raised over his head, the stray tom like a mast in his hands on top. He was moving slowly around the place, as if in a deep Oriental exercise or a dance, the cat investigating the book shelves.

"It's you," Mamie said, frozen by the open door.

The pumpkin stench of the bathroom wafted toward her. The uriney cold rushed in from behind, carrying with it the flap of helicopters. He turned to see her, brought the cat down to his chest. "Hi." He was chewing on a difficult bit of candy, pieces of it stuck in his teeth. He pointed to his cheek, grimacing. "Jujubes," he said. "They play with your mind."

The television burst on: people chanting together, like an anthem for cola. *We are the Undying. We are . . .*

He turned away and lifted the cat up high again, close to the golden moldings of the ceiling. "Cats love this," he said. His arms were long and tireless. In the reach, his shirt had come untucked, and the soft bare skin of his waist flashed like a smile. "Where have you been?"

There was only this world, this looted, ventriloquized earth. If one were to look for a place to die, mightn't it be here? – like some old lesson of knowing your kind and returning. She was afraid, and the afraid, she realized, sought opportunities for bravery in love. She tucked the flower in her blouse. Life or death. Something or nothing. *You want something or nothing?*

She stepped toward him with a heart she'd someday tear the terror from.

Here. But not now.

JOYCE CAROL OATES

☆   ☆   ☆   ☆

# *Where Are You Going,*
# *Where Have You Been?*

*For Bob Dylan*

Her name was Connie. She was fifteen and she had a quick
nervous giggling habit of craning her neck to glance into mirrors,
or checking other people's faces to make sure her own was all
right. Her mother, who noticed everything and knew everything
and who hadn't much reason any longer to look at her own face,
always scolded Connie about it. "Stop gawking at yourself, who
are you? You think you're so pretty?" she would say. Connie
would raise her eyebrows at these familiar complaints and look
right through her mother, into a shadowy vision of herself as she
was right at that moment: she knew she was pretty and that was
everything. Her mother had been pretty once too, if you could
believe those old snapshots in the album, but now her looks were
gone and that was why she was always after Connie.

"Why don't you keep your room clean like your sister?
How've you got your hair fixed – what the hell stinks? Hair
spray? You don't see your sister using that junk."

Her sister June was twenty-four and still lived at home. She
was a secretary in the high school Connie attended, and if that
wasn't bad enough – with her in the same building – she was so
plain and chunky and steady that Connie had to hear her praised
all the time by her mother and her mother's sisters. June did this,
June did that, she saved money and helped clean the house and
cooked and Connie couldn't do a thing, her mind was all filled
with trashy daydreams. Their father was away at work most of
the time and when he came home he wanted supper and he read
the newspaper at supper and after supper he went to bed. He

didn't bother talking much to them, but around his bent head Connie's mother kept picking at her until Connie wished her mother was dead and she herself was dead and it was all over. "She makes me want to throw up sometimes," she complained to her friends. She had a high, breathless, amused voice which made everything she said a little forced, whether it was sincere or not.

There was one good thing: June went places with girlfriends of hers, girls who were just as plain and steady as she, and so when Connie wanted to do that her mother had no objections. The father of Connie's best girlfriend drove the girls the 3 miles to town and left them off at a shopping plaza, so that they could walk through the stores or go to a movie, and when he came to pick them up again at eleven he never bothered to ask what they had done.

They must have been familiar sights, walking around that shopping plaza in their shorts and flat ballerina slippers that always scuffed the sidewalk, with charm bracelets jingling on their thin wrists; they would lean together to whisper and laugh secretly if someone passed by who amused or interested them. Connie had long dark blond hair that drew anyone's eye to it, and she wore part of it pulled up on her head and puffed out and the rest of it she let fall down her back. She wore a pullover jersey blouse that looked one way when she was at home and another way when she was away from home. Everything about her had two sides to it, one for home and one for anywhere that was not home: her walk that could be childlike and bobbing, or languid enough to make anyone think she was hearing music in her head, her mouth which was pale and smirking most of the time, but bright and pink on these evenings out, her laugh which was cynical and drawling at home – "Ha, ha, very funny" – but high-pitched and nervous anywhere else, like the jingling of the charms on her bracelet.

Sometimes they did go shopping or to a movie, but sometimes they went across the highway, ducking fast across the busy road, to a drive-in restaurant where older kids hung out. The restaurant was shaped like a big bottle, though squatter than a real bottle, and on its cap was a revolving figure of a grinning boy who held a hamburger aloft. One night in midsummer they ran across, breathless with daring, and right away someone leaned out a car window and invited them over, but it was just a boy from high school they didn't like. It made them feel good to be able to ignore him. They went up through the maze of parked and cruising cars to the bright-lit, fly-infested restaurant, their faces pleased and expectant as if they were entering a sacred building that loomed out of the night to give them what haven and what blessing they yearned for. They sat at the counter and crossed their legs at the ankles, their thin shoulders rigid with excitement and listened to the music that made everything so good: the music was always in the background like music at a church service, it was something to depend upon.

A boy named Eddie came in to talk with them. He sat backwards on his stool, turning himself jerkily around in semi-circles and then stopping and turning again, and after a while he asked Connie if she would like something to eat. She said she did and so she tapped her friend's arm on her way out – her friend pulled her face up into a brave droll look – and Connie said she would meet her at eleven, across the way. "I just hate to leave her like that," Connie said earnestly, but the boy said that she wouldn't be alone for long. So they went out to his car and on the way Connie couldn't help but let her eyes wander over the windshields and faces all around her, her face gleaming with joy that had nothing to do with Eddie or even this place; it might have been the music. She drew her shoulders up and sucked in her breath with the pure pleasure of being alive, and just at that moment she happened to glance at a face just a few feet from hers. It was a boy with shaggy black hair, in a convertible jalopy painted gold. He stared at her and then his lips widened into a grin. Connie slit her eyes at him and turned away, but she couldn't help glancing back and there he was still watching her. He wagged a finger and laughed and said, "Gonna get you, baby," and Connie turned away again without Eddie noticing anything.

She spent three hours with him, at the restaurant where they ate hamburgers and drank Cokes in wax cups that were always sweating, and then down an alley a mile or so away, and when he left her off at five to eleven only the movie house was still open at the plaza. Her girlfriend was there, talking with a boy. When Connie came up the two girls smiled at each other and Connie said, "How was the movie?" and the girl said, "*You* should know." They rode off with the girl's father, sleepy and pleased, and Connie couldn't help but look at the darkened shopping plaza with its big empty parking lot and its signs that were faded and ghostly now, and over at the drive-in restaurant where cars were still circling tirelessly. She couldn't hear the music at this distance.

Next morning June asked her how the movie was and Connie said, "So-so."

She and that girl and occasionally another girl went out several times a week that way, and the rest of the time Connie spent around the house – it was summer vacation – getting in her mother's way and thinking, dreaming, about the boys she met. But all the boys fell back and dissolved into a single face that was not even a face, but an idea, a feeling, mixed up with the urgent insistent pounding of the music and the humid night air of July. Connie's mother kept dragging her back to the daylight by finding things for her to do or saying suddenly, "What's this about the Pettinger girl?"

And Connie would say nervously, "Oh, her. That dope." She always drew thick clear lines between herself and such girls, and her mother was simple and kindly enough to believe her. Her mother was so simple, Connie thought, that it was maybe cruel to fool her so much. Her mother went scuffling around the house in old bedroom slippers and complained over the telephone to one sister about the other, then the other called up and the two of them complained about the third one. If June's name was mentioned her mother's tone was approving, and if Connie's name was mentioned it was disapproving. This did not really mean she disliked Connie and actually Connie thought that her mother preferred her to June because she was prettier, but the two of them kept up a pretense of exasperation, a sense that they were tugging and struggling over something of little value to either of them. Sometimes, over coffee, they were almost friends, but something would come up – some vexation that was like a fly buzzing suddenly around their heads – and their faces went hard with contempt.

One Sunday Connie got up at eleven – none of them bothered with church – and washed her hair so that it could dry all day long, in the sun. Her parents and sister were going to a barbecue at an aunt's house and Connie said no, she wasn't interested, rolling her eyes, to let her mother know just what she thought of it. "Stay home alone then," her mother said sharply. Connie sat out back in a lawn chair and watched them drive away, her father quiet and bald, hunched around so that he could back the car out, her mother with a look that was still angry and not at all softened through the windshield, and in the back seat poor old June all dressed up as if she didn't know what a barbecue was, with all the running yelling kids and the flies. Connie sat with her eyes closed in the sun, dreaming and dazed with the warmth about her as if this were a kind of love, the caresses of love, and her mind slipped over onto thoughts of the boy she had been with the night before and how nice he had been, how sweet it always was, not the way someone like June would suppose but sweet, gentle, the way it was in movies and promised in songs; and when she opened her eyes she hardly knew where she was, the back yard ran off into weeds and a fence-line of trees and behind it the sky was perfectly blue and still. The asbestos "ranch house" that was now three years old startled her – it looked small. She shook her head as if to get awake.

It was too hot. She went inside the house and turned on the radio to drown out the quiet. She sat on the edge of her bed, barefoot, and listened for an hour and a half to a program called XYZ Sunday Jamboree, record after record of hard, fast, shrieking songs she sang along with, interspersed by exclamations from "Bobby King": "An' look here you girls at Napoleon's – Son and Charley want you to pay real close attention to this song coming up!"

And Connie paid close attention herself, bathed in a glow of slow-pulsed joy that seemed to rise mysteriously out of the music itself and lay languidly about the airless little room, breathed in and breathed out with each gentle rise and fall of her chest.

After a while she heard a car coming up the drive. She sat up at once, startled, because it couldn't be her father so soon. The gravel kept crunching all the way in from the road – the driveway was long – and Connie ran to the window. It was a car she didn't know. It was an open jalopy, painted a bright gold that caught the sun opaquely. Her heart began to pound and her fingers snatched at her hair, checking it, and she whispered, "Christ. Christ," wondering how bad she looked. The car came to a stop at the side door and the horn sounded four short taps as if this were a signal Connie knew.

She went into the kitchen and approached the door slowly, then hung out the screen door, her bare toes curling down off the step. There were two boys in the car and now she recognized the driver: he had shaggy, shabby black hair that looked crazy as a wig and he was grinning at her.

"I ain't late, am I?" he said.

"Who the hell do you think you are?" Connie said.

"Toldja I'd be out, didn't I?"

"I don't even know who you are."

She spoke sullenly, careful to show no interest or pleasure, and he spoke in a fast bright monotone. Connie looked past him to the other boy, taking her time. He had fair brown hair, with a lock that fell onto his forehead. His sideburns gave him a fierce, embarrassed look, but so far he hadn't even bothered to glance at her. Both boys wore sunglasses. The driver's glasses were metallic and mirrored everything in miniature.

"You wanta come for a ride?" he said.

Connie smirked and let her hair fall loose over one shoulder.

"Don'tcha like my car? New paint job," he said. "Hey."

"What?"

"You're cute."

She pretended to fidget, chasing flies away from the door.

"Don'tcha believe me, or what?" he said.

"Look, I don't even know who you are," Connie said in disgust.

"Hey, Ellie's got a radio, see. Mine's broke down." He lifted his friend's arm and showed her the little transistor the boy was holding, and now Connie began to hear the music. It was the same program that was playing inside the house.

"Bobby King?" she said.

"I listen to him all the time. I think he's great."

"He's kind of great," Connie said reluctantly.

"Listen, that guy's *great*. He knows where the action is."

Connie blushed a little, because the glasses made it impossible for her to see just what this boy was looking at. She couldn't decide if she liked him or if he was just a jerk, and so she dawdled in the doorway and wouldn't come down or go back inside. She said, "What's all that stuff painted on your car?"

"Can'tcha read it?" He opened the door very carefully, as if he was afraid it might fall off. He slid out just as carefully, planting his feet firmly on the ground, the tiny metallic world in his glasses slowing down like gelatine hardening and in the midst of it Connie's bright green blouse. "This here is my name, to begin with," he said. ARNOLD FRIEND was written in tar-like black letters on the side, with a drawing of a round grinning face that reminded Connie of a pumpkin, except it wore sunglasses. "I wanta introduce myself, I'm Arnold Friend and that's my real name and I'm gonna be your friend, honey, and inside the car's Ellie Oscar, he's kinda shy." Ellie brought his transistor up to his shoulder and balanced it there. "Now these numbers are a secret code, honey," Arnold Friend explained. He read off the numbers 33, 19, 17 and raised his eyebrows at her to see what she thought of that, but she didn't think much of it. The left rear fender had been smashed and around it was written, on the gleaming gold background: DONE BY CRAZY WOMAN DRIVER. Connie had to laugh at that. Arnold Friend was pleased at her laughter and looked up at her. "Around the other side's a lot more – you wanta come and see them?"

"No."

"Why not?"

"Why should I?"

"Don'tcha wanta see what's on the car? Don'tcha wanta go for a ride?"

"I don't know."

"Why not?"

"I got things to do."

"Like what?"

"Things."

He laughed as if she had said something funny. He slapped his thighs. He was standing in a strange way, leaning back against the car as if he were balancing himself. He wasn't tall, only an inch or so taller than she would be if she came down to him. Connie liked the way he was dressed, which was the way all of them dressed: tight faded jeans stuffed into black, scuffed boots, a belt that pulled his waist in and showed how lean he was, and a white pull-over shirt that was a little soiled and showed the hard small muscles of his arms and shoulders. He looked as if he probably did hard work, lifting and carrying things. Even his neck looked muscular. And his face was a familiar face, somehow: the jaw and chin and cheeks slightly darkened, because he hadn't shaved for a day or two, and the nose long and hawk-like, sniffing as if she were a treat he was going to gobble up and it was all a joke.

"Connie, you ain't telling the truth. This is your day set aside for a ride with me and you know it," he said, still laughing. The way he straightened and recovered from his fit of laughing showed that it had been all fake.

"How do you know what my name is?" she said suspiciously.

"It's Connie."

"Maybe and maybe not."

"I know my Connie," he said, wagging his finger. Now she remembered him even better, back at the restaurant, and her cheeks warmed at the thought of how she sucked in her breath just at the moment she passed him – how she must have looked to him. And he had remembered her. "Ellie and I come out here especially for you," he said. "Ellie can sit in back. How about it?"

"Where?"

"Where what?"

"Where're we going?"

He looked at her. He took off the sunglasses and she saw how pale the skin around his eyes was, like holes that were not in shadow but instead in light. His eyes were like chips of broken glass that catch the light in an amiable way. He smiled. It was as

if the idea of going for a ride somewhere, to some place, was a
new idea to him.

"Just for a ride, Connie sweetheart."

"I never said my name was Connie," she said.

"But I know what it is. I know your name and all about you,
lots of things," Arnold Friend said. He had not moved yet but
stood still leaning back against the side of his jalopy. "I took a
special interest in you, such a pretty girl, and found out all about
you like I know your parents and sister are gone somewheres
and I know where and how long they're going to be gone, and I
know who you were with last night, and your best friend's name
is Betty. Right?"

He spoke in a simple lilting voice, exactly as if he were
reciting the words to a song. His smile assured her that everything was fine. In the car Ellie turned up the volume on his radio
and did not bother to look around at them.

"Ellie can sit in the back seat," Arnold Friend said. He
indicated his friend with a casual jerk of his chin, as if Ellie did
not count and she should not bother with him.

"How'd you find out all that stuff?" Connie said.

"Listen: Betty Schultz and Tony Fitch and Jimmy Pettinger
and Nancy Pettinger," he said, in a chant. "Raymond Stanley
and Bob Hutter — "

"Do you know all those kids?"

"I know everybody."

"Look, you're kidding. You're not from around here."

"Sure."

"But — how come we never saw you before?"

"Sure you saw me before," he said. He looked down at his
boots, as if he were a little offended. "You just don't remember."

"I guess I'd remember you," Connie said.

"Yeah?" He looked up at this, beaming. He was pleased. He
began to mark time with the music from Ellie's radio, tapping
his fists lightly together. Connie looked away from his smile to
the car, which was painted so bright it almost hurt her eyes to
look at it. She looked at that name, ARNOLD FRIEND. And
up at the front fender was an expression that was familiar —
MAN THE FLYING SAUCERS. It was an expression kids had

used the year before, but didn't use this year. She looked at it for
a while as if the words meant something to her that she did not
yet know.

"What're you thinking about? Huh?" Arnold Friend
demanded. "Not worried about your hair blowing around in the
car, are you?"

"No."

"Think I maybe can't drive good?"

"How do I know?"

"You're a hard girl to handle. How come?" he said. "Don't
you know I'm your friend? Didn't you see me put my sign in the
air when you walked by?"

"What sign?"

"My sign." And he drew an X in the air, leaning out toward
her. They were maybe ten feet apart. After his hand fell back to
his side the X was still in the air, almost visible. Connie let the
screen door close and stood perfectly still inside it, listening to
the music from her radio and the boy's blend together. She stared
at Arnold Friend. He stood there so stiffly relaxed, pretending to
be relaxed, with one hand idly on the door handle as if he were
keeping himself up that way and had no intention of ever moving
again. She recognized most things about him, the tight jeans that
showed his thighs and buttocks and the greasy leather boots and
the tight shirt, and even that slippery friendly smile of his, that
sleepy dreamy smile that all the boys used to get across ideas
they didn't want to put into words. She recognized all this and
also the singsong way he talked, slightly mocking, kidding, but
serious and a little melancholy, and she recognized the way he
tapped one fist against the other in homage to the perpetual
music behind him. But all these things did not come together.

She said suddenly, "Hey, how old are you?"

His smile faded. She could see then that he wasn't a kid, he
was much older — thirty, maybe more. At this knowledge her
heart began to pound faster.

"That's a crazy thing to ask. Can'tcha see I'm your own
age?"

"Like hell you are."

"Or maybe a coupla years older, I'm eighteen."

"Eighteen?" she said doubtfully.

He grinned to reassure her and lines appeared at the corners of his mouth. His teeth were big and white. He grinned so broadly his eyes became slits and she saw how thick the lashes were, thick and black as if painted with a black tar-like material. Then he seemed to become embarrassed, abruptly, and looked over his shoulder at Ellie. "*Him*, he's crazy," he said. "Ain't he a riot, he's a nut, a real character." Ellie was still listening to the music. His sunglasses told nothing about what he was thinking. He wore a bright orange shirt unbuttoned halfway to show his chest, which was a pale, bluish chest and not muscular like Arnold Friend's. His shirt collar was turned up all around and the very tips of the collar pointed out past his chin as if they were protecting him. He was pressing the transistor radio up against his ear and sat there in a kind of daze, right in the sun.

"He's kinda strange," Connie said.

"Hey, she says you're kinda strange! Kinda strange!" Arnold Friend cried. He pounded on the car to get Ellie's attention. Ellie turned for the first time and Connie saw with shock that he wasn't a kid either – he had a fair, hairless face, cheeks reddened slightly as if the veins grew too close to the surface of his skin, the face of a forty-year-old baby. Connie felt a wave of dizziness rise in her at this sight and she stared at him as if waiting for something to change the shock of the moment, make it all right again. Ellie's lips kept shaping words, mumbling along with the words blasting his ear.

"Maybe you two better go away," Connie said faintly.

"What? How come?" Arnold Friend cried. "We come out here to take you for a ride. It's Sunday." He had the voice of the man on the radio now. It was the same voice, Connie thought. "Don'tcha know it's Sunday all day and honey, no matter who you were with last night today you're with Arnold Friend and don't you forget it! – Maybe you better step out here," he said, and this last was in a different voice. It was a little flatter, as if the heat was finally getting to him.

"No. I got things to do."

"Hey."

"You two better leave."

"We ain't leaving until you come with us."

"Like hell I am — "

"Connie, don't fool around with me. I mean, I mean, don't fool *around*," he said, shaking his head. He laughed incredulously. He placed his sunglasses on top of his head, carefully, as if he were indeed wearing a wig, and brought the stems down behind his ears. Connie stared at him, another wave of dizziness and fear rising in her so that for a moment he wasn't even in focus but was just a blur, standing there against his gold car, and she had the idea that he had driven up the driveway all right but had come from nowhere before that and belonged nowhere and that everything about him and even the music that was so familiar to her was only half real.

"If my father comes and sees you — "

"He ain't coming. He's at a barbecue."

"How do you know that?"

"Aunt Tillie's. Right now they're – uh – they're drinking. Sitting around," he said vaguely, squinting as if he were staring all the way to town and over to Aunt Tillie's back yard. Then the vision seemed to clear and he nodded energetically. "Yeah. Sitting around. There's your sister in a blue dress, huh? And high heels, the poor sad bitch – nothing like you, sweetheart! And your mother's helping some fat woman with the corn, they're cleaning the corn – husking the corn — "

"What fat woman?" Connie cried.

"How do I know what fat woman. I don't know every goddam fat woman in the world!" Arnold Friend laughed.

"Oh, that's Mrs. Hornby. . . . Who invited her?" Connie said. She felt a little light-headed. Her breath was coming quickly.

"She's too fat. I don't like them fat. I like them the way you are, honey," he said, smiling sleepily at her. They stared at each other for a while, through the screen door. He said softly, "Now what you're going to do is this: you're going to come out that door. You're going to sit up front with me and Ellie's going to sit in the back, the hell with Ellie, right? This isn't Ellie's date. You're my date. I'm your lover, honey."

"What? You're crazy — "

"Yes, I'm your lover. You don't know what that is but you will," he said. "I know that too. I know all about you. But look: it's real nice and you couldn't ask for nobody better than me, or more polite. I always keep my word. I'll tell you how it is, I'm always nice at first, the first time. I'll hold you so tight you won't think you have to try to get away or pretend anything because you'll know you can't. And I'll come inside you where it's all secret and you'll give in to me and you'll love me—"

"Shut up! You're crazy!" Connie said. She backed away from the door. She put her hands against her ears as if she'd heard something terrible, something not meant for her. "People don't talk like that, you're crazy," she muttered. Her heart was almost too big now for her chest and its pumping made sweat break out all over her. She looked out to see Arnold Friend pause and then take a step toward the porch lurching. He almost fell. But, like a clever drunken man, he managed to catch his balance. He wobbled in his high boots and grabbed hold of one of the porch posts.

"Honey?" he said. "You still listening?"

"Get the hell out of here!"

"Be nice, honey. Listen."

"I'm going to call the police—"

He wobbled again and out of the side of his mouth came a fast spat curse, an aside not meant for her to hear. But even this "Christ!" sounded forced. Then he began to smile again. She watched this smile come, awkward as if he were smiling from inside a mask. His whole face was a mask, she thought wildly, tanned down onto his throat but then running out as if he had plastered make-up on his face but had forgotten about his throat.

"Honey—? Listen, here's how it is. I always tell the truth and I promise you this: I ain't coming in that house after you."

"You better not! I'm going to call the police if you – if you don't—"

"Honey," he said, talking right through her voice, "honey, I'm not coming in there but you are coming out here. You know why?"

She was panting. The kitchen looked like a place she had never seen before, some room she had run inside but which wasn't good enough, wasn't going to help her. The kitchen window had never had a curtain, after three years, and there were dishes in the sink for her to do – probably – and if you ran your hand across the table you'd probably feel something sticky there.

"You listening, honey? Hey?"

" — going to call the police — "

"Soon as you touch the phone I don't need to keep my promise and can come inside. You won't want that."

She rushed forward and tried to lock the door. Her fingers were shaking. "But why lock it?" Arnold Friend said gently, talking right into her face. "It's just a screen door. It's just nothing." One of his boots was at a strange angle, as if his foot wasn't in it. It pointed out to the left, bent at the ankle. "I mean, anybody can break through a screen door and glass and wood and iron or anything else if he needs to, anybody at all and specially Arnold Friend. If the place got lit up with a fire, honey, you'd come running out into my arms, right into my arms and safe at home – like you knew I was your lover and'd stopped fooling around. I don't mind a nice shy girl but I don't like no fooling around." Part of those words were spoken with a slight rhythmic lilt, and Connie somehow recognized them – the echo of a song from last year, about a girl rushing into her boyfriend's arms and coming home again —

Connie stood barefoot on the linoleum floor, staring at him. "What do you want?" she whispered.

"I want you," he said.

"What?"

"Seen you that night and thought, that's the one, yes sir. I never needed to look any more."

"But my father's coming back. He's coming to get me. I had to wash my hair first — " She spoke in a dry, rapid voice, hardly raising it for him to hear.

"No, your daddy is not coming and yes, you had to wash your hair and you washed it for me. It's nice and shining and all for me, I thank you, sweetheart," he said, with a mock bow, but again he almost lost his balance. He had to bend and adjust his boots. Evidently his feet did not go all the way down; the boots must have been stuffed with something so that he would seem taller. Connie stared out at him and behind him Ellie in the car, who seemed to be looking off toward Connie's right, into nothing. This Ellie said, pulling the words out of the air one after another as if he were just discovering them, "You want me to pull out the phone?"

"Shut your mouth and keep it shut," Arnold Friend said, his face red from bending over or maybe from embarrassment because Connie had seen his boots. "This ain't none of your business."

"What – what are you doing? What do you want?" Connie said. "If I call the police they'll get you, they'll arrest you—"

"Promise was not to come in unless you touch that phone, and I'll keep that promise," he said. He resumed his erect position and tried to force his shoulders back. He sounded like a hero in a movie, declaring something important. He spoke too loudly and it was as if he were speaking to someone behind Connie. "I ain't made plans for coming in that house where I don't belong but just for you to come out to me, the way you should. Don't you know who I am?"

"You're crazy," she whispered. She backed away from the door but did not want to go into another part of the house, as if this would give him permission to come through the door. "What do you . . . You're crazy, you . . ."

"Huh? What're you saying, honey?"

Her eyes darted everywhere in the kitchen. She could not remember what it was, this room.

"This is how it is, honey: you come out and we'll drive away, have a nice ride. But if you don't come out we're gonna wait till your people come home and then they're all going to get it."

"You want that telephone pulled out?" Ellie said. He held the radio away from his ear and grimaced, as if without the radio the air was too much for him.

"I toldja shut up, Ellie." Arnold Friend said. "You're deaf, get a hearing aid, right? Fix yourself up. This little girl's no trouble and's gonna be nice to me, so Ellie keep to yourself, this ain't your date – right? Don't hem in on me. Don't hog. Don't crush. Don't bird dog. Don't trail me," he said in a rapid meaningless voice, as if he were running through all the expressions he'd learned but was no longer sure which one of them was in style, then rushing on to new ones, making them up with his eyes closed, "Don't crawl under my fence, don't squeeze in my chipmunk hole, don't sniff my glue, suck my popsicle, keep your own greasy fingers on yourself!" He shaded his eyes and peered in at Connie, who was backed against the kitchen table. "Don't mind him, honey, he's just a creep. He's a dope. Right? I'm the boy for you and like I said you come out here nice like a lady and give me your hand, and nobody else gets hurt, I mean, your nice old bald-headed daddy and your mummy and your sister in her high heels. Because listen: why bring them in this?"

"Leave me alone," Connie whispered.

"Hey, you know that old woman down the road, the one with the chickens and stuff – you know her?"

"She's dead!"

"Dead? What? You know her?" Arnold Friend said.

"She's dead —"

"Don't you like her?"

"She's dead – she's – she isn't here any more —"

"But don't you like her, I mean, you got something against her? Some grudge or something?" Then his voice dipped as if he were conscious of rudeness. He touched the sunglasses on top of his head as if to make sure they were still there. "Now you be a good girl."

"What are you going to do?"

"Just two things, or maybe three," Arnold Friend said. "But I promise it won't last long and you'll like me that way you get to like people you're close to. You will. It's all over for you here, so come on out. You don't want your people in any trouble, do you?"

She turned and bumped against a chair or something, hurting her leg, but she ran into the back room and picked up the telephone. Something roared in her ear, a tiny roaring, and she was so sick with fear that she could do nothing but listen to it – the telephone was clammy and very heavy and her fingers groped

down to the dial but were too weak to touch it. She began to
scream into the phone, into the roaring. She cried out, she cried
for her mother, she felt her breath start jerking back and forth in
her lungs as if it were something Arnold Friend were stabbing
her with again and again with no tenderness. A noisy sorrowful
wailing rose all about her and she was locked inside it the way
she was locked inside this house.

After a while she could hear again. She was sitting on the
floor, with her wet back against the wall.

Arnold Friend was saying from the door, "That's a good
girl. Put the phone back."

She kicked the phone away from her.

"No, honey. Pick it up. Put it back right."

She picked it up and put it back. The dial tone stopped.

"That's a good girl. Now you come outside."

She was hollow with what had been fear, but what was now
just an emptiness. All that screaming had blasted it out of her.
She sat, one leg cramped under her, and deep inside her brain
was something like a pinpoint of light that kept going and would
not let her relax. She thought, I'm not going to see my mother
again. She thought, I'm not going to sleep in my bed again. Her
bright green blouse was all wet.

Arnold Friend said, in a gentle–loud voice that was like a
stage voice, "The place where you came from ain't there any
more, and where you had in mind to go is cancelled out. This
place you are now – inside your daddy's house – is nothing but a
cardboard box I can knock down any time. You know that and
always did know it. You hear me?"

She thought, I have got to think. I have to know what to do.

"We'll go out to a nice field, out in the country here where it
smells so nice and it's sunny," Arnold Friend said. "I'll have my
arms tight around you so you won't need to try to get away and
I'll show you what love is like, what it does. The hell with this
house! It looks solid all right," he said. He ran a fingernail down
the screen and the noise did not make Connie shiver, as it would
have the day before. "Now put your hand on your heart, honey.
Feel that? That feels solid too but we know better, be nice to me,
be sweet like you can because what else is there for a girl like you

but to be sweet and pretty and give in? – and get away before her people come back?"

She felt her pounding heart. Her hands seemed to enclose it. She thought for the first time in her life that it was nothing that was hers, that belonged to her, but just a pounding, living thing inside this body that wasn't hers either.

"You don't want them to get hurt," Arnold Friend went on. "Now get up, honey. Get up all by yourself."

She stood.

"Now turn this way. That's right. Come over here to me – Ellie, put that away, didn't I tell you? You dope. You miserable creepy dope," Arnold Friend said. His words were not angry but only part of an incantation. The incantation was kindly. "Now come out through the kitchen to me honey and let's see a smile, try it, you're a brave sweet little girl and now they're eating corn and hotdogs cooked to bursting over an outdoor fire, and they don't know one thing about you and never did and honey you're better than them because not one of them would have done this for you."

Connie felt the linoleum under her feet; it was cool. She brushed her hair back out of her eyes. Arnold Friend let go of the post tentatively and opened his arms for her, his elbows pointing up toward each other and his wrists limp, to show that this was an embarrassed embrace and a little mocking, he didn't want to make her self-conscious.

She put out her hand against the screen. She watched herself push the door slowly open as if she were safe back somewhere in the other doorway, watching this body and this head of long hair moving out into the sunlight where Arnold Friend was.

"My sweet little blue-eyed girl," he said, in a half-sung sigh that had nothing to do with her brown eyes but was taken up just the same by the vast sunlit reaches of the land behind him and on all sides of him, so much land that Connie had never seen before and did not recognize except to know that she was going to it.

TIM O'BRIEN

☆   ☆   ☆   ☆

# The Things They Carried

First Lieutenant Jimmy Cross carried letters from a girl named
Martha, a junior at Mount Sebastian College in New Jersey.
They were not love letters, but Lieutenant Cross was hoping, so
he kept them folded in plastic at the bottom of his rucksack. In
the late afternoon, after a day's march, he would dig his foxhole,
wash his hands under a canteen, unwrap the letters, hold them
with the tips of his fingers, and spend the last hour of light
pretending. He would imagine romantic camping trips into the
White Mountains in New Hampshire. He would sometimes taste
the envelope flaps, knowing her tongue had been there. More
than anything, he wanted Martha to love him as he loved her,
but the letters were mostly chatty, elusive on the matter of love.
She was a virgin, he was almost sure. She was an English major
at Mount Sebastian, and she wrote beautifully about her profes-
sors and room-mates and midterm exams, about her respect for
Chaucer and her great affection for Virginia Woolf. She often
quoted lines of poetry; she never mentioned the war, except to
say, Jimmy, take care of yourself. The letters weighed 10 ounces.
They were signed Love, Martha, but Lieutenant Cross understood that Love was only a way of signing and did not mean
what he sometimes pretended it meant. At dusk, he would
carefully return the letters to his rucksack. Slowly, a bit distracted, he would get up and move among his men, checking the
perimeter, then at full dark he would return to his hole and watch
the night and wonder if Martha was a virgin.

The things they carried were largely determined by necessity.
Among the necessities or near-necessities were P-38 can openers,
pocket knives, heat tabs, wristwatches, dog tags, mosquito

repellent, chewing gum, candy, cigarettes, salt tablets, packets of Kool-Aid, lighters, matches, sewing kits, Military Payment Certificates, C rations, and two or three canteens of water. Together, these items weighed between 15 and 20 pounds, depending upon a man's habits or rate of metabolism. Henry Dobbins, who was a big man, carried extra rations; he was especially fond of canned peaches in heavy syrup over pound cake. Dave Jensen, who practiced field hygiene, carried a tooth-brush, dental floss, and several hotel-sized bars of soap he'd stolen on R&R in Sydney, Australia. Ted Lavender, who was scared, carried tranquilizers until he was shot in the head outside the village of Than Khe in mid-April. By necessity, and because it was SOP, they all carried steel helmets that weighed 5 pounds including the liner and camouflage cover. They carried the standard fatigue jackets and trousers. Very few carried under-wear. On their feet they carried jungle boots – 2.1 pounds – and Dave Jensen carried three pairs of socks and a can of Dr. Scholl's foot powder as a precaution against trench foot. Until he was shot, Ted Lavender carried 6 or 7 ounces of premium dope, which for him was a necessity. Mitchell Sanders, the RTO, carried condoms. Norman Bowker carried a diary. Rat Kiley carried comic books. Kiowa, a devout Baptist, carried an illus-trated New Testament that had been presented to him by his father, who taught Sunday school in Oklahoma City, Oklahoma. As a hedge against bad times, however, Kiowa also carried his grandmother's distrust of the white man, his grandfather's old hunting hatchet. Necessity dictated. Because the land was mined and booby-trapped, it was SOP for each man to carry a steel-centered, nylon-covered flak jacket, which weighed 6.7 pounds, but which on hot days seemed much heavier. Because you could die so quickly, each man carried at least one large compress bandage, usually in the helmet band for easy access. Because the nights were cold, and because the monsoons were wet, each carried a green plastic poncho that could be used as a raincoat or groundsheet or makeshift tent. With its quilted liner, the poncho weighed almost 2 pounds, but it was worth every ounce. In April, for instance, when Ted Lavender was shot, they used his poncho to wrap him up, then to carry him across the paddy, then to lift him into the chopper that took him away.

They were called legs or grunts.

To carry something was to hump it, as when Lieutenant Jimmy Cross humped his love for Martha up the hills and through the swamps. In its intransitive form, to hump meant to walk, or to march, but it implied burdens far beyond the intransitive.

Almost everyone humped photographs. In his wallet, Lieutenant Cross carried two photographs of Martha. The first was a Kodacolor snapshot signed Love, though he knew better. She stood against a brick wall. Her eyes were gray and neutral, her lips slightly open as she stared straight-on at the camera. At night, sometimes, Lieutenant Cross wondered who had taken the picture, because he knew she had boyfriends, because he loved her so much, and because he could see the shadow of the picture-taker spreading out against the brick wall. The second photograph had been clipped from the 1968 Mount Sebastian yearbook. It was an action shot – women's volleyball – and Martha was bent horizontal to the floor, reaching, the palms of her hands in sharp focus, the tongue taut, the expression frank and competitive. There was no visible sweat. She wore white gym shorts. Her legs, he thought, were almost certainly the legs of a virgin, dry and without hair, the left knee cocked and carrying her entire weight, which was just over 100 pounds. Lieutenant Cross remembered touching that left knee. A dark theater, he remembered, and the movie was *Bonnie and Clyde*, and Martha wore a tweed skirt, and during the final scene, when he touched her knee, she turned and looked at him in a sad, sober way that made him pull his hand back, but he would always remember the feel of the tweed skirt and the knee beneath it and the sound of the gunfire that killed Bonnie and Clyde, how embarrassing it was, how slow and oppressive. He remembered kissing her goodnight at the dorm door. Right then, he thought, he should've done something brave. He should've carried her up the stairs to her room and tied her to the bed and touched that left knee all night long. He should've risked it. Whenever he looked at the photographs, he thought of new things he should've done.

What they carried was partly a function of rank, partly of field specialty.

As a first lieutenant and platoon leader, Jimmy Cross carried a compass, maps, code books, binoculars, and a .45-caliber pistol that weighed 2.9 pounds fully loaded. He carried a strobe light and the responsibility for the lives of his men.

As an RTO, Mitchell Sanders carried the PRC-25 radio, a killer, 26 pounds with its battery.

As a medic, Rat Kiley carried a canvas satchel filled with morphine and plasma and malaria tablets and surgical tape and comic books and all the things a medic must carry, including M&Ms for especially bad wounds, for a total weight of nearly 20 pounds.

As a big man, therefore a machine gunner, Henry Dobbins carried the M-60, which weighed 23 pounds unloaded, but which was almost always loaded. In addition, Dobbins carried between 10 and 15 pounds of ammunition draped in belts across his chest and shoulders.

As PFCs or Spec 4s, most of them were common grunts and carried the standard M-16 gas-operated assault rifle. The weapon weighed 7.5 pounds unloaded, 8.2 pounds with its full twenty-round magazine. Depending on numerous factors, such as topography and psychology, the riflemen carried anywhere from twelve to twenty magazines, usually in cloth bandoliers, adding on another 8.4 pounds at minimum, 14 pounds at maximum. When it was available, they also carried M-16 maintenance gear – rods and steel brushes and swabs and tubes of LSA oil – all of which weighed about a pound. Among the grunts, some carried the M-79 grenade launcher, 5.9 pounds unloaded, a reasonably light weapon except for the ammunition, which was heavy. A single round weighed 10 ounces. The typical load was twenty-five rounds. But Ted Lavender, who was scared, carried thirty-four rounds when he was shot and killed outside Than Khe, and he went down under an exceptional burden, more than 20 pounds of ammunition, plus the flak jacket and helmet and rations and water and toilet paper and tranquilizers and all the rest, plus the unweighed fear. He was dead weight. There was no twitching or flopping. Kiowa, who saw it happen, said it was like watching a rock fall, or a big sandbag or something – just boom, then down – not like the movies where the dead guy rolls around and does fancy spins and goes ass over teakettle – not like that, Kiowa said, the poor bastard just flat-fuck fell. Boom. Down. Nothing else. It was a bright morning in mid-April. Lieutenant Cross felt the pain. He blamed himself. They stripped off Lavender's canteens and ammo, all the heavy things, and Rat Kiley said the obvious, the guy's dead, and Mitchell Sanders used his radio to report one US KIA and to request a chopper. Then they wrapped Lavender in his poncho. They carried him out to a dry paddy, established security, and sat smoking the dead man's dope until the chopper came. Lieutenant Cross kept to himself. He pictured Martha's smooth young face, thinking he loved her more than anything, more than his men, and now Ted Lavender was dead because he loved her so much and could not stop thinking about her. When the dustoff arrived, they carried Lavender aboard. Afterward they burned Than Khe. They marched until dusk, then dug their holes, and that night Kiowa kept explaining how you had to be there, how fast it was, how the poor guy just dropped like so much concrete. Boom-down, he said. Like cement.

In addition to the three standard weapons – the M-60, M-16, and M-79 – they carried whatever presented itself, or whatever seemed appropriate as a means of killing or staying alive. They carried catch-as-catch-can. At various times, in various situations, they carried M-14s and CAR-15s and Swedish Ks and grease guns and captured AK-47s and Chi-Coms and RPGs and Simonov carbines and black market Uzis and .38 caliber Smith & Wesson handguns and 66 mm LAWs and shotguns and silencers and blackjacks and bayonets and C-4 plastic explosives. Lee Strunk carried a slingshot; a weapon of last resort, he called it. Mitchell Sanders carried brass knuckles. Kiowa carried his grandfather's feathered hatchet. Every third or fourth man carried a Claymore antipersonnel mine – 3.5 pounds with its firing device. They all carried fragmentation grenades – 14 ounces each. They all carried at least one M-18 colored smoke grenade – 24 ounces. Some carried CS or tear gas grenades. Some carried white phosphorus grenades. They carried all they could bear, and then some, including a silent awe for the terrible power of the things they carried.

In the first week of April, before Lavender died, Lieutenant Jimmy Cross received a good-luck charm from Martha. It was a simple pebble, an ounce at most. Smooth to the touch, it was a milky white color with flecks of orange and violet, oval shaped, like a miniature egg. In the accompanying letter, Martha wrote that she had found the pebble on the Jersey shoreline, precisely where the land touched water at high tide, where things came together but also separated. It was this separate-but-together quality, she wrote, that had inspired her to pick up the pebble and to carry it in her breast pocket for several days, where it seemed weightless, and then to send it through the mail, by air, as a token of her truest feelings for him. Lieutenant Cross found this romantic. But he wondered what her truest feelings were, exactly, and what she meant by separate-but-together. He wondered how the tides and waves had come into play on that afternoon along the Jersey shoreline when Martha saw the pebble and bent down to rescue it from geology. He imagined bare feet. Martha was a poet, with the poet's sensibilities, and her feet would be brown and bare, the toenails unpainted, the eyes chilly and somber like the ocean in March, and though it was painful, he wondered who had been with her that afternoon. He imagined a pair of shadows moving along the strip of sand where things came together but also separated. It was phantom jealousy, he knew, but he couldn't help himself. He loved her so much. On the march, through the hot days of early April, he carried the pebble in his mouth, turning it with his tongue, tasting sea salt and moisture. His mind wandered. He had difficulty keeping his attention on the war. On occasion he would yell at his men to spread out the column, to keep their eyes open, but then he would slip away into daydreams, just pretending, walking barefoot along the Jersey shore, with Martha, carrying nothing. He would feel himself rising. Sun and waves and gentle winds, all love and lightness.

What they carried varied by mission.

When a mission took them to the mountains, they carried mosquito netting, machetes, canvas tarps, and extra bug juice.

If a mission seemed especially hazardous, or if it involved a place they knew to be bad, they carried everything they could. In certain heavily mined AOs, where the land was dense with Toe Poppers and Bouncing Betties, they took turns humping a 28-pound mine detector. With its headphones and big sensing plate, the equipment was a stress on the lower back and shoulders, awkward to handle, often useless because of the shrapnel in the earth, but they carried it anyway, partly for safety, partly for the illusion of safety.

On ambush, or other night missions, they carried peculiar little odds and ends. Kiowa always took along his New Testament and a pair of moccasins for silence. Dave Jensen carried night-sight vitamins high in carotene. Lee Strunk carried his slingshot; ammo, he claimed, would never be a problem. Rat Kiley carried brandy and M&Ms candy. Until he was shot, Ted Lavender carried the starlight scope, which weighed 6.3 pounds with its aluminum carrying case. Henry Dobbins carried his girlfriend's pantyhose wrapped around his neck as a comforter. They all carried ghosts. When dark came, they would move out single file across the meadows and paddies to their ambush coordinates, where they would quietly set up the Claymores and lie down and spend the night waiting.

Other missions were more complicated and required special equipment. In mid-April, it was their mission to search out and destroy the elaborate tunnel complexes in the Than Khe area south of Chu Lai. To blow the tunnels, they carried one-pound blocks of pentrite high explosives, four blocks to a man, 68 pounds in all. They carried wiring, detonators, and battery-powered clackers. Dave Jensen carried earplugs. Most often, before blowing the tunnels, they were ordered by higher command to search them, which was considered bad news, but by and large they just shrugged and carried out orders. Because he was a big man, Henry Dobbins was excused from tunnel duty. The others would draw numbers. Before Lavender died there were seventeen men in the platoon, and whoever drew the number 17 would strip off his gear and crawl in headfirst with a flashlight and Lieutenant Cross's .45-caliber pistol. The rest of them would fan out as security. They would sit down or kneel, not facing the hole, listening to the ground beneath them imagining cobwebs and ghosts, whatever was down there – the tunnel walls squeezing in – how the flashlight seemed impossibly heavy in the hand and how it was tunnel vision in the very strictest sense, compression in all ways, even time, and how you had to wiggle in – ass and elbows – a swallowed-up feeling – and how you found yourself worrying about odd things: Will your flashlight go dead? Do rats carry rabies? If you screamed, how far would the sound carry? Would your buddies hear it? Would they have the courage to drag you out? In some respects, though not many, the waiting was worse than the tunnel itself. Imagination was a killer.

On April 16, when Lee Strunk drew the number 17, he laughed and muttered something and went down quickly. The morning was hot and very still. Not good, Kiowa said. He looked at the tunnel opening, then out across a dry paddy toward the village of Than Khe. Nothing moved. No clouds or birds or people. As they waited, the men smoked and drank Kool-Aid, not talking much, feeling sympathy for Lee Strunk but also feeling the luck of the draw. You win some, you lose some, said Mitchell Sanders, and sometimes you settle for a rain check. It was a tired line and no one laughed.

Henry Dobbins ate a tropical chocolate bar. Ted Lavender popped a tranquilizer and went off to pee.

After five minutes, Lieutenant Jimmy Cross moved to the tunnel, leaned down, and examined the darkness. Trouble, he thought – a cave-in maybe. And then suddenly, without willing it, he was thinking about Martha. The stresses and fractures, the quick collapse, the two of them buried alive under all that weight. Dense, crushing love. Kneeling, watching the hole, he tried to concentrate on Lee Strunk and the war, all the dangers, but his love was too much for him, he felt paralyzed, he wanted to sleep inside her lungs and breathe her blood and be smothered. He wanted her to be a virgin and not a virgin, all at once. He wanted to know her. Intimate secrets: Why poetry? Why so sad? Why that grayness in her eyes? Why so alone? Not lonely, just alone – riding her bike across campus or sitting off by herself in the cafeteria – even dancing, she danced alone – and it was the aloneness that filled him with love. He remembered telling her that one evening. How she nodded and looked away. And how, later, when he kissed her, she received the kiss without returning it, her eyes wide open, not afraid, not a virgin's eyes, just flat and uninvolved.

Lieutenant Cross gazed at the tunnel. But he was not there. He was buried with Martha under the white sand at the Jersey shore. They were pressed together, and the pebble in his mouth was her tongue. He was smiling. Vaguely, he was aware of how quiet the day was, the sullen paddies, yet he could not bring himself to worry about matters of security. He was beyond that. He was just a kid at war, in love. He was twenty-four years old. He couldn't help it.

A few moments later Lee Strunk crawled out of the tunnel. He came up grinning, filthy but alive. Lieutenant Cross nodded and closed his eyes while the others clapped Strunk on the back and made jokes about rising from the dead.

Worms, Rat Kiley said. Right out of the grave. Fuckin' zombie.

The men laughed. They all felt great relief.

Spook city, said Mitchell Sanders.

Lee Strunk made a funny ghost sound, a kind of moaning, yet very happy, and right then, when Strunk made that high happy moaning sound, when he went *Ahhooooo*, right then Ted Lavender was shot in the head on his way back from peeing. He lay with his mouth open. The teeth were broken. There was a swollen black bruise under his left eye. The cheekbone was gone. Oh shit, Rat Kiley said, the guy's dead. The guy's dead, he kept saying, which seemed profound – the guy's dead. I mean really.

The things they carried were determined to some extent by superstition. Lieutenant Cross carried his good-luck pebble.

Dave Jensen carried a rabbit's foot. Norman Bowker, otherwise a very gentle person, carried a thumb that had been presented to him as a gift by Mitchell Sanders. The thumb was dark brown, rubbery to the touch, and weighed 4 ounces at most. It had been cut from a VC corpse, a boy of fifteen or sixteen. They'd found him at the bottom of an irrigation ditch, badly burned, flies in his mouth and eyes. The boy wore black shorts and sandals. At the time of his death he had been carrying a pouch of rice, a rifle, and three magazines of ammunition.

You want my opinion, Mitchell Sanders said, there's a definite moral here.

He put his hand on the dead boy's wrist. He was quiet for a time, as if counting a pulse, then he patted the stomach, almost affectionately, and used Kiowa's hunting hatchet to remove the thumb.

Henry Dobbins asked what the moral was.

Moral?

You know. *Moral*.

Sanders wrapped the thumb in toilet paper and handed it across to Norman Bowker. There was no blood. Smiling, he kicked the boy's head, watched the flies scatter, and said, It's like with that old TV show – *Paladin*. Have gun, will travel.

Henry Dobbins thought about it.

Yeah, well, he finally said. I don't see no moral.

There it *is*, man.

Fuck off.

They carried USO stationery and pencils and pens. They carried Sterno, safety pins, trip flares, signal flares, spools of wire, razor blades, chewing tobacco, liberated joss sticks and statuettes of the smiling Buddha, candles, grease pencils, *The Stars and Stripes*, fingernail clippers, Psy Ops leaflets, bush hats, bolos, and much more. Twice a week, when the resupply choppers came in, they carried hot chow in green mermite cans and large canvas bags filled with iced beer and soda pop. They carried plastic water containers, each with a 2-gallon capacity. Mitchell Sanders carried a set of starched tiger fatigues for special occasions. Henry Dobbins carried Black Flag insecticide. Dave Jensen carried empty sandbags that could be filled at night for added protection. Lee Strunk carried tanning lotion. Some things they carried in common. Taking turns, they carried the big PRC-77 scrambler radio, which weighed 30 pounds with its battery. They shared the weight of memory. They took up what others could no longer bear. Often, they carried each other, the wounded or weak. They carried infections. They carried chess sets, basketballs, Vietnamese–English dictionaries, insignia of rank, Bronze Stars and Purple Hearts, plastic cards imprinted with the Code of Conduct. They carried diseases, among them malaria and dysentery. They carried lice and ringworm and leeches and paddy algae and various rots and molds. They carried the land itself – Vietnam, the place, the soil – a powdery orange-red dust that covered their boots and fatigues and faces. They carried the sky. The whole atmosphere, they carried it, the humidity, the monsoons, the stink of fungus and decay, all of it, they carried gravity. They moved like mules. By daylight they took sniper fire, at night they were mortared, but it was not battle, it was just the endless march, village to village, without purpose, nothing won or lost. They marched for the sake of the march. They plodded along slowly, dumbly, leaning forward against the heat, unthinking, all blood and bone, simple grunts, soldiering with their legs, toiling up the hills and down into the paddies and across the rivers and up again and down, just humping, one step and then the next and then another, but no volition, no will, because it was automatic, it was anatomy, and the war was entirely a matter of posture and carriage, the hump was everything, a kind of inertia, a kind of emptiness, a dullness of desire and intellect and conscience and hope and human sensibility. Their principles were in their feet. Their calculations were biological. They had no sense of strategy or mission. They searched the villages without knowing what to look for, not caring, kicking over jars of rice, frisking children and old men, blowing tunnels, sometimes setting fires and sometimes not, then forming up and moving on to the next village, then other villages, where it would always be the same. They carried their own lives. The pressures were enormous. In the heat of early afternoon, they would remove their helmets and flak jackets, walking bare, which was dangerous but which helped ease the strain. They would often discard things along the route of march. Purely for comfort, they would throw away rations, blow their Claymores and grenades, no matter, because by nightfall the resupply choppers would arrive with more of the same, then a day or two later still more, fresh watermelons and crates of ammunition and sunglasses and woolen sweaters – the resources were stunning – sparklers for the Fourth of July, colored eggs for Easter – it was the great American war chest – the fruits of science, the smokestacks, the canneries, the arsenals at Hartford, the Minnesota forests, the machine shops, the vast fields of corn and wheat – they carried like freight trains; they carried it on their backs and shoulders – and for all the ambiguities of Vietnam, all the mysteries and unknowns, there was at least the single abiding certainty that they would never be at a loss for things to carry.

After the chopper took Lavender away, Lieutenant Jimmy Cross led his men into the village of Than Khe. They burned everything. They shot chickens and dogs, they trashed the village well, they called in artillery and watched the wreckage, then they marched for several hours through the hot afternoon, and then at dusk, while Kiowa explained how Lavender died, Lieutenant Cross found himself trembling.

He tried not to cry. With his entrenching tool, which weighed 5 pounds, he began digging a hole in the earth.

He felt shame. He hated himself. He had loved Martha more than his men, and as a consequence Lavender was now dead, and this was something he would have to carry like a stone in his stomach for the rest of the war.

All he could do was dig. He used his entrenching tool like an ax, slashing, feeling both love and hate, and then later, when it was full dark, he sat at the bottom of his foxhole and wept. It went on for a long while. In part, he was grieving for Ted Lavender, but mostly it was for Martha, and for himself, because she belonged to another world, which was not quite real, and because she was a junior at Mount Sebastian College in New Jersey, a poet and a virgin and uninvolved, and because he realized she did not love him and never would.

Like cement, Kiowa whispered in the dark. I swear to God – boom, down. Not a word.

I've heard this, said Norman Bowker.

A pisser, you know? Still zipping himself up. Zapped while zipping.

All right, fine. That's enough.

Yeah, but you had to see it, the guy just —

I *heard*, man. Cement. So why not shut the fuck *up*?

Kiowa shook his head sadly and glanced over at the hole where Lieutenant Jimmy Cross sat watching the night. The air was thick and wet. A warm dense fog had settled over the paddies and there was the stillness that precedes rain.

After a time Kiowa sighed.

One thing for sure, he said. The lieutenant's in some deep hurt. I mean that crying jag – the way he was carrying on – it wasn't fake or anything, it was real heavy-duty hurt. The man cares.

Sure, Norman Bowker said.

Say what you want, the man does care.

We all got problems.

Not Lavender. No, I guess not, Bowker said. Do me a favor, though.

Shut up?

That's a smart Indian. Shut up.

Shrugging, Kiowa pulled off his boots. He wanted to say more, just to lighten up his sleep, but instead he opened his New Testament and arranged it beneath his head as a pillow. The fog made things seem hollow and unattached. He tried not to think about Ted Lavender, but then he was thinking how fast it was, no drama, down and dead, and how it was hard to feel anything except surprise. It seemed unchristian. He wished he could find some great sadness, or even anger, but the emotion wasn't there and he couldn't make it happen. Mostly he felt pleased to be alive. He liked the smell of the New Testament under his cheek, the leather and ink and paper and glue, whatever the chemicals were. He liked hearing the sounds of night. Even his fatigue, it felt fine, the stiff muscles and the prickly awareness of his own body, a floating feeling. He enjoyed not being dead. Lying there, Kiowa admired Lieutenant Jimmy Cross's capacity for grief. He wanted to share the man's pain, he wanted to care as Jimmy Cross cared. And yet when he closed his eyes, all he could think was Boom-down, and all he could feel was the pleasure of having his boots off and the fog curling in around him and the damp soil and the Bible smells and the plush comfort of night.

After a moment Norman Bowker sat up in the dark.

What the hell, he said. You want to talk, *talk*. Tell it to me. Forget it.

No, man, go on. One thing I hate, it's a silent Indian.

For the most part they carried themselves with poise, a kind of dignity. Now and then, however, there were times of panic, when they squealed or wanted to squeal but couldn't, when they twitched and made moaning sounds and covered their heads and said Dear Jesus and flopped around on the earth and fired their weapons blindly and cringed and sobbed and begged for the noise to stop and went wild and made stupid promises to themselves and to God and to their mothers and fathers, hoping not to die. In different ways, it happened to all of them. Afterward, when the firing ended, they would blink and peek up. They would touch their bodies, feeling shame, then quickly hiding it. They would force themselves to stand. As if in slow motion, frame by frame, the world would take on the old logic – absolute silence, then the wind, then sunlight, then voices. It was the burden of being alive. Awkwardly, the men would reassemble themselves, first in private, then in groups, becoming soldiers again. They would repair the leaks in their eyes. They would check for casualties, call in dustoffs, light cigarettes, try to smile, clear their throats and spit and begin cleaning their weapons. After a time someone would shake his head and say, No lie, I almost shit my pants, and someone else would laugh, which meant it was bad, yes, but the guy had obviously not shit his pants, it wasn't that bad, and in any case nobody would ever

do such a thing and then go ahead and talk about it. They would
squint into the dense, oppressive sunlight. For a few moments,
perhaps, they would fall silent, lighting a joint and tracking its
passage from man to man, inhaling, holding in the humiliation.
Scary stuff, one of them might say. But then someone else would
grin or flick his eyebrows and say, Roger-dodger, almost cut me
a new asshole, *almost*.

There were numerous such poses. Some carried themselves
with a sort of wistful resignation, others with pride or stiff
soldierly discipline or good humor or macho zeal. They were
afraid of dying but they were even more afraid to show it.

They found jokes to tell.

They used a hard vocabulary to contain the terrible softness.
*Greased* they'd say. *Offed, lit up, zapped while zipping.* It wasn't
cruelty, just stage presence. They were actors. When someone
died, it wasn't quite dying, because in a curious way it seemed
scripted, and because they had their lines mostly memorized,
irony mixed with tragedy, and because they called it by other
names, as if to encyst and destroy the reality of death itself. They
kicked corpses. They cut off thumbs. They talked grunt lingo.
They told stories about Ted Lavender's supply of tranquilizers,
how the poor guy didn't feel a thing, how incredibly tranquil he
was.

There's a moral here, said Mitchell Sanders.

They were waiting for Lavender's chopper, smoking the
dead man's dope. The moral's pretty obvious, Sanders said, and
winked. Stay away from drugs. No joke, they'll ruin your day
every time.

Cute, said Henry Dobbins.

Mind blower, get it? Talk about wiggy. Nothing left, just
blood and brains.

They made themselves laugh.

There it is, they'd say. Over and over – there it is, my friend,
there it is – as if the repetition itself were an act of poise, a
balance between crazy and almost crazy, knowing without
going, there it is, which meant be cool, let it ride, because Oh
yeah, man, you can't change what can't be changed, there it is,
there it absolutely and positively and fucking well *is*.

They were tough.

They carried all the emotional baggage of men who might die. Grief, terror, love, longing – these were intangibles, but the intangibles had their own mass and specific gravity, they had tangible weight. They carried shameful memories. They carried the common secret of cowardice barely restrained, the instinct to run or freeze or hide, and in many respects this was the heaviest burden of all, for it could never be put down, it required perfect balance and perfect posture. They carried their reputations. They carried the soldier's greatest fear, which was the fear of blushing. Men killed, and died, because they were embarrassed not to. It was what had brought them to the war in the first place, nothing positive, no dreams of glory or honor, just to avoid the blush of dishonor. They died so as not to die of embarrassment. They crawled into tunnels and walked point and advanced under fire. Each morning, despite the unknowns, they made their legs move. They endured. They kept humping. They did not submit to the obvious alternative, which was simply to close the eyes and fall. So easy, really. Go limp and tumble to the ground and let the muscles unwind and not speak and not budge until your buddies picked you up and lifted you into the chopper that would roar and dip its nose and carry you off to the world. A mere matter of falling, yet no one ever fell. It was not courage, exactly; the object was not valor. Rather, they were too frightened to be cowards.

By and large they carried these things inside, maintaining the masks of composure. They sneered at sick call. They spoke bitterly about guys who had found release by shooting off their own toes or fingers. Pussies, they'd say. Candy-asses. It was fierce, mocking talk, with only a trace of envy or awe, but even so the image played itself out behind their eyes.

They imagined the muzzle against flesh. So easy: squeeze the trigger and blow away a toe. They imagined it. They imagined the quick, sweet pain, then the evacuation to Japan, then a hospital with warm beds and cute geisha nurses.

And they dreamed of freedom birds.

At night, on guard, staring into the dark, they were carried away by jumbo jets. They felt the rush of takeoff. *Gone!* they yelled. And then velocity – wings and engines – a smiling stewardess – but it was more than a plane, it was a real bird, a big sleek silver bird with feathers and talons and high screeching. They were flying. The weights fell off; there was nothing to bear. They laughed and held on tight, feeling the cold slap of wind and altitude, soaring, thinking *It's over, I'm gone!* – they were naked, they were light and free – it was all lightness, bright and fast and buoyant, light as light, a helium buzz in the brain, a giddy bubbling in the lungs as they were taken up over the clouds and the war, beyond duty, beyond gravity and mortification and global entanglements – *Sin loi!* they yelled. *I'm sorry, mother-fuckers, but I'm out of it, I'm goofed, I'm on a space cruise, I'm gone!* – and it was a restful, unencumbered sensation, just riding the light waves, sailing that big silver freedom bird over the mountains and oceans, over America, over the farms and great sleeping cities and cemeteries and highways and the golden arches of McDonald's, it was flight, a kind of fleeing, a kind of falling, falling higher and higher, spinning off the edge of the earth and beyond the sun and through the vast, silent vacuum where there were no burdens and where everything weighed exactly nothing – *Gone!* they screamed, *I'm sorry but I'm gone!* – and so at night, not quite dreaming, they gave themselves over to lightness, they were carried, they were purely borne.

On the morning after Ted Lavender died, First Lieutenant Jimmy Cross crouched at the bottom of his foxhole and burned Martha's letters. Then he burned the two photographs. There was a steady rain falling, which made it difficult, but he used heat tabs and Sterno to build a small fire, screening it with his body, holding the photographs over the tight blue flame with the tips of his fingers.

He realized it was only a gesture. Stupid, he thought. Sentimental, too, but mostly just stupid.

Lavender was dead. You couldn't burn the blame.

Besides, the letters were in his head. And even now, without photographs, Lieutenant Cross could see Martha playing volleyball in her white gym shorts and yellow T-shirt. He could see her moving in the rain.

When the fire died out, Lieutenant Cross pulled his poncho over his shoulders and ate breakfast from a can.

There was no great mystery, he decided.

In those burned letters Martha had never mentioned the war, except to say, Jimmy, take care of yourself. She wasn't involved. She signed the letters Love, but it wasn't love, and all the fine lines and technicalities did not matter. Virginity was no longer an issue. He hated her. Yes, he did. He hated her. Love, too, but it was a hard, hating kind of love.

The morning came up wet and blurry. Everything seemed part of everything else, the fog and Martha and the deepening rain.

He was a soldier, after all.

Half smiling, Lieutenant Jimmy Cross took out his maps. He shook his head hard, as if to clear it, then bent forward and began planning the day's march. In ten minutes, or maybe twenty, he would rouse the men and they would pack up and head west, where the maps showed the country to be green and inviting. They would do what they had always done. The rain might add some weight, but otherwise it would be one more day layered upon all the other days.

He was realistic about it. There was that new hardness in his stomach. He loved her but he hated her.

No more fantasies, he told himself.

Henceforth, when he thought about Martha, it would be only to think that she belonged elsewhere. He would shut down the daydreams. This was not Mount Sebastian, it was another world, where there were no pretty poems or midterm exams, a place where men died because of carelessness and gross stupidity. Kiowa was right. Boom-down, and you were dead, never partly dead.

Briefly, in the rain, Lieutenant Cross saw Martha's gray eyes gazing back at him.

He understood.

It was very sad, he thought. The things men carried inside. The things men did or felt they had to do.

He almost nodded at her, but didn't.

Instead he went back to his maps. He was now determined

to perform his duties firmly and without negligence. It wouldn't help Lavender, he knew that, but from this point on he would comport himself as an officer. He would dispose of his good-luck pebble. Swallow it, maybe, or use Lee Strunk's slingshot, or just drop it along the trail. On the march he would impose strict field discipline. He would be careful to send out flank security, to prevent straggling or bunching up, to keep his troops moving at the proper pace and at the proper interval. He would insist on clean weapons. He would confiscate the remainder of Lavender's dope. Later in the day, perhaps, he would call the men together and speak to them plainly. He would accept the blame for what had happened to Ted Lavender. He would be a man about it. He would look them in the eyes, keeping his chin level, and he would issue the new SOPs in a calm impersonal tone of voice, a lieutenant's voice, leaving no room for argument or discussion. Commencing immediately, he'd tell them, they would no longer abandon equipment along the route of march. They would police up their acts. They would get their shit together, and keep it together, and maintain it neatly and in good working order.

He would not tolerate laxity. He would show strength, distancing himself.

Among the men there would be grumbling, of course, and maybe worse, because their days would seem longer and their loads heavier, but Lieutenant Jimmy Cross reminded himself that his obligation was not to be loved but to lead. He would dispense with love; it was not now a factor. And if anyone quarreled or complained, he would simply tighten his lips and arrange his shoulders in the correct command posture. He might give a curt little nod. Or he might not. He might just shrug and say, Carry on, then they would saddle up and form into a column and move out toward the villages west of Than Khe.

# Aunt Granny Lith

Beth stood in shadows behind her nearest neighbor's house, listening to her husband's drunken laugh. Every fall was the same. Spring rain and summer sun gave a fine field of ear; late frost sweetened the crop. Casey traded half the liquor he made for supplies, and sold enough to fix the truck. His two-week bender brought him to Lil's.

Beth jerked the back door open and stepped through the cramped kitchen to the living room. Casey was slumped on the couch, a mason jar in his hand.

"Hell's bells," Lil said. "Will you look at what the dogs drug in."

"Want a seat?" Casey said.

"I'm not here on invite," Beth said.

"You sure to God ain't," said Lil.

"You know what I come for."

"Not selling Tupperware, I don't reckon." Lil tapped cigarette ash to the floor. "You ain't got much say in my house. Best be leaving while you still yet can."

"Have a drink, Beth," said Casey. "It's the awfullest good I ever did run."

"You got the jar lid?" Beth said.

"Somewheres."

"Put it on tight."

He patted his shirt pockets, then searched his pants. Lil scooted to the edge of the couch, her knees bent, ready to spring. She took a long pull on her cigarette. Her voice was sandstone harsh.

"Casey just might be tired of you."

"If you feel froggy," Beth said, "jump."

Lil flicked the lit cigarette at Beth and leaped from the couch,

fingers hooked into claws. One hand twisted Beth's black hair.
Both women stumbled across the room, knocking the stovepipe
loose from the flue. Creosote dust drifted the air. Lil snatched
the poker, slammed it hard against Beth's hip. Beth staggered,
the low groan in her chest shifting to a growl. She spat in Lil's
face, cocked her fist, swung. Her knuckles split against Lil's face
and the poker clattered across the floor. Lil swayed like a tree at
the final saw cut, mouth open, blank eyes blinking. As she fell,
Beth gripped a handful of her long red hair and yanked. The hair
tore loose, several strands still clinging to a chunk of scalp. Lil's
head bounced. Her jaw was swollen and bloody.

"You won't bushwhack no drunks for a while," Beth said.
"Leastways not mine."

She shoved the hair in her pocket and turned to Casey on the
couch. His mouth hung open, his eyes half shut. She realized
that he wouldn't have been much good to Lil, anyway. Beth
yanked his shirt.

"Beth," he said.

"I'm here."

"My money's on you to clean her plow."

"Help me get you up."

"I can't get no upper."

Beth dragged him to the edge of the couch. Casey braced his
arm around her shoulder, and she helped him out the front door.
He pushed her aside. "You follow the hard way," he said, and
tipped into the darkness, rolling down the slope, laughing and
grunting. His arm smacked the truck door. "First here," he
yelled. "Beth's on shotgun!"

She limped down the hill in moonlight glowing through the
trees. Casey was a dark mound leaning against the truck. She
rapped his nose with her fist.

"Pretty good lick," he said.

"Try and puke."

Casey shoved a finger down his throat.

When he finished, he wiped his mouth against the truck, and
Beth coaxed him into the cab. She drove along the twin-rut road
above the creek. Asleep against the dashboard, Casey looked
angelic, his hands fisted into clubs. His face was broad as a coal

shovel. A hard bump knocked Casey against her and he jerked the steering wheel. The pickup crashed down the hill, bounced over limestone, and plunged into the creek. Bullfrogs abruptly stopped their roaring.

Beth lit a match and leaned to Casey, who snored on the floorboards, short, thick arms pillowing his head. She opened the door and sank her foot into mud. The night sky was spattered white with stars. She found Orion and began walking just left of his lowest sword-star, ignoring the throbbing of her hip. Moonlight glistened on animal prints tipped by frost in the hardened mud. She followed the game path two miles to her property, bridled the mule, and draped Casey's logging chains over its back.

Thirty years before, Casey's first wife died the day after they were married. She'd been walking the property, scouting a garden place, and Casey found her beneath a tree with a broken branch piercing her face. It ran through her eye and into her brain. Casey married again. His second wife suffered a broken neck at the bottom of a steep cliff. Casey began carrying a pistol in his hip pocket, walking with an arm trailed back, hand hovering over the gun. He looked like a sideways-running dog.

A year later, while checking his crawdad traps on Lick Fork Creek, he saw Beth dipping water to carry home. Her denim workshirt clung to her body in damp patches. He offered to haul the buckets and she refused. The next day he came to court her on the front porch. Beth was the only daughter, the last child at home. Casey was the first man who ever made her laugh. When he left, Beth's mother came outside to sit on an upended washtub. Nomey built a cigarette, curled the end of her pants leg, flicked ashes into the cuff.

"What in case he wants to marry me?" Beth said.

"His people stick by theirs."

"They say he's hexed. Two wives done died on him."

"That boy's had a run of bad," Nomey said. "But he ain't full to blame."

"What is?"

"Hard telling."

"It still yet scares me."

Nomey gave Beth a piece of black moly root that she wore on a strip of leather tight above her hips. Two months later Beth announced her wedding. The local preacher refused to marry them saying that he'd already sent two virgins to the grave and wouldn't risk another. Casey hired a preacher from Rocksalt.

Both families crowded the church. Two armed men guarded the door, and two more roamed the dusty parking lot. After the ceremony, several women stayed to pray for Beth, while the men escorted the newlyweds to the small house Casey had built. Beth's brothers carefully searched the house, the chicken house, and the hog pen. She watched them leave at dusk, firing guns into the woods. Casey's arm circled her waist.

"Whatever you want," he said. "It's yours. I got enough put by for a TV set."

"I got what I want," Beth said.

"You stay right by me, hear. There's a shotgun by the door and a pistol at the bed." He patted the buck knife on his hip. "This don't ever come off either."

Beth tipped her head and moved her mouth to his. She stood on her toes until he lifted. Her knees gripped him and he carried her through the living room to the small bed. They rattled it together for a long time.

After Casey was asleep, Beth felt the coarse of his beard stubble. She didn't know when it had grown. He'd shaved for the wedding, and his face had been smooth when they'd entered the house. She remembered her father's beard pricking her face when she was a child. She hadn't known him well before he died. Now she felt as if she knew him better.

She lay on her side admiring the dim outlines of her new house. She couldn't get used to the idea of being married. Nomey had told her it meant being loyal – to a certain point. If he hit her, he lost his claim. If he didn't come home once in a while, Beth could do the same, but she had to be careful. That sort of thing was harder for women than men. Nomey chuckled then and said that most things were, and that's why women were smarter than men. Beth had nodded, not quite understanding.

She rose from bed and looked through the window at the toilet shack above the creek. Come spring she'd lay flat rocks along the path and plant flowers. Beyond the shadowed hulk of a car, its rusted rims on cinder blocks, Beth saw someone scurry into the woods. She left the house and trailed the person to the head of the hollow, where the figure climbed an animal trail slanting up the slope and out the ridge. Beth followed half a mile before crouching behind a poplar to peek over the tree's lowest crotch. Sweat stung the brier scrapes on her face.

A nighthawk swooped to a halt on the ground. The figure bent, cooing to the bird. It was a small woman with ragged clothes, long hair, and shoulders that crooked forward. She crawled past the bird to a large log lying on the earth. She slipped into its hollow opening and the bird sat in front. The sky behind was empty.

Beth backtracked through the woods to the house. Casey was gone. An hour later the front door crashed open. He stood in the doorway, squinting against the light, his shotgun aimed at Beth, his other hand holding the pistol.

"Beth," he grunted.

He pointed the shotgun at the ceiling, carefully thumbing the hammers down. He slid the pistol in a jacket pocket.

"I ought to wear you out," he said. "Didn't I tell you not to go nowhere."

"I saw her, Casey. I followed her."

"Who?"

"I don't know."

Casey stared through the window, his shotgun poised.

"She's gone," Beth said. "Crawled into an old hollow log up on Flatgap Ridge. I thought she was a ghost."

"She might be."

"You know her?"

"Hope not."

"Who is she?"

"Tell me what you seen, Beth."

She sat in a rocking chair built by her grandfather, the wedding gift from her mother. She pushed the chair back and forth to form the rhythm for her words. When she finished, Casey's face was white as birch. His arm veins swelled from squeezing the shotgun, trying to stop the tremble of his hands.

"I thought she was dead," Casey said.

"Who is she?"

Casey leaned the shotgun beside the door and sat on the bed. He rubbed his face.

"The way it was went like this," he said. "Me and Duck Sparker were playing hide-and-seek twenty years ago. It was my turn to hunt. Duck wasn't never too hard to find because he hid in bushes, behind a tree, or in a rock hole. One time he'd been hid for a spell out Flatgap. I saw his hand hanging out of a big old log, same one you seen, I guess. It's been there since my daddy's time.

"I had me a ring whittled out of a buckeye with my initials carved on it and I thought to pull a rusty on Duck. I sneaked up to the log and put that ring on his finger. 'I take you as my wife,' I said, ''til death do us part.' Well, Duck didn't say nothing and I thought he'd fell asleep while hiding. I banged that log and said, 'Wake up and kiss your husband!' The hand moved and an arm followed it out and I seen it wasn't Duck but a little dried-up woman, old as the hills. Her face was awful. She said, 'I'll wait on you.'

"I ran like a scalded pup and never told nobody, not even Duck."

Casey's voice melted into the stillness of the room. Dawn crawled above the farthest ridge and the outside air was day again. Songbirds filled the woods with sound.

"Only thing ever scared me was snakes," he said. "And I've killed my share. But I'm afraid now, Beth. Bad off afraid."

"I'll talk to Nomey this evening. You should sleep."

Casey nodded. He tucked the pistol beneath his pillow and hid the knife in the blankets. "I'll lay on the outside, Beth."

They awoke past noon, pressed tight together, and walked to her mother's. He split firewood while Beth told Nomey what had happened in the night.

"He wants to burn that log," Beth said. "Set a punk fire and smoke her out like a varmint."

Her mother's face set hard into a frown. A striped engineer's hat covered her head.

"I'd not do that," Nomey said. "She might take a notion to do the same to you. Only one woman got the power to be that mean, but I thought the buzzards had her by now."

"You act like you know her."

"Honey, I do," her mother said. "That woman fetched me into this world."

"Who?"

"The last granny-woman in these parts. She caught three hundred babies on this creek. It got close to your time, she'd be waiting in the woods. You could smell her pipe smoke. When the baby started, she'd walk right in the house with nary a word said. Just go to work. She stopped birthing after that hospital got built in Rocksalt. She got withered up like a blight hit her, and disappeared off creation. But sometimes you could smell that pipe strong, like burning cedar chips.

"People said she left her homeplace and went up Flatgap. Long time back, they quarried rock out of a cave up there and when weather pushed down, her fire smoke hung in the trees. I reckon she's still living in that cave. That log just hides the cave hole."

Dusk slipped along the creek, filtering through the trees. Beth rolled a cigarette and held the gumless flap for her mother to lick. Nomey split a wooden match, flared half to light the cigarette, tucked the other piece into her cap.

"It's unreckoning what she might do," Nomey said.

"She never did have a man or kids of her own. Best be nice by her, keep her close."

"How?"

"Two ways, and you ought to pray the first way works. Take and leave food at the mouth of that log every so often. Not so much she'll think you're begging or buying, and not too little either. Three, four ears of corn'd be good. Don't say nothing and don't be scared. Just walk up bold and leave it."

"What's the other way?"

"A whole lot worse." She raised her voice. "Casey! You come in here."

Boots clumped and the door banged. "Chopped enough wood for a month of Sundays," he said.

"You're mine now," Nomey said, "over marrying Beth."

Casey nodded, looking at the floor.

"You listen at me on this. Stay away from Flatgap and leave them guns at the house. You hear me."

"Yes, ma'am."

"There's more to it than you think. I know you're fierce, but this takes another kind. You'll have to be stouter than you ever was. You've got to do what me and Beth tells you."

"I will."

"You swear?"

"I ain't broke my word yet."

Nomey dug in a pocket for a chunk of moly root. "Make a hole in this and wear it," she said. "Now you'uns get home."

For a year, Beth left garden vegetables by the log's mouth. At fall slaughter she took hog: in winter, fresh venison. She missed her cycle and two months later her belly showed. When Casey came home from clearing timber, Beth's eyes were shy. "I've got a secret," she said. "I'm filled with us."

Casey's beard opened in a smile. He hugged her, then released her, frowning. "Did that hurt?"

"You can't squeeze it out that easy. It ain't no bigger than a radish."

They slept with their hands together on Beth's middle. In the morning Casey left to plow while Beth moved through the house, planning for her child. She opened the kitchen window. A breeze carried birdsong in the house, followed by the pungent scent of burnt cedar. She squeezed the moly root and prayed.

The pipe-smoke smell grew stronger every day. After a week, she went to her mother's house and returned by midday. Nomey was right, the other way was worse than bad. Beth waited until the first day of the next full moon, then walked out Flatgap Ridge. Beyond it lay the massive shadow of Shawnee Rock. Beth stopped at the end of the ridge, face damp, fingers clenched. The log opening was dark as night.

"Aunt Granny Lith," Beth said. "I'm calling your name. I want my family left alone. You think we're married to the same man, but we ain't. He lives with me. I'll send him here tonight and you'll have a man for one night, not no more. You're too old to be a wife but you won't die like you were born. You got my word."

Beth stroked her swelling belly and watched a sparrow chase a jay. She turned damp leaves beneath the tree and rooted in the earth. An inch below the surface lay a chestnut with a finger-sized hole. It was brittle, nearly rotten. Beth felt the baby kick.

After supper she told Casey about the cedar smell, what Nomey had said they had to do, and the visit to the log on Flatgap Ridge. Casey finished his salad of wild ramps and cress. His voice was gentle.

"I don't know much on a woman pregnant," he said, "but I've heard it makes your mind take to spinning. Were you sick this morning?"

"You got to go up on Flatgap tonight, by yourself."

"Won't."

"You leave your clothes by the log and you crawl right inside there. It opens to an old cave."

"Ain't about to."

"Remember what Nomey said. You got to listen and do what we say. It's for the baby, your daughter."

Casey laid his fork down and straightened his back in the maple chair. His thick-knuckled hands pressed the table.

"A girl?"

"Nomey took a token on it."

"A token! I'm sick of tokens, Beth. That's all you two can do. Give a man an old piece of root and take his pistol. Go out in the woods and dicker with a log. That ain't my way, Beth. Someone crosses me, I stay crossed. I plow, hunt, and chop. I work, by God. I work!"

"Tokens work, too."

"I never seen one."

"It's knowing more than seeing."

"You ain't the only one knows things. My daddy run animals out of the garden all his life. You can't ask a rabbit to leave your lettuce alone. You got to kill it."

Casey tore a sleeve from his shirt. He lifted a jug of kerosene and stuffed the sleeve in the narrow mouth. He grabbed a fistful of matches from the stove.

"Won't do no good," Beth said. "Even a groundhog's got two or three back doors."

"She ain't no groundhog."

"You'll just make her mad."

"We'll be square, then."

Casey lifted his shotgun and went outside. Beth heard a crash of shattering glass, then the shotgun's roar. Before the echo faded, he fired the other barrel. Ejected shells bounced against the porch. Two more blasts came and Casey stepped inside, bleeding from his forehead.

"Missed," he said.

"Was it her?"

"Biggest nighthawk I ever did see. First step off the porch, it flew at my head. I dropped the coal oil and busted it." He wiped his face and licked the blood. "Never knew a bird to act that way before."

"Come here, Casey." Her voice was low and calm. "I got something to show you."

She rolled the chestnut ring across the table. Casey picked it up carefully. Carved into the shell were his initials.

"Where'd you get this from?"

"Her."

"It ain't right, me going up there."

"You got to."

"You're my wife."

"That's why I can say."

"It's against everything."

"Not if I tell you to."

"I can't."

"It's the only way."

"That don't make it right."

"You gave your word."

Casey smashed the chestnut with his fist. He pounded the shell to tiny pieces, swept them to the floor.

"I can fix your shirt," Beth said.

"Me, too." Casey ripped the other sleeve away. "Nothing wrong with it now."

She embraced him, rocking and moaning low in her throat. At dusk he left the house. The air was white as day from the moon bloated full above the ridge. Beth watched him walk into the night, the first time she'd seen him without a gun.

She melted lye on the stove, stirred in hog tallow and crumbled sage. She ground the broken chestnut and sprinkled the powder in a pot. After it cooled, she coated the tin bottom of a washtub with the mixture and began heating water, waiting without sleep for his return.

Dawn's light angled through the trees, changing dew to ground fog rising from the hollow. Beth stiffened at a sound on the porch. Casey entered, swaying and shirtless. Nail marks gashed his shoulders and dark clots clung to his chest. He shuffled across the floor in unlaced boots.

"Don't look at me," he said.

He threw his pants outside while she poured scalding water in the washtub. Casey crouched in the steam, hugging his knees while Beth scrubbed his body raw. She helped him to bed, where he lay two weeks, chilled and quaking with fever. Nomey came to dress his wounds and fill the house with the smell of snakeroot tea. They changed the sweat-soaked sheets every morning and night.

On the fifteenth day, Casey opened calm eyes.

"Beth," he said.

"I'm here."

He slept again and Nomey left. The next day he sat wrapped in a quilt by the stove.

"Got any tobacco on you?" he said.

"You don't smoke, Casey."

"I'm starting."

She found some butts her mother had left and rolled him a fresh one. When half was gone, he spoke.

"She begged me, Beth. She flat out begged me."

"She shouldn't have."

"No, not that. After that. She begged me after."

"What?"

"To kill her."

He inhaled, watching the smoke stream into the air like water. The cigarette fell. He lowered his face to his hands and cried for a long time.

Beth tethered the mule on the creek bank, walked down to the pickup, and tumbled Casey to the ground. She used a crowbar to pry the seat loose from the truck. She tied him to the seat and hooked the logging chain to a rusty spring. At the top of the hill, she broke a willow switch and whipped the mule. Muscles rippled beneath its hide. Each nostril puffed mist and saliva foamed from its mouth.

"Pull," Beth yelled again and again.

The mule lurched slowly forward. When the seat reached the top of the ridge, Beth wedged a shoulder under Casey's crotch, and lifted him across the animal's back. She tied his wrist to an ankle, knotting the rope tight against the mule's belly. Her clothes were damp with sweat. Casey and the animal formed a black seamless shape in the darkness of the woods. Beth led the mule down the hollow and up the creek. At the wide place where she'd first met Casey, she tossed Lil's hair into the water, and watched it swirl away.

She unloaded him onto the porch and threw a quilt over him. Casey curled on his side, tucking hands between his knees, his breath coming in ragged snorts. Beth undressed and cleaned the bruised wound on her hip. Her face was scratched and her feet ached. She lay in bed, wishing the long night all those years ago had been this easy. It had broken a part of Casey and graveled him up pretty bad. She didn't think about it often but when she did, she knew that what they'd done was right. Their four girls were proof enough, grown now, and gone.

Hours later she woke from Casey's weight on the mattress. Outside, a rooster bellowed to his hens. Casey's face poked pale and slack from the quilt.

"I lost the truck, Beth."

"You'll find it."

"But I came home," he said. "I always come home."

"Lay down now."

She scooted across the tick. Casey fumbled straps and slid his overalls to the floor. Beth spread the quilt over them as he snuggled against her.

"Ain't never stayed a night away but the one, Beth."

"I know."

"Wished I hadn't then."

"I never think about it anymore."

"You didn't kill Lil, did you?"

"No."

"Sometimes I don't think I been much good to you."

"You're here," Beth said.

"I feel kindly rough."

"Still drunk's all. There's one good way to cure that and I don't mean coffee."

She opened her legs and towed Casey until his head lay between her breasts. She groaned as he mashed her hip.

"What's wrong, Beth?"

"Hip."

"Bad hurt?"

"No. Banged it on the corncrib or something."

"You always did hurt too easy."

She smiled at his ear, brushing her fingers along his lower back. He smelled of dirt and moonshine. She lifted her knees to guide him with her thighs.

ROBERT OLMSTEAD

☆ ☆ ☆ ☆

# Cody's Story

Cody and his partner, G. R. Trimble, were loggers. G.R. had a splendid piebald Percheron twitch horse named Buck that stood 18 hands, and Cody had a 100-horsepower fully articulated John Deere skidder equipped with grapple, winch, and arch, that could skid 500 board-feet equivalent of hardwood logs.

The men lived in the horse trailer with Buck. They had bunks and shelves that folded up during transport and down when they set up camp. They had a TV, electric baseboard heat, and a microwave oven. All of these ran off a little Homelite generator they took in swap for some cordwood.

It was a good life for the two gypsy loggers, even in the winter, when on certain nights the dark silence heaved open with the sound of hardwoods cracking and snapping from the cold within their very heartwood. Such nights Cody would sit up bolt straight in bed and curse silently to himself. G.R. was merely thankful it didn't get as cold as it used to in the old days.

G.R. was older than Cody and had a reputation. They say that when he was up in Saskatchewan he got shorted on an overrun of logs once, so he went down to the mill. When reason failed, he threw the sawyer's bird dog down a well, packed up, and left.

People treated G.R. with respect, just in case the story was true. G.R. always responded with great courtesy, cementing in the minds of everyone he met that the story was indeed true. The more kindly he acted, the more convinced they were that he threw the dog down the well. G.R. was a politic man.

Cody was married to a woman in Winchester, New Hampshire. She had a boy from a previous marriage. When the boy was young Cody loved him, but as he grew older and took on the looks of another man, Cody could see in him his wife's first husband, and as the boy grew, it was as if the other man had moved back in. Finally Cody left for the woods with G.R. He seldom got home, but always sent money to their joint account. Being away helped him start to love her again, and by now he'd been in the woods with G.R. so long he'd forgotten why he'd come in the first place.

Their last year together, Cody and G.R. wintered on the leeward side of Monadnock. G.R. opened his money belt and bought a used D-7 to clear the right-of-way. They hewed out a suitable landing on the main haul road. Arterials ran in at up to 20 per cent grades, too steep for most men, but not for Cody and G.R.

Sunday was the only day Cody and G.R. didn't work. They'd hole up in the trailer, where they serviced their saws and sharpened chain while they watched *The Three Stooges* on TV. G.R. would cringe and say "Oh God" whenever Moe raked a crosscut across Curly's noggin, splaying the teeth in opposite directions and making him screech like a cat in heat. Because he was a real stickler on safety, G.R.'s fascination with the Stooges brought him much pain.

"My way or the highway, boy," he'd yell at Cody, when they were in the woods.

"Don't call me boy," Cody would yell back over the roar of the skidder.

"Okay, boy," G.R. would reply, dragging out the last word before disappearing into the trees with the winch line over his shoulder, hooks and choker assemblies bouncing against his chest.

On this Sunday, the first snow of the year had come down country and gripped everything. The generator ran out of gas at about 4 in the morning. The trailer was freezing, the walls coated with sharp white needles of hoarfrost. Buck was blowing billows of hot breath that were crystallizing in the air and coasting to the floor. "Cody boy, get me a beer, would you?" G.R. said from deep inside his blankets.

Cody and G.R. drank beer on Sunday mornings. They

bought the beer on Saturday night when they went grocery shopping because it was against the law to buy it before noon on Sundays. Cody and G.R. liked their beer on Sundays.

Cody reached into the case under his bunk for a beer. He passed it up to G.R. with a can of tomato juice. G.R. took a swallow and refilled it with the juice.

"This one's for you, Buck ol' boy," he said nodding to the horse. "If it weren't for you, we might've froze to death."

Cody tried to go back to sleep, but it was just too damn cold. He burrowed down in his bed covers for his shoes and trousers. Once he was dressed, he started the generator. It was almost 7.30. Cody squeezed his way around some boxes and dished up oats for the horse. Buck swished his tail and snuffed into his feedbag. He was a good horse.

"Boy, that tastes good," G.R. said, staring at the empty beer bottle. "You know, I can't eat breakfast on an empty stomach."

"Sure, G.R. That's a good one," Cody said.

G.R. dressed while Cody cooked eggs, potatoes, and a rasher of bacon in the microwave. The men washed down their breakfast with beer and tomato juice. By 8 o'clock they had their benches, jigs, and files set up. Each had fifteen chains to sharpen. On each chain they had to sharpen the cutters and file the rakers. They turned on the TV and went to work. It was almost time for *The Three Stooges*.

The men worked carefully, side by side, inspecting each link for wear and stress. A snapped chain at high speed could raise hell with a man's will to live.

The only time G.R. ever used another man's saw, he was bucking up frozen hard maple. When he set the saw to the wood, it skated along the tree, cutters clipping off into the air. The chain broke, whipping around his top hand. They saved his hand, but it took two hours to separate the glove, steel, meat, and bone. It was understood they'd each use their own saw and chain. G.R. tied blue ribbon around his chain and Cody used red.

This Sunday the Stooges were going west in a covered wagon with three fat sisters, Faith, Hope, and Charity. The girls made the boys fetch wood and break holes in the ice for water.

Their horses ran off and they were attacked by Indians. The girls made the boys sleep outdoors under a tarp. By morning they were buried in snow.

The high point for G.R. was when Moe got slapped in the face with a limb Curly let go. Moe poked him in the eyes a good one with his fingers.

"Boy, that had to hurt some," G.R. said, rubbing his eyes.

"It's all phony," Cody said. "If he really did that, it'd blind him."

"I'd like to get those boys in the woods for a day," G.R. said. "I bet I could teach them a few things. Snap them in line."

"For Chrissakes, G.R., it's all bullshit. That stuff doesn't really happen."

"It does more than you think, Cody, my boy. More than you think."

Cody finished his chain while G.R. switched the channel to *Meet the Press*. Cody worried about G.R. lately. G.R. didn't seem to have any diversions except the Three Stooges. He talked about them like they were his boys. Cody watched G.R. cringe whenever the boys got hurt and heard him declare revenge whenever they got screwed by someone. Cody knew G.R. was serious when he said he'd like to take the boys out into the woods and teach them how to be loggers.

Cody and G.R. continued to work all morning, sitting in front of the TV. Cody made sandwiches, thick slabs of beef between bread. The men drank and ate and worked while they watched TV.

"We'd best start the engines tonight," Cody said.

"Why?" G.R. asked, cocking his head sideways toward Cody.

"Winter, G.R. Those engines will never start in the morning. Till this weather breaks, we'd best leave them go around the clock."

"Ether, Cody boy, ether."

"Not in this weather, G.R. You'll blow the heads."

The men sat quietly. Buck ate hay and sucked water from his bucket.

"G.R.," Cody said quietly, "you feeling all right?"

G.R. nodded his head without looking at Cody.

"G.R.," Cody said, "we always leave the engines run in this weather. We never use ether."

G.R. nodded his head again.

"I know, Cody. I know. I know."

"G.R., that ain't like you."

"I know, Cody. I been doing that more and more of late. I miss stuff. It's like when I was stationed overseas, Spain. I got up in the middle of the night to take a leak. All the boys were on guard duty. So I'm standing there in the can draining Big Willy, and the whole room starts to go up and down and here I am pissin' all over the walls. I thought I was sick as a dog, so I go back to my bunk figuring I'd better see the doctor. Well, I get back in the barracks and the concrete floor is going in waves just like the ocean. Now I know I'm sick. Two days later I find out it's a goddamn earthquake."

Cody stared at G.R., trying to fit this into what had prompted the conversation. G.R. began to rummage for his mackinaw.

"Where are you going?" Cody asked.

"Let's go take a leak, Cody. The sun's high and fine."

G.R. had no way of knowing, Cody thought, because there were no windows in the trailer. Cody shut off the TV anyway and followed G.R. out the side door. The sun was low on the southern horizon and wouldn't start to climb until after the solstice. Cody dusted off the machines and unlatched the hoods so what sun there was could warm the batteries. G.R. backed Buck out of the trailer and walked him around the landing half a dozen times to limber him up. The horse stepped high, not too pleased with the whole affair.

Cody watched G.R. amble alongside Buck, whose nose was at the same level as the top of G.R.'s head. Snow collected on Buck's fetlocks in hard, round balls. His shoulders alternately bulged and receded and his haunches swayed rhythmically. G.R. picked up the pace. The two of them pranced around the perimeter of the clearing.

Cody had to admit that Buck earned his keep. They used him for gleaning the swamps, holes, and isolated stands for the best tree. Buck was smart. He had the sense to set over whenever he hit a snag. G.R. would set the choker and Cody would be on the haul road yarding the logs. Buck would twitch the logs a long ways up to Cody on his own without a jam.

That horse is the most important thing in G.R.'s life, Cody thought. They'd logged both coasts and as far north as Hudson Bay together. Buck was old, though, and wouldn't last much longer. G.R. knew it, too, and it had to be on his mind.

G.R. brought Buck up to the Cat where Cody was tinkering with the terminals.

"We're a little stiff today, Cody. Gonna be a long winter this year, I'm afraid."

"No longer than any other."

"I meant more by that, Cody. I meant winter would be longer."

"I know, G.R., winter will be longer this year." G.R. backed Buck off and began around the landing again.

"G.R.," Cody yelled, "picket that horse and let's hike up the haul road. There's deer sign up there."

"You go, Cody, I'm going in and watch TV. There's a cowboy movie on."

Cody started up the haul road with his Deerslayer and field glasses. When he reached the first level he climbed the bank and bushwhacked up the mountain. Halfway to the summit he was forced to skirt a 30-foot rock face. When he reached the top, he walked out on the lip where the snow had melted off and the rocks were warm in the sunlight. He sat down, cradling the shotgun in his lap.

Water was trickling from under the snow behind him, fanning out to his right and left in wide arcs coursing across the rock and then dripping off the edge. Night would come, turning the fans into an icy veneer and the drips into icicles.

Far below he could see the blue hull of the trailer and the yellow skidder and crawler on the edge of the landing. They were encircled by G.R.'s and Buck's track. Cody tapped a cigarette on his thumbnail and lit it. He tried to relax, but kept thinking that G.R. was a little different this morning in a vacant sort of way. Men changed, he knew that. He'd seen it before. He himself had felt it, the feeling of something creeping up on you. The woods were full of men who'd sat down and died, men with a full larder and an income. The more willful hadn't waited for death. They took it to her.

Cody sat and smoked. He just had to get away. He turned around and looked at the mountain that rose up behind him. He imagined Larry, Moe, and Curly tumbling down the mountain toward him with a black bear in hot pursuit. He imagined G.R. riding up to save them on Old Buck, waving a double-bit ax over his head. "You did good, boys," he'd tell them. "You always run downhill from a bear because its front legs are short and it can't go so fast."

Cody looked down the mountain again and saw G.R. running in circles. Cody raised his binoculars. G.R. was spelling Cody's name in the snow. He was standing on the loop of the Y, waving his right arm back and forth. Cody waved his arm and then saluted.

Through the binoculars, Cody could see the smile on G.R.'s red face. He could see a tuft of white hair where G.R.'s shirt was open at the neck. Cody felt better sitting on the rock with the sun on his face and G.R. waving at him. He stretched his legs and opened the collar of his own shirt. He lay back on the rocks, sore and tired from the long week's work. He could smell the pine and hemlock in the air. He fell asleep feeling a little relieved.

When Cody woke up, the sun was fading behind a snow-capped mountain to the southwest. Its light played out in deep reds and purples. Cody stood and stretched, aching with cold. He crossed his arms on his chest and shivered. Turning to make his way home, he stepped on an ice patch to his right. He slipped, his body slapping full length against the rock, and began sliding toward the edge. The only sound was the echo of his gun clattering from rock to rock on its way to the ground.

As Cody slid, everything seemed to pause just for him, all mechanisms stopping so as not to divert him from this moment. His body warmed and his thoughts came like pictures, some he'd never seen before. Then he was floating, unable to figure his orientation to the ground below and not all that concerned with whether his head was up or down. There was no rush of air and his breathing seemed easy to him. Just as he began to worry, he was in the top of a blue spruce, dropping through its branches, limbing them with his legs and arms.

Cody locked his arms around a branch, annoyed that this would be more difficult than he thought. He hugged the branch against himself.

For a second it bent under him and held. At that moment the world about him lurched back into gear as if someone had popped a giant clutch. The branch sheared off and he rode it the rest of the way to the ground.

Cody lay there in the dark a long time, then began taking inventory of his body. It was all there and it worked. He began to wonder if what had happened had happened at all. He found his gun and set out for the trailer.

By the time he got there it was dark. He ran a lead cord and trouble light out to the skidder. He worked quickly, fearing the batteries had cooled and the oil had thickened.

He remembered the time G.R. started a fire under one machine to warm it. Those were the days when everything G.R. did was safe, or at least he'd explain that everything he did was safe.

Cody shifted the skidder into neutral range, switched on the ignition, and pressed the starter. The engine chugged and huffed and then fired up in the sharp night air.

Cody backed her up and then drove forward, breaking the tires free of the ice that was forming. He idled her down, checked the fuel, and went in for the night, walking lightly on the balls of his feet.

The trailer was warm and bright. Saw chains were hung on the wall, blue ribbons for G.R., red for Cody. On the same wall were silver hard hats and duckcloth overalls. Cody's supper was in the microwave waiting for the button to be pushed.

G.R. sat on a bale of hay watching *60 Minutes*. He was eating chili dogs and chicken noodle soup. While he chewed his food, his mouth was half open and his jaw popped.

"Where you been, Cody?" G.R. asked.

"Starting up the skidder." Cody didn't recognize his own voice.

"What for?"

"G.R., we leave it run. I already talked to you about it."

Cody ate his supper, lighting up his last cigarette to go along with his meal. He felt confused and lost, as if G.R. were a total stranger who for no reason had robbed him.

"G.R., remember the time you started a fire under that Massey loader to warm it up?"

"Tried and true method, Cody my boy."

"Good, G.R. That's real good," Cody said, shoving a chili dog into his mouth.

"Watch this, Cody. Dan's going to nab this poor bastard for shutting off an old lady's electricity last winter."

"Goddammit, G.R., something's happening and I want to know what the hell it is."

G.R. stood up and turned toward Cody. He craned his neck and puffed out his chest. "I'm losing my edge a little, Cody. That's all. It's damn hard to maintain when you go the way I do."

"That's a crock, G.R."

"No, Cody. I'm feeling it a little. I'm feeling it right now, and if I can't feel it, then I can't do nothing." G.R. sat down.

"Cody, if I ever get too daft to be out in them woods, I want you to shoot me."

"Sure, G.R., right between your goddamn eyes, and then I'll shoot old Buck and carve a niche inside that mountain. I'll set you up on him with your hands wired to the hames. I'll bury you there for some asshole to dig up in the year 3000."

Cody felt his stomach churn. He eyed G.R., sitting only a few feet away, intent on the TV. For a moment he considered packing it in and going home – something had a hold on him. Cody squeezed through to Buck and fed him a couple cubes of sugar. The horse tossed his head and shifted his weight. The whole trailer bounced. Cody put his face and chest against Buck's body. It was warm and moved slowly as Buck breathed.

Cody took out the curry and brush and began to groom him. He combed out the mane, tail, and fetlocks. He curried his coat until it was sleek and shiny. Then he wrapped his arms around the animal's huge legs, hugging and squeezing them.

When he was done, he leaned back against Buck's chest. The horse rested his chin on Cody's head, breathing deeply, the weight of his head growing heavy as he relaxed.

Cody eased out from under the horse and moved to the front of the trailer. G.R. was already in his bunk, asleep. Cody shut off the TV and lights and climbed into his own bunk.

He lay there for a long time. Tomorrow they would be on the far boundary of the cutting unit, into maple and beech. On a concave slope with a wash down the center. It would be an interesting challenge. G.R. would build it up as insurmountable only so that his method of logging would seem that much more amazing. Things would be all right then, Cody thought. Things would be better in the morning.

Buck stamped once and then there was only silence in the trailer. The horse was asleep, his four legs locked into position. Cody relaxed a little more and then he heard G.R. whisper.

"Cody, What's that noise?"

"It's the skidder," Cody said.

"Of course, of course. Better set that idle or you'll foul the jets."

"It'll do for tonight," Cody said, feeling his stomach clench up again and start to swim. He fought back the feeling. He fought back his fears for G.R. and his fears for himself.

"Colder than hell," G.R. said, still whispering. "Might not make it through this one. They'll find us with icicles hanging out our noses."

"G.R., I'm pretty damn cold myself," Cody lied.

"We better do something," G.R. said.

There was a long time when neither spoke. Cody didn't want to but he tried to remember the images he saw while he was falling. Just as he would begin to get a lock on one, it would slip from his mind's grasp and he was left only with an empty feeling. He gave up on the ones he hadn't recognized, but by then he couldn't remember even the ones that had seemed familiar.

Finally G.R. crawled out of his bunk and got in bed with Cody. Cody rolled onto his side and G.R. lined his body behind him. They lay there feeling the warmth of each other's body.

Cody felt better having his friend so close, haunted as he was by his tumble off the cliff.

"Just one thing, Cody boy," G.R. said.

Cody felt G.R.'s chin whiskers scratching against the back of his neck.

G.R. moved closer. "There'll be no kissing on the mouth," he said.

Cody threw back his head, hitting G.R. in the nose, and laughed. G.R. grabbed his hurt nose and began to laugh, too. They laughed and sighed and Cody began to cry, softly so G.R. wouldn't know. He lay on his side, his face inches from the wall. G.R. was behind him, his arms folded and his face was in the corner made by Cody's shoulder and the mattress.

"G.R., I needed you tonight," Cody said.

"Now, Cody, you've got to take charge more."

"Stop it, G.R. Stop it. I almost died tonight," Cody said, his tears too full to hold back. "I almost died on that goddamn mountain." Then he told the whole story, feeling for the first time the pain in his arms and chest.

G.R. didn't say anything for so long that Cody thought he'd fallen asleep. Then he felt G.R.'s hand on his shoulder and heard him speak, as if he were talking to himself. "Is it true, Cody, that your whole life passes before your eyes?"

Cody didn't answer. He only lay there and listened. He heard the John Deere's diesel knocking outside in the night. He imagined a thousand small explosions going off inside its block, like all the scenes he couldn't remember and never would.

# JAYNE ANNE PHILLIPS

☆　☆　☆　☆

# *Home*

I'm afraid Walter Cronkite has had it, says Mom. Roger Mudd always does the news now – how would you like to have a name like that? Walter used to do the conventions and a football game now and then. I mean he would sort of appear, on the sidelines. Didn't he? But you never see him anymore. Lord. Something is going on.

Mom, I say. Maybe he's just resting. He must have made a lot of money by now. Maybe he's tired of talking about elections and mine disasters and the collapse of the franc. Maybe he's in love with a young girl.

He's not the type, says my mother. You can tell *that* much. No, she says, I'm afraid it's cancer.

My mother has her suspicions. She ponders. I have been home with her for two months. I ran out of money and I wasn't in love, so I have come home to my mother. She is an educational administrator. All winter long after work she watches television and knits afghans.

Come home, she said. Save money.

I can't possibly do it, I said. Jesus, I'm twenty-three years old.

Don't be silly, she said. And don't use profanity.

She arranged a job for me in the school system. All day, I tutor children in remedial reading. Sometimes I am so discouraged that I lie on the couch all evening and watch television with her. The shows are all alike. Their laugh tracks are conspicuously similar; I think I recognize a repetition of certain professional laughters. This laughter marks off the half hours.

Finally I make a rule: I won't watch television at night. I will watch only the news, which ends at 7.30. Then I will go to my room and do God knows what. But I feel sad that she sits there alone, knitting by the lamp. She seldom looks up.

Why don't you ever read anything? I ask.

I do, she says. I read books in my field. I read all day at work, writing those damn proposals. When I come home I want to relax.

Then let's go to the movies.

I don't want to go to the movies. Why should I pay money to be upset or frightened?

But feeling something can teach you. Don't you want to learn anything?

I'm learning all the time, she says.

She keeps knitting. She folds yarn the color of cream, the color of snow. She works it with her long blue needles, piercing, returning, winding. Yarn cascades from her hands in long panels. A pattern appears and disappears. She stops and counts; so many stitches across, so many down. Yes, she is on the right track.

Occasionally I offer to buy my mother a subscription to something mildly informative: *Ms.*, *Rolling Stone*, *Scientific American*.

I don't want to read that stuff, she says. Just save your money. Did you hear Cronkite last night? Everyone's going to need all they can get.

Often, I need to look at my mother's old photographs. I see her sitting in knee-high grass with a white gardenia in her hair. I see her dressed up as the groom in a mock wedding at a sorority party, her black hair pulled back tight. I see her formally posed in her cadet nurse's uniform. The photographer has painted her lashes too lushly, too long; but her deep red mouth is correct.

The war ended too soon. She didn't finish her training. She came home to nurse only her mother and to meet my father at a dance. She married him in two weeks. It took twenty years to divorce him.

When we traveled to a neighboring town to buy my high school clothes, my mother and I would pass a certain road that turned off the highway and wound to a place I never saw.

There it is, my mother would say. The road to Wonder Bar.
That's where I met my Waterloo. I walked in and he said, "There
she is. I'm going to marry that girl." Ha. He sure saw me
coming.

Well, I asked, Why did you marry him?

He was older, she said. He had a job and a car. And Mother
was so sick.

My mother doesn't forget her mother.

Never one bedsore, she says. I turned her every fifteen
minutes. I kept her skin soft and kept her clean, even to the end.

I imagine my mother at twenty-three; her black hair, her
dark eyes, her olive skin and that red lipstick. She is growing
lines of tension in her mouth. Her teeth press into her lower lip
as she lifts the woman in the bed. The woman weighs no more
than a child. She has a smell. My mother fights it continually;
bathing her, changing her sheets, carrying her to the bathroom
so the smell can be contained and flushed away. My mother will
try to protect them both. At night she sleeps in the room on a
cot. She struggles awake feeling something press down on her
and suck her breath: the smell. When my grandmother can no
longer move, my mother fights it alone.

I did all I could, she sighs. And I was glad to do it. I'm glad
I don't have to feel guilty.

No one has to feel guilty, I tell her.

And why not? says my mother. There's nothing wrong with
guilt. If you are guilty, you should feel guilty.

My mother has often told me that I will be sorry when she is
gone.

I think. And read alone at night in my room. I read those books
I never read, the old classics, and detective stories. I can get them
in the library here. There is only one bookstore; it sells mostly
newspapers and *True Confessions* oracles. At Kroger's by the
checkout counter I buy a few paperbacks, best sellers, but they
are usually bad.

The television drones on downstairs.

I wonder about Walter Cronkite.

When was the last time I saw him? It's true his face was pouchy, his hair thinning. Perhaps he is only cutting it shorter. But he had that look about the eyes —

He was there when they stepped on the moon. He forgot he was on the air and he shouted, "There . . . there . . . now – We have Contact!" Contact. For those who tuned in late, for the periodic watchers, he repeated: "One small step . . ."

I was in high school and he was there with the body count. But he said it in such a way that you knew he wanted the war to end. He looked directly at you and said the numbers quietly. Shame, yes, but sorrowful patience, as if all things had passed before his eyes. And he understood that here at home, as well as in starving India, we would pass our next lives as meager cows.

My mother gets *Reader's Digest*. I come home from work, have a cup of coffee, and read it. I keep it beside my bed. I read it when I am too tired to read anything else. I read about Joe's kidney and Humor in Uniform. Always, there are human interest stories in which someone survives an ordeal of primal terror. Tonight it is Grizzly! Two teenagers camping in the mountains are attacked by a bear. Sharon is dragged over a mile, unconscious. She is a good student loved by her parents, an honest girl loved by her boyfriend. Perhaps she is not a virgin; but in her heart, she is virginal. And she lies now in the furred arms of a beast. The grizzly drags her quietly, quietly. He will care for her all the days of his life . . . Sharon, his rose.

But alas. Already, rescuers have organized. Mercifully, her boyfriend is not among them. He is sleeping en route to the nearest hospital; his broken legs have excused him. In a few days, Sharon will bring him his food on a tray. She is spared. She is not demure. He gazes on her face, untouched but for a long thin scar near her mouth. Sharon says she remembers nothing of the bear. She only knows the tent was ripped open, that its heavy canvas fell across her face.

I turn out my light when I know my mother is sleeping. By then my eyes hurt and the streets of the town are deserted.

My father comes to me in a dream. He kneels beside me, touches my mouth. He turns my face gently toward him.

Let me see, he says. Let me see it.

He is looking for a scar, a sign. He wears only a towel around his waist. He presses himself against my thigh, pretending solicitude. But I know what he is doing; I turn my head in repulsion and stiffen. He smells of a sour musk and his forearms are black with hair. I think to myself, It's been years since he's had an erection—

Finally he stands. Cover yourself, I tell him.

I can't, he says, I'm hard.

On Saturdays I go to the Veterans of Foreign Wars rummage sales. They are held in the drafty basement of a church, rows of collapsible tables piled with objects. Sometimes I think I recognize the possessions of old friends: a class ring, yearbooks, football sweaters with our high school insignia. Would this one have fit Jason?

He used to spread it on the seat of the car on winter nights when we parked by country churches and graveyards. There seemed to be no ground, just water, a rolling, turning, building to a dull pain between my legs.

What's wrong? he said, What is it?

Jason, I can't . . . This pain—

It's only because you're afraid. If you'd let me go ahead—

I'm not afraid of you, I'd do anything for you. But Jason, why does it hurt like this?

We would try. But I couldn't. We made love with our hands. Our bodies were white. Out the window of the car, snow rose up in mounds across the fields. Afterward, he looked at me peacefully, sadly.

I held him and whispered, Soon, soon . . . we'll go away to school.

His sweater. He wore it that night we drove back from the football awards banquet. Jason made All-State but he hated football.

I hate it, he said. So what? he said, that I'm out there puking in the heat? Screaming "Kill" at a sandbag?

I held his award in my lap, a gold man frozen in midleap. Don't play in college, I said. Refuse the money.

He was driving very slowly.

I can't see, he said, I can't see the edges of the road . . . Tell me if I start to fall off.

Jason, what do you mean?

He insisted I roll down the window and watch the edge. The banks of the road were gradual, sloping off into brush and trees on either side. White lines at the edge glowed up in dips and turns.

We're going to crash, he said.

No, Jason. You've driven this road before. We won't crash.

We're crashing, I know it, he said. Tell me, tell me I'm okay —

Here on the rummage sale table, there are three football sweaters. I see they are all too small to have belonged to Jason. So I buy an old soundtrack, *The Sound of Music*. Air, Austrian mountains. And an old robe to wear in the mornings. It upsets my mother to see me naked; she looks at me so curiously, as though she didn't recognize my body.

I pay for my purchases at the cash register. Behind the desk I glimpse stacks of *Reader's Digest*s. The Ladies Auxiliary turns them inside out, stiffens and shellacs them. They make wastebaskets out of them.

I give my mother the record. She is pleased. She hugs me.

Oh, she says, I used to love the musicals. They made me happy. Then she stops and looks at me.

Didn't you do this? she says. Didn't you do this in high school?

Do what?

Your class, she says. You did *The Sound of Music*.

Yes, I guess we did.

What a joke. I was the beautiful countess meant to marry Captain von Trapp before innocent Maria stole his heart. Jason was a threatening Nazi colonel with a bit part. He should have sung the lead but sports practices interfered with rehearsals. Tall, blond, aged in make-up under the lights, he encouraged sympathy for the bad guys and overshadowed the star. He appeared just often enough to make the play ridiculous.

★

My mother sits in the blue chair my father used for years.

Come quick, she says. Look —

She points to the television. Flickerings of Senate chambers, men in conservative suits. A commentator drones on about tax rebates.

There, says my mother. Hubert Humphrey. Look at him.

It's true. Humphrey is different, changed from his former toady self to a desiccated old man, not unlike the discarded shell of a locust. Now he rasps into the microphone about the people of these great states.

Old Hubert's had it, says my mother. He's a death mask.

That's what he gets for sucking blood for thirty years.

No, she says. No, he's got it too. Look at him! Cancer. Oh.

For God's sake, will you think of something else for once?

I don't know what you mean, she says. She goes on knitting.

All Hubert needs, I tell her, is a good roll in the hay.

You think that's what everyone needs.

Everyone does need it.

They do not. People aren't dogs. I seem to manage perfectly well without it, don't I?

No, I wouldn't say that you do.

Well, I do. I know your mumbo jumbo about sexuality. Sex is for those who are married, and I wouldn't marry again if it was the Lord himself.

Now she is silent. I know what's coming.

Your attitude will make you miserable, she says. One man after another. I just want you to be happy.

I do my best.

That's right, she says. Be sarcastic.

I refuse to answer. I think about my growing bank account. Graduate school, maybe in California. Hawaii. Somewhere beautiful and warm. I will wear few clothes and my skin will feel the air.

What about Jason, says my mother. I was thinking of him the other day.

Our telepathy always frightens me. Telepathy and beyond. Before her hysterectomy, our periods often came on the same day.

If he hadn't had that nervous breakdown, she says softly, do you suppose —

No. I don't suppose.

I wasn't surprised that it happened. When his brother was killed, that was hard. But Jason was so self-centered. You're lucky the two of you split up. He thought everyone was out to get him. Still, poor thing.

Silence. Then she refers in low tones to the few months Jason and I lived together before he was hospitalized.

You shouldn't have done what you did when you went off to college. He lost respect for you.

It wasn't respect for me he lost — He lost his fucking mind if you remember —

I realize I'm shouting. And shaking. What is happening to me?

My mother stares.

We'll not discuss it, she says.

She gets up. I hear her in the bathroom. Water running into the tub. Hydrotherapy. I close my eyes and listen. Soon, this weekend. I'll get a ride to the university a few hours away and look up an old lover. I'm lucky. They always want to sleep with me. For old times' sake.

I turn down the sound of the television and watch its silent pictures. Jason's brother was a musician; he taught Jason to play the pedal steel. A sergeant in uniform delivered the message two weeks before the State Play-Off games. Jason appeared at my mother's kitchen door with the telegram. He looked at me, opened his mouth, backed off wordless in the dark. I pretend I hear his pedal steel; its sweet country whine might make me cry. And I recognize this silent movie – I've seen it four times. Gregory Peck and his submarine crew escape fallout in Australia, but not for long. The cloud is coming. And so they run rampant in auto races and love affairs. But in the end, they close the hatch and put out to sea. They want to go home to die.

Sweetheart? my mother calls from the bathroom. Could you bring me a towel?

Her voice is quavering slightly. She is sorry. But I never know what part of it she is sorry about. I get a towel from the linen closet and open the door of the steamy bathroom. My mother stands in the tub, dripping, shivering a little. She is so small and thin; she is smaller than I. She has two long scars on her belly, operations of the womb, and one breast is misshapen, sunken, indented near the nipple.

I put the towel around her shoulders and my eyes smart. She looks at her breast.

Not too pretty is it, she says. He took out too much when he removed that lump —

Mom, it doesn't look so bad.

I dry her back, her beautiful back which is firm and unblemished. Beautiful, her skin. Again, I feel the pain in my eyes.

But you should have sued the bastard, I tell her. He didn't give a shit about your body.

We have an awkward moment with the towel when I realize I can't touch her any longer. The towel slips down and she catches it as one end dips into the water.

Sweetheart, she says. I know your beliefs are different than mine. But have patience with me. You'll just be here a few more months. And I'll always stand behind you. We'll get along.

She has clutched the towel to her chest. She is so fragile, standing there, naked, with her small shoulders. Suddenly I am horribly frightened.

Sure, I say, I know we will.

I let myself out of the room.

Sunday my mother goes to church alone. Daniel calls me from DC. He's been living with a lover in Oregon. Now he is back East; she will join him in a few weeks. He is happy, he says. I tell him I'm glad he's found someone who appreciates him.

Come on now, he says. You weren't that bad.

I love Daniel, his white and feminine hands, his thick chestnut hair, his intelligence. And he loves me, though I don't know why. The last few weeks we were together I lay beside him like a piece of wood. I couldn't bear his touch; the moisture his penis left on my hips as he rolled against me. I was cold, cold. I huddled in blankets away from him.

I'm sorry, I said. Daniel, I'm sorry please – what's wrong with me? Tell me you love me anyway . . .

Yes, he said, Of course I do. I always will. I do.

Daniel says he has no car, but he will come by bus. Is there a place for him to stay?

Oh yes, I say. There's a guest room. Bring some Trojans. I'm a hermit with no use for birth control. Daniel, you don't know what it's like here.

I don't care what it's like. I want to see you.

Yes, I say. Daniel, hurry.

When he arrives the next weekend, we sit around the table with my mother and discuss medicine. Daniel was a medic in Vietnam. He smiles at my mother. She is charmed though she has reservations; I see them in her face. But she enjoys having someone else in the house, a presence; a male. Daniel's laughter is low and modulated. He talks softly, smoothly: a dignified radio announcer, an accomplished anchorman.

But when I lived with him, he threw dishes against the wall. And jerked in his sleep, mumbling. And ran out of the house with his hands across his eyes.

After we first made love, he smiled and pulled gently away from me. He put on his shirt and went to the bathroom. I followed and stepped into the shower with him. He faced me, composed, friendly, and frozen. He stood as though guarding something behind him.

Daniel, turn around. I'll soap your back.

I already did.

Then move, I'll stand in the water with you.

He stepped carefully around me.

Daniel, what's wrong? Why won't you turn around?

Why should I?

I'd never seen him with his shirt off. He'd never gone swimming with us, only wading, alone, down Point Reyes Beach. He wore long-sleeved shirts all summer in the California heat.

Daniel, I said, You've been my best friend for months. We could have talked about it.

He stepped backwards, awkwardly, out of the tub and put his shirt on.

I was loading them on copters, he told me. The last one was
dead anyway; he was already dead. But I went after him, dragged
him in the wind of the blades. Shrapnel and napalm caught my
arms, my back. Until I fell, I thought it was the other man's
blood in my hands.

They removed most of the shrapnel, did skin grafts for the
burns. In three years since, Daniel made love five times; always
in the dark. In San Francisco he must take off his shirt for a
doctor; tumors have grown in his scars. They bleed through his
shirt, round rust-colored spots.

Face-to-face in bed, I tell him I can feel the scars with my
fingers. They are small knots on his skin. Not large, not ugly.
But he can't let me, he can't let anyone, look: he says he feels wild,
like raging, and then he vomits. But maybe, after they remove
the tumors – Each time they operate, they reduce the scars.

We spend hours at the veterans' hospital waiting for appointments. Finally they schedule the operation. I watch the black-
ringed wall clock, the amputees gliding by in chairs that tick on
the linoleum floor. Daniel's doctors curse about lack of supplies;
they bandage him with gauze and layers of Band-Aids. But it is
all right. I buy some real bandages. Every night I cleanse his back
with a sponge and change them.

In my mother's house, Daniel seems different. He has shaved
his beard and his face is too young for him. I can only grip his
hands.

I show him the house, the antiques, the photographs on the
walls. I tell him none of the objects move; they are all cemented
in place. Now the bedrooms, my room.

This is it, I say. This is where I kept my Villager sweaters
when I was seventeen, and my dried corsages. My cups from the
Tastee Freeze labeled with dates and boys' names.

The room is large, blue. Baseboards and wood trim are
painted a spotless white. Ruffled curtains, ruffled bedspread. The
bed itself is so high one must climb into it. Daniel looks at the
walls, their perfect blue and white.

It's a piece of candy, he says.

Yes, I say, hugging him, wanting him.

What about your mother?

She's gone to meet friends for dinner. I don't think she believes what she says, she's only being my mother. It's all right.

We take off our clothes and press close together. But something is wrong. We keep trying. Daniel stays soft in my hands. His mouth is nervous; he seems to gasp at my lips.

He says his lover's name. He says they aren't seeing other people.

But I'm not other people. And I want you to be happy with her.

I know. She knew . . . I'd want to see you.

Then what?

This room, he says. This house. I can't breathe in here.

I tell him we have tomorrow. He'll relax. And it is so good just to see him, a person from my life.

So we only hold each other, rocking.

Later, Daniel asks about my father.

I don't see him, I say. He told me to choose.

Choose what?

Between them.

My father. When he lived in this house, he stayed in the dark with his cigarette. He sat in his blue chair with the lights and television off, smoking. He made little money; he said he was self-employed. He was sick. He grew dizzy when he looked up suddenly. He slept in the basement. All night he sat reading in the bathroom. I'd hear him walking up and down the dark steps at night. I lay in the dark and listened. I believed he would strangle my mother, then walk upstairs and strangle me. I believed we were guilty; we had done something terrible to him.

Daniel wants me to talk.

How could she live with him, I ask. She came home from work and got supper. He ate it, got up and left to sit in his chair. He watched the news. We were always sitting there, looking at his dirty plates. And I wouldn't help her. She should wash them, not me. She should make the money we lived on. I didn't want her house and his ghost with its cigarette burning in the dark like a sore. I didn't want to be guilty. So she did it. She sent me to college; she paid for my safe escape.

★

Daniel and I go to the Rainbow, a bar and grill on Main Street. We hold hands, play country songs on the jukebox, drink a lot of salted beer. We talk to the barmaid and kiss in the overstuffed booth. Twinkle lights blink on and off above us. I wore my burgundy stretch pants in here when I was twelve. A senior pinched me, then moved his hand slowly across my thigh, mystified, as though erasing the pain.

What about tonight? Daniel asks. Would your mother go out with us? A movie? A bar? He sees me in her, he likes her. He wants to know her.

Then we will have to watch television.

We pop popcorn and watch the late movies. My mother stays up with us, mixing whiskey sours and laughing. She gets a high color in her cheeks and the light in her eyes glimmers up. She is slipping, slipping back and she is beautiful, oh, in her ankle socks, her red mouth and her armor of young girl's common sense. She has a beautiful laughter. She and Daniel end by mock arm wrestling; he pretends defeat and goes upstairs to bed.

My mother hears his door close. He's nice, she says. You've known some nice people, haven't you?

I want to make her back down.

Yes, he's nice, I say. And don't you think he respects me? Don't you think he truly cares for me, even though we've slept together?

He seems to, I don't know. But if you give them that, it costs them nothing to be friends with you.

Why should it cost? The only cost is what you give, and you can tell if someone is giving it back.

How? How can you tell? By going to bed with every man you take a fancy to?

I wish I took a fancy oftener, I tell her. I wish I wanted more. I can be good to a man, but I'm afraid – I can't be physical, not really . . .

You shouldn't.

I should. I want to, for myself as well. I don't think – I've ever had an orgasm.

What? she says, Never? Haven't you felt a sort of building

up, and then a dropping off . . . a conclusion? like something's
over?

No, I don't think so.

You probably have, she assures me. It's not necessarily an
explosion. You were just thinking too hard, you think too much.

But she pauses.

Maybe I don't remember right, she says. It's been years, and
in the last years of the marriage I would have died if your father
had touched me. But before, I know I felt something. That's
partly why I haven't . . . since . . . what if I started wanting it
again? Then it would be hell.

But you have to try to get what you want —

No, she says. Not if what you want would ruin everything.
And now, anyway. Who would want me?

I stand at Daniel's door. The fear is back; it has followed me
upstairs from the dead dark bottom of the house. My hands are
shaking. I'm whispering . . . Daniel, don't leave me here.

I go to my room to wait. I must wait all night, or something
will come in my sleep. I feel its hands on me now, dragging,
pulling. I watch the lit face of the clock: three, four, five. At
seven I go to Daniel. He sleeps with his pillow in his arms. The
high bed creaks as I get in. Please now, yes . . . he is hard. He
always woke with erections . . . inside me he feels good, real,
and I tell him no, stop, wait . . . I hold the rubber, stretch its rim
away from skin so it smooths on without hurting and fills with
him . . . now again, here, yes but quiet, be quiet . . . oh Daniel
. . . the bed is making noise . . . yes, no, but be careful, she . . .
We move and turn and I forget about the sounds. We push
against each other hard, he is almost there and I am almost with
him and just when it is over I think I hear my mother in the
room directly under us – But I am half dreaming. I move to get
out of bed and Daniel holds me. No, he says, stay.

We sleep and wake to hear the front door slam.

Daniel looks at me.

There's nothing to be done, I say. She's gone to church.

He looks at the clock. I'm going to miss that bus, he says.
We put our clothes on fast and Daniel moves to dispose of the

rubber – how? The toilet, no, the wastebasket – He drops it in, bends over, retrieves it. Finally he wraps it in a Kleenex and puts it in his pocket. Jesus, he swears. He looks at me and grins. When I start laughing, my eyes are wet.

I take Daniel to the bus station and watch him out of sight. I come back and strip the bed, bundle the sheets in my arms. This pressure in my chest . . . I have to clutch the sheets tight, tighter –

A door clicks shut. I go downstairs to my mother. She refuses to speak or let me near her. She stands by the sink and holds her small square purse with both hands. The fear comes. I hug myself, press my hands against my arms to stop shaking. My mother runs hot water, soap, takes dishes from the drainer. She immerses them, pushes them down, rubbing with a rag in a circular motion.

Those dishes are clean, I tell her. I washed them last night.

She keeps washing. Hot water clouds her glasses, the window in front of us, our faces. We all disappear in steam. I watch the dishes bob and sink. My mother begins to sob. I move close to her and hold her. She smells as she used to smell when I was a child and slept with her.

I heard you, I heard it, she says. Here, in my own house. Please, how much can you expect me to take? I don't know what to do about anything . . .

She looks into the water, keeps looking. And we stand here just like this.

# *Walking Out*

As the train rocked dead at Livingston he saw the man, in a worn
khaki shirt with button flaps buttoned, arms crossed. The boy's
hand sprang up by reflex, and his face broke into a smile. The
man smiled back gravely, and nodded. He did not otherwise
move. The boy turned from the window and, with the awesome
deliberateness of a fat child harboring reluctance, began struggling to pull down his bag. His father would wait on the
platform. First sight of him had reminded the boy that nothing
was simple enough now for hurrying.

They drove in the old open Willys toward the cabin beyond
town. The windshield of the Willys was up, but the fine cold
sharp rain came into their faces, and the boy could not raise his
eyes to look at the road. He wore a rain parka his father had
handed him at the station. The man, protected by only the khaki,
held his lips strung in a firm silent line that seemed more grin
than wince. Riding through town in the cold rain, open-topped
and jaunty, getting drenched as though by necessity, was – the
boy understood vaguely – somehow in the spirit of this season.

"We have a moose tag," his father shouted.

The boy said nothing. He refused to care what it meant, that
they had a moose tag.

"I've got one picked out. A bull. I've stalked him for two
weeks. Up in the Crazies. When we get to the cabin, we'll build
a good roaring fire." With only the charade of a pause, he added,
"Your mother." It was said like a question. The boy waited.
"How is she?"

"All right, I guess." Over the jeep's howl, with the wind
stealing his voice, the boy too had to shout.

"Are you friends with her?"

"I guess so."

"Is she still a beautiful lady?"

"I don't know. I guess so. I don't know that."

"You must know that. Is she starting to get wrinkled like me? Does she seem worried and sad? Or is she just still a fine beautiful lady? You must know that."

"She's still a beautiful lady, I guess."

"Did she tell you any messages for me?"

"She said . . . she said I should give you her love," the boy lied, impulsively and clumsily. He was at once embarrassed that he had done it.

"Oh," his father said. "Thank you, David."

They reached the cabin on a mile of dirt road winding through meadow to a spruce grove. Inside, the boy was enwrapped in the strong syncretic smell of all seasonal mountain cabins: pine resin and insect repellent and a mustiness suggesting damp bathing-trunks stored in a drawer. There were yellow pine floors and rope-work throw rugs and a bead curtain to the bedroom and a cast-iron cook stove with none of the lids or handles missing and a pump in the kitchen sink and old issues of *Field and Stream*, and on the mantel above where a fire now finally burned was a picture of the boy's grandfather, the railroad telegrapher, who had once owned the cabin. The boy's father cooked a dinner of fried ham, and though the boy did not like ham he had expected his father to cook canned stew or Spam, so he said nothing. His father asked him about school and the boy talked and his father seemed to be interested. Warm and dry, the boy began to feel safe from his own anguish. Then his father said:

"We'll leave tomorrow around ten."

Last year on the boy's visit they had hunted birds. They had lived in the cabin for six nights, and each day they had hunted pheasant in the wheat stubble, or blue grouse in the woods, or ducks along the irrigation slews. The boy had been wet and cold and miserable at times, but each evening they returned to the cabin and to the boy's suitcase of dry clothes. They had eaten hot food cooked on a stove, and had smelled the cabin smell, and had slept together in a bed. In six days of hunting, the boy had not managed to kill a single bird. Yet last year he had known that, at least once a day, he would be comfortable, if not happy. This year his father planned that he should not even be comfortable. He had said in his last letter to Evergreen Park, before the boy left Chicago but when it was too late for him not to leave, that he would take the boy camping in the mountains, after big game. He had pretended to believe that the boy would be glad.

The Willys was loaded and moving by ten minutes to ten. For three hours they drove, through Big Timber, and then north on the highway, and then back west again on a logging road that took them winding and bouncing higher into the mountains. Thick cottony streaks of white cloud hung in among the mountaintop trees, light and dense dollops against the bulking sharp dark olive, as though in a black-and-white photograph. They followed the gravel road for an hour, and the boy thought they would soon have a flat tire or break an axle. If they had a flat, the boy knew, his father would only change it and drive on until they had the second, farther from the highway. Finally they crossed a creek and his father plunged the Willys off into a bed of weeds.

His father said, "Here."

The boy said, "Where?"

"Up that little drainage. At the head of the creek."

"How far is it?"

"Two or three miles."

"Is that where you saw the moose?"

"No. That's where I saw the sheepman's hut. The moose is farther. On top."

"Are we going to sleep in a hut? I thought we were going to sleep in a tent."

"No. Why should we carry a tent up there when we have a perfectly good hut?"

The boy couldn't answer that question. He thought now that this might be the time when he would cry. He had known it was coming.

"I don't much want to sleep in a hut," he said, and his voice broke with the simple honesty of it, and his eyes glazed. He held his mouth tight against the trembling.

As though something had broken in him too, the boy's father laid his forehead down on the steering wheel, against his knuckles. For a moment he remained bowed, breathing exhaustedly. But he looked up again before speaking.

"Well, we don't have to, David."

The boy said nothing.

"It's an old sheepman's hut made of logs, and it's near where we're going to hunt, and we can fix it dry and good. I thought you might like that. I thought it might be more fun than a tent. But we don't have to do it. We can drive back to Big Timber and buy a tent, or we can drive back to the cabin and hunt birds, like last year. Whatever you want to do. You have to forgive me the kind of ideas I get. I hope you will. We don't have to do anything that you don't want to do."

"No," the boy said. "I want to."

"Are you sure?"

"No," the boy said. "But I just want to."

They bushwhacked along the creek, treading a thick soft mixture of moss and humus and needles, climbing upward through brush. Then the brush thinned and they were ascending an open creek bottom, thirty yards wide, darkened by fir and cedar. Farther, and they struck a trail, which led them upward along the creek. Farther still, and the trail received a branch, then another, then forked.

"Who made this trail? Did the sheepman?"

"No," his father said. "Deer and elk."

Gradually the creek's little canyon narrowed, steep wooded shoulders funneling closer on each side. For a while the game trails forked and converged like a maze, but soon again there were only two branches, and finally one, heavily worn. It dodged through alder and willow, skirting tangles of browned raspberry, so that the boy and his father could never see more than 20 feet ahead. When they stopped to rest, the boy's father unstrapped the .270 from his pack and loaded it.

"We have to be careful now," he explained. "We may surprise a bear."

Under the cedars, the creek bottom held a cool dampness

that seemed to be stored from one winter to the next. The boy
began at once to feel chilled. He put on his jacket, and they
continued climbing. Soon he was sweating again in the cold.

On a small flat where the alder drew back from the creek,
the hut was built into one bank of the canyon, with the sod of
the hillside lapping out over its roof. The door was a low dark
opening. Forty or fifty years ago, the boy's father explained, this
hut had been built and used by a Basque shepherd. At that time
there had been many Basques in Montana, and they had run
sheep all across this ridge of the Crazies. His father forgot to
explain what a Basque was, and the boy didn't remind him.

They built a fire. His father had brought sirloin steaks and an
onion for dinner, and the boy was happy with him about that.
As they ate, it grew dark, but the boy and his father had stocked
a large comforting pile of naked deadfall. In the darkness, by
fire-light, his father made chocolate pudding. The pudding had
been his father's surprise. The boy sat on a piece of canvas and
added logs to the fire while his father drank coffee. Sparks rose
on the heat and the boy watched them climb toward the cedar
limbs and the black pools of sky. The pudding did not set.

"Do you remember your grandfather, David?"

"Yes," the boy said, and wished it were true. He remembered
a funeral when he was three.

"Your grandfather brought me up on this mountain when I
was seventeen. That was the last year he hunted." The boy knew
what sort of thoughts his father was having. But he knew also
that his own home was in Evergreen Park, and that he was
another man's boy now, with another man's name, though this
indeed was his father. "Your grandfather was fifty years older
than me."

The boy said nothing.

"And I'm thirty-four years older than you."

"And I'm only eleven," the boy cautioned him.

"Yes," said his father. "And someday you'll have a son and
you'll be forty years older than him, and you'll want so badly for
him to know who you are that you could cry."

The boy was embarrassed.

"And that's called the cycle of life's infinite wisdom," his father said, and laughed at himself unpleasantly.

"What did he die of?" the boy asked, desperate to escape the focus of his father's rumination.

"He was eighty-seven then. Christ. He was tired." The boy's father went silent. Then he shook his head, and poured himself the remaining coffee.

Through that night the boy was never quite warm. He slept on his side with his knees drawn up, and this was uncomfortable but his body seemed to demand it for warmth. The hard cold mountain earth pressed upward through the mat of fir boughs his father had laid, and drew heat from the boy's body like a pallet of leeches. He clutched the bedroll around his neck and folded the empty part at the bottom back under his legs. Once he woke to a noise. Though his father was sleeping between him and the door of the hut, for a while the boy lay awake, listening worriedly, and then woke again on his back to realize time had passed. He heard droplets begin to hit the canvas his father had spread over the sod roof of the hut. But he remained dry.

He rose to the smell of a fire. The tarp was rigid with sleet and frost. The firewood and the knapsacks were frosted. It was that gray time of dawn before any blue and, through the branches above, the boy was unable to tell whether the sky was murky or clear. Delicate sheet ice hung on everything, but there was no wetness. The rain seemed to have been hushed by the cold.

"What time is it?"

"Early yet."

"How early?" The boy was thinking about the cold at home as he waited outside on 96th Street for his school bus. That was the cruelest moment of his day, but it seemed a benign and familiar part of him compared to this.

"Early. I don't have a watch. What difference does it make, David?"

"Not any."

After breakfast they began walking up the valley. His father had the .270, and the boy carried an old Winchester .30–30, with open sights. The walking was not hard, and with this gentle exercise in the cold morning the boy soon felt fresh and fine. Now I'm hunting for moose with my father, he told himself. That's just what I'm doing. Few boys in Evergreen Park had ever been moose hunting with their fathers in Montana, he knew. I'm doing it now, the boy told himself.

Reaching the lip of a high meadow, a mile above the shepherd's hut, they had not seen so much as a magpie.

Before them, across hundreds of yards, opened a smooth lake of tall lifeless grass, browned by September drought and killed by the frosts and beginning to rot with November's rain. The creek was here a deep quiet channel of smooth curves overhung by the grass, with a dark surface like heavy oil. When they had come 50 yards into the meadow, his father turned and pointed out to the boy a large ponderosa pine with a forked crown that marked the head of their creek valley. He showed the boy a small aspen grove midway across the meadow, toward which they were aligning themselves.

"Near the far woods is a beaver pond. The moose waters there. We can wait in the aspens and watch the whole meadow without being seen. If he doesn't come, we'll go up another canyon, and check again on the way back."

For an hour, and another, they waited. The boy sat with his hands in his jacket pockets, bunching the jacket tighter around him, and his buttocks drew cold moisture from the ground. His father squatted on his heels like a country man, rising periodically to inspect the meadow in all directions. Finally he stood up; he fixed his stare on the distant fringe of woods and, like a retriever, did not move. He said, "David."

The boy stood beside him. His father placed a hand on the boy's shoulder. The boy saw a large dark form rolling toward them like a great slug in the grass.

"Is it the moose?"

"No," said his father. "That is a grizzly bear, David. An old male grizzly."

The boy was impressed. He sensed an aura of power and terror and authority about the husky shape, even at 200 yards.

"Are we going to shoot him?"

"No."

"Why not?"

"We don't have a permit," his father whispered. "And because we don't want to."

The bear plowed on toward the beaver pond for a while, then stopped. It froze in the grass and seemed to be listening. The boy's father added: "That's not hunting for the meat. That's hunting for the fear. I don't need the fear. I've got enough in my life already."

The bear turned and moiled off quickly through the grass. It disappeared back into the far woods.

"He heard us."

"Maybe," the boy's father said. "Let's go have a look at that beaver pond."

A sleek furred carcass lay low in the water, swollen grotesquely with putrescence and coated with glistening blowflies. Four days, the boy's father guessed. The moose had been shot at least eighteen times with a .22 pistol. One of its eyes had been shot out; it had been shot twice in the jaw; and both quarters on the side that lay upward were ruined with shots. Standing up to his knees in the sump, the boy's father took the trouble of counting the holes, and probing one of the slugs out with his knife. That only made him angrier. He flung the lead away.

For the next three hours, with his father withdrawn into a solitary and characteristic bitterness, the boy felt abandoned. He did not understand why a moose would be slaughtered with a light pistol and left to rot. His father did not bother to explain; like the bear, he seemed to understand it as well as he needed to. They walked on, but they did not really hunt.

They left the meadow for more pine, and now tamarack, naked tamarack, the yellow needles nearly all down and going ginger where they coated the trail. The boy and his father hiked along a level path into another canyon, this one vast at the mouth and narrowing between high ridges of bare rock. They crossed and recrossed the shepherd's creek, which in this canyon was a tumbling free-stone brook. Following five yards behind his father, watching the cold, unapproachable rage that shaped the line of the man's shoulders, the boy was miserably uneasy because his father had grown so distant and quiet. They climbed over deadfalls blocking the trail, skirted one boulder large as a cabin, and blundered into a garden of nettles that stung them fiercely through their trousers. They saw fresh elk scat, and they saw bear, diarrhetic with late berries. The boy's father eventually grew bored with brooding, and showed the boy how to stalk. Before dusk that day they had shot an elk.

An open and gently sloped hillside, almost a meadow, ran for a quarter mile in quaking aspen, none over 15 feet tall. The elk was above. The boy's father had the boy brace his gun in the notch of an aspen and take the first shot. The boy missed. The elk reeled and bolted down and his father killed it before it made cover. It was a five-point bull. They dressed the elk out and dragged it down to the cover of large pines, near the stream, where they would quarter it tomorrow, and then they returned under twilight to the hut.

That night even the fetal position could not keep the boy warm. He shivered wakefully for hours. He was glad that the following day, though full of walking and butchery and oppressive burdens, would be their last in the woods. He heard nothing. When he woke, through the door of the hut he saw whiteness like bone.

Six inches had fallen, and it was still snowing. The boy stood about in the campsite, amazed. When it snowed 3 inches in Evergreen Park, the boy would wake before dawn to the hiss of sand trucks and the ratchet of chains. Here there had been no warning. The boy was not much colder than he had been yesterday, and the transformation of the woods seemed mysterious and benign and somehow comic. He thought of Christmas. Then his father barked at him.

His father's mood had also changed, but in a different way; he seemed serious and hurried. As he wiped the breakfast pots clean with snow, he gave the boy orders for other chores. They left camp with two empty pack frames, both rifles, and a handsaw and rope. The boy soon understood why his father felt pressure of time: it took them an hour to climb the mile to the meadow. The snow continued. They did not rest until they reached the aspens.

"I had half a mind at breakfast to let the bull lie and pack us straight down out of here," his father admitted. "Probably smarter and less trouble in the long run. I could have come back on snow-shoes next week. But by then it might be 3 feet deep and starting to drift. We can get two quarters out today. That will make it easier for me later." The boy was surprised by two things: that his father would be so wary in the face of a gentle snowfall and that he himself would have felt disappointed to be taken out of the woods that morning. The air of the meadow teemed with white.

"If it stops soon, we're fine," said his father.

It continued.

The path up the far canyon was hard climbing in 8 inches of snow. The boy fell once, filling his collar and sleeves, and the gun-sight put a small gouge in his chin. But he was not discouraged. That night they would be warm and dry at the cabin. A half mile on and he came up beside his father, who had stopped to stare down at dark splashes of blood.

Heavy tracks and a dragging belly mark led up to the scramble of deepening red, and away. The tracks were 9 inches long and showed claws. The boy's father knelt. As the boy watched, one shining maroon splotch the size of a saucer sank slowly beyond sight into the snow. The blood was warm.

Inspecting the tracks carefully, his father said, "She's got a cub with her."

"What happened?"

"Just a kill. Seems to have been a bird. That's too much blood for a grouse, but I don't see signs of any four-footed creature. Maybe a turkey." He frowned thoughtfully. "A turkey without feathers. I don't know. What I dislike is coming up on her with a cub." He drove a round into the chamber of the .270.

Trailing red smears, the tracks preceded them. Within 50 feet they found the body. It was half-buried. The top of its head had been shorn away, and the cub's brains had been licked out.

His father said "Christ," and plunged off the trail. He snapped at the boy to follow closely.

They made a wide crescent through brush and struck back after a quarter mile. His father slogged ahead in the snow, stopping often to stand holding his gun ready and glancing around while the boy caught up and passed him. The boy was confused. He knew his father was worried, but he did not feel any danger himself. They met the trail again, and went on to the aspen hillside before his father allowed them to rest. The boy spat on the snow. His lungs ached badly.

"Why did she do that?"

"She didn't. Another bear got her cub. A male. Maybe the one we saw yesterday. Then she fought him for the body, and she won. We didn't miss them by much. She may even have been watching. Nothing could put her in a worse frame of mind."

He added: "If we so much as see her, I want you to pick the nearest big tree and start climbing. Don't stop till you're 20 feet off the ground. I'll stay down and decide whether we have to shoot her. Is your rifle cocked?"

"No."

"Cock it, and put on the safety. She may be a black bear and black bears can climb. If she comes up after you, lean down and stick your gun in her mouth and fire. You can't miss."

He cocked the Winchester, as his father had said.

They angled downhill to the stream, and on to the mound of their dead elk. Snow filtered down steadily in purposeful silence. The boy was thirsty. It could not be much below freezing, he was aware, because with the exercise his bare hands were comfortable, even sweating between the fingers.

"Can I get a drink?"

"Yes. Be careful you don't wet your feet. And don't wander anywhere. We're going to get this done quickly."

He walked the few yards, ducked through the brush at streamside, and knelt in the snow to drink. The water was painful to his sinuses and bitterly cold on his hands. Standing again, he noticed an animal body ahead near the stream bank. For a moment he felt sure it was another dead cub. During that moment his father called:

"David! Get up here right now!"

The boy meant to call back. First he stepped closer to turn the cub with his foot. The touch brought it alive. It rose suddenly with a high squealing growl and whirled its head like a snake and snapped. The boy shrieked. The cub had his right hand in its jaws. It would not release.

It thrashed senselessly, working its teeth deeper and tearing flesh with each movement. The boy felt no pain. He knew his hand was being damaged and that realization terrified him and he was desperate to get the hand back before it was ruined. But he was helpless. He sensed the same furious terror racking the cub that he felt in himself, and he screamed at the cub almost reasoningly to let him go. His screams scared the cub more. Its head snatched back and forth. The boy did not think to shout for his father. He did not see him or hear him coming.

His father moved at full stride in a slowed laboring run through the snow, saying nothing and holding the rifle he did not use, crossed the last 6 feet still gathering speed, and brought his right boot up into the cub's belly. That kick seemed to lift the cub clear of the snow. It opened its jaws to another shrill piggish squeal, and the boy felt dull relief on his hand, as though his father had pressed open the blades of a spring trap with his foot. The cub tumbled once and disappeared over the stream bank, then surfaced downstream, squalling and paddling. The boy looked at his hand and was horrified. He still had no pain, but the hand was unrecognizable. His fingers had been peeled down through the palm like flaps on a banana. Glands at the sides of his jaw threatened that he would vomit, and he might have stood stupidly watching the hand bleed if his father had not grabbed him.

He snatched the boy by the arm and dragged him toward a tree without even looking at the boy's hand. The boy jerked back in angry resistance as though he had been struck. He screamed at his father. He screamed that his hand was cut, believing his father did not know, and as he screamed he began to cry. He began to feel hot throbbing pain. He began to worry about the blood he was losing. He could imagine the blood melting red holes in the snow behind him and he did not want to look. He did not want to do anything until he had taken care of his hand. At that instant he hated his father. But his father was stronger. He all but carried the boy to a tree.

He lifted the boy. In a voice that was quiet and hurried and very unlike the harsh grip with which he had taken the boy's arm, he said: "Grab hold and climb up a few branches as best you can. Sit on a limb and hold tight and clamp the hand under your other armpit, if you can do that. I'll be right back to you. Hold tight because you're going to get dizzy." The boy groped desperately for a branch. His father supported him from beneath, and waited. The boy clambered. His feet scraped at the trunk. Then he was in the tree. Bark flakes and resin were stuck to the raw naked meat of his right hand. His father said: "Now here, take this. Hurry."

The boy never knew whether his father himself had been frightened enough to forget for that moment about the boy's hand, or whether his father was still thinking quite clearly. His father may have expected that much. By the merciless clarity of his own standards, he may have expected that the boy should be able to hold onto a tree, and a wound, and a rifle, all with one hand. He extended the stock of the Winchester toward the boy.

The boy wanted to say something, but his tears and his fright would not let him gather a breath. He shuddered, and could not speak. "David," his father urged. The boy reached for the stock and faltered and clutched at the trunk with his good arm. He was crying and gasping, and he wanted to speak. He was afraid he would fall out of the tree. He released his grip once again, and felt himself tip. His father extended the gun higher, holding the barrel. The boy swung out his injured hand, spraying his father's face with blood. He reached and he tried to close torn dangling fingers around the stock and he pulled the trigger.

The bullet entered low on his father's thigh and shattered the knee and traveled down the shin bone and into the ground through his father's heel.

His father fell, and the rifle fell with him. He lay in the snow without moving. The boy thought he was dead. Then the boy saw him grope for the rifle. He found it and rolled onto his stomach, taking aim at the sow grizzly. Forty feet up the hill, towering on hind legs, she canted her head to one side, indecisive. When the cub pulled itself up a snowbank from the stream, she coughed at it sternly. The cub trotted straight to her with its head low. She knocked it off its feet with a huge paw, and it yelped. Then she turned quickly. The cub followed.

The woods were silent. The gunshot still echoed awesomely back to the boy but it was an echo of memory, not sound. He felt nothing. He saw his father's body stretched on the snow and he did not really believe he was where he was. He did not want to move: he wanted to wake. He sat in the tree and waited. The snow fell as gracefully as before.

His father rolled onto his back. The boy saw him raise himself to a sitting position and look down at the leg and betray no expression, and then slump back. He blinked slowly and lifted his eyes to meet the boy's eyes. The boy waited. He expected his father to speak. He expected his father to say *Shinny down using your elbows and knees and get the first-aid kit and boil water and phone the doctor. The number is taped to the dial.* His father stared. The boy could see the flicker of thoughts behind his father's eyes. His father said nothing. He raised his arms slowly and crossed them over his face, as though to nap in the sun.

The boy jumped. He landed hard on his feet and fell onto his back. He stood over his father. His hand dripped quietly onto the snow. He was afraid that his father was deciding to die. He wanted to beg him to reconsider. The boy had never before seen his father hopeless. He was afraid.

But he was no longer afraid of his father.

Then his father uncovered his face and said, "Let me see it."

They bandaged the boy's hand with a sleeve cut from the other arm of his shirt. His father wrapped the hand firmly and split the sleeve end with his deer knife and tied it neatly in two places. The boy now felt searing pain in his torn palm, and his stomach lifted when he thought of the damage, but at least he did not have to look at it. Quickly the plaid flannel bandage began to soak through maroon. They cut a sleeve from his father's shirt to tie over the wound in his thigh. They raised the trouser leg to see the long swelling bruise down the calf where he was hemorrhaging into the bullet's tunnel. Only then did his father realize that he was bleeding also from the heel. The boy took off his father's boot and placed a half-clean handkerchief on the insole where the bullet had exited, as his father instructed him. Then his father laced the boot on again tightly. The boy helped his father to stand. His father tried a step, then collapsed in the snow with a blasphemous howl of pain. They had not known that the knee was shattered.

The boy watched his father's chest heave with the forced sighs of suffocating frustration, and heard the air wheeze through his nostrils. His father relaxed himself with the breathing, and seemed to be thinking. He said, "You can find your way back to the hut."

The boy held his own breath and did not move.

"You can, can't you?"

"But I'm not. I'm not going alone. I'm only going with you."

"All right, David, listen carefully," his father said. "We don't have to worry about freezing. I'm not worried about either of us freezing to death. No one is going to freeze in the woods in November, if he looks after himself. Not even in Montana. It just isn't that cold. I have matches and I have a fresh elk. And I don't think this weather is going to get any worse. It may be raining again by morning. What I'm concerned about is the bleeding. If I spend too much time and effort trying to walk out of here, I could bleed to death.

"I think your hand is going to be all right. It's a bad wound, but the doctors will be able to fix it as good as new. I can see that. I promise you that. You'll be bleeding some too, but if you take care of that hand it won't bleed any more walking than if you were standing still. Then you'll be at the doctor's tonight. But if I try to walk out on this leg it's going to bleed and keep bleeding and I'll lose too much blood. So I'm staying here and bundling up warm and you're walking out to get help. I'm sorry about this. It's what we have to do.

"You can't possibly get lost. You'll just follow this trail straight down the canyon the way we came up, and then you'll come to the meadow. Point yourself toward the big pine tree with the forked crown. When you get to that tree you'll find the creek again. You may not be able to see it, but make yourself quiet and listen for it. You'll hear it. Follow that down off the mountain and past the hut till you get to the jeep."

He struggled a hand into his pocket. "You've never driven a car, have you?"

The boy's lips were pinched. Muscles in his cheeks ached from clenching his jaws. He shook his head.

"You can do it. It isn't difficult." His father held up a single key and began telling the boy how to start the jeep, how to work the clutch, how to find reverse and then first and then second. As his father described the positions on the floor shift the boy raised his swaddled right hand. His father stopped. He rubbed at his eye sockets, like a man waking.

"Of course," he said. "All right. You'll have to help me."

Using the saw with his left hand, the boy cut a small forked aspen. His father showed the boy where to trim it so that the fork would reach just to his armpit. Then they lifted him to his feet. But the crutch was useless on a steep hillside of deep grass and snow. His father leaned over the boy's shoulders and they fought the slope for an hour.

When the boy stepped in a hole and they fell, his father made no exclamation of pain. The boy wondered whether his father's knee hurt as badly as his own hand. He suspected it hurt worse. He said nothing about his hand, though several times in their climb it was twisted or crushed. They reached the trail. The snow had not stopped, and their tracks were veiled. His father said:

"We need one of the guns. I forgot. It's my fault. But you'll have to go back down and get it."

The boy could not find the tree against which his father said he had leaned the .270, so he went toward the stream and looked for blood. He saw none. The imprint of his father's body was already softened beneath an inch of fresh silence. He scooped his good hand through the snowy depression and was startled by cool slimy blood, smearing his fingers like phlegm. Nearby he found the Winchester.

"The lucky one," his father said. "That's all right. Here." He snapped open the breach and a shell flew and he caught it in the

air. He glanced dourly at the casing, then cast it aside in the
snow. He held the gun out for the boy to see, and with his
thumb let the hammer down one notch.

"Remember?" he said. "The safety."

The boy knew he was supposed to feel great shame, but he
felt little. His father could no longer hurt him as he once could,
because the boy was coming to understand him. His father could
not help himself. He did not want the boy to feel contemptible,
but he needed him to, because of the loneliness and the bitterness
and the boy's mother; and he could not help himself.

After another hour they had barely traversed the aspen
hillside. Pushing the crutch away in angry frustration, his father
sat in the snow. The boy did not know whether he was thinking
carefully of how they might get him out, or still laboring with
the choice against despair. The light had wilted to something
more like moonlight than afternoon. The sweep of snow had
gone gray, depthless, flat, and the sky warned sullenly of night.
The boy grew restless. Then it was decided. His father hung
himself piggyback over the boy's shoulders, holding the rifle.
The boy supported him with elbows crooked under his father's
knees. The boy was tall for eleven years old, and heavy. The
boy's father weighed 164 pounds.

The boy walked.

He moved as slowly as drifting snow: a step, then time, then
another step. The burden at first seemed to him overwhelming.
He did not think he would be able to carry his father far.

He took the first few paces expecting to fall. He did not fall,
so he kept walking. His arms and shoulders were not exhausted
as quickly as he had thought they would be, so he kept walking.
Shuffling ahead in the deep powder was like carrying one end of
an oak bureau up stairs. But for a surprisingly long time the
burden did not grow any worse. He found balance. He found
rhythm. He was moving.

Dark blurred the woods, but the snow was luminous. He
could see the trail well. He walked.

"How are you, David? How are you holding up?"

"All right."

"We'll stop for a while and let you rest. You can set me

down here." The boy kept walking. He moved so ponderously, it seemed after each step that he had stopped. But he kept walking.

"You can set me down. Don't you want to rest?"

The boy did not answer. He wished that his father would not make him talk. At the start he had gulped for air. Now he was breathing low and regularly. He was watching his thighs slice through the snow. He did not want to be disturbed. After a moment he said, "No."

He walked. He came to the cub, shrouded beneath new snow, and did not see it, and fell over it. His face was smashed deep into the snow by his father's weight. He could not move. But he could breathe. He rested. When he felt his father's thigh roll across his right hand, he remembered the wound. He was lucky his arms had been pinned to his sides, or the hand might have taken the force of their fall. As he waited for his father to roll himself clear, the boy noticed the change in temperature. His sweat chilled him quickly. He began shivering.

His father had again fallen in silence. The boy knew that he would not call out or even mention the pain in his leg. The boy realized that he did not want to mention his hand. The blood soaking the outside of his flannel bandage had grown sticky. He did not want to think of the alien tangle of flesh and tendons and bones wrapped inside. There was pain, but he kept the pain at a distance. It was not *his* hand anymore. He was not counting on ever having it back. If he was resolved about that, then the pain was not his either. It was merely pain of which he was aware. His good hand was numb.

"We'll rest now."

"I'm not tired," the boy said. "I'm just getting cold."

"We'll rest," said his father. "I'm tired."

Under his father's knee, the boy noticed, was a cavity in the snow, already melted away by fresh blood. The dark flannel around his father's thigh did not appear sticky. It gleamed.

His father instructed the boy how to open the cub with the deer knife. His father stood on one leg against a deadfall, holding the Winchester ready, and glanced around on all sides as he spoke. The boy used his left hand and both his knees. He punctured the cub low in the belly, to a soft squirting sound, and sliced upward easily. He did not gut the cub. He merely cut out a large square of belly meat. He handed it to his father, in exchange for the rifle.

His father peeled off the hide and left the fat. He sawed the meat in half. One piece he rolled up and put in his jacket pocket. The other he divided again. He gave the boy a square thick with glistening raw fat.

"Eat it. The fat too. Especially the fat. We'll cook the rest farther on. I don't want to build a fire here and taunt Momma."

The meat was chewy. The boy did not find it disgusting. He was hungry.

His father sat back on the ground and unlaced the boot from his good foot. Before the boy understood what he was doing, he had relaced the boot. He was holding a damp wool sock.

"Give me your left hand." The boy held out his good hand, and his father pulled the sock down over it. "It's getting a lot colder. And we need that hand."

"What about yours? We need your hands too. I'll give you my—"

"No, you won't. We need your feet more than anything. It's all right. I'll put mine inside your shirt."

He lifted his father, and they went on. The boy walked.

He moved steadily through cold darkness. Soon he was sweating again, down his ribs and inside his boots. Only his hands and ears felt as though crushed in a cold metal vise. But his father was shuddering. The boy stopped.

His father did not put down his legs. The boy stood on the trail and waited. Slowly he released his wrist holds. His father's thighs slumped. The boy was careful about the wounded leg. His father's grip over the boy's neck did not loosen. His fingers were cold against the boy's bare skin.

"Are we at the hut?"

"No. We're not even to the meadow."

"Why did you stop?" his father asked.

"It's so cold. You're shivering. Can we build a fire?"

"Yes," his father said hazily. "We'll rest. What time is it?"

"We don't know," the boy said. "We don't have a watch."

The boy gathered small deadwood. His father used the Winchester stock to scoop snow away from a boulder, and they placed the fire at the boulder's base. His father broke up pine twigs and fumbled dry toilet paper from his breast pocket and arranged the wood, but by then his fingers were shaking too badly to strike a match. The boy lit the fire. The boy stamped down the snow, as his father instructed, to make a small ovenlike recess before the fire boulder. He cut fir boughs to floor the recess. He added more deadwood. Beyond the invisible clouds there seemed to be part of a moon.

"It stopped snowing," the boy said.

"Why?"

The boy did not speak. His father's voice had sounded unnatural. After a moment his father said: "Yes, indeed. It stopped."

They roasted pieces of cub meat skewered on a green stick. Dripping fat made the fire spatter and flare. The meat was scorched on the outside and raw within. It tasted as good as any meat the boy had ever eaten. They burned their palates on hot fat. The second stick smoldered through before they had noticed, and that batch of meat fell in the fire. The boy's father cursed once and reached into the flame for it and dropped it and clawed it out, and then put his hand in the snow. He did not look at the blistered fingers. They ate. The boy saw that both his father's hands had gone clumsy and almost useless.

The boy went for more wood. He found a bleached deadfall not far off the trail, but with one arm he could only break up and carry small loads. They lay down in the recess together like spoons, the boy nearer the fire. They pulled fir boughs into place above them, resting across the snow. They pressed close together. The boy's father was shivering spastically now, and he clenched the boy in a fierce hug. The boy put his father's hands back inside his own shirt. The boy slept. He woke when the fire faded and added more wood and slept. He woke again and tended the fire and changed places with his father and slept. He slept less soundly with his father between him and the fire. He woke again when his father began to vomit.

The boy was terrified. His father wrenched with sudden

vomiting that brought up cub meat and yellow liquid and blood
and sprayed them across the snow by the grayish-red glow of
the fire and emptied his stomach dry and then would not release
him. He heaved on pathetically. The boy pleaded to be told what
was wrong. His father could not or would not answer. The
spasms seized him at the stomach and twisted the rest of his body
taut in ugly jerks. Between the attacks he breathed with a wet
rumbling sound deep in his chest, and did not speak. When the
vomiting subsided, his breathing stretched itself out into long
bubbling sighs, then shallow gasps, then more liquidy sighs. His
breath caught and froth rose in his throat and into his mouth and
he gagged on it and began vomiting again. The boy thought his
father would choke. He knelt beside him and held him and cried.
He could not see his father's face well and he did not want to
look closely while the sounds that were coming from inside his
father's body seemed so unhuman. The boy had never been more
frightened. He wept for himself, and for his father. He knew
from the noises and movements that his father must die. He did
not think his father could ever be human again.

When his father was quiet, he went for more wood. He
broke limbs from the deadfall with fanatic persistence and
brought them back in bundles and built the fire up bigger. He
nestled his father close to it and held him from behind. He did
not sleep, though he was not awake. He waited. Finally he
opened his eyes on the beginnings of dawn. His father sat up and
began to spit.

"One more load of wood and you keep me warm from
behind and then we'll go."

The boy obeyed. He was surprised that his father could
speak. He thought it strange now that his father was so concerned
for himself and so little concerned for the boy. His father had not
even asked how he was.

The boy lifted his father, and walked.

Sometime while dawn was completing itself, the snow had
resumed. It did not filter down soundlessly. It came on a slight
wind at the boy's back, blowing down the canyon. He felt as
though he were tumbling forward with the snow into a long
vertical shaft. He tumbled slowly. His father's body protected

the boy's back from being chilled by the wind. They were both soaked through their clothes. His father was soon shuddering again.

The boy walked. Muscles down the back of his neck were sore from yesterday. His arms ached, and his shoulders and thighs, but his neck hurt him most. He bent his head forward against the weight and the pain, and he watched his legs surge through the snow. At his stomach he felt the dull ache of hunger, not as an appetite but as an affliction. He thought of the jeep. He walked.

He recognized the edge of the meadow but through the snow-laden wind he could not see the cluster of aspens. The snow became deeper where he left the wooded trail. The direction of the wind was now variable, sometimes driving snow into his face, sometimes whipping across him from the right. The grass and snow dragged at his thighs, and he moved by stumbling forward and then catching himself back. Twice he stepped into small overhung fingerlets of the stream, and fell violently, shocking the air from his lungs and once nearly spraining an ankle. Farther out into the meadow, he saw the aspens. They were 100 yards off to his right. He did not turn directly toward them. He was afraid of crossing more hidden creeks on the intervening ground. He was not certain now whether the main channel was between him and the aspen grove or behind him to the left. He tried to project from the canyon trail to the aspens and on to the forked pine on the far side of the meadow, along what he remembered as almost a straight line. He pointed himself towards the far edge, where the pine should have been. He could not see a forked crown. He could not even see trees. He could see only a vague darker corona above the curve of white. He walked.

He passed the aspens and left them behind. He stopped several times with the wind rasping against him in the open meadow, and rested. He did not set his father down. His father was trembling uncontrollably. He had not spoken for a long time. The boy wanted badly to reach the far side of the meadow. His socks were soaked and his boots and cuffs were glazed with ice. The wind was chafing his face and making him dizzy. His thighs felt as if they had been bruised with a club. The boy wanted to give up and set his father down and whimper that this had gotten to be very unfair; and he wanted to reach the far trees. He did not doubt which he would do. He walked.

He saw trees. Raising his head painfully, he squinted against the rushing flakes. He did not see the forked crown. He went on, and stopped again, and craned his neck, and squinted. He scanned a wide angle of pines, back and forth. He did not see it. He turned his body and his burden to look back. The snow blew across the meadow and seemed, whichever way he turned, to be streaking into his face. He pinched his eyes tighter. He could still see the aspens. But he could not judge where the canyon trail met the meadow. He did not know from just where he had come. He looked again at the aspens, and then ahead to the pines. He considered the problem carefully. He was irritated that the forked ponderosa did not show itself yet, but not worried. He was forced to estimate. He estimated, and went on in that direction.

When he saw a forked pine it was far off to the left of his course. He turned and marched toward it gratefully. As he came nearer, he bent his head up to look. He stopped. The boy was not sure that this was the right tree. Nothing about it looked different, except the thick cakes of snow weighting its limbs, and nothing about it looked especially familiar. He had seen thousands of pine trees in the last few days. This was one like the others. It definitely had a forked crown. He entered the woods at its base.

He had vaguely expected to join a trail. There was no trail. After 200 yards he was still picking his way among trees and deadfalls and brush. He remembered the shepherd's creek that fell off the lip of the meadow and led down the first canyon. He turned and retraced his tracks to the forked pine.

He looked for the creek. He did not see it anywhere near the tree. He made himself quiet, and listened. He heard nothing but wind, and his father's tremulous breathing.

"Where is the creek?"

His father did not respond. The boy bounced gently up and down, hoping to jar him alert.

"Where is the creek? I can't find it."

"What?"

"We crossed the meadow and I found the tree but I can't find the creek. I need you to help."

"The compass is in my pocket," his father said.

He lowered his father into the snow. He found the compass in his father's breast pocket and opened the flap, and held it level. The boy noticed with a flinch that his right thigh was smeared with fresh blood. For an instant he thought he had a new wound. Then he realized that the blood was his father's. The compass needle quieted.

"What do I do?"

His father did not respond. The boy asked again. His father said nothing. He sat in the snow and shivered.

The boy left his father and made random arcs within sight of the forked tree until he found a creek. They followed it onward along the flat and then where it gradually began sloping away. The boy did not see what else he could do. He knew that this was the wrong creek. He hoped that it would flow into the shepherd's creek, or at least bring them out on the same road where they had left the jeep. He was very tired. He did not want to stop. He did not care any more about being warm. He wanted only to reach the jeep, and to save his father's life.

He wondered whether his father would love him more generously for having done it. He wondered whether his father would ever forgive him for having done it.

If he failed, his father could never again make him feel shame, the boy thought naively. So he did not worry about failing. He did not worry about dying. His hand was not bleeding, and he felt strong. The creek swung off and down to the left. He followed it, knowing that he was lost. He did not want to reverse himself. He knew that turning back would make him feel confused and desperate and frightened. As long as he was following some pathway, walking, going down, he felt strong.

That afternoon he killed a grouse. He knocked it off a low branch with a heavy short stick that he threw like a boomerang. The grouse fell in the snow and floundered and the boy ran up and plunged on it. He felt it thrashing against his chest. He reached in and it nipped him and he caught it by the neck and squeezed and wrenched mercilessly until long after it stopped writhing. He cleaned it as he had seen his father clean grouse and built a small fire with matches from his father's breast pocket and seared the grouse on a stick. He fed his father. His father could not chew. The boy chewed mouthfuls of grouse, and took the chewed gobbets in his hand, and put them into his father's mouth. His father could swallow. His father could no longer speak.

The boy walked. He thought of his mother in Evergreen Park, and at once he felt queasy and weak. He thought of his mother's face and her voice as she was told that her son was lost in the woods in Montana with a damaged hand that would never be right, and with his father, who had been shot and was unconscious and dying. He pictured his mother receiving the news that her son might die himself, unless he could carry his father out of the woods and find his way to the jeep. He saw her face change. He heard her voice. The boy had to stop. He was crying. He could not control the shape of his mouth. He was not crying with true sorrow, as he had in the night when he held his father and thought his father would die; he was crying in sentimental self-pity. He sensed the difference. Still he cried.

He must not think of his mother, the boy realized. Thinking of her could only weaken him. If she knew where he was, what he had to do, she could only make it impossible for him to do it. He was lucky that she knew nothing, the boy thought.

No one knew what the boy was doing, or what he had yet to do. Even the boy's father no longer knew. The boy was lucky. No one was watching, no one knew, and he was free to be capable.

The boy imagined himself alone at his father's grave. The grave was open. His father's casket had already been lowered. The boy stood at the foot in his black Christmas suit, and his hands were crossed at his groin, and he was not crying. Men with shovels stood back from the grave, waiting for the boy's order for them to begin filling it. The boy felt a horrible swelling sense of joy. The men watched him, and he stared down into the hole. He knew it was a lie. If his father died, the boy's mother would rush out to Livingston and have him buried and stand at the grave in a black dress and veil squeezing the boy to her side like he was a child. There was nothing the boy could do about that. All the more reason he must keep walking.

Then she would tow the boy back with her to Evergreen Park. And he would be standing on 96th Street in the morning dark before his father's cold body had even begun to grow alien and decayed in the buried box. She would drag him back, and there would be nothing the boy could do. And he realized that if he returned with his mother after the burial, he would never again see the cabin outside Livingston. He would have no more summers and no more Novembers anywhere but in Evergreen Park.

The cabin now seemed to be at the center of the boy's life. It seemed to stand halfway between this snowbound creek valley and the train station in Chicago. It would be his cabin soon.

The boy knew nothing about his father's will, and he had never been told that legal ownership of the cabin was destined for him. Legal ownership did not matter. The cabin might be owned by his mother, or sold to pay his father's debts, or taken away by the state, but it would still be the boy's cabin. It could only forever belong to him. His father had been telling him *Here, this is yours. Prepare to receive it.* The boy had sensed that much. But he had been threatened, and unwilling. The boy realized now that he might be resting warm in the cabin in a matter of hours, or he might never see it again. He could appreciate the justice of that. He walked.

He thought of his father as though his father were far away from him. He saw himself in the black suit at the grave, and he heard his father speak to him from aside: *That's good. Now raise your eyes and tell them in a man's voice to begin shoveling. Then turn away and walk slowly back down the hill. Be sure you don't cry. That's good.* The boy stopped. He felt his glands quiver, full of new tears. He knew that it was a lie. His father would never be there to congratulate him. His father would never know how well the boy had done.

He took deep breaths. He settled himself. Yes, his father would know somehow, the boy believed. His father had known all along. His father knew.

He built the recess just as they had the night before, except this time he found flat space between a stone back and a large fallen cottonwood trunk. He scooped out the snow, he laid boughs, and he made a fire against each reflector. At first the bed was quite warm. Then the melt from the fires began to run down and collect in the middle, forming a puddle of wet boughs under them. The boy got up and carved runnels across the packed snow to drain the fires. He went back to sleep and slept warm, holding his father. He rose again each half hour to feed the fires.

The snow stopped in the night, and did not resume. The woods seemed to grow quieter, settling, sighing beneath the new weight. What was going to come had come.

The boy grew tired of breaking deadwood and began walking again before dawn and walked for five more hours. He did not try to kill the grouse that he saw because he did not want to spend time cleaning and cooking it. He was hurrying now. He drank from the creek. At one point he found small black insects like winged ants crawling in great numbers across the snow near the creek. He stopped to pinch up and eat thirty or forty of them. They were tasteless. He did not bother to feed any to his father. He felt he had come a long way down the mountain. He thought he was reaching the level now where there might be roads. He followed the creek, which had received other branches and grown to a stream. The ground was flattening again and the drainage was widening, opening to daylight. As he carried his father, his head ached. He had stopped noticing most of his other pains. About noon of that day he came to the fence.

It startled him. He glanced around, his pulse drumming suddenly, preparing himself at once to see the long empty sweep of snow and broken fence posts and thinking of Basque shepherds fifty years gone. He saw the cabin and the smoke. He relaxed, trembling helplessly into laughter. He relaxed, and was unable to move. Then he cried, still laughing. He cried shamelessly with relief and dull joy and wonder, for as long as he wanted. He held his father and cried. But he set his father down and washed his own face with snow before he went to the door.

He crossed the lot walking slowly, carrying his father. He did not now feel tired.

The young woman's face was drawn down in shock and revealed at first nothing of friendliness.

"We had a jeep parked somewhere, but I can't find it," the boy said. "This is my father."

They would not talk to him. They stripped him and put him before the fire wrapped in blankets and started tea and made him wait. He wanted to talk. He wished they would ask him a lot of questions. But they went about quickly and quietly, making things warm. His father was in the bedroom.

The man with the face full of dark beard had telephoned for a doctor. He went back into the bedroom with more blankets, and stayed. His wife went from room to room with hot tea. She rubbed the boy's naked shoulders through the blanket, and held a cup to his mouth, but she would not talk to him. He did not know what to say to her, and he could not move his lips very well. But he wished she would ask him some questions. He was restless, thawing in silence before the hearth.

He thought about going back to their own cabin soon. In his mind he gave the bearded man directions to take him and his father home. It wasn't far. It would not require much of the man's time. They would thank him, and give him an elk steak. Later he and his father would come back for the jeep. He could keep his father warm at the cabin as well as they were doing here, the boy knew.

While the woman was in the bedroom, the boy overheard the bearded man raise his voice:

"He what?"

"He carried him out," the woman whispered.

"What do you mean, carried him?"

"Carried him. On his back. I saw."

"Carried him from where?"

"Where it happened. Somewhere on Sheep Creek, maybe."

"Eight miles?"

"I know."

"*Eight miles?* How could he do that?"

"I don't know. I suppose he couldn't. But he did."

The doctor arrived in half an hour, as the boy was just starting to shiver. The doctor went into the bedroom and stayed five minutes. The woman poured the boy more tea and knelt beside him and hugged him around the shoulders.

When the doctor came out, he examined the boy without speaking. The boy wished the doctor would ask him some questions, but he was afraid he might be shivering too hard to answer in a man's voice. While the doctor touched him and probed him and took his temperature, the boy looked the doctor directly in the eye, as though to show him he was really all right.

The doctor said: "David, your father is dead. He has been dead for a long time. Probably since yesterday."

"I know that," the boy said.

# MARY ROBISON

☆  ☆  ☆  ☆

# *Pretty Ice*

I was up the whole night before my fiancé was due to arrive from the East – drinking coffee, restless and pacing, my ears ringing. When the television signed off, I sat down with a packet of the month's bills and figured amounts on a lined tally sheet in my checkbook. Under the spray of a high-intensity lamp, my left hand moved rapidly over the touch tablets of my calculator.

Will, my fiancé, was coming from Boston on the 6.50 train – the dawn train, the only train that still stopped in the small Ohio city where I lived. At 6.15 I was still at my accounts; I was getting some pleasure from transcribing the squarish green figures that appeared in the window of my calculator. "Schwab Dental Clinic," I printed in a raveled backhand. "Thirty-eight and 50/100."

A car horn interrupted me. I looked over my desktop and out the living-room window of my rented house. The saplings in my little yard were encased in ice. There had been snow all week, and then an ice storm. In the glimmering driveway in front of my garage, my mother was peering out of her car. I got up and turned off my lamp and capped my ivory Mont Blanc pen. I found a coat in the semidark in the hall, and wound a knitted muffler at my throat. Crossing the living room, I looked away from the big pine mirror; I didn't want to see how my face and hair looked after a night of accounting.

My yard was a frozen pond, and I was careful on the walkway. My mother hit her horn again. Frozen slush came through the toe of one of my chukka boots, and I stopped on the path and frowned at her. I could see her breath rolling away in clouds from the cranked-down window of her Mazda. I have never owned a car nor learned to drive, but I had a low opinion of my mother's compact. My father and I used to enjoy big cars,

with tops that came down. We were both tall and we wanted
what he called "stretch room." My father had been dead for
fourteen years, but I resented my mother's buying a car in which
he would not have fitted.

"Now what's wrong? Are you coming?" my mother said.

"Nothing's wrong except that my shoes are opening around
the soles," I said. "I just paid a lot of money for them."

I got in on the passenger side. The car smelled of wet wood
and Mother's hair spray. Someone had done her hair with a
minty-white rinse, and the hair was held in place by a zebra-
striped headband.

"I think you're getting a flat," I said. "That retread you
bought for the left front is going."

She backed the car out of the drive, using the rear-view
mirror. "I finally got a boy I can trust, at the Exxon station," she
said. "He says that tire will last until hot weather."

Out on the street, she accelerated too quickly and the rear of the
car swung left. The tires whined for an instant on the old snow
and then caught. We were knocked back in our seats a little, and
an empty Kleenex box slipped off the dash and onto the floor
carpet.

"This is going to be something," my mother said. "Will sure
picked an awful day to come."

My mother had never met him. My courtship with Will had
all happened in Boston. I was getting my doctorate there, in
musicology. Will was involved with his research at Boston U.,
and with teaching botany to undergraduates.

"You're sure he'll be at the station?" my mother said. "Can
the trains go in this weather? I don't see how they do."

"I talked to him on the phone yesterday. He's coming."

"How did he sound?" my mother said.

To my annoyance, she began to hum to herself.

I said, "He's had rotten news about his work. Terrible, in
fact."

"Explain his work to me again," she said.

"He's a plant taxonomist."

"Yes?" my mother said. "What does that mean?"

"It means he doesn't have a lot of money," I said. "He studies grasses. He said on the phone he's been turned down for a research grant that would have meant a great deal to us. Apparently the work he's been doing for the past seven or so years is irrelevant or outmoded. I guess 'superficial' is what he told me."

"I won't mention it to him, then," my mother said.

We came to the expressway. Mother steered the car through some small windblown snow dunes and down the entrance ramp. She followed two yellow salt trucks with winking blue beacons that were moving side by side down the center and right-hand lanes.

"I think losing the grant means we should postpone the wedding," I said. "I want Will to have his bearings before I step into his life for good."

"Don't wait too much longer, though," my mother said.

After a couple of miles, she swung off the expressway. We went past some tall high-tension towers with connecting cables that looked like staff lines on a sheet of music. We were in the decaying neighborhood near the tracks. "Now I know this is right," Mother said. "There's our old sign."

The sign was a tall billboard, black and white, that advertised my father's dance studio. The studio had been closed for years and the building it had been in was gone. The sign showed a man in a tuxedo waltzing with a woman in an evening gown. I was always sure it was a waltz. The dancers were nearly two stories high, and the weather had bleached them into phantoms. The lettering – the name of the studio, my father's name – had disappeared.

"They've changed everything," my mother said, peering about. "Can this be the station?"

We went up a little drive that wound past a cinderly lot full of flatbed trucks and that ended up at the smudgy brownstone depot.

"Is that your Will?" Mother said.

Will was on the station platform, leaning against a baggage truck. He had a duffle bag between his shoes and a plastic cup of coffee in his mittened hand. He seemed to have put on weight, girlishly, through the hips, and his face looked thicker to me, from temple to temple. His gold-rimmed spectacles looked too small.

My mother stopped in an empty cab lane, and I got out and called to Will. It wasn't far from the platform to the car, and Will's pack wasn't a large one, but he seemed to be winded when he got to me. I let him kiss me, and then he stepped back and blew a cold breath and drank from the coffee cup, with his eyes on my face.

Mother was pretending to be busy with something in her handbag, not paying attention to me and Will.

"I look awful," I said.

"No, no, but I probably do," Will said. "No sleep, and I'm fat. So this is your town?"

He tossed the coffee cup at an oil drum and glanced around at the cold train yards and low buildings. A brass foundry was throwing a yellowish column of smoke over a line of Canadian Pacific boxcars.

I said, "The problem is you're looking at the wrong side of the tracks."

A wind whipped Will's lank hair across his face. "Does your mom smoke?" he said. "I ran out in the middle of the night on the train, and the club car was closed. Eight hours across Pennsylvania without a cigarette."

The car horn sounded as my mother climbed from behind the wheel. "That was an accident," she said, because I was frowning at her. "Hello. Are you Will?" She came around the car and stood on tiptoes and kissed him. "You picked a miserable day to come visit us."

She was using her young-girl voice, and I was embarrassed for her. "He needs a cigarette," I said.

Will got into the back of the car and I sat beside my mother again. After we started up, Mother said, "Why doesn't Will stay at my place, in your old room, Belle? I'm all alone there, with plenty of space to kick around in."

"We'll be able to get him a good motel," I said quickly, before Will could answer. "Let's try that Ramada, over near the new elementary school." It was odd, after he had come all the

way from Cambridge, but I didn't want him in my old room, in
the house where I had been a child. "I'd put you at my place," I
said, "but there's mountains of tax stuff all over."

"You've been busy," he said.

"Yes," I said. I sat sidewise, looking at each of them in turn.
Will had some blackish spots around his mouth – ballpoint ink,
maybe. I wished he had freshened up and put on a better shirt
before leaving the train.

"It's up to you two, then," my mother said.

I could tell she was disappointed in Will. I don't know what
she expected. I was thirty-one when I met him. I had probably
dated fewer men in my life than she had gone out with in a single
year at her sorority. She had always been successful with men.

"William was my late husband's name," my mother said.
"Did Belle ever tell you?"

"No," Will said. He was smoking one of Mother's cigarettes.

"I always liked the name," she said. "Did you know we ran
a dance studio?"

I groaned.

"Oh, let me brag if I want to," my mother said. "He was
such a handsome man."

It was true. They were both handsome – mannequins, a pair
of dolls who had spent half their lives in evening clothes. But my
father had looked old in the end, in a business in which you had
to stay young. He had trouble with his eyes, which were bruised-
looking and watery, and he had to wear glasses with thick lenses.

I said, "It was in the dance studio that my father ended his
life, you know. In the ballroom."

"You told me," Will said, at the same instant my mother
said, "Don't talk about it."

My father killed himself with a service revolver. We never
found out where he had bought it, or when. He was found in his
warm-up clothes – a pullover sweater and pleated pants. He was
wearing his tap shoes, and he had a short towel folded around
his neck. He had aimed the gun barrel down his mouth, so the
bullet would not shatter the wall of mirrors behind him. I was
twenty then – old enough to find out how he did it.

★

My mother had made a wrong turn and we were on Buttles Avenue. "Go there," I said, pointing down a street beside Garfield Park. We passed a group of paper boys who were riding bikes with saddlebags. They were going slow, because of the ice.

"Are you very discouraged, Will?" my mother said. "Belle tells me you're having a run of bad luck."

"You could say so," Will said. "A little rough water."

"I'm sorry," Mother said. "What seems to be the trouble?"

Will said, "Well, this will be oversimplifying, but essentially what I do is take a weed and evaluate its structure and growth and habitat, and so forth."

"What's wrong with that?" my mother said.

"Nothing. But it isn't enough."

"I get it," my mother said uncertainly.

I had taken a mirror and comb from my handbag and I was trying for a clean center-part in my hair. I was thinking about finishing my bill paying.

Will said, "What do you want to do after I check in, Belle? What about breakfast?"

"I've got to go home for a while and clean up that tax jazz, or I'll never rest," I said. "I'll just show up at your motel later. If we ever find it."

"That'll be fine," Will said.

Mother said, "I'd offer to serve you two dinner tonight, but I think you'll want to leave me out of it. I know how your father and I felt after he went away sometimes. Which way do I turn here?"

We had stopped at an intersection near the iron gates of the park. Behind the gates there was a frozen pond, where a single early-morning skater was skating backward, expertly crossing his blades.

I couldn't drive a car, but, like my father, I have always enjoyed maps and atlases. During automobile trips, I liked comparing distances on maps. I liked the words *latitude*, *cartography*, *meridian*. It was extremely annoying to me that Mother had gotten us turned around and lost in our own city, and I was angry with Will all of a sudden for wasting seven years on something superficial.

"What about up that way?" Will said to my mother, pointing to the left. "There's some traffic up by that light, at least."

I leaned forward in my seat and started combing my hair all over again.

"There's no hurry," my mother said.

"How do you mean?" I asked her.

"To get William to the motel," she said. "I know everybody complains, but I think an ice storm is a beautiful thing. Let's enjoy it."

She waved her cigarette at the windshield. The sun had burned through and was gleaming in the branches of all the maples and buckeye trees in the park. "It's twinkling like a stage set," Mother said.

"It is pretty," I said.

Will said, "It'll make a bad-looking spring. A lot of shrubs get damaged and turn brown, and the trees don't blossom right."

I put my comb away and smiled back at Will. For once I agreed with my mother. Everything was in place, the way it was supposed to be, quiet and holding still.

MONA SIMPSON

☆  ☆  ☆  ☆

# *Lawns*

I steal. I've stolen books and money and even letters. Letters are great. I can't tell you the feeling walking down the street with 20 dollars in my purse, stolen earrings in my pocket. I don't get caught. That's the amazing thing. You're out on the sidewalk, other people all around, shopping, walking, and you've got it. You're out of the store, you've done this thing you're not supposed to do, but no one stops you. At first it's a rush. Like you're even for everything you didn't get before. But then you're left alone, no one even notices you. Nothing changes.

I work in the mailroom of my dormitory, Saturday mornings. I sort mail, put the letters in these long narrow cubbyholes. The insides of mailboxes. It's cool there when I stick in my arm.

I've stolen cash – these crisp, crackling, brand-new 20-dollar bills the fathers and grandmothers send, sealed up in sheets of wax paper. Once I got a 50. I've stolen presents, too. I got a sweater and a football. I didn't want the football, but after the package was messed up on the mail table, I had no choice, I had to take the whole thing in my day pack and throw it out on the other side of campus. I found a covered garbage can. It was miles away. Brand-new football.

Mostly, what I take are cookies. No evidence. They're edible. I can spot the coffee cans of chocolate chip. You can smell it right through the wrapping. A cool smell, like the inside of a pantry. Sometimes I eat straight through the can during my shift.

Tampering with the United States mail is a federal crime, I know. Listen, let me tell you, I know. I got a summons in my mailbox to go to the Employment Office next Wednesday. Sure I'm scared.

The university cops want to talk to me. Great. They think,

"suspect" is the word they use, that one of us is throwing out mail instead of sorting it. Wonder who? Us is the others, I'm not the only sorter. I just work Saturdays, mail comes, you know, six days a week in this country. They'll never guess it's me.

They say this in the letter, they think it's out of *laziness*. Wanting to hurry up and get done, not spend the time. But I don't hurry. I'm really patient on Saturday mornings. I leave my dorm early, while Lauren's still asleep, I open the mailroom – it's this heavy door and I have my own key. When I get there, two bags are already on the table, sagging, waiting for me. Two old ladies. One's packages, one's mail. There's a small key opens the bank of doors, the little boxes from the inside. Through the glass part of every mail slot, I can see. The Astroturf field across the street over the parking lot, it's this light green. I watch the sky go from black to gray to blue while I'm there. Some days just stay foggy. Those are the best. I bring a cup of coffee in with me from the vending machine – don't want to wake Lauren up – and I get there at like 7.30 or 8 o'clock. I don't mind it then, my whole dorm's asleep. When I walk out it's as quiet as a football game day. It's 11 or 12 when you know everyone's up and walking that it gets bad being down there. That's why I start early. But I don't rush.

Once you open a letter, you can't just put it in a mailbox. The person's gonna say something. So I stash them in my pack and throw them out. Just people I know. Susan Brown I open, Annie Larsen, Larry Helprin. All the popular kids from my high school. These are kids who drove places together, took vacations, they all ski, they went to the prom in one big group. At morning nutrition – nutrition, it's your break at 10 o'clock for donuts and stuff. California state law, you have to have it.

They used to meet outside on the far end of the math patio, all in one group. Some of them smoked. I've seen them look at each other, concerned at 10 in the morning. One touched the inside of another's wrist, like grown-ups in trouble.

And now I know. Everything I thought those three years, worst years of my life, turns out to be true. The ones here get letters. Keri's at Santa Cruz, Lilly's in San Diego, Kevin's at

Harvard, and Beth's at Stanford. And like from families, their
letters talk about problems. They're each other's main lives. You
always knew, looking at them in high school, they weren't just
kids who had fun. They cared. They cared about things.

They're all worried about Lilly now. Larry and Annie are
flying down to talk her into staying at school.

I saw Glenn the day I came to Berkeley. I was all unpacked and I
was standing there leaning into the window of my father's car,
saying, "Smile, Dad, jeez, at least try, would you?" He was
crying because he was leaving. I'm thinking oh, my God, some
of these other kids carrying in their trunks and backpacks are
gonna see him, and then finally, he drives away and I was sad.
That was the moment I was waiting for, him gone and me alone
and there it was and I was sad. I took a walk through campus
and I'd been walking for almost an hour and then I see Glenn,
coming down on a little hill by the infirmary, riding one of those
lawn mowers you sit on, with grass flying out of the side and
he's smiling. Not at me but just smiling. Clouds and sky behind
his hair, half of Tamalpais gone in fog. He was wearing this
bright orange vest and I thought, fall's coming.

I saw him that night again in our dorm cafeteria. This's the
first time I've been in love. I worry. I'm a bad person, but
Glenn's the perfect guy, I mean for me at least, and he thinks he
loves me and I've got to keep him from finding out about me.
I'll die before I'll tell him. Glenn, okay, Glenn. He looks like
Mick Jagger, but sweet, ten times sweeter. He looks like he's
about ten years old. His father's a doctor over at UC Med.
Gynecological surgeon.

First time we got together, a whole bunch of us were in
Glenn's room drinking beer. Glenn and his room-mate collect
beer cans, they have them stacked up, we're watching TV and
finally everybody else leaves. There's nothing on but those gray
lines and Glenn turns over on his bed and asks me if I'd rub his
back.

I couldn't believe this was happening to me. In high school,
I was always ending up with the wrong guys, never the one I
wanted. But I wanted it to be Glenn and I knew it was going to

happen. I knew I didn't have to do anything. I just had to stay there. It would happen. I was sitting on his rear end, rubbing his back, going under his shirt with my hands.

All of a sudden, I was worried about my breath and what I smelled like. When I turned fourteen or fifteen, my father told me once that I didn't smell good. I slugged him when he said that and didn't talk to him for days, not that I cared about what I smelled like with my father. He was happy, though, kind of, that he could hurt me. That was the last time, though, I'll tell you.

Glenn's face was down in the pillow. I tried to sniff myself but I couldn't tell anything. And it went all right anyway.

I don't open Glenn's letters but I touch them. I hold them and smell them – none of his mail has any smell.

He doesn't get many letters. His parents live across the Bay in Marin County, they don't write. He gets letters from his grandmother in Michigan, plain, even handwriting on regular envelopes, a sticker with her return address printed on it, Rural Route #3, Guns Street, see, I got it memorized.

And he gets letters from Diane, Di, they call her. High school girlfriend. Has a pushy mother, wants her to be a scientist, but she already got a C in Chem 1A. I got an A+, not to brag. He never slept with her, though, she wouldn't, she's still a virgin down in San Diego. With Lilly. Maybe they even know each other.

Glenn and Di were popular kids in their high school. Redwood High. Now I'm one because of Glenn, popular. Because I'm his girlfriend, I know that's why. Not 'cause of me. I just know, okay, I'm not going to start fooling myself now. Please.

Her letters I hold up to the light, they've got fluorescent lights in there. She's supposed to be blond, you know, and pretty. Quiet. The soft type. And the envelopes. She writes on these sheer cream-colored envelopes and they get transparent and I can see her writing underneath, but not enough to read what it says, it's like those hockey lines painted under layers of ice.

I run my tongue along the place where his grandmother

sealed the letter. A sharp, sweet gummy taste. Once I cut my
tongue. That's what keeps me going to the bottom of the bag,
I'm always wondering if there'll be a letter for Glenn. He doesn't
get one every week. It's like a treasure. Cracker Jack prize. But
I'd never open Glenn's mail. I kiss all four corners where his
fingers will touch, opening it, before I put it in his box.

I brought home cookies for Lauren and me. Just a present. We'll
eat 'em or Glenn'll eat 'em. I'll throw them out for all I care.
They're chocolate chip with pecans. This was one good mother.
A lucky can. I brought us coffee, too. I *bought* it.
    Yeah, okay, so I'm in trouble. Wednesday, at 10.30, I got
this notice I was supposed to appear. I had a class, Chem 1C,
pre-med staple. Your critical thing. I never missed it before. I
told Glenn I had a doctor's appointment.
    Okay, so I skip it anyway and I walk into this room and
there's these two other guys, all work in the mailroom doing
what I do, sorting. And we all sit there on chairs on this green
carpet. I was staring at everybody's shoes. And there's a cop.
University cop, I don't know what's the difference. He had this
sagging, pear-shaped body. Like what my dad would have if he
were fat, but he's not, he's thin. He walks slowly on the
carpeting, his fingers hooked in his belt loops. I was watching
his hips.
    Anyway, he's accusing us all and he's trying to get one of us
to admit we did it. No way.
    "I hope one of you will come to me and tell the truth. Not a
one of you knows anything about this? Come on, now."
    I shake my head no and stare down at the three pairs of
shoes. He says they're not going to do anything to the person
who did it, right, wanna make a bet, they say they just want to
know, but they'll take it back as soon as you tell them.
    I don't care why I don't believe him. I know one thing for
sure and that's they're not going to do anything to me as long as
I say no, I didn't do it. That's what I said, no, I didn't do it, I
don't know a thing about it. I just can't imagine where those
missing packages could have gone, how letters got into garbage
cans. Awful. I just don't know.

The cop had a map with X's on it every place they found mail. The garbage cans. He said there was a group of students trying to get an investigation. People's girlfriends sent cookies that never got here. Letters are missing. Money. These students put up Xeroxed posters on bulletin boards showing a garbage can stuffed with letters.

Why should I tell them, so they can throw me in jail? And kick me out of school? Four-point-oh average and I'm going to let them kick me out of school? They're sitting there telling us it's a felony. A federal crime. No way, I'm gonna go to medical school.

This tall, skinny guy with a blond mustache, Wallabees, looks kind of like a rabbit, he defended us. He's another sorter, works Monday/Wednesdays.

"We all do our jobs," he says. "None of us would do that." The rabbity guy looks at me and the other girl for support. So we're going to stick together. The other girl, a dark blonde chewing her lip, nodded. I loved that rabbity guy that second. I nodded too.

The cop looked down. Wide hips in the coffee-with-milk-colored pants. He sighed. I looked up at the rabbity guy. They let us all go.

I'm just going to keep saying no, not me, didn't do it and I just won't do it again. That's all. Won't do it anymore. So, this is Glenn's last chance for homemade cookies. I'm sure as hell not going to bake any.

I signed the form, said I didn't do it, I'm okay now. I'm safe. It turned out okay after all, it always does. I always think something terrible's going to happen and it doesn't. I'm lucky.

I'm afraid of cops. I was walking, just a little while ago, today, down Telegraph with Glenn, and these two policemen, not the one I'd met, other policemen, were coming in our direction. I started sweating a lot. I was sure until they passed us, I was sure it was all over, they were there for me. I always think that. But at the same time, I know it's just my imagination. I mean, I'm a four-point-oh student, I'm a nice girl just walking down the street with my boyfriend.

We were on our way to get Happy Burgers. When we turned

the corner, about a block past the cops, I looked at Glenn and I was flooded with this feeling. It was raining a little and we were by People's Park. The trees were blowing and I was looking at all those little gardens coming up, held together with stakes and white string.

I wanted to say something to Glenn, give him something. I wanted to tell him something about me.

"I'm bad in bed," that's what I said, I just blurted it out like that. He just kind of looked at me, he was nervous, he just giggled. He didn't know what to say, I guess, but he sort of slung his arm around me and I was so grateful and then we went in. He paid for my Happy Burger, I usually don't let him pay for me, but I did and it was the best goddamn hamburger I've ever eaten.

I want to tell him things.

I lie all the time, always have, but I keep track of each lie I've ever told Glenn and I'm always thinking of the things I can't tell him.

Glenn was a screwed up kid, kind of. He used to go in his backyard, his parents were inside the house I guess, and he'd find this big stick and start twirling around with it. He'd dance, he called it dancing, until if you came up and clapped in front of him, he wouldn't see you. He'd spin around with that stick until he fell down dead on the grass, unconscious, he said he did it to see the sky break up in pieces and spin. He did it sometimes with a tire swing, too. He told me when he was spinning like that, it felt like he was just hearing the earth spinning, that it really went that fast all the time but we just don't feel it. When he was twelve years old his parents took him in the city to a clinic to see a psychologist. And then he stopped. See, maybe I should go to a psychologist. I'd get better, too. He told me about that in bed one night. The ground feels so good when you fall, he said to me. I loved him for that.

"Does anything feel that good now?" I said.

"Sex sometimes. Maybe dancing."

Know what else he told me that night? He said, right before we went to sleep, he wasn't looking at me, he said he'd been thinking what would happen if I died, he said he thought how he'd be at my funeral, all my family and my friends from high school and my little brother would all be around at the front and he'd be at the edge in the cemetery, nobody'd even know who he was.

I was in that crack, breathing the air between the bed and the wall. Cold and dusty. Yeah, we're having sex. I don't know. It's good. Sweet. He says he loves me. I have to remind myself. I talk to myself in my head while we're doing it. I have to say, it's okay, this is just Glenn, this is who I want it to be and it's just like rubbing next to someone. It's just like pushing two hands together, so there's no air in between.

I cry sometimes with Glenn, I'm so grateful.

My mother called and woke me up this morning. Ms. I'm-going-to-be-perfect. Ms. Anything-wrong-is-your-own-fault. Ms. If-anything-bad-happens-you're-a-fool.

She says if she has time, she *might* come up and see my dorm room in the next few weeks. Help me organize my wardrobe, she says. She didn't bring me up here, my dad did. I wanted Danny to come along. I love Danny.

But my mother has *no* pity. She thinks she's got the answers. She's the one who's a lawyer, she's the one who went back to law school and stayed up late nights studying while she still made our lunch boxes. With gourmet cheese. She's proud of it, she tells you. She loves my dad, I guess. She thinks we're like this great family and she sits there at the dinner table bragging about us, to us. She Xeroxed my grade card first quarter with my Chemistry A+ so she's got it in her office and she's got the copy up on the refrigerator at home. She's sitting there telling all her friends that and I'm thinking, you don't know it, but I'm not one of you.

These people across the street from us. Little girl, Sarah, eight years old. Maybe seven. Her dad, he worked for the army, some kind of researcher, he decides he wants to get a sex-change operation. And he goes and does it, over at Stanford. My mom goes out, takes the dog for a walk, right. The mother *confides* in her. Says the things she regrets most is she wants to have more children. The little girl, Sarah, eight years old, looks up at my mom and says, "Daddy's going to be an aunt."

Now that's sad, I think that's really sad. My mom thinks it's a good dinner-table story, proving how much better we are than them. Yeah, I remember exactly what she said that night. "That's all Sarah's mother's got to worry about now is that she wants another child. Meanwhile, Daddy's becoming an aunt."

She should know about me.

So my dad comes to visit for the weekend. Glenn's dad came to speak at UC one night, he took Glenn out to dinner to a nice place, Glenn was glad to see him. Yeah, well. My dad. Comes to the dorm. Skulks around. This guy's a *businessman*, in a three-piece suit, and he acts inferior to the eighteen-year-old freshmen coming in the lobby. My dad. Makes me sick right now thinking of him standing there in the lobby and everybody seeing him. He was probably looking at the kids and looking jealous. Just standing there. Why? Don't ask me why, he's the one that's forty-two years old.

So he's standing there, nervous, probably sucking his hand, that's what he does when he's nervous, I'm always telling him not to. Finally, somebody takes him to my room. I'm not there, Lauren's gone, and he waits for I don't know how long.

When I come in he's standing with his back to the door, looking out the window. I see him and right away I know it's him and I have this urge to tiptoe away and he'll never see me.

My pink sweater, a nice sweater, a sweater I wore a lot in high school, was over my chair, hanging on the back of it, and my father's got one hand on the sweater shoulder and he's like rubbing the other hand down an empty arm. He looks up at me, already scared and grateful when I walk into the room. I feel like smashing him with a baseball bat. Why can't he just stand up straight?

I drop my books on the bed and stand there while he hugs me.

"Hi, Daddy, what are you doing here?"

"I wanted to see you." He sits in my chair now, his legs

crossed and big, too big for this room, and he's still fingering the arm of my pink sweater. "I missed you so I got away for the weekend," he says. "I have a room up here at the Claremont Hotel."

So he's here for the weekend. He's just sitting in my dorm room and I have to figure out what to do with him. He's not going to do anything. He'd just sit there. And Lauren's coming back soon so I've got to get him out. It's Friday afternoon and the weekend's shot. Okay, so I'll go with him. I'll go with him and get it over with.

But I'm not going to miss my date with Glenn Saturday night. No way. I'd die before I'd cancel that. It's bad enough missing dinner in the cafeteria tonight. Friday's eggplant, my favorite, and Friday nights are usually easy, music on the stereos all down the hall. We usually work, but work slow and talk and then we all meet in Glenn's room around 10.

"Come, sit on my lap, honey." My dad like pulls me down and starts bouncing me. *Bouncing me.* I stand up. "Okay, we can go somewhere tonight and tomorrow morning, but I have to be back for tomorrow night. I've got plans with people. And I've got to study, too."

"You can bring your books back to the hotel," he says. "I'm supposed to be at a convention in San Francisco, but I wanted to see you. I have work, too, we can call room service and both just work."

"I still have to be back by 4 tomorrow."

"All right."

"Okay, just a minute." And he sat there in my chair while I called Glenn and told him I wouldn't be there for dinner. I pulled the phone out into the hall, it only stretches so far, and whispered. "Yeah, my father's here," I said, "he's got a conference in San Francisco. He just came by."

Glenn lowered his voice, sweet, and said, "Sounds fun."

My dad sat there, hunched over in my chair, while I changed my shirt and put on deodorant. I put a nightgown in my shoulder pack and my toothbrush and I took my chem book and we left. I knew I wouldn't be back for a whole day. I was trying to calm myself, thinking well, it's only one day, that's nothing in my life. The halls were empty, it was 5 o'clock, 5.10, everyone was down at dinner.

We walk outside and the cafeteria lights are on and I see everyone moving around with their trays. Then my dad picks up my hand.

I yank it out. "Dad," I say, really mean.

"Honey, I'm your father." His voice trails off. "Other girls hold their fathers' hands." It was dark enough for the lights to be on in the cafeteria, but it wasn't really dark out yet. The sky was blue. On the tennis courts on top of the garage, two Chinese guys were playing. I heard that *thonk-pong* and it sounded so carefree and I just wanted to be them. I'd have even given up Glenn, Glenn-that-I-love-more-than-anything, at that second, I would have given everything up just to be someone else, someone new. I got into the car and slammed the door shut and turned up the heat.

"Should we just go to the hotel and do our work? We can get a nice dinner in the room."

"I'd rather go out," I said, looking down at my hands. He went where I told him. I said the name of the restaurant and gave directions. Chez Panisse and we ordered the most expensive stuff. Appetizers and two desserts just for me. A hundred and twenty bucks for the two of us.

Okay, this hotel room.

So, my dad's got the Bridal Suite. He claimed that was all they had. Fat chance. Two-hundred-eighty room hotel and all they've got left is this deal with the canopy bed, no way. It's in the tower, you can almost see it from the dorm. Makes me sick. From the bathroom, there's this window, shaped like an arch, and it looks over all of Berkeley. You can see the bridge lights. As soon as we got there, I locked myself in the bathroom, I was so mad about that canopy bed. I took a long bath and washed my hair. They had little soaps wrapped up there, shampoo, may as well use them, he's paying for it. It's this deep old bathtub and wind was coming in from outside and I felt like that window was just open, no glass, just a hole cut out in the stone.

I was thinking of when I was little and what they taught us

in catechism. I thought a soul was inside your chest, this long horizontal triangle with rounded edges, made out of some kind of white fog, some kind of gas or vapor. I could be pregnant. I soaped myself all up and rinsed off with cold water. I'm lucky I never got pregnant, really lucky.

Other kids my age, Lauren, everybody, I know things they don't know. I know more for my age. Too much. Like I'm not a virgin. Lots of people are, you'd be surprised. I know about a lot of things being wrong and unfair, all kinds of stuff. It's like seeing a UFO, if I ever saw something like that, I'd never tell, I'd wish I'd never seen it.

My dad knocks on the door.

"What do you want?"

"Let me just come in and talk to you while you're in there."

"I'm done, I'll be right out. Just a minute." I took a long time toweling. No hurry, believe me. So I got into bed with my nightgown on and wet already from my hair. I turned away. Breathed against the wall. "Night."

My father hooks my hair over my ear and touches my shoulder. "Tired?"

I shrug.

"You really have to go back tomorrow? We could go to Marin or to the beach. Anything."

I hugged my knees up under my nightgown. "You should go to your conference, Dad."

I wake up in the middle of the night, I feel something's going on, and sure enough, my dad's down there, he's got my nightgown worked up like a frill around my neck and my legs hooked over his shoulders.

"Dad, stop it."

"I just wanted to make you feel good," he says, and looks up at me. "What's wrong? Don't you love me anymore?"

I never really told anybody. It's not exactly the kind of thing you can bring up over lunch. "So, I'm sleeping with my father. Oh, and let's split a dessert." Right.

I don't know, other people think my dad's handsome. They say he is. My mother thinks so, you should see her traipsing around the balcony when she gets in her romantic moods, which, on her professional lawyer schedule, are about once a year, thank God. It's pathetic. He thinks she's repulsive, though. I don't know that, that's what I think. But he loves me, that's for sure.

So next day, Saturday – that rabbity guy, Paul's his name, he did my shift for me – we go downtown and I got him to buy me this suit. Three hundred dollars from Saks. Oh, and I got shoes. So I stayed later with him because of the clothes, and I was a little happy because I thought at least now I'd have something good to wear with Glenn. My dad and I got brownie sundaes at Sweet Dreams and I got home by 5. He was crying when he dropped me off.

"Don't cry, Dad. Please," I said. Jesus, how can you not hate someone who's always begging from you.

Lauren had Poly Styrene on the stereo and a candle lit in our room. I was never so glad to be home.

"Hey," Lauren said. She was on her bed with her legs propped up on the wall. She'd just shaved. She was rubbing in cream.

I flopped down on my bed. "Ohhhh," I said, grabbing the sides of the mattress.

"Hey, can you keep a secret about what I did today?" Lauren said. "I went to that therapist, up at Cowell."

"You have the greatest legs," I said, quiet. "Why don't you ever wear skirts?"

She stopped what she was doing and stood up. "You think they're good? I don't like the way they look, except in jeans." She looked down at them. "They're crooked, see?" She shook her head. "I don't want to think about it."

Then she went to her dresser and started rolling a joint. "Want some?"

"A little."

She lit up, lay back on her bed and held her arm out for me to come take the joint.

"So, she was this really great woman. Warm, kind of chubby. She knew instantly what kind of man Brent was." Lauren snapped her fingers. "Like that." Brent was the pool man Lauren had an affair with, home in LA.

I'm back in the room maybe an hour, putting on mascara, my jeans are on the bed, pressed, and the phone rings and it's my dad and I say, "Listen, just leave me alone."

"You don't care about me anymore."

"I just saw you. I have nothing to say. We just saw each other."

"What are you doing tonight?"

"Going out."

"Who are you seeing?"

"Glenn."

He sighs. "So you really like him, huh?"

"Yeah, I do and you should be glad. You should be glad I have a boyfriend." I pull the cord out into the hall and sit down on the floor there. There's this long pause.

"We're not going to end up together, are we?"

I felt like all the air's knocked out of me. I looked out the window and everything looked dead and still. The parked cars. The trees with pink toilet paper strung between the branches. The church all closed up across the street.

"No, we won't, Daddy."

He was crying. "I know, I know."

I hung up the phone and went back and sat in the hall. I'm scared, too. I don't know what'll happen.

I don't know. It's been going on I guess as long as I can remember. I mean, not the sex, but my father. When I was a little kid, tiny little kid, my dad came in before bed and said his prayers with me. He kneeled down by my bed and I was on my back. *Prayers.* He'd lift up my pajama top and put his hands on my breast. Little fried eggs, he said. One time with his tongue. Then one night, he pulled down the elastic of my pajama pants. He did it for an hour and then I came. Don't believe anything they ever tell you about kids not coming. That first time was the biggest I ever had and I didn't even know what it was then. It just kept going and going as if he were breaking me through layers and layers of glass and I felt like I'd slipped and let go and I didn't have myself anymore, he had me, and once I'd slipped like that I'd never be the same again.

We had this sprinkler on our back lawn, Danny and me used to run through it in summer and my dad'd be outside, working on the grass or the hedge or something and he'd squirt us with the hose. I used to wear a bathing suit bottom, no top – we were this modern family, our parents walked around the house naked after showers and then Danny and I ended up both being these modest kids, can't stand anyone to see us even in our underwear, I always dress facing the closet, Lauren teases me. We'd run through the sprinkler and my dad would come up and pat my bottom and the way he'd put his hand on my thigh, I felt like Danny could tell it was different than the way he touched him, I was like something he owned.

First time when I was nine, I remember, Dad and me were in the shower together. My mom might have even been in the house, they did that kind of stuff, it was supposed to be okay. Anyway, we're in the shower and I remember this look my dad had. Like he was daring me, knowing he knew more than I did. We're both under the shower. The water pasted his hair down on his head and he looked younger and weird. "Touch it. Don't be afraid of it," he says. And he grabs my thighs on the outside and pulls me close to him, pulling on my fat.

He waited till I was twelve to really do it. I don't know if you can call it rape, I was a good sport. The creepy thing is I know how it felt for him, I could see it on his face when he did it. He thought he was getting away with something. We were supposed to go hiking but right away that morning when we got into the car, he knew he was going to do it. He couldn't wait to get going. I said I didn't feel good, I had a cold, I wanted to stay home, but he made me go anyway and we hiked 2 miles and he set up the tent. He told me to take my clothes off and I undressed just like that, standing there in the woods. He's the one who was nervous and got us into the tent. I looked old for twelve, small but old. And right there on the ground, he spread my legs open and pulled my feet up and fucked me. I bled. I couldn't even breathe the tent was so small. He could have done anything. He could have killed me, he had me alone on this mountain.

I think about that sometimes when I'm alone with Glenn in my bed. It's so easy to hurt people. They just lie there and let you have them. I could reach out and choke Glenn to death, he'd be so shocked, he wouldn't stop me. You can just take what you want.

My dad thought he was getting away with something but he didn't. He was the one who fell in love, not me. And after that day, when we were back in the car, I was the one giving orders. From then on, I got what I wanted. He spent about twice as much money on me as on Danny and everyone knew it, Danny and my mom, too. How do you think I got good clothes and a good bike and a good stereo? My dad's not rich, you know. And I'm the one who got to go away to college even though it killed him. Says it's the saddest thing that ever happened in his life, me going away and leaving him. But when I was a little kid that day, he wasn't in love with me, not like he is now.

Only thing I'm sad about isn't either of my parents, it's Danny. Leaving Danny alone there with them. He used to send Danny out of the house. My mom'd be at work on a Saturday afternoon or something or even in the morning and my dad would kick my little brother out of his own house. Go out and play, Danny. Why doncha catch some rays. And Danny just went and got his glove and baseball from the closet and he'd go and throw it against the house, against the outside wall, in the driveway. I'd be in my room, I'd be like dead, I'd be wood, telling myself this doesn't count, no one has to know, I'll say I'm still a virgin, it's not really happening to me, I'm dead, I'm blank, I'm just letting time stop and pass, and then I'd hear the sock of the ball in the mitt and the slam of the screen door and I knew it was true, it was really happening.

Glenn's the one I want to tell. I can't ever tell Glenn.

I called my mom. Pay phone, collect, hour-long call. I don't know, I got really mad last night and I just told her. I thought when I came here, it'd just go away. But it's not going away. It makes me weird with Glenn. In the morning, with Glenn, when it's time to get up, I can't get up. I cry.

I knew it'd be bad. Poor Danny. Well, my mom says she might leave our dad. She cried for an hour, no jokes, on the phone.

How could he *do* this to me, she kept yelping. To her. Everything's always to her.

But then she called an hour later, she'd talked to a psychiatrist already, she's kicked Dad out, and she arrives, just arrives here at Berkeley. But she was good. She says she's on my side, she'll help me, I don't know, I felt okay. She stayed in a hotel and she wanted to know if I wanted to stay there with her but I said no, I'd see her more in a week or something, I just wanted to go back to my dorm. She found this group. She says, just in San Jose, there's hundreds of families like ours, yeah, great, that's what I said. But there's groups. She's going to a group of other thick-o mothers like her, these wives who didn't catch on. She wanted me to go to a group of girls, yeah, molested girls, that's what they call them, but I said no. I have friends here already, she can do what she wants.

I talked to my dad, too, that's the sad thing, he feels like he's lost me and he wants to die and I don't know, he doesn't know what he's doing. He called in the middle of the night.

"Just tell me one thing, honey. Please tell me the truth. When did you stop?"

"Dad."

"Because I remember once you said I was the only person who ever understood you."

"I was ten years old."

"Okay, okay. I'm sorry."

He didn't want to get off the phone. "You know, I love you, honey. I always will."

"Yeah, well."

My mom's got him lined up for a psychiatrist, too, she says he's lucky she's not sending him to jail. I *am* a lawyer, she keeps saying, as if we could forget. She'd pay for me to go to a shrink now, too, but I said no, forget it.

It's over. Glenn and I are, over. I feel like my dad's lost me everything. I sort of want to die now. I'm telling you I feel terrible. I told Glenn and that's it, it's over. I can't believe it either. Lauren says she's going to hit him.

I told him and we're not seeing each other anymore. Nope.

He said he wanted to just think about everything for a few days.
He said it had nothing to do with my father but he'd been feeling
a little too settled lately. He said we don't have fun anymore, it's
always so serious. That was Monday. So every meal after that, I
sat with Lauren in the cafeteria and he's there on the other side,
messing around with the guys. He sure didn't look like he was
in any kind of agony. Wednesday I saw Glenn over by the
window in this food fight, slipping off his chair and I couldn't
stand it, I got up and left and went to our room.

But I went and said I wanted to talk to Glenn that night, I
didn't even have any dinner, and he said he wanted to be friends.
He looked at me funny and I haven't heard from him. It's, I
don't know, seven days, eight.

I know there are other guys. I live in a dorm full of them, or
half full of them. Half girls. But I keep thinking of Glenn 'cause
of happiness, that's what makes me want to hang on to him.

There was this one morning when we woke up in his room,
it was light out already, white light all over the room. We were
sticky and warm, the sheet was all tangled. His room-mate, this
little blond boy, was still sleeping. I watched his eyes open and
he smiled and then he went down the hall to take a shower.
Glenn was hugging me and it was nothing unusual, nothing
special. We didn't screw. We were just there. We kissed, but
slow, the way it is when your mouth is still bad from sleep.

I was happy that morning. I didn't have to do anything. We
got dressed, went to breakfast, I don't know. Took a walk. He
had to go to work at a certain time and I had that sleepy feeling
from waking up with the sun on my head and he said he didn't
want to say goodbye to me. There was that pang. One of those
looks like as if at that second, we both felt the same way.

I shrugged. I could afford to be casual then. We didn't say
goodbye. I walked with him to the shed by the Eucalyptus
Grove. That's where they keep all the gardening tools, the rakes,
the hoes, the mowers, big bags of grass seed slumped against the
wall. It smelled like hay in there. Glenn changed into his uniform
and we went to the North Side, up in front of the chancellor's
manor, that thick perfect grass. And Glenn gave me a ride on the
lawn mower, on the handlebars. It was bouncing over these little

bumps in the lawn and I was hanging on to the handlebars, laughing. I couldn't see Glenn but I knew he was there behind me. I looked around at the buildings and the lawns, there's a fountain there, and one dog was drinking from it.

See, I can't help but remember things like that. Even now, I'd rather find some way, even though he's not asking for it, to forgive Glenn. I'd rather have it work out with him, because I want more days like that. I wish I could have a whole life like that. But I guess nobody does, not just me.

I saw him in the mailroom yesterday, we're both just standing there, each opening our little boxes, getting our mail – neither of us had any – I was hurt but I wanted to reach out and touch his face. He has this hard chin, it's pointy and all bone. Lauren says she wants to hit him.

I mean, I think of him spinning around in his backyard and that's why I love him and he should understand. I go over it all and think I should have just looked at him and said I can't believe you're doing this to me. Right there in the mailroom. Now when I think that, I think maybe if I'd said that, in those words, maybe it would be different.

But then I think of my father – he feels like there was a time when we had fun, when we were happy together. I mean, I can remember being in my little bed with Dad and maybe cracking jokes, maybe laughing, but he probably never heard Danny's baseball in his mitt the way I did or I don't know. I remember late in the afternoon, wearing my dad's navy-blue sweatshirt with a hood and riding bikes with him and Danny down to the diamond.

But that's over. I don't know if I'm sorry it happened. I mean I am, but it happened, that's all. It's just one of the things that happened to me in my life. But I would never go back, never. And what hurts so much is that maybe that's what Glenn is thinking about me.

I told Lauren last night. I had to. She kept asking me what happened with Glenn. She was so good, you couldn't believe it, she was great. We were talking late and this morning we drove down to go to House of Pancakes for breakfast, get something good instead of watery eggs for a change. And on the way, Lauren's driving, she just skids to a stop on this street, in front of this elementary school. "Come on," she says. It's early, but there's already people inside the windows.

We hooked our fingers in the metal fence. You know, one of those aluminum fences around a playground. There were pigeons standing on the painted game circles. Then a bell rang and all these kids came out, yelling, spilling into groups. This was a poor school, mostly black kids, Mexican kids, all in bright colors. There's a Nabisco factory nearby and the whole air smelled like blueberry muffins.

The girls were jump-roping and the boys were shoving and running and hanging on to the monkey bars. Lauren pinched her fingers on the back of my neck and pushed my head against the fence.

"Eight years old. Look at them. They're eight years old. One of their fathers is sleeping with one of those girls. Look at her. Do you blame her? Can you blame her? Because if you can forgive her you can forgive yourself."

"I'll kill him," I said.

"And I'll kill Glenn," Lauren says.

So we went and got pancakes. And drank coffee until it was time for class.

I saw Glenn yesterday. It was so weird after all this time. I just had lunch with Lauren. We picked up tickets for Talking Heads and I wanted to get back to the lab before class and I'm walking along and Glenn was working, you know, on the lawn in front of the Mobi Building. He was still gorgeous. I was just going to walk, but he yelled over at me.

"Hey, Jenny."

"Hi, Glenn."

He congratulated me, he heard about the NSF thing. We stood there. He has another girlfriend now. I don't know, when I looked at him and stood there by the lawn mower, it's chugging away, I felt the same as I always used to, that I loved him and all that, but he might just be one of those things you can't have. Like I should have been for my father and look at him now. Oh,

I think he's better, they're all better, but I'm gone, he'll never have me again.

I'm glad they're there and I'm here, but it's strange, I feel more alone now. Glenn looked down at the little pile of grass by the lawn mower and said, "Well, kid, take care of yourself," and I said, "You too, 'bye," and started walking.

So you know what's bad, though, I started taking stuff again. Little stuff from the mailroom. No packages and not people I know anymore.

But I take one letter a Saturday, I make it just one and someone I don't know. And I keep 'em and burn 'em with a match in the bathroom sink and wash the ashes down the drain. I wait until the end of the shift. I always expect it to be something exciting. The two so far were just everyday letters, just mundane, so that's all that's new, I-had-a-pork-chop-for-dinner letters.

But something happened today, I was in the middle, three-quarters way down the bag, still looking, I hadn't picked my letter for the day, I'm being really stern, I really mean just one, no more, and there's this little white envelope addressed to me. I sit there, trembling with it in my hand. It's the first one I've gotten all year. It was my name and address, typed out, and I just stared at it. There's no address. I got so nervous, I thought maybe it was from Glenn, of course, I wanted it to be from Glenn so bad, but then I knew it couldn't be, he's got that new girlfriend now, so I threw it in the garbage can right there, one of those with the swinging metal door, and then I finished my shift. My hands were sweating, I smudged the writing on one of the envelopes.

So all the letters are in boxes, I clean off the table, fold the bags up neat and close the door, ready to go. And then I thought, I don't have to keep looking at the garbage can, I'm allowed to take it back, that's my letter. And I fished it out, the thing practically lopped my arm off. And I had it and I held it a few minutes, wondering who it was from. Then I put it in my mailbox so I can go like everybody else and get mail.

ROBERT STONE

☆  ☆  ☆  ☆

# *Helping*

One gray November day, Elliot went to Boston for the afternoon. The wet streets seemed cold and lonely. He sensed a
broken promise in the city's elegance and verve. Old hopes
tormented him like phantom limbs, but he did not drink. He had
joined Alcoholics Anonymous fifteen months before.

Christmas came, childless, a festival of regret. His wife went
to Mass and cooked a turkey. Sober, Elliot walked in the woods.

In January, blizzards swept down from the Arctic until the
weather became too cold for snow. The Shawmut Valley grew
quiet and crystalline. In the white silences, Elliot could hear the
boards of his house contract and feel a shrinking in his bones.
Each dusk, starveling deer came out of the wooded swamp
behind the house to graze his orchard for whatever raccoons had
uncovered and left behind. At night he lay beside his sleeping
wife listening to the baying of dog packs running them down in
the deep moon-shadowed snow.

Day in, day out, he was sober. At times it was almost
stimulating. But he could not shake off the sensations he had felt
in Boston. In his mind's eye he could see dead leaves rattling
along brick gutters and savor that day's desperation. The brief
outing had undermined him.

Sober, however, he remained, until the day a man named
Blankenship came into his office at the state hospital for counseling. Blankenship had red hair, a brutal face, and a sneaking
manner. He was a sponger and petty thief whom Elliot had seen
a number of times before.

"I been having this dream," Blankenship announced loudly.
His voice was not pleasant. His skin was unwholesome. Every
time he got arrested the court sent him to the psychiatrists and
the psychiatrists, who spoke little English, sent him to Elliot.

Blankenship had joined the Army after his first burglary but had never served east of the Rhine. After a few months in Wiesbaden, he had been discharged for reasons of unsuitability, but he told everyone he was a veteran of the Vietnam War. He went about in a tiger suit. Elliot had had enough of him.

"Dreams are boring," Elliot told him.

Blankenship was outraged. "Whaddaya mean?" he demanded.

During counseling sessions Elliot usually moved his chair into the middle of the room in order to seem accessible to his clients. Now he stayed securely behind his desk. He did not care to seem accessible to Blankenship. "What I said, Mr. Blankenship. Other people's dreams are boring. Didn't you ever hear that?"

"Boring?" Blankenship frowned. He seemed unable to imagine a meaning for the word.

Elliot picked up a pencil and set its point quivering on his desk-top blotter. He gazed into his client's slack-jawed face. The Blankenship family made their way through life as strolling litigants, and young Blankenship's specialty was slipping on ice cubes. Hauled off the pavement, he would hassle the doctors in Emergency for pain pills and hurry to a law clinic. The Blankenships had threatened suit against half the property owners in the southern part of the state. What they could not extort at law they stole. But even the Blankenship family had abandoned Blankenship. His last visit to the hospital had been subsequent to an arrest for lifting a case of hot-dog rolls from Woolworth's. He lived in a Goodwill depository bin in Wyndham.

"Now I suppose you want to tell me your dream? Is that right, Mr. Blankenship?"

Blankenship looked left and right like a dog surrendering eye contact. "Don't you want to hear it?" he asked humbly.

Elliot was unmoved. "Tell me something, Blankenship. Was your dream about Vietnam?"

At the mention of the word "Vietnam," Blankenship customarily broke into a broad smile. Now he looked guilty and guarded. He shrugged. "Ya."

"How come you have dreams about that place, Blankenship? You were never there."

"Whaddaya mean?" Blankenship began to say, but Elliot cut him off.

"You were never there, my man. You never saw the goddamn place. You have no business dreaming about it! You better cut it out!"

He had raised his voice to the extent that the secretary outside his open door paused at her word processor.

"Lemme alone," Blankenship said fearfully. "Some doctor you are."

"It's all right," Elliot assured him. "I'm not a doctor."

"Everybody's on my case," Blankenship said. His moods were volatile. He began to weep.

Elliot watched the tears roll down Blankenship's chapped, pitted cheeks. He cleared his throat. "Look, fella . . ." he began. He felt at a loss. He felt like telling Blankenship that things were tough all over.

Blankenship sniffed and telescoped his neck and after a moment looked at Elliot. His look was disconcertingly trustful; he was used to being counseled.

"Really, you know, it's ridiculous for you to tell me your problems have to do with Nam. You were never over there. It was me over there, Blankenship. Not you."

Blankenship leaned forward and put his forehead on his knees.

"Your troubles have to do with here and now," Elliot told his client. "Fantasies aren't helpful."

His voice sounded overripe and hypocritical in his own ears. What a dreadful business, he thought. What an awful job this is. Anger was driving him crazy.

Blankenship straightened up and spoke through his tears. "This dream . . ." he said. "I'm scared."

Elliot felt ready to endure a great deal in order not to hear Blankenship's dream.

"I'm not the one you see about that," he said. In the end he knew his duty. He sighed. "Okay. All right. Tell me about it."

"Yeah?" Blankenship asked with leaden sarcasm. "Yeah? You think dreams are friggin' boring!"

"No, no," Elliot said. He offered Blankenship a tissue and

Blankenship took one. "That was sort of off the top of my head. I didn't really mean it."

Blankenship fixed his eyes on dreaming distance. "There's a feeling that goes with it. With the dream." Then he shook his head in revulsion and looked at Elliot as though he had only just awakened. "So what do you think? You think it's boring?"

"Of course not," Elliot said. "A physical feeling?"

"Ya. It's like I'm floating in rubber."

He watched Elliot stealthily, aware of quickened attention. Elliot had caught dengue in Vietnam and during his weeks of delirium had felt vaguely as though he were floating in rubber.

"What are you seeing in this dream?"

Blankenship only shook his head. Elliot suffered a brief but intense attack of rage.

"Hey, Blankenship," he said equably, "here I am, man. You can see I'm listening."

"What I saw was black," Blankenship said. He spoke in an odd tremolo. His behavior was quite different from anything Elliot had come to expect from him.

"Black? What was it?"

"Smoke. The sky maybe."

"The sky?" Elliot asked.

"It was all black. I was scared."

In a waking dream of his own, Elliot felt the muscles on his neck distend. He was looking up at a sky that was black, filled with smoke-swollen clouds, lit with fires, damped with blood and rain.

"What were you scared of?" he asked Blankenship.

"I don't know," Blankenship said.

Elliot could not drive the black sky from his inward eye. It was as though Blankenship's dream had infected his own mind.

"You don't know? You don't know what you were scared of?"

Blankenship's posture was rigid. Elliot, who knew the aspect of true fear, recognized it there in front of him.

"The Nam," Blankenship said.

"You're not even old enough," Elliot told him.

Blankenship sat trembling with joined palms between his

thighs. His face was flushed and not in the least ennobled by pain. He had trouble with alcohol and drugs. He had trouble with everything.

"So wherever your black sky is, it isn't Vietnam."

Things were so unfair, Elliot thought. It was unfair of Blankenship to appropriate the condition of a Vietnam veteran. The trauma inducing his post-traumatic stress had been nothing more serious than his own birth, a routine procedure. Now, in addition to the poverty, anxiety, and confusion that would always be his life's lot, he had been visited with irony. It was all arbritrary and some people simply got elected. Everyone knew that who had been where Blankenship had not.

"Because, I assure you, Mr. Blankenship, you were never there."

"Whaddaya mean?" Blankenship asked.

When Blankenship was gone, Elliot leafed through his file and saw that the psychiatrists had passed him upstairs without recording a diagnosis. Disproportionately angry, he went out to the secretary's desk.

"Nobody wrote up that last patient," he said. "I'm not supposed to see people without a diagnosis. The shrinks are just passing the buck."

The secretary was a tall, solemn redhead with prominent front teeth and a slight speech disorder. "Dr. Sayyid will have kittens if he hears you call him a shrink, Chas. He's already complained. He hates being called a shrink."

"Then he came to the wrong country," Elliot said. "He can go back to his own."

The woman giggled. "He *is* the doctor, Chas."

"Hates being called a shrink!" He threw the file on the secretary's table and stormed back toward his office. "That fucking little zip couldn't give you a decent haircut. He's a prescription clerk."

The secretary looked about her guiltily and shook her head. She was used to him.

Elliot succeeded in calming himself down after a while, but the image of black sky remained with him. At first he thought he would be able to simply shrug the whole thing off. After a few minutes, he picked up his phone and dialed Blankenship's probation officer.

"The Vietnam thing is all he has," the probation officer explained. "I guess he picked it up around."

"His descriptions are vivid," Elliot said.

"You mean they sound authentic?"

"I mean he had me going today. He was ringing my bells."

"Good for Blanky. Think he believes it himself?"

"Yes," Elliot said. "He believes it himself now."

Elliot told the probation officer about Blankenship's current arrest, which was for showering illegally at midnight in the Wyndham Regional High School. He asked what Probation knew about Blankenship's present relationship with his family.

"You kiddin'?" the PO asked. "They're all locked down. The whole family's inside. The old man's in Bridgewater. Little Donny's in San Quentin or somewhere. Their dog's in the pound."

Elliot had lunch alone in the hospital staff cafeteria. On the far side of the double-glazed windows, the day was darkening as an expected snowstorm gathered. Along Route 7, ancient elms stood frozen against the gray sky. When he had finished his sandwich and coffee, he sat staring out at the winter afternoon. His anger had given way to an insistent anxiety.

On the way back to his office, he stopped at the hospital gift shop for a copy of *Sports Illustrated* and a candy bar. When he was inside again, he closed the door and put his feet up. It was Friday and he had no appointments for the remainder of the day, nothing to do but write a few letters and read the office mail.

Elliot's cubicle in the social-services department was windowless and lined with bookshelves. When he found himself unable to concentrate on the magazine and without any heart for his paperwork, he ran his eye over the row of books beside his chair. There were volumes by Heinrich Muller and Carlos Casteneda, Jones's life of Freud, and *The Golden Bough*. The books aroused a revulsion in Elliot. Their present uselessness repelled him.

Over and over again, detail by detail, he tried to recall his conversation with Blankenship.

"You were never there," he heard himself explaining. He was trying to get the whole incident straightened out after the fact. Something was wrong. Dread crept over him like a paralysis. He ate his candy bar without tasting it. He knew that the craving for sweets was itself a bad sign.

Blankenship had misappropriated someone else's dream and made it his own. It made no difference whether you had been there, after all. The dreams had crossed the ocean. They were in the air.

He took his glasses off and put them on his desk and sat with his arms folded, looking into the well of light from his desk lamp. There seemed to be nothing but whirl inside him. Unwelcome things came and went in his mind's eye. His heart beat faster. He could not control the headlong promiscuity of his thoughts.

It was possible to imagine larval dreams traveling in suspended animation undetectable in a host brain. They could be divided and regenerate like flatworms, hide in seams and bedding, in war stories, laughter, snapshots. They could rot your socks and turn your memory into a black-and-green blister. Green for the hills, black for the sky above. At daybreak they hung themselves up in rows like bats. At dusk they went out to look for dreamers.

Elliot put his jacket on and went into the outer office, where the secretary sat frowning into the measured sound and light of her machine. She must enjoy its sleekness and order, he thought. She was divorced. Four redheaded kids between ten and seventeen lived with her in an unpainted house across from Stop & Shop. Elliot liked her and had come to find her attractive. He managed a smile for her.

"Ethel, I think I'm going to pack it in," he declared. It seemed awkward to be leaving early without a reason.

"Jack wants to talk to you before you go, Chas."

Elliot looked at her blankly.

Then his colleague, Jack Sprague, having heard his voice,

called from the adjoining cubicle. "Chas, what about Sunday's games? Shall I call you with the spread?"

"I don't know," Elliot said. "I'll phone you tomorrow."

"This is a big decision for him," Jack Sprague told the secretary. "He might lose twenty-five bucks."

At present, Elliot drew a slightly higher salary than Jack Sprague, although Jack had a Ph.D. and Elliot was simply an M.S.W. Different branches of the state government employed them.

"Twenty-five bucks," said the woman. "If you guys have no better use for twenty-five bucks, give it to me."

"Where are you off to, by the way?" Sprague asked.

Elliot began to answer, but for a moment no reply occurred to him. He shrugged. "I have to get back," he finally stammered. "I promised Grace."

"Was that Blankenship I saw leaving?"

Elliot nodded.

"It's February," Jack said. "How come he's not in Florida?"

"I don't know," Elliot said. He put on his coat and walked to the door. "I'll see you."

"Have a nice weekend," the secretary said. She and Sprague looked after him indulgently as he walked toward the main corridor.

"Are Chas and Grace going out on the town?" she said to Sprague. "What do you think?"

"That would be the day," Sprague said. "Tomorrow he'll come back over here and read all day. He spends every weekend holed up in this goddamn office while she does something or other at the church." He shook his head. "Every night he's at AA and she's home alone."

Ethel savored her overbite. "Jack," she said teasingly, "are you thinking what I think you're thinking? Shame on you."

"I'm thinking I'm glad I'm not him, that's what I'm thinking. That's as much as I'll say."

"Yeah, well, I don't care," Ethel said. "Two salaries and no kids, that's the way to go, boy."

★

Elliot went out through the automatic doors of the emergency bay and the cold closed over him. He walked across the hospital parking lot with his eyes on the pavement, his hands thrust deep in his overcoat pockets, skirting patches of shattered ice. There was no wind, but the motionless air stung; the metal frames of his glasses burned his skin. Curlicues of mud-brown ice coated the soiled snowbanks along the street. Although it was still afternoon, the street lights had come on.

The lock on his car door had frozen and he had to breathe on the keyhole to fit the key. When the engine turned over, Jussi Björling's recording of the Handel Largo filled the car interior. He snapped it off at once.

Halted at the first stoplight, he began to feel the want of a destination. The fear and impulse to flight that had got him out of the office faded, and he had no desire to go home. He was troubled by a peculiar impatience that might have been with time itself. It was as though he were waiting for something. The sensation made him feel anxious; it was unfamiliar but not altogether unpleasant. When the light changed he drove on, past the Gulf station and the firehouse and between the greens of Ilford Common. At the far end of the common he swung into the parking lot of the Packard Conway Library and stopped with the engine running. What he was experiencing, he thought, was the principle of possibility.

He turned off the engine and went out again into the cold. Behind the leaded library windows he could see the librarian pouring coffee in her tiny private office. The librarian was a Quaker of socialist principles named Candace Music, who was Elliot's cousin.

The Conway Library was all dark wood and etched mirrors, a Gothic saloon. Years before, out of work and booze-whipped, Elliot had gone to hide there. Because Candace was a classicist's widow and knew some Greek, she was one of the few people in the valley with whom Elliot had cared to speak in those days. Eventually, it had seemed to him that all their conversations tended toward Vietnam, so he had gone less and less often. Elliot was the only Vietnam veteran Candace knew well enough to chat with, and he had come to suspect that he was being probed for the edification of the East Ilford Friends Meeting. At that time he had still pretended to talk easily about his war and had prepared little discourses and picaresque anecdotes to recite on demand. Earnest seekers like Candace had caused him great secret distress.

Candace came out of her office to find him at the checkout desk. He watched her brow furrow with concern as she composed a smile. "Chas, what a surprise. You haven't been in for an age."

"Sure I have, Candace. I went to all the Wednesday films last fall. I work just across the road."

"I know, dear," Candace said. "I always seem to miss you."

A cozy fire burned in the hearth, an antique brass clock ticked along on the marble mantel above it. On a couch near the fireplace an old man sat upright, his mouth open, asleep among half a dozen soiled plastic bags. Two teenage girls whispered over their homework at a table under the largest window.

"Now that I'm here," he said, laughing, "I can't remember what I came to get."

"Stay and get warm," Candace told him. "Got a minute? Have a cup of coffee."

Elliot had nothing but time, but he quickly realized that he did not want to stay and pass it with Candace. He had no clear idea of why he had come to the library. Standing at the checkout desk, he accepted coffee. She attended him with an air of benign supervision, as though he were a Chinese peasant and she a medical missionary, like her father. Candace was tall and plain, more handsome in her middle sixties than she had ever been.

"Why don't we sit down?"

He allowed her to gentle him into a chair by the fire. They made a threesome with the sleeping old man.

"Have you given up translating, Chas? I hope not."

"Not at all," he said. Together they had once rendered a few fragments of Sophocles into verse. She was good at clever rhymes.

"You come in so rarely, Chas. Ted's books go to waste."

After her husband's death, Candace had donated his books

to the Conway, where they reposed in a reading room inscribed to his memory, untouched among foreign-language volumes, local genealogies, and books in large type for the elderly.

"I have a study in the barn," he told Candace. "I work there. When I have time." The lie was absurd, but he felt the need of it.

"And you're working with Vietnam veterans," Candace declared.

"Supposedly," Elliot said. He was growing impatient with her nodding solicitude.

"Actually," he said, "I came in for the new Oxford *Classical World*. I thought you'd get it for the library and I could have a look before I spent my hard-earned cash."

Candace beamed. "You've come to the right place, Chas, I'm happy to say." He thought she looked disproportionately happy. "I have it."

"Good," Elliot said, standing. "I'll just take it, then. I can't really stay."

Candace took his cup and saucer and stood as he did. When the library telephone rang, she ignored it, reluctant to let him go. "How's Grace?" she asked.

"Fine," Elliot said. "Grace is well."

At the third ring she went to the desk. When her back was turned he hesitated for a moment and then went outside.

The gray afternoon had softened into night, and it was snowing. The falling snow whirled like a furious mist in the headlight beams on Route 7 and settled implacably on Elliot's cheeks and eyelids. His heart, for no good reason, leaped up in childlike expectation. He had run away from a dream and encountered possibility. He felt in possession of a promise. He began to walk toward the roadside lights.

Only gradually did he begin to understand what had brought him there and what the happy anticipation was that fluttered in his breast. Drinking, he had started his evenings from the Conway Library. He would arrive hung over in the early afternoon to browse and read. When the old pain rolled in with dusk, he would walk down to the Midway Tavern for a remedy. Standing in the snow outside the library, he realized that he had contrived to promise himself a drink.

Ahead, through the storm, he could see the beer signs in the Midway's window warm and welcoming. Snowflakes spun around his head like an excitement.

Outside the Midway's package store, he paused with his hand on the door-knob. There was an old man behind the counter whom Elliot remembered from his drinking days. When he was inside, he realized that the old man neither knew nor cared who he was. The package store was thick with dust; it was on the counter, the shelves, the bottles themselves. The old counterman looked dusty. Elliot bought a bottle of King William Scotch and put it in the inside pocket of his overcoat.

Passing the windows of the Midway Tavern, Elliot could see the ranks of bottles aglow behind the bar. The place was crowded with men leaving the afternoon shifts at the shoe and felt factories. No one turned to note him when he passed inside. There was a single stool vacant at the bar and he took it. His heart beat faster. Bruce Springsteen was on the jukebox.

The bartender was a club fighter from Pittsfield called Jackie G., with whom Elliot had often gossiped. Jackie G. greeted him as though he had been in the previous evening. "Say, babe?"

"How do," Elliot said.

A couple of the men at the bar eyed his shirt and tie. Confronted with the bartender, he felt impelled to explain his presence. "Just thought I'd stop by," he told Jackie G. "Just thought I'd have one. Saw the light. The snow . . ." He chuckled expansively.

"Good move," the bartender said. "Scotch?"

"Double," Elliot said.

When he shoved 2 dollars forward along the bar, Jackie G. pushed one of the bills back to him. "Happy hour, babe."

"Ah," Elliot said. He watched Jackie pour the double. "Not a moment too soon."

For five minutes or so, Elliot sat in his car in the barn with the engine running and his Handel tape on full volume. He had driven over from East Ilford in a Baroque ecstasy, swinging and swaying and singing along. When the tape ended, he turned off the engine and poured some Scotch into an apple-juice container to store providentially beneath the car seat. Then he took the tape and the Scotch into the house with him. He was lying on the sofa in the dark living room listening to the Largo, when he heard his wife's car in the driveway. By the time Grace had made her way up the icy back-porch steps, he was able to hide the Scotch and rinse his glass clean in the kitchen sink. The drinking life, he thought, was lived moment by moment.

Soon she was in the tiny cloakroom struggling off with her overcoat. In the process she knocked over a cross-country ski, which stood propped against the cloakroom wall. It had been more than a year since Elliot had used the skis.

She came into the kitchen and sat down at the table to take off her boots. Her lean, freckled face was flushed with the cold, but her eyes looked weary. "I wish you'd put those skis down in the barn," she told him. "You never use them."

"I always like to think," Elliot said, "that I'll start the morning off skiing."

"Well, you never do," she said. "How long have you been home?"

"Practically just walked in," he said. Her pointing out that he no longer skied in the morning enraged him. "I stopped at the Conway Library to get the new Oxford *Classical World*. Candace ordered it."

Her look grew troubled. She had caught something in his voice. With dread and bitter satisfaction, Elliot watched his wife detect the smell of whiskey.

"Oh God," she said. "I don't believe it."

Let's get it over with, he thought. Let's have the song and dance.

She sat up straight in her chair and looked at him in fear.

"Oh, Chas," she said, "how could you?"

For a moment he was tempted to try to explain it all.

"The fact is," Elliot told his wife, "I hate people who start the day cross-country skiing."

She shook her head in denial and leaned her forehead on her palm and cried.

He looked into the kitchen window and saw his own distorted image. "The fact is I think I'll start tomorrow morning by stringing head-high razor wire across Anderson's trail."

The Andersons were the Elliots' nearest neighbors. Loyall Anderson was a full professor of government at the state university, 30 miles away. Anderson and his wife were blond and both of them were over 6 feet tall. They had two blond children, who qualified for the gifted class in the local school but attended regular classes in token of the Andersons' opposition to élitism.

"Sure," Elliot said. "Stringing wire's good exercise. It's life-affirming in its own way."

The Andersons started each and every day with a brisk morning glide along a trail that they partly maintained. They skied well and presented a pleasing wholesome sight. If, in the course of their adventure, they encountered a snowmobile, Darlene Anderson would affect to choke and cough, indicating her displeasure. If the snowmobile approached them from behind and the trail was narrow, the Andersons would decline to let it pass, asserting their statutory right-of-way.

"I don't want to hear your violent fantasies," Grace said.

Elliot was picturing razor wire, the Army kind. He was picturing the decapitated Andersons, their blood and jaunty ski caps bright on the white trail. He was picturing their severed heads, their earnest blue eyes and large white teeth reflecting the virginal morning snow. Although Elliot hated snowmobiles, he hated the Andersons far more.

He looked at his wife and saw that she had stopped crying. Her long elegant face was rigid and lipless.

"Know what I mean? One string at Mommy and Daddy level for Loyall and Darlene. And a bitty wee string at kiddie level for Skippy and Samantha, those cunning little whizzes."

"Stop it," she said to him.

"Sorry," Elliot told her.

Stiff with shame, he went and took his bottle out of the cabinet into which he had thrust it and poured a drink. He was aware of her eyes on him. As he drank, a fragment from old Music's translation of *Medea* came into his mind. "Old friend, I have to weep. The gods and I went mad together and made

things as they are." It was such a waste; eighteen months of
struggle thrown away. But there was no way to get the stuff
back in the bottle.

"I'm very sorry," he said. "You know I'm very sorry, don't
you, Grace?"

The delectable Handel arias spun on in the next room.

"You must stop," she said. "You must make yourself stop
before it takes over."

"It's out of my hands," Elliot said. He showed her his empty
hands. "It's beyond me."

"You'll lose your job, Chas." She stood at the table and
leaned on it, staring wide-eyed at him. Drunk as he was, the
panic in her voice frightened him. "You'll end up in jail again."

"One engages," Elliot said, "and then one sees."

"How can you have done it?" she demanded. "You promised
me."

"First the promises," Elliot said, "and then the rest."

"Last time was supposed to be the last time," she said.

"Yes," he said, "I remember."

"I can't stand it," she said. "You reduce me to hysterics."
She wrung her hands for him to see. "See? Here I am, I'm in
hysterics."

"What can I say?" Elliot asked. He went to the bottle and
refilled his glass. "Maybe you shouldn't watch."

"You want me to be forbearing, Chas? I'm not going to be."

"The last thing I want," Elliot said, "is an argument."

"I'll give you a fucking argument. You didn't have to drink.
All you had to do was come home."

"That must have been the problem," he said.

Then he ducked, alert at the last possible second to the missile
that came for him at hairline level. Covering up, he heard the
shattering of glass, and a fine rain of crystals enveloped him. She
had sailed the sugar bowl at him; it had smashed against the wall
above his head and there was sugar and glass in his hair.

"You bastard!" she screamed. "You are undermining me!"

"You ought not to throw things at me," Elliot said. "I don't
throw things at you."

He left her frozen into her follow-through and went into the

living room to turn the music off. When he returned she was
leaning back against the wall, rubbing her right elbow with her
left hand. Her eyes were bright. She had picked up one of her
boots from the middle of the kitchen floor and stood holding it.

"What the hell do you mean, that must have been the
problem?"

He set his glass on the edge of the sink with an unsteady
hand and turned to her. "What do I mean? I mean that most of
the time I'm putting one foot in front of the other like a good
soldier and I'm out of it from the neck up. But there are times
when I don't think I will ever be dead enough – or dead long
enough – to get the taste of this life off my teeth. That's what I
mean!"

She looked at him dry-eyed. "Poor fella," she said.

"What you have to understand, Grace, is that this drink I'm
having" – he raised the glass toward her in a gesture of salute –
"is the only worthwhile thing I've done in the last year and a
half. It's the only thing in my life that means jack shit, the closest
thing to satisfaction I've had. Now how can you begrudge me
that? It's the best I'm capable of."

"You'll go too far," she said to him. "You'll see."

"What's that, Grace? A threat to walk?" He was grinding his
teeth. "Don't make me laugh. You, walk? You, the friend of the
unfortunate?"

"Don't you hit me," she said when she looked at his face.
"Don't you dare."

"You, the Christian Queen of Calvary, walk? Why, I don't
believe that for a minute."

She ran a hand through her hair and bit her lip. "No, we
stay," she said. Anger and distraction made her look young. Her
cheeks blazed rosy against the general pallor of her skin. "In my
family we stay until the fella dies. That's the tradition. We stay
and pour it for them and they die."

He put his drink down and shook his head.

"I thought we'd come through," Grace said. "I was sure."

"No," Elliot said. "Not altogether."

They stood in silence for a minute. Elliot sat down at the

oilcloth-covered table. Grace walked around it and poured herself
a whiskey.

"You are undermining me, Chas. You are making things
impossible for me and I just don't know." She drank and winced.
"I'm not going to stay through another drunk. I'm telling you
right now. I haven't got it in me. I'll die."

He did not want to look at her. He watched the flakes settle
against the glass of the kitchen door. "Do what you feel the need
of," he said.

"I just can't take it," she said. Her voice was not scolding but
measured and reasonable. "It's February. And I went to court
this morning and lost Vopotik."

Once again, he thought, my troubles are going to be obviated
by those of the deserving poor. He said, "Which one was that?"

"Don't you remember them? The three-year-old with the
broken fingers?"

He shrugged. Grace sipped her whiskey.

"I told you. I said I had a three-year-old with broken fingers,
and you said, 'Maybe he owed somebody money.'"

"Yes," he said, "I remember now."

"You ought to see the Vopotiks, Chas. The woman is young
and obese. She's so young that for a while I thought I could get
to her as a juvenile. The guy is a biker. They believe the kid
came from another planet to control their lives. They believe this
literally, both of them."

"You shouldn't get involved that way," Elliot said. "You
should leave it to the caseworkers."

"They scared their first caseworker all the way to California.
They were following me to work."

"You didn't tell me."

"Are you kidding?" she asked. "Of course I didn't." To
Elliot's surprise, his wife poured herself a second whiskey. "You
know how they address the child? As 'dude.' She says to it,
'Hey, dude.'" Grace shuddered with loathing. "You can't imagine! The woman munching Twinkies. The kid smelling of
shit. They're high morning, noon, and night, but you can't get
anybody for that these days."

"People must really hate it," Elliot said, "when somebody tells them they're not treating their kids right."

"They definitely don't want to hear it," Grace said. "You're right." She sat stirring her drink, frowning into the glass. "The Vopotik child will die, I think."

"Surely not," Elliot said.

"This one I think will die," Grace said. She took a deep breath and puffed out her cheeks and looked at him forlornly. "The situation's extreme. Of course, sometimes you wonder whether it makes any difference. That's the big question, isn't it?"

"I would think," Elliot said, "that would be the one question you didn't ask."

"But you do," she said. "You wonder. Ought they to live at all? To continue the cycle?" She put a hand to her hair and shook her head as if in confusion. "Some of these folks, my God, the poor things cannot put Wednesday on top of Tuesday to save their lives."

"It's a trick," Elliot agreed, "a lot of them can't manage."

"And kids are small, they're handy and underfoot. They make noise. They can't hurt you back."

"I suppose child abuse is something people can do together," Elliot said.

"Some kids are obnoxious. No question about it."

"I wouldn't know," Elliot said.

"Maybe you should stop complaining. Maybe you're better off. Maybe your kids are better off unborn."

"Better off or not," Elliot said, "it looks like they'll stay that way."

"I mean our kids, of course," Grace said. "I'm not blaming you, understand? It's just that here we are with you drunk again and me losing Vopotik, so I thought why not get into the big unaskable questions." She got up and folded her arms and began to pace up and down the kitchen. "Oh," she said when her eye fell upon the bottle, "that's good stuff, Chas. You won't mind if I have another? I'll leave you enough to get loaded on."

Elliot watched her pour. So much pain, he thought; such

anger and confusion. He was tired of pain, anger, and confusion; they were what had got him in trouble that very morning.

The liquor seemed to be giving him a perverse lucidity when all he now required was oblivion. His rage, especially, was intact in its salting of alcohol. Its contours were palpable and bleeding at the borders. Booze was good for rage. Booze could keep it burning through the darkest night.

"What happened in court?" he asked his wife.

She was leaning on one arm against the wall, her long, strong body flexed at the hip. Holding her glass, she stared angrily toward the invisible fields outside. "I lost the child," she said.

Elliot thought that a peculiar way of putting it. He said nothing.

"The court convened in an atmosphere of high hilarity. It may be Hate Month around here but it was buddy-buddy over at Ilford Courthouse. The room was full of bikers and bikers' lawyers. A colorful crowd. There was a lot of bonding." She drank and shivered. "They didn't think too well of me. They don't think too well of broads as lawyers. Neither does the judge. The judge has the common touch. He's one of the boys."

"Which judge?" Elliot asked.

"Buckley. A man of about sixty. Know him? Lots of veins on his nose?"

Elliot shrugged.

"I thought I had done my homework," Grace told him. "But suddenly I had nothing but paper. No witnesses. It was Margolis at Valley Hospital who spotted the radiator burns. He called us in the first place. Suddenly he's got to keep his reservation for a campsite in St. John. So Buckley threw his deposition out." She began to chew on a fingernail. "The caseworkers have vanished – one's in LA, the other's in Nepal. I went in there and got run over. I lost the child."

"It happens all the time," Elliot said. "Doesn't it?"

"This one shouldn't have been lost, Chas. These people aren't simply confused. They're weird. They stink."

"You go messing in anybody's life," Elliot said, "that's what you'll find."

"If the child stays in that house," she said, "he's going to die."

"You did your best," he told his wife. "Forget it."

She pushed the bottle away. She was holding a water glass that was almost a third full of whiskey.

"That's what the commissioner said."

Elliot was thinking of how she must have looked in court to the cherry-faced judge and the bikers and their lawyers. Like the schoolteachers who had tormented their childhoods, earnest and tight-assed, humorless and self-righteous. It was not surprising that things had gone against her.

He walked over to the window and faced his reflection again. "Your optimism always surprises me."

"My optimism? Where I grew up our principal cultural expression was the funeral. Whatever keeps me going, it isn't optimism."

"No?" he asked. "What is it?"

"I forget," she said.

"Maybe it's your religious perspective. Your sense of the divine plan."

She sighed in exasperation. "Look, I don't think I want to fight anymore. I'm sorry I threw the sugar at you. I'm not your keeper. Pick on someone your own size."

"Sometimes," Elliot said, "I try to imagine what it's like to believe that the sky is full of care and concern."

"You want to take everything from me, do you?" She stood leaning against the back of her chair. "That you can't take. It's the only part of my life you can't mess up."

He was thinking that if it had not been for her he might not have survived. There could be no forgiveness for that. "Your life? You've got all this piety strung out between Monadnock and Central America. And look at yourself. Look at your life."

"Yes," she said, "look at it."

"You should have been a nun. You don't know how to live."

"I know that," she said. "That's why I stopped doing counseling. Because I'd rather talk the law than life." She turned to him. "You got everything I had, Chas. What's left I absolutely require."

"I swear I would rather be a drunk," Elliot said, "than force myself to believe such trivial horseshit."

"Well, you're going to have to do it without a straight man," she said, "because this time I'm not going to be here for you. Believe it or not."

"I don't believe it," Elliot said. "Not my Grace."

"You're really good at this," she told him. "You make me feel ashamed of my own name."

"I love your name," he said.

The telephone rang. They let it ring three times, and then Elliot went over and answered it.

"Hey, who's that?" a good-humored voice on the phone demanded.

Elliot recited their phone number.

"Hey, I want to talk to your woman, man. Put her on."

"I'll give her a message," Elliot said.

"You put your woman on, man. Run and get her."

Elliot looked at the receiver. He shook his head. "Mr. Vopotik?"

"Never you fuckin' mind, man. I don't want to talk to you. I want to talk to the skinny bitch."

Elliot hung up.

"Is it him?" she asked.

"I guess so."

They waited for the phone to ring again and it shortly did.

"I'll talk to him," Grace said. But Elliot already had the phone.

"Who are you, asshole?" the voice inquired. "What's your fuckin' name, man?"

"Elliot," Elliot said.

"Hey, don't hang up on me, Elliot. I won't put up with that. I told you go get that skinny bitch, man. You go do it."

There were sounds of festivity in the background on the other end of the line – a stereo and drunken voices.

"Hey," the voice declared, "Hey, don't keep me waiting, man."

"What do you want to say to her?" Elliot asked.

"That's none of your fucking business, fool. Do what I told you."

"My wife is resting," Elliot said. "I'm taking her calls."

He was answered by a shout of rage. He put the phone aside for a moment and finished his glass of whiskey. When he picked it up again the man on the line was screaming at him. "That bitch tried to break up my family, man! She almost got away with it. You know what kind of pain my wife went through?"

"What kind?" Elliot asked.

For a few seconds he heard only the noise of the party. "Hey, you're not drunk, are you, fella?"

"Certainly not," Elliot insisted.

"You tell that skinny bitch she's gonna pay for what she did to my family, man. You tell her she can run but she can't hide. I don't care where you go – California, anywhere – I'll get to you."

"Now that I have you on the phone," Elliot said, "I'd like to ask you a couple of questions. Promise you won't get mad?"

"Stop it!" Grace said to him. She tried to wrench the phone from his grasp but he clutched it to his chest.

"Do you keep a journal?" Elliot asked the man on the phone. "What's your hat size?"

"Maybe you think I can't get to you," the man said. "But I can get to you, man. I don't care who you are, I'll get to you. The brothers will get to you."

"Well, there's no need to go to California. You know where we live."

"For God's sake," Grace said.

"Fuckin' right," the man on the telephone said. "Fuckin' right I know."

"Come on over," Elliot said.

"How's that?" the man on the phone asked.

"I said come on over. We'll talk about space travel. Comets and stuff. We'll talk astral projection. The moons of Jupiter."

"You're making a mistake, fucker."

"Come on over," Elliot insisted. "Bring your fat wife and your beat-up kid. Don't be embarrassed if your head's a little small."

The telephone was full of music and shouting. Elliot held it away from his ear.

"Good work," Grace said to him when he had replaced the receiver.

"I hope he comes," Elliot said. "I'll pop him."

He went carefully down the cellar stairs, switched on the overhead light, and began searching among the spiderwebbed shadows and fouled fishing line for his shotgun. It took him fifteen minutes to find it and his cleaning case. While he was still downstairs, he heard the telephone ring again and his wife answer it. He came upstairs and spread his shooting gear across the kitchen table. "Was that him?"

She nodded wearily. "He called back to play us the chain saw."

"I've heard that melody before," Elliot said.

He assembled his cleaning rod and swabbed out the shotgun barrel. Grace watched him, a hand to her forehead. "God," she said. "What have I done? I'm so drunk."

"Most of the time," Elliot said, sighting down the barrel, "I'm helpless in the face of human misery. Tonight I'm ready to reach out."

"I'm finished," Grace said. "I'm through, Chas. I mean it."

Elliot rammed three red shells into the shotgun and pumped one forward into the breech with a satisfying report. "Me, I'm ready for some radical problem-solving. I'm going to spray that no-neck Slovak all over the yard."

"He isn't a Slovak," Grace said. She stood in the middle of the kitchen with her eyes closed. Her face was chalk white.

"What do you mean?" Elliot demanded. "Certainly he's a Slovak."

"No he's not," Grace said.

"Fuck him anyway. I don't care what he is. I'll grease his ass."

He took a handful of deer shells from the box and stuffed them in his jacket pockets.

"I'm not going to stay with you, Chas. Do you understand me?"

Elliot walked to the window and peered out at his driveway. "He won't be alone. They travel in packs."

"For God's sake!" Grace cried, and in the next instant bolted for the downstairs bathroom. Elliot went out, turned off the porch light and switched on a spotlight over the barn door. Back inside, he could hear Grace in the toilet being sick. He turned off the light in the kitchen.

He was still standing by the window when she came up behind him. It seemed strange and fateful to be standing in the dark near her, holding the shotgun. He felt ready for anything.

"I can't leave you alone down here drunk with a loaded shotgun," she said. "How can I?"

"Go upstairs," he said.

"If I went upstairs it would mean I didn't care what happened. Do you understand? If I go it means I don't care anymore. Understand?"

"Stop asking me if I understand," Elliot said. "I understand fine."

"I can't think," she said in a sick voice. "Maybe I don't care. I don't know. I'm going upstairs."

"Good," Elliot said.

When she was upstairs, Elliot took his shotgun and the whiskey into the dark living room and sat down in an armchair beside one of the lace-curtained windows. The powerful barn light illuminated the length of his driveway and the whole of the back yard. From the window at which he sat, he commanded a view of several miles in the direction of East Ilford. The two-lane blacktop road that ran there was the only one along which an enemy could pass.

He drank and watched the snow, toying with the safety of his 12-gauge Remington. He felt neither anxious nor angry now but only impatient to be done with whatever the night would bring. Drunkenness and the silent rhythm of the falling snow combined to make him feel outside of time and syntax.

Sitting in the dark room, he found himself confronting Blankenship's dream. He saw the bunkers and wire of some long-lost perimeter. The rank smell of night came back to him, the dread evening and quick dusk, the mysteries of outer darkness: fear, combat, and death. Enervated by liquor, he began to cry. Elliot was sympathetic with other people's tears but ashamed of his own. He thought of his own tears as childish and excremental. He stifled whatever it was that had started them.

Now his whiskey tasted thin as water. Beyond the lightly frosted glass, illuminated snowflakes spun and settled sleepily on weighted pine boughs. He had found a life beyond the war after all, but in it he was still sitting in darkness, armed, enraged, waiting.

His eyes grew heavy as the snow came down. He felt as though he could be drawn up into the storm and he began to imagine that. He imagined his life with all its artifacts and appetites easing up the spout into white oblivion, everything obviated and foreclosed. He thought maybe he could go for that.

When he awakened, his left hand had gone numb against the trigger guard of his shotgun. The living room was full of pale, delicate light. He looked outside and saw that the storm was done with and the sky radiant and cloudless. The sun was still below the horizon.

Slowly Elliot got to his feet. The throbbing poison in his limbs served to remind him of the state of things. He finished the glass of whiskey on the windowsill beside his easy chair. Then he went to the hall closet to get a ski jacket, shouldered his shotgun, and went outside.

There were two cleared acres behind his house; beyond them a trail descended into a hollow of pine forest and frozen swamp. Across the hollow, white pastures stretched to the ridge-line, lambent under the lightening sky. A line of skeletal elms weighted with snow marked the course of frozen Shawmut Brook.

He found a pair of ski goggles in a jacket pocket and put them on and set out toward the tree line, gripping the shotgun, step by careful step in the knee-deep snow. Two raucous crows wheeled high overhead, their cries exploding the morning's silence. When the sun came over the ridge, he stood where he was and took in a deep breath. The risen sun warmed his face and he closed his eyes. It was windless and very cold.

Only after he had stood there for a while did he realize how tired he had become. The weight of the gun taxed him. It seemed infinitely wearying to contemplate another single step in the snow. He opened his eyes and closed them again. With sunup the world had gone blazing blue and white, and even with his tinted goggles its whiteness dazzled him and made his head ache. Behind his eyes, the hypnagogic patterns formed a monsoon-heavy tropical sky. He yawned. More than anything, he wanted to lie down in the soft, pure snow. If he could do that, he was certain he could go to sleep at once.

He stood in the middle of the field and listened to the crows. Fear, anger, and sleep were the three primary conditions of life. He had learned that over there. Once he had thought fear the worst, but he had learned that the worst was anger. Nothing could fix it; neither alcohol nor medicine. It was a worm. It left him no peace. Sleep was the best.

He opened his eyes and pushed on until he came to the brow that overlooked the swamp. Just below, gliding along among the frozen cattails and bare scrub maple, was a man on skis. Elliot stopped to watch the man approach.

The skier's face was concealed by a red-and-blue ski mask. He wore snow goggles, a blue jumpsuit, and a red woolen Norwegian hat. As he came, he leaned into the turns of the trail, moving silently and gracefully along. At the foot of the slope on which Elliot stood, the man looked up, saw him, and slid to a halt. The man stood staring at him for a moment and then began to herringbone up the slope. In no time at all the skier stood no more than 10 feet away, removing his goggles, and inside the woolen mask Elliot recognized the clear blue eyes of his neighbor, Professor Loyall Anderson. The shotgun Elliot was carrying seemed to grow heavier. He yawned and shook his head, trying unsuccessfully to clear it. The sight of Anderson's eyes gave him a thrill of revulsion.

"What are you after?" the young professor asked him, nodding toward the shotgun Elliot was cradling.

"Whatever there is," Elliot said.

Anderson took a quick look at the distant pasture behind him and then turned back to Elliot. The mouth hole of the professor's mask filled with teeth. Elliot thought that Anderson's teeth were quite as he had imagined them earlier. "Well, Polonski's cows are locked up," the professor said. "So they at least are safe."

Elliot realized that the professor had made a joke and was smiling. "Yes," he agreed.

Professor Anderson and his wife had been the moving force behind an initiative to outlaw the discharge of firearms within the boundaries of East Ilford Township. The initiative had been defeated, because East Ilford was not that kind of town.

"I think I'll go over by the river," Elliot said. He said it only to have something to say, to fill the silence before Anderson spoke again. He was afraid of what Anderson might say to him and of what might happen.

"You know," Anderson said, "that's a bird sanctuary over there now."

"Sure," Elliot agreed.

Outfitted as he was, the professor attracted Elliot's anger in an elemental manner. The mask made him appear a kind of doll, a kachina figure or a marionette. His eyes and mouth, all on their own, were disagreeable.

Elliot began to wonder if Anderson could smell the whiskey on his breath. He pushed the little red bull's-eye safety button on his gun to Off.

"Seriously," Anderson said, "I'm always having to run hunters out of there. Some people don't understand the word 'posted.'"

"I would never do that," Elliot said. "I would be afraid."

Anderson nodded his head. He seemed to be laughing. "Would you?" he asked Elliot merrily.

In imagination, Elliot rested the tip of his shotgun barrel against Anderson's smiling teeth. If he fired a load of deer shot into them, he thought, they might make a noise like broken china. "Yes," Elliot said. "I wouldn't know who they were or where they'd been. They might resent my being alive. Telling them where they could shoot and where not."

Anderson's teeth remained in place. "That's pretty strange," he said. "I mean, to talk about resenting someone for being alive."

"It's all relative," Elliot said. "They might think, 'Why should he be alive when some brother of mine isn't?' Or they might think, 'Why should he be alive when I'm not?'"

"Oh," Anderson said.

"You see?" Elliot said. Facing Anderson, he took a long step backward. "All relative."

"Yes," Anderson said.

"That's so often true, isn't it?" Elliot asked. "Values are often relative."

"Yes," Anderson said. Elliot was relieved to see that he had stopped smiling.

"I've hardly slept, you know," Elliot told Professor Anderson. "Hardly at all. All night. I've been drinking."

"Oh," Anderson said. He licked his lips in the mouth of the mask. "You should get some rest."

"You're right," Elliot said.

"Well," Anderson said, "got to go now."

Elliot thought he sounded a little thick in the tongue. A little slow in the jaw.

"It's a nice day," Elliot said, wanting now to be agreeable.

"It's great," Anderson said, shuffling on his skis.

"Have a nice day," Elliot said.

"Yes," Anderson said, and pushed off.

Elliot rested the shotgun across his shoulders and watched Anderson withdraw through the frozen swamp. It was in fact a nice day, but Elliot took no comfort in the weather. He missed night and the falling snow.

As he walked back toward his house, he realized that now there would be whole days to get through, running before the antic energy of whiskey. The whiskey would drive him until he dropped. He shook his head in regret. "It's a revolution," he said aloud. He imagined himself talking to his wife.

Getting drunk was an insurrection, a revolution – a bad one. There would be outsize bogus emotions. There would be petty moral blackmail and cheap remorse. He had bullied Anderson with his violence and unhappiness, and Anderson would not forgive him. There would be damn little justice and no mercy.

Nearly to the house, he was startled by the desperate

feathered drumming of a pheasant's rush. He froze, and out of instinct brought the gun up in the direction of the sound. When he saw the bird break from its cover and take wing, he tracked it, took a breath, and fired once. The bird was a little flash of opulent color against the bright-blue sky. Elliot felt himself flying for a moment. The shot missed.

Lowering the gun, he remembered the deer shells he had loaded. A hit with concentrated shot would have pulverized the bird, and he was glad he had missed. He wished no harm to any creature. Then he thought of himself wishing no harm to any creature and began to feel fond and sorry for himself. As soon as he grew aware of the emotion he was indulging, he suppressed it. Pissing and moaning, mourning and weeping, that was the nature of the drug.

The shot echoed from the distant hills. Smoke hung in the air. He turned and looked behind him and saw, far away across the pasture, the tiny blue-and-red figure of Professor Anderson motionless against the snow. Then Elliot turned again toward his house and took a few labored steps and looked up to see his wife at the bedroom window. She stood perfectly still, and the morning sun lit her nakedness. He stopped where he was. She had heard the shot and run to the window. What had she thought to see? Burnt rags and blood on the snow. How relieved was she now? How disappointed?

Elliot thought he could feel his wife trembling at the window. She was hugging herself. Her hands clasped her shoulders. Elliot took his snow goggles off and shaded his eyes with his hand. He stood in the field staring.

The length of the gun was between them, he thought. Somehow she had got out in front of it, to the wrong side of the wire. If he looked long enough he would find everything out there. He would find himself down the sight.

How beautiful she is, he thought. The effect was striking. The window was so clear because he had washed it himself, with vinegar. At the best of times he was a difficult, fussy man.

Elliot began to hope for forgiveness. He leaned the shotgun on his forearm and raised his left hand and waved to her. Show a hand, he thought. Please just show a hand.

He was cold, but it had got light. He wanted no more than the gesture. It seemed to him that he could build another day on it. Another day was all you needed. He raised his hand higher and waited.

# AMY TAN

☆ ☆ ☆ ☆

# *Rules of the Game*

I was six when my mother taught me the art of invisible strength. It was a strategy for winning arguments, respect from others, and eventually, though neither of us knew it at the time, chess games.

"Bite back your tongue," scolded my mother when I cried loudly, yanking her hand toward the store that sold bags of salted plums. At home, she said, "Wise guy, he not go against wind. In Chinese we say, Come from South, blow with wind – poom! – North will follow. Strongest wind cannot be seen."

The next week I bit back my tongue as we entered the store with the forbidden candies. When my mother finished her shopping, she quietly plucked a small bag of plums from the rack and put it on the counter with the rest of the items.

My mother imparted her daily truths so she could help my older brothers and me rise above our circumstances. We lived in San Francisco's Chinatown. Like most of the other Chinese children who played in the back alleys of restaurants and curio shops, I didn't think we were poor. My bowl was always full, three five-course meals every day, beginning with a soup full of mysterious things I didn't want to know the names of.

We lived on Waverly Place, in a warm, clean, two-bedroom flat that sat above a small Chinese bakery specializing in steamed pastries and dim sum. In the early morning, when the alley was still quiet, I could smell fragrant red beans as they were cooked down to a pasty sweetness. By daybreak, our flat was heavy with the odor of fried sesame balls and sweet curried chicken crescents. From my bed, I would listen as my father got ready for work, then locked the door behind him, one-two-three clicks.

At the end of our two-block alley was a small sandlot

playground with swings and slides well-shined down the middle with use. The play area was bordered by wood-slat benches where old-country people sat cracking roasted watermelon seeds with their golden teeth and scattering the husks to an impatient gathering of gurgling pigeons. The best playground, however, was the dark alley itself. It was crammed with daily mysteries and adventures. My brothers and I would peer into the medicinal herb shop, watching old Li dole out onto a stiff sheet of white paper the right amount of insect shells, saffron-colored seeds, and pungent leaves for his ailing customers. It was said that he once cured a woman dying of an ancestral curse that had eluded the best of American doctors. Next to the pharmacy was a printer who specialized in gold-embossed wedding invitations and festive red banners.

Farther down the street was Ping Yuen Fish Market. The front window displayed a tank crowded with doomed fish and turtles struggling to gain footing on the slimy green-tiled sides. A hand-written sign informed tourists, "Within this store, is all for food, not for pet." Inside, the butchers with their blood-stained white smocks deftly gutted the fish while customers cried out their orders and shouted, "Give me your freshest," to which the butchers always protested, "All are freshest." On less crowded market days, we would inspect the crates of live frogs and crabs which we were warned not to poke, boxes of dried cuttlefish, and row upon row of iced prawns, squid, and slippery fish. The sanddabs made me shiver each time; their eyes lay on one flattened side and reminded me of my mother's story of a careless girl who ran into a crowded street and was crushed by a cab. "Was smash flat," reported my mother.

At the corner of the alley was Hong Sing's, a four-table café with a recessed stairwell in front that led to a door marked "Tradesmen." My brothers and I believed the bad people emerged from this door at night. Tourists never went to Hong Sing's, since the menu was printed only in Chinese. A Caucasian man with a big camera once posed me and my playmates in front of the restaurant. He had us move to the side of the picture window so the photo would capture the roasted duck with its head dangling from a juice-covered rope. After he took the picture, I told him he should go into Hong Sing's and eat dinner. When he smiled and asked me what they served, I shouted, "Guts and duck's feet and octopus gizzards!" Then I ran off with my friends, shrieking with laughter as we scampered across the alley and hid in the entryway grotto of the China Gem Company, my heart pounding with hope that he would chase us.

My mother named me after the street that we lived on: Waverly Place Jong, my official name for important American documents. But my family called me Meimei, "Little Sister." I was the youngest, the only daughter. Each morning before school, my mother would twist and yank on my thick black hair until she had formed two tightly wound pigtails. One day, as she struggled to weave a hard-toothed comb through my disobedient hair, I had a sly thought.

I asked her, "Ma, what is Chinese torture?" My mother shook her head. A bobby pin was wedged between her lips. She wetted her palm and smoothed the hair above my ear, then pushed the pin in so that it nicked sharply against my scalp.

"Who say this word?" she asked without a trace of knowing how wicked I was being. I shrugged my shoulders and said, "Some boy in my class said Chinese people do Chinese torture."

"Chinese people do many things," she said simply. "Chinese people do business, do medicine, do painting. Not lazy like American people. We do torture. Best torture."

My older brother Vincent was the one who actually got the chess set. We had gone to the annual Christmas party held at the First Chinese Baptist Church at the end of the alley. The missionary ladies had put together a Santa bag of gifts donated by members of another church. None of the gifts had names on them. There were separate sacks for boys and girls of different ages.

One of the Chinese parishioners had donned a Santa Claus costume and a stiff paper beard with cotton balls glued to it. I think the only children who thought he was the real thing were too young to know that Santa Claus was not Chinese. When my turn came up, the Santa man asked me how old I was. I thought it was a trick question; I was seven according to the American formula and eight by the Chinese calendar. I said I was born on

March 17, 1951. That seemed to satisfy him. He then solemnly asked if I had been a very, very good girl this year and did I believe in Jesus Christ and obey my parents. I knew the only answer to that. I nodded back with equal solemnity.

Having watched the other children opening their gifts, I already knew that the big gifts were not necessarily the nicest ones. One girl my age got a large coloring book of biblical characters, while a less greedy girl who selected a smaller box received a glass vial of lavender toilet water. The sound of the box was also important. A ten-year-old boy had chosen a box that jangled when he shook it. It was a tin globe of the world with a slit for inserting money. He must have thought it was full of dimes and nickels, because when he saw that it had just ten pennies, his face fell with such undisguised disappointment that his mother slapped the side of his head and led him out of the church hall, apologizing to the crowd for her son who had such bad manners he couldn't appreciate such a fine gift.

As I peered into the sack, I quickly fingered the remaining presents, testing their weight, imagining what they contained. I chose a heavy, compact one that was wrapped in shiny silver foil and a red satin ribbon. It was a twelve pack of Life Savers and I spent the rest of the party arranging and rearranging the candy tubes in the order of my favorites. My brother Winston chose wisely as well. His present turned out to be a box of intricate plastic parts; the instructions on the box proclaimed that when they were properly assembled he would have an authentic miniature replica of a World War II submarine.

Vincent got the chess set, which would have been a very decent present to get at a church Chistmas party, except it was obviously used and, as we discovered later, it was missing a black pawn and a white knight. My mother graciously thanked the unknown benefactor, saying, "Too good. Cost too much." At which point, an old lady with fine, white, wispy hair nodded toward our family and said with a whistling whisper, "Merry, merry Christmas."

When we got home, my mother told Vincent to throw the chess set away. "She not want it. We not want it," she said, tossing her head stiffly to the side with a tight, proud smile. My brothers had deaf ears. They were already lining up the chess pieces and reading from the dog-eared instruction book.

I watched Vincent and Winston play during Christmas week. The chessboard seemed to hold elaborate secrets waiting to be untangled. The chessmen were more powerful than old Li's magic herbs that cured ancestral curses. And my brothers wore such serious faces that I was sure something was at stake that was greater than avoiding the tradesmen's door to Hong Sing's.

"Let me! Let me!" I begged between games when one brother or the other would sit back with a deep sigh of relief and victory, the other annoyed, unable to let go of the outcome. Vincen at first refused to let me play, but when I offered my Life Savers as replacements for the buttons that filled in for the missing pieces, he relented. He chose the flavors: wild cherry for the black pawn and peppermint for the white knight. Winner could eat both.

As our mother sprinkled flour and rolled out small doughy circles for the steamed dumplings that would be our dinner that night, Vincent explained the rules, pointing to each piece. "You have sixteen pieces and so do I. One king and queen, two bishops, two knights, two castles, and eight pawns. The pawns can only move forward one step, except on the first move. Then they can move two. But they can only take men by moving crossways like this, except in the beginning, when you can move ahead and take another pawn."

"Why?" I asked as I moved my pawn. "Why can't they move more steps?"

"Because they're pawns," he said.

"But why do they go crossways to take other men? Why aren't there any women and children?"

"Why is the sky blue? Why must you always ask stupid questions?" asked Vincent. "This is a game. These are the rules. I didn't make them up. See. Here. In the book." He jabbed a page with a pawn in his hand. "Pawn. P-A-W-N. Pawn. Read it yourself."

My mother patted the flour off her hands. "Let me see book," she said quietly. She scanned the pages quickly, not reading the foreign English symbols, seeming to search deliberately for nothing in particular.

"This American rules," she concluded at last. "Every time people come out from foreign country, must know rules. You not know, judge say, Too bad, go back. They not telling you why so you can use their way go forward. They say, Don't know why, you find out yourself. But they knowing all the time. Better you take it, find out why yourself." She tossed her head back with a satisfied smile.

I found out about all the whys later. I read the rules and looked up all the big words in a dictionary. I borrowed books from the Chinatown library. I studied each chess piece, trying to absorb the power each contained.

I learned about opening moves and why it's important to control the center early on; the shortest distance between two points is straight down the middle. I learned about the middle game and why tactics between two adversaries are like clashing ideas; the one who plays better has the clearest plans for both attacking and getting out of traps. I learned why it is essential in the endgame to have foresight, a mathematical understanding of all possible moves, and patience; all weaknesses and advantages become evident to a strong adversary and are obscured to a tiring opponent. I discovered that for the whole game one must gather invisible strengths and see the endgame before the game begins.

I also found out why I should never reveal "why" to others. A little knowledge withheld is a great advantage one should store for future use. That is the power of chess. It is a game of secrets in which one must show and never tell.

I loved the secrets I found within the sixty-four black and white squares. I carefully drew a handmade chessboard and pinned it to the wall next to my bed, where at night I would stare for hours at imaginary battles. Soon I no longer lost any games or Life Savers, but I lost my adversaries. Winston and Vincent decided they were more interested in roaming the streets after school in their Hopalong Cassidy cowboy hats.

On a cold spring afternoon, while walking home from school, I detoured through the playground at the end of our alley. I saw a group of old men, two seated across a folding table playing a game of chess, others smoking pipes, eating peanuts, and watching. I ran home and grabbed Vincent's chess set, which was bound in a cardboard box with rubber bands. I also carefully selected two prized rolls of Life Savers. I came back to the park and approached a man who was observing the game.

"Want to play?" I asked him. His face widened with surprise and he grinned as he looked at the box under my arm.

"Little sister, been a long time since I play with dolls," he said, smiling benevolently. I quickly put the box down next to him on the bench and displayed my retort.

Lau Po, as he allowed me to call him, turned out to be a much better player than my brothers. I lost many games and many Life Savers. But over the weeks, with each diminishing roll of candies, I added new secrets. Lau Po gave me the names. The Double Attack from the East and West Shores. Throwing Stones on the Drowning Man. The Sudden Meeting of the Clan. The Surprise from the Sleeping Guard. The Humble Servant Who Kills the King. Sand in the Eyes of Advancing Forces. A Double Killing Without Blood.

There were also the fine points of chess etiquette. Keep captured men in neat rows, as well-tended prisoners. Never announce "Check" with vanity, lest someone with an unseen sword slit your throat. Never hurl pieces into the sandbox after you have lost a game, because then you must find them again, by yourself, after apologizing to all around you. By the end of the summer, Lau Po had taught me all he knew, and I had become a better chess player.

A small weekend crowd of Chinese people and tourists would gather as I played and defeated my opponents one by one. My mother would join the crowds during these outdoor exhibition games. She sat proudly on the bench, telling my admirers with proper Chinese humility, "Is luck."

A man who watched me play in the park suggested that my mother allow me to play in local chess tournaments. My mother smiled graciously, an answer that meant nothing. I desperately wanted to go, but I bit back my tongue. I knew she would not let me play among strangers. So as we walked home I said in a small voice that I didn't want to play in the local tournament. They would have American rules. If I lost, I would bring shame on my family.

"Is shame you fall down nobody push you," said my mother.

During my first tournament, my mother sat with me in the front row as I waited for my turn. I frequently bounced my legs to unstick them from the cold metal seat of the folding chair. When my name was called, I leapt up. My mother unwrapped something in her lap. It was her *chang*, a small tablet of red jade which held the sun's fire. "Is luck," she whispered and tucked it into my dress pocket. I turned to my opponent, a fifteen-year-old boy from Oakland. He looked at me, wrinkling his nose.

As I began to play, the boy disappeared, the color ran out of the room, and I saw only my white pieces and his black ones waiting on the other side. A light wind began flowing past my ears. It whispered secrets only I could hear.

"Blow from the South," it murmured. "The wind leaves no trail." I saw a clear path, the traps to avoid. The crowd rustled. "Shhh! Shhh!" said the corners of the room. The wind blew stronger. "Throw sand from the East to distract him." The knight came forward ready for the sacrifice. The wind hissed, louder and louder. "Blow, blow, blow. He cannot see. He is blind now. Make him lean away from the wind so he is easier to knock down."

"Check," I said, as the wind roared with laughter. The wind died down to little puffs, my own breath.

My mother placed my first trophy next to a new plastic chess set that the neighborhood Tao society had given to me. As she wiped each piece with a soft cloth, she said, "Next time win more, lose less."

"Ma, it's not how many pieces you lose," I said. "Sometimes you need to lose pieces to get ahead."

"Better to lose less, see if you really need."

At the next tournament, I won again, but it was my mother who wore the triumphant grin.

"Lost eight piece this time. Last time was eleven. What I tell you? Better off lose less!" I was annoyed, but I couldn't say anything.

I attended more tournaments, each one farther away from home. I won all games, in all divisions. The Chinese bakery downstairs from our flat displayed my growing collection of trophies in its window, amidst the dust-covered cakes that were never picked up. The day after I won an important regional tournament, the window encased a fresh sheet cake with whipped-cream frosting and red script saying "Congratulations, Waverly Jong, Chinatown Chess Champion." Soon after that, a flower shop, headstone engraver, and funeral parlor offered to sponsor me in national tournaments. That's when my mother decided I no longer had to do the dishes. Winston and Vincent had to do my chores.

"Why does she get to play and we do all the work," complained Vincent.

"Is new American rules," said my mother. "Meimei play, squeeze all her brains out for win chess. You play, worth squeeze towel."

By my ninth birthday, I was a national chess champion. I was still some 429 points away from grand-master status, but I was touted as the Great American Hope, a child prodigy and a girl to boot. They ran a photo of me in *Life* magazine next to a quote in which Bobby Fischer said, "There will never be a woman grand master." "Your move, Bobby," said the caption.

The day they took the magazine picture I wore neatly plaited braids clipped with plastic barrettes trimmed with rhinestones. I was playing in a large high school auditorium that echoed with phlegmy coughs and the squeaky rubber knobs of chair legs sliding across freshly waxed wooden floors. Seated across from me was an American man, about the same age as Lau Po, maybe fifty. I remember that his sweaty brow seemed to weep at my every move. He wore a dark, malodorous suit. One of his pockets was stuffed with a great white kerchief on which he wiped his palm before sweeping his hand over the chosen chess piece with great flourish.

In my crisp pink-and-white dress with scratchy lace at the

neck, one of two my mother had sewn for these special occasions, I would clasp my hands under my chin, the delicate points of my elbows poised lightly on the table in the manner my mother had shown me for posing for the press. I would swing my patent leather shoes back and forth like an impatient child riding on a school bus. Then I would pause, suck in my lips, twirl my chosen piece in midair as if undecided, and then firmly plant it in its new threatening place, with a triumphant smile thrown back at my opponent for good measure.

I no longer played in the alley of Waverly Place. I never visited the playground where the pigeons and old men gathered. I went to school, then directly home to learn new chess secrets, cleverly concealed advantages, more escape routes.

But I found it difficult to concentrate at home. My mother had a habit of standing over me while I plotted out my games. I think she thought of herself as my protective ally. Her lips would be sealed tight, and after each move I made, a soft "Hmmmmph" would escape from her nose.

"Ma, I can't practice when you stand there like that," I said one day. She retreated to the kitchen and made loud noises with the pots and pans. When the crashing stopped, I could see out of the corner of my eye that she was standing in the doorway. "Hmmmmph!" Only this one came out of her tight throat.

My parents made many concessions to allow me to practice. One time I complained that the bedroom I shared was so noisy that I couldn't think. Thereafter, my brothers slept in a bed in the living room facing the street. I said I couldn't finish my rice; my head didn't work right when my stomach was too full. I left the table with half-finished bowls and nobody complained. But there was one duty I couldn't avoid. I had to accompany my mother on Saturday market days when I had no tournament to play. My mother would proudly walk with me, visiting many shops, buying very little. "This my daughter Wave-ly Jong," she said to whoever looked her way.

One day after we left a shop I said under my breath, "I wish you wouldn't do that, telling everybody I'm your daughter." My mother stopped walking. Crowds of people with heavy bags pushed past us on the sidewalk, bumping into first one shoulder, then another.

"Aiii-ya. So shame be with mother?" She grasped my hand even tighter as she glared at me.

I looked down. "It's not that, it's just so obvious. It's just so embarrassing."

"Embarrass you be my daughter?" Her voice was cracking with anger.

"That's not what I meant. That's not what I said."

"What you say?"

I knew it was a mistake to say anything more, but I heard my voice speaking. "Why do you have to use me to show off? If you want to show off, then why don't you learn to play chess?"

My mother's eyes turned into dangerous black slits. She had no words for me, just sharp silence.

I felt the wind rushing around my hot ears. I jerked my hand out of my mother's tight grasp and spun around, knocking into an old woman. Her bag of groceries spilled to the ground.

"Aii-ya! Stupid girl!" my mother and the woman cried. Oranges and tin cans careened down the sidewalk. As my mother stooped to help the old woman pick up the escaping food, I took off.

I raced down the street, dashing between people, not looking back as my mother screamed shrilly, "Meimei! Meimei!" I fled down an alley, past dark, curtained shops and merchants washing the grime off their windows. I sped into the sunlight, into a large street crowded with tourists examining trinkets and souvenirs. I ducked into another dark alley, down another street, up another alley. I ran until it hurt and I realized I had nowhere to go, that I was not running from anything. The alleys contained no escape routes.

My breath came out like angry smoke. It was cold. I sat down on an upturned plastic pail next to a stack of empty boxes, cupping my chin with my hands, thinking hard. I imagined my mother, first walking briskly down one street or another looking for me, then giving up and returning home to await my arrival. After two hours, I stood up on creaking legs and slowly walked home.

The alley was quiet and I could see the yellow lights shining from our flat like two tiger's eyes in the night. I climbed the sixteen steps to the door, advancing quietly up each so as not to make any warning sounds. I turned the knob; the door was locked. I heard a chair moving, quick steps, the locks turning – click! click! click! – and then the door opened.

"About time you got home," said Vincent. "Boy, are you in trouble."

He slid back to the dinner table. On a platter were the remains of a large fish, its fleshy head still connected to bones swimming upstream in vain escape. Standing there waiting for my punishment, I heard my mother speak in a dry voice.

"We not concerning this girl. This girl not have concerning for us."

Nobody looked at me. Bone chopsticks clinked against the inside of bowls being emptied into hungry mouths.

I walked into my room, closed the door, and lay down on my bed. The room was dark, the ceiling filled with shadows from the dinnertime lights of neighboring flats.

In my head, I saw a chessboard with sixty-four black and white squares. Opposite me was my opponent, two angry black slits. She wore a triumphant smile. "Strongest wind cannot be seen," she said.

Her black men advanced across the plane, slowly marching to each successive level as a single unit. My white pieces screamed as they scurried and fell off the board one by one. As her men drew closer to my edge, I felt myself growing light. I rose up into the air and flew out the window. Higher and higher, above the alley, over the tops of tiled roofs, where I was gathered up by the wind and pushed up toward the night sky until everything below me disappeared and I was alone.

I closed my eyes and pondered my next move.

STEPHANIE VAUGHN

☆ ☆ ☆ ☆

# Dog Heaven

Every so often that dead dog dreams me up again.

It's twenty-five years later. I'm walking along 42nd Street in Manhattan, the sounds of the city crashing beside me – horns, gearshifts, insults – sombody's chewing gum holding my foot to the pavement, when that dog wakes from his long sleep and imagines me.

I'm sweet again. I'm sweet-breathed and flat-limbed. Our family is stationed at Fort Niagara, and the dog swims his red heavy fur into the black Niagara River. Across the street from the officers' quarters, down the steep shady bank, the river, even this far downstream, has been clocked at 9 miles per hour. The dog swims after the stick I have thrown.

"Are you crazy?" my grandmother says, even though she is not fond of dog hair in the house, the way it sneaks into the refrigerator every time you open the door. "There's a current out there! It'll take that dog all the way to Toronto."

"The dog knows where the backwater ends and the current begins," I say, because it is true. He comes down to the river all the time with my father, my brother MacArthur, or me. You never have to yell the dog away from the place where the river water moves like a whip.

Sparky Smith and I had a game we played called knockout. It involved a certain way of breathing and standing up fast that caused the blood to leave the brain as if a plug had been jerked from the skull. You came to again just as soon as you were on the ground, the blood sloshing back, but it always seemed as if you had left the planet, had a vacation on Mars, and maybe stopped back at Fort Niagara half a lifetime later.

There weren't many kids my age on the post, because it was

a small command. Most of its real work went on at the missile batteries flung like shale along the American–Canadian border. Sparky Smith and I hadn't been at Lewiston-Porter Central School long enough to get to know many people, so we entertained ourselves by meeting in a hollow of trees and shrubs at the far edge of the parade ground and telling each other seventh-grade sex jokes that usually had to do with keyholes and door-knobs, hot dogs and hot-dog buns, nuns, priests, preachers, schoolteachers, and people in blindfolds.

When we ran out of sex jokes, we went to knockout and took turns catching each other as we fell like a cut tree toward the ground. Whenever I knocked out, I came to on the grass with the dog barking, yelping, crouching, crying for help. "Wake up! Wake up!" he seemed to say. "Do you know your name? Do you know your name? My name is Duke! My name is Duke!" I'd wake to the sky with the urgent call of the dog in the air, and I'd think, Well, here I am, back in my life again.

Sparky Smith and I spent our school time smiling too much and running for office. We wore mittens instead of gloves, because everyone else did. We made our mothers buy us ugly knit caps with balls on top – caps that in our previous schools would have identified us as weird but were part of the winter uniform in upstate New York. We wobbled onto the ice of the post rink, practicing in secret, banged our knees, scraped the palms of our hands, so that we would be invited to skating parties by civilian children.

"You skate?" With each other we practiced the cool look.

"Oh, yeah. I mean, like I do it some – I'm not a racer or anything."

Every morning we boarded the Army-green bus – the slime-green, dead-swamp-algae-green bus – and rode it to the post gate, past the concrete island where the MPs stood in their bulletproof booth. Across from the gate, we got off at a street corner and waited with the other Army kids, the junior-high and high-school kids, for the real bus, the yellow one with the civilian kids on it. Just as we began to board, the civilian kids – there were only six of them but eighteen of us – would begin to sing the Artillery song with obscene variations one of them had invented. Instead of "Over hill, over dale," they sang things like "Over boob, over tit." For a few weeks, we sat in silence watching the heavy oak trees of the town give way to apple orchards and potato farms, and we pretended not to hear. Then one day Sparky Smith began to sing the real Artillery song, the booming song with caissons rolling along in it, and we all joined in and took over the bus with our voices.

When we ran out of verses, one of the civilian kids, a football player in high school, yelled, "Sparky is a *dog's* name. Here Sparky, Sparky, Sparky." Sparky rose from his seat with a wounded look, then dropped to the aisle on his hands and knees and bit the football player in the calf. We all laughed, even the football player, and Sparky returned to his seat.

"That guy's just lucky I didn't pee on his leg," Sparky said.

Somehow Sparky got himself elected homeroom president and me homeroom vice president in January. He liked to say, "In actual percentages – I mean in actual per capita terms – we are doing much better than the civilian kids." He kept track of how many athletes we had, how many band members, who among the older girls might become a cheerleader. Listening to him even then, I couldn't figure out how he got anyone to vote for us. When he was campaigning, he sounded dull and serious, and anyway he had a large head and looked funny in a knit cap. He put up a homemade sign in the lunchroom, went from table to table to find students from 7-B to shake hands with, and said to me repeatedly, as I walked along a step behind and nodded, "Just don't tell them that you're leaving in March. Under no circumstances let them know that you will not be able to finish out your term."

In January, therefore, I was elected homeroom vice president by people I still didn't know (nobody in 7-B rode our bus – that gave us an edge), and in March my family moved to Fort Sill, in Oklahoma. I surrendered my vice presidency to a civilian girl, and that was the end for all time of my career in public office.

Two days before we left Fort Niagara, we took the dog, Duke, to Charlie Battery, 14 miles from the post, and left him with the mess sergeant. We were leaving him for only 6 weeks, until we could settle in Oklahoma and send for him. He had stayed at Charlie Battery before, when we visited our relatives in Ohio at Christmastime. He knew there were big meaty bones at Charlie Battery, and scraps of chicken, steak, turkey, slices of cheese, special big-dog bowls of ice cream. The mess at Charlie Battery was Dog Heaven, so he gave us a soft, forgiving look as we walked with him from the car to the back of the mess hall.

My mother said, as she always did at times like that, "I wish he knew more English." My father gave him a fierce manly scratch behind the ear. My brother and I scraped along behind with our pinched faces.

"Don't you worry," the sergeant said. "He'll be fine here. We like this dog, and he likes us. He'll run that fence perimeter all day long. He'll be his own early-warning defense system. Then we'll give this dog everything he ever dreamed of eating." The sergeant looked quickly at my father to see if the lighthearted reference to the defense system had been all right. My father was in command of the missile batteries. In my father's presence, no one spoke lightly of the defense of the United States of America – of the missiles that would rise from the earth like a wind and knock out (knock out!) the Soviet planes flying over the North Pole with their nuclear bombs. But Duke was my father's dog, too, and I think that my father had the same wish we all had – to tell him that we were going to send for him, this was just going to be a wonderful dog vacation.

"Sergeant Mozley has the best mess within five hundred miles," my father said to me and MacArthur.

We looked around. We had been there for Thanksgiving dinner when the grass was still green. Now, in late winter, it was a dreary place, a collection of rain-streaked metal buildings, standing near huge dark mounds of earth. In summer, the mounds looked something like the large grassy mounds in southern Ohio, the famous Indian mounds, softly rounded and benignly mysterious. In March, they were black with old snow. Inside the mounds were the Nike missiles, I supposed, although I didn't know for sure where the missiles were. Perhaps they were hidden in the depressions behind the mounds.

★

Once during "Fact Monday" in Homeroom 7-B, our teacher, Miss Bintz, had given a lecture on nuclear weapons. First she put a slide on the wall depicting an atom and its spinning electrons.

"Do you know what this is?" she said, and everyone in the room said, "An atom," in one voice, as if we were reciting a poem. We liked "Fact Monday" sessions because we didn't have to do any work for them. We sat happily in the dim light of her slides through lectures called "Nine Chapters in the Life of a Cheese" ("First the milk is warmed, then it is soured with rennet"), "The Morning Star of English Poetry" ("As springtime suggests the beginning of new life, so Chaucer stands at the beginning of English poetry"), and "Who's Who Among the Butterflies" ("The monarch – *Danaus plexipus* – is king"). Sparky liked to say that Miss Bintz was trying to make us into third-graders again, but I liked Miss Bintz. She had high cheekbones and a passionate voice. She believed, like the adults in my family, that a fact was something solid and useful, like a penknife you could put in your pocket in case of emergency.

That day's lecture was "What Happens to the Atom When It Is Smashed." Miss Bintz put on the wall a black-and-white slide of four women who had been horribly disfigured by the atomic blast at Hiroshima. The room was half darkened for the slide show. When she surprised us with the four faces of the women, you could feel the darkness grow, the silence in the bellies of the students.

"And do you know what this is?" Miss Bintz said. No one spoke. What answer could she have wanted from us, anyway? She clicked the slide machine through ten more pictures – close-ups of blistered hands, scarred heads, flattened buildings, burned trees, maimed and naked children staggering toward the camera as if the camera were food, a house, a mother, a father, a friendly dog.

"Do you know what this is?" Miss Bintz said again. Our desks were arranged around the edge of the room, creating an arena in the center. Miss Bintz entered that space and began to move along the front of our desks, looking to see who would answer her incomprehensible question.

"Do you know?" She stopped in front of my desk.

"No," I said.

"Do you know?" She stopped next at Sparky's desk.

Sparky looked down and finally said, "It's something horrible."

"That's right," she said. "It's something very horrible. This is the effect of an atom smashing. This is the effect of nuclear power." She turned to gesture at the slide, but she had stepped in front of the projector, and the smear of children's faces fell across her back. "Now let's think about how nuclear power got from the laboratory to the scientists to the people of Japan." She had begun to pace again. "Let's think about where all this devastation and wreckage actually comes from. You tell me," she said to a large crouching boy named Donald Anderson. He was hunched over his desk, and his arms lay before him like tree limbs.

"I don't know," Donald Anderson said.

"Of course you do," Miss Bintz said. "Where did all of this come from?"

None of us had realized yet that Miss Bintz's message was political. I looked beyond Donald Anderson at the drawn window shades. Behind them were plate-glass windows, a view of stiff red-oak leaves, the smell of wood smoke in the air. Across the road from the school was an orchard, beyond that a pasture, another orchard, and then the town of Lewiston, standing on the Niagara River 7 miles upstream from the long row of red-brick Colonial houses that were the officers' quarters at Fort Niagara. Duke was down the river, probably sniffing at the reedy edge, his head lifting when ducks flew low over the water. Once the dog had come back to our house with a live fish in his mouth, a carp. Nobody ever believed that story except those of us who saw it: me, my mother and father and brother, my grandmother.

Miss Bintz had clicked to a picture of a mushroom cloud and was now saying, "And where did the bomb come from?" We were all tired of "Fact Monday" by then. Miss Bintz walked back to where Sparky and I were sitting. "You military children," she said. "You know where the bomb comes from. Why don't you tell us?" she said to me.

Maybe because I was tired, or bored, or frightened – I don't know – I said to Miss Bintz, looking her in the eye, "The bomb comes from the mother bomb."

Everyone laughed. We laughed because we needed to laugh, and because Miss Bintz had all the answers and all the questions and she was pointing them at us like guns.

"Stand up," she said. She made me enter the arena in front of the desks, and then she clicked the machine back to the picture of the Japanese women. "Look at this picture and make a joke," she said. What came next was the lecture she had been aiming for all along. The bomb came from the United States of America. We in the United States were worried about whether another country might use the bomb, but in the whole history of the human species only one country had ever used the worst weapon ever invented. On she went, bombs and airplanes and bomb tests, and then she got to the missiles. They were right here, she said, not more than 10 miles away. Didn't we all know that? "You know that, don't you?" she said to me. If the missiles weren't hidden among our orchards, the planes from the Soviet Union would not have any reason to drop bombs on top of Lewiston-Porter Central School.

I had stopped listening by then and realized that the pencil I still held in my hand was drumming a song against my thigh. Over hill, over dale. I looked back at the wall again, where the mushroom cloud had reappeared, and my own silhouette stood wildly in the middle of it. I looked at Sparky and dropped the pencil on the floor, stooped down to get it, looked at Sparky once more, stood up, and knocked out.

Later, people told me that I didn't fall like lumber, I fell like something soft collapsing, a fan folding in on itself, a balloon rumpling to the floor. Sparky saw what I was up to and tried to get out from behind his desk to catch me, but it was Miss Bintz I fell against, and she went down, too. When I woke up, the lights were on, the mushroom cloud was a pale ghost against the wall, voices in the room sounded like insect wings, and I was back in my life again.

"I'm so sorry," Miss Bintz said. "I didn't know you were an epileptic."

★

At Charlie Battery, it was drizzling as my parents stood and talked with the sergeant, rain running in dark tiny ravines along the slopes of the mounds.

MacArthur and I had M&Ms in our pockets, which we were allowed to give to the dog for his farewell. When we extended our hands, though, the dog lowered himself to the gravel and looked up at us from under his tender red eyebrows. He seemed to say that if he took the candy he knew we would go, but if he didn't perhaps we would stay here at the missile battery and eat scraps with him.

We rode back to the post in silence, through gray apple orchards, through small upstate towns, the fog rising out of the rain like a wish. MacArthur and I sat against opposite doors in the back seat, thinking of the loneliness of the dog.

We entered the kitchen, where my grandmother had already begun to clean the refrigerator. She looked at us, at our grim children's faces – the dog had been sent away a day earlier than was really necessary – and she said, "Well, God knows you can't clean the dog hair out of the house with the dog still in it."

Whenever I think of an Army post, I think of a place the weather cannot touch for long. The precise rectangles of the parade grounds, the precisely pruned trees and shrubs, the living quarters, the administration buildings, the PX and commissary, the nondenominational church, the teen club, snack bar, the movie house, the skeet-and-trap field, the swimming pools, the runway, warehouses, the officers' club, the NCO club. Men marching, women marching, saluting, standing at attention, at ease. The bugle will trumpet reveille, mess call, assembly, retreat, taps through a hurricane, a tornado, flood, blizzard. Whenever I think of the clean squared look of a military post, I think that if one were blown down today in a fierce wind, it would be standing again tomorrow in time for reveille.

The night before our last full day at Fort Niagara, an arctic wind slipped across the lake and froze the rain where it fell, on streets, trees, power lines, rooftops. We awoke to a fabulation of ice, the sun shining like a weapon, light rocketing off every surface except the surfaces of the Army's clean streets and walks.

MacArthur and I stood on the dry, scraped walk in front of our house and watched a jeep pass by on the way to the gate. On the post, everything was operational, but in the civilian world beyond the gate power lines were down, hanging like daggers in the sun, roads were glazed with ice, cars were in ditches, highways were impassable. No yellow school buses were going to be on the roads that morning.

"This means we miss our very last day in school," Mac-Arthur said. "No goodbyes for us."

We looked up at the high, bare branches of the hard maples, where drops of ice glimmered.

"I just want to shake your hand and say so long," Sparky said. He had come out of his house to stand with us. "I guess you know this means you'll miss the surprise party."

"There was going to be a party?" I said.

"Just cupcakes," Sparky said. "I sure wish you could stay the school year and keep your office."

"Oh, who cares!" I said, suddenly irritated with Sparky, although he was my best friend. "Jesus," I said, sounding to myself like an adult – like Miss Bintz maybe, when she was off duty. "Jesus," I said again. "What kind of office is home-goddamn-room vice president in a crummy country school?"

MacArthur said to Sparky, "What kind of cupcakes were they having?"

I looked down at MacArthur and said, "Do you know how totally ridiculous you look in that knit cap? I can't wait until we get out of this place."

"Excuse me," MacArthur said. "Excuse me for wearing the hat you gave me for my birthday."

It was then that the dog came back. We heard him calling out before we saw him, his huge woof-woof. "My name is Duke! My name is Duke! I'm your dog! I'm your dog!" Then we saw him streaking through the trees, through the park space of oaks and maples between our house and the post gate. Later the MPs would say that he stopped and wagged his tail at them before he passed through the gate, as if he understood that he should be stopping to show his ID card. He ran to us, bounding across the crusted, glass-slick snow – ran into the history of our family, all the stories we would tell about him after he was dead. Years and years later, whenever we came back together at the family dinner table, we would start the dog stories. He was the dog who caught the live fish with his mouth, the one who stole a pound of butter off the commissary loading dock and brought it to us in his soft bird dog's mouth without a tooth mark on the package. He was the dog who broke out of Charlie Battery the morning of an ice storm, traveled 14 miles across the needled grasses and frozen pastures, through the prickly frozen mud of orchards, across backyard fences in small towns, and found the lost family.

The day was good again. When we looked back at the ice we saw a fairyland. The red-brick houses looked like ice castles. The ice-coated trees, with their million dreams of light, seemed to cast a spell over us.

"This is for you," Sparky said, and handed me a gold-foiled box. Inside were chocolate candies and a note that said, "I have enjoyed knowing you this year. I hope you have a good life." Then it said, "P.S. Remember this name. Someday I'm probably going to be famous."

"Famous as what?" MacArthur said.

"I haven't decided yet," Sparky said.

We had a party. We sat on the front steps of our quarters, Sparky, MacArthur, the dog, and I, and we ate all the chocolates at 8 o'clock in the morning. We sat shoulder to shoulder, the four of us, and looked across the street through the trees at the river, and we talked about what we might be doing a year from then. Finally, we finished the chocolates and stopped talking and allowed the brilliant light of that morning to enter us.

Miss Bintz is the one who sent me the news about Sparky four months later. BOY DROWNS IN SWIFT CURRENT. In the newspaper story, Sparky takes the bus to Niagara Falls with two friends from Lewiston-Porter. It's a searing July day, 100 degrees in the city, so the boys climb down the gorge into the river and swim in a place where it's illegal to swim, 2 miles downstream from the Falls. The boys Sparky is tagging along with — they're both student-council members as well as football players, just the kind of boys Sparky himself wants to be – have sneaked down to this swimming place many times: a cove in the bank of the river, where the water is still and glassy on a hot July day, not like the water raging in the middle of the river. But the current is a wild invisible thing, unreliable, whipping out with a looping arm to pull you in. "He was only 3 feet in front of me," one of the boys said. "He took one more stroke and then he was gone."

We were living in civilian housing not far from the post. When we had the windows open, we could hear the bugle calls and the sound of the cannon firing retreat at sunset. A month after I got the newspaper clipping about Sparky, the dog died. He was killed, along with every other dog on our block, when a stranger drove down our street one evening and threw poisoned hamburger into our front yards.

All that week I had trouble getting to sleep at night. One night I was still awake when the recorded bugle sounded taps, the sound drifting across the Army fences and into our bedrooms. Day is done, gone the sun. It was the sound of my childhood in sleep. The bugler played it beautifully, mournfully, holding fast to the long, high notes. That night I listened to the cadence of it, to the yearning of it. I thought of the dog again, only this time I suddenly saw him rising like a missile into the air, the red glory of his fur flying, his nose pointed heavenward. I remembered the dog leaping high, prancing on his hind legs the day he came back from Charlie Battery, the dog rocking back and forth, from front legs to hind legs, dancing, sliding across the ice of the post rink later that day, as Sparky, Mac-Arthur, and I played crack-the-whip, holding tight to each other, our skates careening and singing. "You're AWOL! You're AWOL!" we cried at the dog. "No school!" the dog barked back. "No school!" We skated across the darkening ice into the sunset, skated faster and faster, until we seemed to rise together into the cold, bright air. It was a good day, it was a good day, it was a good day.

JOY WILLIAMS

☆ ☆ ☆ ☆

# *Train*

Inside, the Auto-Train was violet. Both little girls were pleased because it was their favorite color. Violet was practically the only thing they agreed on. Danica Anderson and Jane Muirhead were both ten years old. They had traveled from Maine to Washington, DC, by car with Jane's parents and were now on the train with Jane's parents and 109 other people and 42 automobiles on the way to Florida where they lived. It was September. Danica had been with Jane since June. Danica's mother was getting married again and she had needed the summer months to settle down and have everything nice for Dan when she saw her in September. In August, her mother had written Dan and asked what she could do to make things nice for Dan when she got back. Dan replied that she would like a good wall-hung pencil sharpener and satin sheets. She would like cowboy bread for supper. Dan supposed that she would get none of these things. Her mother hadn't even asked her what cowboy bread was.

The girls explored the entire train, north to south. They saw everyone but the engineer. Then they sat down in their violet seats. Jane made faces at a cute little toddler holding a cloth rabbit until he started to cry. Dan took out her writing materials and began writing to Jim Anderson. She was writing him a postcard.

"Jim," she wrote, "I miss you and I will see you any minute. When I see you we will go swimming right away."

"That is real messy writing," Jane said. "It's all scrunched together. If you were writing to anyone other than a dog, they wouldn't be able to read it at all."

Dan printed her name on the bottom of the card and embellished it all with X's and O's.

"Your writing to Jim Anderson is dumb in about twelve different ways. He's a *golden retriever*, for Godssakes."

Dan looked at her friend mildly. She was used to Jane yelling at her and expressing disgust and impatience. Jane had once lived in Manhattan. She had developed certain attitudes. Jane was a treasure from the city of New York currently on loan to the state of Florida where her father, for the last two years, had been engaged in running down a perfectly good investment in a marina and dinner theater. Jane liked to wear scarves tied around her head. She claimed to enjoy grapes and brown sugar and sour cream for dessert more than ice cream and cookies. She liked artichokes. She *adored* artichokes. She *adored* the part in the New York City Ballet's *Nutcracker Suite* where the Dew Drops and the candied Petals of Roses dance to the "Waltz of the Flowers." Jane had seen the *Nutcracker* four *times*, for Godssakes.

Dan and Jane and Jane's mother and father had all lived with Jane's grandmother in her big house in Maine all summer. The girls hadn't seen that much of the Muirheads. The Muirheads were always "cruising." They were always "gunk-holing," as they called it. Whatever that was, Jane said, for Godssakes. Jane's grandmother had a house on the ocean and knew how to make pizza and candy and sail a canoe. She called pizza 'za. She sang hymns in the shower. She sewed sequins on their jeans and made them say grace before dinner. After they said grace, Jane's grandmother would ask forgiveness for things done and left undone. She would, upon request, lie down and chat with them at night before they went to sleep. Jane was crazy about her grandmother and was quite a nice person in her presence. One night, at the end of summer, Jane had had a dream in which men dressed in black suits and white bathing caps had broken into her grandmother's house and taken all her possessions and put them in the road. In Jane's dream, rain fell on all her grandmother's things. Jane woke up weeping. Dan had wept too. Jane and Dan were friends.

The train had not yet left the station even though it was two hours past the posted departure time. An announcement had just been made that said that a two-hour delay was built into the train's schedule.

"They make up the time at night," Jane said. She plucked the postcard from Dan's hand. "This is a good one," she said. "I think you're sending it to Jim Anderson just so you can save it yourself." She read aloud, "This is a photograph of the Phantom Dream Car crashing through a wall of burning television sets before a cheering crowd at the Cow Palace in San Francisco."

At the beginning of the summer, Dan's mother had given her 100 dollars, four packages of new underwear and three dozen stamped postcards. Most of the cards were plain but there were a few with odd pictures on them. Dan's mother wanted to hear from her twice weekly throughout the summer. She had married a man named Jake, who was a carpenter. Jake had already built Dan three bookcases. This seemed to be the extent of what he knew how to do for Dan.

"I only have three left now," Dan said, "but when I get home, I'm going to start my own collection."

"I've been through that phase," Jane said. "It's just a phase. I don't think you're much of a correspondent. You wrote, 'I got sunburn, Love, Dan' . . . 'I bought a green Frisbee. Love, Dan' . . . 'Mrs. Muirhead has swimmer's ear. Love, Dan' . . . 'Mr. Muirhead went water-skiing and cracked his rib. Love, Dan' . . . When you write to people you should have something to say."

Dan didn't reply. She had been Jane's companion for a long time, and was wearying of what Jane's mother called her "effervescence."

Jane slapped Dan on the back and hollered, "Danica Anderson, for Godsakes! What is a clod like yourself doing on this fabulous journey!"

Together, the girls made their way to the Starlight Lounge in Car 7 where Mr. and Mrs. Muirhead told them they would be enjoying cocktails. They hesitated in the car where the train's magician was with his audience, watching him while he did the magic silks trick, the cut and restored handkerchief trick, the enchanted salt shaker trick, and the dissolving quarter trick. The audience, primarily retirees, screamed with pleasure.

"I don't mind the tricks," Jane whispered to Dan, "but the junk that gets said drives me crazy."

The magician was a young man with a long spotted face. He did a lot of card forcing. Again and again, he called the card that people chose from a shuffled deck. Each time that the magician was successful, the audience participant yelled and smiled and in general acted thrilled. Jane and Dan passed on through.

"You don't really choose," Jane said. "He just makes you think you choose. He does it all with his pinky." She pushed Dan forward into the Starlight Lounge where Mrs. Muirhead was on a banquette staring out the window at a shed and an unkempt bush which was sliding slowly past. She was drinking a martini. Mr. Muirhead was several tables away talking to a young man wearing jeans and a yellow jacket. Jane did not sit down. "Mummy," she said, "can I have your olive?"

"Of course not," Mrs. Muirhead said, "it's soaked in gin."

Jane, Dan in tow, went to her father's table. "Daddy," Jane demanded, "why aren't you sitting with Mummy? Are you and Mummy having a fight?"

Dan was astonished at this question. Mr. and Mrs. Muirhead fought continuously and as bitterly as vipers. Their arguments were baroque, stately, and although frequently extraordinary, never enlightening. At breakfast, they would be quarreling over an incident at a cocktail party the night before or a dumb remark made fifteen years ago. At dinner, they would be howling over the fate, which they called by many names, which had given them one another. Forgiveness, charity and cooperation were qualities unknown to them. They were opponents *pur sang*. Dan was sure that one morning, Jane would be called from her classroom and told as gently as possible by Mr. Mooney, the school principal, that her parents had splattered one another's brains all over the lanai.

Mr. Muirhead looked at the children sorrowfully and touched Jane's cheek.

"I am not sitting with your mother because I am sitting with this young man here. We are having a fascinating conversation."

"Why are you always talking to young men?" Jane asked.

"Jane, honey," Mr. Muirhead said, "I will answer that." He took a swallow of his drink and sighed. He leaned forward and said earnestly, "I talk to so many young men because your mother won't let me talk to young women." He remained hunched over, patting Jane's cheek for a moment, and then leaned back.

The young man extracted a cigarette from his jacket and

hesitated. Mr. Muirhead gave him a book of matches. "He does automobile illustrations," Mr. Muirhead said.

The young man nodded. "Belly bands. Pearls and flakes. Flames. All custom work."

Mr. Muirhead smiled. He seemed happier now. Mr. Muirhead loved conversations. He loved "to bring people out." Dan supposed that Jane had picked up this pleasant trait from her father and distorted it in some perversely personal way.

"I bet you have a Trans Am yourself," Jane said.

"You are so-o-o right," the young man said. "It's ice-blue. You like ice-blue? Maybe you're too young." He extended his hand showing a large gaudy stone in a setting that seemed to be gold. "Same color as this ring," he said.

Dan nodded. She could still be impressed by adults. Their mysterious, unreliable images still had the power to attract and confound her, but Jane was clearly not interested in the young man. She demanded much of life. She had very high standards when she wanted to. Mr. Muirhead ordered the girls ginger ales and the young man and himself another round of drinks. Sometimes the train, in the mysterious way of trains, would stop, or even reverse, and they would pass unfamiliar scenes once more. The same green pasture filled with slanty light, the same row of clapboard houses, each with the shades of their windows drawn against the heat, the same boats on their trailers, waiting on dry land. The moon was rising beneath a spectacular lightning and thunder storm. People around them were commenting on it. Close to the train, a sheen of dark birds flew low across a dirt road.

"Birds are only flying reptiles, I'm sure you're all aware," Jane said suddenly.

"Oh my God, what a horrible thought!" Mr. Muirhead said. His face had become a little slack and his hair had become somewhat disarranged.

"It's true, it's true," Jane sang. "Sad but true."

"You mean like lizards and snakes?" the young man asked. He snorted and shook his head.

"*Glorified* reptiles certainly," Mr. Muirhead said, recovering a bit of his sense of time and place.

Dan suddenly felt lonely. It was not homesickness, although she would have given anything at that moment to be poking around in her little aluminum boat with Jim Anderson. She wouldn't even be living any longer in the place she thought of as "home." The town was the same but the place was different. The house where she had been a little tiny baby and had lived her whole life belonged to someone else now. Over the summer, her mother and Jake had bought another house which Jake was going to fix up.

"Reptiles have scales," the young man said, "or else they are long and slimy."

Dan felt like bawling. She could feel the back of her eyes swelling up like cupcakes. She was surrounded by strangers saying crazy things, and had been for quite some while. Even her own mother said crazy things in a reasonable way that made Dan know she was a stranger too. Dan's mother told Dan everything. Her mother told her she wouldn't have to worry about having brothers or sisters. Her mother discussed the particular nature of the problem with her. Half the things Dan's mother told her, Dan didn't want to know. There would be no brothers and sisters. There would be Dan and her mother and Jake, sitting around the house together, caring deeply for one another, sharing a nice life together, not making any mistakes.

Dan excused herself and started toward the lavatory on the level below. Mrs. Muirhead called to her as she approached and handed her a folded piece of paper. "Would you be kind enough to give this to Mr. Muirhead?" she asked. Dan gave Mr. Muirhead the note and went down to the lavatory. She sat on the little toilet as the train rocked along and cried.

After a while, she heard Jane's voice saying, "I hear you in there, Danica Anderson. What's the matter with you?"

Dan didn't say anything.

"I know it's you," Jane said. "I can see your stupid shoes and your stupid socks."

Dan blew her nose, pushed the button on the toilet and said, "What did the note say?"

"I don't know," Jane said. "Daddy ate it."

"He ate it!" Dan exclaimed. She opened the door of the stall and went to the sink. She washed her hands and splashed her face with water. She giggled. "He really ate it?"

"Everybody is looped in that Starlight Lounge," Jane said. Jane patted her hair with a hairbrush. Jane's hair was full of tangles and she never brushed hard enough to get them out. She looked at Dan by looking in the mirror. "Why were you crying?"

"I was thinking about your grandma," Dan said. "She said that one year she left the Christmas tree up until Easter."

"Why were you thinking about my grandma!" Jane yelled.

"I was thinking about her singing," Dan said, startled. "I like her singing."

In her head, Dan could hear Jane's grandmother singing about Death's dark waters and sinking souls, about Mercy Seats and the Great Physician. She could hear the voice rising and falling through the thin walls of the Maine house, borne past the dark screens and into the night.

"I don't want you thinking about my grandma," Jane said, pinching Dan's arm.

Dan tried not to think of Jane's grandma. Once, she had seen her fall coming out of the water. The beach was stony. The stones were round and smooth and slippery. Jane's grandmother had skinned her arm and bloodied her lip.

The girls went into the corridor and saw Mrs. Muirhead standing there. Mrs. Muirhead was deeply tanned. She had put her hair up in a twist and a wad of cotton was noticeable in her left ear. The three of them stood together, bouncing and nudging against one another with the motion of the train.

"My ear is killing me," Mrs. Muirhead said. "I think there's something they're not telling me. It crackles and snaps in there. It's like a bird breaking seeds in there." She touched the bone between cheekbone and ear. "I think the doctor I was seeing should lose his license. He was handsome and competent, certainly, but on my last visit, he was vacuuming my ear and his secretary came in to ask him a question and she put her hand on his neck. She stroked his neck, his secretary! While I was sitting there having my ear vacuumed!" Mrs. Muirhead's cheeks were flushed.

The three of them gazed out the window. The train must

have been clipping along, but things outside, although gone in an instant, seemed to be moving slowly. Beneath a street light, a man was kicking his pick-up truck.

"I dislike trains," Mrs. Muirhead said. "I find them depressing."

"It's the oxygen deprivation," Jane said, "coming from having to share the air with all these people."

"You're such a snob, dear," Mrs. Muirhead sighed.

"We're going to supper now," Jane said.

"Supper," Mrs. Muirhead said. "Ugh."

The children left her looking out the window, a disconsolate, pretty woman wearing a green dress with a line of frogs dancing around it.

The dining car was almost full. The windows reflected the eaters. The countryside was dim and the train pushed through it.

Jane steered them to a table where a man and woman silently labored over their meal.

"My name is Crystal," Jane offered, "and this is my twin sister, Clara."

"Clara!" Dan exclaimed. Jane was always inventing drab names for her.

"We were triplets," Jane went on, "but the other died at birth. Cord got all twisted around his neck or something."

The woman looked at Jane and smiled.

"What is your line of work?" Jane persisted brightly.

There was silence. The woman kept smiling, then the man said, "I don't do anything, I don't have to do anything. I was injured in Vietnam and they brought me to the base hospital and worked on reviving me for forty-five minutes. Then they gave up. They thought I was dead. Four hours later, I woke up in the mortuary. The Army gives me a good pension." He pushed his chair away from the table and left.

Dan looked after him, astonished, a cold roll raised halfway to her mouth. "Was your husband really dead for all that while?" she asked.

"My husband, ha!" the woman said. "I'd never laid eyes on that man before the 6.30 seating."

"I bet you're a professional woman who doesn't believe in men," Jane said slyly.

"Crystal, how did you guess! It's true, men are a collective hallucination of women. It's like when a group of crackpots get together on a hilltop and see flying saucers." The woman picked at her chicken.

Jane looked surprised, then said, "My father went to a costume party once wrapped from head to foot in aluminum foil."

"A casserole," the woman offered.

"No! A spaceman, an alien astronaut!"

Dan giggled, remembering when Mr. Muirhead had done that. She felt that Jane had met her match with this woman.

"What do you do!" Jane fairly screamed. "You won't tell us!"

"I do drugs," the woman said. The girls shrank back. "Ha," the woman said. "Actually, I test drugs for pharmaceutical companies. And I do research for a perfume manufacturer. I am involved in the search for human pheromones."

Jane looked levelly at the woman.

"I know you don't know what a pheromone is, Crystal. To put it grossly, a pheromone is a smell that a person has that can make another person do or feel a certain thing. It's an irresistible signal."

Dan thought of mangrove roots and orange groves. Of the smell of gas when the pilot light blew out on Jane's grand-mother's stove. She liked the smell of the Atlantic Ocean when it dried upon your skin and the smell of Jim Anderson's fur when he had been rained upon. There were smells that could make you follow them, certainly.

Jane stared at the woman, tipping forward slightly in her seat.

"Relax, will you, Crystal, you're just a child. You don't even *have* a smell yet," the woman said. "I test all sorts of things. Sometimes I'm part of a control group and sometimes I'm not. You never know. If you're part of the control group, you're just given a placebo. A placebo, Crystal, is something that is nothing, but you don't know it's nothing. You think you're getting something that will change you or make you feel better or healthier or more attractive or something, but you're not really."

"I know what a placebo is," Jane muttered.

"Well that's terrific, Crystal, you're a prodigy." The woman removed a book from her handbag and began to read it. The book had a denim jacket on it which concealed its title.

"Ha!" Jane said, rising quickly and attempting to knock over a glass of water. "My name's not Crystal!"

Dan grabbed the glass before it fell and hurried after her. They returned to the Starlight Lounge. Mr. Muirhead was sitting with another young man. This young man had a blond beard and a studious manner.

"Oh, this is a wonderful trip!" Mr. Muirhead said exuberantly. "The wonderful people you meet on a trip like this! This is the most fascinating young man. He's a writer. Been everywhere. He's putting together a book on cemeteries of the world. Isn't that some subject? I told him anytime he's in our town, stop by our restaurant, be my guest for some stone crab claws."

"Hello," the young man said to the girls.

"We were speaking of Père-Lachaise, the legendary Parisian cemetery," Mr. Muirhead said. "So wistful. So grand and romantic. Your mother and I visited it, Jane, when we were in Paris. We strolled through it on a clear crisp autumn day. The desires of the human heart have no boundaries, girls. The mess of secrets in the human heart are without number. Witnessing Père-Lachaise was a very moving experience. As we strolled, your mother was screaming at me, Jane. Do you know why, honey-bunch? She was screaming at me because back in New York, I had garaged the car at the place on East 84th Street. Your mother said that the people in the place on East 84th Street never turned the ignition all the way off to the left and were always running down the battery. She said that there wasn't a soul in all of New York City who didn't know that the people running the garage on East 84th Street were idiots who were always ruining batteries. Before Père-Lachaise, girls, this young man and I were discussing the Panteón, just outside of Guanajuato in Mexico. It so happens that I am also familiar with the Panteón. Your mother wanted some tiles for the foyer so we went to Mexico. You stayed with Mrs. Murphy, Jane. Remember? It was Mrs. Murphy who taught you how to make egg salad. In any case, the Panteón is a walled cemetery, not unlike the Campo Santo in Genoa, Italy, but the reason everybody goes there is to see the mummies. Something about the exceptionally dry air in the mountains has preserved the bodies and there's a little museum of mummies. It's grotesque of course, and it certainly gave me pause. I mean it's one thing to think we will all gather together in a paradise of fadeless splendor like your grandma thinks, lamby-lettuce, and it's another thing to think as the Buddhists do that latent possibilities withdraw into the heart at death, but do not perish, thereby allowing the being to be reborn, and it's one more thing, even, to believe like a Goddamn scientist in one of the essential laws of physics which states that no energy is ever lost. It's one thing to think any of those things, girls, but it's quite another to be standing in that little museum looking at those miserable mummies. The horror and indignation were in their faces still. I almost cried aloud, so vivid was my sense of the fleetingness of this life. We made our way into the fresh air of the courtyard and I bought a package of cigarettes at a little stand which sold postcards and films and such. I reached into my pocket for my lighter and it appeared that my lighter was not there. It seemed that I had lost my lighter. The lighter was a very good one that your mother had bought me the Christmas before, Jane, and your mother started screaming at me. There was a very gentle, warm rain falling, and there were bougainvillea petals on the walks. Your mother grasped my arm and reminded me that the lighter had been a gift from her. Your mother reminded me of the blazer she had bought for me. I spilled buttered popcorn on it at the movies and you can still see the spot. She reminded me of the hammock she bought for my fortieth birthday, which I allowed to rot in the rain. She recalled the shoulder bag she bought me, which I detested, it's true. It was somehow left out in the yard and I mangled it with the lawnmower. Descending the cobbled hill into Guanajuato, your mother recalled every one of her gifts to me, offerings both monetary and of the heart. She pointed out how I had mishandled and betrayed every one."

No one said anything. "Then," Mr. Muirhead continued, "there was the Modena Cemetery in Italy."

"That hasn't been completed yet," the young man said hurriedly. "It's a visionary design by the architect Aldo Rossi. In our conversation, I was just trying to describe the project to you."

"You can be assured," Mr. Muirhead said, "that when the project is finished and I take my little family on a vacation to Italy, as we walk, together and afraid, strolling through the hapless landscape of the Modena Cemetery, Jane's mother will be screaming at me."

"Well, I must be going," the young man said. He got up.

"So long," Mr. Muirhead said.

"Were they really selling postcards of the mummies in that place?" Dan asked.

"Yes, they were, sweetie-pie," Mr. Muirhead said. "In this world there is a postcard of everything. That's the kind of world this is."

The crowd was getting boisterous in the Starlight Lounge. Mrs. Muirhead made her way down the aisle toward them and with a deep sigh, sat beside her husband. Mr. Muirhead gesticulated and formed words silently with his lips as though he was talking to the girls.

"What?" Mrs. Muirhead said.

"I was just telling the girls some of the differences between men and women. Men are more adventurous and aggressive with greater spatial and mechanical abilities. Women are more consistent, nurturent and aesthetic. Men can see better than women, but women have better hearing," Mr. Muirhead said.

"Very funny," Mrs. Muirhead said.

The girls retired from the melancholy regard Mr. and Mrs. Muirhead had fixed upon one another, and wandered through the cars of the train, occasionally returning to their seats to fuss in the cluttered nests they had created there. Around midnight, they decided to revisit the game car where earlier, people had been playing backgammon, Diplomacy, anagrams, crazy eights and Clue. They were still at it, variously throwing down queens of diamonds, moving troops through Asia Minor and accusing Colonel Mustard of doing it in the conservatory with a wrench.

Whenever there was a lull in the playing, they talked about the accident.

"What accident?" Jane demanded.

"Train hit a Buick," a man said. "Middle of the night." The man had big ears and a tattoo on his forearm.

"There aren't any good new games," a woman complained. "Haven't been for years and years."

"Did you fall asleep?" Jane said accusingly to Dan.

"When could that have happened?" Dan said.

"We didn't see it," Jane said, disgusted.

"Two teenagers escaped without a scratch," the man said. "Lived to laugh about it. They are young and silly but it's no joke to the engineer. The engineer has a lot of paperwork to do after he hits something. The engineer will be filling out forms for a week." The man's tattoo said MOM and DAD.

"Rats," Jane said.

The children returned to the darkened dining room where *Superman* was being shown on a small television set. Jane instantly fell asleep. Dan watched Superman spin the earth backward so he could prevent Lois Lane from being smothered in a rock slide. The train shot past a group of old lighted buildings. SEWER KING, a sign said. When the movie ended, Jane woke up.

"When we lived in New York," she said muzzily, "I was sitting in the kitchen one afternoon doing my homework and this girl came in and sat down at the table. Did I ever tell you this? It was the middle of the winter and it was snowing. This person just came in with the snow on her coat and sat right down at the table."

"Who was she?" Dan asked.

"It was me, but I was old. I mean I was about thirty years old or something."

"It was a dream," Dan said.

"It was the middle of the afternoon, I tell you! I was doing my homework. She said, 'You've never lifted a finger to help me.' Then she asked me for a glass with some ice in it."

After a moment, Dan said, "It was probably the cleaning lady."

"Cleaning lady! Cleaning lady for Godssakes, what do you know about cleaning ladies!"

Dan felt her hair bristle as though someone were running a comb through it back to front, and realized she was mad, madder than she'd been all summer, for all summer she'd only felt humiliated when Jane was nasty to her.

"Listen up," Dan said, "don't talk to me like that anymore."

"Like what," Jane said cooly.

Dan stood up and walked away, leaving Jane sitting there, not realizing what had happened to her. Jane was saying, "The thing I don't understand is how she ever got into that apartment. My father had about a dozen locks on the door."

Dan sat in her seat in the quiet, dark coach and looked out at the dark night. She tried to recollect how it seemed dawn happened. Things just sort of rose out, she guessed she knew. There was nothing you could do about it. She thought of Jane's dream in which the men in white bathing caps were pushing all her grandma's things out of the house and into the street. The inside became empty and the outside became full. Dan was beginning to feel sorry for herself. She was alone, with no friends and no parents, sitting on a train between one place and another, scaring herself with someone else's dream in the middle of the night. She got up and walked through the rocking cars to the Starlight Lounge for a glass of water. After 4 a.m. it was no longer referred to as the Starlight Lounge. They stopped serving drinks and turned off the electric stars. It became just another place to sit. Mr. Muirhead was sitting there, alone. He must have been on excellent terms with the stewards because he was drinking a Bloody Mary.

"Hi, Dan!" he said.

Dan sat opposite him. After a moment she said, "I had a very nice summer. Thank you for inviting me."

"Well, I hope you enjoyed your summer, sweetie," Mr. Muirhead said.

"Do you think Jane and I will be friends forever?" Dan asked.

Mr. Muirhead looked surprised. "Definitely not. Jane will not have friends. Jane will have husbands, enemies, and lawyers."

He cracked ice noisily with his white teeth. "I'm glad you enjoyed your summer, Dan, and I hope you're enjoying your childhood. When you grow up, a shadow falls. Everything's sunny and then this big goddamn *wing* or something passes overhead."

"Oh," Dan said.

"Well, I've only heard that's the case actually," Mr. Muirhead said. "Do you know what I want to be when I grow up?" He waited for her to smile. "When I grow up I want to become an Indian so I can use my Indian name."

"What is your Indian name?" Dan asked, smiling.

"My Indian name is 'He Rides a Slow Enduring Heavy Horse.'"

"That's a nice one," Dan said.

"It is, isn't it?" Mr. Muirhead said, gnawing ice.

Outside, the sky was lightening. Daylight was just beginning to flourish on the city of Jacksonville. It fell without prejudice on the slaughter houses, Dairy Queens and courthouses, on the car lots, sabal palms and a billboard advertisement for pies.

The train went slowly around a long curve, and looking backward, past Mr. Muirhead, Dan could see the entire length of it moving ahead. The bubble-topped cars were dark and sinister in the first flat and hopeful light of the morning.

Dan took the three postcards she had left out of her bookbag and looked at them. One showed Thomas Edison beneath a banyan tree. One showed a little tar-paper shack out in the middle of the desert in New Mexico where men were supposed to have invented the atomic bomb. One was a "quicky" card showing a porpoise balancing a grapefruit on the top of his head.

"Oh, I remember those," Mr. Muirhead said, picking up the "quicky" card. "You just check off what you want." He read aloud, "*How are you? I am fine ( ) lonesome ( ) happy ( ) sad ( ) broke ( ) flying high ( )*" Mr. Muirhead chuckled. He read, "*I have been good ( ) no good ( ). I saw The Gulf of Mexico ( ) The Atlantic Ocean ( ) The Orange Groves ( ) Interesting Attractions ( ) You in My Dreams ( ).*"

"I like this one," Mr. Muirhead said, chuckling.

"You can have it," Dan said. "I'd like you to have it."

"You're a nice little girl," Mr. Muirhead said. He looked at his glass and then out the window. "What do you think was on that note Mrs. Muirhead had you give me?" he asked. "Do you think there's something I've missed?"